The
MX Book
of
New
Sherlock
Holmes
Stories

Part LI
The True Sherlock Holmes:
England's Greatest Hero
(1897-1901)

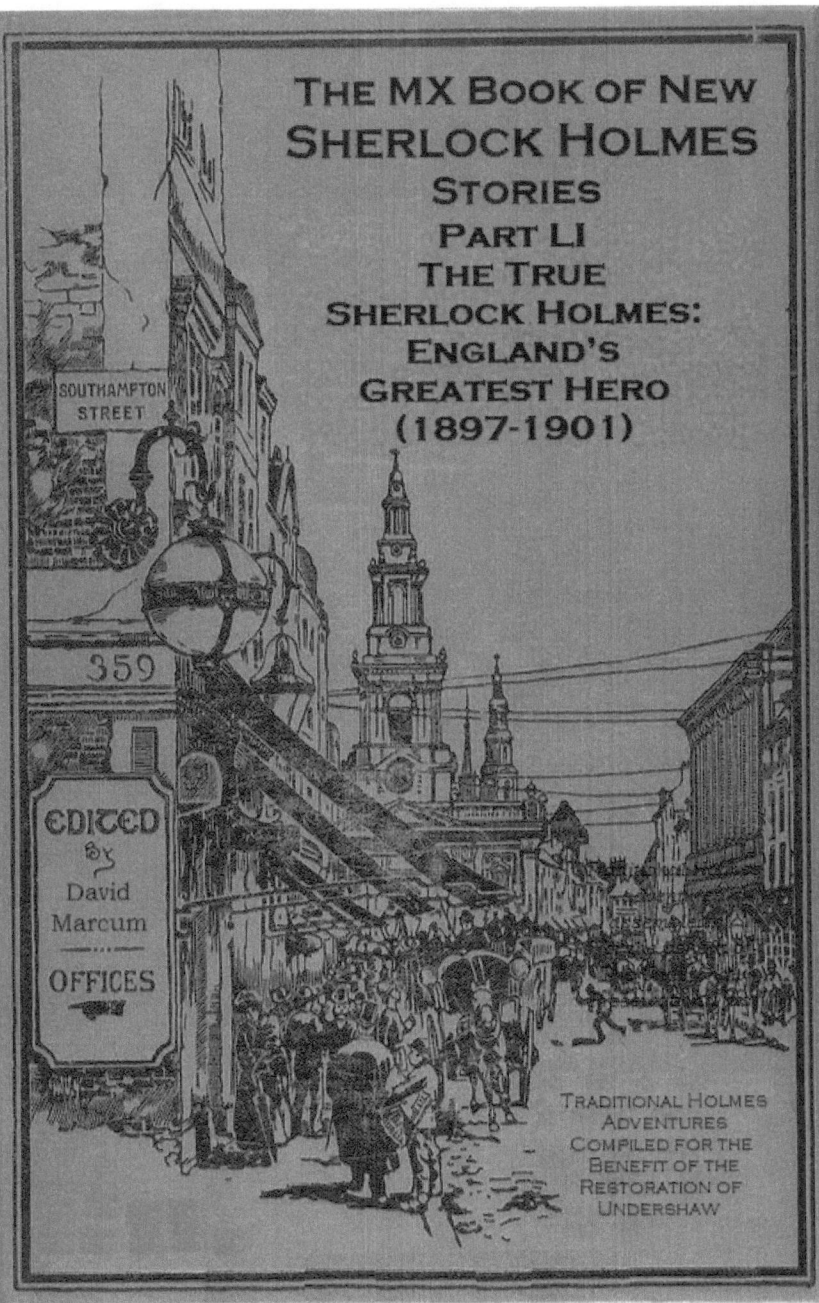

THE MX BOOK OF NEW
SHERLOCK HOLMES
STORIES
PART LI
THE TRUE
SHERLOCK HOLMES:
ENGLAND'S
GREATEST HERO
(1897-1901)

SOUTHAMPTON
STREET

359

EDITED
By
David
Marcum

OFFICES

TRADITIONAL HOLMES
ADVENTURES
COMPILED FOR THE
BENEFIT OF THE
RESTORATION OF
UNDERSHAW

ISBN Hardback 978-1-80424-691-7
ISBN Paperback 978-1-80424-692-4
AUK ePub ISBN 978-1-80424-693-1
AUK PDF ISBN 978-1-80424-694-8

Published in the UK by
MX Publishing
335 Princess Park Manor, Royal Drive,
London, N11 3GX
www.mxpublishing.co.uk

David Marcum can be reached at:
thepapersofsherlockholmes@gmail.com

Cover design by Brian Belanger
www.belangerbooks.com and *www.redbubble.com/people/zhahadun*

Internal Illustrations by Sidney Paget

CONTENTS

Foreawords

Adventures

(Continued on the next page . . . .)

(Continued on the next page . . . .)

These additional adventures are contained in

Part XLIX – The True Mr. Sherlock Holmes:
England's Greatest Hero (1880-1888)

Part L – The True Sherlock Holmes:
England's Greatest Hero (1889-1896)

(Continued on the next page . . . .)

**Part LII – The True Sherlock Holmes:
England's Greatest Hero (1902-1923)**

(Continued on the next page . . . .)

The MX Book of New Sherlock Holmes Stories
Parts I – LII (2015-2025) contain the following:

(Continued on the next page . . . .)

(Continued on the next page . . . .)

PART V – Christmas Adventures

(Continued on the next page . . . .)

PART VI – 2017 Annual

(Continued on the next page . . . .)

The Unwelcome Client – Keith Hann
The Tempest of Lyme – David Ruffle
The Problem of the Holy Oil – David Marcum
A Scandal in Serbia – Thomas A. Turley
The Curious Case of Mr. Marconi – Jan Edwards
Mr. Holmes and Dr. Watson Learn to Fly – C. Edward Davis
Die Weisse Frau – Tim Symonds
A Case of Mistaken Identity – Daniel D. Victor

PART VII – Eliminate the Impossible: 1880-1891
Foreword – Lee Child
Foreword – Rand B. Lee
Foreword – Michael Cox
Foreword – Roger Johnson
Foreword – Melissa Farnham
Foreword – David Marcum
No Ghosts Need Apply (A Poem) – Jacquelynn Morris
The Melancholy Methodist – Mark Mower
The Curious Case of the Sweated Horse – Jan Edwards
The Adventure of the Second William Wilson – Daniel D. Victor
The Adventure of the Marchindale Stiletto – James Lovegrove
The Case of the Cursed Clock – Gayle Lange Puhl
The Tranquility of the Morning – Mike Hogan
A Ghost from Christmas Past – Thomas A. Turley
The Blank Photograph – James Moffett
The Adventure of A Rat. – Adrian Middleton
The Adventure of Vanaprastha – Hugh Ashton
The Ghost of Lincoln – Geri Schear
The Manor House Ghost – S. Subramanian
The Case of the Unquiet Grave – John Hall
The Adventure of the Mortal Combat – Jayantika Ganguly
The Last Encore of Quentin Carol – S.F. Bennett
The Case of the Petty Curses – Steven Philip Jones
The Tuttman Gallery – Jim French
The Second Life of Jabez Salt – John Linwood Grant
The Mystery of the Scarab Earrings – Thomas Fortenberry
The Adventure of the Haunted Room – Mike Chinn
The Pharaoh's Curse – Robert V. Stapleton
The Vampire of the Lyceum – Charles Veley and Anna Elliott
The Adventure of the Mind's Eye – Shane Simmons

PART VIII – Eliminate the Impossible: 1892-1905
Foreword – Lee Child
Foreword – Rand B. Lee
Foreword – Michael Cox
Foreword – Roger Johnson
Foreword – Melissa Farnham

(Continued on the next page . . . .)

Part IX – 2018 Annual (1879-1895)

(Continued on the next page . . . .)

(Continued on the next page . . . .)

Part XII: Some Untold Cases (1894-1902)

PART XIII: 2019 Annual (1881-1890)

(Continued on the next page . . . .)

PART XIV: 2019 Annual (1891 -1897)

(Continued on the next page . . . .)

(Continued on the next page . . . .)

The Adventure of the Headless Lady – Tracy J. Revels
Angelus Domini Nuntiavit – Kevin P. Thornton
The Blue Lady of Dunraven – Andrew Bryant
The Adventure of the Ghoulish Grenadier – Josh Anderson and David Friend
The Curse of Barcombe Keep – Brenda Seabrooke
The Affair of the Regressive Man – David Marcum
The Adventure of the Giant's Wife – I.A. Watson
The Adventure of Miss Anna Truegrace – Arthur Hall
The Haunting of Bottomly's Grandmother – Tim Gambrell
The Adventure of the Intrusive Spirit – Shane Simmons
The Paddington Poltergeist – Bob Bishop
The Spectral Pterosaur – Mark Mower
The Weird of Caxton – Kelvin Jones
The Adventure of the Obsessive Ghost – Jayantika Ganguly

Part XVII – Whatever Remains . . . Must Be the Truth (1891-1898)

Foreword – Kareem Abdul-Jabbar
Foreword – Roger Johnson
Foreword – Steve Emecz
Foreword – David Marcum
The Violin Thief (*A Poem*) – Christopher James
The Spectre of Scarborough Castle – Charles Veley and Anna Elliott
The Case for Which the World is Not Yet Prepared – Steven Philip Jones
The Adventure of the Returning Spirit – Arthur Hall
The Adventure of the Bewitched Tenant – Michael Mallory
The Misadventures of the Bonnie Boy – Will Murray
The Adventure of the *Danse Macabre* – Paul D. Gilbert
The Strange Persecution of John Vincent Harden – S. Subramanian
The Dead Quiet Library – Roger Riccard
The Adventure of the Sugar Merchant – Stephen Herczeg
The Adventure of the Undertaker's Fetch – Tracy J. Revels
The Holloway Ghosts – Hugh Ashton
The Diogenes Club Poltergeist – Chris Chan
The Madness of Colonel Warburton – Bert Coules
The Return of the Noble Bachelor – Jane Rubino
The Reappearance of Mr. James Phillimore – David Marcum
The Miracle Worker – Geri Schear
The Hand of Mesmer – Dick Gillman

Part XVIII – Whatever Remains . . . Must Be the Truth (1899-1925)

Foreword – Kareem Abdul-Jabbar
Foreword – Roger Johnson
Foreword – Steve Emecz
Foreword – David Marcum
The Adventure of the Lighthouse on the Moor (*A Poem*) – Christopher James
The Witch of Ellenby – Thomas A. Burns, Jr.

(Continued on the next page . . . .)

Part XIX: 2020 Annual (1882-1890)

(Continued on the next page . . . .)

The Adventure of the Matched Set – Peter Coe Verbica
When the Prince First Dined at the Diogenes Club – Sean M. Wright
The Sweetenbury Safe Affair – Tim Gambrell

(Continued on the next page . . . .)

Part XXII: Some More Untold Cases (1877-1887)

(Continued on the next page . . . .)

The Dundas Separation Case – Kevin P. Thornton
The Broken Glass – Denis O. Smith

(Continued on the next page . . . .)

Part XXV: 2021 Annual (1881-1888)

(Continued on the next page . . . .)

(Continued on the next page . . . .)

Mrs. Crichton's Ledger – Tim Gambrell
The Adventure of the Not-Very-Merry Widows – Craig Stephen Copland
The Son of God – Jeremy Branton Holstein
The Adventure of the Disgraced Captain – Thomas A. Turley
The Woman Who Returned From the Dead – Arthur Hall
The Farraway Street Lodger – David Marcum
The Mystery of Foxglove Lodge – S.C. Toft
The Strange Adventure of Murder by Remote Control – Leslie Charteris and Denis Green
        (Introduction by Ian Dickerson)
The Case of The Blue Parrot – Roger Riccard
The Adventure of the Expelled Master – Will Murray
The Case of the Suicidal Suffragist – John Lawrence
The Welbeck Abbey Shooting Party – Thomas A. Turley
Case No. 358 – Marcia Wilson

Part XXVIII: More Christmas Adventures (1869-1888)
Foreword – Nancy Holder
Foreword – Roger Johnson
Foreword – Steve Emecz
Foreword – Emma West
Foreword – David Marcum
A Sherlockian Christmas (A Poem) – Joseph W. Svec III
No Malice Intended – Deanna Baran
The Yuletide Heist – Mark Mower
A Yuletide Tragedy – Thomas A. Turley
The Adventure of the Christmas Lesson – Will Murray
The Christmas Card Case – Brenda Seabrooke
The Chatterton-Smythe Affair – Tim Gambrell
Christmas at the Red Lion – Thomas A. Burns, Jr.
A Study in Murder – Amy Thomas
The Christmas Ghost of Crailloch Taigh – David Marcum
The Six-Fingered Scoundrel – Jeffrey A. Lockwood
The Case of the Duplicitous Suitor – John Lawrence
The Sebastopol Clasp – Martin Daley
The Silent Brotherhood – Dick Gillman
The Case of the Christmas Pudding – Liz Hedgecock
The St. Stephen's Day Mystery – Paul Hiscock
A Fine Kettle of Fish – Mike Hogan
The Case of the Left Foot – Stephen Herczeg
The Case of the Golden Grail – Roger Riccard

(Continued on the next page . . . .)

Part XXIX: More Christmas Adventures (1889-1896)

Part XXX: More Christmas Adventures (1897-1928)

(Continued on the next page . . . .)

The Adventure of the Chained Phantom – J.S. Rowlinson
Santa's Little Elves – Kevin Thornton
The Case of the Holly-Sprig Pudding – Naching T. Kassa
The Canterbury Manifesto – David Marcum
The Case of the Disappearing Beaune – J. Lawrence Matthews
A Price Above Rubies – Jane Rubino
The Intrigue of the Red Christmas – Shane Simmons
The Bitter Gravestones – Chris Chan
The Midnight Mass Murder – Paul Hiscock

Part XXXI: 2022 Annual (1875-1887)
Foreword – Jeffrey Hatcher
Foreword – Roger Johnson
Foreword – Steve Emecz
Foreword – Emma West
Foreword – David Marcum
The Nemesis of Sherlock Holmes (A Poem) – Kelvin I. Jones
The Unsettling Incident of the History Professor's Wife – Sean M. Wright
The Princess Alice Tragedy – John Lawrence
The Adventure of the Amorous Balloonist – I.A. Watson
The Pilkington Case – Kevin Patrick McCann
The Adventure of the Disappointed Lover – Arthur Hall
The Case of the Impressionist Painting – Tim Symonds
The Adventure of the Old Explorer – Tracy J. Revels
Dr. Watson's Dilemma – Susan Knight
The Colonial Exhibition – Hal Glatzer
The Adventure of the Drunken Teetotaler – Thomas A. Burns, Jr.
The Curse of Hollyhock House – Geri Schear
The Sethian Messiah – David Marcum
Dead Man's Hand – Robert Stapleton
The Case of the Wary Maid – Gordon Linzner
The Adventure of the Alexandrian Scroll – David MacGregor
The Case of the Woman at Margate – Terry Golledge
A Question of Innocence – DJ Tyrer
The Grosvenor Square Furniture Van – Terry Golledge
The Adventure of the Veiled Man – Tracy J. Revels
The Disappearance of Dr. Markey – Stephen Herczeg
The Case of the Irish Demonstration – Dan Rowley

Part XXXII: 2022 Annual (1888-1895)
Foreword – Jeffrey Hatcher
Foreword – Roger Johnson
Foreword – Steve Emecz

(Continued on the next page . . . .)

Part XXXIII: 2022 Annual (1896-1919)

(Continued on the next page . . . .)

(Continued on the next page . . . .)

Part XXXVI: "However Improbable . . . ." (1897-1919)

(Continued on the next page . . . .)

(Continued on the next page . . . .)

(Continued on the next page . . . .)

Part XLI: Further Untold Cases (1877-1892)

Part XLII: Further Untold Cases (1894-1922)

(Continued on the next page . . . .)

Part XLIII: 2024 Annual (1874-1888)

(Continued on the next page . . . .)

Boxing Day, Brother Mine – Gretchen Altabef
The Case of Colonel Warburton's Madness – Jane Rubino
The Exploited Assassins – David Marcum
The Case of the Missing Docker – Jonathan Schneer

Part XLIV: 2024 Annual (1889-1897)
Foreword – Daniel Stashower
Foreword – Roger Johnson
Foreword – Emma West
Foreword – Steve Emecz
Foreword – David Marcum
"Moriarty" (A Poem) – Kevin Patrick McCann
The Disputed Debutante – I.A. Watson
The Deaths on the Edge of Standish Woods – Stephen Herczeg
The Disappeared Doctor – Paula Hammond
The Adventure of Heirloom Necklace – Tracy J. Revels
The Case of the Ignoble Cuckold – Tom Turley
The Midsummer Murders – Paul A. Freeman
The Adventure of the Absentee Officer – Daniel Lenois
A Bucket's Worth of Help – David Marcum
Magic Squares – Marcia Wilson
The Adventure of the Moving Pictures – Shane Simmons
Death of a Mudlark – David MacGregor
The Adventure of the Serpent's Head – Arthur Hall
The Adventure of the Aged Actor – Tracy J. Revels
The Stratford Street Lodgers – Naching T. Kassa
The Other Woman – Susan Knight
The Adventure of the Surrey Revenant – Alan Dimes
A Generous Helping of Deceit – DJ Tyrer
Hollingbourne Grange – Mike Chinn
The Professor's Assistant – Chris Chan
The Mysterious Death of the Russian Anarchist – Jonathan Schneer
A Matter of ABC – Susan Knight
The Taverne Emerald – Alan Dimes

Part XLV: 2024 Annual (1898-1917)
Foreword – Daniel Stashower
Foreword – Roger Johnson
Foreword – Emma West
Foreword – Steve Emecz
Foreword – David Marcum
"Heaven's Guise" (A Poem) – Alisha Shea
The Adventure of the Awakened Mummy – Tracy J. Revels
The Adventure of the Unknown Traitor – Arthur Hall
The Yorkshire Chieftain – Robert Stapleton

(Continued on the next page . . . .)

Part XLVI: Occupants of the Canonical Realm (1861-1889)

(Continued on the next page . . . .)

Part XLVII: Occupants of the Canonical Realm (1890-1898)

Part XLVIII: Occupants of the Canonical Realm (1899-1924)

(Continued on the next page . . . .)

Part XLIX: The True Mr. Sherlock Holmes – England's Greatest Hero (1880-1888)

Part L: The True Mr. Sherlock Holmes – England's Greatest Hero (1889-1996)

(Continued on the next page . . . .)

Part LI: The True Mr. Sherlock Holmes – England's Greatest Hero (1897-1901)

(Continued on the next page . . . .)

The Box – Robert Stapleton
A Puzzle in Porphyry – DJ Tyrer
The Adventure of the Fearful Printer – Arthur Hall
The Prophecies of the Brahan Seer – Paul D. Gilbert
The Clockmaker's Fate – Mike and Arianna Fox
The Wages of Loyalty – Mike Adamson
Death of an Uncommon Man – Geri Schear
The Adventure of the Long Arm – Alan Dimes

Part LII: The True Mr. Sherlock Holmes – England's Greatest Hero (1902-1923)

Foreword – Bonnie MacBird
Foreword – Roger Johnson
Foreword – Emma West
Foreword – Steve Emecz
Foreword – David Marcum
The Adventure of the Disgraced Baron – Derrick Belanger
Sherlock Holmes: The End? (A Poem) – Joseph W. Svec III
Holmes the Hunter – Susan Knight
The Adventure of the Live Burial – Shane Simmons
Phantom of the Operetta – Tim Newton Anderson
The Ambassador's Dilemma – Peter Coe Verbica
The Adventure of the Dreaming Dragon – Josh Reynolds
The Disappearing Detective – J. Lawrence Matthews
The Adventure of the Unfinished Case – John McNabb
The Interrupted Retirements – Don Rowley
The Adventure of the Longest Case – I.A. Watson
The Clue of the Undamaged Stones – David Marcum
The Sound of the Grand's Piano – Paul Hiscock
The Adventure of the Fearless Postman – Andrew Salmon
The Adventure of the Cheapside Secret – Steven Philip Jones
The Adventure of the King's Code – Mike Chinn
His Longest Case – Martin Daley
The Bohemian Corporal– Orlando Pearson
The Riddle of the Sphinx – Liz Hedgecock
The Case of the One-Armed Crabbe – Roger Riccard
The Mystery of the Graveyard Angel – Adrian Middleton
The Adventure of the Wonderful Things – Craig Janacek
Epilogue: A Travel-Worn and Battered Tin Dispatch Box – David Marcum

The following contributors appear
in the companion volumes:
The True Sherlock Mr. Holmes –
England's Greatest Hero
Part XLIX – (1880-1888)
Part L – (1889-1896)
Part LII – (1902-1923)

A Thousand Cunning Windings
by David Marcum

". . . a thousand cunning windings . . . ." So said Mr. Sherlock Holmes in "The Final Problem" to describe the path he traced when cornering Professor James Moriarty. But that phrase can also apply to over one-thousand brilliant Holmes adventures in *The MX Book of New Sherlock Holmes Stories*, now finishing at fifty-two massive volumes . . . . .

Know this from *The Gospel* of The Church of the Traditional Canonical Sherlock Holmes:

> *"In the beginning was The Canon, and it was good.*
> *But it was not enough."*

> – *The Book of Holmes*, (Chapter I, Verses 1-2)

And if that isn't clear enough, Verses 3 and 4 continue:

> *"Verily, verily, I say unto thee: There have*
> *NEVER been enough traditional and*
> *Canonical Holmes adventures.*
> *There NEVER will be."*

And as Dickens wrote, *"This must be distinctly understood, or nothing wonderful can come of the story I am going to relate."*

The initial original Canonical (and pitifully few) Sixty Tales were just the merest glimpse into the long lives of Sherlock Holmes and Dr. John H. Watson. Those Canonical adventures served as the main structural fibers of *The Great Holmes Tapestry*, but there were so many empty spaces in between that needed filling in order to reveal a full and vivid image. This is accomplished by way of post-Canonical adventures called *pastiches.*

The Canon relates sixty events across a period from 1874 ("The Gloria Scott") to 1914 ("His Last Bow") – from when Sherlock Holmes was twenty years old to when he was sixty. Forty years. But consider that most of those cases just take a day or so, or sometimes only a few hours. Forty years is approximately 14,600 days, and yet the total on-page narrative of most of the Canonical cases, when tallied, equals around six months – three days here, two here, and approximately one month for *The Hound*. (Even the off-stage events of The Great Hiatus, nearly three years in duration, is just a fraction of forty years.) There is so much more between 1874 and 1914 that is left undescribed – not to mention whatever happened in Holmes and Watson's lives before 1874 and after 1914.

And even though The Canon is the core of The Great Holmes Tapestry, the stories that make up this core were chosen by Watson as representative examples of Holmes's skills – they were not necessarily his greatest triumphs or "best" cases. Watson had thousands of recorded adventures from which to choose when selecting for publication, and he had reasons for what he picked . . . and for what he suppressed. *What about all of those other cases that weren't published in Watson's lifetime?*

That's where the Post-Canonical Chroniclers step in . . . .

"Apart from what you have told me,
can you give me any further
information about the man?"
– Sherlock Holmes
"The Illustrious Client"

In 2015, we knew less about Mr. Sherlock Holmes than we do now, for back then, there were over one-thousand fewer of his adventures that had been revealed to the curious public. Don't misunderstand – there were still quite a few post-Canonical Holmes narratives in 2015, but they were harder to find, *and there were not enough.*

". . . we must hunt for this man's secrets."
– Sherlock Holmes
"The Illustrious Client"

Growing up, I had the very-common experience of discovering and reading The Canon, and re-reading it, and then realizing with crushing disappointment that the ride was seemingly at an end. I was fortunate to discover Holmes in 1975, at age ten, just one year after Nicholas Meyer had ignited the current and still-burning Sherlockian Golden Age with his discovery of the lost manuscript for *The Seven-Per-Cent Solution* (1974). While it was flawed – the implications that Moriarty was not evil, and that the Great Hiatus did not occur, were obviously grafted onto Watson's original manuscript by some later Moriarty heir to posthumously rehabilitate the evil Professor's reputation – this book revealed the basic but staggering truth that Watson's stories *did not have to cross the First Literary Agent's desk to be both accepted and amazing.*

The hunt was on to locate Watson's other missing narratives, filling in all the gaps and spaces between what we know from The Canon. Meyer continued by finding an exponentially better second Watsonian manuscript, *The West End Horror* – and the dam holding back the release of these various historic documents was washed away forever.

> *"But that is not enough, Mr. Holmes."*
> – Lord Bellinger, Prime Minister
> "The Second Stain"

In the following years, I tracked down, collected, read, and chronologicized almost every existing traditional Canonical Holmes adventures – *but there were not enough.* And in the early 2000's, I noticed a disturbance in the Holmesian Force: Several media adaptations that incorrectly placed Holmes in Modern Times began popping up. One in particular gained a lot of traction, painting Holmes as a broken sociopathic murderer. That would be fine if it stopped there, for there have been a lot of insulting works over the years that similarly attacked Holmes – the worst up to that point being Michael Dibdin's *The Last Sherlock Holmes Story* (1978), in which Holmes was presented as a gleeful Jack the Ripper, whose death was arranged by Watson.

> *"We must not lose sight of our main inquiry."*
> – Sherlock Holmes
> "The Naval Treaty"

I was dismayed when aspects of this modernized sociopathic Holmes began creeping into what were supposed to be traditional Canonical adventures, as presented by people who should have known better: In these "traditional" adventures, supposedly Canonical Holmes now had a "mind palace". Watson's wound was psychosomatic. Mrs. Hudson was the widow of a drug dealer. Irene Adler was a dominatrix. Mary Watson was a secret agent assassin. And people were adapting to this – accepting this – as if maybe Holmes *had always been a sociopath*, or that Watson *really wasn't wounded*, if one just read The Canon a little more closely. Many said, "It's okay – as long as this attracts new people to Sherlock Holmes, who cares how they get there?" But they were all showing up with the expectation and looking for hints that Irene Adler really was a dominatrix, or that James Moriarty was . . . whatever that was supposed to be.

I became increasingly . . . shall we say *peeved*. And then I became motivated – a fiery motivation that has only increased every day since.

I little dreamed the strange shape
which that campaign was destined to take.
– Dr. John H. Watson
"Charles Augustus Milverton"

One night in early 2015, I had a dream, and it abruptly awakened me. If I'd gone back to sleep, I might have forgotten it, but instead I went ahead and got up, as it was nearly time to arise anyway. And I kept thinking about that very-vivid vision.

I had dreamed that I'd edited a book of new Holmes stories, along the lines of *The Mammoth Book of Sherlock Holmes Stories* (1997), or the many volumes that Martin H. Greenberg co-edited with a number of other people over several decades – new Holmes stories, set in the correct time, indistinguishable from the Canonical tales that originally appeared in *The Strand.*

"*. . . we must take our own line of action.*"
– Sherlock Holmes
"The Disappearance of Lady Frances Carfax"

That morning before going to work, I looked around at my Holmes collection – now nearly 5,000 volumes, but somewhat less then – and saw a number of authors represented there that I'd love to invite. Later that morning, I emailed Publisher Extraordinaire Steve Emecz with the idea, and he was willing. (Steve has always been most supportive of various project ideas.) I had no idea that I'd started something that would be a huge part of my life for the next ten years . . . .

That email is on the next page . . . .

David Marcum   Jan 22, 2015, 9:40 AM   ☆   ☺   ↩   ⋮
to Steve ▾

Steve,

This is the idea I had for a future book. I was literally dreaming about it when I woke up this morning.

I would like to contact a specific list of authors (see below) – who I would pick because they write well and who write the kinds of Holmes stories that I would want to read – and have each one of them pen a Holmes short story.

The volume would be along the lines of all of those anthologies that have come before, such as *The Mammoth Book, Holmes for the Holidays, Murder in Baker Street,* etc. Like *The Mammoth Book,* I would arrange the stories by chronological date, and not by a perceived author importance.

I would be the editor, and I would format it. (As you know, I have strict standards.) I would ask that each story be 5,000-8,000 words in length, much like stories from the Canon. The stories would be traditional and Canonical Holmes only, as narrated by Watson. The characters would be in standard settings, and it would be like when authors were writing *Star Trek* novels, and they were told that they could use the characters, but essentially put them back as they found them when they were done. There would be no weird Alternate Universe or present-day stuff, no Holmes-is-the-Ripper, nothing where Watson is at Holmes's funeral or vice-versa, etc. Essentially nothing that shockingly contradicts what is in the Canon.

I would contact each author personally to explain the project and request a submission. That way other authors who didn't get to play wouldn't necessarily get their feelings hurt, since it would go on behind the scenes and the book would simply appear as a finished product.

Each author would retain the rights to his or her story, for use in a future collection of their own. To avoid the question of who gets what, royalties would go to Undershaw, or some other good cause of your choosing.

Also, it would generate some new Holmes stories that I would get to read, and that would be great!

If eight participated, it would be a pretty good nice book. If more played, so much the better. We could even consider doing two versions, the standard paperback, and possibly a collectible hardcover – that would be your call, of course.

So, what do you think? I think I could put this together fairly easily, once the stories arrived. It would be a lot of fun, and it would be something really cool for MX as well.

I await your thoughts....

David

  . . . and if you can't easily read it, I wrote:

January 22, 2015 9:40 a.m.

Steve,

This is the idea I had for a future book. I was literally dreaming about it when I woke up this morning.

I would like to contact a specific list of authors (see below) – who I would pick because they write well and who write the kinds of Holmes stories that I would want to read – and have each one of them pen a Holmes short story.

The volume would be along the lines of all of those anthologies that have come before, such as The Mammoth Book, Holmes for the Holidays, Murder in Baker Street, *etc. Like* The Mammoth Book, *I would arrange the stories by chronological date, and not by a perceived author importance.*

I would be the editor, and I would format it. (As you know, I have strict standards.) I would ask that each story be 5,000-8,000 words in length, much like stories from the Canon. The stories would be traditional and Canonical Holmes only, as narrated by Watson. The characters would be in standard settings, and it would be like when authors were writing Star Trek novels, and they were told that they could use the characters, but essentially put them back as they found them when they were done. There would be no weird Alternate Universe or present-day stuff, no Holmes-is-the-Ripper, nothing where Watson is at Holmes's funeral or vice-versa. etc. Essentially nothing that shockingly contradicts what is in the Canon.

I would contact each author personally to explain the project and request a submission. That way other authors who didn't get to play wouldn't necessarily get their feelings hurt, since it would go on behind the scenes and the book would simply appear as a finished product.

Each author would retain the rights to his or her story, for use in a future collection of their own. To avoid the question of who gets what, royalties would go to Undershaw, or some other good cause of your choosing.

Also, it would generate some new Holmes stories that I would get to read, and that would be great!

If eight participated, it would be a pretty good nice book. If more played, so much the better. We could even consider doing two versions, the standard paperback, and possibly a collectible hardcover – that would be your call, of course.

So, what do you think? I think I could put this together fairly easily, once the stories arrived. It would be a lot of fun, and it would be something really cool for MX as well.

I await your thoughts . . . .

David

"We must define the situation a little more clearly."
– Sherlock Holmes
"The Red Circle"

When Steve approved, I also emailed a couple of Sherlockian friends, and their opinions were positive. So I started sending out invitations – and I was very clear: The books could have no actual supernatural solutions. There might be some element of *"What was that . . . ?"* at the end of the story – perhaps Watson looks back as they drive away and sees a mythical creature after all – but the crime could not have been caused by the creature. No real vampires or wolfmen or actual Jekyll-Hyde transformations. No aliens or Old Gods or intelligent brain-mutating parasites. Although one naysayer who is bored with The Canon and favors pure Holmes-versus-Actual Supernatural Creatures later sneered at these "Scooby Doo solutions", Holmes stated it exactly right: *"No ghosts need apply."*

Likewise, there could be no anachronistic elements. "Mind palaces" and other such incorrect modern references were forbidden. Technology had to agree with the year in which the story took place – with absolutely no Steampunk. The story itself had to fit into the Holmes and Watson chronology. For instance, close reading of The Canon shows that Watson only had a practice during those years when he was married. Watson's residences when living away from Baker Street – Paddington and Kensington and Queen Anne Street – had to be correct for the period in which the story occurred.

Finally, there could be no aspects of parody. People had been calling Our Heroes things like *Hairlock Combs* and *Fetlock Jones* since the late 1800's. It wasn't funny then, and it isn't funny now.

"We must strike while the iron is hot."
– Sherlock Holmes
"The Cardboard Box"

When I started sending invitations, I was afraid that no one would respond, so I kept widening the net. I went through my entire Holmes collection, looking for pasticheurs and finding ways to contact them. Then, to my amazement, I had the first positive reply – from Lyndsay Faye, who wrote back within a few hours of my initial email, stating: *"I'd be happy to – when do you need it by?"*

Wow – this thing might happen after all.

"Well, I think we must wait
for a little more material."
– Sherlock Holmes
"The Red Circle"

I'd been worried that there would be no interest, and I'd also thought that, at best, the final result might be a one-volume paperback of maybe twelve stories – if I was lucky. So I kept sending more invitations, and getting more replies from people saying that they were in. Then . . . the first story arrived, from Luke Benjamen Kuhns, and I first experienced that brand-new thrill – that *addiction* – of receiving new Holmes stories in my inbox.

"Our material is rapidly accumulating."
– Sherlock Holmes
"The Dancing Men"

As 2015 progressed, word spread about this new project, and an increasing number of people wanted to join the party. I began receiving more emails and more stories, and pretty soon it became apparent that this was going to be a really big book. Maybe too big for just one book . . . .

"We will confine ourselves for the present
with your permission to this very
interesting document."
– Sherlock Holmes
The Hound of the Baskervilles

Over several months, Steve Emecz and I worked out book lengths and sizes, and he was receptive when I shared that I thought it would become a two-volume set. And he was still receptive when that grew to three volumes. By late Summer 2015, the set had grown to 63 stories – more tales than in The Canon.

"We need certainly to muster all our resources."
– Sherlock Holmes
"The Five Orange Pips"

From the beginning, the royalties from this project have gone to support the restoration of Undershaw, one of Sir Arthur Conan Doyle's former homes. For a number of years, the site had been in disrepair, and was more recently in danger of being torn down or cut up into private dwellings, disrespecting the historical significance of the place. A movement had helped to save Undershaw, and Steve Emecz and MX

Publishing had been part of that, having published several previous volumes whose royalties had also helped the site.

> *"Now, we must make the best use of our time . . . ."*
> – Sherlock Holmes
> "The Speckled Band"

Now the building was saved, having recently been purchased by the nearby Stepping Stones School for special needs children – and Steve suggested that the royalties from the new books go to the school. This only made the project more popular with the contributors.

The three volumes were published in Autumn 2015, and I was very fortunate to be able to travel to England – my second Holmes Pilgrimage – to attend a launch party high on a festive outdoor deck atop one of London's noted skyscrapers – at the location of Steve's then-employer. And then I returned home, and things settled down for a week or so . . . but it wasn't long before I started receiving emails about when to contribute to the *next book . . . .*

> *"Why should you go further in it?*
> *What have you to gain from it?"*
> – Sherlock Holmes
> "The Red Circle"

Next book? Next book! I'd had no plans for anything past the first three books. But receiving new Holmes stories by email *was* an addiction, and people wanted to contribute – both former and new pasticheurs – and others wanted to read further volumes with stories about the True Holmes, and most of all, *there are never enough traditional Canonical Holmes adventures. Never enough.*

> *"We must begin again."*
> – Sherlock Holmes
> "The Disappearance of Lady Frances Carfax"

So I wrote to Steve and explained, and we decided upon one more book – or maybe we decided on one new book per year. (I can't remember exactly.) In any case, I announced it, and more stories arrived, and Part IV, published in Spring 2016, had twenty-one stories. And then came the questions about the *next* volume . . . .

> *"We must begin from a different angle."*
> – Sherlock Holmes
> "The Illustrious Client"

It became apparent that there were so many contributors anxious to reach into Watson's Tin Dispatch Box, and also so many readers who were *starving* for more traditional Canonical adventures, that we could produce a lot more than one book per year – so it was decided to have a Spring *Annual*, and an Autumn themed volume. And 2016's themed Autumn volume was *Christmas Adventures* – 30 stories, (It's still one of the most popular of the series. We did another three-volume Christmas set in 2021.)

"We must hustle and put the thing through."
– Sherlock Holmes
"The Three Garridebs"

By then, the pattern was set. I would announce a "Call for Submissions" about six months before publication of a particular set – the *Annuals* in Spring, and themed books in Autumn – such as Christmas, and Untold Cases, and seemingly-supernatural-but-not-really. More and more stories would arrive, necessitating that we eventually grew to six volumes per year – three for the *Annuals*, and three for the themed sets. I was usually reading new stories for the next set while also finishing final edits for the current set, and by the time the current set was published, fresh to the excited reading public, it was far in my rear-view mirror as I edited the new stories.

"We will raise as much as we can in money . . . ."
– John Ferrier
A Study in Scarlet

In September 2016, the Stepping Stones School at Undershaw held their grand opening, and my deerstalker and I were invited as special guests (representing Holmes and Pasticheurs) because of the books' connection to the school. It was my own Holmes Pilgrimage No. 3. At that time – and since then as well – I was told that while the money raised for the school was substantial and useful – over $135,000 as I write this foreword – the more important aspect of the books' association was that they raised awareness of the school all over the world.

"We will have some indication as to
where the document has gone."
– Sherlock Holmes
"The Second Stain"

There were a number of milestones as the books progressed. A set of six volumes, taken from the early anthologies, were published in India by

Jaico. A single volume was translated and sold in Japan. Phil Growick, an initial contributor, had the brilliant idea of taking Holmes stories and assigning them to different artists – each of whom would produce a painting related to that tale, and all for charity. He published four different volumes of *The Art of Sherlock Holmes*, and almost all of the stories in those books were taken directly from *The MX Book of New Sherlock Holmes Stories*. He even had a gallery showing for one set of paintings, and more were planned before COVID shut things like that down. And contributor Sean Wright – who co-wrote (with Michael Hodel) *Enter the Lion* (1979), one of the best post-Canonical adventures way back in the late 1970's, not long after the current Sherlockian Golden Age commenced – suggested a volume of stories from this series that were contributed by members of the BSI – and thus *An Investee's Anthology* was published in 2022.

"... *he has done a considerable amount of writing lately* . . ."
– Sherlock Holmes
"The Red-Headed League"

During his lifetime, the late Philip K. Jones compiled an amazing database of post-Canonical stories – approximately 16,000 of them at the time of his passing, not long after the first MX anthology volumes were published. If one disregards the number of parodies and non-traditional non-Canonical stories that he included, then there are approximately 10,000 traditional and Canonical adventures listed – a fairly complete list up to that time. Since then, *The MX Book of New Sherlock Holmes Stories*, with these final four volumes, has 1,063 stories – or approximately ten percent (10%) of the other traditional and Canonical adventures ever written. Additionally, these books have had over 200 contributors world-wide. Some authors wrote a single story, while others have stepped up and contributed dozens – to my everlasting gratitude.

"*We must each try our own way and see what comes of it.*"
– Sherlock Holmes
"Wisteria Lodge"

I never cease to be amazed at the directions taken by the different contributors. From the common point of the traditional Canon, stories in these books may be comic or tragic. One might find a cozy murder or a strict police procedural murder investigation – or no murder at all. Holmes might investigate a stolen document or jewel – or something that ends up completely crime-free. The setting might be a British city or the countryside, or another country or continent. Holmes's client might be a businessman or a criminal, or a little old lady or Royalty. He might work for a private interest, or as an agent of the Government. The adventure might be a complicated swindle or a ghost story or a spy mission. The tale may be cerebral, or filled with breakneck action. Holmes might progress steadily from one witness to another, or he may be settled in to unlock a mysterious puzzle or code. Holmes might solve the crime from his armchair, or – as he says in *A Study in Scarlet* –"*Now and again a case turns up which is a little more complex. Then I have to bustle about and see things with my own eyes.*"

> "*I should wish to go further into this matter.*
> *It interests me.*"
> – Professor Presbury
> "The Creeping Man"

Another wonderful thing to me that occurred along the way was that these books gave some people their first opportunities to be published authors, and they went on to write more stories – about Holmes, and in other areas too. Some authors used these books as a "prompt" – reminders every six months to write more Holmes stories so that, as these accumulated, they would have enough to be collected into their own books. There have been quite a few volumes of these "children" of the MX anthologies.

> "*. . . we will go out together and see what we can do.*"
> – Sherlock Holmes
> "The Norwood Builder"

One of the best stories of a "child" of these books was the creation and success of Derrick and Brian Belanger's *Belanger Books*. I first "met" Derrick when he reviewed one of my own books, and we became email friends. He was among the very first group of authors that I invited when I had the idea for the anthologies, and his contribution was his first written Holmes adventure. I "met" his brother, Brian, when he took over as MX's cover artist after the untimely passing of the previous artist. (I've since seen them several times on those occasions when I've attended the yearly Sherlock Holmes Birthday Weekend in New York.)

After Derrick had a taste of writing about Holmes, he and Brian had an idea: To form their own publishing company. I had an email from Derrick in August 2015 – a month or so before the first MX anthologies were published – asking me if I'd be involved in their publishing venture, and I've been thrilled to be associated with them ever since. I've edited over two-dozen books for them, and they've published both of my Solar Pons short story collections, with another on the way.

Belanger Books has published many Holmes anthologies since its inception, including several volumes in their anthology series *Sherlock Holmes: A Year of Mystery*. They have themed Holmes collections related to Poe and Lovecraft and H.G. Wells. There are sets devoted to The Early Years and The Denarian Years, and The Great Hiatus and World War I, and the Montague Street days Before Watson. There are Canonical sequels and team-ups with Solar Pons and other Great Detectives and Female Detectives, and stories centered around the Theatre.

I'm thrilled that Belanger Books came into being, and I believe that it was directly because of Derrick's initial involvement in *The MX Book of New Sherlock Holmes Stories*, and the joy he found when writing his first Holmes adventure. More important, I'm also thrilled that Belanger Books has gone on to be one of the two most-respected and important Sherlockian publishers ever – the other being MX Publishing. Both companies work together very closely to support each other's projects and charities, and spread the True Sherlockian Word far and wide. I'm very proud to be associated with both MX Publishing and Belanger Books.

> *"I cannot really see how we can get*
> *much further than our present position."*
> – Sherlock Holmes
> "Silver Blaze

In 2023, one of the MX contributors wrote, asking me what the future plans were for the series. He wanted to keep contributing for as long as the books continued, and he wanted to keep collecting every volume too, but he wondered how many stories that meant he'd need to write over the years, and how much extra bookshelf space he'd require. His email set me to thinking about an end game . . . .

> *"I think that we have gathered all that we can."*
> – Sherlock Holmes
> "The Priory School"

I'd joked before that the books should fittingly go to Part MX – Volume 1,010 for those who don't speak Roman Numeral – but sadly that wasn't realistic. When I started considering, we were then up to forty-two volumes, and I wondered if we could reach fifty – which seemed like a good number upon which to stop. If we had three Spring volumes in 2024, (Parts 43, 44, and 45), and three in the Autumn (Parts 46, 47, and 48), then we could reach fifty with just two volumes in Spring 2025. If the stories kept arriving at the usual rate, we would have over 1,000 of them upon reaching the Spring 2025 volumes. And personally, 2025 would be ten years since the books began in 2015 – a milestone – and personally I would turn sixty – my own milestone.

"We must prepare for the worst."
– Sherlock Holmes
"The Disappearance of Lady Frances Carfax"

The same person who had asked me about the books' future warned me that strictly limiting the final set to two volumes might be a mistake, as a lot of people would certainly want to participate at the end, but I was adamant: Fifty was a solid and pleasing number, and I would close the door. But that person – it was Kevin Thornton – was correct: Enthusiasm was high, and we were going to need extra volumes. I didn't want to increase to fifty-one – there's nothing pleasing about that number – but fifty-two felt good. There are fifty-two cards in a deck, and fifty-two weeks in a year – and an ambitious reader could read one volume of this series per week for an entire year. (I highly recommend this as a self-improvement activity, and would like to hear from whomever completes this Noble Quest.)

"In over a thousand cases I am not aware that
I have ever used my powers upon the wrong side."
– Sherlock Holmes, "The Final Problem"

As I write this foreword to the final volumes, I'm currently finishing the final editing process. As mentioned, I've been thrilled to receive new Holmes stories nearly every day for the last decade, and I'm going to miss that incredibly – although I will now have more free time to read other things, without my spare minutes and hours being devoted to printed-out stories on 8½ x 11-inch paper and with an editing pen in hand. I've also enjoyed being something of a Sherlockian influencer, able to nudge the Sherlockian ship in directions that I wanted it to go . . . .

"Then we must take that as our working hypothesis."
– Sherlock Holmes
"The Bruce-Partington Plans"

Not long after I first discovered Holmes in 1975 – before I'd even read all of The Canon – my parents gifted me with William S. Baring-Gould's incredible *Sherlock Holmes of Baker Street* (1962), the amazing biography of Holmes that establishes so many things – his birth date and background, his *other* older brother Sherrinford, his upbringing and schooling, his travels in America as an actor, his relationship with Irene Adler and his son, and the circumstances of his death. (That's right – as a historical figure, he wasn't immortal.) I don't agree with everything Baring-Gould posited, but I concur with much of it, and it was a great jumping off place when constructing my own 1,200-page (and ever-growing) Holmes Chronology.

> *"Well, we will take it as a working hypothesis*
> *for want of a better."*
> – Sherlock Holmes
> "The Man with the Twisted Lip"

As the editor of these fifty-two volumes – and a few dozen more as well for MX and Belanger Books, I've been able to nudge the ship in the direction I believe to be correct, encouraging certain ideas that I hope will become even more established in the reading consciousness as time goes on, in the same way that Baring-Gould's ideas have found popular footing. For instance, whenever the question came up, I encouraged contributors to reinforce the idea that Holmes lived at No. 24 Montague Street (as first discovered by Sherlockian Michael Harrison) before moving to Baker Street. I arranged the stories of each set in chronological order, and in the order to match what I believe is the correct chronology. I firmly aver that Holmes wore a deerstalker, and that he wore it in town and also the country. (Anyone who would shoot *V.R.* into his wall with a hair-trigger pistol would not be concerned by fashion dictates. He would dress as needed in useful clothing to go to work at a moment's notice.) Thus, he wears a deerstalker in these thousand-plus stories.

> *"We must look for consistency."*
> – Sherlock Holmes
> "The Problem of Thor Bridge"

These books helped to further establish that Holmes retired to Hodcombe Farm at Beachy Head on the Sussex Coast. Study of The Canon reveals that Watson had *three* wives – not two, not seven – and these books strengthen that conclusion. There is now much additional evidence, by way of these books, that Nero Wolfe was Holmes's son, and Solar Pons was his nephew. We know a great deal more about The Great Hiatus than what was revealed in "The Empty House", and we also know why Holmes "retired" in 1903, and more about what he was up to in those years leading to World War I and "His Last Bow".

"Their cumulative effect is certainly considerable,
and yet each of them is quite possible in itself."
– Dr. John H. Watson
"The Abbey Grange"

While these books are coming to a close, there are already plans for other similar volumes, although they will not be the size of the MX anthologies, and they will be one-time projects with much-less rigorous editing demands. But one thing will not change: The new books will absolutely stick to what made the original MX volumes so successful: *Firm adherence to the Canonical model.* Holmes will not be substituting for Van Helsing or Doctor Who. He will not be a sociopathic murderer with a "mind palace", and he will not be a joke, or realize halfway through and adventure that he's a character in someone's book, or be covered in tattoos while paying off a prostitute in the doorway of a modern-day Manhattan brownstone. These new books (when they arrive), as well as all fifty-two volumes (and over one-thousand stories) of *The MX Book of New Sherlock Holmes Stories,* hold to a basic premise: They were all generated by a desire for more traditional Canonical adventures – *and there are never enough traditional Canonical Holmes adventures.*

* * * * *

"Of course, I could only
stammer out my thanks."
– The Unhappy John Hector McFarlane
"The Norwood Builder"

As always when one of these collections is finished, I want to thank with all my heart my incredible, patient, brilliant, kind, and beautiful wife of almost thirty-seven years, Rebecca – Every single day I'm more stunned at how lucky I am than the day before! – and our amazing, funny, creative, and wonderful son, and my friend, Dan (with whom I was able to share a multi-week Holmes Pilgrimage No. 4 around England and Scotland in Spring 2024). I love you both, and you are everything to me!

With each new set of the MX anthologies, some things got easier, and there were also new challenges. For several years, the stresses of real life have been much greater on all of us than when this series started. Through all of this, the amazing contributors have pulled truly amazing works from the Tin Dispatch Box. I'm more grateful than I can express to every contributor who has donated both time and royalties to this ongoing project. It's amazing what we've accomplished.

Finally, I cannot express how thankful I am to all of those who keep buying these books and making them the largest and most popular Sherlockian anthology ever.

I'm so glad to have gotten to know so many of you through this process. It's an undeniable fact that Sherlock Holmes authors are the *best* people!

I wish especially thank the following:

☐ *Steve Emecz* – From my first association with MX in 2013, I saw that MX (under Steve Emecz's leadership) was *the* fast-rising superstar of the Sherlockian publishing world. Connecting with MX and Steve Emecz was personally an amazing life-changing event for me, as it has been for countless other Sherlockian authors. It has led me to write many more stories, and then to edit books, along with unexpected additional Holmes Pilgrimages to England – none of which might have happened otherwise. By way of my first email with Steve, I've had the chance to make some incredible Sherlockian friends and play in the Holmesian Sandbox in ways that I would have never dreamed possible.

Through it all, Steve has been one of the most positive and supportive people that I have ever known.

From the beginning, Steve has let me explore various Sherlockian projects and open up my own personal possibilities in ways that otherwise would have never happened. Thank you, Steve, for every opportunity!

☐ *Roger Johnson* – From his immediate support at the time of the first volumes in this series to the present, I can't imagine Roger not being part of these books. His Sherlockian knowledge is exceptional, as is the work that he does to further the cause of The Master. But even more than that, both Roger and his wife, Jean Upton, are simply the finest and best of people, and I'm very lucky to know both of them – even though I don't get to see them nearly as often as I'd like. I look forward to getting back over to the Holmesland sooner rather than later and visiting with them again, but in the meantime, many thanks for being part of this.

☐ *Brian Belanger* –I initially became acquainted with Brian when he took over the duties of creating the covers for MX Books, and I found him to be a great collaborator, and wonderfully creative too. I've worked with him on many projects with MX and Belanger Books, which he co-founded with his brother Derrick Belanger, also a good friend. Along with MX Publishing, Derrick and Brian have absolutely locked up the Sherlockian publishing field with a vast amount of amazing material. The old dinosaurs must be trembling to see every new and worthy Sherlockian project, one after another after another, that these two companies create. Luckily MX and Belanger Books work closely with one another, and I'm thrilled to be associated with both of them. Many thanks to Brian for all he does for both publishers, and for all he's done for me personally.

☐ *Bonnie MacBird* – I first met Bonnie in 2013, during my Holmes Pilgrimage No. 1, when I was joining Roger Johnson and Jean Upton for lunch at The Sherlock Holmes Pub, and they brought Bonnie along. I didn't know she was famous then – just that she was a very nice lady. After lunch and an extensive exploration of the Holmes exhibit, Roger guided us on the route taken by Holmes and Watson, as described in "The Empty House", from Cavendish Square to Camden House in Baker Street. Later that evening, Bonnie attended my first book signing at the Sherlock Holmes Hotel in Baker Street. I saw her again in 2015 at the launch party of the MX anthologies, and then several times after that at Sherlockian gatherings in Indiana and New York. In the meantime, we've stayed in touch by email.

During our first meeting, along the way of the "Empty House" walk, she rather shyly stated that she was working on writing a pastiche. I hinted that I'd like to read it, but no such luck – until *Art in the Blood* was published in 2015 and I was able to read it as my book-of-choice while in London for Holmes Pilgrimage No. 2 – the first of her very successful Holmes series from HarperCollins. Bonnie has been an incredible supporter of these books from the very beginning, and I'm thrilled and thankful that she is a part of them for the final volumes.

And finally, last but certainly *not* least, thanks to **Sir Arthur Conan Doyle**: Author, doctor, adventurer, and the Founder of the Sherlockian Feast. Honored, and present in spirit.

As I always note when putting together an anthology of Holmes stories, the effort has been a labor of love. Looking back over ten years, this has never wavered. These adventures are just part of the many tiny threads woven into the ongoing Great Holmes Tapestry, continuing to grow and grow, for there can *never* be enough stories about the man whom Watson described as *"the best and wisest . . . whom I have ever known."*

David Marcum
March 4th, 2025
The 144th Anniversary of
the monumental first day of the
Jefferson Hope Murder Investigation

Questions or comments
may be addressed to David Marcum at
thepapersofsherlockholmes@gmail.com.

Foreword
by Bonnie MacBird

Well, here it is. Bringing it on Holmes, editor and Sherlockian scholar extraordinaire David Marcum presents the final volumes of his magnificent series for MX publishing, which has brought 52 volumes of over 1,000 stories by Holmesian writers from all over the planet – from the famous to the newly fledged, all writing from the heart and from the mind, reflecting our hero: Mr. Sherlock Holmes. This series has taken in more than $134,000 in support of the Undershaw school for special needs children.

You hold in your hands the last of these volumes, representing over ten years of David Marcum's creative life. He's diligently read, edited, championed, and also beautifully added to this astonishing collection of ongoing adventures of our heroes.

All of these works have been traditional, in emulation of that genius storyteller Sir Arthur Conan Doyle, whom we happily acknowledge here as the mastermind. He has enthralled thousands of readers for more than 130 years. His craft seems so effortless (until you try your hand at it), his prose both brisk and evocative, and even "cinematic", although most of it predates cinema. His wit is crisp, his insights subtle, his characters unforgettable.

How wise that he chose as the storytelling "voice" that of the pragmatic, energetic man of action, John Watson, who doesn't waste words on endless scenic detail or overweening innuendo but, by golly, gets cracking on with the story.

And how exquisitely drawn is Sherlock Holmes, with just enough mystery to the man himself to make us insatiably curious! He is acknowledged as the first superhero of popular fiction, but with no supernatural trappings. He seems to work miracles – but its sheer intelligence, knowledge, stamina, reasoning . . . and let's not forget . . . artistry that are his superpowers. He is a scientist, a logician, and an artist who sees what others do not. Of course, there's also a facility with baritsu, boxing, and single stick when needed.

Ah, the aspiration these stories awaken! Could we not be more like Holmes or Watson with practice, with learning? And wouldn't we be a better person if so?

But setting aside inspirational qualities of these stories, we must also acknowledge the absolute crazy fun they provide, and even more so, the comfort. In a world fraught with conflict and violence, with ignorance and prejudice, these stories amuse and entertain as they bring us close to characters who demonstrate what our world needs most – rational, fact-based critical thinking, courage, and friendship. Armed with those, these two men stand side by side to fight evil and win. Always win.

And at the end, we find ourselves fireside, once again at 221b. And so very glad to be there. Thank you, David and MX. And thank you, Sir Arthur.

Bonnie MacBird
Author, *The Sherlock Holmes Adventure Series*
for HarperCollins
February 2025

"Let me recommend this book – one of the most remarkable ever penned."
by Roger Johnson

That, you'll remember, was Sherlock Holmes's opinion of *The Martyrdom of Man* by William Winwood Reade (1838-1875), who was pithily defined by the *Dictionary of National Biography, 1885-1900* as "*traveller, novelist and controversialist*". The *DNB* noted of the book so remarkably endorsed by Holmes: "*in this work the author does not attempt to conceal his atheistical opinions*". S.C. Roberts, in the very first issue of *The Sherlock Holmes Journal*, observed that "*Holmes, with his social moodiness, his artistic temperament and his queer intellectual interests, had no doubt re-acted against the conventional beliefs of his squirearchical family and Winwood Reade's book was exactly the work that would catch him on the rebound.*"

Reade was an extraordinary man, who led an extraordinary life. The same could be said of Sherlock Holmes, of course, though his life was considerably longer. It was fairly early in their partnership that he urged John Watson to read *The Martyrdom of Man*. If the Good Doctor did so, he probably didn't accept Reade's statement that: "*The soul must be sacrificed; the hope in immortality must die.*" And if Holmes's own opinion at the time matched Reade's, we know that it did become more positive. Consider his discourse on the moss rose in the case of "The Naval Treaty":

> "*What a lovely thing a rose is!*"
> *He walked past the couch to the open window, and held up the drooping stalk of a moss-rose, looking down at the dainty blend of crimson and green. It was a new phase of his character to me, for I had never before seen him show any keen interest in natural objects.*
> "*There is nothing in which deduction is so necessary as in religion,*" *said he, leaning with his back against the shutters. "It can be built up as an exact science by the reasoner. Our highest assurance of the goodness of Providence seems to me to rest in the flowers. All other things, our powers our desires, our food, are all really necessary for*

23

our existence in the first instance. But this rose is an extra. Its smell and its colour are an embellishment of life, not a condition of it. It is only goodness which gives extras, and so I say again that we have much to hope from the flowers."

That has nothing to do with the case in hand – not directly, at any rate. The intention was probably to encourage his client Percy Phelps to a more optimistic attitude, but Holmes's observations are surely sincere, however unexpected. And no one, surely, can doubt the sincerity of his admonition to the tragic Eugenia Ronder:

We had risen to go, but there was something in the woman's voice which arrested Holmes's attention. He turned swiftly upon her.
"Your life is not your own," he said. "Keep your hands off it."
"What use is it to anyone?"
"How can you tell? The example of patient suffering is in itself the most precious of all lessons to an impatient world."

Detective stories didn't begin when Arthur Conan Doyle wrote *A Study in Scarlet*. Among the Baker Street sleuth's predecessors were the Chevalier C. Auguste Dupin, protagonist of three short stories by Edgar Allan Poe, Emile Gaboriau's Monsieur Lecoq of the French Sûreté, Inspector Bucket in *Bleak House* and Sergeant Cuff in *The Moonstone* – creations respectively of Charles Dickens and Wilkie Collins. Their exploits are still read and enjoyed more than a century-and-a-half later. But who now reads, for example, *The Boy Detective, or The Crimes of London* by Edward Ellis, the apparently endless exploits of Deadwood Dick by Edward L. Wheeler, or those of Jack Harkaway by Bracebridge Hemyng?

Even though he ranked the Holmes Saga low among his literary work, Conan Doyle achieved something remarkable: Fifty-six short stories and four novels, of genuine quality. At first, the detective appears to be essentially one-dimensional, but as we and Dr. Watson come to know him better, we realise that this is a character of real depth. It isn't merely the excitement of the crime and the solution that keep us reading and re-reading – there's also the fascination of his personality – and not only his but the admirable Doctor's as well. *

Even before the last remnants of copyright in the Canonical Holmes stories finally expired, there was a considerable output of parody and pastiche. Parody has different aims and different rules, but pastiche requires fidelity to the substance, the style and the spirit of the original, and that fidelity is too often missing – especially since the expiration of the Conan Doyle copyright – and the ability to post pretty much anything online. As they used to say, *"Never mind the quality, feel the width!"*

Fortunately, that does not apply to this book and its predecessors. David Marcum has worked tirelessly with his many authors to ensure that these new tales of Sherlock Holmes and John H. Watson are up to scratch.

And don't forget that none of the contributors will receive any financial reward, as the proceeds from the publication will go to the upkeep of Undershaw, the house that Arthur Conan Doyle had built for himself and his family near Hindhead in Surrey. Since 2016 it has been home to the Undershaw School, providing care and education for children aged eight to nineteen with Autistic Spectrum Disorder and associated learning needs.

Roger Johnson
BSI, ASH
February 2025

---

*   Watson has so often and so unjustly been depicted as an idiot, especially on film! That will probably continue, but eventually, I hope, it will only be for comedic purposes.

An Ongoing Legacy
for Sherlock Holmes
by Steve Emecz

Undershaw
Circa 1900

Fifty two is a wonderful number of volumes to complete the world's largest-ever Sherlock Holmes anthology. It's unlikely we will ever see another collection like this, with over twohundred Holmes authors participating. It has taken ten years and a mammoth amount of editing from David Marcum to gift the world more than one-thousand new, traditional stories.

As many have commented – the fifty-six short stories and four novellas that Sir Arthur penned was painfully few for the dedicated fan, and wading through the myriad of pastiches on offer is difficult for those yearning for more Conan Doyle. *The MX Book of New Sherlock Holmes Stories* is a haven for those wanting an extension to The Canon in a very similar voice to ACD.

Whilst the collection draws to a close, our work continues with multiple resulting projects coming from this huge set of stories. We come together on 17th May, 2025 at Undershaw to celebrate in person with David and many of the participating authors – and hopefully many of you online too. We'll raise a glass to Sir Arthur, who would no doubt be proud with what we all together have been able to achieve.

Steve Emecz
February 2025

The Doyle Room at Undershaw
Partially funded through royalties from
The MX Book of New Sherlock Holmes Stories

A Word from Undershaw
by Emma West

Undershaw
September 9, 2016
Grand Opening of the Stepping Stones School
(Now *Undershaw*)
(Photograph courtesy of Roger Johnson)

It is with immense gratitude that I write the final words from Undershaw for this last publication of *The MX Book of New Sherlock Holmes Stories*, a collection compiled in support of Undershaw's restoration.

These stories have not only entertained us, but have also played a vital role in transforming the lives of our students. Thanks to the generosity of MX Publishing, we have been able to maintain this historic building while developing an inspiring learning environment for 102 students with Special Educational Needs and Disabilities.

Our partnership with MX Publishing has enriched our school community, offering opportunities and experiences that may otherwise have been out of reach for many of our students. Undershaw stands as a beacon of creativity, learning, and success – fitting for a place so closely linked to the literary legacy of Sir Arthur Conan Doyle.

As we mark this milestone – 52 volumes in the series – we also look forward to celebrating with "A Soirée with Sherlock Holmes", a special event dedicated to the great detective and his creator. Led by MX

Publishing, the evening will include a wonderful auction, streamed around the globe, with proceeds directly benefiting our students. These funds will support the creation of a cutting-edge media lab, complete with state-of-the-art computers, cameras, editing software, and a green screen, allowing our budding writers to bring their stories to life in print and on the screen.

Undershaw is more than just a historic site – it is a place where storytelling, imagination, and creativity thrive. The legacy of Sherlock Holmes continues to inspire our students, equipping them with skills for the future while fostering a lifelong love of literature. We are incredibly fortunate to be part of this ongoing journey and deeply grateful for our enduring partnership with MX Publishing. Their unwavering support has helped change the lives of countless young people.

Though the final volumes of this incredible collection, the impact of these stories – and the generosity behind them – will live on. The pages may close on this chapter, but the spirit of Sherlock Holmes, and the difference this series has made, will remain. Thanks to the unwavering support of MX Publishing and their community of authors and readers, Undershaw will continue to inspire generations to come, ensuring that the Great Detective's legacy is not only preserved, but carried forward into the future.

With heartfelt thanks and appreciation,

Emma West
Headteacher
February 2025

"Undershaw" Hindhead, Conan Doyle's House.

Editor's *Caveats*

When these anthologies first began back in 2015, I noted that the authors were from all over the world – and thus, there would be British spelling and American spelling. As I explained then, I didn't want to take the responsibility of changing American spelling to British and vice-versa. I would undoubtedly miss something, leading to inconsistencies, or I'd change something incorrectly.

Some readers are bothered by this, made nervous and irate when encountering American spelling as written by Watson, and in stories set in England. However, here in America, the versions of The Canon that we read have long-ago has their spelling Americanized, so it isn't quite as shocking for us.

Additionally, I offer my apologies up front for any typographical errors that have slipped through. As a print-on-demand publisher, MX does not have squadrons of editors as some readers believe. The business consists of three part-time people who also have busy lives elsewhere – Steve Emecz, Sharon Emecz, and Timi Emecz – so the editing effort largely falls on the contributors. Some readers and consumers out there in the world are unhappy with this – apparently forgetting about all of those self-produced Holmes stories and volumes from decades ago (typed and Xeroxed) with awkward self-published formatting and loads of errors that are now prized as very expensive collector's items.

I'm personally mortified when errors slip through – ironically, there will probably be errors in these *caveats* – and I apologize now, but without a regiment of professional full-time editors looking over my shoulder, this is as good as it gets. Real life is more important than writing and editing – even in such a good cause as promoting the True and Traditional Canonical Holmes – and only so much time can be spent preparing these books before they're released into the wild. I hope that you can look past any errors, small or huge, and simply enjoy these stories, and appreciate the efforts of everyone involved, and the sincere desire to add to The Great Holmes Tapestry.

And in spite of any errors here, there are more Sherlock Holmes stories in the world than there were before, and that's a good thing.

David Marcum
Editor

Sherlock Holmes (1854-1957) was born in Yorkshire, England, on 6 January, 1854. In the mid-1870's, he moved to 24 Montague Street, London, where he established himself as the world's first Consulting Detective. After meeting Dr. John H. Watson in early 1881, he and Watson moved to rooms at 221b Baker Street, where his reputation as the world's greatest detective grew for several decades. He was presumed to have died battling noted criminal Professor James Moriarty on 4 May, 1891, but he returned to London on 5 April, 1894, resuming his consulting practice in Baker Street. Retiring to the Sussex coast near Beachy Head in October 1903, he continued to be associated in various private and government investigations while giving the impression of being a reclusive apiarist. He was very involved in the events encompassing World War I, and to a lesser degree those of World War II. He passed away peacefully upon the cliffs above his Sussex home on his 103rd birthday, 6 January, 1957.

Dr. John Hamish Watson (1852-1929) was born in Stranraer, Scotland on 7 August, 1852. In 1878, he took his Doctor of Medicine Degree from the University of London, and later joined the army as a surgeon. Wounded at the Battle of Maiwand in Afghanistan (27 July, 1880), he returned to London late that same year. On New Year's Day, 1881, he was introduced to Sherlock Holmes in the chemical laboratory at Barts. Agreeing to share rooms with Holmes in Baker Street, Watson became invaluable to Holmes's consulting detective practice. Watson was married and widowed three times, and from the late 1880's onward, in addition to his participation in Holmes's investigations and his medical practice, he chronicled Holmes's adventures, with the assistance of his literary agent, Sir Arthur Conan Doyle, in a series of popular narratives, most of which were first published in *The Strand* magazine. Watson's later years were spent preparing a vast number of his notes of Holmes's cases for future publication. Following a final important investigation with Holmes, Watson contracted pneumonia and passed away on 24 July, 1929.

Photos of Sherlock Holmes and Dr. John H. Watson courtesy of Roger Johnson

The
MX Book
of
New
Sherlock
Holmes
Stories

Part LI
The True Sherlock Holmes:
England's Greatest Hero
(1897-1901)

Finding Holmes
by Christopher James

F lung from a passing car, *The Memoirs of Sherlock Holmes*
is splintered at the roadside. Two-hundred pages
dandruff the hard shoulder. The cover's gone, already
scavenged by a crow. Broken down, with nothing else
to do, I piece it together under the lamp of the moon.
I gather the stories: Rescuing "Silver Blaze", "The Crooked Man"
and "Reigate Squire"; reuniting Watson and Holmes.
On the opposite verge, I see a man watching me,
perhaps Conan Doyle himself, between life and death,
beside a stranded coach. Our shadows are shrouded
with frost. Maps of London form in the clouds.
Now the road from Brighton has become Baker Steet;
stars are street lamps gleaming in rain. By the time
I see the flashing amber, I'm missing only the last page.
Conan Doyle holds it up. Only he knows how this will end.

The Adventure of the
Man No One Mourned
by Tracy J. Revels

"**M**r. Holmes, it is my duty to my late uncle to hire you to find his murderer. However, sir, I must be frank with you . . . *I am in great hopes that you fail.*"

My friend and I shared a curious glance. Holmes rose from his chair and filled his pipe, then took his time lighting it. Our early morning guest – a man of perhaps forty years, simply dressed, with dark hair and wide, honest features – sat patiently, turning his hat around in his hands.

"Mr. Weldon, I confess myself confused. If you do not wish to know the truth of your relative's passing, then why come to me? And why present me – " Here Holmes tapped the cheque the gentleman had placed on the table. " – with a generous retainer?"

"Please do not think me mad, sir. I am merely honoring his last wish, made to me on my final visit with him. He requested you by name, and even gave me this note, already signed and made out, asking me only to supply the proper date."

Holmes shook his head. "I am flattered, I suppose, and shall try to honor his confidence in my abilities. But first, tell me why you don't wish his murderer discovered."

"Because, frankly, if ever a man deserved to be murdered, it was Julius Zane!"

"Good Heavens," I puffed. "You should be more discreet, Mr. Weldon – or someone might think you killed him."

The gentleman nodded. "I am aware of that, Doctor. But I know that Mr. Holmes prefers to hear the truth in such matters. And anything less would be dishonest. I am a historian by trade, a private tutor. I despise the act of making people better than they were in life, just because they are deceased. I am certain that no one will wear mourning for my uncle. Instead, they will wish him a speedy trip to Hell."

Holmes settled back into his chair. "I am now thoroughly intrigued. Give us your story, Mr. Weldon."

"My uncle and my mother were siblings, the last in the line of a family that had dwindled both in numbers and in fortune from the days when its scions served in Tudor and Stuart courts. Mother and Uncle Julius were raised together at Zane Hall, which is a mere hour from London. They were orphaned when Mother was twenty and Uncle was twenty-five.

45

Mother had wed my father, Mark Weldon, and moved to London. Uncle came into the family estate and took possession of the property. Mother told me in the first year of their shared bereavement she feared Uncle would need to sell the old pile, as he was unprepared to earn enough money to preserve it. Uncle had been a dolt of a student, barely finishing an elementary course of study and never progressing to advanced work. He had no career and no profession, beyond lazing about the great hall and bullying the servants. Mother worried he would starve.

"But then the most remarkable thing happened: Uncle grew wealthy! He began sporting the accoutrements of a lord of the manor: Fine clothes, a new carriage, and an enlarged staff. Uncle claimed he had invested the meager cash aspect of his inheritance wisely in various colonial ventures. Perhaps, Mother said, she had overlooked some innate shrewdness on his part.

"I should add that sudden abundance did not engender a charitable nature in Uncle. As a lad, I imagined him as a dragon, curled around a horde of gold and gems, and woe be it to any mortal who asked him to share. Mother retained many friends in the village who informed her that Uncle did not attend church, nor did he subscribe to any of the agencies that helped the poor. He made Mr. Scrooge, before his ghostly visitations, seem warm and generous.

"Then another astonishing thing happened. Though I was quite young, I recall how startled Mother was to receive a note from her brother, saying he had taken on a ward, an orphaned infant named David. It was as if he had gone shopping in London and returned with a child rather than a pipe or coat! A few days later, a nurse was hired to help care for the baby, and little more was said about it. Mother assumed her brother wanted an heir, but not the trouble of a wife.

"David was a happy, playful child, but a small one who was slow to put on height or flesh. Uncle Julius encouraged him to exercise and romp to build up his bird-like frame. The year I was ten and David five, I spent much of the summer at Zane Hall. What a little rascal David was! We had a merry time and Miss Helen Dolittle, little David's nurse, was as kind and loving as any mother might be. I was sad to leave them for school in autumn.

"It was the following winter that the unthinkable occurred. David received a fine pair of skates that Christmas. The holiday week was frigid, and a pond on the property had frozen. Of course, Uncle forbid David to venture onto the pond alone, but the Boxing Day morning was so bright and beautiful, and all the adults were so sluggish, that the boy could not resist slipping out to enjoy his new plaything." Mr. Weldon barely suppressed a groan. "The ice was not as sturdy as it appeared."

46

"And this tragedy transformed your uncle?" Holmes asked.

"Sir, it unhinged him. The news reached us early that morning, and we hurried to Zane Hall. As we entered, we heard screams – Uncle had turned his grief and rage upon the nurse. He beat her savagely. If we had not burst in on the scene, I fear he might have killed poor Miss Helen. As it was, Mother gave her enough money to immediately leave Uncle's employment, while Father restrained Uncle, who was screeching every vile name a man might call a woman, blaming her for allowing David to slip out of the nursery."

"A terrible story," Holmes said.

"In the years since, Uncle Julius has brought a half-dozen frivolous lawsuits against his country neighbors and pressed ancient ancestorial claims that turned poor, honest people off their land. He has found ways to spoil every church treat or Christmas celebration. He abused his servants until he had but a single housekeeper and her son with him when he died.

"And now I come to the end of my story. My parents passed away six months ago, within days of each other. I was surprised to find, after my mother's funeral, a card from Uncle, expressing what appeared to be sincere condolences and asking me to come and see him, stating – truthfully – that we were the only family left to one another. I had not set foot at Zane Hall since David's death, and Mother had, for all purposes, broken ties with her sibling due to his cruelty to the nurse. I knew of Uncle's black reputation through gossipy letters Mother had shared with me over the years. I considered declining the invitation, but I admit I was lonely. Thinking perhaps I could affect some positive change on Uncle, I agreed to come during the month of May, when my tutoring duties were slack."

"No sooner had I arrived than I regretted it. Zane Hall was falling apart, desperately in need of repairs. Uncle's food was poor, his wine heavily watered. He screeched at Mrs. Ross, his housekeeper, a poor woman who has suffered terribly, and more than once cursed at her son, Teddy, who takes care of the stables and the grounds. At sundown, Uncle led me to the rear of his estate, a place very near the pond where poor David drowned. Much to my surprise, I saw a kind of shrine there, a marble temple twice the size of a gardening shed. Inside, behind locked bars, was a statue of the lost child, a figure in plaster, done in mimicry of Michealangelo's most famous work. Sadly, whoever had attempted to copy the master artist . . . Well, perhaps this was his first commission, for it was grotesque. Standing on a low pedestal, the statue was life-sized, but rough and ill-proportioned, rather lumpy in places, with a strange kind of fringed skirt on the body, instead of a modest fig leaf. The face might have been that of a puppet in a Punch and Judy show, with a gaping grin that left one feeling disquieted and uneasy.

"'What do you think?' Uncle demanded, unlocking the gate and bidding me to look closer. There was just room for the two of us to stand inside the structure. A skylight was directly above the figure. I thought how ghastly it must be in moonlight. 'Well?' he prodded.

"'It is . . . unique,' I said. 'I am glad it gives you comfort,' I added, very quickly, assuming something more was required.

"'If only I had longer to be comforted by it.'

"'What do you mean?'

"He settled on a little bench inside the temple and drew a blanket over his shoulders. 'I feel it in my bones . . . I am going to be murdered.'

"'Who has threatened you?'

"'No one – but I sense the danger. The blow will soon fall. I have not long to live.' Uncle Julius sighed and looked toward the statue. 'You are now, of course, my heir – but you have done nothing to deserve that position. Therefore, I shall not tell you, directly, what you need to know.'

"Mr. Holmes, imagine my shock. I could hardly have come to his house when my mother didn't believe him to be proper company for me. Yet he went on at some length, blaming me for abandoning him, saying how much he would have enjoyed sharing his treasures with me in his lifetime, if I hadn't been such an ungrateful wretch who never visited him. I bore it longer than I should.

"'This is nonsense – and it is cruel. Believe what you want about me, Uncle. You do not owe me a farthing!'

"He scowled. 'I have none other to leave my fortune to. But you will have to search for the source of my wealth! Let us see if your profession does you any good.'

"And with that, sir, he rose and ushered me from the shrine, locking the gate behind him. Had it not been so late, I would have departed that evening, but the good Mrs. Ross bid me to stay at least through breakfast. The next morning, she filled me with as hearty a meal as her improvised stores would allow. Uncle met me at the door and gave me an envelope, with the cheque and the instructions that you should be brought in to solve his murder. I bid him a cool farewell, thinking he was barking mad, and I shouldn't see him again for many years. Three weeks passed, and yesterday, he was indeed found dead – though not slain."

"He died in bed?" I asked.

"No – he was found, just at sunrise, halfway between the temple to David's memory and his own back door. The doctor said, judging by the stiffness of the corpse, that Uncle had succumbed sometime around midnight."

"How was he dressed?" Holmes asked.

"In his nightshirt and slippers, but with his old coat – which hung on a peg by the door – thrown over his bedclothes."

"No one heard him leave the house?"

"Uncle retired at ten, his usual hour, and the housekeeper and her boy at eleven. Neither one heard a door open, nor any disturbance on the rear lawn."

"No screams or shouts?"

"None."

"Footprints?"

"It has been quite dry, so the ground is hard. Uncle's form faced the house, at the edge of his garden, but he had lost one of his slippers, which laid a yard or so behind him."

"Any light?"

"A lantern, which had been extinguished when he fell."

Holmes leaned back in his chair, closing his eyes. "What is your opinion of the housekeeper and her lad?"

"Good, honest folks. The lady is kindness personified, even if she is difficult to look at."

"What do you mean?" Holmes asked.

"She was badly burned in a fire in her youth. Half of her face is twisted and scarred, and she has but one eye. Her voice is harsh and low, also an effect of the blaze, and she wears a kind of wimple, much like a nun, for she has no hair from the conflagration. She is, however, a gentle soul and was as concerned for my comfort as if I were the Prince of Wales. Her boy is perhaps fourteen or so, tall and slender, very attentive to his work."

Holmes nodded. "Let us return to your uncle. What was the doctor's opinion?"

"Death from old age and unusual exertion. No one could imagine why he had gone out, especially as the night was unusually cold for the last of May."

"Has he been buried?"

"The service is to be held today at one." Mr. Weldon shifted about nervously. "I had intended to merely send you a letter, and this payment, as a formality. But then something occurred, and I knew I must come to you in person."

"And what was that?"

"I arrived at Zane Hall yesterday, about eight in the morning, just as Uncle's body was being removed to the undertakers' establishment. I assured Mrs. Ross that she and her son were welcome to stay until things could be sorted, and she was most gracious. While she prepared luncheon,

I sent her lad out to run errands for me, then I walked outside, tracing Uncle's final steps. I saw nothing at first except the hard ground where Uncle had died. And then – for what reason I am not certain – I walked on another eighty yards or so until I reached the temple. I glanced through the bars and received a severe shock.

"Mr. Holmes, the door was unlocked, and the statue was gone. Its pedestal remained, there was fine white dust and broken plaster on the ground, and within the shrine I saw the imprint of one bare foot – as if the statute had loosened itself from the platform, and simply walked away."

We arrived just in time to attend the funeral of Mr. Julius Zane. Besides his nephew and ourselves, the housekeeper and her son were the only mourners. The vicar's words were brief and decidedly uninspired, and the coffin was borne away to the churchyard by the undertaker and his assistants. Clods of earth were soon shoved atop it, making a sad, hollow sound.

Mrs. Ross stood with us as her son went to fetch the carriage. I noticed that Holmes observed both her and her boy very closely, though as the lady's face was covered in a suitably heavy veil, I doubted he could discern her countenance.

"Where were you before you came to Zane Hall, Mrs. Ross?"

"In York, sir."

"And your late husband – was he also in service?"

"No, sir. He was the ship's pursuer on the *Highland Maid*."

Holmes and I exchanged a sorrowful glance. The vessel had gone down in the North Sea three years previously.

"My sympathies. Only one more question: How was it that you came here, to work for Mr. Zane?"

"It was through the late Mrs. Weldon," she said, and our companion gave a start. "She heard of my sad plight through some mutual friends. Mr. Weldon, your mother bid me to never to tell you, for – "

The gentleman smiled. "She was keeping a watch on the old sinner, through you? Please don't feel abashed, Mrs. Ross. That is just the type of thing she would conspire to do."

"She was charitable to me, sir. A saint upon this earth."

We chatted about inconsequential matters until we reached the Hall, where Mrs. Ross provided us with a nourishing repast since we had missed our luncheon. Holmes sat for so long without moving his silverware that I worried something was amiss on his plate.

"No, Watson, the food is excellent. I am taken with the portrait on the wall behind you. Mr. Weldon, you are a historian. Tell me who she is. I'd wager five pounds that is an original Holbein."

Our host chuckled. "I wouldn't like to take your money, Mr. Holmes. It is by one of his apprentices, which is a pity, because if it were a Holbein, it would be worth quite a lot of money. It might even be that fortune Uncle claimed to possess."

I rose to examine the picture in its gilded frame. It showed a winsome girl dressed in red silk, her neck and fingers dripping in pearls and precious stones. A diamond tiara graced her flowing golden tresses. A knowing, almost sultry smile tugged at her lips.

"It is a study of Queen Catherine Howard, done in proposed coronation robes," Weldon said.

"Proposed?" I asked.

"Have you forgotten your history?" Holmes chuckled. "She was the naughty queen, who cuckolded Henry VIII with one of his courtiers, and thus lost her chance to be formally crowned. 'I die a queen, but I would rather die the wife of Culpeper,' she said, immediately before she was beheaded. Or so some chronicles tell us."

"A dubious claim at best," Weldon said, "but that is getting into the *minutia* of my profession. "

"How did such a work come into the family?" Holmes asked.

"In 1541, Lady Zane was a confidant of Queen Catherine. She was supposed to follow the Queen on a royal progress, but suffered a terrible fall from a horse and was forced to return to Zane Hall to recuperate. The Queen sent this portrait, along with some books and a little dog, as tokens of affection, to urge a speedy recovery. Before my ancestress could even hobble about on a cane, however, the queen was arrested and executed for infidelity."

"A great misfortune," Holmes mused, "especially if Lady Zane was a chaste and religious woman, instead of a bawd like Lady Rochford, who aided the queen in her indiscretions. But I digress. I presume the photograph, upon the mantel, is your uncle's ward?"

"Yes, that is David. The picture was made only a month before his death."

Holmes rose and took down the silver frame, studying the image. "Let us go to the shrine, immediately," he said, ignoring the fact that neither of us had completed our meal, and his was largely untouched upon his plate. "An idea has occurred to me. Let us see if it bears fruit."

Weldon led us through the kitchen to a small courtyard, pointing to the small stables and assorted out buildings. There was a garden off to our right, with a line of turned up earth. Teddy Ross was busy polishing some tack in the courtyard, and Holmes halted, then strolled over to him.

"Your flowers are lovely."

"Thank you, sir," he answered, with a tip of his hat.

"I see a patch of turned up earth. What are you planting?"

"I'm preparing rose beds. Mr. Zane had a row of roses, just there, but they were withered and blighted. It felt right to begin anew."

"It seems a lot of work for one young man. Does your mother assist you?"

"Oh no, sir – even if she wished to putter about, her skin is much too sensitive. There is a little boy, Jonesy by name, who lives in a cottage just down the path, beyond the pond. I fetch him whenever I need an extra hand."

"Mr. Zane sanctioned this, and paid him?"

Teddy shook his head. "Mr. Zane was far too stingy to – I'm sorry, I didn't mean to be disrespectful. He would never have approved it, but Jonesy is a scamp who is always hungry. I bribe him with extra sweets."

Holmes indulged in a full, rich laugh and slapped the boy's shoulder. "A true British entrepreneur! Carry on!"

Weldon, who had observed this exchange with a scowl, dropped his voice to a low whisper as we began to walk toward the shrine.

"Surely you don't suspect that boy of any wrongdoing?"

"He seems a bright young fellow," Holmes said lightly. "Now remind me, Weldon – you said the gate to the shrine was unlocked when you discovered the statue missing. Where did you find the key?"

"In what I presume to be its usual place, in Uncle's study. I relocked the shrine immediately and have kept the key in my pocket ever since."

"Excellent. Let us see what the temple can tell us."

The structure was a strange memorial, in the form of a miniature Parthenon, with the late child's name engraved upon the pediment. Weldon opened the gate, but Holmes gestured for us to remain outside. He balanced on his toes, as light as a dancer, careful not to disturb the floor, which was littered with broken bits of plaster and fine white powder. There was a single footprint, and though it was somewhat smeared, I could just make out the small swirl of toes and a heel. Holmes pulled out his lens, then touched a finger to the white substance on the marble floor.

"Ah – just as I thought – not plaster, but flour."

"*Flour!*" Weldon exclaimed.

Holmes motioned toward the more solid chunks. "These are indeed bits of plaster, from where the statue was wrenched from its dais. But the rest is flour, of an unusually fine texture. And what might this be?"

My friend moved to the low bench at the rear of the shrine, picking up a bit of red-and-blue fabric.

"No mystery there," Weldon said. "Uncle left a blanket, to wrap up in, when he came out to mourn. He put it around his shoulders on the afternoon we spoke, and dropped it when we departed."

"Ah, but did it also contain these items?"

Holmes pulled two articles from the crumpled pile of wool, holding them aloft. One was a pair of boy's trousers, the other a rather dirty flannel shirt.

"I presume they were David's," Weldon said. "Mrs. Ross told me the boy's clothes and toys have been preserved. Perhaps he treated them as relics."

"Then I have seen all I require here," Holmes said, folding the clothing and tucking the items under his arm. "Be sure to lock the gate. Now, Mr. Weldon, it strikes me that you could be of great assistance."

"How so?"

"Have Teddy drive you to the village and speak with the residents, especially the shopkeepers. I need to know more of your uncle's movements. When was the last time he visited the grocer's, or the butcher's establishment? When was his final telegram sent, and where was it directed? I presume he had a solicitor. Perhaps that gentleman can tell you more about his latest lawsuit. You mentioned there was conflict with the neighbors."

"I shall be glad to do so, but I fear it will take some time."

"Watson and I can manage on our own. There was a public house – The Sleeping Swan, I believe? We shall meet there for supper at eight, to compare notes. Send Teddy back to Zane Hall around seven, and we shall come to the pub in your carriage."

Weldon nodded and hurried off to find Teddy. Holmes directed me toward the footpath, which wove around the tragic pond and on through an ancient forest.

"Holmes," I said, "I have been your friend long enough to recognize a goose chase! Why did you send your client off on one?"

"Watson, recall his very words to me . . . *He wishes me to fail in my quest.* Or, more particularly, he doesn't wish to know the identity of the murderer. Therefore, I seek to spare him, while honoring the obligation to the late Mr. Zane. Let us put some questions to Teddy's assistant."

Another half-mile brought us to a modest cottage. An elderly woman, her face puffy and her eyes red from weeping, opened the door. Holmes greeted her with a smile.

"Good afternoon, Madam. We are historical researchers from London and – Dear me, someone sounds quite ill."

A harsh, painful cough echoed the dimness of the home. The woman wrung her hands together.

"My little grandson, sir – here to spend the summer with me, and – "
More painful noises rose over her words. "Oh, what shall I do? He needs a doctor, and I have not a shilling to spare. I will have to send for his father, who is in Scotland, and – "

"I am a doctor," I said. "I will be happy to advise you."

She seized my arm so vigorously I nearly stumbled. The boy was lying on a cot, behind a tattered curtain. He tried to crawl beneath the covers, but I was able to coax him to sit up and let me take his pulse and peer into his throat, then place my palm on his forehead.

"No more than a summer cold, I think, but we shouldn't allow it to remain untreated. Tea with lemon and honey will be needed. He will also require some medical powders to help him rest."

"But I have no money!"

"Please allow me to assist," Holmes said, pressing a guinea into her hand. "He reminds me of my own boy. Watson can write out a prescription which the local apothecary will fill. We shall both be glad to stay with Master – "

"Jonesy, sir," the boy whispered.

"A fine name! We will stay with you until your grandmother's return."

The old woman nodded, blessed us a thousand times, and hurried off toward the village. The little sufferer looked relieved to see his elder depart.

"She fusses so . . . Are you gents really from London? Have you ever met the Queen?"

"I have indeed made that Gracious Lady's acquaintance," Holmes said, as casually as if discussing an aged auntie. "She is rarely in residence at Buckingham Palace, however. She prefers to be at Windsor, where she often visits the resting place of her husband, the late Prince Consort, and gazes upon his effigy. Perhaps you understand, Master Jonesy . . . and even know of someone who also visited a special place, to look upon the image of a lost loved one."

The lad suddenly wiggled back down in the covers, drawing them up to his eyes.

"Jonesy," Holmes said, very gently, "I am going to perform a magic trick. I will tell you exactly what you did that was very naughty." Holmes sat at the foot of the bed, his eyes narrowing. "Two nights ago, you left your grandmother dozing and went to Zane Hall, where you met with Teddy Ross. You planned a bit of fun at the old Mr. Zane's expense. When you reached the temple, Teddy had already opened the iron bars, and the statute of David was removed."

"Oh no, sir! It was there!"

I started. My friend rarely erred in his little recitations. Holmes arched a skeptical eyebrow. The boy dropped the cover from his face and grinned.

"I had to help him move the statue! He had it loose from the pedestal, but then we had to carry it off."

"To the hole you two had dug in the garden?"

"Just so!"

Holmes offered me a sly wink. "Afterward, you removed your clothes. It must have been uncomfortable standing there with no attire, as if you had just stepped from the bath."

"He gave me a little apron to wrap around my waist. It was rather nippy on the backside, though."

"And how did it feel when he dumped the sacks of flour over your head?"

"It tickled. It made me sneeze!" The boy had clearly warmed to his tale. "Teddy put me in a pose and told me to hold still. Then he went and threw rocks at the old gent's bedroom window. A minute later, he came running back, saying Mr. Zane was walking out. 'Remember,' he said, 'when he comes to the bars, open your eyes and moan loudly.'"

"And did you?"

"Yes, sir – just as he said. I thought it was good sport." The lad's face suddenly became solemn. "I heard Mr. Zane come up and exclaim that the bars were ajar. I opened my eyes and made a loud noise, waving my arms a bit. The gent gave an awful shriek and started galloping away. I jumped down and looked out, and I saw him fall and Teddy jump out from behind a bush and hurry up to him. I started to go to them, but Teddy shouted at me that Mr. Zane had fainted, and I should run home quickly and not tell anyone what we had done. Teddy said he would bring my clothes to me later. I took off like a racehorse, and I was all the way to the pond when I realized I could hardly go home covered in flour. I dove into pond to get clean."

"Which explains how you caught cold," I said, reaching out to ruffle his hair.

"Yes, sir. Grandmother was still asleep, and I pulled on my nightshirt and got into bed without her knowing I'd been out. But the next morning I was shaking and coughing and blowing my nose. When she finally thinks to ask where my clothes are, I'm sure to get in trouble."

Holmes smiled and removed the boy's attire from inside his coat. "Here is your reward for being honest with us."

"Oh, thank you, sir! You've spared me a whipping!"

"Holmes," I said, as we made our way back to Zane Hall, "I must confess I find myself rather disappointed."

55

"How do, Watson?"

"I had begun to suspect something diabolical – not supernatural, of course, but a human form of evil – had conspired to end the old man's life. To learn it was nothing more than the tragic outcome of a boyish prank! This will not go down as one of your more interesting cases!"

"Perhaps you should reserve that judgement until the case is at an end, which it is not. One more interview needs to be conducted."

He gestured with his cane toward the house. I shook my head.

"The poor mother will be devastated to learn that her boy's folly has killed a man."

Holmes said nothing. A few moments later, we entered, and Holmes requested Mrs. Ross to join us in the dining room, beneath the gaze of Queen Catherine Howard's portrait.

"Madam," he said, without any soothing preamble, "I must put a few questions to you. I wish you to know that your future, and Teddy's, hinges upon your honesty."

"Sir, I do not – "

"All I require is a shovel to complete my case against your son. Once I unearth the plaster statue of David, I will prove Teddy is responsible for your employer's death. A conversation with the grocer – who sold you the fine and expensive white flour, hardly an item that either a boy or a stingy employer would purchase – will confirm your complicity."

The lady took a step, staggered, and tugged at her wimple. She turned away from us, her entire body shaking.

"Madame," Holmes continued, his voice suddenly gentle, "David, your older son, has been avenged."

I confess that my jaw dropped. Holmes rose, took the photograph of the deceased boy, and placed it on the table.

"The resemblance is remarkable. Not only does the child share your long nose, but he greatly favors his half-brother, Teddy, though your living child is far more robust." Holmes pulled out a chair, and with a studied courtliness handed Mrs. Ross into it before resuming his seat. "You are David's mother, and David's death was not an accident."

"Your reputation is well-deserved," the lady finally said. "I can do nothing but tell you my story and throw myself and my son upon your mercy.

"I was one of Zane's first servants when he inherited the hall, a lowly scullery maid. He came into my room and assaulted me one night, telling me that should I report his abuse, no one would believe me, and he would turn my poor widowed mother out of her cottage on his estate. I fled his service the next day and went to London, where in due time I learned I was with child. My mother was so distraught – she chose to believe I had taken a lover in defiance of our strict religious faith – that she sickened and died. Someone – a false friend – told Zane of my condition, and when David was but a month old, Zane arrived at my miserable dwelling. I awakened from a weary nap to find Zane looming over my son's cradle.

"'I see the child is male, and healthy,' he sneered. 'My status requires an heir, but I have no use for a wife. I will take him as a ward, and in time adopt him. You may follow, to be his nursemaid, if you agree to never speak of his origin. I warn you, if you reject my offer now, it will not be repeated.'

"I considered screaming, but none in that filthy lodging house would have raised a hand to assist me. I was nearly starving, barely able to give my child nourishment. I consented because I felt I had no choice – I was nothing but a poor, ignorant, helpless girl who had given birth to a child out of wedlock. I feared if I said no, I would soon be dead, and my son in the grave beside me. I bowed my head and accepted Zane's conditions.

"For five years, my life was miserable, but at least David thrived, and I remained at his side, able to love and care for him. Zane never abused me again, though I always slept with a dagger beneath my pillow. As David grew, Zane became more demanding of him . . . My child was always delicate, and Zane sought to toughen him with sports and exercise. That Christmas, David didn't wish for skates. He was afraid of the pond in winter, for he had witnessed a sheep falling through the ice and perishing. But Zane insisted it was safe. The morning after Christmas, I heard Zane dragging David out before the dawn, to 'take his exercise' with his new gift. My son was crying and pleading that it was too cold, he didn't wish to go. I threw on a wrapper and met them in the hall, but Zane ordered me back into my room, saying a woman had no place in manly excursions.

"Zane forced David onto the ice, and when it broke, Zane didn't go to his son's aid. Instead, he came back and raised the alarm, as if he had just discovered David was missing. He blamed David's death on the child being impulsive and disobedient, and on me for not preventing him from leaving the nursey."

"How are you certain Zane didn't try to save his son?" I asked.

The lady wiped at a tear. "Zane was a coward. And he couldn't swim. His clothes were completely dry when he came inside and began to shout that David was gone from the nursery. Shall I continue?"

Holmes nodded solemnly. "Please do."

"I fainted upon learning the truth. But when I recovered, I went into the study, where Zane was drinking, and lost all control of my senses, screaming that I would turn him in to the authorities. It was foolish of me, but I was wild with grief. I even rushed at him with my dagger, but he easily punched me in the face and took it from me. He then seized a riding crop and began to beat me. He would have killed me had the Weldons and their son not arrived when they did. Mrs. Weldon took me aside and listened to my tale. I couldn't tell if she believed me – why should she take the word of a disgraced servant over that of her brother? But she gave me enough money to escape the horrors of Zane Hall. I dared not linger to attend David's funeral, for fear Zane would have me arrested."

"Years passed. I was blessed to meet a fine man, James Ross, a carriage driver at Wildlocke, an estate in Sussex. He found me a position in service there, and in time we were married and had Teddy. I never told James about David, only that my life before meeting him had been painful and tragic – good man that he was, he never asked for further explanation.

"Four years ago, there was a tragedy at Wildlocke, a fire in the stables. James bravely ran inside, to rescue the horses. I was helping the rest of the servants form a bucket brigade. I was closest to a wall, which suddenly crumpled, knocking me to the ground beneath it. When I awakened, I was an object of pity, and my husband was dead. But the master of Wildlocke was a good, kind man who paid for doctors and the hospital, and established an annuity for me, so I might live quietly and never need work again.

"It was while I recovered that Teddy came across an old trunk of mine, which contained a picture of David. He begged me to tell him who this child was, noting that he and the boy were so alike. I revealed everything that I had kept hidden and, in doing so, felt anger burn inside me, as hot as the fire that had destroyed half my face and stolen my beloved husband. Teddy was outraged as well, and to amuse ourselves through long hours of my healing, we spun fantasies of how we might murder Zane.

"At last, we made a plan – I was now unrecognizable to anyone who had known me in the past, and Teddy was a total stranger. We came to Zane Hall eight months ago and simply knocked on the door, claiming to be impoverished servants seeking positions. We had decided that if we were hired, it was a signal, that Heaven blessed our cause. Zane was alone – he had just driven away a butler and a maid – and he gave not a glance to our false references but hired us instantly when we agreed to accept rather low wages. Mrs. Weldon knew nothing of it, of course, and all I shared with others was a lie. I had plotted ways to poison Zane, or drown him, but in the end, I couldn't lift my hand to take his life. I told my son we should leave. Teddy proposed the scheme to have his friend impersonate the statute, saying that at least he would have the satisfaction of giving a bad man a good scare. I don't believe for a moment Teddy intended the fright to be fatal – nor would he willingly have done anything to cause trouble for Jonesy. That, I swear upon my soul, is the truth. If you must arrest someone, please let it be me! Just allow my boy to flee – I will gladly hang in his place."

Sherlock Holmes shook his head. "Madame," he said, "let me propose another solution . . . ."

"Mr. Holmes, Doctor Watson – I was beginning to think you had forgotten me and . . . My word, you seem to have been doing a bit of farming!"

This exclamation was well founded, for despite our precautions in removing jackets and rolling up sleeves, we were both quite filthy and disheveled from our labors. We looked, and no doubt smelled, more like village rustics than proper London gentlemen.

"We have been industrious today," Holmes cheerfully agreed. "Two orders of fish and chips wouldn't go amiss, along with a pair of pints."

For almost an hour we feasted and drank, with Holmes regaling his client with amusing stories of other adventures. A few of the tales were truthful, though quite embellished. At last, Holmes consulted his watch.

"It grows late, so I will no longer delay in completing my task. Mr. Weldon, you hired me in fulfillment of your uncle's last wishes, to discover the identity of his murderer. I have done so."

Weldon gasped. "Uncle Julius *was* murdered?"

"As surely and intentionally as if shot or stabbed in the heart, and yet no human hand touched him. However, as I understand the charge, I am also under no obligation to *reveal* the name of his killer to you."

Our client had leaned forward in eager anticipation, but now he fell back against the wooden booth.

"Why . . . yes, that is true."

"Therefore, I need not turn the murderer over to any authority for prosecution."

"But then how – ?"

"Watson is my witness to the solution of the crime. If you will accept his word as a gentleman that justice has been done, the matter is resolved."

"Why, of course. But . . . can you at least tell me *why* Uncle was killed?"

"The murder was an intensely personal matter, related to your uncle's manifold wickedness. In this case, the line is so thin between vengeance and an Act of God that I think we do well not to quibble over it. Can you agree?"

"Yes," Weldon said, sighing as if some great burden had been lifted from his shoulders. "I will say no more about the matter."

"Excellent. Then let us celebrate the solution of the second mystery."

"Second mystery?" Weldon murmured, as Holmes signaled for the barmaid to remove the plates and glasses. "I was not aware there was another question."

"Were you not curious as to where you uncle procured his wealth, and where he might have hidden it from you?"

Holmes placed a canvas bag upon the table, gesturing for Weldon to open it.

"Rather dirty, I fear, but a careful cleaning will restore what remains to its former glory. Surely the item is familiar?"

Weldon reached into the bag, moving slowly, as if he expected to find a serpent within. He started when his fingers touched metal. He pulled the object free, gasping in shock, turning it over and over in his hands.

"Why, it's Queen Catherine's tiara! From the portrait!"

"Sent as a gift to your ancestress. Afterward, it vanished," Holmes said, "for three centuries. Perhaps an earlier heir hid it in some secret panel during a time of civil turmoil. Wherever it was secreted, the knowledge of it was lost, or surely by now more than a quarter of its diamonds would be missing. My deduction is that your uncle discovered it shortly after inheriting the property. Being careful not to raise suspicions, he harvested the jewels slowly, selling them in London whenever he needed an influx of cash, while claiming the funds came from wise investments. There are fourteen diamonds remaining."

"But where was it?"

"Hidden inside the statue of David, which perhaps explains why the piece was so twisted and malformed, as Zane had to chisel out and then reshape portions of it each time he removed a single diamond. Once we retrieved the statue – No, I shall not tell you where we found it! – we destroyed it in the process of retrieving the tiara. However, you can now commission a more appropriate memorial to David's memory."

"But how on earth did you guess it?"

Holmes shook his head. "I never guess. I felt certain Zane had found something of great value within the house, based on your description of how quickly his financial status improved. The painting, as well as his taunting of you about using your profession, made the connection. Misers, in my experience, enjoy putting their wealth before the nose of one who may never enjoy it. Your description of David's plaster statue as ill-formed and lumpy immediately suggested that in the decades since the child's passing, the memorial was tampered with – and instantly, I imagined its use as the hiding place for Zane's precious artefact." Holmes tapped his temple. "Imagination is central to the detective's craft, and to the historian's as well."

Weldon pulled out a handkerchief and mopped his brow.

"Sir, this . . . this is astonishing. It means – I hardly know how to say it, but there is a lady – Christiana – I love her, yet – We dared not wed because I earned so little money – and now – !" His hands were quivering too hard to grasp the precious artifact. It rattled onto the table. "Mr. Holmes, just one more thing: Are you certain the villain who killed my uncle knows nothing of this and will never harm me or my dear future wife, in pursuit of it?"

Holmes and I exchanged a knowing glance, both of us thinking how Mrs. Ross and Teddy were already on their way toward Edinburgh, where the lad hoped to eventually enroll in medical school.

"I guarantee your safety," Holmes said. "My heartiest congratulations upon your impending nuptials. A warm bath at Baker Street beckons, and we have just time to catch the evening train . . . though as malodorous as Watson is, we may be forced to travel in third class!"

The Case of the
Three Cufflinks
by Steve Lockley

In all the years I have known my friend Mr. Sherlock Holmes, there have been many times when I thought he would never find the solution to a problem, but he has never failed in his task, as far as I'm aware.

I have been sure to record details of his cases, a number of which have appeared in issues of *The Strand* magazine, but there have been a few which Holmes thought too trivial to be worth mentioning. While at no point did he attempt to suppress or censor my writing, he clearly felt that some investigations had little or no merit. There were also cases presented to him that held his interest even if there was no loss to the person with the problem, no death, no great element of law-breaking, and yet the puzzle had left the potential client uneasy.

Holmes rarely accepted payment for such cases as these, as many took little more than an hour or two of his time, often without him even needing to leave Baker Street. One such matter involved the widow of a military man I had known during my own service, and I confess that I was instrumental in bringing the matter to his attention. In truth, I had hoped to solve the mystery myself, but had reached the conclusion that a solution was impossible to find. I suppose I was hoping that Holmes would agree with my assessment, despite how much I wanted the woman to find peace of mind.

I hadn't met Mrs. Anson before the day she called on me in Baker Street. Holmes was pursuing an interest of his own and not expected to return before late that evening at the earliest. There was always the possibility that he would not put in an appearance until the following day. Such were his habits at times. I was taking the opportunity to catch up on my reading of some medical journals. More than one of them had been mutilated by the removal of an article, doubtless something that had caught Holmes's interest. When Mrs. Hudson announced that I had a visitor and ushered the woman inside, she seemed to know me, though I was sure I had never set eyes on her before that moment.

"Dr. Watson," the woman said, holding one hand well out in front of her in greeting. "My husband thought very highly of you, and often remarked on your exploits when he followed them in *The Strand*."

It took me a moment to realise just who her husband might have been. "Major Anson?" I asked cautiously.

"That's correct, though sadly he is no longer with us."

"I'm so sorry to hear that, Mrs. Anson." I said, memories of the man now coming back to me with no difficulty at all. "He was a fine fellow."

"Thank you, Doctor. He often said that he owed the later years of his life to you and your skill with a needle."

I remembered vividly the injuries he had sustained in battle. I had done my best to save his life, and his leg, though I was sure that there would have been long-lasting effects from his injuries. "I am so glad that he had a life after his trauma," I said. "So many didn't."

"Indeed," she replied, and then fell silent, as if unsure of how to ask whatever she had come to discuss. I gave her a moment to gather her thoughts.

"I received a note a few days ago," she started eventually. "From Asprey's. It said that the item my husband had ordered from them was ready for collection. I immediately thought that he had perhaps ordered something for my birthday."

"A quite reasonable assumption," I said. Asprey's was indeed amongst the finest jewellers in the country. While it would have been tinged with sadness, I was sure it would have brought her solace, a reminder of a long and happy marriage.

"But it wasn't for me," she said and dabbed a handkerchief to the corner of one eye. My mind raced with possibilities I didn't wish to consider. Although it had been some years since I had spent any time in the company of her late husband, he had seemed devoted to his wife. I suspected that whatever I said next was unlikely to be the right response, and so I waited for her to explain.

"It was a cufflink," she said. "Identical to a pair he already owned. They had been left to him by his father."

I started to consider all the possibilities. "Perhaps he had lost one, and had a replacement made, only to later find the missing one." That seemed the most likely, but when I suggested it, Mrs. Anson didn't think so.

"That was my first thought too," she said, "but when I returned home, I found that he still had both in the case in which he always kept them. He always took such great care of them," she added. "He valued them far more than any of the medals he won for his service in the army."

"He was a very brave man," I said, and there was no doubt in my mind that it was true. "I've known many officers that were happy to send men into battle while waiting at the rear, watching their men fall from a place of safety. That was never the case with your husband. He wouldn't ask his men to do anything he wasn't prepared to do himself. That was what made him both loved and respected."

She smiled. "That's very kind of you to say so, but I am sure that there are many others who did the same, and I include those who tended to the injuries of the fallen."

She reached across and placed a hand on mine. It was only a fleeting moment of tenderness, but it was matched by the glint of a tear in her eye.

"I admit that I am at a loss to explain why Major Anson might have commissioned an extra cufflink. I take it that Asprey's were unable to shed any light on the matter?"

"The gentleman who discussed the matter with my husband wasn't available when I collected the order. He's in Amsterdam at the moment, and won't return for a few days." She reached inside her handbag and produced two small boxes, one of which bore the Asprey's name, the other blank. She opened the latter first to reveal a pair of cufflinks with what appeared to be blue sapphires, each set in a rectangular gold cartouche. They were indeed beautiful things.

"These were in my late husband's bedside drawer. That is the box in which he always kept them." She passed it over, but before I had the opportunity to take a closer look, she opened the other box to reveal a link that appeared identical to the first. "This is the one I collected from Asprey's."

"If it's only a few days before the gentleman returns from Amsterdam, he may have the answers you are looking for."

"Let us hope so," she said. "But there is an extra element to the mystery."

"Oh? And what might that be?"

"The gentleman at Asprey's said that someone else tried to claim the single cufflink only a day or so before I received the note to say it was ready for collection. It was a man who appeared to have been down on his luck."

For a moment I was lost for words. Who else could possibly have known about it? "I trust they sent him away with a flea in his ear."

"They told him he would have to return with the receipt they had given to my husband."

"How strange," I said. "Did they inform the police of the matter?"

"I believe not," she answered. "They said that as no crime had been committed, they didn't wish to involve the authorities. But that was when they wrote the letter to me to say that the item was ready for collection."

I nodded in understanding. A reputable company like Asprey's would rather not have its clients see the police coming and going.

"What would you like me to do?" I asked, suspecting that I already knew the answer.

"I was rather hoping that you might solve the riddle, Doctor Watson. I have been unable to sleep with this preying on my mind. My lawyer has been a great help in resolving other matters, but there are still so many things for me to deal with, and this is just one more burden. I know that you have helped Mr. Sherlock Holmes in the past, and am sure that you are in a better position to gain answers than I."

I assured her that I would do what I could, but wasn't convinced that it would be possible to answer all of her questions. My hopes lay with the person in Asprey's who had taken the order to make the new cufflink, and the possibility that the Major had told him the reason for requesting it.

As she got up to leave, she noticed an invitation to a regimental dinner I had left on the mantelpiece. It was only then that I realised that I would almost certainly have seen the Major there, had he still been alive.

"Will you be attending?" she asked. "Please say you will."

I was a little taken aback by her sudden outburst, but I told her that indeed I would.

"Thank goodness," she said. "At least I will know someone there."

"You will be attending?" I asked, a little surprised.

"I will. A number of the wives of officers who are no longer with us have been invited to attend in their husband's place. When the organisers heard about my husband, they extended the offer to me in his stead. I rather suspect that we women will be shunted off into another room once the meal is over so that you men may share your war stories without troubling our delicate ears." She at least raised a smile at the latter comment.

As she left, she gave me the note she had received from Asprey's stating that the cufflink was ready for collection. I was still examining it and the three cufflinks, trying to find any differences, when Holmes returned from his excursion. I was pleased to see that he showed no sign of having visited one of the opium dens, which had been my greatest concern. At first, he seemed to pay no attention to what I was doing, instead falling into his armchair with a heavy sigh.

"There are times, Watson, when I despair at the matters the detectives at Scotland Yard consider to be baffling, and I include Inspector Lestrade in that category."

"Had to put one of them in his place today, did you?" I laughed. I was being facetious, but Holmes took it as an acknowledgement of his superior faculties.

He turned in his chair to face me, one arm hooked across the back of the chair. "I see you've had a visitor," he said.

I set the note down and gave him my full attention. I had already decided that I would probably need to ask his advice, and it was likely to come unbidden if I simply gave him the time and opportunity. It appeared to have come sooner than I had anticipated.

"I suppose you've deduced that from the fact that I'm examining things that weren't here when you left earlier?"

"On the contrary. I caught the faint trace of rosewater when I entered the room, a fragrance I am sure neither you nor Mrs. Hudson is in the custom of wearing." He paused for a moment and gave the slightest of smiles before continuing. "From that, I assume your visitor was a woman, probably of middle age. The fact that the perfume was still in the air meant that she left only recently, and was probably the same woman I saw getting into a cab as I approached from the end of the street. As she was a woman alone, and you never consult patients from these rooms, you are already acquainted with her, or with a close member of her family."

Not once during his stream of statements did he look in my direction, seeming to be disinterested in the objects on the table in front of me.

"She left some objects with you, no doubt of sentimental value, and as I caught sight of them when I came into the room, I take them to be cufflinks, though there appears to be one missing. As it seems unlikely that you would be consulted simply about a missing cufflink, there is a greater mystery at the heart of the matter. But why would she consult you rather than the police – or me? It can only mean she thinks that it might turn out to have a simple explanation, and couldn't bear the embarrassment. How am I doing so far?"

This time he barely paused for breath before adding, "I assume these cufflinks belonged to her late husband, who you served alongside in the army. Perhaps you even saved his life, though I must admit that the latter is a mere possibility."

It was only then that he looked in my direction, and while his look could be described as self-satisfied, and he didn't need me to confirm that he was right in every respect, he was still looking for me to respond. I took a breath, then related the details of the meeting that had taken place, doing my best to leave not a single detail out, no matter how trivial it might seem. Only when I had finished did he join me at the table, magnifying glass at the ready.

"Do you mind?" he asked, motioning towards the cufflinks as he sat down opposite me. I pushed the two boxes towards him and watched in silence as he examined each one in turn, replacing them in the same position.

"This one," he said, pointing to the Asprey's box, "is the new one, though it's nearly identical to the other two. While there are minor differences between each of them, as you would expect in any item made by hand, this one bears the current hallmark, while the other two are dated as almost fifty years old. Despite that, however, all three were made by Asprey's, and the level of workmanship is identical, though it's hard to believe that they could have been made by the same hand given the time that has passed. I suspect that an expert in the field might be able to recognise the differences, but they are outside my area of expertise. The obvious answer would be that your client's husband – "

"She isn't my client," I interrupted. "She's the widow of a man I admired."

"Yes, yes, of course," he said with a wave of his hand. "The obvious answer is that Major Anson lost one of his cufflinks and ordered a replacement to be made. By the time of his death, and before the work had been completed, he had found the missing item."

"That was my thinking too," I said, relieved that he had reached the same conclusion, but then crestfallen with his next statement.

"But if a man had lost a cufflink and wanted a replacement made, wouldn't he have taken them to the jeweller in the box in which he usually kept them in? Why would he still have his original cufflinks at home?"

"Sentimental reasons?" I suggested.

"Sentiment? Well, I suppose that's more your area than mine, but in this case, I don't think it would be the actions of a man with a rational mind. No, his widow has reasons for concern."

"Concern?"

"It may be nothing, but this is a mystery that deserves due attention."

"I don't see what we can do until the man at Asprey's returns," I said. "We just have to wait and speak to him then."

"But he isn't the only member of staff there who has been involved in this matter. There is also whoever dealt with the mystery man who tried to claim the new cufflink."

"Do you think that's important?"

"Almost certainly. This man, whoever he was, knew that the cufflink was there. And at that time, not even the major's wife was aware of that. The question is: How did he know?"

Not for the first time, I felt stupid that I hadn't thought of this myself. Of course, this was a bigger mystery than why the major had ordered the replacement to be made in the first place.

"We'll visit them first thing in the morning," Holmes said. "It will be too late to see anyone now. In the meantime, we must consider what other courses of action we might take."

He returned to his armchair after retrieving his pipe and the Persian slipper from where it hung beside the fireplace. I knew better than to interrupt him when he was deep in concentration, and took the opportunity to take one last look at the cufflinks before I closed the two boxes. At least it was just tobacco he had turned to.

The following morning found us in New Bond Street, at the premises of Asprey's within minutes of them opening their doors for the day. It took only the matter of a minute or two to determine which of the men behind the counter had dealt with the person who had tried to claim the cufflink.

"I was taken aback that the gentleman knew that we had been working on the piece for Major Anson. I have to admit that he didn't look like the kind of client we usually have on these premises, if you understand me, sir."

The corners of Holmes's lips twitched. "Perhaps you could describe him for us."

"Well, sir, I'm not sure that I paid that much attention to him."

"Please try," Holmes said, clearly trying to hold back his impatience.

"He wasn't a young man, sir. Perhaps in his fifties, though I could not say so with any certainty. His hair and beard were dark and unkempt, and he wore a greatcoat, even though the weather was fairly clement. The coat had seen better days, and while I am not particularly familiar with that specific garment, I suspected it might have been of the sort issued to a military man. One thing I did notice was that he kept his hands thrust in his pockets, his shoulders hunched over. If I were to guess, sir, I would describe him as a gentleman down on his luck."

"Bravo," said Holmes. "You use the word 'gentleman'. Was that word well-chosen? Or is it simply a habit of your trade."

"Oh no, sir. That's why I said I thought he was down on his luck. He was polite and well-spoken. An educated person. Not a man born to the streets, if you understand what I mean, sir."

Holmes thanked him effusively after he had established that the man who had accepted the order for the replacement, who the attendant referred to as "Young Mr. Asprey", was due to return the following day.

"What do you make of that?" Holmes asked as we walked along New Bond Street. I had expected him to hail a cab, but he seemed determined to walk. It was barely a mile-and-a-half, and it was a pleasant day, so I welcomed the opportunity, provided that he didn't go marching off at a pace I might have difficulty keeping up with. Fortunately, he seemed to be more-than-happy to take his time.

"I don't know what to make of it," I said. "Perhaps the man overheard the Major when he placed the order."

"Possible, but unlikely," Holmes said. "The mystery man doesn't sound like a regular visitor to New Bond Street, and I'm sure he would have been noticed."

"I suppose," I said. "But that doesn't really tell us why the Major ordered the cufflink in the first place."

"On the contrary. I think it tells us everything."

"Really?" I said, stopping in my tracks.

"Oh, there are still a few loose ends," Holmes said, "but I see no reason why we might not tie them all up before young Mr. Asprey returns from his trip to the Continent. Do you mind continuing to Baker Street without me? I have an errand to run, but if anyone calls asking for me, please ask them to wait. I shouldn't be more than an hour or two."

Without waiting for a reply, he turned on his heels and cut down one of the side streets, leaving me standing open-mouthed for a moment before I continued on my way. Clearly, Holmes had something in his head that he didn't feel the need to share with me, but if he was going to concern himself with the mystery man in the great coat, I would keep my thoughts fixed on why the Major would have had the cufflink made in the first place. It might not be possible to get the answer until Mr. Asprey returned, but that didn't mean I couldn't consider all the possibilities. I determined that, as soon as I returned to Baker Street, I would take the opportunity to set them all down on paper and follow Holmes's abiding principles.

I had barely been at the table in our rooms for more than half-an-hour, the cufflinks in front of me once more and my notebook open, when Mrs. Hudson knocked on the door.

"There's a visitor for Mr. Holmes," she said, though she didn't seem particularly happy about it.

"Ah," I said. "I understand that he is expected. Holmes will be back shortly, and he asked me to make sure that his visitor waited for him. Best send him up."

Mrs. Hudson pursed her lips and gave a huff before leaving the room. I heard her soft and steady footsteps on the stairs as she made her way down, an exchange of voices, followed by a thunder of feet as someone hurried upstairs. I wasn't surprised when the newcomer burst into the room to announce himself as one of those street Arabs that Holmes called upon from time to time.

"Well, well, if it isn't young Wiggins," I said. "And what brings you here in such a hurry?"

"Wotcha, Doctor Watson," the boy panted. "Mister 'Olmes is looking for some information. Said 'e would pay double if one of us got back 'ere before him."

"And what information might that be?"

"Ah, that's for Mister 'Olmes's ears only."

"Nonsense," I said. "How much has he promised you?"

"Seven bob if I got 'ere with the information before 'e got back."

Seven shillings? I couldn't imagine Holmes offering him that much money, no matter what he had been asked to discover. And if I was being completely honest, I didn't trust the boy and his gang as much as Holmes did.

"Then I suppose you had better sit down," I said, offering him one of the chairs at the table. Mrs. Hudson would never forgive me if I allowed him to sit in one of the armchairs. "Would you like a glass of water?"

"Wouldn't mind a beer," Wiggins replied, a cheeky grin across his face. I was about to berate him when I heard the front door open, soon followed by the unmistakable sound of Holmes taking the stairs two at a time.

"Wiggins!" he proclaimed when he entered. "I was rather hoping you would be waiting for me. What news?"

"Found him," Wiggins said, thrusting out his chest with pride.

"Already?"

"I know where 'e'll be at seven tonight."

"And that is good enough for us, isn't it Watson?"

"Is it?" I said. "I don't even know who we're talking about."

"Why, the man who tried to claim the cufflink, of course. So where might we find him?"

"Near The Blind Beggar, Whitechapel. There's a warehouse they use as like a church. They bribe people in with food. 'E's been there for the last few nights. One of the boys reckons that 'e beds down for the night not far from there."

Holmes retrieved a number of coins from his pocket and dropped them into the boy's hand. "Meet us outside The Blind Beggar at a quarter-to-seven and lead us to this warehouse, and I'll give you the rest then."

"Need me to bring any of the boys?"

"I don't think that will be necessary. Thank you again for your assistance."

"See you later," Wiggins said then headed out, the coins jangling in his pocket.

"Are you going to tell me what this is all about?" I asked. "And who this mystery man is?"

"All in good time," Holmes smiled as he dropped into his chair and reached for his pipe.

"But this is the man who visited Asprey's?" I asked.

"Indeed it is," Holmes said. "And now I need you to pay a visit to Mrs. Anson before this evening. I need to know if she's received an unexpected delivery recently."

"Delivery? What kind of delivery?"

70

"That would be telling," Holmes replied. "But tell her to hang onto it – or better still, bring it back with you. I suspect it will be needed very soon."

Holmes could be infuriating at times. He clearly knew far more than he was letting on. It was so frustrating when he kept things like this from me, but I was happy to play my part. I was still no further forward with my own list of possibilities as far as the cufflink was concerned, and perhaps the walk would do me good.

Mrs. Anson was surprised to see me, but welcomed me into her home, offering me refreshments. I wanted to address the matter at hand without delay.

"Do you have news?" she asked when she had shown me into the sitting room filled with mementoes of her late husband's exploits, including a portrait of him in full dress uniform above the fireplace.

"Not yet, but Holmes expects to learn more this evening."

"Mr. Holmes is involved? There really was no need for that, surely? I just needed to understand what had happened to give me peace of mind."

"When Holmes gets an idea into his head," I said, "it's impossible to dislodge it."

"So what can I do for you, Doctor Watson?"

"It's actually Sherlock Holmes who has sent me," I said. "He would like to know if you've received any unexpected parcels since your husband's death."

She said that she hadn't, but then a curious look passed across her face. "Well, there has been one thing," she added. "I've been meaning to return it, but somehow . . . ."

A tear sprang to her eye, and I did my best to reassure her, but I'm not sure that it made any difference. "These things take time," he said. "Is there anything I can do to help?"

"Oh, could you, Doctor Wason? That would be so kind. Let me get it."

She rose to her feet and hurried out of the room, leaving me surrounded by all the memories the major had left behind – the record of a career of great bravery. Mrs. Avery returned only a few moments later with a bulky parcel wrapped in brown paper, with only enough torn away to reveal its contents.

"It's a new uniform," she said. "I assume he had ordered it for the dinner, but I can't think why he needed it, as his dress uniform is still in pristine condition, hanging in his closet. Could you possibly return it for me and explain the circumstances?"

"Of course. It would be my pleasure." I stood and took the parcel from her, barely giving it a glance.

"And could you provide me with any news you may have in your investigation? I would feel a lot happier if you were able to identify the would-be thief who tried to obtain my husband's cufflinks. That is another mystery now weighing on my mind."

"I hope we will have news this evening, if all goes as Holmes expects, but I would hate to make any promises."

"Please, Doctor, if you learn anything, anything at all, please let me know in the morning."

"Of course I will. I'll call on you with an update, whether we have success or not."

"Thank you so much," she said and showed me out.

I returned to Baker Street to find our rooms filled with a fug of smoke. I set the parcel down and opened the windows, keen to let the product of Holmes's pipe out, and some fresh air in.

"I see that my suspicion was correct," Holmes said, launching himself out of his chair. He bent to examine the package without moving it from its resting place on the table. "Have you opened it?"

"Not at all," I told him. "And neither had Mrs. Anson. But it appears to be a replacement dress uniform for the major, ready for the dinner."

"Oh, I think you'll be surprised when you open it," Holmes said.

"Open it?"

"Of course. How else are you going to know what's inside?"

"But I can see what it is," I said.

"No. You are making an assumption based on seeing a piece of what is inside, and the person to whom the package is addressed. Open it."

I started to worry at the knot in the string, but then Holmes handed me a pocketknife with one of its many blades exposed. In a fraction of the time it would have taken me to release the knots, I had the package open. I folded the blade back and returned it before I completely unwrapped it.

"I don't understand," I said as I unfolded it. "They must have sent the wrong uniform."

I held up the jacket and saw that this wasn't intended for the major. It wasn't even a uniform for his regiment.

"There is of course another possibility," said Holmes.

"And what might that be?"

"There's time enough for that later," Holmes said. "First, we have other matters to attend to. I'm sure you will piece it all together as the night wears on. For now, we need to get ourselves into place in plenty of time. There might even be the opportunity to find something to eat while we wait."

The mention of food reminded me that there was an emptiness in my stomach, as I hadn't eaten since breakfast. Somehow the hours had slipped away.

Holmes had insisted that I wear my old coat, the nearest piece of clothing I had to looking rough and worn out, while he had something from his seemingly endless supply of working men's attire. While we attracted one or two glances from the drinkers in The Blind Beggar, we didn't seem to be gathering excessive attention. Holmes pointed me in the direction of an unoccupied table and went to the bar where a wary-looking harridan stood in attendance. He joined me just a couple of minutes later, carrying two foaming glasses of beer.

"Two pies on their way," he said, to my relief, as he set the glasses down. More than once he had been frustrated by the way my stomach dictated my day, but today he seemed to be particularly considerate.

"About the uniform," I said, and saw a twinkle in his eye as he regarded me over the rim of his glass.

"You've had a thought?" he said.

"The uniform was clearly not intended for the major. It's for the wrong regiment, and I could be wrong, but I suspect it would have been a little on the small side for him."

"Go on," Holmes said as our pies arrived.

"Clearly the uniform belongs to someone else."

"Obviously," he said as I cut into my pie.

"Beef-and-oyster," I said, my mouth suddenly watering. "Good choice."

Holmes laughed. "It's the only pie they do. But please, go on. What else can we say about the uniform?"

"There has been a mistake, and it was sent to the major in error."

"And how might that happen?"

"Perhaps his own uniform was being repaired and the two had been mixed up." In truth, the idea only came to me as I was speaking, summoned up largely by the thought of some stain at a previous dinner.

"That is certainly possible," said Holmes. "Did the major's widow say that his own uniform was missing?"

"Not at all. She mentioned that it's still hanging in his closet, in pristine condition. She didn't know why he had ordered another."

I was still wondering about that when the street door opened and closed, but I couldn't see if anyone had left. Or arrived, given the number of people standing near the bar and obscuring my view. Holmes pulled out his pocket watch briefly then turned to the door to see Wiggins making his way towards us. There were a few shouts and jeers at the boy's presence, but it all seemed good-natured.

"I've just seen 'im, Mr. 'Olmes," the boy said. "'E's gone inside the church already."

"Very good," Holmes said. "As you've come in to tell me this, I assume you've left someone on watch?"

"I 'ave," he said. "I know you said you didn't need me to bring any of the others, but they sometimes come down 'ere for sport, like."

"Hmm, breaking windows and throwing penny bangers no doubt," said Holmes without any sign of condemnation, but Wiggins looked crestfallen as if ashamed that their secret was out.

"How long is he usually inside?" I asked, not wishing to feel left out.

"'Alf-an-'our maybe," Wiggins said. "They get a bowl of broth and a piece of bread, but they 'ave to stay for prayers an' 'ymns an' that."

"A heavy price," Holmes laughed. "But we cannot risk losing our quarry."

"But you haven't touched your pie," I said, hurriedly finishing my own. Holmes pushed the plate in Wiggins's direction, and in an instant, it was as if it had never been there.

The warehouse was less than a matter of yards away, and Wiggins led us to where one of his confederates was keeping watch from the shadows. A trickle of men were making their way inside, being welcomed at the doorway by a uniformed gentleman that I recognised as belonging to the army of Salvationists led by the self-titled General William Booth.

Wiggins led us into the shadows where a smaller boy was waiting for us.

"'E's still inside," the boy said. "There's at least thirty of 'em in there now. You need me to 'ang around?"

Wiggins glanced at Holmes before he told him that he wouldn't be needed. Then he reached in his pocket and produced the pie Holmes had given him. The boy's eyes lit up, showing only the slightest hint of disappointment when Wiggins instructed him to share it with the others.

"Is our quarry's hidey-hole far from here?" Holmes asked, his eyes firmly fixed on the warehouse doors as they closed. Clearly, it wouldn't be easy for anyone to just slip away easily once they had eaten. I supposed that made it unlikely that the man Holmes was looking for would be leaving any time soon, but if all the men left together it might prove more difficult to pick out one man in particular, especially as neither of us had seen him before, but Holmes seemed confident enough. Wiggins gave him directions that suggested an area that Holmes was more familiar with than I, and then received another coin or two for his trouble before being sent on his way.

"Wouldn't it have been better if Wiggins had stayed with us?" I suggested.

"I think not. Two of us might follow him without difficulty, especially if we already know his likely destination, but three? And one of them a young urchin? Unlikely, I fear. We would attract too much attention. All we have to do is wait."

I couldn't help but think that we could have waited inside the alehouse. Instead, we stood in near silence as the flotsam and jetsam of humanity drifted past us, most of them unaware of our presence. A couple made their way towards the warehouse, but then turned away when they saw that the doors were already closed.

After a while, the sound of discordant singing came from the warehouse, and eventually its doors opened again and what was at first a trickle of men leaving soon became a flood. I hadn't thought there would be quite so many people in there.

"There's our man," Holmes said, grabbing my arm and pointing. How he managed to pick out the stranger amongst the crowd I had no idea, but there was a certainty in his voice. I couldn't even be sure which man he meant until the crowd thinned a little as they broke off in twos and threes, making it easier to spot what was unmistakeably an army greatcoat. He walked with a sight stoop, his hands thrust in his pockets, just as the man in Asprey's had described. Still holding my arm, Holmes tugged me out of the shadows, and we set off after him. We didn't have far to go before the man we were following had shed the others.

"A moment of your time, if you please, Captain Anson," Holmes called out to my surprise, and all three of us stopped in our tracks. The man ahead of us didn't turn at first, and I wondered if he was about to try to make his escape through the gaps between buildings on either side of the street, but eventually, he turned to face us.

"What do you want?" the man demanded, his hands still thrust in his pockets, his shoulders hunched. He seemed more wary than confrontational.

"To carry out your brother's wishes," Holmes said.

Brother? My mouth fell open in surprise and I could only watch as Holmes closed the distance to the man in the greatcoat, his left hand held out in greeting. It was only when the stranger did the same and shook it that I realised what I was looking at.

Within the hour, all three of us were back in Baker Street. We had stopped long enough to gather the man's few possessions from the ramshackle old boat shed down by the river that he had been calling home. I had been full of questions, but Holmes had insisted that the man should be allowed the opportunity to tell his story in his own time, and while Mrs. Hudson had given the man a disapproving look, she had said nothing when we took him upstairs.

"I really don't know where to start," the man said. He spoke as if even those words were hard to say.

"Why don't I tell you what we know?" Holmes said. "Then you can tell me if we've left anything out."

The man nodded and I saw a familiar look in his eye. I had seen it in enough patients who had suffered in conflict and were still haunted by their experiences. I felt the need to reassure him, but Holmes had already begun to reel off the litany of facts that he had deduced or discovered.

"You are Captain James Anson, brother of the late Major Henry Anson. You were injured in a conflict in India, and were presumed dead, though obviously your body wasn't retrieved."

I should have known. I looked at the man again I could see the similarity to his brother. He was younger, and had obviously lived a much tougher life in recent years, but there was a clear family resemblance.

"Someone cared for your wounds," Holmes continued. "Someone with at least a rudimentary knowledge of medicine. Your recovery may have taken some time, but you chose not to try to find your way back to your regiment, or to return to England immediately. Something must have changed to make you return . . . ."

"Amrit Singh," Anson said, a tear forming in his eye. "The man who saved me was called Amrit Singh. He found me when I was close to death, but he saved my life. Even when I was recovering, I knew that I owed him everything."

"But something changed that," Holmes said, clearly unable to hold back. "I assume that Amrit Singh died."

Anson nodded. "He was killed trying to protect me from a group of locals who had discovered that he was harbouring me. I managed to make my escape, abandoning my uniform with the exception of my greatcoat, which kept me warm when I slept under the stars."

I wanted to hear the story of how he had managed to return eventually to England, but that offered no interest to Holmes.

"According to one of my young associates, you have been in London for at least a month, which suggests you made contact with your brother quite soon after your return," Holmes said. "And yet you continued to sleep rough."

"My brother wanted to take me in, but I wouldn't let him. I hadn't lived in civilised society for so long and needed a little time to simply be, without being asked so many questions, and so many pairs of eyes on me."

"And yet you agreed to accompany your brother to a regimental dinner as his guest," Holmes said.

"It was his idea. He said it would give me a date by which I would give up the life I had been living. But how did you know?"

76

"He ordered a new uniform, one that was clearly not for himself. And of course you knew about the cufflink . . . ."

My interest perked up at this. Had Holmes solved that puzzle too? I suppose I should never have doubted that.

"They belonged to our father, and he wanted me to have one of them, a sort of welcome home gift. I told him that was a ridiculous idea but when he offered to have a copy of one made for me, I accepted."

"But why only one?" I blurted out, almost without thinking. "What use is that?"

There was a look of surprise on Holmes's face, but the other man simply looked down for a moment, in shame or embarrassment, then stood up and removed his coat. It was only then that I realised that the sleeve of his right arm remained tucked into its pocket, and it became obvious that his right hand had been amputated well above the wrist. I realized that the man's bent stance had hidden from me what was obvious to Holmes.

An hour later, the three of us were in Mrs. Anson's sitting room. She had fussed over the man she had thought long dead, unable to fathom how or why her late husband had kept the news of his brother's resurrection a secret from her. Perhaps he had been waiting for the right moment to tell her, but that had been taken from him before the chance had arisen.

Once she had brought her shock and surprise under control, she became a whirlwind of activity, issuing orders to the housekeeper, who seemed more than capable of dealing with the situation. It didn't take the two women long to determine that the new arrival was to stay with them and which room he was to be allocated. What he was going to eat for his supper, despite his protestations, and what might need to be arranged the following day. She also insisted that I check the condition of Captain Anson's stump, even though it had long since healed. He was a lucky man on many counts.

"I believe our work here is done," said Holmes. "They have no further need of us."

It was getting late as we made our way back to Baker Street, and the number of cabbies plying their trade much reduced. While there was a chill in the air, there seemed no threat of rain, and so we walked while I pressed Holmes on how he had reached his conclusions.

"You were on the right track with the cufflink," he said, "though you fell short in the process of elimination. You didn't consider all the possible reasons why a single cufflink might be required."

"Ah, the only person who might need a single cufflink could be a one-armed man," I said, though for whose benefit I wasn't sure.

"Indeed. And if you recall, the sales assistant we spoke to in Asprey's said that he walked somewhat hunched over and kept his hands thrust into his pockets, despite the weather, Didn't that strike you as odd?"

I had to admit, to myself at least, that it hadn't. "But how on earth did you know that it was his brother, when by all accounts, he was dead?"

"That was an even more obvious matter," Holmes said. "These cufflinks held a sentimental value over and above their intrinsic value, so it seemed certain that the new one was for someone close, perhaps a family member."

"Which led you to the possibility that the brother was actually still alive."

"It had to be a possibility," Holmes said, "a possibility that could not be eliminated. And so I set Wiggins and the ever-useful Baker Street Irregulars on the case, searching for a one-armed man who was new to the city, while I examined the Major's family background. I have to admit that we struck lucky with how quickly they were able to locate him, and then to identify him. It seems that such things are a fascination to young boys."

Pease Poison Cold
by Marcia Wilson

Ian Clarke was in extraordinary good health, but like many hypochondriacs, failed to appreciate it. He was also of the stripe of man "born bad", and this also explained his unusually long lifespan. This unfortunate situation lasted until the very end, when he failed to come down for his usual seven a.m. breakfast of eggs and Blake's Authentic Remedy. His housekeeper, a stout child of the Harris, was alarmed when two minutes passed without his arrival or even a bellow promising to beat her black and blue. Mr. Clarke, she insisted, was never anything but on the dot.

"And there I found him, like you see him there."

Inspector Lestrade looked at the dead man lying half inside his bed-clothes, and back at the housekeeper. The two of them had recognised each other at first glance: Practical and grim defenders of their territories. Neither was willing to budge an inch in sacrifice of their boundaries. Since his was the strange death of Mr. Clarke and hers was the entirety of the Clarke Building, both wholly expected their horns to lock sooner or later.

Gentleman that he was, Lestrade let her go first. "My men will be very careful with him, Mrs. Morrison." And because marriage had taught him something of politics: "Have you any recommendations as to where we should look?"

The plump woman's eyes narrowed, suspicious at this uncharacteristic display of good common sense among the police, but he was a plainclothes, wasn't he? Perhaps they were different. She had met him respectfully at the door, turned over her heavy key-ring, and told them where the master had kept the keys for his special rooms. No, she didn't have any of those keys. He had them on his neck on a chain. Yes, it was that chain he was holding.

"I can't tell a lie, Mr. Lestrade. I was afraid this day would come. Mr. Clarke was taking too many things in his mouth that wasn't food, and it cost him dreadfully."

"You mean his purse?"

"Aye, his purse and more of his health. It wasn't so bad when I started work some twenty-year 'go, but every year there's been more of the pills, more of the drops, more of the salts . . . more of everything that wasn't plain good food or drink."

Of such details, cases are built. Lestrade was writing this down as fast as his shorthand would permit. "And you think his death is unnatural, Mrs. Morrison."

"I most certainly do." Her voice could have cut glass. Behind her and across the hall, a constable froze like a guilty child before the marm.

I wish Gregson had taken this case, Lestrade thought wearily. *But no, he's working on the Mill murders, and isn't he happy to let me have 'this little problem, Ratty'.*

"I apologise for forcing you to repeat yourself, Mrs. Morrison, but I must be correct. You called for a Bobby when you found him this way, and you said – ?"

"I said he was too careful of it to be natural."

Lestrade hesitated. "And yet you said you weren't surprised?"

"I thought he would lose his fortune to the medicines and die on the streets." she admitted.

"Oh."

"And . . . ." For the first time, a crack in the proper old face. "He never made a mistake in his doses, Mr. Lestrade. He wasn't careless. Nobody but him touched his things. All locked up. I didn't have the keys. It was all his property and I'm no thief and I won't have anyone say so. I won't have it."

"Go on."

"It wouldn't be a mistake in his doses. But there are the doses themselves . . . ."

"The doses themselves – ?" Lestrade repeated.

"I shouldn't say more." She bit her lip and looked away. An old bruise marked her jaw.

Bother, and just when the conversation was getting interesting. "Well, if you aren't certain, that's a good idea," Lestrade agreed blandly. "If you think of something, don't hesitate to tell me or one of my men. They'll see right to it."

The doses themselves? The little man rubbed his chin as the housekeeper quietly set herself down in a chair. Polite and respectful, and if he didn't mistake the glint in her eye, she had personal experience with how nasty a copper could be – a *bad* copper, he corrected in his mind. There were too many to count, and made the work harder for the likes of him.

This is just likely one of these mayfly cases, like Mr. Holmes says – short but briefly unusual.

Think of the devil and you'll see his horns soon enough. The Clarke House was less than two minutes' walk from 221b Baker Street. If Mr.

Holmes were out in this rare fine weather, he would be hopping over for certain. Best accept that now and solve this case quickly.

Lestrade tapped his pencil against his jaw thoughtfully as he peered about with a suspicious eye. This was a clean house – and he had seen many of them in London. The House-Proud made eternal war on grime, but there was something else about it that drew his eye . . . unpleasantly.

It was the same old, sad story. Mrs. Morrison might not like the suffering of her employment, but she was at least ruler of her household, and women often gave up much more in the name of some freedom. Still . . . .

He wandered slowly through the little sitting room with its green stone fireplace and the office directly across the narrow hall. There were cupboards and wall-shelves, a clever closet set inside the staircase, and even some of the steps had pull-outs. *Haven't seen those in years!* Mirrors and framed pictures, glasses so clean you could fall in them, and the carpet was fading evenly from too much aggressive pounding and cleaning, not in the middle from wear and tear of shoes.

There isn't a lot here, he realised, and something was making him gradually more uneasy, for even the paper flowers in the vases had the look of being long-term residents. The polish glowed brightly and the wall-paper was gently brushed with tender hands, but this was a house that wasn't putting money into upkeep. Tiny stitches in the pale lilac curtain, the threads cobbled from the hemline itself. A sniff proving the oil for the chairs was handmade.

It wasn't until he saw PC Weber – the big Wendish – hunch his shoulders and turn slightly as he walked down the hallway to give his report that he recognised the strangeness for what it was. The rooms and hall and all the spaces were small enough that he, a small man, was beginning to feel cramped.

Lestrade had honestly never experienced this sensation in a house before, and he didn't like it one bit. It was too odd, too alien. On the other hand, he could enjoy imagining Sherlock Holmes here. Would be like sending a stork into a maze, wouldn't it?

The absent smile on his lips lasted as long as it took him to reach the next door – *A-ha! The Master's key fits that. Let's see – and pull it open.*

He stood, staring.

"PC Weber."

"Yes, sir?"

"Ask Mrs. Morrison if she would mind coming here and answering a question."

"Yes, sir."

"Yes, Mr. Lestrade?"

Lestrade knew it was rude, but he couldn't quite trust himself to look the woman in the face. "Mrs. Morrison, was your employer taking all of these . . . remedies?"

The woman took his question literally and pushed gently past him to examine the small bath. Floor to ceiling, glass bottles gleamed under the exorbitant glow of their own electric bulb in the ceiling. There were small wooden boxes marked in a broad variety of languages, but the numbers were easily enough ciphered. There were tubes, a rack of measuring-spoons, dosing cups, egg cups, three types of brandy, and each with their drinking-glass. There was this and much more. An ordinary bath had been gutted like a deer and remade into something scientifically nightmarish, not unlike Mary Shelley's monster had been made of once-ordinary human parts.

"To the best of my knowing, Mr. Lestrade – Yes, he was taking all of these here."

"Thank you, Mrs. – Here." Lestrade felt his heart skip. "I beg your pardon, did you say 'here'?"

"Yes, all of these here."

Lestrade swallowed. "And there is more?"

"Yes."

"Where?"

She told him.

Then, when the little policeman remembered to blink before his eyes dried up, he bowed his head in defeat and told Weber to take a quick walk over to Baker Street and see if Mr. Holmes might possibly be disposed to come and comment.

". . . And then I sent for you."

Sherlock Holmes's reaction to the house had been almost disappointing. He stepped carefully down the hallway with an unthinking hunch of his shoulders like they were all doing and paused for Dr. Watson to follow. Watson, the older of the two and a bit broader, had a wry expression stamped so deep under his mustaches it bordered on rudeness.

"My apologies, Doctor. If I had known you were there, I would have included you in the invitation."

"I believe I would have been here regardless." Watson shook his head and looked up, then down, and side to side at the microcosm of chemistry in the walls. "He was an occasional patient of mine, but not enough that I could say I knew him well . . . ."

"I would like to know the fellows who could say that . . ." Holmes murmured. That was exactly what Lestrade was thinking.

"Lived alone, didn't like to leave his house, played the market, and gained wealth off his mining shares like an oyster collects another layer of pearl." Lestrade lifted his shoulders, unsure if he should be impressed at the rewards of sloth, or disgusted that a man of means lived so . . . meaninglessly.

"But . . . you said . . . there's a room like this on each *floor*?" Watson was trying very hard to keep his expression on the polite sides of horror and astonishment. Honest men are usually terrible at this sort of thing, but since sharing his lodgings with Holmes, Lestrade felt the man was improving.

"I didn't believe it either, not until I saw it for myself. He didn't want to run out, she said."

"Run out of what?" Watson blurted without thinking. "Did he anticipate an epidemic that selectively attacked chemists?"

"If so, he clearly foiled that malady . . . ." Holmes cleaned the tip of his walking stick with his clean gloves and tapped it against the wall gently. He did this several times, up and down the length of the short hall that connected the front door with the office, sitting room, closet, and back room leading to the kitchen and pantry. Lestrade had already tapped for hollow spots.

"Mrs. Morrison says he put a completely new layer of wall in the house about ten years ago." Lestrade told him. "He was afraid of draughts."

"That would explain why the bottom of the front door is clad in India-rubber." Holmes mused. "I'm seeing a great deal of funds sunk into this project."

"He was wealthy enough for that." Watson shuddered. "Inspector, I assure you all my treatments were properly documented. I can even tell you the names of his chemists."

"*Chemists*, did you say?" Holmes frowned, and his unnerving grey eyes opened fully.

His reaction was hardly surprising. Families had one chemist, and they stuck to them religiously, through thick and thin, handing them down through the generations. To go to more than one was barely imaginable. Lestrade had already seen the papers to prove Watson's words, and he could hardly countenance the evidence of his eyes.

It's because this is an allegedly respectable man, he thought sourly. *On the wrong side of Lambeth, I wouldn't even raise an eyebrow.* He glanced about Mr. Clarke's office again, but other than an atrocious portrait of the man, and an even worse oil of dogs chasing a disproportionate stag, there was nothing to provide illumination.

"A moment, gentlemen." Holmes lifted his hand. "Lestrade, is there a place here where we may retire after seeing the body?"

"This office should do. I've found nothing that shouldn't be here. And I'll take you upstairs now."

Mr. Clarke's body was still in its original pose, half-in and half-out of a taffy-twist of linens. The bedroom was still smallish, but larger than the rest. Inset wall shelves displayed an almost tasteful array of books, art baubles, and . . . what appeared to be a collection of ceramic pill-cutting tablets. Strangest of all was an almond-shaped bowl filled halfway with children's sweets. For the first time, there was the sign of some frivolousness, some frailty that said a human being had lived here. Lestrade felt a headache coming, and he didn't think it was from their close quarters with a dead man.

"If you'd like to do the honours, Dr. Watson?" The little man smiled around the throb in his temple.

Watson was happy to oblige. The limbs had stiffened during the night and the blood was pooling in the low portions. Still, this was unmistakably the same man whose portrait hung in the office.

Watson duly poked, prodded, and palpitated the corpse for answers while the other two men watched and occasionally asked him to check this or move that. The young man – Lestrade felt he could still call him a young man, compared to himself – was growing more and more puzzled the further he went.

Finally, he stood with a grimace and a fist on his leg and cricked his shoulders back.

"Gentlemen, this man has almost none of the smell of death upon him. His pallor is typical of his chronic anaemia, and his lower intestines are distended. There are masses. It's too early to rule out any one cause. It could be anything from cancer of the bowel to an abnormality.

"However, if this were cancer, I am positive the signs would be obvious."

"We can deliver him to the surgeons if you are both satisfied." Lestrade had been hoping Watson would say something different, but the man was right.

"Who is your coroner now?"

"I believe Old Haggarty."

"If that is the Haggerty I know, that man has a fine eye for detail and no patience for fools."

"There's more than one Haggerty?" Lestrade looked horrified at the thought. "I think you *do* know him. Congratulations. He has all my men in terror. But I say, he knows his work back and forth."

"Excellent," said Holmes. "If I may, Lestrade, these quarters are close. I should like to examine before the wagon arrives." He pulled out his notebook and pencil.

Watson and Lestrade stepped out with PC Weber, standing duty in the doorway. Mrs. Morrison, he reported, had retired to her room and was writing a letter to her brother about his earlier offer to move in with her.

"She picked up his directions, drugs, my samples and receipts and bills for him more than not." Watson confided. "He was often indisposed." His mouth set. "*I didn't know,*" he whispered, so Lestrade knew he had seen her jaw.

"*Can't say I'm wasting my tears,*" Lestrade whispered back, and said out loud, "Anaemia?"

"That, and troubles with his potassium, and yes, excessive sugar in his blood. There were times when I thought London would run out of iron pills."

Holmes rejoined them and looked like he very much wished to smoke. Lestrade took them all back down to the office, where smoking was clearly permitted, and Holmes had already searched for clues.

"My receipts are in yellow paper, with a blue edge on top," Watson reminded them as if this fact had suddenly changed.

"That does make it simpler." Lestrade had pulled the dead man's files from his desk and was leafing through an intimidatingly neat and rigid system of alphabetization and dates. "Why do you do that, Doctor? The paper's got to be much more expensive."

"It is easier to read yellow paper than white, and my patients tend to be stubborn and will not admit their eyes are sensitive." Watson didn't look at his companion. Holmes blandly regarded the ceiling plaster.

"Dear Heavens, I thought you were joking." Lestrade stared. "I thought too much iron was dangerous!" Holmes peered over his shoulder and whistled.

"It is! When I stopped dispensing, he said he would simply visit my colleagues for more. And then the potassium deficiency. There was no point in writing him for a nostrum's pills when dried fruit would have easily sufficed, but he claimed digestive troubles." Watson's fingers tapped angrily on his legs. "I did my best by him, but he only listened to my diagnosis when convenient. He would happily have spent a pound on a pill when a bowl of groats and compote would have stood him better."

Lestrade started from sorting papers. "Prescriptions from Dr. Shannon."

Holmes grimaced and Watson swore, before catching himself and glancing about in case Mrs. Morrison was in earshot.

"That . . . *quack!*"

The doctor shot to his feet and tried to pace in the small room. He wasn't successful. Holmes silently helped Lestrade separate Watson's receipts from the stack.

"I don't see anyone else, if that gives you comfort."

"It does not!"

"At least the late Doctor Shannon is out of our hands and before the Final Judge." Lestrade really didn't like seeing Watson's ire up. His temper was rare, but the type that made one think of old folk-tales of ball lightning rolling through a house during a storm.

"And he is there," Watson bit out, "because he was too clever for his own good and made a bosh of trying to poison Holmes!" As if they needed reminding, he pointed at Holmes for good measure.

"I never fail to be thankful when a criminal is caught in his own trap, Watson. And I'm more interested in the fact that these receipts are clearly dated past Shannon's own death. Clarke must have paid handsomely for so many future prescriptions."

"For quackery and catholicons! Snail oils, mermaids-tears and – " Watson yanked up a paper and snarled at it, "Shilajit! Where in London could he have gotten *shilajit*!"

"I don't even know what that is." Lestrade was startled. He looked to Holmes for answers, but Holmes shook his head, just as mystified. "Right, I'll ask. What is it?"

"I've no idea, and I don't believe anyone does. It oozes out of rocks in the mountains of Afghanistan." Watson came out of his mood enough to notice they were staring at him. "If he was getting 'care' from Shannon, I'm only surprised he lived so long!" They watched as he breathed through his nose until his colour faded to normal. "Holmes, an autopsy must be quick about it. Perhaps my patient died of his own indiscretions, or something we don't know, but there is too good of a chance . . . ."

"I hear the wagon now, Doctor." Lestrade rose to his feet. "Mr. Holmes?"

"I should like to reserve the right to return later, after I have had the chance to study the data."

"You have it."

The next events were the unremarkable, just tedious procedures that are the lot and suffering of a British policeman in service to Crown and Justice. Mr. Clarke's mortal remains were taken for *post mortem* examination. Dr. Watson accompanied the body with his field report. Holmes stayed behind with Lestrade but popped off repeatedly, haring into different directions – outside, to the neighbors, praising Mrs. Morrison's mouser, and pinning the beat constable against the wall to pelt him with questions. As a rank-holding officer, Lestrade *could* have possibly told Holmes to back off, but PC Gilbert was a cocky sort, and it would do him good to be up against things he didn't understand more often.

"You keep coming up here."

Holmes didn't turn at Lestrade's voice. He continued to stare at the bed, empty of its master like a cast seed-pod.

"Clarke wasn't a man I shall mourn. Nevertheless, it would be annoying if Shannon is a posthumous murderer on top of his other murders."

Lestrade edged closer into the small room. "Any other man would just be glad he escaped his clutches."

"You make him sound like a kraken, Lestrade. He was just a cold heart with no concern for his victims."

"And I've seen more of 'em than I'll ever count." Lestrade paused. "I didn't get much more out of Mrs. Morrison. She was already planning to retire in a few months. She had no motive. He put a little aside for her bank account, I suspect to buy her silence as to the truth of his character. You know the type, Mr. Holmes. As long as she's accepting his money, she won't say a word against him.

"He was certainly prepared for his death."

"Always thought he was dying."

"Eventually he was right."

"Good Lord, would ye look at that noo."

Watson had chosen to go with the body for an extra reason: His old teacher of the cadaver, he who told Watson he would make a fine cutter "someday, pr'haps, and chew tha' ginger before ye swoon, Laddie," was indeed the same Dr. Haggerty cutting open the corpse in examination. Teacher and Pupil nodded at each other in fraternal unity, and time slipped backwards when Haggerty grinned up one side as he always did, and pushed the tray of instruments at him. "You may as well make yourself useful, young Watson," he said, as he often had.

At least this time Watson wasn't a callow student feeling a sore head from too much celebrating with the Blackheaths the night before.

"Well, been a long time." Haggerty said after his knife neatly split the skin from navel to collar-bone.

Watson thought he meant their last meeting. "You're looking well."

"Noo tha', ye good-harted mooncalf." Haggerty chuckled. "Look younder, Laddie. Och, did ye not notice no death-cloud?"

"I thought it was strange and worth noting to the police."

"Hope for ye yet, Laddie. Here, look at this prize plumbing!" And he tugged aside the assortment of intestines.

Watson looked, confident he would see nothing he would be unprepared to see. Casual surgery and the horrors of war had taught him intestines constricted and moved, sometimes long after the heart ceased. The large chain of lumps inside the gut tracts weren't his expectations.

"Might want to hold your nose." Haggerty shook his head as he poised a scalpel. "Man's constipated to the end of his days, but we maun' be thorough and confirm, aye?"

Watson agreed with him in principle, but there were days when going the full length were less than joyful occasions and he said so.

Haggerty cackled. "Best pay heed, this is what happens when you don't eat yer proper oats and kale!" And he made his first cut. The layers of intestine fell away, but not, as the shocked doctors saw, to reveal a foul mass of blocked excrement.

Former teacher and former student studied the subject in stone silence at length, then looked at each other. They looked at the dead man again. Watson really wished he could say something, but as the former pupil and a guest in the man's own kingdom, it was his duty to let Haggerty have the honour.

Besides, Haggerty had never once disappointed his students with his pithy comments.

Haggerty didn't disappoint. He swallowed, cleared his throat, and swallowed again.

"Me mam's fruitcake wasn't that cheery."

"He swallowed *what*?" Lestrade gaped. "Are you sure?"

"If I weren't, Haggerty would be." Watson's eyes still held a gleam of dazed wonder.

"Food-colouring and clay."

"And elevated levels of lead. And sugar. It was poorly digested."

"But at least it was digested . . . ." Lestrade tugged his hat off and gripped the brim. "That poor fellow, but . . . Look, I'm not stupid, but I understand none of this!"

Sherlock Holmes had listened to the report without saying a word, though his eyebrows had tried to climb into his high browline a few times while he tapped tobacco into a traveler's pipe. Watson was a better storyteller than even he knew.

"Iron and potassium and sugar," he muttered to himself. "Watson, what is your doctor's diagnosis for the information at hand?"

"For the information at hand?" Watson was relieved he wasn't asked to imagine things. "He was taking too much iron, which causes severe constipation. He refused fruit which would have helped him digest the iron, and he was consistently low in potassium. His sugar levels were queer. He seemed sensitive to it, but my tests weren't consistent. I had a suspicion he was ignoring my diet and slipping the sweets and the man was . . . something of a stranger to discipline."

To strangers, John H. Watson was being professional in his summary.

To the men that knew him, John H. Watson loathed and despised his old patient as a despicable worm and cad and unmanly freak of nature.

"Good thing he inherited the gold mines," Lestrade opined. "I'm not sure he *could* have worked."

"His affairs were in order." Holmes reminded them. "There were no known reasons why anyone, even Shannon, would have wanted to kill him." As Watson groaned, the detective held up a pile, his gaze apologetic.

"I am sorry, Watson, but Shannon was making himself very comfortable at your patient's expense. He had a nice little contract where Clarke had his concoctions sent over."

"Even if they did deserve each other," Lestrade said in words that brooked no doubt they had, "you can't tell me he died because his guts stopped working."

Holmes lowered his head in thought for a long minute. "Ask Mrs. Morrison to come here, just one last time."

The old woman had managed a bit of powder on her face and was facing them with a bit more confidence than last time. Her hands clasped neatly before her as she listened to Sherlock Holmes.

"Now that you mention it, Mr. Holmes, he had been ordering a lot of Dr. Shannon's Digestive Comfits."

"I've never heard of them."

"Yes, Dr. Shannon had developed a new kind of comfit. Said he'd exclusively made digestive sweets that were lower in sugar, so he could eat more of them. That's what he said."

"That is interesting. Are there any left?"

"I'm surprised to say there are. They're all up in that bowl by his bedside. Always nibbling away at the sugar pease, like a child who never had a sore tum."

Lestrade thought that *excessively* ironic but managed not to say that.

"Lestrade, if I may have some of these pease? I don't believe I'll need all of them."

"Hmm!"

True to his word, Holmes had taken only a handful of the sweets. They were indeed the sort of candy sold cheaply at the confectionaries'.

Odd-sized little flattened balls of sugar colored brightly in red, green, and yellow, and a few bone-white.

"Perhaps we should test for poisons." Lestrade offered uneasily. "I'm not sure that green is natural."

"It's at least partially sap-green dissolved in brandy." Watson frowned. "But that has been hard to find of late."

"I don't even know what sap-green is."

"Buckthorn."

"Lestrade, I must ask your patience. This test will take several days."

"But you can be positive of the result?"

"If we have the expected result."

"All right, but I'll be taking a few of these to my own chemists. I don't like those colours."

"Very well, and let us see what we shall find."

Lestrade took his portion to the chemists down at the Yard and was satisfied, if that was the proper word, that the treats were at least partially poisonous. He also had to pass Gregson in the hall, who naturally sneered at him for holding a bowl of children's sweets.

"Feeling sweet today, Ratty?"

"Sweeter than you, you bitter old man."

"Lacks elegance!" Gregson called after him.

Lestrade slammed the door behind him. Professor Stanislas jumped from his station over a frightening glass forest of instruments.

"Elegance?"

"Nothing. What have you found? I finally got permission to bring the rest of these over." He waved the candies sourly.

"Oh, excellent. We might need them just in case."

"Just in case of what?"

"Took a little ammonia and poured it right over the green ones," explained Professor Stanislas. "A little is all it took. The liquid turned blue as the sky. Only copper would do this."

"And what about the rest?"

"Dropped them in sulphuretted hydrogen!" Stanislas said proudly, and thrust a vile looking beaker of a repulsive blackish-brown under his nose. "Muriatic acidulation! That's lead, sure enough!"

"And this is enough to kill a grown man?"

Stanislas' face fell. "A grown man? Well . . . perhaps? If he ate a great deal of them."

"How much would a great deal be?" Lestrade's frail hopes crashed.

"You'd have to eat about as much as . . . ." The chemist indicated a space about as big as half-a-loaf of bread. "But it could poison a man," he called after the dejected detective, "if that's all he ate for a few days!"

Lestrade didn't think even Clarke was that indulgent. And to make things worse, he just *knew* Gregson was waiting to taunt him when he left the floor.

"Ah, Lestrade!" Holmes beamed. "Come in! I'm about to top off my little experiment! What did your man say?"

"He said sweets are bad for rats." Lestrade snarled. "I mean – never mind. He found some nasty things.

"Lead and copper. Enough for a stomach-ache, but he said there might be something else in the works, or in the man's health to do more." He passed over a copy of the file, and Holmes read through the neat lines with a nod.

"Good man! Very well, here we are. Did you bring your pipe?"

"Yes, I brought my pipe! But why, I ask you," Lestrade waved the stem at his host's proud and extensive collection of dreadful smoking-implements. "Don't you have enough?"

"Oh, but this needs to be your very own pipe for it to work. Watson, if you would do the honours?"

"I'm afraid there's little to tell," Watson confessed with an awkward cough. "I simply followed my orders and boiled the sugar pease in a staggering amount of boiling water until they fell to particles. Then, I set the solution aside in the quietest corner of the room with a lid, and let it sit undisturbed."

Lestrade looked at the crucible in question, but he didn't think for one moment there was such a thing as a quiet corner in those rooms.

"After the second day, we felt it had settled enough to decant the liquid, and I did this to the best of my ability. The sludge was allowed to evaporate until it acquired a puttylike consistency, and then Holmes and I set it here."

Curious despite himself, Lestrade poked at the pale stuff with a finger. It was mostly white, with a greyish look that might have come from the leftover colouring-agents. "Very well, and what is it?"

"For this, I ask that you take your pipe and fill it, and we shall all sit and smoke and talk while we wait for the next step."

Someday, I'm going to just tell him he's absolutely barking, Lestrade promised to himself one more time, but he knew he had made this promise too long and too often for it to have any value left. But there was no rushing one of Mr. Holmes's tricks, and it was a pleasant evening for a visit and a chat. The three settled down and spent an enjoyable half-hour smoking and talking about how their various professions altered their views of London.

Lestrade's pipe was a simple thorn, a cheap thing bought from a stall. He didn't think anything of it when the bowl grew hot, but Holmes's grey eyes positively glowed when he saw him trade the pipe from one hand to the next.

"Excellent!" He said. "Lestrade, while we are watching, pop in a bit of that stuff on the hot coal."

"Well, all right, but I'm not puffing it!" Lestrade followed his directions and held the bowl in his hands. Three heads bent over, studying the matter.

It happened quickly. The lump became a hard bricklike chunk that Lestrade would have recognized in his sleep.

"Cornish clay." He scowled. "Are you telling me – Oh, no! It was the sweets. They're low in sugar but absolutely full of clay!"

"Clay poisoning was once far more common than it is in these enlightened days." Holmes's smile fairly split his face. "As an organic chemist, I can tell you it was a leading cause of low potassium and anemia in our fathers' time."

Watson sighed sadly. "That isn't all it was. People used to be addicts to it. It caused lead poisoning, muscle atrophy, and death from nutritional deficit."

"Shannon had been giving him these . . . poisoned treats to do what? Keep him under control?"

"I doubt it was that simple. Clarke paid well for a doctor who obeyed his wishes over his health. He doubtless assured Shannon that he would follow his directions regarding the sweets, but as Watson assures us, he lacked self control. It wasn't just that he was eating the clay candies. He ate far too many of them over the course of several weeks. The clay bound his intestines and contributed to his death, yes, but the combination of the clay, lead, and copper was a guaranteed poison, even if one component alone was insufficient."

"So . . . what you're saying is, Clarke died a death of his own making, as much as Shannon did in his." Lestrade could only shake his head. "And you had to use my pipe for this?"

"Do *not*," Watson interjected darkly in front of Holmes, "smoke from *any* of these pipes here, Lestrade. I keep mine in my room." His glare at his friend was . . . unfriendly.

"Even so, Lestrade, I should think you would be grateful for the closure to this little case and in this particular matter."

Lestrade thought about it. And then he smiled.

"Penny for your thoughts, Friend Lestrade?" Holmes murmured.

"I was just thinking of Gregson tomorrow, when I bring in the case." Lestrade said with relish. "He'll say, *'Isn't it a bit difficult for you, Ratty? You know I'm always glad to help a man in need.'*

"And I," Lestrade said around his laughter, "am going to say, *'Excellent, Gregson. Just put it in your pipe and smoke it!'*"

NOTES

> "Pease pudding and saveloys, what next is the question?
> Rich gentlemen have it boys – in-di-gestion."

"Food, Glorious Food" from the Broadway musical and film, *Oliver!*

So goes one of the two times Americans encounter this mass noun, or uncountable noun, for *peas*. In general, it is used to talk about pease pudding (hot, cold, and in the pot nine days old), the same way we say "oatmeal" instead of "just oats", but there was a darker encounter of this word, and it was aligned with innocent children's sweets.

In his 1820 classic, *A Treatise on Adulterations of Food*, Friedrich C. Accum denounced the scandal of casual poisoners who made confectionaries in the shape of small sweet spheres or pellets. Called "sugar pease", they were usually white with occasional bright colors, and they were made cheaper and sold dearer by mixing the sugar and starch up with white clay. It was potential poison, and children were the frequent victims as they had smaller bodies and constitutions, less capable of throwing off the damages of eating large amounts of clay and the toxic elements used to add appealing colors. Sadly, the candy was all too easy to make and sell.

Clay-eating is its own interesting topic, found around the world. In moderation, it is harmless and even beneficial, but excessive amounts can lead to a combination of problems as in *Pease Porridge Cold*. Humans can develop an addiction for clay, and this makes simple avoidance complicated. Cornish clay, or pipe-clay, was used the most among London food counterfeiters. It was fine, and adulterated everything from sugar, desserts, cornstarch, and flours.

The Adventure of the Vanished Uncle

by Arthur Hall

The door of our sitting room closed softly as our landlady, Mrs. Hudson, withdrew. The young man who she had just announced as "Mr. Daniel Worth" faced us uncertainly, until my friend, the consulting detective Mr. Sherlock Holmes, bade him approach.

"I think you will find the basket chair comfortable, Mr. Worth. I am Sherlock Holmes, and this is my friend and colleague, Doctor John Watson. Your hesitation is quite unnecessary, I assure you, for anything that you wish to tell us will remain within these walls."

The gentleman, who I judged to be about thirty years of age, had allowed himself to become rather portly, so that his rather vivid waistcoat appeared stretched across his body. I noticed marks of strain, or concern, around his eyes.

"Thank you, Mr. Holmes," he replied as he settled himself. "I appreciate that you have consented to see me so quickly, since my telegram was sent only yesterday."

"It reached me soon after I concluded another matter, and so I was free to respond. But I see that you are troubled by your nerves. Perhaps a restorative might help." He turned to me. "Watson, a brandy for our new client, if you please."

I rose and poured from the crystal decanter. Mr. Worth accepted the glass with good grace and emptied it with two swallows. The harsh spirit appeared to have a calming effect almost at once.

"Now," continued Holmes, "I would be grateful if you would tell us of your problem. Leave out no detail, however small it may seem to you. All I know of you at this moment is that you are a green-grocer and you have come to us today from Highgate."

"The fact is . . . ." Our client faltered as he realised what my friend had said. "But I have not confided to either of you gentlemen of my profession or my place of residence!"

"But you have neglected to remove the Underground ticket from the top pocket of your morning-coat. Also, the stains on your palms definitely result from much handling of tomatoes, oranges, and probably other fruits."

"Why, yes. Of course." Confusion slowly left his expression.

"Pray tell what it is that troubles you, then."

Mr. Worth shifted in his chair and brushed back a stray lock of black hair. "I am worried for my uncle, Mr. Septimus Merrett. He has disappeared from the face of the earth."

Holmes nodded. "Why do you believe this?"

"Because I haven't heard from him for a week, when he usually calls on me every two or three days, and because of his disclosures at our last meeting."

"They concerned something of importance?"

"Indeed. I should explain that my uncle and his business partner, Mr. Jacob Virney, ran a fruit importing concern until a few months ago, when they both retired."

"Was that how you became a green-grocer?" I interjected.

"It was. They were my principal, but not my only, suppliers of exotic fruits and vegetables. They it was who originally set me up in the trade, about five years ago."

"So what was it that concerned you so about your uncle's revelations?" Holmes asked, I thought with a trace of impatience at my interruption.

"I am sorry to say that Mr. Virney died only weeks after entering retirement. Like myself, he was unmarried and without offspring. He therefore left his not-inconsiderable fortune, mostly from the sale of the business, to my uncle who, already having enough for his own needs, set about giving large portions of it away to various individuals. He mentioned some of the recipients in a note, which he accidentally left when we last separated."

"Do you still have it?"

Mr. Worth shook his head. "I had no reason to suppose at the time that I would need it, but I have an excellent memory."

"Then kindly give these details, as best you can recall them, to Doctor Watson. Also your address, when you leave."

"I will, most certainly."

"So it was since he began this distribution that your uncle disappeared?" Holmes resumed.

"Yes. He had already given to those mentioned in the note, and was about to embark on a crusade to enrich the remainder, which were known only to himself."

A few moments of silence passed between us. Holmes wore a thoughtful expression as the cries of a coachman, urging his horse to greater efforts, reached us from the street below.

"Is your uncle usually inclined to such excessive philanthropy?" Holmes enquired then.

Our client shrugged. "He has been known to act in such a manner now and then, though never on such a scale as this before."

"But then he has never previously possessed such an abundance of wealth, I suppose?"

"Exactly."

Holmes came to a decision. "Very well. I will look into this on your behalf. Pray describe your uncle's appearance, giving special attention to any peculiarities that this may entail."

"He is tall and extremely thin." Mr. Worth took a moment to assemble his recollection. "He has apparently been that way for his entire life, despite a considerable appetite. His hair is almost gone, revealing a red patch in the centre of his skull. He habitually wears *pince-nez*, and is inclined to stutter when speaking quickly."

"Thank you, Mr. Worth," Holmes said in conclusion, rising to his feet. "Pray allow Doctor Watson to record your remaining details, then I think we need detain you no longer. I believe I can promise you that you will be hearing from us very soon."

With that, my friend approached the window, where he adopted a contemplative posture as I made notes to Mr. Worth's dictation. Soon we were alone again, and I asked Holmes for his observations.

"First," he replied as he resumed his seat, "I was struck by our client's coincidental resemblance to Valleurin."

"That name is unknown to me."

"Ah, of course it would be, since the enquiry took place while I lived in Montague Street. Valleurin was a professional assassin from Paris, in England to dispose of Mr. Michael Stiller, a prominent naturalist who lived in Kent. Who it was that wished this man's death or why was never discovered, but the murder was committed in a most unusual way."

He fell into silence then, drawing on a Turkish cigarette and surrounding himself with clouds of fragrant smoke. I waited until it became apparent that he intended to say nothing more.

"Pray continue," I entreated. "How did Valleurin carry this out? Was he caught and punished?"

He consigned the scant remainder of his cigarette to an ashtray. "I do apologise for my distraction, Watson. I had begun to reflect on Mr. Worth's problem. As for Valleurin, it was known that he meticulously studied his victims before acting against them. In this instance, he knew that his intended victim was in the habit of keeping a king cobra in a vivarium beside his bed. One night, he visited Mr. Stiller's house in the early hours, climbing a drainpipe until he was able to slide the half-open window to its fullest extent. Using a catapult, he then fired a single shot, a piece of lead, that shattered the side of the vivarium tank, releasing its deadly occupant. The noise woke Mr. Stiller instantly, and his terrified movements attracted the creature with fatal results. You see the beauty of the crime, Watson? There was no weapon, nor any indication that the man's death was anything but the result of an accident. He would surely have been acquitted in a court of law."

"Valleurin escaped then? He never faced justice for his misdeeds?"

"Not in the usual sense. I had been engaged to offer some measure of protection to the absent-minded Mr. Stiller, and had learned of Valleurin's intentions. I knew him already by reputation, and was aware that he was responsible for at least eight deaths in England and France within the preceding six months. I followed him to Mr. Stiller's house that night, but had no way of knowing how he intended to carry out his task. I stood not far from him as he opened the window and would have shot him in the leg had he attempted to enter the room, but I was quite unprepared for his subsequent approach. When I realised that he was about to beat a hasty retreat I knew he had already forestalled me, but I could not in good conscience allow him to continue his murderous career."

"So, you arrested him?" I ventured.

"It was unnecessary. Before he could descend, he fell from the drainpipe, and on examination I saw that his neck was broken."

"Most convenient," I acknowledged, feeling certain that Holmes had somehow ensured that the assassin met a justifiable end.

"But I digress," he continued in this most unusually talkative manner. "We were discussing the enquiry brought to us by Mr. Worth. It seems that the two most likely explanations for Mr. Septimus Merrett's disappearance are that he was waylaid and taken prisoner by some person who knew of his good fortune, or that he himself suddenly decided to temporarily cease his philanthropy in order to indulge his own tastes. I see from your notes that his solicitors are Hicks and Birchwood of Westminster, and that he dealt with Mr. Jonathan Darraway. Perhaps, if we call there after luncheon, we may be granted an interview."

Mr. Darraway turned out to be an elderly and amiable fellow, not given to the inscrutable and indifferent traits that I have experienced during my dealings with many of his profession. He smiled at us across his desk, his monocle glinting from the reflection of the dull light outside.

"I am delighted to meet you gentlemen," he said with a jovial air. "Your activities are often in the newspapers, Mr. Holmes, though I suspect that Scotland Yard's achievements are actually yours in many instances." He turned his attention to me. "Your accounts, Doctor Watson, are also familiar to me. I would very much prefer to think that you do not exaggerate."

"You can be assured of it, sir," said I.

The solicitor rubbed his hands together. "Wonderful! Now, gentlemen, how can I assist you?"

"We have been approached by a client who fears that his uncle has disappeared," Holmes began. "The uncle's name is Mr. Septimus Merrett, who we understand is a client of yours."

Mr. Darraway nodded at once. "Indeed, that is so. We have acted for him many times over the years. He has mentioned Mr. Daniel Worth, who must be your client, often when making occasional bequests. Mr. Merrett always struck me as a most generous fellow."

"Quite so. Mr. Worth is anxious regarding his uncle's welfare, since their regular appointments have not been kept."

"Dear me," Mr. Darraway fingered his moustache that was so light in colour to be almost invisible. "What can have happened to the man? I am aware that his gifts to three individuals, in addition to his nephew, were paid to them by him in cash, since he remarked that he was about to withdraw a large sum for that purpose when I informed him of the extent of his good fortune, but as to the others that were to benefit, I know nothing."

Holmes read from my notes. "Pray tell me, are these the beneficiaries that you know of?"

The solicitor leaned forward in his chair, adjusting his monocle. "I believe they are, Mr. Holmes. I recall that Mr. Merrett seemed excited in a way, or perhaps relieved, that he was to pay these people. It was as if he owed each of them a long-standing debt."

"Can you bring to mind anywhere that Mr. Merrett is likely to have retreated, perhaps for a short while as he considers where the remainder of his money would best be bestowed?"

"I regret that I cannot."

"And you are quite sure that no further individual was mentioned by him?" I asked.

Mr. Darraway shook his head slowly. "I am sorry, gentlemen. To the best of my recollection, my client confided no more to me than we have discussed today."

Holmes rose, and I did also.

"Then nothing remains other than to convey our thanks to you, sir. You have been most helpful."

"It has, I do assure you gentlemen, been a pleasure."

We left the rather poorly lit and cramped office to find that the sky had darkened with gathering clouds.

"An amiable fellow I think," I said, "but I cannot see that we have learned much from him."

"We at least have verified some of our client's assertions." My friend half-turned his head and adopted a serious expression. "Watson, when we arrived in Westminster, I was unsure as to whether the carriage behind our hansom was following. I am now sure that this was so, because it waited near the solicitor's office and has resumed a slow pursuit as we seek a cab. No, do not look around. It is enough for now that we are aware of it."

We returned to Baker Street and Mrs. Hudson's shepherd's pie with me feeling slightly uncomfortable because of the unwelcome scrutiny. Holmes seemed quite unaffected, but peered from our sitting room window before we ate to ensure that our follower was still nearby. It was well into the evening before the carriage departed.

I slept well that night, but Holmes was still pacing in his room as consciousness slipped away.

The next morning found us both enjoying our breakfast. Holmes actually cleared his plate, and I deduced from this that he had decided upon a course of action since he would have confined himself to a pot of strong coffee otherwise.

"I assume we are to begin visiting Mr. Merrett's beneficiaries," I ventured when we were about to leave the table.

"Since the morning post has as yet failed to arrive, we may as well begin," he answered. "Are you free to accompany me?"

"I am."

"Excellent." He crossed to the window. "I see that our follower is late, if he is attending at all."

Holmes explained that we were to visit Mr. George Trench, who was on the list furnished by our client. I saw no sign of our pursuer as we neared Kensington.

It was Mr. Trench himself who admitted us to his rooms in a house which must once have been a splendid building, but had since suffered long neglect.

"Oh, do come in gentlemen," he said on hearing our introduction and the purpose of our visit. "I suppose I can spare you a few minutes." He appeared mildly confused. "Damned if I can see what a consulting detective could want with me, though."

Holmes and I glanced at each other and followed our host into a spacious but not well-furnished room. We weren't invited to sit, nor to partake of any refreshments, but Mr. Trench lowered himself immediately onto a worn armchair.

"The fellow you mentioned," he began at once, "called to see me one day last week. I forget which day it was, but he brought with him a substantial gift of money. He said he felt that he owed me something from an incident which took place some time ago, and it took me a few minutes to call it to mind."

"What occurred," asked Holmes, "on that occasion?"

Mr. Trench gave a little shrug. "It was quite unintentional. I was taking a stroll along Kensington High Street when a carriage sped by, far too close to the pavement. I heard later that the driver seemed to have died suddenly while whipping up the horse, so control was lost. Anyhow, Mr. Merrett narrowly missed being struck, and blundered into me as he jumped out of the way. Somehow, the fellow adopted the notion that I had saved his life – which I did not – and wished to reward me for it. He was drunk at the time, I suppose."

"Did you explain to him his mistake?" I enquired.

Our host gave me a look such as you would reserve for someone suddenly afflicted by madness.

"Good Heavens, no! I had no great need of the money of course, but a little more is always useful when one gambles. I accepted his generosity, told him what a pleasure it was to have made his acquaintance, and sent him on his way, as one would."

By this time, I had decided that Mr. Trench wasn't a fellow I would care to include among my friends. I would have thought him not much more than twenty-five, and far from the well-to-do gentleman of the impression he intended to suggest. His superior attitude I found repugnant, and the casual manner with which he had treated us was almost offensive. I had noticed, as Holmes certainly would have, the faded curtains, scratched paintwork and threadbare carpet that told of a man of little means. From his bearing and accent, I deduced that he was of an aristocratic family, possibly disowned by them, and had subsequently ruined himself at the tables.

"I had thought," he continued, "that you gentlemen were connected with my benefactor, and had possibly brought an additional sum. I did suggest to Mr. Merrett that this might be fitting for some future time. After all, what is a man's life worth? You cannot put upon it a price."

"Mr. Merrett is missing," Holmes said, ignoring the question. "Is there anything you can tell us that might aid us in tracing his whereabouts? Some remark he might have made regarding his intentions for the immediate future, perhaps?"

Mr. Trench considered, but not for long. "No. As I told you, I can't say I know the fellow. It was a surprise to me when he called to pay me."

"Then we will bid you good morning, Mr. Trench."

We rose as one and left, leaving him surrounded by a disappointed air.

"Odious fellow," I said as we sought a cab.

"I suspect," Holmes remarked, confirming my own supposition, "that he has been recognised by his family as an idler and a parasite and dismissed from their company. Some of those who are long-established wouldn't like their name associated with one who would squander their wealth."

When our hansom reached Baker Street, my friend requested that I inform our landlady that he would be late for lunch and remained in the cab. In our sitting room, I indulged myself with a brandy and began work on my patient notes that had been somewhat neglected of late.

Mrs. Hudson entered to enquire if I knew how much longer Holmes was likely to be, and I answered that I did not, but the moment she returned to the kitchen I heard a cab come to rest below, followed by our front door opening and slamming shut. I heard him bounding up the stairs and he entered with a flourish.

"Holmes!" I exclaimed. "I will tell Mrs. Hudson – " I ceased at once because I saw that his face was bruised. "Are you all right? What has happened to you?"

He brushed away my concern, hanging up his hat and coat and seating himself at the table at once.

"Do not concern yourself. I have at least had some unexpected exercise."

"What has occurred, then?"

"I'll explain in a moment. First let us partake of the excellent steak-and-kidney pie that I could smell as I entered. I hear Mrs. Hudson on the stairs now."

It was on clearing our plates and awaiting the fruit-and-cream dessert that I alone consumed completely that he told me that his intention had been to seek out some of his informants.

"I eventually discovered one fellow I wanted in an inn on the King's Road," he announced. "After meeting Mr. Trench, I formed the opinion that he was probably lacking in scruples enough to have a hand in detaining Mr. Merrett, with a view to extracting from him the remainder of his funds. As it happened, my supposition was quite wrong, but I had felt it worth pursuing."

I nodded. "And the bruises on your face?"

"That came from the blackguard who has lately followed us. I was aware that he was still with me as I searched on foot. He attacked me in an alley and I fought off his knife thrusts with my stick. Disarmed, he resorted to his fists, but thought better of it. I pursued him into the street where he ran in front of a dray laden with barrels, which tumbled from the cart when the driver pulled up swiftly. My would-be assassin was trapped beneath them, and so will not be a threat to anyone again. The driver was shocked and bewildered, so I called upon a passing constable to help."

"Was your assailant known to you?"

"I saw his face and noted his singular peculiarities, but I couldn't put a name to him. Doubtless my index will inform me further."

We rose from the table and Holmes checked his index.

"Did you discover the identity of the man who attacked you?" I asked.

Holmes replaced the volume. "His name is – or was – Rupert Carstairs, a known assassin against whom a crime has never been proved. The capital is well rid of him."

I moved towards my armchair, but saw that Holmes had other intentions.

"If you would care to accompany me," he said, "I will next visit the second name on the list, Mr. Willian Jeavon, this afternoon."

We arrived in Knightsbridge within the hour.

Holmes rapped upon the door of a house rather less imposing than the others in a pleasant tree-lined street. At first there was no reply, but we heard movement within as he was about to repeat the summons.

"Mr. Jeavon has experienced an injury, I perceive," he remarked before the door was opened.

"You deduced that because he has taken an extraordinarily long time to answer the door." I ventured.

"Not entirely. As soon as we could hear his approach, I noted that the sounds were uneven, such as someone with a pronounced limp would make. He seems to move quite quickly however, so we may surmise that he has lived with his condition for long enough to become at least partially accustomed to it."

"Then why was his response not more immediate?"

"Doubtless he has difficulty rising from his armchair, or there may be any number of other reasons."

At that moment the door swung open, revealing a man I judged to be about forty years of age who leaned heavily upon a wooden crutch. He looked at us enquiringly until Holmes introduced us and explained our purpose, then smiled broadly and bade us enter.

"Mr. Merrett is an extraordinary man," he pronounced when we were seated in his sitting room and had refused tea. "He called upon me with a most generous gift. I was born in this house and have lived here all my life, but since the death of my parents, it has been a constant struggle to pay the rent. Thanks to him the place will soon be mine. I cannot express my gratitude sufficiently."

"Would you be kind enough to explain how you came to receive this sum?" Holmes asked.

Our host's smile suddenly lost some of its warmth. "There is nothing dishonest involved here, I hope. Surely the money cannot have come into

Mr. Merrett's possession dishonestly?"

"Not at all."

"Then kindly explain the reason for your question."

"Mr. Merrett seems to have disappeared," I stated. "We are attempting to trace him to ease the concern of his nephew," said I.

Holmes said nothing, but I saw that he was studying Mr. Jeavon's expression closely.

"I do hope there is no cause for alarm," said our host. "Perhaps he has taken a holiday, because of his new-found wealth, or visited a relative who lives far away. I am sure there is a simple explanation."

Holmes nodded. "We are anxious to confirm that this is so. Pray tell us then, how he came to bestow this gift upon you."

"Some months ago, we shared a carriage on the Glasgow Express. We got to talking, and I told him of the charity that I often contribute to, an organisation that exists for the benefit of disabled ex-railway workers such as myself. Mr. Merrett was impressed enough to request my address, with the promise that he would donate a substantial sum if certain negotiations turned out as expected. Apparently they did, for I received a visit from him and the sum that I have already described."

"Quite so. Can you recall from your conversation, then, any indication of Mr. Merrett's future intentions? Kindly mention even the smallest hint, for it is often those that lead to greater conclusions."

Mr. Jeavon spent a few moments in contemplation. "No, I cannot remember that we spoke of any such thing. We spoke mostly of other railway journeys and the unfamiliar varieties of fruit that are now imported, but that is all."

I noted a curious look on Holmes's face as we rose to leave. We bade Mr. Jeavon good afternoon and left. As we walked towards the High Street in search of a hansom, my friend appeared deep in thought.

"That man isn't all that he seems," I said to intrude upon his reverie.

"I am aware of that, but how did you reach that conclusion?"

"He spoke of using Mr. Merrett's money to buy the house, and yet the promise made on the train was for the money to be donated to the charity he mentioned."

"Indeed." He raised his stick and a passing cab came to a halt ahead. "But there is more involved here. As soon as I set eyes on Mr. Jeavon, I knew I had seen him before. Or perhaps I have seen his photograph in the dailies. Let us return to Baker Street, and we will see what can be discovered."

Surprisingly, my friend was in no great hurry to do anything but consume a glass of fine porter on returning to our sitting room. I assumed this was because the appearance of Mrs. Hudson with our dinner was imminent, and the good lady served us with roast lamb moments after we had drained our glasses.

"I recommend that you busy yourself with the evening edition of *The London News*." Holmes advised when our meal was over. "I will join you presently, after I've settled some things to my satisfaction."

He then immersed himself in his index, and I anticipated an evening of little conversation. I was pleasantly surprised when he gave a cry of triumph less than half-an-hour later.

"Ha! I knew it! Our friend Mr. Jeavon had indeed featured in the newspapers. His claim to have worked on the railways is false, since he was released from Newgate Prison less than a year ago."

I sat up straight in my armchair, lowering the newspaper. "What was his crime?"

"One of the lowest that there is: *Blackmail*. I wonder what actually occurred in that railway coach. Did Mr. Merrett accidentally disclose something that he would have preferred to remain hidden? From what we know of him, it would have seemed unlikely. Still, humanity is an infinite puzzle, and people are often not as they appear. I think Lestrade will be appreciative when I direct his attention to this."

When Holmes appeared to have finished his observations, I seized upon a moment of silence to request that he lifted his ban on the publication of several past enquiries. He considered for a few moments before answering.

"I was about to refuse, Watson," he said then. "but on reflection, the deaths of both Lord Boltonmere and Miss Marie Baccour have been reported during the past month, so I suppose you might consider inflicting your over-dramatised accounts of their activities upon the public."

"Thank you."

From there we talked for a while about the rising threat from Imperial Germany, until we agreed that it was time to retire.

As we left the room, he reminded me. "In the morning, we'll take a cab to Mayfair to visit the last person on Mr. Worth's list. If Miss Andrea Milton can throw no light on Mr. Merrett's disappearance, we're forced to divert our investigation to a different direction."

We then wished each other goodnight, and I went up to my room wondering what Holmes had in mind.

I rose to find Holmes already prepared for the day ahead. Breakfast was over swiftly, and I sensed that he had learned something more from his index that he hadn't yet shared with me. That, I concluded, would explain both his unusually bright early-morning disposition and the reappearing but faint smile of triumph on his lips as he reminded me, "I don't anticipate the need to be armed today, but there is a remote likelihood, so kindly keep your service revolver on your person."

I drank the last of my coffee and pushed away my cup. "It's rarely far from my side these days."

"Stout fellow!" He pushed back his chair and rose quickly, full of enthusiasm for what was to come. I felt convinced that he now perceived this to be the end of our investigation, but I didn't ask him to elaborate since it has always been his custom to inform me at the time he considered most appropriate, and I knew he wouldn't depart from that.

We paused in our journey at a Post Office, from where Holmes despatched a telegram. Once again our destination was a district that is affluent and most pleasant to the eye. Our cab deposited us in a short Mayfair street of old but sturdily built houses. As the hansom departed, Holmes scarcely took time to look around us before striding up a paved path amidst an immaculate lawn that was edged by roses.

"Do not contribute to the discussion more than necessary. Observe closely the lady's response to my questions."

Moments after he had rapped upon the door, a maid appeared. Holmes gave the young girl his card, and we waited.

We were bidden to enter almost immediately and shown onto a high-ceilinged drawing room with elegant furnishings. The tall windows looked out upon a garden that was a carpet of flowers of many species and colours, and an extremely beautiful woman reclined upon a chaise longue awaiting us.

"Good morning, gentlemen," she said as she rose to greet us. Indicating the surrounding armchairs, she bade us be seated as she resumed her position.

"I am aware of your profession, Mr. Holmes," she began before we could speak, "but I cannot imagine how it has brought about a crossing of our paths. Curiosity, therefore, compelled me to grant you this interview."

"There is no mystery to it, Miss Milton," my friend replied. "We are engaged upon an enquiry regarding a gentleman who has suddenly disappeared from his home and his usual haunts, for the purpose of allaying the concerns of his relatives and friends."

She adopted an expression of what seemed to me exaggerated surprise. I thought that she could be no more than thirty years of age, her hair fashioned exquisitely and her costume of the deepest blue.

"And who would that be, pray?"

"Mr. Septimus Merrett, who we believe you have met twice recently. We have been informed that you were a beneficiary of a sum of money from him."

"You are correct, in part. The first occasion of our meeting was to

106

make an arrangement whereby I advanced a large sum to Mr. Merrett, and the second was to effect his repayment. Other than those times, I knew nothing of him."

"Most strange," Holmes said after a moment. "We were led to believe him to be a man of adequate means."

"Of his financial position, or anything else about him, I know nothing."

"You had never met Mr. Merrett, before lending him this amount?"

She shifted, against the cushions. "Never. I have said as much."

"It strikes me as extraordinary that you would have committed so much to a stranger."

I noticed that a tiny red patch had appeared, just below her eyes on each side of her face.

"You find it unusual, only because you do not know me."

Holmes smiled faintly. "Much to the contrary, Madam. I know far more about you than you think."

A different expression came into her eyes. Fear, or curiosity, perhaps.

"What do you mean?" she retorted. "Explain yourself, sir."

"Isn't it true that you are in fact the wife of Rupert Carstairs, who is a rather clumsy killer for hire on occasion? No, do not bother to deny it. I knew it as I entered this room, for the fragrance of your quite unusual perfume was also on your husband's clothes when he attempted to halt my investigation with my murder after apparently following my client when I was consulted. Oh, I see that you have been somewhat worried that he hasn't returned to you. I can assure you that he never will."

A stillness had come over her, but I could see no tears or indication of regret for her loss.

"You killed him," she said coldly.

"Not so. He ran from our altercation and was struck by barrels falling from a cart. Tell me, was his attack upon me his own decision, or did you have a hand in it?"

She didn't answer Holmes's question. "A breath of an exotic fragrance will not convict me, and you have no other proof."

"There you are in error. When I tore the mask from your husband's face I did not recognise him, but I did remember that the top of his left ear was missing. The framed photograph displayed on the occasional table over there near your fireplace shows an identical disfigurement."

"That is enough!" Miss Milton – or as she really was, Mrs. Carstairs – got to her feet quickly and confronted us. "You have been quite clever, Mr. Holmes, but it has led you to your destruction. This is an old house, with a large vault adjoining the cellar. That is where Rupert and I deposited the body of Mr. Septimus Merrett when we realised the extent of the wealth he carried with him. You and Doctor Watson will join him there shortly, and will never be found, because no one ever enters the place."

I saw that she had produced a tiny pistol from the folds of her dress. Holmes stepped sideways, shielding me from her sight. Nevertheless, I had no time to draw my revolver, but as she raised her weapon I picked up a cushion from the chaise longue and hurled it at her face. It went wide but distracted her for an instant, long enough for Holmes to wrench the pistol from her grasp. Other than a hostile glare she showed no emotion, but shook her head in resignation and resumed her seat at the same moment that a furious beating upon the front door began. I heard the maid run to answer and then a brief hurried exchange, before Inspector Hopkins and two burly constables rushed into the room.

"I see that you have the situation well in hand, Mr. Holmes," he said breathlessly. "Were your suspicions justified?"

"Completely," my friend replied as he relinquished the pistol. "Everything has been revealed to my satisfaction. This tiny weapon is capable of killing at short range, but Doctor Watson and I have managed to avert our demise. If you would escort Mrs. Carstairs to Scotland Yard, we will call in later to furnish the details."

After little more conversation, the inspector placed handcuffs on her wrists. With the constables, he left shortly after.

"Holmes," I said now that we were alone, "it's clear to me that you learned much from your index and your informers that you haven't seen fit to confide in me. Who is this woman?"

"Her original name I do not know," he confessed. "But I have discovered that she has a criminal history of long standing. While consulting my index, I realised that a number of unsolved crimes were committed by the same woman using different identities. Eventually she met and married Mr. Rupert Carstairs while retaining a previous name for the purposes of earning her living. This took the form of frequenting the various gambling dens around the capital. She would befriend anyone who had won a large sum and either dispose of them or somehow cheat them of their winnings. As you observed, she appears to have profited greatly from her activities. By her own admission, she conspired with her husband to murder Mr. Merrett, and so will surely face the hangman."

"A sad fate for such a beautiful woman."

He gave me a mildly sympathetic look. "Watson, how often have I told you that the outward appearance is rarely an indication of the true person? Beneath her beauty is the heart of a devil, make no mistake."

Two months later Holmes's prediction was proven correct, as Mrs. Carstairs was hanged. The true reason for Mr. Merrett's visit to her was never discovered, since to the last, she refused to divulge it.

Murder in Grasmere
by David MacGregor

I suppose, by exercising my imagination to its utmost, that I could conjure up a more unpleasant way to start the day. Perhaps a roaring conflagration sweeping down Baker Street in such a fashion as to put the Great Fire of London in 1666 to shame. Perhaps the cries of newsboys heralding a Mongol Invasion on the south coast of England. Still, being summoned to the bedside of Muriel Higgins at an ungodly hour of the morning by her doting husband was bad enough. When I opened the door to see the bald head and squinting green eyes of Mortimer Higgins, not a word needed to be exchanged between us. I immediately fetched my trusty black medical bag and dutifully followed him down three streets to attend to the spectacularly hypochondriacal Mrs. Higgins and pull her once again from death's door.

In the past year, she had contrived, in her own mind, to contract not only bubonic plague and dengue fever, but also gout, diphtheria, and tuberculosis. Fortunately, my soothing bedside manner and the occasional administration of headache powder had inspired a brisk recovery on all of these occasions. I had long since given up any hope of convincing her that her various ailments existed almost entirely in her own mind, because I finally realized the root cause behind all of her assorted crises. Her episodes, bouts, and bad turns were all simply a way of giving her patient husband reasons to dote on her more than he already did. He would stand patiently at the foot of the bed, a small smile on his face, as I examined the invalid from head to foot and invariably prescribed a strong cup of tea and a nice walk in the park. They were an odd pair to be sure, but they had settled on the kind of marriage that suited them both, and that was that.

My mood was by no means improved when I emerged from their flat to find that it had begun to rain, although not in earnest. Eschewing the possibility of hailing a hansom cab, I simply quickened my step and soon found myself slightly out of breath as I ascended the steps up to our rooms. By this point, my friend Sherlock Holmes was already up and staring out our window onto Baker Street with a pensive expression on his face. He didn't bother to acknowledge my arrival in the slightest – not when I took a few moments to put on some dry clothes, not when Mrs. Hudson kindly brought in a pot of fresh tea, and not when I ventured to the window myself to see what he might be looking at. It was only when I had made myself comfortable in my armchair that he deigned to speak, laconically remarking, "May I take it that you have once again heroically rescued Mrs. Higgins from death's door?"

"You may," I returned, but I was still in such a peevish state of mind that I couldn't be bothered to ask Holmes how he had managed to come to that quite accurate conclusion with not a word from me.

Still, without even a glance in my direction, Holmes continued, "Mr. Higgins is possessed of a rather distinctive knocking style – three normal taps followed by two more solid blows to our door. I then watched as you returned on foot to our rooms, so your excursion was short enough to not require a cab. You were slightly damp as you came in, but not drenched through, which confirmed that your walk was a short one, and the presence of your medical bag indicated you had been called out on professional duties."

"Bravo," I muttered, and it was only then that Holmes turned from the window.

"Oh dear," he said. "I fear that I have begun to bore my dutiful chronicler with my rather tiresome deductive observations. I'm merely keeping in practice, dear fellow."

"For what?" I answered. "We haven't had an interesting case in the past two months."

This elicited an amused chuckle from Holmes. "My word. The good doctor is most definitely out of sorts on this damp summer day. Perhaps this might change your mood."

With that, Holmes dropped a telegram into my lap, and I picked it up to read:

> Murder most foul in Grasmere. Lepidopterist dead. Please come if possible.
>
> Willadsen

"Grasmere?" I looked up at Holmes. "That's in the Lake District."

"Geographically correct," he answered.

"And a lepidopterist is someone who studies and collects butterflies."

"Watson, your early morning house-call has honed your wits to a razor's edge."

At this, I felt what little energy I had ebb out of me. Mrs. Higgins had started the job, and now Holmes's sarcastic remark had finished it. I couldn't expect an apology from Holmes, but recognizing that he had gone a bit too far, Holmes proceeded to tap me gently on the shoulder, then topped off my cup of tea. Raising it to my lips, I decided to give him one more chance to offer something more than a clipped and unhelpful reply.

111

"Do you know this Willadsen?"

"I do," answered Holmes. "Alan Willadsen. Quite an amiable young chap that cut his policing teeth with six months as a London constable, but who fancied himself as a poet more than anything else. When the opportunity arose to take a position in Grasmere, he was off like a shot, no doubt hoping that the salutary atmosphere which inspired both Wordsworth and Coleridge would guide his pen as well. He's been up there nearly two years now, and for all I know this may be the first crime he has encountered in that famously pastoral setting."

"So then," I asked, "are you going to Grasmere?"

"I don't see why not," said Holmes. "I have a consultation with Mycroft tomorrow evening regarding a delicate situation unfolding in Amsterdam, but in the meantime a brief trip north would not be amiss. The train from Euston Station departs for Oxenholme in the Lake District in one hour. We'll have to switch trains to make our way to Windermere, after which it will have to be a cab to Grasmere."

"'*We'll*'?" I had snatched at the only word I had really heard.

"If I might have the pleasure of your company," said Holmes. "Mind you, if Mrs. Higgins looks likely to take a turn for the worse, I'll understand perfectly if you prefer to stay in London."

I only heard those last few words dimly, as I had already made my way to my bedroom to pack quickly for the adventure ahead. *Grasmere!* I had heard the name, of course, but had never had the privilege of visiting there in person. It was a small-enough village, but its reputation as a hub of literary activity in the early part of the nineteenth century put it on a par with any other city in England, save London itself. There was no time for me to do a quick review of the Lake District and its various celebrated inhabitants, but a long train ride with Holmes would doubtless leave me a veritable fount of information in the next few hours. Truth be told, Holmes and I made an excellent pair in this regard. He enjoyed regaling me with examples of his admittedly prodigious knowledge, and I marveled at all of the events and personalities of which I had only the most perfunctory knowledge.

It was only as we settled into our seats as the train puffed away quietly in Euston Station, that I began to have some misgivings regarding just how informed Holmes might be on the literary giants associated with the Lake District. They were, after all, poets, and poetry wasn't a topic likely to play a significant role in the life of a consulting detective. On the other hand, he was Holmes, and it appeared to me on more than one occasion that he had somehow assembled his vast warehouse of knowledge almost by osmosis. Merely put him in a room with *The Twelve Caesars* by Suetonius and an hour later he would be able to write a treatise on the life of the

Emperor Tiberius. This was patently ridiculous, of course, but Holmes's offhand remarks on subjects as diverse as the religious practices of the Aztecs and the life cycle of the duck-billed platypus had amazed me upon more than one occasion.

It was only as the train began to pick up speed on its way out of London that I looked across at Holmes with raised eyebrows and he instantly took my meaning, shaking his head in response.

"I'm afraid that my knowledge of the Lake District and its famous poets is rudimentary at best. I was rather hoping you might fill me in. You are the writer, after all."

"Writer, yes," I replied, a feeling of disappointment settling over me. "Poet, no. I'm afraid it's a literary form that never quite caught my fancy."

"Ah, well," Holmes turned his gaze out the window. "I do know that Thomas De Quincey was a frequent visitor to Grasmere. Perhaps we can take some inspiration from him."

"What?" I answered, a faint feeling of alarm running through me. "The author of *Confessions of an English Opium-Eater*? Surely not."

"No, no, nothing of the kind." Holmes pulled out his pipe and began to tamp it down. "Some years after overcoming his laudanum addiction, De Quincey published a trilogy of essays whose subject matter is much more in line with my own interests: *On Murder Considered as One of the Fine Arts*. Let us hope that the crime Willadsen has for us is of some interest, perhaps even venturing into the artistic realms so enthusiastically described by De Quincey."

"He was enthusiastic about murder?"

"Well, his principal intent was to satirize the aesthetic theory of Immanuel Kant, but De Quincey did describe Cain, the first murderer recorded in the Bible, as '*a man of first-rate genius*'. We shall see if the same level of genius has recently visited Grasmere."

The remainder of our journey north passed uneventfully, although the sun burst through the clouds about an hour after leaving London, promising a pleasant day ahead in the Lake District. At length, Holmes and I clambered into a cab in Windermere for the last leg of our excursion, which would take us the final nine miles to Grasmere. I had managed to pick up a map of the Lake District at the Oxenholme rail station, so that as we continued north, I was able to fill Holmes in on the various sites and scenery. After passing over the Troutbeck Bridge, we gradually turned west, and soon found ourselves almost on the banks of Lake Windermere itself, before passing through Ambleside and Rydal, then finding the River Rothay on our left before finally entering the bucolic village of Grasmere. As our cab came to a halt, Holmes immediately leapt out as I sat in a kind

113

of daze, still endeavouring to take in the stupefying amount of beauty I had just witnessed.

Too much time in London had accustomed me to a hard world of buildings and business, and crowds of people hurrying to their next destination with nary a glance at their fellow humans. The rhythm of the city was like a steam-hammer metronome, all hustle and bustle, the affairs of Empire requiring a pace and energy that left no time for pause or reflection. But the Lake District was the antithesis of London. Gentle peaks rose next to softly burbling waters. The puffy white forms of sheep dotted hillsides, and the rare person that was seen moved with all the leisure of a Highland cow exploring a fresh field of clover. We entered Grasmere itself via a winding road framed by ancient stone walls, to the sound of joyous school children in their bright blue sweaters chasing a ball across an emerald field of grass. It was, quite simply, a world of almost unbearable beauty.

"Murder, Watson." I came to with a start, seeing Holmes's face staring at me from outside the cab.

"Right, of course." I scrambled to collect my things. "Murder."

The cab had come to a halt outside the extremely modest Grasmere Police Station, and a moment later we were in the even more modest office of Chief Constable Alan Willadsen, who rose to greet us. He was a young man, perhaps not even thirty, with dark brown eyes and an apparently untamable cowlick in his light blond hair. His hands fluttered, his eyes shifted back and forth, and he gave every appearance of a man for whom the past few hours had been the most stressful of his life.

"Mr. Holmes! Dr. Watson! Thank you so much for coming! Thank you! Please sit down. If you would care to sit. Or we can stand. I'm entirely at your disposal whether we stand or sit. Thank you so much for coming!"

Holmes and I exchanged a glance, then Holmes reached for one of the plain wooden chairs next to the desk and I followed his lead.

"Perhaps we'll just sit a moment," began Holmes, "so you can fill us in on what's happened."

"Excellent!" Willadsen took his chair behind the desk. "That way we're all sitting. Most excellent, indeed. Yes."

Willadsen licked his dry lips as his gaze flickered between Holmes and myself.

"Calm yourself, Willadsen. What's done is done. Watson and I will do our best to assist you as best we can."

"Thank you! Yes indeed! Excellent! Most excellent! Thank you so much for coming!"

114

As Willadsen lapsed into silence, Holmes leaned across the desk and grasped Willadsen by the wrist, "I want you to get a hold of yourself and tell us what has happened. Your telegram said there had been a murder."

Swallowing hard, Willadsen only nodded, so Holmes continued. "Do you know who was murdered?"

"I do, yes," answered Willadsen. "Indeed, I do. Yes."

"Would you care to share the name of the unfortunate individual with us?"

"Mr. Percy Cholmondeley." Even uttering the name stirred Willadsen to new heights of agitation. He rose from his chair and began pacing behind it, wringing his hands. "Mr. Holmes, I pride myself on being a good Chief Constable. In my time in Grasmere, I have located or retrieved no fewer than two-dozen lost pets. If I do say so myself, my familiarity with everyone in the village enables me to break up almost any pub fight with no damage to the participants or the pub itself. And just last month I was able to solve the mystery of the disappearing gingerbread. But this . . . ."

Willadsen turned to us and spread his hands in supplication.

Holmes rose from his chair. "Perhaps if you could take us to the location of the crime."

"Yes. The location. Yes, indeed. It isn't too far from here."

True enough, a walk of not more than five minutes was all that was needed to leave any trace of human activity behind us. As we entered a small copse of trees, Willadsen's pace slowed, and he gestured with his head that Holmes and I should venture deeper into the woods. Not fifty yards further on we came upon a most jarring sight. Two butterfly nets lay next to what I presumed was the murder victim, who was leaning against a tree and had been covered by a rough tarpaulin. Keeping his distance behind us, Willadsen explained the scene to us.

"I put the tarpaulin over him, Mr. Holmes," began Willadsen. "I didn't know what else to do. Then I sent a telegram to you."

"You left the body unguarded?" asked Holmes. At a helpless shrug from Willadsen, Holmes continued. "Who discovered him?"

"Jamie Goodison. Smart lad. Just turned ten years old last week. On his way to school, he took this way as a short-cut and . . . found what he found. He came straight to me, or at least he said he did. I told him not to tell anyone."

"And judging by what footprints I can observe, he has obeyed your injunction," said Holmes. "Curious. A lad of that age would usually be frantic to tell his friends about such a discovery."

"Mr. Holmes . . ." Willadsen hesitated. "The poor boy was traumatized. He could barely speak when he came to me. And when he led me back here, I understood why. I knew right away that it was Mr. Cholmondeley, but . . . ." Willadsen trailed off with a shake of his head.

"Very good, Willadsen," said Holmes. "Just stay where you are while Watson and I examine the body."

Being careful with every step he took, Holmes approached the slouched form as I followed behind him. With infinite care, he lifted the tarpaulin and pulled it from the corpse, revealing a sight that will stay with me until the day I die. It was a heavy-set man of some sixty years of age, grey hair, with two flasks on the ground next to him, as well as some birding glasses nestled in his lap. A collecting box for butterflies was nearby, and it was here that the vision veered into the obscene and fantastical. His killing jar, one made of clear glass with a mass of what appeared to be white cotton wool stuffed into the bottom, had been tied to the poor man's face by a leather cord, covering both his mouth and nose. Worse than this, the loose tarpaulin which had covered him hadn't deterred various insects from descending upon his corpse for an easy meal. Even as Holmes and I looked on, various flies and ants were entering and leaving his eye sockets, and I observed Holmes's jaw clench as he took in this grotesque vision.

Ever the master of even the most disturbing situation, Holmes spoke without even turning. "Willadsen, I want you to fetch a cart or barrow so that we may convey Mr. Cholmondeley to the local doctor's office, where we might examine him more closely."

The words were scarcely out of Holmes's mouth before the sounds of the rapidly retreating Willadsen had faded into silence. Kneeling next to the corpse, Holmes quickly determined that both of the flasks were empty, as was the box for collecting butterflies. He then carefully examined the leather cord knotted around the killing jar, before using his penknife to cut it and remove it from Cholmondeley's face. Holmes waved his hand gently over the open top of the jar, cautiously sniffing the air.

"Potassium cyanide," he announced. "A popular means of disposing of insects among entomologists, but lethal to any living organism."

"In this case, Mr. Cholmondely," I added.

"An ugly way to die," said Holmes, "but the absence of any signs of struggle would indicate the following sequence of events: Mr. Cholmondeley armed himself for his butterfly hunting expedition with his weapons of choice, but having little success, decided to sit down beneath this tree and drown his sorrows from his two flasks."

Holmes picked up one of the flasks and sniffed at the opening.

"Gin," he announced, "which apparently caused Mr. Cholmondeley to fall into an alcohol-induced slumber. It was then that some unknown passerby happened upon this scene and decided to relieve Mr.

Cholmondeley of all his earthly troubles with the weapon at hand – a jarful of cyanide."

"Do you think the murder could possibly have been premeditated?" I asked.

"Not at all. Observe that this piece of leather cord used to secure the jar previously served to hang the birding glasses around Mr. Cholmondeley's neck. Our enterprising murderer simply took advantage of the materials at hand."

"Who would do such a thing?" I asked.

"Who indeed?" answered Holmes, pulling out his magnifying lens as he crouched down. "Let us see if a closer examination of the ground reveals anything."

Some ten minutes later, Holmes rose to his full height with a grumble. "Thanks to his substantial girth, Mr. Cholmondeley's tracks are relatively easy to follow. I was also able to detect traces of what must be Willadsen's movements. Beyond that, nothing. The ground is simply too firm to retain any other impressions."

It was at that moment that we heard sounds of Willadsen returning with a cart to transport the body, and Holmes turned to me. "We shall have to enquire as to whether Mr. Cholmondeley had any known enemies or individuals who might benefit from his untimely demise. That can wait until we have had an opportunity to examine the body further. Not to impugn the abilities of rural practitioners, Watson, but if you could possibly assist in that examination, I would be most grateful."

Less than an hour later, the late Mr. Cholmondeley had been laid out on an examination table and I had been joined in the task of conducting the *post-mortem* by the elderly Dr. Spencer, whose contribution to the effort consisted largely of circling the table and muttering, "It's a bad business."

Chief Constable Willadsen refused to enter the room and was pacing up and down the corridor, while Holmes stood off to the side of the corpse and offered brief comments and suggestions regarding any recent abrasions, checking beneath the man's fingernails, and so on. In the end, we found nothing remarkable and settled on what had appeared to be apparent from the first – Mr. Cholmondeley had died from inhaling the vapours of his own killing jar.

Following this, Holmes thought it might be best to settle Willadsen's nerves with a libation or two at The Grasmere Arms, and after half-an-hour, it was a visibly relaxed Willadsen who answered Holmes's query as to whether Mr. Cholmondeley had any enemies. With a gentle shake of his head and another sip from his glass, Willadsen launched into his narrative.

"Where to begin, Mr. Holmes? The man seemed to positively revel in the discomfort and pain of others. As best as I have been able to determine, he came into a small inheritance in Newcastle and moved here shortly thereafter. That was about a year ago. Apparently, he took a fancy to the sisters who run the Grasmere Gingerbread Shop, Agnes and Irene Nelson, but when they both rejected his attentions, his moral character began to decline. He began drinking more and more heavily, and took up the pursuit of butterfly hunting as a hobby. No one here seriously believed he had any interest in butterflies, but he used it as an excuse to traipse all over other people's property at all hours of the day. I can't tell you the number of complaints I've had about ruined cabbage patches and trampled rose bushes. I would try talking to him and I've fined him on several occasions for trespassing, but he would simply pay the fine and carry on as before. We almost came to blows at one point."

"Really?" Holmes looked across the table at Willadsen. "What manner of mischief caused that? Not a ruined field of daffodils, I hope."

Willadsen smiled at Holmes's remark, then began reciting Wordsworth from memory:

> *I wandered lonely as a cloud*
> *That floats on high o'er vales and hills,*
> *When all at once I saw a crowd,*
> *A host, of golden daffodils.*

Holmes softly applauded this brief recitation, before asking, "And your own poetic efforts. How are they coming along?"

Giving Holmes a rueful smile, Willadsen shook his head. "Doggerel, Mr. Holmes. The best I can manage is poorly rhymed doggerel. I have come to realize that it is one thing to appreciate beauty, but quite another to express it eloquently. I would just as soon move back to London save for the fact that . . . Well, I'm sure you would agree that Grasmere does have its charms."

With that, Willadsen pulled a small notebook from his coat and set it before Holmes. "I don't know if this will be any help, but this is a record of all the disturbances in Grasmere since my arrival. Nothing of much consequence, as you will see, but please note the sheer number of incidents that involved Mr. Cholmondeley."

"Excellent, Willadsen." Holmes picked up the notebook and began leafing through it, his eyes scanning quickly every page. After a few moments of this, Holmes glanced up. "I note that the Grasmere Gingerbread Shop appears to be the scene of a number of recent altercations."

"Perhaps that's too strong a word," answered Willadsen. "Mr. Cholmondeley was in the habit of getting liquored up and then appearing in the shop just as they were closing. As I mentioned, he seemed to take great pleasure if he could somehow inconvenience or otherwise harass practically anyone in the village. But the principal target of his venom centered on the Gingerbread Shop, which is run by the two sisters who had rejected his advances. Lately, he had even begun making highly inappropriate comments to their niece, who is recently arrived in Grasmere and works in the shop as well."

"How recently?" asked Holmes.

"Two months ago. Apparently, her father died in a fishing accident on the Irish Sea, and it was her two aunts who very kindly took her in."

"Ah," Holmes closed the notebook, "then perhaps we might venture to this Gingerbread Shop to see what else we can learn. But before we do that, let me ask you, Willadsen: Have you formed any theory as to Mr. Cholmondeley's demise?"

"I have, Mr. Holmes, but I hesitate to even mention it for fear you will consider it too absurd to be remotely possible."

"Not at all," answered Holmes. "In my profession, I have found it necessary to be open to even the most far-fetched theories until they have been proven false. What are you thinking?"

"I'm thinking . . . ." Willadsen drained the remains of his glass and took a deep breath. "I'm thinking suicide."

Without looking I could almost feel Holmes's eyebrows arching upward. "Indeed? I will admit that's as bold a theory as I have ever encountered. What, pray tell, leads your suspicions in that direction?"

"With all due respect to the dead," continued Willadsen, "Mr. Cholmondeley was the most unpleasant human being I have ever encountered. It was as if some kind of evil worm writhed in his brain morning, noon, and night. When he saw beauty his first instinct was to destroy it."

"Hence his hobby of catching butterflies," I added.

"But not for science, nor even to admire their aesthetic beauty in death," returned Willadsen. "Simply to kill. To deprive others of their beauty, and the butterflies themselves of their very lives."

"Very well," said Holmes, "but how does all that lead to a man deciding to not only kill himself, but to try and make it appear as if he was murdered?"

"I'm not going to pretend I can understand his motivation completely," answered Willadsen, "but I was thinking about the issue as I waited for you and Dr. Watson to arrive from London. It occurred to me that if Mr. Cholmondeley had recently been diagnosed with some form of fatal malady, or if he himself suspected that his end was near, he would be mortified at the thought of going out with a whimper, as it were. Instead, he would concoct some form of monstrous scheme to inflict pain and misery even after he was gone. He would stage his own death, with the hope of making it appear that he had been murdered, with some perfectly innocent person then being convicted of the crime and quite possibly hanged."

"So that Mr. Cholmondeley would have his last laugh from the grave," I added.

"Exactly, Dr. Watson! That is precisely the sort of person he was."

Holmes leaned back in his chair and observed both Willadsen and me for some time as I saw his eyes shifting back and forth. At length, he rose from his chair and announced, "I fancy some gingerbread. Watson, can I tempt you at all?"

"Absolutely!" I answered, feeling more than a bit peckish.

Willadsen had risen from his chair at Holmes's words, and I could see an expression of excited anticipation in his face. "I'll take you straight there!" he announced. "As I mentioned to you, the shop is run by two sisters, Agnes and Irene Nelson, and it's their niece Euphemia who helps them out minding the counter. Given their unpleasant dealings with Mr. Cholmondeley, I thought it best to inform them of his demise, but swore them to secrecy regarding the matter."

This earned a sound of disapproval from Holmes, "Willadsen, in the future I would encourage you to follow the advice of Benjamin Franklin, who once astutely observed, 'Three can keep a secret, if two of them are dead.' But what's done is done. Please be so kind as to lead the way."

Our ensuing brisk two-minute stroll through town was accompanied by a few curious stares, so it was apparent that news of the murder had begun to make its way around the village. Whether this was due to the young boy who found the body, the doctor with whom I had conducted the *post-mortem*, or the Nelson sisters was impossible to guess, but murder has a way of making itself known, especially in small communities like Grasmere. We soon found ourselves entering the Grasmere Gingerbread Shop, and as we did so the counter-girl looked up at us in surprise, then returned her attention to the customer in front of her. She was a tiny thing, somewhere in her twenties, scarcely over five feet tall, and possessed of flaming red hair and bright blue eyes. Her cheeks and nose were dappled with freckles, and her familiarity with Willadsen was clearly evident as she relieved the customer of sixpence and then boxed up some gingerbread and speedily tied it up with butcher's string before turning her full attention on us.

"Alan!" she exclaimed. "How lovely to see you! And you've brought friends!"

"Indeed, I have!" answered Willadsen. "Euphemia, may I introduce you to Sherlock Holmes and his colleague, Dr. Watson. They've come from London to help . . . Well, to – "

"Meddle in our affairs?" boomed a feminine voice from the back of the shop. This was immediately followed by the appearance of not one, but two formidable ladies who came strolling towards us with expressions like thunder, eyeing Holmes and me up and down the whole while. This then, was presumably Irene and Agnes Nelson, the purveyors of the Grasmere Gingerbread Shop, and their ample forms spoke of their dedication to sampling their product on what I presumed was a daily basis. They were clearly anything but pleased to see us, as Willadsen began wringing his hands nervously and began to explain.

"They're . . . Well, what's happened with . . . I thought perhaps consulting with an experienced authority in such matters . . . I thought that . . . ." Willadsen trailed off feebly, and there followed a prolonged silence broken only when one of the sisters wiped her hands on her apron and launched into a sustained monologue, aided and abetted by her sister who chimed in with "*Ayes*" and "*That's right*" whenever the first sister required a breath to continue speaking.

"Percy Cholmondeley was a monster who deserved what happened to him, and there's no one in Grasmere about to mourn the death of a wicked man that we're well rid of . . . *Aye, that's right* . . . From the moment he came here, he wasn't right in the head, and not a day passed that he didn't make himself more unwelcome . . . *Absolutely, aye* . . . even propositioning both Irene and me on the very same day and skulking away like a whipped dog when we told him what we thought of him . . . *Too true, that* . . . Then when poor Phemie arrived here after the death of her father, it wasn't more than a few days before that evil man started looking at her in a way we did not like . . . *No, we did not* . . . and it was only Alan coming into the shop just last Thursday, was it Thursday? . . . *Aye, so it was* . . . that Mr. Cholmondeley was overstaying his welcome here and Alan gave him quite a talking to which we were happy to see . . . *So we were* . . . and Mr. Cholmondeley shook his finger at us and told us – well, I wouldn't like to say what he actually said . . . *No, no* . . . but it was very threatening, you best believe it, and he told us we'd be singing a different tune once he became our landlord, which gave both Irene and me quite a shock . . . *So it did* . . . and now that he's dead I say let the Devil take his soul and may he burn in eternity . . . *Aye, absolutely.*"

As this dual soliloquy came to a close, I wasn't quite sure how either Holmes or me would respond, so it was with some relief that I realized that Euphemia was holding out small pieces of gingerbread to both of us.

"Would you care for a sample?" she asked, as if her aunts' impassioned speech had never occurred. Holmes and I both took her offering and, as Holmes popped the piece of gingerbread in his mouth, I saw him savouring it with an air of appreciation that was uncommon to him when it came to the matter of food. At length, Holmes gave a satisfied sigh.

"Remarkable," he began. "Quite, quite delicious. I would describe its texture as being somewhere between a biscuit and a cake, and managing to be both sweet and pleasantly spicy at the same time thanks to an abundance of ground ginger, although I believe I detect notes of cinnamon and nutmeg as well. Truly unique. Unlike any gingerbread I have ever encountered. My congratulations, ladies. It's a rare thing in life to experience perfection, but that is what your gingerbread is. Your recipe is perfection and nothing less."

With that, the thundercloud expressions of both sisters dissipated in an instant, and sunny smiles lit up both of their faces.

"Oh, it isn't our recipe . . . *No, no* . . . It was our Aunt Sarah who invented it . . . *Back in 1854 it was* . . . Not that she opened this shop right away . . . *No, she didn't* . . . but people loved it so much and kept asking her to make it . . . *Aye, they did* . . . Tourists would come here and then take our gingerbread back to the bigger cities, so now here we are . . . *Aye, here we are.*"

This was followed by an awkward pause, after which one of the sisters turned to Euphemia. "Well, don't just stand there. Get these lovely gentlemen some more gingerbread."

Holmes held up his hands. "No, no, we couldn't possibly – "

"You can and you will . . . *With our compliments* . . . How many pieces would suit you?"

"Then perhaps just two or three small pieces to take with us back to London," answered Holmes.

With that, the lightning fingers of Euphemia went to work and within seconds Holmes held in his hands a box of gingerbread and we were back out on the street with the highly discombobulated Willadsen.

"Did I hear you right, Mr. Holmes? You're planning on returning to London immediately?"

"Yes, I'm afraid so. Watson and I shall spend the night at the Grasmere Inn, but then must begin our journey back south in the morning. However, I do have one question for you. The sisters failed to go into specifics, so I will ask you directly: What was the nature of your most recent unpleasant interaction with Mr. Cholmondeley?"

This was a question that clearly discomfited Willadsen, and he hemmed and hawed for a moment before answering. "As you might appreciate, Mr. Holmes, a man in my position does come in for a reasonable amount of abuse from the local populace, especially young men in their cups late in the evening. I'm used to it and accept it with as much good nature as I can manage. However, when I see a perfectly innocent person being subjected to such abuse, I simply cannot abide it. After making a drunken spectacle of himself with the sisters, I felt the need to intervene so that they could close up the store. I thought that would be the end of it, but – "

"To point a finer point on it," said Holmes, "you came upon Mr. Cholmondeley speaking inappropriately to Euphemia Nelson."

The colour immediately rose in Willadsen's face as he cleared his throat. "That I did. Miss Nelson was on her way home, and Mr. Cholmondeley caught up with her just outside the postmaster's. I will not repeat what I overheard, but once I had seen Euphemia on her way – yes, Mr. Cholmondeley and I had a rather spirited exchange, which ended with him threatening me in no uncertain terms."

"Would the postmaster be able to confirm this?" asked Holmes.

"I expect so, yes."

"Perhaps there was another witness or two in the vicinity?"

"I can't recall very clearly . . . I was in a somewhat heated frame of mind, Mr. Holmes, but quite possibly, yes."

At this, Holmes turned his eyes down the street and we became aware that several of the good citizens of Grasmere had gathered and were staring in our direction.

"Apparently, news of the death of Mr. Cholmondeley is spreading rapidly," said Holmes.

"Good Lord!" I detected a note of panic in Willadsen's voice. "This will make its way to Windermere, and who knows where else?"

"Then you must prepare yourself for the arrival of the press, Willadsen," I offered. "Take it from me, they live for bizarre cases like this. In fact, the more macabre, the better."

"Mr. Holmes . . . ." I could see Willadsen desperately trying to gather his scattered thoughts, ". . . could you possibly . . . if you might be able to . . . with all of your experience, perhaps you could handle any questions."

"As Chief Constable," began Holmes, "the press will be most interested in your opinion. Besides, as I mentioned, Watson and I will be returning to London, as I have an appointment with my brother Mycroft tomorrow evening."

"But Mr. Holmes! The murder! Can you offer me any kind of guidance at all?"

"Call on me at our hotel in the morning before we leave. I shall then give you my opinion on the matter. Come along, Watson."

As was typical of Holmes, his long stride soon outpaced my own, and in truth I slowed my pace even further to take in the spectacular vista surrounding me. The sun was setting behind verdant hills, the sky has turned various shades of violet and orange, and the gentlest of summer zephyrs brought a fresh breeze to my cheeks. Life was beautiful, even if my thoughts were of a much more dismal shade. It was abundantly evident that Willadsen was smitten with the young Euphemia, and every leering remark to which Cholmondeley had subjected the poor girl had fired the rage building in Willadsen's heart. The threats to the Nelson sisters and his own well-being had only stoked those flames, and when the opportunity presented itself to rid the community of Cholmondeley, Willadsen had taken it. By the time I got to our hotel room, Holmes had already lit a pipe and was deep in thought as wisps of smoke made their way to the ceiling.

"Well, Watson, what do you make of it?"

Knowing that Holmes would ask me this, I had my answer ready. "Suicide, obviously. Just as Willadsen deduced. No question about it."

Holmes stared at me, then removed his pipe from his mouth. "Fascinating. Would you care to explain further?"

"Come now, Holmes. We both know very well what really happened."

"Enlighten me."

"Chief Constable Willadsen may be a failure as a poet, but he could return to London and make his way onto any West End stage he pleased. Whether it be Shakespeare or Gilbert and Sullivan, I feel certain he would excel in any role. The man is a consummate actor. His apparent nerves and squeamishness since we arrived have been an act first to last."

"Then he is our murderer?"

"Of course! Did he have the motive? Most assuredly. The fact that he is quite taken with Euphemia Nelson is obvious, so he would feel duty-bound to protect her honour. Then he was threatened in public by Mr. Cholmondeley in front of witnesses. This would come out at any inquest, as would the fact that the ground immediately around Cholmondeley's body showed signs of only two pairs of footprints – the victim's and Willadsen's."

"I follow you so far," said Holmes, "but why would he summon me from London to investigate the crime if he was the perpetrator?"

"What greater proof of his innocence could there be than calling in Sherlock Holmes? *Would a guilty man do such a thing? Of course not. Therefore, he must be innocent.* That's what he's counting on, and I say we play along, rather than send the poor man to the gallows."

"Hmm . . . ." Holmes rose from his chair and produced his penknife. With an easy motion he cut the string on the gingerbread box, opened it, and offered me a slice. "Perhaps a piece of gingerbread might clear your thoughts."

"Then you don't agree?" I asked.

"I do not."

"Are you suggesting – ?" My thoughts were in a whirl as I tried to reorder the sequence of events in some manner that would make sense. And then, it all came to me in a rush, the way a magnifying lens may gather the gentle rays of the sun and focus them into a searing pinpoint of light. "The Nelson sisters! Of course! Not only did Cholmondeley threaten them, but he threatened their niece as well! Quite rightly, they decided that the air of Grasmere would be decidedly sweeter without the odious presence of Mr. Cholmondeley. They chanced upon the opportunity to murder him and took full advantage of it!"

"A plausible theory," began Holmes, "and I assure you that I shouldn't wish to fall afoul of the formidable Nelson sisters, but again no."

"Why not?"

"I would draw your attention to the curious incident of the footprints at the murder scene." As I gazed at Holmes in mystification, he continued. "As you rightly observed, the heavy-set Cholmondeley left his footprints and the lightly built Willadsen left only faint traces. Both sisters being nearer in size to Cholmondeley than Willadsen, presumably they would have left clear footprints as well. But we're forgetting one more presence at the scene: Young Jamie Goodison, the ten-year-old boy who found the body. Not a sign of him anywhere, for the simple reason that he is only a child and too small and light to leave any impression on the earth."

"You don't think he had anything to do with it, do you?" I asked.

"Of course not. But cast about in your mind for any other person we encountered today who would be too small and light to leave any kind of footprint behind."

"Euphemia!" I gaped at Holmes. "Surely not! She's such a tiny thing."

"A tiny thing who is madly in love with Willadsen, a fact that he has yet to fully appreciate. She had the motive, saw her opportunity, and took it."

"But how can you say such a thing? She was pleasant enough to Willadsen, but she was pleasant enough to us as well. There was nothing said between them that would indicate any kind of intense passion on her part."

"Love may speak its mind," continued Holmes, "as so many poets have expressed with great eloquence, but passion goes beyond words. If you had observed closely, when young Euphemia looked at Willadsen, there arose at the base of her throat a slight blushing effect, a capillary response to his presence quite out of her control. For all of our pretensions, human beings are still animals, and that response in the female signals to the male that his attentions will be most welcome."

"For God's sake, Holmes – "

"You may take it from me, she didn't stray far when Willadsen rescued her from Cholmondeley's attentions outside the postmaster's. When she witnessed the confrontation between the two men, her reaction would have been one of absolute fury, wanting nothing more than to fly to the defense of the man with whom she is in love. However, being a woman and not possessed of the size or strength to physically assault Cholmondeley, she could only fume in impotent anger . . . until Providence itself put the drunk and unconscious Cholmondeley in her path only days later. It was a Heaven-sent opportunity, and it was an opportunity that she took."

I shook my head at Holmes's words. "I see where you're coming from, but I'm sorry, I'm just not convinced."

"No? Observe." Holmes took the string that had been used to tie up the gingerbread box and set it before me. He then drew from his pocket the leather cord that had secured the killing jar to Cholmondeley's face and put it next to the string. "I would draw your attention to the knots."

Looking at both of the knots, it was instantly apparent that they were identical, as Holmes continued. "There are a variety of knots favoured by fishermen. This is known as the Palomar Knot, prized for the speed with which it can be executed. As we learned, Euphemia Nelson's late father was a fisherman, and I have no doubt that she learned this at her father's knee. Quite practical when tying up packages . . . and for other uses."

I looked up at Holmes, then down at the two knots, the truth of Holmes's words settling into me. A moment later, Holmes had swept both the string and the leather cord into his pocket.

"It has been a long day for both of us, Watson, and not without its exertions. We've an early rise, and a long journey before us tomorrow, so I propose that we retire early. I'll have a word with Willadsen before we depart."

Exhausted as I was thanks to my early morning with Mrs. Higgins, I still had trouble dropping off to sleep. The implications of everything Holmes had said weighed heavily on me, and the vision of the insects

126

crawling in and out of Mr. Cholmondeley's eye sockets wasn't one to encourage peaceful slumber. Still, I clearly managed to fall asleep, because I awoke to Holmes shaking me gently by the shoulder as morning light streamed through the window.

"Our cab awaits, old boy. Shift yourself and we'll be on our way."

"Have you spoken to Willadsen?" I asked.

Holmes glanced out our window. "It would appear he has been unavoidably detained. No matter. In fact, the fewer words, the better."

Ten minutes later, Holmes and I exited the hotel to find our cab just outside, along with a sizable crowd of people awaiting our appearance. Sure enough, Chief Constable Willadsen had been encircled by assorted townsfolk, and I spied the Nelson sisters and their niece Euphemia standing off to the side as three gentlemen of the press approached Holmes with their notebooks open and pencils ready. As expected, word of Mr. Cholmondeley's gruesome demise had spread beyond Grasmere, and would doubtless spread further in the coming days. Holmes stopped the three newspapermen in their tracks with a raised hand.

"Gentlemen, as much as I would like to tarry and answer all of your questions, I'm afraid that my friend Dr. Watson and I have a train to catch in Windermere. However, I will make a short statement related to this case and my findings. It was Chief Constable Willadsen who contacted me to request my assistance, and when I enquired as to his opinion of the case, he stated that he felt that Mr. Cholmondeley had died by his own hand with the intended purpose of making it appear as if he had been murdered. Shortly after this, I questioned my colleague Dr. Watson on the same point and found that he agreed with Chief Constable Willadsen's view of the case. Having examined all of the available evidence and given the matter my due consideration, I feel quite confident in issuing my own verdict, which coincides with that of my colleagues – Mr. Cholmondeley died by suicide. Nothing more, nothing less."

A buzz of excitement went around the assembled crowd as the gentlemen from the press scribbled frantically in their notebooks, and a moment later Holmes and I were in our cab. Motioning Willadsen to approach, Holmes had a quiet word in his ear, and then we were off at a pace calculated to get us to Windermere in time to catch our train back to London. It had all happened so fast that I was only able to manage my first question when we were a good way down the road.

"What did you say to Willadsen?"

"Nothing much. Just a gentle word of encouragement regarding his prospects with Euphemia Nelson."

"The murderess."

"The very same. I suspect she would rank quite high in Thomas De Quincey's assessment of various murderers throughout history. As De Quincey wrote, '*If once a man indulges himself in murder, very soon he comes to think little of robbing, and from robbing he comes next to drinking and Sabbath-breaking, and from that to incivility and procrastination.*' Let us hope that Miss Euphemia Nelson's indulgence doesn't lead her down such a dark path."

I sat back in my seat for a moment, looking out at the passing scenery, then felt duty-bound to state the readily obvious. "Holmes, we have sanctioned the murder of Percy Cholmondeley."

"Indeed we have. And what of it? I am interested in only two things – truth and justice. We were able to discover the truth, and I am satisfied that the actions of Miss Nelson were justified. Justice is not the sole province of bewigged old men in courtrooms, Watson. Justice belongs to all of us. It is when good people stand by and let wickedness prosper that any civilization begins its inexorable decline. Miss Nelson may have been motivated by her tender feelings for Willadsen, but she struck a blow for all of the inhabitants of Grasmere. Let us hope that when we are put in a similar position, that we would do likewise."

"All the same, I suspect that the English legal community would take exception to your point of view."

"The wealthy and powerful men of England devoted to protecting the interests of other wealthy and powerful men? No doubt. But that is not justice, and it would be a heresy against the truth to declare it as such. Am I suggesting anarchy? By no means. But a society in which every member feels they have a vested interest in justice taking place? Yes. A thousand times yes. So I have no compunction in saying that I hope Miss Nelson and Chief Constable Willadsen have many pleasant gingerbread-filled years ahead of them."

At this, I couldn't help but smile, and to my astonishment Holmes proceeded to reach into his pocket to retrieve two pieces of Grasmere gingerbread wrapped in paper. He handed one of the pieces to me and we raised our gingerbread in a toast.

"To the happy couple," announced Holmes.

"Hear, hear!" I agreed.

And with that, we both fell silent and devoted our attention to the quite excellent gingerbread of Grasmere.

The Case of the
Bryniau Witch Tower
by Paula Hammond

Holmes wandered around our rooms with his chin upon his chest, packing and repacking his pipe, with an attitude of weary forbearance. Eventually, pipe still unlit, he threw himself into his armchair and began thumbing through the morning papers.

He hummed tunelessly as he read, clearly finding nothing of interest in either the daily news or *The Police Gazette*. "It's no use," he finally said. "London has become too weary for words. One day I will write a monograph on the correlation between crime and temperature, for it's clear that as soon as the mercury rises, the criminal classes become absolute fools. There isn't a single crime, intrigue, or rumor here that a pudding-head like Lestrade couldn't muddle his way through."

"It *is* unseasonably hot for July," I ventured.

"What it is, is damnably dull! Honestly, Watson, if things don't improve, we may have to go on holiday, or something equally horrible," he replied theatrically.

"Sadly, the state of my finances means I'll be staying in London for the whole season." I sighed. I'd been itching to escape the smoky fog and noise of the city for weeks, but voicing my predicament sent me into quite the funk.

"Oh, my dear fellow!" Holmes exclaimed, sounding contrite. "You should have said something. Come!" he cried, jumping up with one of his characteristic bursts of energy. "My own finances are healthy enough for two. Choose somewhere, and we'll be off this very morning."

I suspected that Holmes's idea of paradise was to spend the entire summer, blinds half-drawn, pipe wedged between his lips, so I was reluctant to let such an unexpected offer pass by.

I had just read an advertisement in *The Morning Chronicle* for a delightful-sounding place on the Welsh coast. So it was that, within the hour, we were headed to Euston and, from there to Llandudno – which the marketing men had nicknamed "*The Queen of Welsh Watering Places*".

Our journey was so peaceful that I soon drifted into a sound sleep. One moment I was watching the sun rising over the patchwork of towns and factories that littered the English countryside, and the next, it seemed, our train was steaming along the coast, where sand and the fretful waves of the Irish Sea, unfolded before us.

Llandudno is named for Saint Tudno, one of the seven sons of Seithenyn, whose failure to maintain the sea defenses led to the drowning of his kingdom. In an attempt to atone for the sins of his father, Tudno established a small church on a huge limestone outcrop, known as the Great Orme's Head. A thousand years later, modern engineering has paved and terraced Tudno's massive rock, but it still dominates the town. Indeed, we saw the Great Orme long before Llandudno itself came into view.

The tourists who flock to this picturesque resort will tell you that the name, *Great Orme*, comes from the Norse meaning "*Great Wrym*", and there was something distinctly dragonish in its appearance. It loomed large over the town, its "head" the most prominent feature, with its body curling around the peninsula. Wrapped as it was in a heavy mist, the effect was quite striking.

By the time our train had pulled into the station, I was eager to see what other delights our destination had to offer. I had been yearning to feel the wind in my hair, and hear the crunch of shingle under my boots, and it was with a spring in my step that I alighted into the smoke-filled station.

The striking structure was perhaps four or five years old, and looked determinedly modern when compared to the smaller, provincial stations we'd seen en route. Red Ruabon bricks and finialed iron columns supported a vast glass canopy, which trapped both heat and steam within, creating a veritable Turkish bath.

The station's five platforms were filled with trains arriving and departing, and between them rushed an assortment of travelers and holiday-makers, all dressed for the summer, with their cares packed neatly away.

Between Platforms Two and Three ran a cobbled road, designed to allow hansoms to line up alongside the carriages, and it was there that we quickly found a cab.

We hadn't had time to make plans, or even pick a hotel, but after consulting the driver, we determined that The King's Head Public House would suit us very nicely, being on the edge of town, and close to the headland that the advertisement had made so much capital of.

"I have a suspicion," Holmes remarked to the ruddy-faced driver, "that my companion would rather walk. If you could deliver our luggage to the inn and secure us two rooms, we'd be very much obliged. But for now, where is this famous Great Orme that my friend is so keen to view?"

"Are you sure?" I asked Holmes, knowing that he neither shared my appreciation for nature, nor unwarranted exercise.

"My dear fellow," he replied, "based on the way you've been prowling around Baker Street, I'm fairly certain that should you spend another moment indoors – even if said indoors should prove to be deliciously cool and well-sprung – you're likely to explode. Besides, train carriages tend not to be designed for those with long limbs, and I could do with unknotting my legs.

"Well, it's a lovely day, mind," the driver intoned in a wonderfully sing-song accent. "As for *Y Gogarth*," he said, using what I assumed was the Welsh name for the hill, "you can't miss it." He gestured up and west, where the looming shadow of the Great Orme was perfectly visible through the station's glass canopy. "Cross the tree-lined avenue and take any road. They all lead up, eventually. It's quite a gentle walk, with plenty of places to stop and admire the view."

The man's instructions proved to be exact, and soon we were ascending the Orme with the sun on our faces, and a sea-breeze in our nostrils.

Before long, however, I was breathing hard and leaning into my cane. "Good Heavens!" I panted regarding the ever steepening road ahead with alarm. "I've climbed mountain passes in Peshawar that were less arduous than this!"

"Gentle indeed!" my companion laughed. "I'm beginning to suspect that Welshmen are part goat."

We ploughed on, feeling great sympathy for the poor pack animals we passed, who had been pressed into service hauling necessaries up and down the hill.

After thirty minutes of stumbling over a pathway rutted with the grooves of carriage wheels and the imprint of hobnails, we suddenly came to a row of stone cottages. And there, standing in the little garden, watering a row of potted plants, was Peter Jones, formerly of Scotland Yard.

It had been over six years since we'd encountered Inspector Jones, and at a glance, he seemed little changed. On closer inspection, he appeared leaner and fitter than the man who had been with us on that long vigil to apprehend John Clay in the bowls of the City and Suburban Bank.

He greeted us warmly, with a brisk handshake and a smile of delight.

"Well, as I live and breathe, if it isn't Mr. Holmes and Doctor Watson!"

"Country living suits you, Jones!" I exclaimed, genuinely pleased to see our old sparring-partner looking so well.

"They do say that!" the old police dog chuckled before waving us inside, where we found the little house delightfully compact and homey.

Jones invited us to sit while a woman, who he introduced as his sister, busied around, offering us tea and a type of flat scone made with currents, called a "Welsh cake".

Encouraged by Jones, I piled my plate high, and followed his example in liberally spreading the cakes with jam and butter. Thus provided with a much-needed – albeit much-delayed – breakfast, we settled down to get our breath.

"You retired then, Jones?" I asked.

"In a manner of speaking. After thirty years at the Yard, I had the chance to collect a pension which was equal to thirty-fiftieths of the pay. My baby sister, Nerys, had not long since lost her husband, and there was an opening for an inspector here. Well, I was starting to feel a little long in the tooth for chasing villains, and thirty-fiftieths pay is a little tight to live on in London, so it seemed a fine time to move back."

We made small talk for long enough for my legs to forget the steepness of the hill, then headed back out to attempt the summit.

"Very obliged for the refreshments, Jones," Holmes said, as we waved our farewells, "and should you need anything at all, we'll be staying in The King's Head."

My friend had once called Jones "an absolute imbecile". I prided myself on not being quite such an idiot.

"So, how long have you known that Jones was in Wales?" I asked, finding it hard to feel as annoyed as I should, with such spectacular views unfolding before us.

My friend gave me a sheepish grin. "Since last year, but remember: It was your choice to come here . . . ."

I shot him my best disapproving look. "And I suppose it was pure coincidence that I happened upon *The Morning Chronicle* and its pages – creased just so – fell open at a quarter-page advertisement for Inspector Jones's new beat?"

Holmes gave a small, embarrassed cough. "Sorry. Guilty as charged. But come, now, my dear Watson. You would have manfully gone through the whole summer without a break had I not determined that Llandudno could offer us both a much-needed respite. What is it Monsieur Taine says? '*We travel to change, not to change a place, but to change ideas.*'"

I wasn't about to let him off the hook. "And I suppose your spiderish networks told you exactly where the inspector could be found? Although knowing he would be watering his plants exactly as we walked past is a remarkable piece of prestidigitation, even for you!"

"There is such a thing as co-incidence, you know," Holmes replied, sounding abashed. "Although, had we not been so lucky, I imagine I'd have been compelled to knock for a glass of water . . . ."

"Well, don't think I'm going to forgive you so easily!"

He looked so shamefaced that I couldn't help but smile and soon, we were both chuckling heartily. It wasn't until we had climbed over the headland, that the beauty of the scene stopped all further laughter.

The sun was high now and there, before us, lay the sparkling sea. Small sail boats bobbed up and down on the horizon while overhead, curlew called mournfully to their mates.

I did not know what the scientific explanation was for the curious way the rays of sun broke through the clouds, like spotlights illuminating the land below, but in that moment, I fancied that Wales itself was telling me "*Here. You may take your rest here.*"

And rest I did.

Late afternoon had turned to early evening by the time we left the soft heather and scent of wild flowers behind, to begin our descent.

Soon, we were back on the same dust track we had ascended and before us, once again, lay the little row of miner's cottages where we had met Jones.

Suddenly Holmes let out a low cry. "Ho! What's this?"

It was some time before I spotted what Holmes's eagle-eyes had seen. There, silhouetted in the doorway of his cottage, stood Jones and a uniformed officer, deep in conversation.

The young constable gave a little start as we approached. I saw his face, pale and serious, and something in his attitude made my heart sink.

Holmes lengthened his stride, and it wasn't long before he had joined the conclave. As for myself, my knees protested horribly at the steepness of the track, and by the time I had caught up, it was clear that Holmes had already learned the reason for the solemn expressions and hushed tones.

"It's bad, Watson," he said, in a voice heavy with tension. He looked at Jones, who turned to give me the full weight of his regard.

"Mr. Holmes has already explained that you're in sore need of a sabbatical, but if you can help, it's a doctor we need now."

"You surely have doctors on call?" Holmes sounded so defensive that I instantly forgave him his previous machinations.

"This is a holiday town. On a warm weekend like this, every doctor is run off his feet setting bones and treating sunstroke. And none of them – not even the coroner – is *Doctor Watson*." He gave such weight to those final words that I felt myself blush.

"I really am so sorry, my dear fellow," Holmes said.

"Nonsense. Jones, Constable, I'm entirely at your disposal. If the fates have put us here, then let us do what we can."

There's nothing more wretched than a young woman in the full flush of life who has made that final climb up the golden staircase. As a doctor, I knew death in all its forms. Many times, it comes as a blessed release. For others, it's a painless journey. This young lady's death was neither of those things.

Enfys Tegwen was a lively, popular girl. She worked as a shop assistant, sang in the chapel choir, and sent money home to her elderly father in Bala every week.

Enfys lodged with two other girls in an attic room above Arthur's General Store, where all three worked.

That Saturday, she had asked for a day's leave to visit her sick father. The girl had no other relatives, so the store's owner readily agreed. She was away all day, and all night.

Saturday closing wasn't until half-past-eight, and Enfys's co-workers didn't get home until nine. When they rose the next morning for chapel, she still hadn't returned, which surprised them as she was diligent about attending. After chapel, the girls walked on the promenade, then along the pier, stretching out those little pleasantries as long as possible, as people do when they have the luxury of a free day, without any spare money to spend.

They returned to their lodgings around three, which is when they found their friend's body, curled up on her bed, dead.

She'd been sick – violently so, several times. Her dress and the bedsheets were bloodied and, from the position of her body, it was clear that she had suffered violent convulsions in the moments leading up to her death.

She was so pale, and there was so much blood, that it was clear she'd bled to death in this sad, little garret. But what had caused her to bleed in such a dramatic fashion? That was the question that occupied me.

I already had my suspicions, but a glass and an empty tin on the bedside table confirmed them. Inside both was the residue of a white powder – and it was this which revealed the lady's tragic story.

I handed it to Jones. "Hmm, sweets?" he said, looking at the label. "But Pollards aren't Welsh. They're based in Leamington Spa. My old Da always swore by their toffee. Had to order it for him by mail. Not cheap." He peered into the tin, sniffing experimentally. "Well that's not toffee, that for sure."

"I'll have to do some tests to be certain, but I've vouch its diachylon or similar."

"Lord!" the inspector whispered, clearly sensible of my meaning.

While I worked, Holmes prowled the room, looking for all those tiny details that would help piece together the poor girl's last moments.

134

"Mmm . . . we've been lucky. The black paint on the boards is relatively new. There's little scuffing beyond this patch, between the bed and the door. See here: The marks from two sets of shoes. One is a lady's walking boot, the other are a pair of men's lightweight dress shoes."

His face was almost pressed against the floorboards. Yet from his expression, it seemed that whatever patterns had revealed themselves to him, they were not as clear as he would have wished.

"The scuffs are confused, seeming to lead from the door to the bed, then back again. Was there a struggle? Was the lady dragged to the bed, and held down? Indentations on the mattress suggest that someone did indeed hold her down. You'll have noted the bruises around her wrists, Doctor, as well as the strands of red hair on the collar of her dress. Note that neither of her roommates are red-haired."

He paused, looking absorbed. "But what does this diachylon have to do with her death, Watson? It's it's a simple household medicament – No?"

As a student, I'd seen women admitted to Barts in desperate condition as the result of what was termed a "backstreet abortion". It happened more often than we men would like to admit, and not always to unmarried women. Such procedures were dangerous, but no more so than the purgatives and abortifacients advertised, quite publicly, for their ability to resolve "female irregularities".

"You're quite right. Ordinarily, diachylum is used to make plasters to treat cuts and sores. It's part of every housewife's medicine cabinet. However, as many women have discovered, *diachylum* is a preparation of white lead. In sufficiently large doses, it causes headaches, vomiting, and miscarriages."

If the lady had taken it willingly, then I would have reported this as a tragic accident. Exsanguination as the result of a miscarriage. The family need not be further distressed by the details. But Holmes had raised an interesting point: Did someone force Enfys to digest the contents of this tin? If so, he or she may not have intended her murder, but murder it was.

Notwithstanding their distress, the girls waiting outside the attic room proved to be sensible and thoughtful witnesses.

Jones quickly ascertained that Enfys had, as they termed it, been "visiting with a young gentleman" for at least four months. Neither girl knew his name, nor had seen him. She often stayed away overnight, too, implying some secret tryst.

Enfys herself had let slip scant clues as to the identity of her mystery caller. He was, according to Judy Meredith, "free with his money", for in the last month she'd seen Enfys in two new dresses, and wearing "a rainbow brooch".

"These dresses," Holmes asked, "would be the navy blue one and the yellow one, in her trunk?"

"That's right."

"And this brooch – there are pin marks on her dress, but it isn't here in the room. When did you last see her wearing it?"

"Why, she hasn't taken it off since she was gifted it," the doe-eyed girl called Nia replied, adding for clarification that, "Enfys means 'rainbow' in Welsh."

"I see. Would one have to be a Welsh-speaker to know that?"

"I should think so, sir."

"And what else did you notice? Please, think carefully."

"A couple of times," Judy commented, "I caught her crying. I knew she was very keen on this gent, but she'd seen him walking out with some young widow, and she worried that she was too plain, too poor, and was sure to lose him."

"What sort of man would do that?" Jones said with a flush of tenderness that was surprising in such an old Scotland Yard bulldog. "Playing a pretty girl like that. Shameful!"

"What sort of a man? Hmm," Holmes replied, distractedly. "Let us see what we have so far, shall we? He's a liberal gift-giver. However, the dresses he bought are second or third-hand. You can see where they have been re-cut. His shoes were likely costly but have been much repaired – the imprint of patches are quite visible on the boards. So he's a man who wishes to impress, but has limited resources, or spends beyond his means.

"Shoe size generally is proportional to height, so he is at least six foot tall. He's a Welsh-speaker, has red-hair, and wears a signet ring on the middle finger of his right hand – the mark left by it can be seen on the poor girl's wrist. And the brooch – I wonder if the lady returned it, or was it taken? Regardless, it's surely unusual enough to trace."

"Ho!" Jones cried. "No need! We have him! There's only one man in town who fits that description: Granville Baughn!" He said it like a curse. "The family business is the sort of big, dirty industry we have in Wales: Mines, and quarries, and the like. They're hardworking people who've done well for themselves. Not as well as some, but they're respectable and ambitious. They place great hopes on Granville, who is their only child and, frankly, Mr. Holmes, a stain on their good name. He's a reputation as a drinker, a gambler, a profligate. Spends freely, and not afraid to borrow when funds run low. He wants something, he takes it. That's said to include other men's wives.

"He's been arrested a score of times – nothing that stuck. I couldn't say if he has a good lawyer, or we have bad police, but he seems to have a charmed life. No matter how many drunken brawls, no matter how many accusations of fraud or theft, he's never held to account. But we have him here, Mr. Holmes. We have him here!"

"I'm not so sure," Holmes answered, quietly.

"Oh?"

"Just this: Diachylum is freely available from any pharmacy, yet it was sold or given to Granville in this tin. That suggests that the person who gave it to him was trying to disguise it as something else."

"But Enfys must have known what the tin contained," I said. "Why else would she struggle so?"

"If we assume that the lady wanted to keep the child, but Granville Baughn did not, then that's quite a sound assumption, Doctor. But what if we look at the evidence another way? The scuffs on the floor . . . Let us suppose they lead from the bed to the door. So the lady takes the powder, and falls ill. Granville may have been assisting her, rather than compelling her – trying to help her to a doctor, perhaps? She takes a turn for the worse, so he drags her back to the bed. The indentations on the mattress, the bruises around her wrists – she was convulsing. In that instance, would you not attempt to hold someone down to stop them from injuring themselves?"

"Are you suggesting that neither Granville nor Enfys knew what was in the tin?"

"Why else would you disguise its contents?"

"Why, indeed?"

"Look, Mr. Holmes, we have Granville bang to rights on this!" Jones interjected. "Why, the boy could have bought the diachylon himself, and put it in this tin to pretend it was some harmless thing."

"But the lady struggled!" I said.

"Did she now? Or maybe when he saw how sick she was, he tried for a doctor, as Mr. Holmes suggested." Jones nodded to the constable who had been diligently guarding the door to the attic room. "Williams, I want you to head over to the Imperial. Granville keeps rooms there. Grab a couple of extra constables on the way and bring him to the station. I'll be along shortly."

"Of course, it's your case, Inspector," Holmes commented, "but even if Granville is our man, there are still too many questions that need to be answered. Tell me, Watson: How widely known are the effects of diachylon?"

"Most married ladies would know of it. Would Granville? Unlikely. It's hardly spoken of in polite company."

"I see. By-the-by, Jones, who might single ladies, with no mothers to consult, go to for help with such things hereabouts?"

Jones is a big man but as Holmes spoke, he suddenly seemed to deflate. "Oh, Lord! Dinah Davis!"

"And who is Dinah Davis?" Holmes asked, his keen eyes shining.

"Only the local witch, Mr. Holmes. Only the bloomin' local witch! She lives in an old ruin, close to Thomas Barker's antimony mine."

"How interesting" Holmes murmured. "Did you know that antimony is used to harden lead?"

We were seated in a hansom heading towards a place Jones called the Bryniau Watch Tower – a seventeenth-century structure built to warn coastal communities of Barbary slavers. The area was made up of ancient smallholdings nestled amongst medieval ruins, lying just outside the town.

"So, Jones," Holmes said, his voice steady and sober, "tell me about witches."

"It's embarrassing, but the truth is that there's many in these parts who still take this sort of thing very seriously. You see, there's always been cunning folk in Wales that people go to with their problems."

"What sort of problems?"

"Oh, women's things, mainly."

"In the past," I said by way of explanation, "most communities would have a wise woman of some sort – skilled in herbalism, traditional medicine. Someone to deliver babies and such . . . ."

"That's right, Doctor. Only there's no 'in the past' about it. Wales has always been a bit more inclined towards the magical and the mystical. They burnt witches in England. In Wales, they gave them good silver and their thanks. Indeed, the Welsh like their cunning folk, and while we're a proudly Christian country, there's a barely town of village where you won't find one still plying their trade. Good folk, mostly, but some really do deserve the name 'witch'!"

"You can't be serious?" I spluttered.

Holmes nodded thoughtfully. "Oh, I think, my dear Watson, you underestimate how hard it is to shake off beliefs that have been part of life for thousands of years. Why, I've recent accounts in my files of people being sent to the Assizes for hiring witches, of men and women accused of witchcraft – even murdered for it. As Jones says, many of these cunning folk are simply blessed with a little medical know-how. But others play on much older superstitions. Perhaps they even believe in it themselves."

"Witchcraft isn't on the statue books any longer?" I remarked, not at all sure that was actually the case.

"True, although it is illegal for persons to pretend or profess to tell fortunes, or to use any subtle craft, means, or device to deceive and impose. This Davis woman, Jones: Does she claim to be a witch?"

"Not openly, but it's known that she's the person to go to for charms, potions, and the like."

"There's a great deal of difference between making herbal remedies and deliberately causing hurt." Holmes said, quietly. "Which is it? After all, not everyone can afford a doctor. As for love potions – Well, if the price of hope is a ha'penny concoction, what harm is there in that?"

"I agree and, until today, I've had no reason to believe Davis is anything other than an inoffensive old woman, trading rose-water charms for gin money."

"And women's problems?"

"Let's just say that no one has gone out of their way to draw my attention to such things. And I haven't gone out of my way to look into it. But if you're right, and Davis did supply Enfys with the powder, well . . . the law is the law."

"Do you intend to arrest her?" I asked.

In lieu of an answer, Jones rapped on the cab's roof, as a signal for the driver to stop.

In London, our night skies are so clouded in smoke that one can rarely see the stars. In this corner of Wales, however, the sky was bright, and the gleaming stars cast a golden glow over the hillside.

We were only a few miles from the garish jollity of the holiday town, but the land felt positively primitive. Bats and owls flapped overhead, mice and voles skittered across our feet, and the eyes of animals – wild and domestic – shone at us out of the gloom.

Jones warned us to watch our feet, as once we were off the road, the "going would get tricky" – and so it was.

A rabbit hole brought me down, hard. Jones himself stumbled and swore as he fought to untangle his legs from the brambles and wild gorse. A wind rose, howling in our ears, tugging at our hair, and with it came a chill that felt like the icy fingers of some ancient Celtic spirit, angry at being disturbed.

Nature fought us, and every step we took seemed a struggle. Had I been a superstitious man, I might have looked up at the watch tower and shuddered to think on the witch who lived there who, even now, was listening to our approach.

Only Holmes – as sure-footed as ever – seemed immune to the curious atmosphere of the place. He set his aquiline features to the wind and ploughed on, clambering over the piles of tumbled-down rocks with enviable ease.

We were close enough now to see the old ruin – and how cunningly it had been re-purposed.

It was a round, rubble-stone affair, about twenty foot in height and perhaps the same in internal diameter. The northeast wall was missing, but a hovel built of drystone had been set against it.

A roof constructed of timber and a simple bramble thatch covered the whole. The lower levels had been smeared with pitch, presumably to proof it against the elements. The upper stage of the tower revealed a window, covered in some kind of sail cloth, and in it was set a storm lantern, its bright orange flame busily bobbing against the elements.

Dinah Davis had clearly heard us coming. She met us at the door of the hovel, where she stood, buffeted by the wind, tying a tall black hat over a shock of dark, unruly curls.

Dressed in the traditional Welsh costume of hat, petticoat-like skirt, and woolen cloak, she looked like a picture-book witch come to life.

She could have been anywhere between forty to fifty years old, yet her face was so pinched, and her skin so sallow, that she looked much older.

She regarded us with large, dark eyes, arms folded defensively across her chest. Her greeting was warm enough, but her smile made it no further than her mouth, which was pursed and thin.

The front of the hovel was so low that all three of us had to bend to enter. It was a sorry sort of dwelling. A pair of chairs and table were set beside the door. Further in, against the tower's far wall, was a tiny bed, another chair, and a pair of old sea chests.

Makeshift wooden shelves virtually filled the wall of the tower, where books fought for space with rows and rows of old sweet jars and tins. Labels were attached to each one describing the contents in a neat, cursive script.

"We've come to speak to you about Enfys Tegwen," Jones said.

"Then speak," Davis replied.

"May we?" the inspector gestured to the tower end of the house. "It would be more comfortable for us all if we could sit."

"Do as you will." The lady took off her hat and headed for the little bed, where she positioned herself, while Holmes and I carried the chairs through.

Thus seated, Jones began.

"We've reason to believe that you were recently visited by Enfys Tegwen and Granville Baughn. Can you tell us why they came to see you?"

"No secret to it. Baughn had ruined another young girl and expected me to help him keep his good name."

"And did you?"

140

"I did nothing for him."

"Don't lie to me now, Dinah!"

"Pssh!" the old lady hissed, clearly irritated. "Don't you 'Dinah' me! It's 'Miss Davis' to you, and I may be many things, but I'm no liar. You can ask Enfys yourself."

Jones took a deep breath. "I'm afraid that Miss Tegwen isn't in a position to speak to anyone anymore."

I saw Davis give a little start. For a moment I thought the news had rendered her speechless. Then she suddenly exploded into a paroxysm of rage.

Dinah Davis was barely four foot tall, and as thin as a switch, but in that moment she seemed to fill the room.

She leapt to her feet. The light from the flickering lanterns, set on either side of the tower, cast elongated shadows on the walls, so that it seemed there was an ever growing army of old ladies. They bobbed and whirled around the room, and in the centre of the maelstrom stood Dinah Davis, her back ramrod straight, fists clenched, her unblinking eyes aflame.

"No, no, no! Say it isn't true! Say it isn't true?" She repeated the same phrases several times, her tiny frame shaking so much that I feared she would give herself an apoplexy.

"My dear Miss Davis," Holmes said, in that gentle way he has, "please, sit. Calm yourself."

Davis looked at Holmes as though she was searching for something in his cool, grey eyes. I do not know what she found, but she held his gaze for longer than I would have found comfortable. As she did so, her breathing slowed, and the color began to return to her face.

"We're sorry to be the bringer of bad news," Holmes began. "You mentioned that he had 'ruined another girl'. Had he been to see you before?"

"No. Most girls in trouble will go their mother, or an older married friend, but poor Enfys had no one."

"Tell us," Holmes said, his eyes still fixed on Davis, his face a mask.

The old witch smoothed her skirts, pulled her cloak around her shoulders, and began:

"This was Saturday, just after ten in the morning. I'd never seen either of them before, but I knew Granville. Knew the sort of man he was. All charm and talk – He will tell a girl what she wants to hear. Anything she's foolish enough to believe. Oh, how they coddle and cajole, these little princes. '*Rich in will, weak in willpower*' – These *liars! Deceivers! Palterers!*"

As she spoke, her voice rose, and her eyes took on a far-away look.

In the closeness of that ancient tower, her words echoed strangely and their rhythm had a curious effect on me. I recalled reading Tacitus's account of Rome's Legions arriving on the Isle of Anglesey, only to find themselves facing an army of wild-haired Druids, throwing curses into the wind. Davis had something of that. An attitude both primitive and knowing. I felt the hair on the back of my neck prickle and a shudder came, unbidden.

For a moment, it seemed that Davis was lost to us in some Druidic past. Then, with a blink of those huge eyes, she was back.

The lady herself didn't seem to know that her mind had wandered, and resumed her account, quite unaware of the curious impact it had had on her listeners.

"He put on a good show, I'll say for him. Lots of talk about 'being too young to start a family yet' and 'wanting to do right by his intended'. I didn't believe a word of it.

"I asked him to leave us so that we women could speak freely. She told me, straight – Granville had persuaded her to come, but she wanted to keep the baby. I can see her now: Pitiful child, so trusting. 'He wants to do things right' she said. 'He's says we'll have plenty of time for a family later, but his parents will think badly of me if I go to the altar pregnant.'"

"So Granville had made her an offer of marriage?"

"That's what she believed."

Holmes fished around in the voluminous pockets of his sack coat and produced the Pollard's tin. He asked Davis to look inside it.

"Have you ever," he asked, "given anyone such a substance?"

"If a lady is out of order, and not too far along, then hellebore, savin, tansy, or pennyroyal will restore the courses. That's what I would recommend. *Recommend*, mind," she added, looking pointedly at Jones.

"So you gave her nothing?"

"I didn't say that. I gave her a powder to help with the baby – and instructions on how to take it."

"A restorative?" I asked.

"Exactly that."

"Tell me, Miss Davis: How did Baughn react when you told him Miss Tegwen wanted to keep the child. Was he angry?" Jones asked the question, but I could see Holmes's eyes, fixed on Davis.

"He said they would go home and talk some more. That he would abide by her decision. But I was afraid for the girl."

"You thought he would harm her?" Holmes queried.

"I didn't say so."

142

"No, Miss Davis, I notice that you're very careful about what you say. So I'll repeat the question: Did you think that Mr. Baughn posed a danger to Miss Tegwen?"

Miss Davis didn't reply immediately. Instead, she wrapped her hands around herself in a curious manner, appearing, once again, to be elsewhere. Then, as before, she blinked those remarkable eyes, and seemed to remember herself. "I think," she said, in a voice that was brittle and hard, "that people like Mr. Baughn always pose a danger to people like Miss Tegwen."

With that, the interview was at an end and we were ejected back onto the hillside wherein lay the bones of the long dead.

"Well, that's that" Jones commented, as we trudged back down the slope towards the waiting cab. "It looks like Baughn's our man."

"Oh, indeed?" Holmes sniffed. "You don't find anything strange about Miss Davis's statement?"

"She's a strange women, to be sure, and there may be a case to answer about her wider activities. But it's clear to me that Baughn didn't want this child and, having failed to procure what he needed from Davis, likely consulted with one of his other women about how to deal with it. Maybe that rich widow of his? We'll know more once we get to the station."

"Clear? No it isn't clear, Inspector. Nothing is clear, apart from the fact that Dinah Davis might be 'many things, but not a liar'. Isn't that what she said?"

"Exactly!" Jones huffed. "She told us the truth."

"No. She didn't lie. There's a difference."

"Now look here, Mr. Holmes, you have your methods. They're a little too theoretical and fantastical for me, but you've always been a great help to the police, so if you've something on your mind that has a bearing on this case, then out with it."

Holmes answered Jones's question answered with another: "What do you know of her? This supposed witch? What's her history?"

"Lord knows! Some say she's an educated woman. Worked in one the fashionable Midland towns as a governess. Fell on hard times, and came home to Wales. That's the story."

"Well," Holmes observed, "she writes with an educated hand and has an interesting library for a women in such dire straits,"

"Indeed," I added. "Not many living as she does could quote Shakespeare."

"Ah, thank you, Doctor!" Holmes replied. "There seemed something familiar about '*rich in will*', but it's a very long time since I studied the Bard."

Back in the hansom, Holmes sank back in his seat, consumed by his thoughts – and I was left alone with mine. So dark were they that I was pleased, once again, to see the lights of the seaside town and hear the cheery voices of the holiday-makers as they passed by, taking in the night air.

I still couldn't shake off the image of Dinah Davis, railing to the gods about Granville Baughn. Or was it Baughn that she referenced? At that moment, I looked at Holmes, and I knew that he, too, had come to the same realization. And, for the second time since we had become embroiled in this case, my heart sank.

Granville Baughn lay on the slab on the little parish mortuary. It felt strange to finally see someone who had been spoken of so freely, and with such ill will, but here he was.

He had a shock of shoulder-length red hair, a pale face, and looked so painfully young that it took my breath away to see him. I was reminded immediately of Wallis's painting of *The Death of Chatterton* – the romantic poet who had poisoned himself with arsenic in a fit of despair.

Baughn had been found by the constables who had been sent to detain him, his throat slashed by a cut-throat razor discovered beside him. He had left no note, and the door-man spoke of him arriving at the Imperial in a state of such distress that he'd ignored the familiar greetings of the hotel's other long-term residents.

He had been dead long enough for *rigor* to have set in. "That puts the time of death not long after Enfys's," I noted.

It was with some difficulty that we prized open the clenched fist that lay on his chest, over his heart. It contained the golden rainbow brooch that he had given to Enfys. It was such a sad sight that I felt tears come, unbidden, and was forced to step away to collect myself.

"Have you read William James, Watson?" Holmes uttered *sotto voce*, sounding much as I felt. "Interesting fellow. American. He wrote about how ideas, feelings, and sensations, both present and past, cohere into the experience of what he calls 'a continuous self'. For Dinah Davis, the past – her past – is ever present, and when she saw Enfys, she saw herself. You noticed the way she talked, how she cradled *something* – something small, something needing her protection. And how none of that seemed to have anything to do with Granville or Enfys.

"This lady has been poorly used – so poorly used that she fled from her life to hide away, here, in Wales. I imagine, Inspector, that should we look for traces of Dinah Davis in Leamington Spa, we would fill in the gaps of this tragic tale. Jones – you did say that she'd lived in the

Midlands? I wonder what happened to her baby? The baby that ruined her life."

"And made her determined that no other young girl should have to endure the shame of being an unmarried mother?"

"That's exactly it, Watson. What was it she called the powder that she gave to Miss Tegwen? A *'restorative'* – something to restore health and well-being. Which, to her, meant restoring Enfys to her previous condition. I believe she had no ill-intent. She simply couldn't believe in Granville. She'd been too injured by her own past."

Jones had sent constables to arrest Davis as soon as he had heard the news about Granville. He now stood, coat lapels turned up, hands deep in his pockets, puffing out little plumes of chill mortuary air like a miniature steam engine. "Lord, but this is a mess!" he repeated, for the sixth time since we'd arrived.

"Dinah told us that Granville and Enfys intended to go home and talk. We must assume that he did, indeed, decide to abide by her decision to keep the child. He must have encouraged her to drink the powder – thinking it a tonic for the baby. Imagine his horror. His terror. His guilt! He couldn't have known what would happen should he have gotten the dose of the 'tonic' even slightly wrong. And what of Davis? The most I can charge her with is supplying poison with intent to procure a miscarriage. Should I do that, then every desperate woman will pushed to take even more desperate actions. But the law *is* the law."

"I think Dinah Davis would be far better in a medical institute than a criminal one," I sniffed, suddenly feeling very tired.

Jones nodded. "You may be right at that, Doctor."

It had been almost ten hours since we'd arrived in this beautiful holiday resort. Our bags still lay, unclaimed, in The King's Head, our beds unused. "There are times when what one needs most in the whole world is a pipe, a brandy, and some convivial company," I mused, to no one in particular.

Jones looked first to myself and then to Holmes. "Sorry to say that Wales is dry on Sundays," he replied. "But I do have a pack of Grousemoor tobacco, a bottle of fine brandy, and a garden with the best views in the whole of Llandudno, should you consider an old Scotland Yard dullard like myself convivial enough."

I looked at Holmes and Jones, suddenly feeling a rush of affection for all those times that Baker Street had been my bulwark against the world. No matter how dire, no matter how tragic the events that overtook us, I knew I could always rely on the warmth of the companionship I found there.

145

Holmes was right. Sometimes you needed a change of place to change your perspective.

"I think, Inspector," I replied, smiling, "that might be exactly what the Doctor ordered."

NOTES

1. Saint Tudno is the patron saint of Llandudno He founded the original parish church on the Great Orme in the Sixth Century. The present twelfth-century church stands on the same site.
2. Watson is quite right. The "modern" station, parts of which still stand, was built in 1892, replacing a much older structure.
3. Etruria Marl clay is found in the Ruabon area of Wales. Its discovery heralded the beginning of mass tile and terracotta production. So-called Ruabon bricks get their rich red color from the clay's high iron content.
4. The King's Head, named after King William IV (1765-1837), is the only pub surviving from "*old Llandudno*" before the development of the modern resort.
5. Hippolyte Taine (1828-1893) was a French historian, critic, and philosopher.
6. London police were one of the earliest professions to have a pension. Police paid a premium out of their own wages, in the hope that it would induce men to join and remain in the service, which was a poorly paid profession.
7. Leamington Spa water is a mild laxative. Spa water toffees were taken for a similar effect.
8. For most of history, abortion has been commonplace. Even amongst the early Puritan settlers to America, *abortifacients* were so widely known and used that Benjamin Franklin included a well-known recipe for one in his book, *The American Instructor, Or, Young Man's Best Companion* from 1759. In 1803, the first specific British law to deal with abortion made it punishable by the death penalty. The 1861 law removed the death penalty, but made administering drugs or using instruments to procure abortion punishable by life in prison. Despite this, many products were sold under the promise of "*restoring female regularity*", "*removing obstructions*", and dealing with "*delayed periods*". One 1897 advertisement for Beechams's Powders appeared in the *Christian Herald* with the motto: "*Worth a guinea a box . . . for all bilious and nervous disorders . . . and female ailments.*"

    When a water source became polluted by lead, causing a spate of miscarriages, diachylon, which was known to contain white lead, became a popular choice. Such products, as well as backstreet abortions, remained a fact of life for working class women until abortion was legalized in 1967. These highly dangerous products and procedures killed many thousands of women who, like poor Enfys, bled to death, or died of infections. Others were left infertile. Diachylon had the added danger of lead poisoning if it was used too often.
9. In England and Scotland, around five-thousand women were sentenced to death for witchcraft. Only five witches were executed in Wales, where "cunning folk" were indeed largely well-regarded unless they caused harm. Those who were killed appeared to have fallen foul of the powerful and the wealthy.

10. Barbary pirates terrorized coastal communities in the Mediterranean, Britain, and Ireland for almost two-hundred-and-fifty years, beginning in the seventeenth century. The Bryniau Watch Tower is believed to be the remains of a tower built to give coastal communities advance warning of pirate attacks. Its remains are still visible today. *Bryniau* means "*hill*" in Welsh. It's pronounced "*brin-y-I*" with a rolling "*R*".
11. The 1824 Vagrancy Act outlawed persons pretending or professing to be able to use magical powers. Accusations of witchcraft continued to appear in legal records throughout the 1850's and 1860's. The last witch trial in Britain happened in 1944.
12. Psychologist William James coined the term "stream of thought" in 1890. His interest was in the "wandering mind", and how our internal stream of consciousness can be used to explore "the mind within".
13. "*Rich in Will*" comes from Shakespeare's *Sonnet 135*.
14. The battle Tacitus wrote of happened in 60 CE, between Druids on the Isle of Anglesey and the troops of General Suetonius Paulinus.

The author, who moved to Wales in 2023, lives on Bryniau Road,
and the Bryniau Tower can be seen from the end of her street.
This photo was made during a walk given by the
Great Orme Exploration Society (GOES), of which she is a member.

The Mystery of the
Authentic Mystic
by William Todd

A bitter, early autumn wind rattled the windows of 221b Baker Street and, judging by the brooding colour of the sky, rain – which had been intermittent the entire day – was threatening to start once again. I had settled into an overstuffed chair at one of the windows, reading *The Times*, while my friend, Sherlock Holmes, stood warming himself by the fire and smoking his clay pipe. The weather had been rather miserable of late. The close, damp fog, mixed with the insufferable pollutants of thousands of chimneys, gave the October sky a jaundiced hue, which in turn gave all the inhabitants of London a jaundiced disposition – no one worse than Holmes.

"Do you feel like a night out?" I asked to break the silence. "We can get some dinner at Simpson's, and Wagner is playing at Covent Garden."

Holmes gave a long draw from his pipe and waved the statement off. "No, I need stimulation of a different variety. Besides," he went on, "Simpson's has a new chef whose preference in fowl preparation seems to consistently err on the side of leather."

He turned and pointed his pipe at me to bring home the point. "Do you know what poultry tastes like when it is overcooked? You should be so lucky not to."

I shrugged. "Simpson's isn't the only place in which to dine. Or we could just eat in and go to Covent Garden after."

My friend began to pace the room as he always did when he hadn't an investigation into which he could sink his proverbial teeth. Lestrade's cases were such that Holmes's unique abilities weren't needed, and no interesting private matters had graced our rooms for longer still.

It is during these idle times that I rather worried for my friend. Throughout these extended lethargies, he often turned to his needle. He hadn't partaken of his seven-per-cent solution in quite some time, but I still worried that the urge might one day overtake him once more.

It is also during these times that I openly admit trying all the harder to give him something to do. If my friend wouldn't see through my ruse, it might be a task all the easier to accomplish, but Holmes not only saw the ploy, but took offense at my effort.

A remonstration was percolating on his lips when there was a knock at our door.

"Come!" Holmes shouted as he stared me down, and I, for my part, couldn't hide a wry smile.

Mrs. Hudson came in bearing a card on a silver platter.

Holmes snatched it and read the inscription.

"Shall I see him up?" Mrs. Hudson asked.

"Yes, yes, please," Holmes replied with some anxiousness in his voice. "We cannot keep . . . '*Mr. Archibald Ramsay*'," he read from the card, "waiting in such dreadful weather."

"I'm not so frightful a person as to keep him waiting outside, Mr. Holmes," Mrs. Hudson replied with some offense. "The gentleman is in the entryway."

He shooed her out. "Then please show him up!"

He then handed me the card. "What do you make of it?" he asked. "Quickly, before he enters and ruins our little exercise."

I turned it over in my hand. "Thick stock, expensive font, embellishments in the corners. I would say a man of some means, at the very least. It has a bit of a smudge on the back, and the edges aren't crisp. If I didn't know any better, I would say he has already used this calling card on several occasions." I looked up at Holmes. "Possibly a man of some wealth who has in the recent past come upon hard times, such that he has to re-use his cards."

Holmes shot me a ghost of a smile and said, "Very good. I daresay Lestrade wouldn't have given the card much thought at all, although I might lean more towards thrift for reasons I cannot explain now. It may not give us the reason for his visit, but it gives us a starting point from which to judge the story we are about to hear."

There was a knock, and Mrs. Hudson opened the door wide for the gentleman to step through. He was middle-aged with thinning brown hair that had been slightly whipped up in the gusts outside. He was somewhat stocky and had long, bushy side-whiskers and a mustache that was their equal. His robust cheeks were red from exertion and chill.

Mrs. Hudson was about to leave us to discuss the man's interest in seeking us, but Holmes put up a finger, silently asking her to wait.

"Mr. Ramsay, I am Sherlock Holmes, and this is my friend and colleague, Dr. Watson. Please, come in. Would you care for some tea?"

"None for me, thank you," he replied in a rich baritone.

At that, he silently waved Mrs. Hudson her leave, to which she shot me a look of exasperation and sighed.

I, for my part, only shrugged. It wasn't out of indifference to what one might perceive as Holmes's discourteousness, but out of a realization that his lack of tact seemed as involuntary as scratching an itch. I have discovered over the years that there seemed to be a direct correlation between his level of abuse and how fond he was of someone. With that being the judge, it was obvious he was quite fond of Mrs. Hudson.

Perceiving a small quiver in our guest's hand, I asked, "Would you like something stronger to take the chill off? Brandy, perhaps?"

"Now, I wouldn't say no to that," he replied, stepping deeper into the room. "Thank you."

As I fetched the brandy decanter and poured the man a glass, Holmes offered him a seat and began. "Pray, what brings you out in such wretched weather, especially all the way from . . . Cornwall. Plymouth, perhaps? And you have just arrived and come straight here, instead of finding a hotel room, either because you are frugal with your money, or haven't the funds to afford both a ticket to London and a room. I deduce the former. However, my colleague fears it is the latter."

The man shot me a look of amazement.

"He does that quite often," said I. "It is his own little parlour trick."

"You're right on every point, Mr. Holmes. As to my funds," he coughed with some embarrassment, "I have been told I'm a bit tight-fisted, I have. Better to have it and not need it than need it and not have it, I always say. But how did you know? How did you know any of it before the fact?"

I gave the man his drink.

A smile of amusement brushed briefly across my friend's lips. "It is quite simple. When I tell you, you should be embarrassed by its simplicity. First and easiest, where you are from – your accent. You have a distinct West Country accent, and I daresay anyone with ears could have deduced that much. What made me waver, if it must be called that, was because your speech doesn't possess the typical quick Cornish cadence, so I would surmise you live closer to the Devonshire border than, say, to Penzance.

"I take pride in my familiarization with the *Bradshaw* and know the train from Plymouth should have delivered you to Paddington approximately twenty-five minutes ago. Allowing for several minutes of jostling through the crowds in the station before emerging onto Praed Street, a quick walk in the inclement weather, and you will arrive on our stoop.

"Lastly, the time difference from the train's arrival and your appearance at our doorstep does not allow for the procurement of a hotel room, so I deduced you came directly from the station."

Here, Mr. Ramsay spoke up. "Could I not have arrived on an earlier train?"

"You could have . . . but did not, as evidenced by your damp trouser leg and the significant creasing in both the knees and elbows of your suit. Had you arrived on an earlier train and purchased a hotel room first, you would have also no doubt changed your suit after such a long ride, and the creasing in the knees and elbows would have been minimal."

With a flourishing wave of his long arm, Holmes added, "Please tell me if I have missed anything."

The man smiled. "You are certainly the man I have heard and read so much about." He looked himself over. "Unfortunately, when I made up my mind that I should consult you, I had no time to pack any overnight bag, and what you see before you, creases and all, is what I came to London with."

"A fresh press," I replied, "and you shall be right as rain."

"And Doctor," he went on, "I daresay your use of the term *parlour trick* is most deductive, as well." He settled back in the chair and took a large swill from the glass. "It isn't me, you see, but my younger sister, Maggie, for whom I have come to ask your help. She is a new widow of just under a year. Her husband, Thomas, left her a tidy sum to live out her days as comfortable as such funds will allow."

"How much?" Holmes asked.

"Fifteen-thousand pounds. Now, only twelve."

I raised my eyebrows in shock. "That is a significant expenditure in less than a year."

"Indeed," he replied with vigour. "My sister has never been as economical as I am, but she doesn't squander money either. That was a true enough statement until she met Madame Trevellin." He sighed. "Maggie is interested in this psychic, tarot card, palm-reading hullabaloo. She is determined to contact her husband from the Great Beyond." He looked at Holmes wide-eyed. "And she swears this woman has succeeded!"

"In what way has she . . . *succeeded*?" my friend asked with obvious incredulity.

The man drank down the last of the brandy and leaned forward in the chair. "It isn't like the accounts read in the popular press. You know – in darkened rooms with floating tables and confederates hiding behind curtains with bells and whistles and the like. No, no, Madame Trevellin takes Maggie to the beach, and they lay out a blanket. They sit on the blanket and this medium does some incantations over her. She allows Maggie to ask one question."

Holmes raised a brow. "Only one? Interesting. Go on."

"Once the question is asked, Madame Trevellin does some more incantations, and then they lift the blanket and dig in the sand underneath. After some digging, they find a bottle with a note inside. And the note reveals the answer to her question."

"What kind of questions is she allowed to ask?"

"Whatever Maggie wants. They can be as general or specific as she likes. 'Are you here? Who am I speaking to? Where are you? What is it like there?' But as the sessions went on, Maggie began asking more personal questions. 'When is your birthday? What is your favorite color?' Things such as that just to make sure it was indeed her Thomas she was speaking to. Every time they uncovered a bottle with a note in it, and each time the paper revealed the correct answer."

Holmes leaned forward eagerly, one brow slightly raised in either interest or cynicism. "And she is prompted in no way by this medium in what question she may ask?"

"None whatever," Ramsay replied with a dismissive wave of his hand. "She is free to submit whatever question she may ask, and is prevailed upon in no way by the medium."

"Interesting. Is it always at the same spot, same beach?"

"Same beach, yes, but that was Maggie's pick because it was her and Thomas's favorite place. She swears it's never in the same place, but always on the same stretch of beach. I was worried about the drain on her funds, so I went with her to one of these . . . whatever you call them at the beach. Madame Trevellin didn't seem to mind in the least. She even let me ask the question as proof, and by George it was right! I brought it along to show you."

He pulled from his pocket a folded piece of foolscap and handed it to Holmes. In what appeared to be a trembling hand was written in large, black letters *Billacombe Brook*.

Holmes furrowed his brow. "What was the question?"

Mr. Ramsay smiled, but it didn't hide the fear in his eyes. "I asked this spirit of Thomas what we did on the Saturday before he died. And the answer, the answer you see there, was absolutely correct." His face turned pale. "We had never fished Billacombe Brook together before. That was the first time. Before that, we always fished the Plym. Had I not seen the note for myself, I wouldn't have believed it! I mean I still don't believe it, but I'll not lie: I am having kittens over it!"

"Were there others fishing nearby?" I asked.

"No, so far as I know. I saw no one but us, but there may have been some up or downstream."

Holmes examined the paper. Other than a few wrinkles and the folds, it looked unremarkable.

He resumed his normal repose of leaning back languidly in his chair. "I do not usually take on cases of the occult, as there are official bodies that routinely investigate possible counterfeit mediums, though I use the word *possible* loosely, as I am quite certain they are all counterfeits. But this case has some interesting bits on which to digest. Pray, when did money start changing hands?"

"After about a month-and-a-half. At first, they would get together once a week. When it seemed as if Maggie was completely convinced, it became twice a week. Then, Thomas started adding to his notes about giving money to charity. And this is what puzzles me, Mr. Holmes – she hasn't given so much as a ha'penny to the woman, only to these 'needy causes', as Madame Trevellin calls them."

"They are Madame Trevellin's recommendations?"

"Yes."

My friend stood, and Mr. Ramsay and I followed suit.

"There won't be another train to Plymouth until tomorrow morning," Holmes replied, "so if you could see your way to part with a little money and get a hotel room, Mr. Ramsay, we shall all leave tomorrow morning, and see what we can do about this Madame Trevellin. Watson, please bring your medical bag with you. I prefer having your services at the ready when dealing with the recently widowed."

He then handed Mr. Ramsay back his calling card, and, with a blush on his full cheeks, the man took it and placed it back in his suit pocket.

We picked up Mr. Ramsay in his now-pressed suit at the Langham Hotel the next morning. His red-rimmed eyes betrayed a sleepless night, and worry deepened the crow's feet at the corners of his eyes. It was only too obvious that with no one to look after the well-being of his sister, it would now fall to Mr. Ramsay, and the anxiety of that responsibility was palpable on his face.

We left on the 8:30 a.m. Great Western from Paddington to Plymouth. It was early afternoon when we alighted the carriage at the station. A man in livery colors walked up to us and Mr. Ramsay introduced him. "This is Bradford. He'll take your luggage. I hope you don't object to staying with me. It is only me. Never married, you see, so I wouldn't mind the company for as long as your stay needs be."

Holmes gave a small nod. "That would be most welcome. And can you arrange a meeting with your sister as soon as is convenient for her?"

The man smiled. "I thought you'd want to get right to it, so I sent her a telegram yesterday to expect us about now. Would you rather go straightway or drop off your things first?"

"Now, if the preference is mine to make," Holmes replied.

The weather on the southwest coast was indeed much better than in London. The sun shone brightly in the sky, warming the skin, and the air, clean and slightly crisp, was heaven in the lungs.

We made the widow's home in fifteen minutes. It was in a lovely large Queen Anne style with a steep, cross-gable roof and an intricately spindled porch that wrapped around the front and one side of the house.

We were shown into a lovely home, in whose entryway were myriad photographs and watercolours of meadows and mountainscapes, running along both sides of the hallway ahead of us. A writing desk was tucked into a small alcove under the staircase to our right, which itself was sentried with potted ferns on either of the landing.

The manservant, Carrivick, showed us into the drawing room. There, a lady in black mourning attire rose from some needlework and greeted us with a crooked smile that seemed at once to also border on a frown at one end.

Mr. Ramsay introduced us. "Maggie, this is Sherlock Holmes and his colleague, Dr. Watson. I told you about them."

Holmes gave a slight bow, and I said, "Good afternoon."

"Gentlemen," Ramsay went on, "this is my sister, Mrs. Maggie Penhaligon."

The widow was a slightly plump, rosy-cheeked woman of approximately fifty years of age. Her sandy hair, streaked with wide bands of grey, was severely bunched at the top of her head – so much so that I could only guess at the number of pins it must have taken to keep it all in place.

"Gentlemen," she started in a rather husky voice. "My brother Archie has somehow decided that I need some 'assistance' in a matter I had hitherto not known needed it – my acquaintance Madame Trevellin, whom I consider a close, personal friend. I can assure you, as my brother can attest since he was there on one occasion, that as a psychic medium, she is completely authentic."

Holmes gave the woman a thin smile and replied, "Mrs. Penhaligon, we don't wish to authenticate anyone or anything . . . as yet. We are here merely to ascertain some facts, nothing more. Once we establish those facts and put them forth, you may do with them what you please."

She looked to one and the other of us, and her features softened, although, as with her brother, her cheeks remained coloured, as if afflicted with rosacea. "Please, take a seat, and ask whatever you like."

Mr. Ramsay sat on the sofa next to his sister, and Holmes and I both took the other two soft highbacks on the other side of the hearth, crackling with a fire just large enough to give the room a warm, comfortable feel.

Holmes began. "Your brother has given us an overview of the events that began shortly after the death of your husband."

"If you are referring to when, exactly, I began to see Madame Trevellin, yes, about three months afterward. I have seen her nearly every week since then."

"And you haven't paid her for her . . . services." It was a statement more than a question.

"That isn't entirely correct," she replied. "My first dealing with her was after a reading in her home. That is where she conducts most of her business. It was the first time I had met her, and since she makes her living by her gifts, naturally I paid her. However, once we struck up a friendship, I haven't paid one shilling, and she hasn't asked. Surely, you have taken on cases purely for the love of your profession – or have the newspapers' accounts of your activities been incorrect?" She gave a little triumphant grin.

Holmes's features remained expressionless, and he replied placatingly, "You are very correct, and you are lucky to have such a friend to help you during this very trying period. But you have given to some 'charities' at her behest, have you not?"

"Yes, but none have anything to do with her."

"Are they somehow related to psychical endeavours?"

"They are, but they are not *her* endeavours. They are regional organizations that deal in astrological and psychical research."

"I see. And you post these donations yourself, or do you give them to Madame Trevellin to post?"

Her face pinched. "I am not an idiot, Mr. Holmes! Of course I post them myself."

Holmes flashed her a quick smile, but not one of amusement. "And do you happen to have the names of these organizations?"

Here, Mr. Ramsay spoke up, probably more to diffuse the tension than be of any assistance. "I asked her in the telegram to have the list prepared."

Holmes smiled mildly. "That was most thoughtful and expedient of you, Mr. Ramsay. Let me assure you that I am not paid by the hour."

His cheeks turned more crimson than they already were. "Uh, hem, yes, of course."

"Nonetheless, time wasted is time lost, and although it would have been but a moment more, I do appreciate your forethought."

The smile that spread across his face was much the same as his sister's – one couldn't tell one way or the other whether they were elated or upset. I suspected here the former.

With a little sigh of annoyance, the widow said, "Archie, can you hand them the paper I prepared – on the side table beside you?"

156

Ramsay did as instructed and handed Holmes the sheet, which he studied momentarily before passing it for me to see. Three businesses were listed: The Southwest Institute for Psychical Research, The National Trust for the Occult, and The Bristol Foundation for the Advancement of the Occult.

I made note of their names then returned the paper to my friend, who then folded it and slipped it into the pocket of his frock coat.

"Tell me about your husband," Holmes went on. "How did he die?"

The thought of talking about her husband, even the events of his passing, seemed to lighten her features. She straightened her back on the sofa and replied, "His poor heart gave out one day at work." She splayed her arms in front of her. "He just slumped over at his desk, poor soul. They said it was quick and painless, which is some consolation. Not everyone is so fortunate."

Multiple medical journal monograms on the subject notwithstanding, if it had been a coronary thrombosis, it may have been quick but was certainly not painless. However, the pain of death is often downplayed to spare loved ones the reality of it.

"Did he have a known heart condition?" I asked.

"He did, for about five years, I think." She withdrew a handkerchief from her sleeve and dabbed her eye. "His profession ordained that he administer dictates to others, but he rarely adhered to doctor's orders himself, especially where abstention from food and drink were concerned. He always knew someday his heart would be the death of him."

"And what was your husband's profession?" Holmes went on.

"Thomas works . . . *worked* in the apothecary at the Royal Naval Hospital. He was the chief chemist on staff, overseeing the dispensing of medication to almost twelve-hundred patients."

"I daresay even for a chief chemist he must have been paid quite handsomely to bequeath so much money and such a beautiful home."

The woman eyed my friend sourly, debating whether to take offense at the statement, but she chose to let it go and replied levelly, "His salary was adequate, although I always felt not quite on par for such a very important and prestigious position within the hospital. However, his family was of some means themselves, and left him this house, along with a little sum. He was an only child, you see."

Getting to the heart of the matter, Holmes then asked, "And how did you happen to be introduced to Madame Trevellin?"

She gave a little shrug. "I had known *of* her for some time. She is the sister of one of the junior chemists under Thomas at the hospital. His name is Oscar. They moved here from Aberdeen about three years ago. Her

157

husband and his wife had both died in a train accident, so all they have now is each other.

"At the funeral, seeing how utterly overcome with grief I was, Oscar gave me her card and told me, if I wished it, I could communicate with my Thomas. A few months afterward, I had worked up enough courage to give it a go. I was lonely – we have no children, you see – so with some reluctant hope, I attended a seance in her home with some others."

She dabbed her eyes again and took a long, slow breath to control and arrange her thoughts. "I wasn't convinced at first." She gave us both a look of understanding. "I know what is said about this kind of thing in certain circles, and I daresay I had my own doubts at first. But she was right on so many things. I had a hard time believing she hit home on so many things by pure chance." She gave a little shrug of her shoulders. "Even so, she saw my hesitancy, so she asked me if there was a special place where Thomas and I liked to go. I told her Tinside Beach, and she agreed to meet me there for a more intimate meeting to channel my Thomas."

She gave a breath as to continue, but Holmes gently interrupted her. "Pray tell, when you subsequently met her there, did you offer where to sit on the beach or did she?"

She thought for a moment. "I believe it was by mutual agreement, but I believe I played more of the lead, and she followed. The days of swimming in the surf for me and my husband had long passed, so we always sat up in the dryer sand by the changing huts, and it was in this general area where Madame Trevellis and I always pitched our blanket."

Nodding to Mr. Ramsay, Holmes said, "Your brother has explained that you never sat in the same place twice."

"That's correct," she agreed.

"Who chose where to sit on each subsequent meeting?"

"Why I did, of course."

"And it is completely arbitrary?"

"I believe so," she answered with some incredulity.

"But always in the same general area?"

"As I have said. Thomas and I ourselves always sat in the same general area. It offers a most beautiful spot in which to look out over the bay."

"Do you have another reading with Madame Trevellin planned?" he asked.

She smiled anxiously. "In two days, weather permitting."

"At what time?"

"At nine in the morning. She prefers mornings, as we are less likely to be disturbed."

Holmes put his hands together and leaned forward in his chair. "I don't wish to trouble you any more than need be, Mrs. Penhaligon, but I assume your husband had a study?"

She nodded. "It is as he left it. I cannot bring myself to alter it in any way. It was his . . . his sanctum."

Mr. Ramsay patted his sister gently on the arm. Thankfully, she was dabbing her eyes again and didn't see my friend roll his eyes.

There was a brief silence while she gathered herself before Holmes asked in a veiled sarcasm of which I was luckily enough to be the only one to sense, "I apologize for what you must feel is a monumental intrusion to your privacy, but may we see it? I assure you we will touch nothing. I would like to just get a sense of the man, if I may."

Annoyance rose on her cheeks. "If it were anyone but Archie's misgivings that had you here, I would have you stricken from my home. Nonetheless . . . ." She rose and replied, "I shall show you his study, and I hope that will be the last of it, Mr. Holmes."

We followed her across the hallway to a well-appointed study with bountiful bookcases stuffed with all manner of titles, mostly relating to chemistry, and medical and apothecarial matters. In front of a large, latticed window overlooking the back garden stood a large mahogany desk. It was overrun with open books, loose papers – some scattered on the floor – a desk lamp, and a crystal inkwell and pen.

Holmes walked slowly around the room with his hands clasped behind his back, taking in everything with a critical eye, but true to his word touched nothing. He looked out the window casually then turned to the desk, noticing a blank area on the otherwise cluttered surface. It was directly in front of the chair.

He looked up at Mrs. Penhaligon and pointed at the spot. "Pray, what was here?"

"He always left that spot clear for his journal. He mostly worked out equations and formulations and such for work, but he also wrote in it as well – appointments, reminders, little asides. He was a rather dry man in direct conversation, but possessed a profound wit on paper, given enough time to wrap his mind around an idea."

"Do you know where his journal is now?"

She shrugged. "At the dispensary, I should think. As I said, he used it mostly for work, and some very difficult formulations were in it. I cannot remember when last I saw it. I have enough memories with what is already here to worry about whether it is ever given back. It will no doubt be of better use there, anyway."

"I am sure you are correct, Madame."

Holmes then gave her a brief smile of conclusion and said, "I believe we have seen all that needs to be seen. Thank you for your time, Mrs. Penhaligon. This has been most illuminating."

"Have you formed an opinion yet as to the *bona fides* of Madame Trevellin?" she asked as we exited the room.

"There are a few threads that I would like to untangle before I make any suppositions one way or another. I will say only this: If I cannot find a way of contradicting any of the evidence already given, then this woman has been blessed with a gift far more profound than any *mere* ability of deduction I may possess. Now, if you will permit me, I shall put some theories to the test and have an answer, hopefully before your next session."

She waved him off and said smugly, "Take all the time you need. Your bill isn't being paid from my purse. But I believe you will have wasted your time and Archie his money – for once – when all is said and done." She gave a smile of satisfaction and added, "Of course, I would love to tell Madame Trevellin that even the great Sherlock Holmes had to acquiesce to her powers."

Holmes held his tongue with difficulty. He disguised a sigh of frustration by giving a slight nod of courtesy and said, "Then we shall take our leave. If nothing else, we will have partaken in a much-needed respite from the dreadful London air."

Once outside, Holmes said, "I beg your pardon, Mr. Ramsay, but I believe I would like to change our previously agreed-upon arrangements. We don't wish to prevail upon you any more than we already have. We shall get some rooms at a hotel and use that as a base of operations for our stay."

"If you think it best," he replied ruefully.

"Do not fret, Mr. Ramsay," Holmes replied with a mixture of humour and annoyance. "Our hotel bill will be paid from our private funds, not yours. It is just that we sometimes come and go at odd hours, and I don't wish to disrupt your household routine. Not to mention, we may end up staying over a bit longer once this little affair has been completed. I must admit the weather is most agreeable and a clarion call to my faculties."

With that, the man's face brightened, and his step quickened as we made our way to his waiting carriage. "I believe I know just the place that will add to the enjoyment of your extended stay, should you wish it.

The Duke of Cornwall Hotel was a grand gothic structure, and a bit over-styled for Holmes's Bohemian tastes. The autumn weather had lifted both our spirits to the point of allowing a little extravagance after leaving the cold fog and rain of London, so we both heartily agreed when it was suggested by Mr. Ramsay.

We procured our rooms and, after unpacking, discussed the situation as he saw it.

"You don't really think that you will be unable to expose this woman as a fraud, surely?" I said, sitting at the writing desk in the corner of the room.

Holmes's face turned grave. "I shall have to find irrefutable evidence. Mrs. Penhaligon seems completely unwavering in her conviction of the woman's legitimacy. Otherwise, I fear they will divest her of every last shilling in her possession. The change in weather shall no doubt also affect the pace at which she is stripped of her wealth. This next meeting may be the one where she is convinced to hand over everything she owns." He shook his head nominally. "And she seems quite content in doing so."

He lit a cigarette and leaned up against the windowsill, looking out at the sunny sky with the season's colours just beginning to stain the landscape. Frustration was obvious on his face. There were times when Sherlock Holmes did not suffer fools gladly. This was one of those times.

He blew out a sigh of irritation and said, "There is a certain part of me that almost wishes it to happen."

I was taken aback. "Holmes! How can you say such a thing?"

He pointed a long finger at me. "Even if she doesn't know the *how* of the fraudulence, she should at least understand the *what* and the *why*. What is it? A cunning deception. Why is it being done? To rob her of her inheritance. Her own brother sees it for what it is. People who choose to be so easily beguiled and refuse to listen to reason deserve the fruit of their labors!"

"Being pinched for a few pounds is one thing. Certainly, that would serve as a good lesson learned. But fifteen-thousand pounds . . . ? And some deceptions are so elaborately planned, the actors in the game so good at their craft, they can fool all but the most brilliant."

My friend nodded reluctantly and finally conceded, "You are right, of course. I'm thankful you are at my side to keep me grounded, Watson, or I might let the whole of England suffer in their ignorance. It is a very hard thing indeed to save people from themselves!"

"If anyone needed saving from themselves," said I, "it is Mrs. Penhaligon. She is absolutely convinced of the woman's ability."

Holmes nodded. "I am convinced of her ability, as well. Still, what that ability is differs greatly from that of the widow's idea of it. They have performed a most clever deception, and that is the one thing that draws me to this case and keeps me here." He gave a quickly disappearing grin, nodded to the window, and added, "That, and the weather, of course."

"They?" I queried. "She has a confederate?"

"Certainly. You heard the widow say that Madame Trevellin's brother is the one who offered her the card at the funeral. He is undoubtedly part of the deception."

"How do you think those answers are being placed into the bottles?" I asked. "And correct answers at that," I reminded. "I have to say that has me puzzled."

He furrowed his brow. "Myself as well. Yet, the answer may lie in the fact the widow is only allowed one question."

"Yes, but the question is random and at the widow's choosing. And," I pointed out, "Mrs. Penhaligon also chooses where to lay the blanket. What are the odds that Madame Trevellin and her accomplice pick both the right place to sit *and* the correct answer to a question she has yet to ask?"

The gouges at the bridge of his nose deepened. "Presently, I am at a loss."

He thought silently for a moment, staring out the window into the distance. "This is most definitely a three-pipe problem. I am without the presence of my pipe and the time in which to smoke it! We must prove their fraudulence and do so quickly ."

"How shall we proceed, knowing that if they get any indication they are being investigated, they will almost certainly disappear before we can do anything about it?"

"The weather is fine, and we have a few hours yet of sunlight. I believe a visit to Tinside Beach is in order".

We found a hansom and soon after arrived at the beach. After we made our way down a winding, sandy path with high grass on either side, we were rewarded with a beautiful view of Plymouth Sound, with Rame Peninsula stretching across the waterway to our right. There were many people out enjoying the sunny weather, but a brisk, cool wind was whipping up the surf, so the crowds weren't as large as they might have otherwise been.

The changing huts, in all their blues and reds and yellows, stretched out along the grassline to our immediate right. A few couples were sitting on blankets, enjoying the late afternoon sun, and one gentleman erupted in laughter when, nearer the waterline, an unfortunate lady's hat was almost extricated from her head in a particularly vicious gust of wind. Only her hatpins saved its complete loss.

We surveyed the expanse of the beach momentarily before Holmes began walking, slowly at first, darting his head this way and that, first at the changing huts, then at the water, then back down at the sand at his feet, and lastly, at the grassy dunes behind the huts. He would quicken his step then stop suddenly and repeat the process over again, to which I followed suit. He said nothing, but his keen eyes seemed to scrutinize every grain of sand.

His observations then took us through the high grass dunes behind the huts. Through all this he was silent, and seemed to find nothing that piqued his interest.

After several minutes we found ourselves back in front of the huts. Holmes turned to me and said, "Stay here while I inspect inside."

I remained where I was, about twenty feet or so away from the nearest hut, while Holmes entered each one. After less than a minute, I could hear him pounding on the walls and stomping around. He would then leave the beach hut and enter the next, following the same routine.

As the distance between us increased as he inspected each subsequent hut, I assumed we wanted me to follow, keeping the same distance between us. Each time, all was quiet for a while, and then the pounding and stomping would begin again. I suspected he wanted to know whether one might be heard inside while sitting on a blanket nearby.

When he exited the last one, seeing that I had followed him, he smiled. "You did wonderful, Watson! My apologies for not asking you to follow me. I assumed you would."

"I could hear you pounding and stomping in each hut. Is that what you were ascertaining? Whether someone could be heard inside the beach huts?"

"No," was his only reply.

"Did you find anything of worth?"

"Not to my liking. A few loose floorboards and nothing more."

I looked around us at the expanse of sand and water. "The beach didn't seem to offer up any clues," I lamented.

"Not so," he replied. "Even the lack of clues is a clue itself."

"Where do we go from here?"

Holmes offered up a wry smile. "We go back to the hotel, change, and have what I hope is at least a more palatable dinner than what Simpson's has been offering of late."

I found Holmes the next morning in a suffocating fog, as he sat cross-legged on his bed, a cigarette between his teeth in almost a trance-like state, with both the paper with the ethereal answer to Mr. Ramsay's question and the paper with the names of the charities Mrs. Penhaligon had given laid out before him on the cover. I had found him in this position during many investigations over the years. It was an unhealthy attitude, to say the least, but it did bring about resolution, more often than not.

"How on earth can you breathe in this miasma?" I remonstrated as I opened a window. "Any guests passing by might make the mistake that the room is on fire."

He pulled the cigarette from his mouth. "If you can inhale the worst London has to offer, this should be refreshing by contrast."

"I assume you have been up all night, pondering."

"This case has some interesting conundrums which needed a bit more thought. And like this room with the window now open, the fog of it is beginning to lift."

"Care to enlighten?"

"I shall keep my musings close to my vest," he replied, "for the time being."

"What shall be our plan of attack for today?"

"We shall separate. I would like you to visit Mrs. Penhaligon again and ask if you may accompany her to her session with Madame Trevellin tomorrow. Insist upon it. Tell her that you wish to have your skepticism allayed. Tell her you are more open-minded than am I, and watching the session may perhaps change your attitude on the matter." He pointed his cigarette at me. "Do not leave there until you have her assurances. And to the best of your ability, make sure she understands that in no way should she reveal to Madame Trevellin your true motives."

"That shouldn't be too difficult a task to accomplish. She seems eager to prove Trevellin's legitimacy. What will you do?"

"I am going to look into the charities. I doubt it will be a straightforward matter. The boards of those charities must be verified, however convoluted the trail is. My hope is to find the one thread that will lead back to Trevellin. If I run into any difficulties, I'll leave a message with the front desk. I'll do my best to be back in time for your session, but proceed, regardless."

While Holmes was off investigating the charities, I procured a hansom back to Widow Penhaligon's, to ask permission to accompany her to her session. Since her brother had attended one, she didn't think that Madame Trevellin would mind. I made her promise to refer to me only as a friend who is interested in the occult. And to use my Christian name, John, instead of Dr. Watson. By this time in Holmes's career, even my name, as his colleague and chronicler, was fairly well-known. I reminded her that if Madame Trevellin was a real medium, she wouldn't mind such an intrusion, and in fact, word of mouth was apropos to proselytizing such a gift. If she were a fraud, knowing she caught the attention of Sherlock Holmes might cause Madame Trevellin's sudden disappearance, and with her all the money she had fleeced from not only the widow, but others as well.

164

There were some fears that needed a delicate remedy, however. She had feared that, as a medium, Madame Trevellin might have foreknowledge of the deception and thus ruin their friendship irreparably. Or Thomas might relay in his ghostly note that this was all a deception. I had to convince her, which wasn't an easy task, that those on the Other Side didn't possess omniscience (at least from my minimal knowledge of the subject matter), so it was unlikely they would have any knowledge of me . . . or Sherlock Holmes, for that matter.

With a mighty effort, I finally convinced her of the efficacy of the plan, but I did have misgivings that she might give away the duplicity, whether inadvertent or otherwise.

She asked me to join her for luncheon, and I stayed on in the capacity of a physician, explaining to her in some detail her husband's health issues before he died, and I even treated her for some minor irritations of gout while I was there. For me, it was a needed distraction from the talk over the last two days of all things occult.

When I returned to the hotel, a message was waiting for me at the front desk.

Watson,

> *Leaving for Bristol to check on charities there. A few clues are presenting themselves regarding the charities and the Trevellins, but nothing definitive thus far. There are a few trifles beginning to appear, and the train ride might help me turn these* minutiae *into a workable theory upon which we may act. Until that happens, we are no further along than at the end of our conversation with Mrs. Penhaligon yesterday.*

> *Play along with tomorrow's ruse to the best of your ability. All the while, observe – do not just see. Listen – do not just hear. Mrs. Penhaligon's financial future and possibly her life may depend entirely upon how convincing you are. We shall reconvene as soon as I return. I do not know how long I shall be absent, but if I am not back by tomorrow morning, good luck.*

Holmes

This was the first time Holmes had mentioned a fear of bodily injury, but over the years we had seen much worse devastation waylaid for much less money, so it wasn't surprising the possibility was there.

The rest of the day was spent in nervous introspection about what might transpire the next morning. I didn'teven have the stomach to enjoy either a nice meal or the pleasant autumn weather.

I took a cab to Mrs. Penhaligon's home at eight the next morning. The widow and I chatted for a few minutes while the carriage was in its final preparations, and we were off by eight-twenty. The air was chilled, but a cloudless, blue sky stretched out before us.

"I am never in a hurry to get there," the lady said after some silence. "I always arrive before her. I believe it is her way of proving that the area had in no way been prepared before my arrival."

"It does seem that Madame Trevellin goes out of her way to make sure her abilities are trusted," I confirmed.

She gave me a look of controlled exasperation. "I am only doing this to prove that she is exactly who she says she is. I understand the skepticism. I just wish Archie would just leave me to my beliefs, as I do his."

I gave her a weak smile and did my best to not sound patronizing. "I'm sure he does what he does out of brotherly love."

She scoffed. "Familial ties don't give one the right to meddle."

"He only wishes to make sure your legacy remains intact."

"My legacy," she replied coldly, "is mine to do with as I please."

I couldn't help but acknowledge inwardly that this woman was by far the least appreciative of Sherlock Holmes's help of any previous client, although, strictly speaking, Mr. Ramsay was our patron. If I had truly understood the depth in which this woman was entrenched in such beliefs, I would have tried to talk my friend out of taking the case altogether. Nonetheless, all we could do now was see it through to whatever end awaited us.

As warned, Madame Trevellin arrived ten minutes later than we.

We alighted our carriages together and stood at the grassline between the thoroughfare and the beach huts on the other side of the dunes. I judged Madame Trevellin to be close to forty. She was a somewhat attractive woman, thin, but not severely so, with black hair braided up tightly from a pronounced widow's peak. She had piercing, ice-blue eyes, a long, straight nose with an intellectual flare of the nostril, and full, feminine lips. Her only detriments were acute angles to her jaw and chin which subtracted somehow from her beauty. The severity of her jawline seemed to accentuate any emotion given with her mouth, either in smile or frown, making her seem happier or angrier than perhaps were her true emotions.

Mrs. Penhaligon introduced us. "Madame Trevellin, this is John, an acquaintance of mine. John, this is Madame Trevellin."

166

I smiled and took her hand gently, but she grabbed my hand firmly and closed her eyes, momentarily, which caught me unawares. I did my best not to pull my hand away and let play out whatever it was she was doing.

"My apologies," she finally said in a throaty voice, letting go of my hand. "I have no control over what the spirits tell me and when they wish to say it. When they speak, I must listen."

"Maggie has told me much about you," I replied. "I must say, I'm intrigued."

She looked from one to the other of us then gave me her full attention. "Funny, she hasn't mentioned you at all."

"I am an old friend, just over from Sussex," I lied. "I haven't been over this way in quite some time, so I thought I would pay my respects. I regret I couldn't get away for Thomas's funeral."

"And what brings you here now?" she asked with a little smile.

I returned a cheeky one, playing along as Holmes had asked. "I was rather hoping you might tell me that."

"A disbeliever," she stated more than asked.

"Let us just say open-minded with some reservations."

"And watching Mrs. Penhaligon's session will convince you?"

"I don't know what will convince me, but I am willing to allow for the possibility."

She nodded to the widow. "Then let us see what answer to Mrs. Penhaligon's question today reveals." She gave me a dark look and added, "I am not certain even that shall suffice."

We walked down to the beach single file with the widow first, then Madame Trevellin, and I took up the rear, carrying the blanket.

Once we made the beach, Madame Trevellin said, "Let us join hands. Mrs. Penhaligon will arbitrarily choose a spot, and we shall lay out the blanket."

We did as we were told, and after we had just passed the fifth beach hut, our steps became slower, and finally, Mrs. Penhaligon stopped. She looked around. "I believe this is where I would like to stop today."

Madame Trevellin nodded, "As you wish. Doctor, if you would please hand me the blanket, I shall lay it down."

My heart skipped a beat, "How . . . how did you know I was a doctor?" I asked, amazement awash on my face.

"It is my business to know what others do not," she said cryptically.

Was she playing with me? Did she know my true identity? Being in the business of knowing what others do not was a statement my friend had made on more than one occasion. It was practically verbatim.

She went on as a way of explanation, "As I said, I have no control over when the spirits speak to me . . . or what they tell me. In the strictest sense, I didn't *know* you were a doctor. I was told, and I trust completely what the spirits tell me."

"And they told you I was a doctor?" At this, I cast a glance at the widow.

She beamed triumphantly and put up her hands. "I haven't spoken to Madame Trevellin since our last session, upon my word!"

I looked around the beach, which was empty at this hour, and then looked upon the severe smile of the woman, which now seemed unnerving. I shook my head and handed her the blanket, which she, in turn, laid out.

I wished at that point to have the rational mind of Sherlock Holmes to look upon for grounding. I never believed in the occult, but unless some trickery was somehow revealed, possibly deception by the widow herself, I couldn't otherwise account for the woman's preternatural knowledge.

"Please, everyone sit," Madame Trevellin said. "John to the north, Maggie to the east, and I shall sit to the south."

We sat in a triangular pattern on the blanket.

"Now, hold hands and close your eyes in prayer, thinking about a beloved you would like to channel."

We did as instructed. Madame Trevellin began to mumble under her breath in an unfamiliar tongue. She leaned back, pulling us with her, and then leaning forward, making our outstretched arms go slack. Left, then right, then back, then forward again, all the while chanting the strange incantations.

"There are two people coming through," she said breathlessly. "Thomas and – and a woman."

I opened my eyes just enough to see the furrowed brow on her face as if trying to understand. Her lips were locked in a thin line, making her lower jaw look as sharp as a razor.

"*M*", she suddenly blurted. "*Margaret, Marjory, Mary . . . Yes, Mary. A Mary is here.*"

I gasped and found myself whispering, "Mary?" My wife, whom I had met during one of our investigations, had died a few years prior, during the time in which I had presumed my friend dead at the hands of Professor Moriarty, and her passing was still a point of severe grief at times.

I opened my eyes completely and found Madame Trevellin staring openly at me, her blue eyes dulled by sadness. "She wishes to speak to you, but I'm afraid that is all I can give at this point, John. Thomas's spirit is stronger, and he doesn't wish to share with you the time he has with his wife. Perhaps another time . . . ."

My shoulders slumped, and I looked upon an ebullient Mrs. Penhaligon, who seemed to radiate her triumph. She could tell by my shocked countenance that Madame Trevellin had been correct.

There was a silence – as if for my benefit, to let the reality of her statement and all it implied sink in. How could she have known? Could she truly be what she claimed?

Turning from me to the widow, Madame Trevellin asked softly, "Thomas is waiting. What do you wish to ask?"

Where was Holmes? I needed him now more than ever! I didn't know how much more of this I could take. My mind was now entirely taken by Mary.

Mrs. Penhaligon cut across my thoughts in a voice that seemed at once cutting and magnanimous, "My dear," she said, speaking to the presence of her dead husband, "I know you endured much to get what you wanted in life. Most didn't see the hard work you put into your profession to give us the life we had, but I did. Even the money you inherited was hard-earned by your father and his before him. I don't take lightly the responsibility for it bestowed upon me at your death. I cannot believe it was all meant just for me. You were too charitable a person to leave it to the greed of just one person."

She took a deep breath and sobbed, a deep, genuine sorrow. "I am lonely without you, Tom. I miss you so much. I want to continue our meetings, however fleeting they may be. I can feel your hand upon my cheek, even if I cannot see it. I feel your presence, and it brings me such comfort that even Madame Trevellin cannot truly understand the peace it brings me. As small as these gestures may be, I can only have them with the help of Madame Trevellin. I want these meetings to continue, and I am prepared to share all we have to do so. Darling, this isn't an easy thing to ask, but I want to know if you feel the same. Should I . . . should I share the wealth of your estate with Madame Trevellin, and continue our life here, in these little moments, until I can finally be reunited with you there forever?"

I couldn't hide my shock. With one question she was going to divest herself of everything she owned.

"Are you sure that is prudent?" I asked.

The widow glared at me. "How much more proof do you need?" she exclaimed.

I looked upon Madame Trevellin. "Surely, you will decline such an offer!"

If eyes could laugh, the woman was surely mocking me with her cold, even stare. "Mrs. Penhaligon isn't asking me, Doctor. She is asking her husband. Who better to seek such guidance?"

169

She closed her eyes once more. "Let us see if we can get an answer," she said, and then began chanting, this time accompanied by a slight shuddering of her shoulders. This lasted for some time. Suddenly, she let go of our hands, slumped over onto the blanket, and let out a heavy sigh.

"I believe Thomas has responded," she said breathlessly as she pushed herself up off the blanket. "Shall we see what the answer is?"

We all stood, and the medium pushed aside the blanket and began to dig in the sand.

I took that time to search our surroundings. I saw no one. No Holmes, no police. He must have been detained in Bristol longer than anticipated. I half-expected to have another message stating as such waiting for me once I returned to the hotel.

There was a little gasp of delight by the widow as Madame Trevellin, at last, pulled a bottle from the sand. Within it was a rolled-up piece of paper. She fished it out with some excitement of her own, unfurled it, and read aloud, "'*Madame Trevellin is a . . . .*'" She didn't finish the statement, only looked at the paper in confusion.

I snatched it from her hands and read aloud with a smile slowly spreading across my features, "'*Madame Trevellin is a fraud and is quite possibly complicit in the murder of Mr. Thomas Penhaligon. S.H.*'"

Once the note had been read, Holmes pushed open the nearest beach hut triumphantly and stepped out. At almost the same time, a constable and a man dressed in tweed appeared from the tall grass behind the hut and all three surrounded us.

"I apologize, Watson," my friend said, sporting a smile of amusement. "I couldn't resist giving our Madame Trevellin a little taste of her own medicine."

"You! You!" The woman let out an ear-piercing scream of lamentation.

"Madame Trevellin," Sherlock Holmes started, "this is Inspector Havarin of the Plymouth Constabulary, and Constable Crabtree."

The constable gave her a polite smile before he grabbed her by her arm, and the inspector said, "Lucy Meacham, I am arresting you on multiple accounts of obtaining money under false pretenses."

"Lucy Meacham?" Mrs. Penhaligon bemoaned, looking from the constable to my friend.

"That is her real name," Holmes replied dryly. "You didn't expect a player in a game such as this to use her real name, did you?"

"Where is Oscar?" she spat. "Where is my brother!"

"Your brother was kind enough to give up the use of his beach hut early this morning for my sake, and is now awaiting your arrival at the Plymouth Constabulary."

She scowled at him, setting her sharp jawline even sharper. "I shall get you for this, Sherlock Holmes! If it is the last thing I do, I shall get you for this!"

"Shall you accost me from The Great Beyond?" Holmes asked with droll humour. "Once they exhume Mr. Penhaligon's body and prove poisoning – that, sadly, will be your only recourse."

"Poison?" the widow asked sharply, tears now streaming down her face. "My husband was poisoned?"

Holmes nodded gravely. "I am afraid it's almost a certainty. You have been a victim of a most-cunning game of fraud which began with the murder of your husband for the purpose of cleaning you of every penny you have, after which they were going to disappear. They have done it on at least three other occasions – twice in Wales, and once in Scotland before settling down here. Additional investigation may uncover more."

I looked upon the dejected countenance of the widow and asked, "Shall we see you home, Mrs. Penhaligon? I'm sure you must have many questions that my friend would be more than willing to answer."

She sighed in resignation. "The only thing I wish is to be left alone." She blinked back tears. "Thank you, all the same, Doctor. And you, as well, Mr. Holmes. I feel much the fool."

"They are masters of their craft," my friend replied. "They have fooled many people, praying on grief that often overrides one's other, more rational, emotions."

Detective Havarin said to Mrs. Penhaligon, "I shall accompany Miss Meacham to the station. Then, if it's all right with you, I'll look upon you at home. There are some questions I need answered, and I'm sure you will have some as well."

"Of course," she sobbed.

She began a slow, dejected walk back to her waiting carriage.

The detective, noticing the blanket crumpled in the sand at our feet, picked it up and began to fold it as he sloughed through the sand to catch up with the widow. He said something softly to her, no doubt some words of comfort – if there could be such a thing given such devastating news. They then walked back up the sandy path together with the constable and Miss Meacham, still spewing obscenities, following behind.

Suddenly, Holmes and I were the only ones left on the beach.

"Come, Watson," he said with a revelatory twinkle in his eyes, "let me show you how this little ruse was accomplished."

I followed my friend to the beach hut from which he had just appeared. He opened the door, and with a sweep of his long arm asked, "What do you see?"

The hut was utterly empty, and I said as much.

"A cursory look would seem to vindicate your appraisal," he replied. "That appraisal would be incorrect."

He stepped inside, while I stayed in the open doorway.

"Remember my remarking about the loose floorboards?"

"I remember, yes."

"Those loose floorboards were my first clue. Some huts had them, some did not, but the ones that did, the floorboards were loose in the exact same spot."

I shrugged my shoulders. "These huts are left to the mercy of the elements. I would expect some degree of degradation with the salt spray and winds."

"I agree, but chance alone would not account for the loosening of the exact floorboard in each hut."

He shot me a sardonic grin. "And then there is this." He pulled up the floorboard, revealing a length of what looked like flexible hydraulic tubing that disappeared into the sand under the hut."

"What on earth is that?" I asked.

"They were clever by half, I give them that," Holmes said. Then, from within the tubing itself, he pulled out what could only be described as a flexible length of a bore cleaner with the far end slightly smaller than the diameter of the tubing itself. When entirely extracted from the tubing, it was approximately twenty feet in length.

I looked from the hut to where the three of us had been sitting on the blanket, and I judged it to be about the same length.

"How did they do it?" I asked.

"Go over to where you had been sitting on the blanket, and I shall show you."

I did as instructed and knelt at the hole Madame Trevellin had dug.

"I'm ready," I yelled to my friend.

After some time, I began to see the sand move, and suddenly, a rolled-up piece of paper popped up through the sand. I cleared away the sand from that area and finally found the end of the tubing with the bore cleaner popped out at the end.

I unrolled the paper, and on it Holmes had written: *This is how*.

He emerged from the hut and continued his elucidation as he joined me on the beach. "They would come the night before and set up where the next day's session would take place. They would run the hydraulic tubing, used for its strong but flexible construction and larger diameter, from the nearest beach hut to the agreed upon spot, loosely attach the end of the tube to the lip of the bottle, and cover everything with sand. Lucy Meacham's brother would hear the question asked by the widow, write the answer on the paper, roll it up, and push it through the tubing and into the

172

bottle at the other end with the bore brush. He would then pull all the tubing gently back through the sand, leaving only the bottle behind with the answer to her question inside. I suspect she would always have Mrs. Penhaligon sit with her back to the hut in case there was any shifting of the sand when he pulled the hose back. They buried it far enough down that I doubt there would have been anything noticeable anyway."

There were still some questions needing answers before I was sufficiently satisfied. "How did her brother know the answers to the questions?"

"From the deceased's missing journal. From a logical point of view, it would have just about everything one needed to answer most questions. It was on his person when her brother was arrested late last evening when he was setting up for today's session." He then held up a finger. "And he worked with Mr. Penhaligon in the hospital apothecary. Certainly, many topics would have been breached throughout a normal workday, and they worked together for some time – three years if he gained employment as soon as they arrived in Plymouth. Between the two, they could have garnered more than enough information to answer just about any question asked."

"But how were they able to stop in the exact spot needed to find the bottle?" I asked perplexed. "No amount of intricate planning would have mattered if they hadn't stopped at precisely the right spot.

"The power of suggestion," my friend replied with a wry grin. "I did the same to you when we initially came down to the beach."

I furrowed my brow. "I don't understand."

"When we walked along, whenever I slowed my pace, you did the same. When I stopped you stopped, and then I asked where we should start our investigation, and you said right where we had stopped. It was a quite natural reaction. You thought you were making the decision where to begin, but it was I who had actually decided. You just followed my lead, whether you realized it or not."

Then the realization came to me in an epiphany. "And today, when we were walking along, we were all holding hands. We were just following Madame Trevellin's – "

"Lucy Meacham."

"Yes, yes, Lucy Meacham. We just followed her lead without ever realizing it."

"I was watching through a crack in the doorway of the hut, and although you couldn't see it, I could see that Miss Meacham began to squeeze Mrs. Penhaligon's hand ever so slightly as they approached the designated spot. The widow mistook the pressure as an unconscious indication that they were closing in on Thomas's energy, so although it was Mrs. Penhaligon's choice where to stop and lay out the blanket, she was going by Meacham's indications they were where they needed to be to talk to the widow's husband."

"And the charities?" I queried.

"All good lies must have an element of truth in them to be successful. As it turns out, the charities are legitimate and have no ties to the Meachams in any way. That was how the widow was lured in completely – by the one truth that was told. They were perfectly happy to give up a few thousand pounds to gain several times that amount in return."

"What an incredible deception," said I. "How were you able to figure it out?"

"The beach huts and their proximity to the women on every occasion was the most obvious clue," my friend replied. "I am familiar with some similar forms of street magic due to some early cases I investigated before we met."

"So, you knew how it was done?"

"I didn't say that," he corrected. "All I needed to know was where to look for the deception. The 'how' one can then see with his own eyes once he knows where to look. In this case, I had only to wait for the confederate to show himself and begin to set the stage for the show, and he was literally caught in the act."

My features fell at one thing that had yet to be explained. "She knew about Mary. How do you explain that?"

"I cannot," he said dolefully. "Except to say that some deceptions run very deep indeed. The Meachams more than likely had allies in many different places, bought off for information that could be used in their ruse. It is entirely possible that Mr. Ramsay had a member of his staff who was a paid informant and warned the Meachams we were being brought down to investigate." He shrugged. "I daresay, the public probably knows more about us and our histories than we would care to admit. In any case, if they were warned, they had at least a few days to look into our pasts and use that knowledge to their advantage."

"Why wouldn't they have just left town then?" I asked. "Surely, they would have had to know we would find them out."

Sherlock Holmes smiled. "Arrogance is a very cruel mistress. It can be the keystone in pulling off such an intricate deception, but it can also fool even its possessor into believing in the power of his own lie."

Holmes smiled and inhaled deeply. "Come, Watson. Let us give Mr. Ramsay the news. Then, we can return to the beach and imbibe more of the sunshine and cool sea air."

"You read my mind," I replied cheekily.

Sherlock Holmes and the
Female Detective
by Susan Knight

Holmes was wool-gathering, staring disconsolately out of our upstairs window, in the hope, I suppose, that a new engrossing puzzle was about to arrive on our doorstep. He had been like this for nigh on an hour, and I feared that all-too-soon his glance would stray to the box where he kept his cocaine and syringes. If the day had been in any way clement, I should have suggested a bracing walk in Regent's Park. But it was damp, with that November chill that seems to seep into one's very bones.

"You should get a hobby, Holmes," I said, raising my head from the article I was reading on the intriguing new science of psychology. "Chess, perhaps."

"Chess!" he snorted. "And who, pray, would I play with? You? I'd beat you every time, so where would be the challenge in that?"

I ignored the insult, attributing it to the frustrations of inactivity.

"You could always play against yourself," I replied. "Then you would have only a fifty-fifty chance of winning."

"Pah! Watson. I suppose you consider that very witty."

I grinned, but before I could think up a suitable response, a light tap sounded on the door.

"I didn't hear anyone arrive below, Watson," Holmes said. "Did you?"

"No," I replied. "It's probably Mrs. Hudson, asking when we want our tea."

It was, indeed, our estimable landlady, but her request was not as expected.

"Mr. Holmes," she said, "my seamstress is here, and she has a problem which perhaps you might help her with."

"Your seamstress!"

I am afraid Holmes's disdain sounded all too clearly in his tone. Or did he imagine he was about to be asked to help with hemming a skirt?

"It's a distressing matter, but not without interest for you, I think," Mrs. Hudson continued. "If you would only consent to meet with Lottie and hear what she has to say – "

"Let her come then." Holmes waved a hand, sighing. Anything to dispel the boredom of the afternoon.

The woman in question must have been lurking on the stairs right behind Mrs. Hudson, for she stepped forward immediately: A small, worn-looking person in her thirties, someone you wouldn't look at twice if you passed her in the street, plainly dressed in a grey serge jacket and skirt.

"Thank you so much for seeing me, Mr. Holmes," she said in a surprisingly deep, melodious voice that shook a little. "You see, I am driven mad with worry for poor Mrs. Flowerdew."

"Before anything else, please be seated," Holmes said, somewhat brusquely, "and Mrs. Hudson, perhaps you would be so kind as to bring us all a pot of tea. It is already nearly four of the clock, and Watson is parched."

Quite untrue, though tea is always welcome. Our landlady withdrew, closing the door behind her.

"Now," Holmes continued, the woman having perched herself on one of our harder chairs, "please explain."

"It's rather delicate." She glanced at me.

"Dr. Watson is my friend and colleague and utterly discreet. You may speak freely in front of both of us."

I smiled reassuringly at her, my curiosity, I confess, already a little aroused.

"Very well. Best if I start from the beginning, Dr. Watson, Mr. Holmes, sirs. My name is Charlotte Booth and I am, as Martha . . . Mrs. Hudson . . . told you, a seamstress by trade, and in that capacity have been engaged on several occasions by a Mrs. Alfred Flowerdew, of the borough of Lewisham. However, I am a widow, and the income generated by such work is insufficient to support myself and my young son, and so I supplement it by helping the police."

"The police?" Holmes sounded surprised. "In what capacity?"

"I sometimes work as a searcher, sir. You see, when women suspected of theft are arrested, they have to be searched. Of course, male officers cannot possibly with propriety conduct such examinations, so they call on the likes of me." She paused and her face lit up in a rare smile. "You'd be astonished, gents, at the some of the places where such women conceal their loot. In their hats and hair, in their mouths, in their garments – puff sleeves are much favoured for ease of concealment. Even in their stays and other under-garments."

I nodded. I had heard of the practice of employing women in this capacity before.

"That was how I started off, as a searcher, but since those early days, I have been more often engaged to follow known miscreants, to try and catch them perpetrating a criminal act. The police like me because I look ordinary and can pass unnoticed through a crowd, or enter a shop without

176

arousing suspicion. In that way, I have brought several vicious folk to justice."

"It sounds quite dangerous," I said.

"Yes, Doctor, it can be," she replied. "I have been struck several times and stabbed once, although happily only in my shoulder."

A brave young woman!

"Most interesting," Holmes remarked with a yawn. "But how is this relevant to the case of Mrs. . . . er . . . Flowerdew?"

"Not directly, although I have also been engaged by a certain well-established private detective agency, when they require the gathering of information to be used in divorce or similar cases of a domestic nature. As a seamstress, you see, it is easy for me to be admitted quite legitimately into households where I can keep my eyes and ears open."

"And it is in this regard that you have attended Mrs. Flowerdew?"

"Oh no, sir. Mrs. Flowerdew simply wished for me to make a dress for her. As I mentioned, this wasn't the first time she has requested my services. If I say so myself, gents, and as Mrs. Hudson can tell you, I'm a skilled and prompt worker, and my gowns are of the highest quality. In addition, you know, I charge less than many others."

"Yes, yes."

I could see that Holmes was getting impatient. Would the woman ever come to the point? And no need to advertise her services to us, for, after all, we were hardly likely to be ordering garments from her, now or in the future.

"Well, you see, sirs, Mrs. Flowerdew," she continued, "is a pretty little lady of maybe forty or so years of age. Maybe nearer fifty, to be exact. She has always been very pleasant to me and, in the past, as I thought, happy enough with her life, although childless. However, when I visited her this last time, three weeks ago, I was quite shocked by her appearance. Wan and thin, the roses drained from her cheeks. I asked her if she was all right but she merely said that she hadn't been well. I noticed, too, that a new housekeeper had been appointed, a flashy-looking person to my eye, one I should rather have seen flaunting herself on the stage in some low theatrical establishment than working in a respectable home in the suburbs. When I asked what had happened to the previous housekeeper, a homely, comfortable body named Elsie Chambers, Mrs. Flowerdew simply said that Alfred – that's Mr. Flowerdew – had found her work deficient and that this Alice Penn was like to prove much more satisfactory."

Charlotte Booth paused. She was clearly trying to master her emotions.

"When I returned, two weeks later with the finished garment for her to try, I was met at the front door by this same Alice Penn. She was quite rude and abrupt, and wouldn't admit me, saying that Mrs. Flowerdew was indisposed and not able for visitors. She almost snatched the dress from me, telling me that she would give it to her mistress and that payment would be arranged. I explained that it needed to be fitted on the lady herself in case minor adjustments had to be made. She just muttered "Another time," and almost slammed the door on me. I didn't like it, Mr. Holmes. I didn't like it at all."

"Is that it?" Holmes asked, lying back in his chair, his eyes closed. "Is that what is worrying you?"

"There's more," she answered, perhaps a little put out by his attitude. "This morning, I attempted another visit but with the same result. Dismissed on the doorstep – and still not paid, by the way – so I decided on a ruse I had employed before, when investigating possible . . . pardon me . . . marital infidelities. I concealed myself in an alleyway opposite the house and waited. Luckily, I have learned patience and wasn't inclined to abandon my vigil, even after two hours in the cold and damp. The wait was rewarded at last when I observed Alice Penn leave the house. To my dismay, I saw that she was wearing the very dress I had made for her mistress!"

"My God!" I exclaimed. "Something's very wrong there."

Charlotte Booth nodded. "You may well say so, Dr. Watson, sir," she replied. "When I was certain she was gone, I approached the house again, but this time made my way to the back, where I knew the kitchen door to be situated. I was ready with an excuse to give to the cook or to any servant I should meet, but to my astonishment there was no one about, even though the back door stood open. Moreover, the place showed strong signs of neglect. Dirty dishes and empty bottles of beer and gin were strewn everywhere, and there was a rank smell. I'd be quite mortified if I let my place fall into rack and ruin like that." She paused, no doubt reimagining the shocking scene.

"Please continue," Holmes said.

"Yes, sir . . . I'm getting there. I cautiously made my way into the body of the house, but again met with no one. I thought that was very strange, Very strange, indeed. Wouldn't you think so?"

I nodded encouragingly.

"So then, having climbed the stairs to the room I knew to be Mrs. Flowerdew's, I knocked on the door and called out her name. At first there was no reply. I knocked again and this time heard a faint murmur, which I understood to be permission to enter. However," she paused for dramatic effect, "the door was locked fast."

At that moment, a tap on our own door caused us all to jump. Well, I did at least. However, it was only Mrs. Hudson with a tray of tea, and, I was delighted to observe, some freshly made drop scones.

"It's a shocking tale, isn't it?" she remarked. Clearly the seamstress had already apprised her of the circumstances regarding this Mrs. Flowerdew.

"Had the lady locked herself in?"" I asked.

"Not at all. She managed to creep to the door and spoke to me through the keyhole. It seems she had been imprisoned in the room by her husband and the fearsome Alice. Imprisoned, sirs!" She shook her head. "All the other servants had been dismissed. 'They are trying to poison me, Lottie!' the poor lady told me. 'I have stopped eating what they give me, but fear I am not long for this world anyway.'"

Charlotte Booth shook her head some more. "You can imagine how horrified I was to hear that. I tried to find a key to open the door and, having failed that, to break it down, to no avail. All I could do was to promise her to return with help. That is why I have come to you, Mr. Holmes. Mrs. Hudson is always singing your praises."

"I am most gratified to hear it," Holmes replied, nodding an acknowledgement to our landlady. "However, Mrs. Booth, this is surely a matter for the police."

"You would think so, wouldn't you?" The seamstress gave a bitter smile. "The trouble is that Mr. Alfred Flowerdew *is* the police. He is the District Inspector at the station in Lewisham. No use reporting it there, Mr. Holmes. I've seen over and over again how the members of the force stick up for each other. They wouldn't pay attention to the likes of me."

"But in a clear case of at least marital cruelty such as this . . ." I ventured.

"Mrs. Booth is right to be wary, Watson." Holmes interjected. "Alfred Flowerdew has only to say that his wife is mad – which, pardon me, Madam, may well be the case." He was sitting straighter now, his interest excited at last. "But that, of course, cannot justify inhumane treatment."

"I don't think her mad, sir, or, if she is, he and his trollop have made her so," the seamstress remarked shortly.

"You'll look into it, won't you, Mr. Holmes?" Mrs. Hudson said, offering 'round the plate of drop scones. I was the only one to partake.

"If your suspicions and those of the lady concerned are correct," Holmes told the seamstress, "there is no time at all to be lost. Mrs. Flowerdew says she isn't eating, but, while the body can sustain life for several weeks without food, as I know from my own researches, she will die very quickly if she isn't taking liquids. And if she is drinking anything at all, then of course poison can be administered that way as well as any other." He frowned. "Of course, the whole business may yet be a figment of a troubled mind . . . ."

Charlotte Booth looked to interrupt but Holmes held up a finger to restrain her.

"Nonetheless," he continued, "in the light of what you have told me regarding the dismissal of the servants and the neglected state of the house, plus the very telling fact of this Alice Penn having the impudence to wear the very same dress you made for her mistress, I am inclined to believe you that evil deeds are afoot in the Flowerdew household." He stood up. "I shall therefore ask you, Mrs. Booth, to accompany myself and Dr. Watson to Lewisham." He turned to me. "I particularly wish you to be present, Watson, in your capacity as a doctor, so bring your medical bag with you."

I nodded.

"It is too late this evening, I fear," Holmes continued. "Inspector Flowerdew will no doubt be on his way home shortly, and I particularly wish him not to be there when we arrive. Let us meet early tomorrow morning at Charing Cross Station. Say just before eight, since I seem to recall that the Lewisham train leaves on the hour."

Good Lord! Had the man even memorised the suburban train timetables?

"Oh, thank you, sir!" Charlotte Booth exclaimed. "Thank you so very much!" Whereupon she at last helped herself to a scone.

It was a strange-looking trio that made the journey the next morning from Charing Cross to Lewisham. Myself – the professional man of means, the doctor with his leather case. The seamstress in her plain and slightly shabby grey suit. The labouring man in his filthy greatcoat, sporting an equally dirty brimmed hat and big scuffed boots. Charlotte Booth had to look twice or thrice at this apparition before realising that it was Holmes.

It proved impossible to discuss our plans just then, however, for, although we had found a compartment to ourselves, at the very last minute a prosperous-looking middle-aged gentleman and his wife joined us. At the sight of Holmes, they clearly wished to withdraw again, but too late. The train was already in motion. The wife cowered against her husband, who shot reproving glances at my friend and muttered about a waste of a first-class ticket when forced to travel with those persons who by rights merited only third-class.

180

Holmes grinned at them, baring long stained teeth, which made the lady wife cower even more. At the next stop, the couple hastily alighted, no doubt to find more acceptable travelling companions.

When the train started up again, Holmes, having already discussed the matter with me, conveyed his plan of action to Charlotte Booth.

"In case the whole matter is a simple misunderstanding, Dr. Watson will first attempt to gain access to the lady, on foot, he will say, of concern about her well-being. If the housekeeper is caring of her mistress, she may admit him. At least her attitude can be judged from her response."

"She will not admit him," Charlotte Booth replied. "I would bet my life on it."

"Your life!" Holmes smiled. "That's quite a wager, my dear."

"You will soon see." The seamstress folded her arms, a grim expression on her face.

"In that case, I shall call to the house offering my services as a handy-man."

"Do you think that will work, sir?" She looked sceptical.

"Holmes has quite a way with the ladies," I remarked, "when he wants to get around them."

Charlotte Booth looked even more sceptical, but Holmes laughed.

"Well, thank you, Watson," he said. "I am flattered. But even if Alice Penn proves unimpressed with my undoubted charms, I am sure that I can inveigle my way into the house somehow."

"So what do I do?" Mrs. Booth asked.

"You will wait patiently, as you have told us you have often had occasion to do before. Then, if we have to force the issue, your presence will be invaluable in reassuring the poor lady."

If the seamstress was disappointed in her reduced role, she didn't show it, but nodded agreement.

The Flowerdew residence in Wivenhoe Place was a medium-sized, end-of-terrace house with a sizable garden to one side. Apart from the somewhat overgrown nature of this latter, the place looked perfectly respectable. One could hardly conceive of anything shocking occurring behind those unimpeachable red bricks. When I expressed surprise that a policeman, even a District Inspector, could afford a house like this, the seamstress replied that she understood the money came from Mrs. Flowerdew's inheritance.

"Of course, with her gone, it would be all his," Charlotte Booth added drily.

"Which it is anyway under current law," I added.

She shook her head. "Such injustice. A woman's wealth should be her own."

I agreed heartily. However, this was neither the time nor the place to discuss the rights of women.

Walking up to the front door, I rapped firmly upon it with a brass knocker in the somewhat tarnished form of a lion's head. There being no answer, I tried again. Eventually, a young woman opened it. She looked as if I had roused her from sleep, even though it was already past nine o'clock. Her dress had been hastily donned, the bodice half-buttoned, and her fair hair was unkempt. Attractive in a slatternly way, she regarded me through heavy-lidded, unfriendly eyes.

"Yes?"

"Good morning," I said, politely raising my hat. "My name is Dr. Sacker. Apologies for calling unannounced, but I have been approached by a friend of Mrs. Flowerdew who, understanding her to be sick, is most worried about her. She requested me to see if I could assist in the lady's recovery in some way."

Alice Penn, for assuredly it was she, looked puzzled by my speech.

"Who did you say you are?" she asked.

"Dr. Sacker," I repeated, Holmes and I having judged it safer for me not to use my real name. It was admittedly unlikely that the young woman would be acquainted with my published accounts of Holmes's adventures, but no need to take the risk.

"Mrs. Flowerdew has her own doctor." Spoken uncompromisingly.

"I see. I am very pleased to hear that. But, to reassure Mrs. Flowerdew's friend, may I request the name of my colleague?" I asked.

"You may not," and Alice Penn slammed the door shut in my face.

It was no more than we had expected and as Charlotte Booth had predicted. We would have to employ the next stage of the plan.

I removed with the seamstress to a nearby pastry shop while Holmes, not wishing to call too soon after my visit, in case it aroused the housekeeper's suspicions, engaged to keep watch on the house. With any luck, Alice Penn might decide to go out, as she had done before.

It was a long and dreary wait in the shop. Despite my fondness for sweets, there is a limit to the number of jam tarts that even I can comfortably consume, while Charlotte Booth sat rather miserably over a single cup of cold tea. I am sure the little waitress, who hovered hopefully at our table, was most intrigued. Maybe she took me for a member of that class of well-heeled gentlemen who prey on young women, although the seamstress, with her worn looks and plain garb, would hardly fit the usual type of victim.

182

Although distracted with worry for her friend, with nothing else to talk about, she opened up to me about her life, and about the little boy, Matthew, who was the centre of her world – a rascal, she said fondly, of seven years. Her late husband had been a police constable, who had died young of consumption.

"All those nights in the wet, the fog," she complained. "I reckon that's what did it for him, Dr. Watson, sir."

It was through her connection with the Force that she had been recruited as a searcher.

"They've been good to me, Doctor, I'll say that for them. Without the extra work, I don't know how I should have managed."

"But I think you told us that you've also been employed by some private detective agencies."

"Yes, indeed. Though I have to say that I am not always happy with what I have to do. Spying on unfaithful wives to provide evidence in divorce cases, and the like. Quite often the poor woman is trapped in a horrible marriage to start with, so you can well understand her wanting to find a bit of happiness elsewhere, can't you?"

I made a non-committal murmur.

"No, Doctor," she continued, "I prefer hunting down the real villains – the thieves and cutpurses. The really rotten eggs."

"You're quite the lady detective," I said, laughing.

She blushed and suddenly became quite pretty.

"Oh, I'm no lady, I'm afraid, sir. I wouldn't presume. As for being a detective, I suppose I am in some small way. After all, I have brought quite a number of blackguards to justice." She paused, thoughtfully. "Monty Crowe, the forger. Mrs. Casper, the fraudulent fortune-teller. Belle McGregor, the baby farmer. Sam Briggs, the butcher's assistant who murdered his employer and chopped him up into prime cuts."

"Good Heavens!" I said, startled.

"Yes, that Sam Briggs was a really nasty piece of work. It was him as stabbed me in the shoulder, trying to make his escape, but we caught him anyway." She smiled at the recollection. "You know what, Doctor? In my opinion, it would be no bad thing if the police force allowed women to be officially employed. One day, perhaps."

I nodded. I do not share the prejudice that deems women too delicate or mentally unfit for police work. Many females of my acquaintance are at least as able, enterprising, and practical as males, and often, more so. The young woman in front of me was certainly a case in point.

Eventually, after two or more hours, the pastry shop door opened to admit Holmes, even more disreputable-looking than before, if that were possible. The little waitress was wide-eyed when he sat himself down at our table. Her head shook like a nodding doll's as she took his order for a big pot of tea – "Scalding hot, if you please." – and a portion of pie and mash.

The seamstress and I were of course impatient to hear what had transpired but Holmes held up a hand to forestall our questions.

"All in good time," he announced, much to my astonishment. "I am in dire need of some sustenance first." Food is usually incidental to his investigations, if he even remembers to eat at all.

A steaming plate having been set down in front of him, he set to with an unwonted appetite and relish.

"A fine pie," he even called out to the little waitress, who bobbed and blushed.

At last, with a sigh, he sat back in his chair and shook his head.

"That woman," he said. "A vampire if ever I saw one."

"Alice Penn?" I asked.

"Who else? I was lucky to get out of there alive."

He recounted how he had called to the house in the guise of an odd-job man, informing Alice that some tiles were loose on the roof and that it was also probable, given the autumnal weather and the abundance of trees near the house, that the guttering would need clearing of dead leaves.

"It had occurred to me that, if I could get a ladder, I could perhaps see into Mrs. Flowerdew's bedroom and find out if all was well with her."

Alice had studied him for a few moments and apparently liked what she saw. After all, despite the rough clothes, Holmes was still a fine looking man, with, at that moment, a touch of the gypsy about him. I could understand how a woman like Alice Penn might find him attractive.

"I don't know if we have a ladder, Jim," she had said, Jim being the name Holmes had given her, "but I expect I could find something for you to do."

She brought him into the house. Then, into the kitchen, where she offered him some beer. He could see that she was glad of company, while he was happy to draw her out, in case he should learn something of note.

It soon transpired that she wasn't at all content with the situation in which she found herself.

"I'm not used to domestic work, Jim," she had said. The state of the kitchen alone attesting the truth of that. "I never thought it would be skivvy stuff like this when I gave up the job at the Alhambra."

So Charlotte Booth had been quite correct, imagining Alice to have been on the stage. Apparently, she been a singer and dancer in one of Shoreditch's notorious establishments.

"Fred and his mates turned up one night," she had laughed. "We thought it was a raid at first, but they was just punters like the others. Fred took quite a shine to me, and kept coming back. Then he suggested I come and live with him here. Well, I thought it would be a good move, seeing as how life in the theatre is uncertain, 'specially when a girl starts getting on a bit."

She had looked at him coyly and expectantly, so Holmes had felt obliged to insist that, in his eyes, she was a fine young piece of work.

"What about . . . er . . . Fred's wife?" he had ventured.

"Oh, her." Alice was dismissive. "He told me that she was on her last legs . . . ."

"And is she?" Holmes had asked.

"The old bitch is hanging on and on and meantime, here am I, stuck with Fred and no nearer being his new missus than ever." She had sighed and offered him some more beer, partaking freely herself, Holmes only pretending to do so.

"So," he had asked, "where is the woman of the house now? Is she home?"

Alice had smiled lasciviously at him.

"Why d'you want to know? Want to know if the coast's clear, is that it, darling?" She had leaned forward and stroked his hand. "You don't need to worry about her none, Jimmy."

Her intention couldn't have been clearer, and I chuckled at Holmes's patent horror in recalling it.

"How did you escape?" I asked

"Barely. I suggested I return later with a ladder, as a cover in case of suspicious neighbours. 'Good idea,' she had said. 'And if the old man comes back unexpected, you can use it to climb out the bedroom window.' Laughing heartily."

"So you found out nothing," Charlotte said, somewhat tight-lipped.

"I wouldn't say that, Mrs. Booth. The fact that Alice is bored to death might well prove useful to us. I noticed several dog-eared copies of yellow-backed sensational literature lying about, a translation of Paul de Kock among others – a sign of someone who craves excitement in her own life. If necessary, we might play on this susceptibility of hers."

"But what about Mrs. Flowerdew?" Charlotte was clearly frustrated at Holmes's lack of progress. "The poor woman might be at death's door."

"I could hardly force the issue just then." Holmes replied. "What! Would you have had me knock Alice unconscious and search the house?"

Charlotte Booth shrugged.

"So will you go back?" I asked. "With a ladder?"

Holmes shuddered. "I suppose I must. However, Watson, I rely on you to save me if necessary. In any case, I shall insist on clearing the gutters first. With luck, that way I shall learn all that is necessary regarding Mrs. Flowerdew."

Applying to the little waitress, who was still hovering, all agog, he discovered the location of the nearest ironmonger's shop, from which he was hoping to hire a suitable ladder for the afternoon. This time, we accompanied him, and it was lucky that we did, for the available ladder was of such an unwieldy height and weight, it was impossible for one man easily to carry it.

Once again, heads turned in the street to observe the strange procession that we made, the scruffy labourer and the respectable gentleman manhandling a long wooden ladder, followed by the seamstress, carrying my doctor's bag.

Having arrived at Wivenhoe Place, Holmes had to struggle alone the last part of the way, while Charlotte Booth and I ambled slowly past the house. From a discreet distance, we observed how Holmes dragged the ladder round the back, where Charlotte had told him Mrs. Flowerdew's bedroom was situated.

It wasn't long, however, before we heard a female voice raised in shrill anger. To intervene or not? The plucky seamstress made the decision for me.

"It'll be quite in order for me to call in, Doctor, since I haven't yet been paid for the dress I made." Whereupon she took herself off hot-foot, while I lingered uncertainly on the front doorstep.

I was endeavouring to hear what was happening, and so didn't notice a giant of a man approaching until he was upon me.

"What the devil are you doing here?" he asked.

From his uniform and general demeanour, I assumed this must be District Inspector Alfred Flowerdew himself, inopportunely returned.

"I am Dr. Sacker," I spluttered as he loomed above me, burly and red-faced. "I have been asked to examine your sick wife."

"Examine my wife! Who asked you? Not me anyway. Some meddling nosy parker, I suppose."

"A friend of Mrs. Flowerdew's." I replied. "Hearing of her indisposition, she was worried about her."

"A friend? My wife has no friends. Not anymore." He shook his head, as if sorrowfully. "You're wasting your time, here, Doctor. She's gone quite barmy. Locked herself in her room."

"If I could just see her . . . ."

"She won't admit you. Mad as a hatter, I tell you."

Shouts and cries from the back of the house drew his attention from me, and he hastened thither, muttering "What the devil!" again. I followed after.

Rounding the corner of the house, a bizarre sight confronted us. Holmes was holding for dear life on to an upper window frame, while Alice Penn was shaking the ladder he was on, and Charlotte Booth was trying to pull her away.

"Alice!" shouted the District Inspector. "What in Hell's name's going on here!"

"I caught a thief for you, Fred, trying to break in," she called back to him. She glanced at me. "Blimey, there's a whole bleedin' gang of 'em."

"No, no," I said. "I can explain."

Flowerdew rounded on me.

"You're in it, too, are you?"

Over his shoulder, I saw Holmes shake his head at me.

"No," I said. "Nothing of the sort. I know nothing of this man. As I said, I am a doctor that Mrs. Booth here asked to check on her friend."

"And I'm no thief, neither!" the seamstress piped up. "If there's a thief around here, it's her!" pointing at Alice. "Wearing the dress I made for her mistress and not paying for it neither."

Alice left the ladder be and advanced threateningly on the seamstress, now standing next to me.

"Say that again! Say again that I'm a thief, if you dare."

She raised her hands as if ready to claw Charlotte's eyes out.

"Now, now, Alice," Flowerdew said. "Calm down. There's quite clearly been a misunderstanding here . . . ." His tone was suddenly appeasing, "See, Mrs. Booth, my dear, my wife gave the dress to Alice here . . . Poor Florrie. She's bedridden, now and won't be wearing dresses ever again, I'm afraid." He sniffed as if overcome with emotion. So if we have forgotten to pay you, Mrs. Booth . . . ." He reached into his inside pocket and drew out a wallet. "How much?"

"You going to pay her, Fred, after what she said about me?" Alice's voice was hard.

"Just leave it be, woman." He took out a coin. "Here's a guinea for you."

"A guinea!" Alice screeched. "Far too much."

Charlotte Booth took the money.

"Thank you, sir," she said with dignity.

"As for the other matter . . . ." Flowerdew spun round. "What the Hell?"

For Holmes was nowhere to be seen.

"That was a near thing!"

The two of us safely back in Baker Street, Charlotte Booth having returned home to her little son. Holmes was chuckling over a pipe and a restorative glass of single malt whisky.

"Good you were able to provide a distraction, Watson, or I'd be languishing in Lewisham Prison by now."

"I'm just sorry for the poor ironmonger, missing his ladder. You realise that you are a *de facto* thief, after all?"

"I'll make sure the ladder is returned to the shop. But we have more urgent business to attend to. I wasn't able to see into Mrs. Flowerdew's bedroom, for the curtains were drawn closed, and before I could attempt an entry, Alice Penn arrived on the scene like a vengeful Fury."

"So we still have no notion as to the true condition of the lady?"

"Unfortunately, not . . . Did you feel that Flowerdew's grief was genuine, Watson?"

"Crocodile tears, to my mind. He changed his tune too quickly, yet still wouldn't admit me to see her."

"There is no alternative, then. We shall have to enter covertly."

"Break in, you mean."

"Precisely."

I sighed. "One of these days you'll go too far."

"No, Watson. One of these days *we'll* go too far . . . Have some more whisky. It's very good. Glenlivet as drunk by Queen Victoria."

The following morning saw Holmes, Charlotte Booth, (who had insisted on being present,) and myself with my doctor's bag, back at the pastry shop. The little waitress was pleased to see us – but frowned in puzzlement at the sight of Holmes, now dressed as himself. I could almost guess at her thoughts – that he looked vaguely familiar but that she couldn't quite place him.

We had watched Flowerdew depart earlier for work, but Holmes reckoning that Alice Penn wouldn't rouse herself quite so soon, we had retreated to the comfort of the shop. This time, not leaving things to chance, the woman was to be lured from the house by a ruse we reckoned she would find irresistible.

"Here he comes," Holmes said with satisfaction, as a grimy urchin entered the pastry shop, one of the Wiggins clan from among the Baker Street Irregulars.

The little waitress started to shoo him out, but Holmes told her with a reassuring smile that the boy was with him and asked her to bring over a big plate of jam tarts and a mug of tea. She shook her head wonderingly as she piled the pastries on to a plate.

"Well?" Holmes asked.

188

"Went like a dream, Guv," young Wiggins reported. "I telled 'er like wot you said. That a fine gentleman 'ad given me a penny to deliver the note and the rose. She tooked both, smelt the rose and read the note and smiled and said, 'Tell the gent: Yes.'"

"I knew she would fall for it in her vanity," Holmes told us. "In her boredom and thirst for adventure."

"Whatever did the note say?" asked Charlotte Booth, who hadn't been present when Holmes and I – Holmes more than I, in truth – had hatched the plan on the previous evening.

"It purports to be from a secret admirer, who observed her on stage at the Alhambra and who has long wished to make her further acquaintance," I told her. "He writes that if Alice is willing to meet him, to learn something greatly to her advantage, he will send a hansom forthwith to pick her up. To avoid compromising her in the sight of the neighbours and to reassure her as to his honourable intentions, a lady in his employ of irreproachable character and mature years will accompany her to his office."

Charlotte looked confused. "What lady?"

"Mrs. Hudson, of course!" I laughed. "She was delighted to be involved in the enterprise, and is prepared to lead the woman a merry dance."

"I hope Martha will be safe!" Charlotte said. "That Alice Penn isn't a woman to be trifled with. If she suspects anything, it'll surely go bad for poor Martha."

"Don't worry," Holmes replied. "The hansom driver is in on the plot as well. He will be ready to rush to Mrs. Hudson's rescue if necessary, though I am sure it will not come to that."

"I sincerely hope not," the seamstress remarked.

We waited in the pastry shop until a certain cab passed by, slowing slightly. This allowed us to observe Mrs. Hudson nodding almost imperceptibly at us through the window, to signal the all-clear. We paid the little waitress forthwith. She seemed sorry to see us go and urged us to "Come again soon, won't you, gents and lady."

Young Wiggins answered that he would if there were any more jam tarts going begging.

"Cheeky," the little waitress said.

Now there were four of us making our way to Wivenhoe Place, including the boy, whose face was become even more grubby, smeared as it was with a considerable quantity of raspberry jam. His job now would be to keep watch and warn us if anyone approached the house. To this end, he sat himself down by the garden wall and played jacks with pebbles.

Meanwhile, Charlotte and I went up to the front door, as before, to see if anyone else was home, I rapped sharply with the brass lion knocker. There being no answer, we followed Holmes round to the back of the house. This time, the kitchen door was locked fast. The ladder, meanwhile, was lying flat on the ground.

"What now?" asked Charlotte Booth. "Will we have to give up? Or climb up?"

"Not at all," I said, as Holmes removed a little case of instruments from his pocket, his housebreaking kit.

"Oh my Lord!" the seamstress exclaimed. "We'll be sent to prison, the lot of us."

Holmes worked quickly and skilfully, and soon the door creaked open.

"Don't worry, Mrs. Booth," he said. "As you can see, the door is open and, if anyone should ask, that's how we found it."

We entered without stealth, as if we had every right to be there, just in case there happened, after all, to be someone in the house. However, all was quiet. Too quiet for my taste, and I hoped we were in time to save poor Mrs. Flowerdew.

I had been prepared for disorder, but the state of the kitchen utterly appalled me. Clear it was that no effort had been made to wash or tidy for a long time, or even clear away the rotting remains of meals. Droppings indicated the presence of mice, or worse. I wondered that the District Inspector could bear it until I mused that he probably never set foot in that part of the house. Indeed, as we progressed further, the signs of neglect were less evident, though a film of grey dust coated most surfaces. Up the unswept stairs we climbed, Charlotte Booth leading the way.

"This is her room," she said, and tried the door handle. It was still locked.

"Mrs. Flowerdew . . . Florrie . . ." she called. "It's Lottie. Are you there? Can you open the door?"

Silence.

She called again.

Still silence.

We looked at each other. Holmes again extracted his wallet of instruments and set to work. A satisfying click at last, and the door opened on a wave of fetid air.

An unearthly yowl greeted us. Bulging green eyes shone out at us from the darkness. Poor Charlotte Booth clutched at my arm in terror, but it was nothing supernatural. Our eyes adjusting, we could discern a ginger cat standing there, its hair on end. The creature was skin and bones and clearly starving.

"Oh, the poor thing!" Charlotte said.

Beyond this apparition, darker blocks in the general murk signalled furniture, and the seamstress hastened to what had to be the bed.

"She isn't here," she said, dismayed.

Holmes pulled open the heavy curtains, letting a sulphurous light illuminate the room through filthy windows. It was true. The bed, sheets stained and tossed, was empty.

"Watson, quick!" Holmes called. "Over here."

What I had taken to be a heap of rags, proved to be a tiny woman huddled under the window ledge.

"Is she alive?" Charlotte asked.

"Just about," I said, examining her. "Fetch some water, if you please."

"Not that," Holmes added sharply as Charlotte reached for a jug on the dresser. "Fresh water from the kitchen."

I pulled the stinking sheets from the bed and then gently picked up Mrs. Flowerdew and laid her on the mattress, which thankfully wasn't in too horrid a state. I chafed her limbs to restore some circulation, muttering reassuring words until Charlotte returned with a mug of water. I dipped a clean handkerchief into it and then wetted the lady's mouth. At first she failed to respond, but finally, to my relief, she licked her lips and half-opened anaemic eyes.

"Here's Lottie, my dear," I said to her in soft tones, "and I'm Doctor Watson, come to look after you. You are safe now."

I gave her more water, in small sips. She murmured something.

"What is it?"

"Cl . . . Cleo . . . pat . . . ra . . . ."

"Cleopatra? Queen of Egypt."

She nodded. Mad, after all. I looked at Holmes.

"I imagine," he said, "that she means the cat. There is a C emblazoned on the disc hanging round her neck."

Mrs. Flowerdew nodded again, clearly agitated.

"Cleo will be just fine," Charlotte told her. "I'll get her something to drink and eat, and you too, Florrie dear."

"Not from that kitchen," Holmes replied, reaching again into his pocket and drawing out a small paper package. "Here is one of Mrs. Hudson's drop scones. That will do, won't it, Watson?"

"Perfect," I said, taking the scone and breaking off a tiny morsel. "Too much at once could be harmful, but it was foresighted of you to bring it, Holmes."

I chided myself that I hadn't thought to do the same.

Suddenly we heard a thunderous noise on the stairs and two large constables rushed into the room.

"The game's up, me boyos!" one shouted, brandishing his truncheon.

"Whatever do you mean, Officer?" Holmes replied, calmly and languidly.

The two men, taking in the scene before them at last, looked confused.

"We was told there was thieves breakin' in," the other said.

"Do we look like thieves to you?"

Young Wiggins crept in behind the constables.

"I couldn't stop 'em, Mr. 'Olmes," he said. "They come in like greased lightnin', so they done."

"No harm, Wiggins," Holmes said. "I was about to call for the police myself."

"Sherlock 'Olmes, is it?" said the first constable. "I've 'eard of you."

"No doubt," my friend replied.

"I've "heard of 'im," the constable told the other, younger man. "'E's a detective, 'e is, but not with the po-leece. Private geezer."

"So what you up to then, Mister Private Detective?" the younger one asked. "This 'ere's our Super's place, in case you don't know it."

"I'm well aware of that, Constable," Holmes replied. "And I trust you will return forthwith to Lewisham Station and arrest your Super at once."

The men stood with their mouths hanging open.

"Wha'?"

"For the attempted murder of his wife. He has imprisoned her here and, having failed to poison her, has been letting her starve to death."

"It's a joke," said the younger one.

The other looked at Mrs. Flowerdew – I was still allowing her morsels of scone and sips of water – the state of her, of the bed, of the room.

"Well, I'll be – !" He was lost for words.

More thunderous steps sounded on the stairs. This time it was none other than Alfred Flowerdew himself. Despite what they had just heard of him, the two constables stood to attention.

"What the devil is going on here?" The man looked about to explode with rage, his apoplectic complexion purple. "They told me my place was being robbed!"

"We got a call at the station from a neighbour who saw people entering illegally," the younger constable told him.

"And you didn't think to convey that information to me?" Flowerdew growled.

"We couldn't find you, sir, so we come over as fast as we could . . . and found . . . these people."

Flowerdew looked at me, eyes so narrowed that they all but disappeared into his fleshy cheeks. "You, Doctor! Don't you ever give up? Didn't I tell you my wife was mad? Told you that she locked herself in and refused to eat."

"If she locked herself in, where's the key?" I asked. "If she's refused to eat, why's she eating now?"

"Because she's mad, that's why," He pushed his face up close to mine. "She's probably hidden the key." He looked round as if the thing might suddenly materialise. "Where's Alice?" he added.

"Gone out," I told him.

He grinned, suddenly relaxed. "So that's why my wife's locked in. For her own safety, d'you see. We can't have her wandering about the house by herself in the state she's in, can we?"

"You're changing your tune," Holmes said. "And just look at the state she's in."

We all did. At the poor shrunken woman, in her filthy night dress, trembling in terror.

"She needs calm and quiet," I said sternly. "Please all go downstairs and continue your discussion there. And Mrs. Booth, perhaps you could call for an ambulance. Mrs. Flowerdew is in a very bad way. She must be taken to hospital as quickly as possible."

"By what right – ?" the District Inspector started to say, but, catching the cold eyes of his constables upon himself, never finished his sentence, and, instead, meekly took himself out of the room with the others.

"Thank you, Doctor," his wife spoke softly. "Thank you ever so much." Then she grinned triumphantly. "Know what I did?" she asked. "I licked the window."

"What!" I exclaimed, fearing again for her sanity.

"They didn't know . . . There was water on the window and I licked it."

Condensation! That's why we found her where we did. I smiled back at her. "Clever girl," I said, and she giggled.

Upstairs with my patient, I missed the excitement below, although some of the ruckus was faintly audible. It was only later, however, after Mrs. Flowerdew had been safely dispatched by ambulance to my old alma mater of St. Bartholomew's, that I received a detailed description of what had transpired. Holmes, Charlotte Booth, and I had returned to Baker Street with Mrs. Hudson, who was bursting with news of her own adventure.

Our landlady recounted how the impatient Alice, at first full of anticipation and questions about her supposed secret admirer, which Mrs. Hudson had fielded as well as she could, all too soon became suspicious.

"We were already on the Sevenoaks Road when she demanded to be brought home," Mrs. Hudson recounted. "At first I tried to cajole her into continuing on, but she became quite aggressive, accusing me of kidnap, and, to be honest, gentlemen, I quite feared for my safety, so I instructed Higgins, the driver, to bring us back. At least Alice seemed to accept my claim to know nothing very much, that I was some simple old soul who had been hired to escort her."

"While you were upstairs, Watson, she burst in on us in a red rage," Holmes said, clearly relishing the memory, "though I think she was too angry to be fully aware of our presence. She made for Flowerdew and started punching and scratching him, accusing him of organising the note, the hansom, and the whole wasted journey. 'I suppose,' she screeched, 'you wanted to get rid of me now, the way you've got rid of your wife!' She really thought Mrs. Hudson was taking her to be killed and disposed of in the hop fields of Kent. The product of reading too much sensational fiction! Always a bad idea."

"But how did Flowerdew react when she accused him like that?" I asked. "In front of his constables, too?"

"He shouted back that he knew nothing about any of it. That it was all her doing – that he was ignorant of any plot to kill his wife, having assumed her to be under Alice's tender care. Nothing, he claimed, could have shocked him more than seeing his wife's abject condition . . . ."

Holmes smiled sardonically. "Of course, no one was taken in for a minute by that, not even his dim-witted constables. But while they were arresting him, Alice tried to slip away. Only for the quick-thinking of Mrs. Booth here, she might even have succeeded. Charlotte chased her out into the garden and flattened her into the briar patch."

"That I should have liked to see," I said.

"You should have, Doctor," Mrs. Hudson said, glancing fondly at her friend. "Lottie was the heroine of the hour."

"All the same," the seamstress responded, "I could have wished to have avoided the briars. Apart from being scratched to pieces myself, it ruined the lovely dress Alice was wearing. The one I had made for Mrs. Flowerdew."

One month later, and quite recovered, and with her husband and the dreadful Alice locked away, the lady herself was back home in Wivenhoe Place. Sterling work had been done in cleaning and freshly decorating the house in advance of her arrival by the previous housekeeper, Elsie

Chambers and the rest of the reinstated staff. There was one addition to the number: Charlotte Booth had moved in as Mrs. Flowerdew's companion, with little Matthew become the favoured surrogate grandchild. Charlotte has continued to work as a seamstress, but only for certain clients such as Mrs. Hudson. As for her other role, she has virtually retired from that, though I overheard her mention to Holmes that if he was ever in need of a female detective to help in his investigations, he would know where to come.

NOTE

This story was inspired by an absorbing new study, *The Mysterious Case of the Victorian Female Detective*, by Sara Lodge (Yale, 2024)

The Case of the Puzzled Postman
by Naching T. Kassa

The New Year of 1898 was but days away when I awoke that cold December morning. I dressed and, upon entering the sitting room, found my friend, Mr. Sherlock Holmes, in a chair before the fire. As he motioned me into the room, I noticed a gentleman seated upon the settee. The fellow seemed a jovial sort, possessing a rosy, rather weathered countenance, and wispy brown hair. His left eye seemed somewhat swollen and purpled, as though he'd recently been injured.

"Ah, Watson," Holmes said. "This is Mr. Hezekiah Bardleship. He has just arrived and has a story he would like to relate. Mr. Bardleship, you need not fear speaking before my friend. I can vouch for his discretion."

"Oh, there's no secret in what I have to say," the fellow said. "And I've read all of Dr. Watson's stories, I know he'll do me justice. I'm not worried about what others might think of my strange experience, Mr. Holmes. The constabulary seems to have no interest in it, anyway. That's why I've brought my troubles to you."

"And these troubles . . . they occurred two days ago? You were attacked while delivering the post."

Bardleship stared at Holmes, his mouth agape. "Have you spoken with the police?"

"Regarding the matter? No, I have not."

"Then . . . how could you know this? It wasn't important enough for the papers."

"Your face is mildly bruised. The skin has yellowed near your eye, indicating you were struck there only two days ago. Your scuffed and worn shoes are those of a man who walks much of the day. Only a policeman or a postman would show such wear in his shoes. Upon seeing your trousers, I knew you to be a postman. They are part of your uniform. And though you changed the coat, you did not change the trousers."

Bardleship shook his head. "You amaze me, Mr. Holmes. Everything you say is true. It's clear I've come to the right man." He leaned toward Holmes. "It isn't the attack which worries me, sir. I was robbed, true, but only a few coins were taken. It is Miss Abigail Lakewood and Mrs. Julia Winthrop for whom I fear."

Holmes leaned back in his chair and steepled his fingers. "Tell us everything, Mr. Bardleship. Every detail, no matter how insignificant, is of interest to me."

"If that is the case, then I should tell you about all the strange incidents which proceeded the assault – the ones which began just before the death of Mrs. Jane Lakewood and have continued ever since.

"Mrs. Lakewood is – *was* – an elderly woman on my route. She was the mother of Abigail and Julia, and she lived on the ground floor at 262 Clapham High Street. She owned the lease, you see. Bought it after the death of her husband. For the past ten years, she has greeted me at her door and spoken with me at least once a day. I have delivered both good and bad news to her – from the birth of her niece in Cornwall to the death of her brother in Surrey.

"A little over a month ago, just before I knocked on her door, I heard shouting behind it. Mrs. Lakewood answered the door, her expression like a thundercloud. She snatched the letters from my hand and then disappeared inside again. It was most unlike her. She'd always been such a gentle thing. Raised her two daughters quite alone, after her husband died, and I'd never heard her say one cross word to them – or anyone for that matter. So it was quite a shock to hear her voice raised and see her so furious. It made me wonder who could have angered her so.

"I'm ashamed to say I'd overheard a bit of the conversation. Mrs. Lakewood accused the man she argued with of being a 'liar' and a 'vulture'. She said she'd tell Abigail all about it, and then she'd ordered the man from the house."

"Did you hear this fellow's response?" Holmes asked.

Bardleship shook his head. "I couldn't. The man only murmured. It was a low sound, so I never made out a word."

"Did the man ever leave the house?"

"I saw no one leave."

Holmes paused, his brow furrowed.

"Is Miss Abigail Lakewood the elder or younger daughter?" he asked.

"The younger. She's trained as a nurse. Julia is the elder. Rather flighty, that one."

"How so?"

"Four months ago, the girls went to Yorkshire - visiting relatives, I'm told – and Julia met the new vicar of Hawes. The next thing you know, she's married to the man. Then Abigail left London for Yorkshire to live with Julia at the vicarage in Hawes. Their mother wasn't too pleased at first. She was an old-fashioned sort, and even though the man's a vicar, she didn't trust him. Thought Julia should've had a longer engagement.

But Abigail soon brought her around. I suspect that's why Abigail moved into the vicarage with them – to watch Julia for her mother."

"What is the vicar's name?"

"Mr. John Winthrop. I've met the man only once, but he seems a good enough fellow."

"Were the daughters on good terms with their mother?"

"They wrote to her twice a week. And Abigail returned to London once a month."

"Were there servants in Mrs. Lakewood's household?"

"No. She lived quite frugally after her husband died. The girls helped her when they were young, but she did most of the work herself."

"Did she take in lodgers?"

"Yes, but the last one moved out six months ago. No one had taken the rooms since. She lived there quite alone."

"What of the neighbors?"

"Well . . . Mrs. Lakewood never was one for entertaining. She kept to herself mostly. She did have one friend, however, a Mrs. Partridge who lives down the street. The woman's a frightful gossip. I often wondered what use Mrs. Lakewood had for her."

"Did you return to Mrs. Lakewood's home?"

"I did. The next day. It was quiet behind the door when I came to deliver, and when Mrs. Lakewood came out, she acted as though nothing had happened. We chatted for a bit and then she said, 'I do apologize for the scene I made yesterday.'

"'Think nothing of it,' said I. 'Whoever he was, he must've deserved it. You're the kindest lady in the world, and no mistake.'

"'Oh, Mr. Bardleship, you'll make me blush! He deserved everything he got. But I shouldn't have treated you the way I did.'"

"That was all she said. I didn't ask her for any more. But I can't help thinking now I should have.

"I didn't see her the next few days, and I did get a bit worried. When Monday came around, I resolved I would knock on her door until she answered, but it turns out there was no need. She opened the door the moment I reached it, as though she'd been waiting for me.

"'Hello, Mrs. Lakewood,' says I. "Where have you been?'

"'I've been ill,' says she. 'Since Friday. I'm well enough now, though.'

"I noticed then how ill she really looked. Her face had gone pale, and there were shadows under her eyes. She leaned against the doorjamb as though she had little strength.

"'Mr. Bardleship, could I ask a favor of you?'

"'Yes.'

"'I'd like to give you a letter to post. But I don't want it posted right away. I'd like you to wait three days. And then, if I ask for it back, I'd like you to give it to me.'

"It was a strange request, Mr. Holmes. And though I wanted to do as she asked, I knew I couldn't. I suppose you'd say I'm a bit of a pedant when it comes to the post. I value my work, and I never break the rules.

"I have many regrets, Mr. Holmes. And I can't help but think my devotion to the rules might have contributed to what happened later. She had it in her hand, held it out to me, and I refused to take it. Told her to wait three days and give it to me then.

"She nodded, and as I turned to go, she called me back."

"'Mr. Bardleship,' said she.

"I faced her.

"'I love my children.' She said this last bit rather hopelessly.

"'I'm sure you do.'

"I thought, for a moment, she might say something else, but instead, she shut the door. That was three days ago and the last time I saw her alive. She passed that very night. Her daughter, Abigail, found her when she came to visit on Tuesday."

Holmes rose from his chair and paced the room. "To whom was the letter addressed?" he asked.

Bardleship paused, a finger to his upper lip. At last, he said, "The only thing I remember is it was addressed to a gentleman. I couldn't quite make out the address – most of it was hidden by her hand, and I could only make out the word '*Yard*'. But the name was '*S. Hopkins*' – '*S. Hopkins of Yard*'."

Holmes paused, an eager light in his eyes. Like a hunting dog, he had suddenly caught the scent.

"Is that all you remember of the envelope?"

"It was an inexpensive one. Commonly used."

"What of the return address?"

"It was hers. Written in her hand."

"And Mrs. Lakewood's death . . . was it a natural one?"

"Mrs. Partridge went to visit on Tuesday and Abigail told her Mrs. Lakewood had died. Passed from her illness, I expect. The funeral is tomorrow. I will, of course, attend."

Holmes ceased his pacing and, taking the cherry-wood pipe from off the mantel, peered into the bowl. He then withdrew a pinch of shag from the Persian slipper.

"What events occurred following the lady's passing?"

"They were strange, Mr. Holmes, and there were several of them. The first one took place just two days after Mrs. Lakewood's death."

"That would be Wednesday. Yesterday."

"Yes. I was coming up Clapham High Street when I happened to spy a young man dashing across the road toward Mrs. Lakewood's house. He ducked inside before I got a good look at him, but I did notice he was a young man with spectacles and a bowler hat. I thought he might be another one of Mrs. Lakewood's relatives, one I hadn't met, and so I decided to pay my respects.

"The man didn't open the door, but Abigail did. I hadn't seen her in some time, but I knew her all the same. She's blonde, you see. Julia's hair is red.

"I gave her my condolences and she nodded. Unable to speak, I expect. The more I spoke to her, the worse I felt. I told her of the letter and how I wished I'd posted it.

"And then, she did the strangest thing. She glanced over her shoulder, into the house, and then stepped out and shut the door.

"'Mr. Bardleship,' said she. 'The letter . . . was it addressed to me?'

"'No. It was not.'

"'You're certain it wasn't? Perhaps it was addressed under another name?'

"She glanced back at the door, and I swear Mr. Holmes, her face betrayed her fear. She was frightened, and no mistake."

"'What was the name, Mr. Bardleship? I must know.'

"I told her Mr. Holmes, same as I told you. Then, she said, 'That is the name! The very name under which Mother said she would write to me! No doubt the address belongs to Dr. Hopkins, my old employer, in Mason's Yard. But you mustn't take it there, Mr. Bardleship. If you find the letter, you must bring it straight to me. That is, unless another postman has taken the letter?'

"'No, Miss. I'm the only postman on this street.'

"She glanced back at the door once more, then lowered her voice and said, 'Mother wouldn't tell me what was in it – said I would know soon enough. I never received anything from her, though, and then, the next I knew . . . .' Here she paused overcome with emotion. 'Mr. Bardleship, I must have that missive.'

"'If it is in the post, you shall,' I said. 'You have my word.'

"Someone called Abigail's name then, a man's voice, undoubtedly that of the young man I had seen. Abigail's face went white as she reentered the house.

"'Who is that?' I asked as she turned.

"'My cousin.'

"'Cousin?'

"'He is my mother's nephew.'"

200

"'Nephew?'"

"'I'm afraid I must go. Remember the promise you have made.'

"And with those words, she hurried into the house.

"I must admit Mr. Holmes, the entire experience struck me as ominous. I had never before heard of this cousin, and if Mrs. Lakewood had possessed a nephew, he was quite unknown to me. I considered knocking upon the door once more and confronting those inside, but it seemed a foolish notion. Other than the manner in which Miss Abigail had greeted me and spoken of the mysterious letter, I had no evidence of misdeeds.

"I returned to the street and my rounds. Once I had finished my deliveries, I made my way home. I live in Kenwyn Street and I'll often cut through an alley or two to save time."

"The same alleys?" Holmes asked. "Or do you vary your route home?"

"The same ones."

Holmes nodded and waved a hand, encouraging our guest to continue.

"The last alley I entered is between two abandoned buildings. There are squatters there, but none who've ever troubled me. I strode down it easily enough, but when I reached the end of it, someone struck me from behind. I fell face first and my eye got the worst of it, I'm afraid – though it might have been worse. At the very least, there was snow upon the ground. I struck it instead of bare stone.

"When I woke, I found a lady kneeling beside me. She smiled at me gently, and for a moment, I thought it was Miss Abigail. But then, I saw her ginger hair, and I knew it was her sister, Julia."

"'Are you quite well, Mr. Bardleship?' she asked, concern written upon her handsome face.

"My head ached and I could only mutter my reply. 'I was attacked, Miss Julia.'

"It was then I noticed my coat had been torn and my satchel had vanished. Every one of my pockets had been turned out, and whatever coin I had upon me had been stolen.

"'I – I've been robbed!'

"'We must inform the police at once. Fear not, Mr. Bardleship. We do have this. John, do you have the satchel?'

"A man – I assume it was her husband because he wore a vicar's collar – approached with it in hand. My satchel was covered with mud and had also been torn.

"'We found it in the street,' Julia explained. 'We wondered from whence it came, and that is how we found you. Do you need a doctor? You don't look well.'

201

"I rose to my feet and rubbed the back of my head. 'I've a lump and a bit of a headache, but naught else.'

"'Well, you mustn't stay here,' said she. "We shall take you home. Where do you live?"

"I pointed down the road. 'The little house just there.'

"'Are you quite certain you don't need a doctor? John could fetch him.'

"'Oh, no. A good night's sleep will solve all my ills. I'll be right as rain in the morning.'

"'Then you must allow us to take you home. John, will you help him into the coach, please?'

"They insisted on taking me home. Even loaded me into their coach and drove me the short distance. Then, the vicar helped me to bed and spoke soft words of comfort. Then, they must've thought me sleeping, for they whispered a few words before going out the door.

"'He's after the letter,' said she. 'He's beaten Mr. Bardleship because of it. We must find it, John. Before he injures another soul.'

I could scarcely close my eyes after they'd gone. I remembered the expression on Miss Abigail's face and it chilled me to think of her in danger. I knew it must be the cousin who'd attacked me. They had as much as said so. I resolved I would visit the constabulary and tell them all I knew."

"The vicar and his wife didn't inform the police?"

"That is what I learned when I arrived at Scotland Yard this morning. No one had heard of me or the robbery. To me, it is further proof of how Miss Julia and the others fear her cousin. Worse still, though the robbery was taken quite seriously, the inspector at the Yard didn't think a whispered conversation warranted investigation. He said it was more likely I had been attacked by a vagrant than a gentleman I had never met."

"Who was this inspector?"

"I believe his name was Jones."

"Athelney?"

"Yes! That was the name."

"A rather unimaginative fellow."

"That is why I have come to you, Mr. Holmes?"

"And what of the address? Did you go to the offices of Dr. Hopkins in Mason's Yard?"

"I did. But I found no one there. It looked as though the doctor had moved on, for no one had been there for quite some time."

"How did you know this?"

"By the dust in the window. And the fact there was no post in the slot."

Holmes nodded.

The postman shifted on the settee and sighed. "I fear for the ladies, Mr. Holmes, and would be most grateful if you looked into the matter. I don't have much, but I do have a few coins salted away – "

Holmes waved a dismissive hand and rose from his chair. "Tut, tut, Mr. Bardleship! You have given me a very interesting problem, indeed. The work shall be its own reward. I will what I can."

"Very good! How may I be of service?"

"Continue your rounds. Send a telegram should you notice anything strange at the house."

"I will. I bid you good day, Mr. Holmes. And good hunting."

When our client had gone, Holmes grabbed for his hat and coat, and rushed from the room.

Two hours passed before he returned. He strode in, his eyes bright.

"I have been to Clapham High Street," he said. "And I have spent a profitable afternoon in the company of Mrs. Emma Partridge. Bardleship has neglected a good resource there. He might have learned more had he visited her. The woman is a veritable fount of information. I know more about Clapham High Street than I could've wished."

"You learned of Mrs. Lakewood?"

"And her daughters, and the vicar. More importantly, I have learned a great deal about the cousin. His name is Edward Magee, and he has only just arrived at the Lakewood home. The fellow lives in Edinburgh. He's a schoolmaster."

"Only just arrived? But Bardleship said he'd overheard the man arguing before the lady died."

"If you recall, our client couldn't identify the man he heard. The voice was little more than a murmur. He supposed it to be Mr. Magee."

"Then . . . with whom did Mrs. Lakewood argue?"

"That is the question. Mrs. Lakewood didn't mention the argument to Mrs. Partridge. And she heard nothing of it from her usual sources. It seems Bardleship was the only one privy to the disagreement. According to Mrs. Partridge, the one with which Mrs. Lakewood argued couldn't have been the sisters or the vicar. They arrived the same day as their cousin, Mr. Magee. She did, however, confide a few interesting facts. Would it surprise you to know the sisters and their cousin are the sole heirs to the Lakewood fortune?"

"Fortune? What fortune?"

"Bardleship was correct when he described Mrs. Lakewood as a frugal woman. Her husband had been insured for over fifty-thousand pounds and, upon his death, she came into a great fortune. She bought the house and kept the remainder in the Bank of England.

"The second thing she revealed to me was that Mrs. Lakewood feared for her life. She believed someone wished her dead, but she wouldn't reveal who, not even to Mrs. Partridge. When I mentioned the letter, she showed no knowledge of it."

"She didn't give it to Mrs. Partridge, then?"

"No. And the fact she didn't has given me the final clue as to the identity of the recipient, as well as the address. The letter, if it was posted, will be in his possession very soon. I have telegraphed him – Is this his reply? It seems he has received the telegram sooner than I expected."

Holmes motioned to the window. A boy had rushed up to the door and given Mrs. Hudson a missive. Moments later, she appeared in our rooms and handed not one, but two telegrams, to Holmes.

"This is from Bardleship," he said. Frowning, he tossed it over to me.

"*No funeral tomorrow,*" I read aloud. "*Small burial tonight. St. Peter's Church.*"

"Much has changed since I visited Clapham High Street. Mrs. Partridge didn't have this news when last I spoke with her." He opened the other telegram and read it quickly. Instead of handing it to me, he thrust it into his pocket. "Our time is running short," said he. "And there is danger for one involved. We can no longer wait upon a return message. Come, we must go and speak to the man ourselves."

I hurried into my coat and hat and then rushed into the street after Holmes. He called for a cab and, moments later, we were whisked through London.

"The moment Bardleship revealed what he had seen on the letter, I knew who the recipient must be. Mrs. Partridge confirmed as much when she told me she hadn't seen the letter and knew nothing of it. If she wouldn't confide in her best friend, then she trusted no one near her with the information the letter contained."

"Then . . . she would trust a stranger with the information?"

"Excellent!" he said. "And what stranger could be trusted with such a missive?"

I considered the question for several minutes. "It would depend upon what is in the message. If it were a medical question, the recipient would be a doctor."

"Yes, it would be a professional man."

"Then it must be a change of will, and the recipient a solicitor."

"You have diverted from the trail, but you are on the track. Perhaps, the address will reveal to you what I already know."

"Mason's Yard?"

"Perhaps a different Yard. Come, we have arrived at our destination."

We alighted before a building I knew well.

204

"Scotland Yard? Then Mrs. Lakewood wrote to a constable? The thought came to me in a thrice and I could scarcely believe I had been so stupid.

"She wrote to an *inspector*! *S. Hopkins* could only be Stanley Hopkins."

"Capital! It is indeed Stanley Hopkins. Let us see if he is in."

Unfortunately, the good inspector was not in. The sergeant on duty, a large man with a florid face, informed us Hopkins had gone out earlier that afternoon and wasn't expected back until the morrow. The man was most affable and could say without a doubt that, though Holmes's telegram had arrived, there was no letter from a Mrs. Lakewood. Holmes scribbled a note on a sheet of foolscap and handed it to the sergeant.

"Please ensure the inspector receives this when he returns."

"Yes, sir, I will. I'll give it to him the moment he comes in."

Holmes fell silent as we departed the Yard. He hailed a cab and when we had climbed aboard and pulled away, he said, "If the letter hasn't arrived, it was never sent."

"Why did she make such a request of Bardleship?" I asked. "Why wait three days?"

"One may theorize, but one will never know the truth without the missing facts. The contents of the letter will reveal all. It must be hidden in the house. If it is, that is where we must go. But first, we must return to Baker Street. I must collect a few items, just as you must collect your revolver."

The sky had gone dark by the time we reached Clapham High Street. Holmes directed the cab driver past No. 262 and toward a nearby alley. We alighted there.

Snow had fallen during our visit to the Yard, cloaking the world in white and leaving the road deserted. We left the alley and walked down toward the Lakewood house, keeping to the shadows. Holmes carried his dark lantern in one hand, but didn't light it.

"That is Mrs. Partridge's home just there," Holmes said, indicating a small brick home just off the road. "It is why we move through the darkness. It would be better if she didn't see us. I'm uncertain of how she shares her information. She may divulge our presence to those who shouldn't be aware of it."

We reached the house we sought but moments later. It stood, a lonely sentinel, on the wintry street.

"Hopkins' letter is somewhere within," Holmes said.

"And if it isn't?" I asked. "Perhaps, this Magee has already found it."

"I don't believe anyone has found it. If they had, the funeral would've taken place on the morrow as planned. They wouldn't have decided upon a hurried burial in the evening. No, they are going to flee – flee before the letter reaches its intended recipient."

"They?"

Holmes didn't answer my query. He had crept up to the back door and removed his collection of lockpicks from the pocket of his coat, along with a few matches. He lit the dark lantern and studied the lock for several seconds. Then, with a chuckle, he turned the handle. The door swung open.

"They didn't take the trouble to lock it," said he, rising to his feet. "Judging by the impressions in the snow here, they have had a wagon at the back of the house. It has come empty and departed with a full load."

I stared at the tracks, which seemed to me indecipherable.

"The wagon tracks are deeper when they leave than when they've come," he explained. "It seems they are moving house."

He stepped inside and I followed.

The room we entered proved to be the kitchen. Several crates stood upon the table, stacked in neat rows. The place seemed bare, and when I happened to open a drawer, I found it empty.

"They've certainly wasted no time," I said, glancing up at Holmes. "You're correct. Everything has been packed away."

"As I said," he replied, studying an address upon one of the boxes, "they're in a great hurry to leave. These crates aren't bound for Hawes. They are to be delivered to a shop in Portobello Road."

"A shop? Why would Magee send them there?"

"Watson," he said with a sigh, "just as it is a capital mistake to theorize without data, it is also a mistake to accept the prejudices of a witness. You have accepted Bardleship's opinion as fact. It should be clear to you by now who the culprits are and where the true danger lies."

"If it isn't Magee, then who could it be? Surely you aren't accusing the vicar."

"I telegraphed the vicarage after seeing Mrs. Partridge. This is the telegram I received in return." He withdrew it from his pocket and handed it to me."

"'*Vicar in Hawes recently dismissed from his post*,'" I read aloud. "'*Post achieved through fraudulent means. Real name Milton Jeffers not Winthrop.*'"

I glanced up at Holmes. "Milton Jeffers, the confidence man? He is known for impersonating clergymen!"

"He also works his way into the homes of elderly women and cajoles – or threatens – them into giving him their money. He was, undoubtedly, the man who accosted Bardleship in the alley near Kenwyn Street. Do you not find it strange the couple didn't keep their promise and inform the police of the robbery? That they *happened* upon the scene after the attack?

Further, did you also notice, throughout his narrative, Bardleship only mentioned the vicar speaking once? In a whisper? He is rather quiet for a supposed clergyman. No, I believe the reason is clear: He feared Bardleship would recognize his voice."

"Then it was he who argued with Mrs. Lakewood."

"It would seem so."

"I can scarcely believe it."

"That a man could impersonate a clergyman? Why, I myself have done it, on more than one occasion."

A terrible thought came to my mind.

"Holmes, the ladies – "

"What of them?"

"They are in the company of that blackguard! They could be in danger."

"They are not," Holmes replied. "For one simple reason. They are his cohorts."

Before I could reply, he moved into the dining room. Crates sat willy-nilly about the floor and the dining table, if there had been one, had already been removed.

"I have suspected them from the first," Holmes said. "Mrs. Lakewood's distrust extended to everyone but Inspector Hopkins at Scotland Yard."

"But she mentioned Abigail in the argument with the vicar. And Abigail said – "

"She said the letter had been addressed to her under another name. In fact, believe she is working hand-in-hand with her sister and brother-in-law."

"To what end?"

"To deceive Mr. Magee and rob him of his inheritance. Perhaps his life. Which is why we must find the letter. If it is important enough they should run, it may be the very thing which sends them to prison."

Holmes passed through the foyer and the stairway which led to the first floor. We entered another hall which led to a small, half-empty parlor.

"It seems they haven't finished with this room as yet," Holmes observed.

Open crates stood near one wall and some of the items in the room had been packed in it. A chair stood by the fireplace and dark curtains covered the window on the southern side of the room. Near the window, in the corner, I spied a writing desk. It was a fine piece, fashioned from mahogany in the Rococo style, though a trifle out of place in the modest room. Various papers covered it and the floor below.

"They have searched this," Holmes said, "However, they couldn't find the keys. The locked drawers have been forced. See where the wood has splintered?"

I stared at the drawers, the ink bottle, the blotter, the pens, the opened correspondence transfixed to the paper spindle, the ledger filled with Mrs. Lakewood's neat handwriting, and a letter opener. Nothing there seemed to lend a clue.

"How will we find something they have not?" I asked. "When they've had every opportunity to find it? Why, it could be inside something they've already packed away."

Holmes had studied the entirety of the room, his gaze returned to the desk.

He knelt and gathered the papers from off the floor, studying each one. When he had finished with a page, he set it in a pile on the carpet.

"They must have searched through these," I said, as I gathered pages from the desk.

Holmes held up a hand and I fell silent. Seconds later the creak of carriage wheels sounded in the street. For a moment, I thought they might stop at the door, but they continued on and soon faded into the distance.

"We must hurry," Holmes said.

He continued his perusal of the pages and then tossed them aside in disgust.

"We must think as she would. She was a clever woman. The only thing which marred her good sense was her trust in her children. When she no longer trusted them, she hid the letter in a place they would never think to find it. Ah! I have been a fool!" He slapped a hand to his forehead. "It has been before us all this time. She hasn't hidden the letter. She has placed it in plain view for all to see."

He lifted the paper spindle from off the desk and removed the envelopes fixed to it. One had not been opened. It was addressed to Stanley Hopkins.

Something fell to the floor above us, and I startled at the sound. Holmes and I stood still, watching the ceiling of the parlor. After several seconds of silence, Holmes pressed his finger to his lips and, placing the letter in his pocket, hurried out of the room.

When we reached the foyer, we rushed up the staircase leading to the first floor. At the landing, we entered a dark hall. A door stood to our right, and when Holmes tried it, he found it locked.

Withdrawing his tools once more, he worked at unlocking the door. Within seconds, the lock clicked open and we were inside.

In the dim light of the dark lantern, we found a young man lying upon the floor, his arms and legs bound. He lay near a small bed and must've fallen from it, producing the sound we had heard. I rushed to his side. A quick examination revealed he was not dead. His body spasmed, and I marked the rigidity of his neck, arms and legs. There was a slight cyanosis about his lips and the condition horrified me.

"Strychnine," I cried. "He is fading."

"Can he be saved."

"I will do my best."

"Then I count him a lucky man. Let us remove him from this house before they return."

We lifted him from the floor and with Holmes under one arm and I under the other, we helped him from the room.

Holmes's dark lantern provided little light as we descended the stairs and several times, I felt we might trip upon them and tumble down, earning broken necks for our trouble. I was much relieved when we reached the bottom.

My relief was short-lived. The creak of carriage wheels filled the air once more. This time, they didn't pass by. They stopped.

Footsteps approached the door.

"Watson, your revolver," Holmes said. I handed it to him as I became Magee's sole support.

Holmes closed the dark lantern, plunging us into darkness.

Seconds passed. A key turned in the lock and the door swung open. A man entered, lantern in hand.

"Hopkins!" Holmes cried and rushed forward to shake his hand. "You received my message?"

"Sergeant Wilson is a great admirer of yours, Mr. Holmes. And of you, Doctor," Hopkins said with a grin. "He delivered your message to me personally and I went to St. Peter's right away. I've taken the ladies into custody, but the bounder escaped."

"Blast. Well, it can't be helped. At most, we have saved Mr. Magee. He has been poisoned and needs more medical attention than we can provide."

"MacGregor! Leeson!" Hopkins shouted. "This man needs a hospital!" The constables came through the door on a run and quickly took my charge from me.

"What of the ladies?" Hopkins asked.

"Bring them in, Hopkins," Holmes said, turning the gas up. "Bring them in."

Moments later, Mrs. Winthrop and Miss Lakewood stepped into the foyer. Julia Winthrop, a proud and haughty woman, entered first. She stood before us, glowering at Hopkins. Miss Abigail Lakewood came in second, her gaze on the floor. Tears flowed down her cheeks.

"Mr. Hopkins," Mrs. Winthrop began, "I have asked you once, and I will ask you again. What is the meaning of this? And why are these . . . *people* . . . in our mother's home?"

"I must apologize, Madame," Holmes said smoothly. "I am here at the request of Mr. Bardleship."

"The postman?" Mrs. Winthrop said. "Whatever could he want?"

"He believed you to be in danger, just as your mother was. He thought your cousin, Mr. Magee, to be your tormentor. He was mistaken, as you intended him to be. You wished him to suspect Mr. Magee, to cover your own crime."

"What crime?"

"The murder of your mother."

"My mother died in her sleep. Abigail found her in the bedroom."

"Hopkins, when you arrived at St. Peter's Church, had the burial been completed?"

"No. I did as you requested."

"Very good. I think you will find Mrs. Lakewood has been poisoned with a strychnine derivative – the same as given to Mr. Magee. If we hadn't found him, he might soon have suffered a similar fate."

"Inspector, really! How dare you have this person suggest such things to me! He is no policeman!"

"You are quite correct, Mrs. Winthrop. My name is Sherlock Holmes."

Mrs. Winthrop's face grew pale. When she saw the envelope Holmes removed from his pocket, she blanched.

"I believe you've been searching for this," Holmes said. He opened it and upon opening the letter, read:

Mr. Hopkins,

You do not know me. My name is Jane Lakewood and I live at 262 Clapham High Street. I heard your name from a friend of mine. She says you are a fine constable, far better than most.

I am uncertain of what to call you. Whether it should be Inspector or Mister. Please, excuse me if I have addressed you wrongly.

This is a difficult letter to write. I have agonized over it, wondering if it should ever come to you. Or if I should simply destroy it.

A woman should not think such things of her children, but in recent weeks I have been forced to. Mr. Winthrop, my daughter Julia's husband, has threatened me in my own home and attempted to force me into signing my fortune over to him. He is a thief who would steal my home and my very livelihood. But he does not act on his own accord. He is but a pawn in a much larger game, one which I fear, I must lose.

I trusted my daughter. Believed she would care for me and protect me from hideous persons such as he. I was wrong.

My daughter is not the woman I thought she was. She came in the guise of an angel, but has shown a devil's face. I have no proof, but I believe she is slowly killing me. I have no strength, not even the small amount needed to leave this house.

But what if I am wrong? What if she is helping me and I have misunderstood? If I am wrong, if she is an angel, then you shall never see this letter. However, if she is everything I think she is, then I have died and she is my murderer.

I pray the former, for I still love my child.

Most sincerely and with fervent hope,

Mrs. Jane Lakewood

Mrs. Winthrop's entire demeanor changed during this reading. Her haughty bearing grew humble and cowed.

"It wasn't me!" she protested. "You mustn't believe it was me! It was *her*! She planned it all. She's the one who fed Mother the strychnine – "

"Quiet, Julia," Abigail snarled. Her transformation, the exact opposite of her sister's, shocked all but Holmes into silence. She stared at him in contempt, her manner like ice, the tears still upon her cheeks bearing witness to her falseness.

"You killed your own mother?" I cried. "Why?"

Miss Lakewood turned her gaze on me and through those eyes, I glimpsed the cruel and withered heart beneath. "I grew tired of waiting," she replied. "And I could not suffer sharing a fortune with a cousin I scarcely know."

"Mr. Bardleship was your unwitting pawn," Holmes said. "First, you planted the seed of Magee's guilt in his mind by pretending to fear the young man. Then, when you learned of the letter with Mr. Bardleship, you had your brother-in-law attack and search him. He found nothing, of course. Tell me: Was it your idea that he and your sister should act as saviors and divert the postman's attention to Magee with their whispered

211

conversation? As clever as your false vicar is, it doesn't quite match his style."

"An interesting narrative, Mr. Holmes," Miss Lakewood said. "I wonder how you will prove it. The letter doesn't mention which daughter. It could well be my sister of whom she speaks."

Mrs. Winthrop screeched and lunged at Miss Lakewood. Hopkins quickly grasped hold of the older woman and held her back.

"I'm sure it will be proved," Holmes replied. "Your sister and Mr. Jeffers – Yes, I know his identity. – will no doubt make excellent witnesses once he is apprehended. Come, Watson. It is not yet seven and the air, not unlike Miss Lakewood, is sharper than a serpent's tooth. Perhaps, the fire at Baker Street and a glass of brandy will stave off this cold."

The Uncle's Cryptic Clues
by David Marcum

"I expected your . . . office . . . to be a bit more . . . impressive." The young man's tongue darted out to lick his lips, and he tried to explain further. "I mean – this. It' so . . . unassuming." He cleared his throat and started to stand. "I apologize. I must have received the wrong information. I meant to visit your office, and obviously this is your residence."

Our visitor, J. Danforth Hutton, looked to the left and right around our sitting room. It didn't take him very long, as the space was only about twenty feet wide, and fifteen or so deep. It was no different than any similar room that could be found in that type of house all over London. Known as a "two up, two down", the first floor consisted of a sitting room with two tall windows overlooking the street in front, and the back half was the stairwell and a bedroom – in this case, Sherlock Holmes's room. My own bedroom was one flight up.

I recalled when I first saw this sitting room, on the second day of January 1881. I was not long returned from the war in Afghanistan, and grateful for the opportunity to have found affordable and comfortable rooms. I'd had no thoughts then that it wasn't impressive enough for, despite its modest size, it was soon a veritable museum of curiosities, with a chemistry table in one corner, shelves groaning with books – both professionally published volumes and hand-assembled scrapbooks – and an overwhelming number of fascinating criminal relics, such as a small porcelain leprechaun which had been coated with a sticky poison, and a polished human femur seamlessly joined to a polished mahogany pole to form a most unique walking stick, and an unassuming little collection of teacups, gathering dust on the back of a table. Each – as I was told – had been used in different successful cases of murderous poisoning. The fact that Holmes now possessed them testified that none of the murderers had escaped justice. Some men collect butterflies – Holmes sought criminals. "A pin, a cork, and a card, and we add him to the Baker Street collection!" he would sometimes say with a laugh.

Now, thanking our landlady, Mrs. Hudson, for fresh coffee and motioning to our uncertain visitor that he should sit back down, Holmes said, "Our little agency has not yet seen the necessity to take separate offices." There was a twinkle in his eyes as he leaned back in his chair and observed young Hutton, seated between us in a basket chair across from a cold fireplace, the morning light from the window behind Holmes illuminating the lad's smooth and care-free features. "Since I first began offering my services here, this location has been more-than-sufficient. Having an office staff, and maintaining a waiting room and consulting rooms and all the trappings of such a business like some sort of Harley Street specialist, would only be an unnecessary distraction. Much of what is discussed here is of a confidential nature."

The young man simply blinked, as if considering what he'd been told before committing to his next reaction or response. Meanwhile, it gave me a chance to more closely observe the prospective client.

Over the years, since first accepting the offer to share lodgings with Holmes in Baker Street, and then beginning to take note of his methods, I had attempted to improve my own observational skills. And there were several occasions where I had noticed this or that odd fact that saved my friend and me from some unwanted grief. The unmistakable odor of an unexploded bomb. A misshapen coat that concealed an undeclared weapon. A sudden flight of birds from an otherwise peaceful-looking copse that signified a likely ambush. But even after all those years, I understood that I still had far to go.

I knew that Holmes had seen all that I had, and certainly more. I was satisfied to note that Hutton looked to be in his early twenties, sturdy and possessing solid rude health, and right handed. He was somewhat careless with his moderately expensive attire, his necktie askew and a few picks and loose threads upon his coat, but that could be attributed to his wide-eyed callowness. His handshake had revealed that he had no acquaintance with manual labor, while he did have the long-term ink-stains of a man who wrote extensive pieces by hand.

"I did recognize this as a residential-type structure when I arrived," Hutton explained, "but I supposed that the building was just the modest front entrance for something larger – that it opened to a building on the adjacent street, and I would be led through to something a bit . . . umm, nicer to the rear." He smiled apologetically. "Oh dear. Have I put my foot in my mouth?"

"Just a little," smiled Holmes. "Your heart was in the right place, I think. How old are you?"

"Twenty-one." Hutton took a deep breath. "Just the other day. That's why I'm here."

"Because of your birthday?" asked Holmes with mock surprise.

"Because of my inheritance," Hutton replied. "Although that isn't related to my birthday, which just happened to be the other day. Oh, I'm confusing things. Perhaps I should explain."

Holmes gestured for him to continue. "Please do."

214

Hutton took a sip of the coffee, spent part of a moment to order his thoughts, and then began.

"I'm an orphan," he stated. "My parents died when I was ten – a railway accident near Basingstoke. They were returning from the West Country – just the two of them. Father was a civil engineer, and did work for the Royal Navy, and it was something of a working holiday for the two of them. It was the only time that I recall that they went away together without taking me along. I had remained in London. I've always wondered if Father had a premonition to leave me behind . . . ."

"You are an only child?" Holmes asked.

Hutton nodded and took another sip. "During my parents' trip, I stayed with my Uncle Jonah, my father's older brother. Actually, we – Father, Mother, and me – had all lived with him for several years before that, upon our return to London from the Continent.

"Uncle's house is at the top of Mayfair – No. 57 Green Street. It originally belonged to my grandparents, and when they died thirty years ago, they left it to Uncle Jonah – that is, Jonah Hutton – as he was the older son, along with the substantial part of their fortune – and it was substantial. It still is, I suppose, although I've never had much cause to consider it until recently. Having that to tide him over, Uncle never really had to work, and he settled into an idle life, pursuing his interests in writing and drawing. He was never very good, I suppose, but it helped him to while away his life – although I don't know if he was ever very happy. He never seemed so. He did manage to have a few of his novels published when he was younger, but they didn't create a ripple. Rather, he established a connection with some publisher-type who produced the physical books from my uncle's works in exchange for an infusion of Uncle's cash into the publisher's business. But there was nothing dishonest about it, and it gave my uncle some joy. He was always proud to point to the little bookshelf where his books were kept in a place of honor, and he felt that it gave him some footing to claim that he was an *Author* – with a capital *A* – whenever he would attend local literary society meetings."

On some occasions, Holmes displayed impatience when a client didn't drive straight for the point, but on that summer morning, with no urgent business on hand and memories of the previous evening's Wagner concert still echoing in his mind, he seemed inclined toward tolerance.

"My father," continued Hutton, "although just as loved by his parents, was left a substantially smaller inheritance, and he had to find a career – which suited him, because he was smart and hard-working, and would have never settled for sitting around and doing nearly nothing like my uncle. In fact, Father always said it was his parents' greatest gift to him not to have burdened him with the money that sustained my uncle's idleness.

"When I was very small, the three of us – Father, Mother, and me – traveled all over in relation to Father's job. Up and down the British Isles, and to America, and on the Continent. When in London we would stay with Uncle Jonah, and after our permanent return here, we moved in with him. All was well, never a cross word, and after my parents were killed, I remained with my uncle – it simply seemed to be understood – and he finished raising me to adulthood.

"I attended university, obtaining a place at Camford in my father's old school, but I'm sad to say that maybe there is too much of my uncle in me, because I couldn't settle down to my studies, having more interest in pursuing my own literary and artistic interests than the rigid coursework required to follow in my father's more-technical footsteps. After a couple of years, I left school and, a year ago, moved back here, to London. I had an allowance from Uncle, and found my own rooms in Bloomsbury where I could write. I've had a few things published to good reviews – just minor pieces, you understand – but I have the sense that I can make my name with a lot of hard work and patience.

"Over the last year, I tried to visit Uncle as much as I could, but you know how it is – the days fill up, and then the weeks, and there's always next week with the best of intentions. All the while, while I didn't know it, he was becoming more and more ill, and just a week ago, last Wednesday, a couple of days before my birthday, he died."

"Your birthday was on Friday?"

Hutton nodded. "I was able to see him, at the very last – the day before, on Tuesday. Word was sent to me by the old couple who served as his butler and housekeeper, and I went 'round to the house. Uncle was weak, but glad that I was there. He could barely talk, but he was very serious – he knew he was running out of time. He explained that I was his heir – this wasn't a surprise – but then he said that he wasn't going to make it easy for me. He didn't offer a better explanation than that, and I didn't press him. I don't know if he meant to tell me more or not, but he fell asleep then, and that was all I had from him before he passed. Then, two days ago, on Monday, I met with Uncle's attorney, a chap named Harrell who has an office in Lincoln's Inn Fields. He gave me a . . . well, a clue is the best way to describe it. I have a week to solve the riddle – starting from the time Harrell put it into my hand – returning to his office by noon next Monday, delivering something or other to him, some object, or the house in Mayfair will be sold and the entire estate will go to charity."

Hutton took another sip of coffee, now surely gone cold. "I'd never met this Harrell fellow before last Monday – never heard of him, actually

– but he told me that he'd been Uncle's lawyer for years. He told me in confidence that, as Uncle's attorney, he'd had an obligation to draw up the conditions as requested by my uncle, to arrange the test, and to do so in the best and tightest legal manner possible, and for that he apologized. He would have to strictly follow the conditions, and he also said that he had no idea what the riddle meant – that hadn't been explained to him – but he would know the object when it was placed into his hand, fulfilling Uncle's requirement."

"I went away with my head spinning, returning not to my own rooms, but instead to the empty old house."

"Empty, you say?" interrupted Holmes. "What of the staff?"

"Oh, they had already gone. It was just the old couple, Mr. and Mrs. Linkous. They were there for years, and I'd known them all my life. But they each received a legacy from Uncle and had wanted to move on immediately – or so Lawyer Harrell told me."

Holmes nodded and waved for Hutton to continue.

"I wandered through the house for hours that first day, trying unsuccessfully to get a line on what my uncle was thinking. Eventually, I went back to my own apartment in Bloomsbury, but I couldn't sleep. That was on Monday, and I spent all of yesterday – Tuesday – in a similar fog, roaming around the empty house. Another day wasted. It was only early this morning, when noticing the newspaper and the story about how you were responsible for clearing up the murder of a salesman in a house down in Sotheby, that I realized you might be able to help me. Some say that you like odd puzzles like this."

"Some do, I expect," replied Holmes. "Might I see this odd clue to which you referred?"

"What? Oh, certainly." And he fished in his waistcoat pocket, pulling out a much-folded and abused sheet of paper.

Holmes took it, looked at both front and back, holding it to the light, and then under careful examination by way of his magnifying glass.

"That's a copy Harrell made for me – that's his handwriting and paper. It was taken directly from Uncle's will that he signed on his deathbed a few days before . . . before he was gone. No secret messages or invisible ink there – just that mysterious jumble of words."

Holmes, with a gleam of interest in his eyes, passed the sheet across to me. I confess that I was dumbfounded.

hftpvcnlqodxehdbfoqlokqoveyxnIrfeqwogocfnzgkvbt

"Do you have any idea what it means?" I asked, handing it back to Holmes. Hutton shook his head. "No, but whatever it says is the key to my inheritance."

Holmes was intently staring at the string of letters, his heavy dark brows pulled into a concentrated frown. Finally he shook his head and looked up. "Was your uncle fond of puzzles and riddles – and had he ever made use of codes before?"

"Not to my knowledge. He did read a great deal, however, and many things fascinated him."

Holmes took a deep breath. "I've made a study of cryptology and, at first glance, this doesn't resemble any complex code that I recognize. It certainly isn't a simple substitution – *Z* for *A*, *Y* for *B*, and so on. It may be based upon a specific word or phrase. Was there some word that your uncle used regularly – something that he'd know that *you* would know?"

Hutton frowned, his gaze drifting into concentrated reminiscence. Then he shook his head. "Nothing special. Sometimes he said 'Eureka!' or 'Brilliant!', but not to the point that I'd specifically associate those words with him.

Holmes nodded and returned his gaze to the sheet. After a moment he gave up. "No, those two words don't generate any sort of easy solution. I didn't expect that they would. May I keep this sheet?" When Hutton nodded, Holmes straightened in his chair. "I believe that Dr. Watson and I will need to speak to the attorney – Harrell. If you would leave his address, as well as your own information – ? Thank you. We shall be in touch – hopefully with good news."

The young man seemed surprised that we were suddenly at the end of the interview. I suspect that he'd pictured spending a greater amount of time at 221b, answering more of Holmes's questions and trying to guess what word or phrase would unlock the secret message. But such was not Holmes's way and, within a few moments, J. Danforth Hutton had departed. I watched from the window as he turned southwest, likely back toward Bloomsbury, and then looked back to Holmes, who had arisen and was preparing to depart.

"Will you join me?" he asked. "This may be of interest for a few hours."

I nodded. "Certainly of more interest than that fish-monger's problem last week," I said with a smile. "He almost seemed angry that you solved it so quickly – as if he wasn't getting his money's worth, in spite of the positive resolution to the affair that you provided."

"Mr. Waddell is an old acquaintance," Holmes explained, taking his fore-and-aft cap from the rack, "and I would have expected nothing else from him. Perhaps if you knew how I first met him, and the desperate hide-

and-seek game that I had to play between here and Stoke-on-Trent in order to find his thieving brother and unfaithful wife, you'd understand why he takes that attitude." And he then told me the story during the cab ride, finishing just as we pulled to a stop outside Harrell's legal chambers.

We stepped to the pavement in front of a shabby brick building on the north side of Lincoln's Inn Fields. On the tenant plaque, I noted that all but one of the metal plates were rather new, indicating that these lawyers had recently moved in. Only one name, T. Claiborne Harrell's, indicating residence on the top floor, showed signs of long occupancy. The other newer plates were polished with pride. Harrell's was not so, being badly weathered over a period that was certainly decades instead of merely years.

We climbed the narrowing flights to the top floor, and the building became warmer with each upward level. Although just mid-morning, the early summer sun was already warming the old red bricks.

A knock upon the door prompted a distant and gruff, "Come in!" We entered a windowless anteroom, dark and illuminated only by the light of an office beyond. Although my eyes hadn't adjusted, and were somewhat affected by the bright office doorway opposite where we stood, I could see that the front room had a desk, piled high with files, and a number of cabinets, some with the drawers pulled open and emptied.

There was a scrambling sound from the opposite doorway, and a lean tall figure appeared, silhouetted against the light. "Yes? It will be that desk and the cabinets, and then the furniture in the inner office as well."

We stepped forward and, seeing us more clearly, the figure retreated – not to lead us through, but more out of nervousness. I could understand his viewpoint. From where he stood, we were two shadows advancing slowly toward him. But we continued to move steadily into the office, where all of us could now look upon one another.

We faced an exceedingly thin man in his early sixties. Like so many of his physical type, he leaned forward like a construct of sticks and tensioned wires, his bony head perched on the end of a long sinewy neck, and dipped downward as if he were a carrion bird. His arms were folded and held up to his breastbone, where his long fingers were intertwined, not below his long pointed chin, as if he were about to pray over his next meal like some sinister minister. He was dressed well-enough in a nice wool suit of an older style, and it did something to moderate the overall effect he projected, though in spite of his clothing, I somehow seemed to see him in a musty Dickensian outfit, as if he were a younger Ebenezer Scrooge, still undergoing his full transition into a miser, and several decades before his Christmas encounter with a series of grim ghosts.

219

"Yes? Yes? What can I do for you? The office is closed – permanently. Are you hear about the furniture?"

Holmes shook his head, introducing us. "I am Sherlock Holmes, a consulting detective, and this is my associate, Dr. John Watson. We have been retained to look into the matter of J. Danforth Hutton's curious inheritance."

The man blinked, markedly, and then once again, as he considered our presence. "Yes. Well. Indeed." Then he seemed to relax a bit, unloosening his fingers and waving a hand to one side and then the other.

"Many apologies, gentlemen," he said. "You catch me at an awkward moment. I'm in the middle of closing down my practice. I'm retiring, you see. Mr. Hutton's uncle, Jonah, was my very last client. He was a dear old friend, and I only remained in practice to finish up his final affairs. He left a generous bequest for me, you see, something of a recompense for helping him manage his accounts and such for so many years – since 1884, to be exact – all the way through to the bitter end, poor fellow. Now I'll be able to travel as I'd always hoped."

He peered at us. "I thought you were the furniture men, here to collect the desks, chairs, cabinets, and shelves."

"We won't take much of your time," said Holmes. He looked beyond Harrell toward the inner office. "May we have a seat? You can tell us about the odd clue left by Jonah Hutton for his nephew?"

Harrell didn't look too pleased, but he gestured us toward a pair of heavy wooden chairs, and then he went around his large desk and sat down, the only window in the office behind him leaving his face in shadow while we were well-lit. It was an old trick, and an effective one. In fact, Holmes had the same arrangement in our sitting room, with his back to one of the windows, while the client sat in a chair somewhat facing him, looking into the light. My chair in the sitting room was opposite Holmes, so I also faced the window. *Perhaps,* I thought, without much sincerity, *my own deductive abilities might be significantly heightened if I was able to fully see the clients too, instead of squinting.* Then I had to admit to myself, *Not very likely.*

"The clue," prompted Holmes. "When was it added to the will?"

"Not long before Jonah died. He called me late the week before, with new instructions – to revise the will, and leave a blank space in the middle where he could handwrite the clue. I told him that I wasn't sure it would be legal – adding a holographic segment to a typewritten document – but he insisted. I offered to type in the clue, but he insisted on writing it himself just before he signed the will."

"And you hurried to accommodate him, I take it? To complete the will, as his health was failing."

"I did. He telephoned me several times to make sure I was working on it – and he had his butler and housekeeper, Mr. and Mrs. Linkous, call me once or twice as well. They'd been with him for many years. He insisted that they be his witnesses. He also left them a sizeable bequest – a thousand pounds each."

"How large is the estate?"

Here the attorney became rather reticent for a moment, but I couldn't blame him. Finally he said, "Sizeable. Let us use that word to describe it."

"You knew Mr. Hutton a long time," said Holmes. "How would you describe him? Eccentric?"

Harrell rubbed his thin jaw. "That fits," he said. "He's always had his own ideas – and sometimes I would have to talk him away from the bad ones. I remember once during the Boer War, he hear something from Lord Carnarvon that convinced him of the need to invest in a bicycle factory, because he'd worked out to his own satisfaction that there would be a need for them in South Africa, and that quickly and cheaply produced and shipped bicycles would be a way to quickly make a financial killing."

"Possibly he recognized something that others did not," I said, and the lawyer frowned.

"It would have been a waste of his money," he responded gruffly. "And I had a professional responsibility to preserve his capital to the best of my ability."

"Can you give any further examples of his personality?" asked Holmes.

"Jonah Hutton was a pleasant-enough fellow when things went his way – but he often sulked and got down in the dumps when they didn't. He had a negativity about him that seeped through in whatever he did – in his amateur art and writing, and mostly in conversations and his dealings with other people. He could never simply be happy, or wish you 'Good morning'. It was always, 'Good morning – although it looks like rain is coming.' Or 'The veal was good last night – which was a surprise, since anything from that butcher is usually mostly inedible.' That sort of thing – always a dark lining to every cloud. Is that what you're looking for, Mr. Holmes?"

"Possibly. It's still early days."

"Not so early. I gave Danforth notice on Monday morning, and now it's already been – " He glanced at the wall clock. " – approximately forty-eight hours. He has just five days left."

Holmes crossed his legs. "Do you *want* Mr. Hutton to succeed?" he asked bluntly.

Harrell was silent for a long. Although his face was shadowed to us, I could see that Harrell's mouth was tightened in irritation – and the lines

221

upon his face showed that to be his normal countenance. "I'm not sure that it was in the spirit of Jonah Hutton's last request that Danforth hire consultants."

"Indeed," replied Holmes. "And was there specific language in the will that prevented such an arrangement?"

"Well, no, but Jonah wanted the lad to think his own way through the problem – to use his intelligence and *earn* the inheritance." Harrell frowned at him. "I see what you're doing, you know – trying to find out how Jonah's mind worked, to break that code. Well, as I said, I'm not so sure that it's ethical for me to help you do so. As the deceased's legal representative, it was my duty to follow his wishes, and to make the legal instrument expressing them as tight and foolproof as possible."

"And yet," countered Holmes with a smile, "it sounds as if you neglected to include a specific requirement that Danforth Hutton solve the clue without any outside assistance."

Harrell didn't speak for a moment, and then he folded his fingers and placed his hand before him on his desk, as if willing himself to sit very still.

Holmes continued. "Do you not consider it an intelligent action when, finding that the task was beyond him, Mr. Hutton had sense enough to hire workmen who *could* complete the job successfully? It's no different than if he needed work on his pipes and hired a plumber instead of doing it himself."

"Well, yes, I suppose so. But still – "

"May we see the will?"

Harrell shrugged. "The document is already placed with the proper officials – filed on Monday just after I spoke with Danforth. I don't have it. Now – " He stood abruptly, as if he were some long-legged mantis suddenly unfolding in preparation for leaping away. " – as you can see, there is much to do here, and – "

At that moment, there was a knock on the outer door and, without comment, Harrell quickly left us, walking through to other office, a look of sudden relief upon his face. We heard the front door open, some muted conversation, and then a middle-aged fat man and two lanky workers followed Harrell back into the office.

"The furniture men are here," Harrell said to us. "If you don't mind . . . ?" He was clearly glad that the interview was ending.

We stood and thanked him, and then walked out. I thought that I saw Holmes and the fat man exchange a subtle look, but then we were in the hall, the office door shut behind us, and I realized just how quickly our visit to the attorney had passed.

"Now, Watson," said Holmes when we'd descended the narrow stairs and stood in the sunny street, "I have several tedious visits to make. I can offer you the choice of joining me, or returning to Baker Street until I have something to report."

"If it's all the same to you," I replied, "I would just as soon accompany you. My schedule just now is singularly devoid of activity."

"A fine way of describing it," Holmes said. "Then, knowing that we might not have an opportunity later, I recommend that we find some nearby lunch. Do you still enjoy visiting The Ship? A solid old tavern, just around the corner, and I think it will suit us down to the ground."

And it did, having been a favorite of mine since my student days. Holmes led me west along the wide pavement, past a large furniture van inscribed with *Burger Furnishings*, and then north through the small passage that was Gate Street. There, just at the turning where an alley leads on north to High Holborn, was the little pub, still in operation since its long-ago opening. As we found a seat, Holmes and I discussed some of the history of the place: Built in the mid-1500's during the height of the Reformation, it had been a secret place of safety for beleaguered Catholics. More recently, it had been designated a Masonic lodge in the late 1700's. As we waited for our food, Holmes pointed out various signs and symbols indicating the Masonic connection. "They believe they are being subtle and mysterious," he said with a silent laugh, and then he recounted a little affair there during his Montague Street days when he'd accidentally exposed the affairs of a Government agent. "It took me the better part of a week to make things right."

Over our excellent beef-and-mushroom pies, and with tall glasses of cider, Holmes shared his thoughts. "It is – shall we say – *curious* that Harrell is retiring just now, but then again, it could be perfectly natural. After we eat, we'll stroll around to Somerset House and get a look at that will."

"And then – ? The house in Green Street."

"That too. But first I want to speak with Alexander Burger – the moving man that was in Harrell's office. He's an old acquaintance."

"I thought that you two seemed to recognize one another. What do you think he can tell you?"

"I'm not sure – probably nothing, but he seemed as if he were trying to convey something to me."

We settled up and then walked south half-a-mile or so, passing along the western edge of Lincoln's Inn Fields and then through a tangle of streets until we reached and crossed the Strand. Holmes walked with confidence into Somerset House, leading me promptly to the Probate Office. The old white-whiskered man behind the counter, introduced to me as Mr. Fairlop, greeted him fondly, and in a trice had the document in question placed before us.

I didn't pretend to know what I was looking for, but I did my best to be observant, nonetheless. Holmes *hmm*'d to himself several times, looking at the simple two-page will for quite a while, turning it and holding it up to the light. Then he pulled out the sheet with the clue that Hutton had given him that morning. After another moment, let me have a closer look at the will. "What do you see?" he asked.

I stated that all I saw for sure was that the curious clue, shakily handwritten in a wide spot left for it on the second sheet, accurately matched what had been copied letter-for-letter and given to young Hutton. "What else should I see?"

"Well, look at the part referencing our new acquaintance, Harrell."

I read it again. "He received a ten-thousand pound bequest. Possibly excessive, but he had been the man's lawyer for over twenty years – and one presumes that he was doing a good job to have held the position for so long."

"Look deeper."

"Well, there's the dead man's signature on the second page, and also two witnesses – Mr. and Mrs. Linkous. I suppose that's legal? A husband and wife, employees of the dead man, acting as witnesses?"

Holmes nodded. "Anything else?"

Then I saw what he meant – the conditions of solving the clue. "If Hutton doesn't solve the riddle within a week, all assets are turned over to charity – but no specific charities are defined, and the entire process of distribution is under Harrell's direction, with no oversight."

"Not necessarily illegal," elaborated Holmes, "but certainly there's opportunity for mischief. Harrell might establish an entity to make *himself* as the charity, and there would be no legal rejoinder. There's also no instrument defined to make Harrell account for where the money goes. Do you see anything else?"

I didn't, and said so. "Ah well," replied Holmes, "there are a couple of other items, but perhaps one needs to be a bit more seasoned to spot them – or jaded and suspicious." He raised his voice. "Did you see them, Mr. Fairlop?"

The old man, who had never wandered very far, replied promptly. "I did, lad. But the attorney of record certified the document, so it's on him, until someone complains. We just receive and preserve documents here. We don't initiate investigations. In the meantime, we'll guard that document for its legal purpose – or if it should someday become evidence."

Holmes nodded. "The latter, I think. And this attorney, Harrell – Have you ever seen anything shady from him before?"

"Never at all, ever. Never heard of him, actually. This is certainly the first time he's ever submitted a will." He lowered his voice conspiratorially. "I did verify that much, Doctor. I thought that there might someday be a question arise from this document – the irregularities, you know, and the sizable fortune attached to it."

I looked back at the two pages, but couldn't see what Holmes or Fairlop were referencing. It was true that the conditions were odd, and questionable that the dissemination of the assets was vague and left under the lawyer's control, but then again, the rooms around me, filled with countless similar legal documents going back centuries, probably had many with the same vague conditions, leaving much in the power of the originating lawyers with no oversight or threat of punishment if criminal mischief occurred. *What was I missing?*

Holmes refused to elaborate and, with thanks to the smiling old man, we went outside and found a cab to take us east, into Commercial Street in Whitechapel, where we soon entered the used furniture business of Mr. Alexander Burger.

Up close, I could see that the fat man hadn't achieved his stout frame from too much eating. Rather, he came by it naturally, for it was obvious he was the physical type that, if was lined up with any of his forebears, would match their solid and heavy low-slung frames. He greeted Holmes with cool respect, and shook my hand when we were introduced.

"You have something to tell me?" asked Holmes as we stood in the wide open shop area at the front of the building's ground floor. Around us, men, women, and couples moved silently like aimless fish in a bowl, swimming amongst the furniture, looking at price information posted on cards atop each piece before moving on. A couple of salesmen stood off to the side, patient but predatory expressions in their eyes, ready to assist or transact when the need arose.

"Sorry to imply so," said Burger, with a faint Germanic accent. I had noticed that the sign over the front of his store – *Burger Furnishings* – was aged though well cared for. Seeing that the place looked relatively successful made me think that Burger had done all right.

"When I saw you there," continued Burger, "I knew that there's no smoke without fire. I don't have any information for you, that I know of, but if you want to ask me questions, or perhaps search the furniture? It's just been unloaded in the back . . . ."

"No need for that," Holmes said, "But I will ask a few questions. When did you get the call about purchasing Harrell's furniture?"

"Let's see. Would've been last Wednesday – a week ago."

"The day Jonah Hutton died," I said. "That was fast."

"Wouldn't know about that," replied Burger. "But it's taken me this long to see about getting back there."

"Back there? To the lawyer's office? Today was your second visit?"

"That's right. I went around a week ago, the day he called, and told him what I'd pay for the furniture. It was awkward, as it seemed to me as if the office was shutting down most unexpected-like. There was a mousy little fellow in the outer office – a clerk – who could barely keep from shedding a tear. He mentioned several times about how long he'd worked there, and he'd just found out that morning that the office was closing. 'What am I to do?' he asked me, as if I could tell him, and telling me 'I had no plans to retire just now. What shall I do?' I felt badly for him, but I had to work out the details with Harrell – what I would take, how much I'd pay, when I'd be by to pick it up.

"I took a couple of the boys with me this morning, and you saw – Harrell wasn't nearly ready. Papers stacked everywhere, files still in the cabinets, books on the shelves. He apologized after you left – said he'd let his clerk go late last week, when he should have kept him a few more days to help clean out the office." Burger turned over his big calloused hands. "That's all I know, Mr. Holmes. I gave him a fair price for the furniture – less what he already owed me for moving the old couple out of the house in Mayfair – and my lads emptied the desks and shelves and cabinets, right onto the floor, and made quick work of loading them up. We settled up and left. As I said, the furniture is back in the warehouse if you'd like to have a look."

"No need for that, Alexander," answered Holmes. "But what's this about moving an old couple from a house in Mayfair?"

Burger nodded. "That's right. I'd never heard of this lawyer, but he called up and said that he needed to take care of some business quickly, including helping an old couple move from a house in Mayfair, where they'd been servants for years, until their master recently died. One of his clients, he said. We went over there later that day. Both the old husband and wife were upset, but they seemed to understand that their master had died just that day – the undertaker was taking him out, even as we carried out the old couple's few belongings – and it was over and done with quick-like."

"Do you happen to have their address – where you took the old couple's belongings?"

Burger nodded. "I'll get it for you."

He went into a small windowed office along the back wall, and when I started to speak, Holmes held up a hand to hush me.

226

"Here it is," said Burger upon his return. "A little house in Lambeth – the old lady's sister lives there."

"Thank you. And one other thing: Do you recall the name of the lawyer's clerk?"

"Hmm . . . *Dunwoody.* That's it. Don't remember his first name, though."

"That should be enough. I appreciate the information. There are several nuggets there that I can use. Now, are you on the telephone, I believe? I saw the number painted on the side of your van . . . ."

Burger led him into the office, and Holmes was soon speaking with someone. Then he made two other quick telephone calls. In the meantime, I had a short conversation with Burger, who seemed to think the world of Holmes. In the years since I'd known him, I'd encountered many like that, all around London, all benefiting from some help or service from the Baker Street consulting detective.

Shortly thereafter, Holmes rejoined us, thanking Burger, and then we were back in Commercial Street, hailing a cab.

"I reached Danforth Hutton," Holmes explained. "We're meeting him at the house in Green Street to have a look, along with a few other people, if we're lucky. I feel as if the solution to this riddle can only be approached with an understanding of Jonah Hutton. He left the clue with the belief that his nephew would understand."

"I wonder if there's any actual fortune to find," I noted. "There seems to rising suspicion about Claiborne Harrell and his actions."

"Possibly, but we ought not convict the fellow quite yet. I'll admit that the situation contrived by the will has dubious aspects, and those two circumstances I mentioned related to the will document are certainly indicative, but it could still be a set of circumstances that, while questionable from one angle, becomes innocent when taking a different perspective by way of a single step to the left or right. No, let us set aside the lawyer for the present, and take a look at the riddle instead."

It was a good thing that we'd taken time to eat lunch, because the rest of our afternoon was given over to solving Jonah Hutton's curious puzzle. We reached No. 57 Green Street around the same time as Danforth Hutton. He led us to the front door and pulled out his key. As he did so, Holmes stated, "You mentioned this morning that the housekeeper and butler had already moved before you spent time searching the house."

"That's right. They each received a legacy from Uncle, and Mr. Harrell told me that they had chosen to leave immediately. It rather hurt my feelings, as I've known them since childhood, but I understood that they were upset, and I assumed that they would get in touch with me soon, when things had settled down."

"We've been told," Holmes explained, "that their move was rather sudden and upsetting – and instigated by Mr. Harrell on the day your uncle died."

"What? I don't understand. I thought – "

"You can ask them about it yourself, hopefully soon. I've made arrangements to have them brought here from their new lodgings in Lambeth – assuming that they can be easily found." Holmes paused, having one more question to ask.

"When you visited Mr. Harrell's office two days ago, did you find it rather topsy-turvy?"

Hutton nodded. "That's right. He explained that he was closing up shop – that Uncle had been his last client, and that he was now ready to travel."

Holmes nodded, having confirmed that fact.

No. 57 was a tidy place, five floors (counting the attic level), and a basement that could be reached through an areaway guarded by a spiked iron fence. The doorway was on the right of the narrow building, in an arched recess reached by a five shallow marble steps. The bottom three floors, along with the basement, had lovely bow windows, one atop the other, on the left side of the building and, altogether, the house presented a most appealing dwelling. But when we stepped inside, there was already the faintest hint of abandonment, even though the owner had only been dead a week, and his nephew had just been there the day before.

Holmes immediately moved into action, walking left and into the front room, something of a parlour, and pulling back the drapes from the bow window. Then he paused to look around, as if considering where to search first.

Hutton started to say something, but I held up a hand. "Best to let him approach it in his own way," I explained.

After watching Holmes examine that room, and then hearing him as he moved through the rest of the house, I was considering asking Hutton about a cup of tea when the doorbell rang. Opening it, I found a heavy-set man in his forties, standing there with an older couple, both of them clearly nervous.

As I shut the door, the older man touched a finger to his worn cloth cap. "Afternoon, sir. Wilfred Deaver, at your service, with a delivery for Mr. Holmes – this husband and wife here, direct from Lambeth."

I heard Holmes approach from behind. "Ah, Deaver. Very good. Mr. and Mrs. Linkous? Please come in. Mr. Danforth Hutton is here and – Ah, here he is. Mr. Hutton – please take care of your old friends, would you? Perhaps a cup of tea while we wait for Mr. Dunwoody? Excellent."

As Hutton shuffled the older couple inside, Holmes turned to the man on the stoop. "Thank you, Deaver. Please wait – there may be some more work for you."

"As you like, Mr. Holmes." And he turned, stepped down to the street, and walked toward a plumber's van with his name painted on the side.

Closing the door, Holmes said softly, "Deaver has done a few errands for me in the past, down Lambeth way. He seemed the best bet to quickly locate Mr. and Mrs. Linkous and bring them to us."

"Have you found anything useful?" I asked.

"Looking around the house, I begin to have a sense of the late Jonah Hutton," Holmes replied, "and I see some light. But before I set about solving the riddle, I want to hear from the other involved parties. Ah!" he added as the sound of an automobile was heard, drawing up in Green Street.

We reopened the door to see a worn Winton stopping just outside. A heavily built man wearing dark spectacles was stepping from the driver's seat. He was strong-looking and firmly in middle-age. He walked around and helped a man of similar age, but of starkly different and weaker appearance, out of the vehicle.

"Right this way, Mr. Dunwoody," rumbled the big man, helping the little clerk toward the door.

"Excellent, Barker!" said Holmes to the former. "Any problems?"

"Not a one. A few telephone calls to a couple of lawyers that I know, and I had Dunwoody's information in no time. I went around and picked him up right away."

"And that other little matter?"

"I have men on it now."

"Wonderful. It's a pleasure doing business with you. Would you care to stay for the *denouement*?"

"With pleasure. Wouldn't miss it."

"Hello, Barker," I said, offering my hand.

"Doctor," he replied with a nod, returning my grip. "I trust you're well."

"Very much so. And you?"

Barker nodded. "Very well, thank you." He was a private detective with whom Holmes occasionally worked. My friend regularly called him, "My hated rival upon the Surrey shore," but it was meant with good-natured affection, and the two men had a deep respect for one another.

"Mr. Dunwoody," said Holmes, reaching for the man's hand and shaking it firmly. "Thank you for taking time to join us. Watson – Would you take Mr. Dunwoody inside while I catch Barker up?"

I agreed and left them talking on the pavement, wishing that someone would catch *me* up – although I suspected that such would be the case very shortly.

In the front room, Hutton was already serving tea to the former butler and housekeeper, having apparently insisted that they take chairs as guests instead of functioning as former servants. He spoke to Dunwoody politely, giving the tense little man some tea as well. At first I wondered why they seemed to be strangers, and then I recalled that Dunwoody had been retired by Harrell the previous week, before Hutton had been called in to receive his uncle's clue. I was offered tea as well, and though I'd had the notion just a few minutes ago that I'd like a cup, I declined. Then Holmes and Barker joined us.

"Thank you all for coming. I felt that this would be best handled by getting everyone together in one place for some quick answers." He then introduced himself, along with Barker and me. "Mr. and Mrs. Linkous, you, of course, know Mr. Hutton."

"That we do," said Linkous fondly, while his wife looked on proudly, as if he were her own grandchild.

"I'm sorry," said Hutton to both of them. "I didn't know that you were leaving so soon, but I was certain that we would soon regain contact with one another. I – "

"Please, Mr. Hutton," interrupted Holmes. Then: "Mr. Dunwoody, this is Mr. Hutton, who is the heir to Mr. Jonah Hutton."

The former clerk looked more closely at Hutton, and then nodded with no apparent change of expression, which – at least to me – indicated that he knew enough about Jonah Hutton's affairs to recognize the name and to have no strong feelings one way or another about the young man.

"Let us be about our business." Holmes said, turning to Mr. and Mrs. Linkous. "You were both let go rather quickly."

They nodded, and Mrs. Linkous replied, with sudden tears in her eyes, "It was so sudden – the very day the master died! And then there was no service for him – " Her husband reached and patted her hand.

"That was my uncle's wish," explained Hutton. "For no service, I mean. He'd always insisted that he simply be immediately cremated. That occurred on the day after his death, and at some point, I plan to scatter his ashes – when I can figure out where he would like to rest – and then I'll have a memorial service. You will both be invited, of course."

"Were you aware of the strange clue that Mr. Hutton wished to be included in his will?" Holmes asked the older couple.

They nodded. "He made sure that we saw it," explained Mr. Linkous, "and that we saw him adding it to the second page of the will before we witnessed it."

Holmes pulled out the folded sheet that Danforth Hutton had given him that morning. Showing it to both Mr. and Mrs. Linkous, he asked, "And was this the clue?"

They studied it and then nodded. "To the best of our knowledge, yes," said Mr. Linkous. "It is a curious jumble isn't it? I can't swear that it's exactly the same."

Holmes pivoted to Dunwoody. "And do you agree?"

The old man leaned forward, reading the letters and moving his lips. "It is. Or I believe so."

"And you know of the conditions of the . . . shall we say *test*, where there is a specific time within which Mr. Hutton is required to solve the riddle?"

"I am," Dunwoody replied. "One year."

Hutton stood abruptly. "One *year*? A *year*? But . . . I was told that I only had one *week*! I saw the will – it says one *week*!"

Dunwoody shook his head. "No, no. I prepared the document myself, on my own typewriter, from Mr. Harrell's drafted notes, per Mr. Jonah Hutton's instructions. It clearly stated that you had one *year* to solve the riddle from the time you were informed of it."

"Which," explained Holmes, "was why Mr. Harrell promptly retired you – so that when he filed an altered will, with the allowed time changed from a *year* to a *week*, you wouldn't be there to contradict him. Not knowing Mr. Harrell, but seeing that he was willing to play this dangerous game to steal Jonah Hutton's fortune, I propose, Mr. Dunwoody, that you're very fortunate you haven't been run down by a stray vehicle sometime in the last week to further ensure your silence. But perhaps I credit Mr. Harrell with more malice than he deserves."

The little old man blanched, becoming even more ill-looking than before.

"That's what you saw on the will when we examined it at the Probate Office," I said. "That the time limit had been changed."

"Not exactly. There was no indication of erasures or alterations of the word '*days*'. Instead, what I observed was that the specified time limit was mentioned but once – on the *first* page of the will, while the riddle itself, as well as the signatures of both Jonah Hutton and the witnesses, Mr. and Mrs. Linkous, were on the *second* page – so only the first page had to be revised and swapped out to change the conditions. And that page had, in fact, been swapped. The typing on the first page was clearly different from that of the second – as done by a two-finger typist, and not someone, like Mr. Dunwoody here, who regularly types with all ten fingers. You'll have noted the callosities on Mr. Dunwoody's fingers which confirm this. The typing on the first sheet, while skillful, showed entirely different characteristics from the typing on the second sheet. Clearly, two different typists had prepared the two different sheets."

"The first page was also slightly different from the second in that it was less-yellowed, as if taken from a different and newer set of blank sheets. I also noticed," Holmes said, holding up the sheet with the handwritten clue, "that this page provided by Harrell to Mr. Hutton, where the clue was copied from the will, was the same type of paper as the swapped first sheet. When Harrell wrote this for you, Mr. Hutton, did he retrieve the blank sheet from his desk?"

"He did."

"And that would be where he also pulled a sheet when he retyped the first page of the will."

"And then," I noted, "Mr. and Mrs. Linkous had to be moved along so they couldn't comment on any irregularities that they might have also observed."

"I expect so. You've both already received your thousand-dollar inheritances?" Holmes asked them.

They nodded. "The day we were moved out," replied the lady.

"Interesting, as that was *before* the document was even officially filed, let alone approved. Harrell may have paid you out of his own pocket – but more likely from the dead man's accounts in his care – in order to move you away from what he was planning."

"But he still had to notify Mr. Hutton about the will and the conditions," I said, "because with such a fortune involved, he couldn't simply steal it. He had to find a way to legally take control."

"Exactly. He hoped that Mr. Hutton would try and fail to solve the clue, giving up in the week that had been falsely allotted."

"Surely this is enough to have the entire will thrown out," said Barker, after silently taking in the direction of the discussion. "The case is solved."

"One would think," agreed Holmes, "and it's enough to have Harrell arrested as well. You're having him watched?"

"As instructed," said Barker. "With all his affairs winding up, as you've indicated, and with him thinking he's going to get away with it, he might decide to bolt, but he won't get far."

Hutton, who had remained standing the whole time, seemed stunned when considering what had happened so quickly. "So that's it, then? There's no need to solve the riddle?"

"Not so fast," replied Holmes. "Although the time limit was changed from a year to a week, we know that your uncle did truly intend for you to solve the riddle. That was still a condition of his will, and it could still be enforced. No, I think it's better to go ahead and solve it right now, while we're all here, and get this over with, instead of letting it drag on until next summer."

"Then . . . then you know the solution?" Hutton looked at Holmes with wonder in his eyes.

"I believe so – or at least enough to begin on the right track." He turned to the former butler and housekeeper. "Do you know what the hidden object is? What Mr. Hutton is supposed to find to gain his inheritance?"

The looked at one another. Then the old man said, "I . . . we think it was a small key – with a paper tag upon it."

"Excellent!" He looked at all of us. "I can tell you that the clue to figuring out the coded message is in this room. Do any of you see it?"

We all looked around, everyone in a different direction, hoping that something obvious would present itself.

The room was eccentrically decorated, with a number of odd sculptures scattered about on low tables and shelves. Likewise, the walls were filled with many artworks of dubious quality, likely painted by the dead man, in small frames hanging from nails in the wall, and larger works hanging by wire from a rather deep picture rail running around the ceiling.

Mixed in through all of these works were a variety of homilies and sayings, tired clichés all of them, written in varying styles and presented in frames of different materials and sizes. *You can lead a horse to water, but you can't make him drink* was framed on one wall. Another motto, *Life is like pounding water in a mortar*, had been crocheted and framed and hung by the door to the front hallway. *The grass is always greener on the other side of the fence* was painted over the doorway leading into the hall, and *Two steps forward, three steps back* was inscribed in large and lovely calligraphic letters upon the mantelpiece bricks over the fireplace. *It's better to be safe than sorry* was framed near the big bow window, and *It's just the tip of the iceberg* was in a frame standing on a table near one of the chairs. *Curiosity killed the cat. You can't have it both ways. You have to walk before you can run.* I noticed that, when viewed in a certain mindset, there was a similar subtle negative shading to each statement, hints of discouragement, and I commented upon it.

Hutton nodded. "That was Uncle's way – there was always something *disappointed* about him – as if he expected the worst."

Both Mr. and Mrs. Linkous nodded. "He'd say things like, *'There's always rain with the rainbow.'* Poor man – he had so much, and could never truly be happy."

I pointed to one, stenciled on the wall near the fireplace. "*'No news is good news.'* How is that negative?"

Hutton laughed and shook his head. "Uncle's interpretation was that '*No news*' – that is, no news of any sort at all – is *ever* good news. He used to rant about 'How can people offer that statement as a comfort – telling them that none of the news they receive will be good?'"

I turned to Holmes. "Is that it?" I asked. "Is there something to these statements that serves as the clue – that has allowed you to understand the dead man's intent?"

Holmes nodded. "Being here and seeing these credos and mottos – and one specifically – that so displayed the nature of the dead man were the clues that led me to understand the solution the riddle."

Then to Hutton he said, "Tell me – was the back bedroom on the first floor that of your uncle?"

"It was."

"Then I suggest we adjourn there."

There was a sense of electric anticipation, along with complete and utter mystified confusion, as our entire company relocated, climbing the steps to the first floor and entering the large rear bedroom. It was rather dim, despite the south-facing window, as drapes were partially closed. Barker walked over and threw them wide, while Holmes was busy turning on couple of electric lamps upon a nearby table.

Holmes looked at Hutton. "The electric power is still on."

Hutton nodded. "Mr. Harrell agreed to it – for a while – while I conducted my search."

"Mr. Linkous," said Holmes, turning to the old butler, "is there a step-ladder available? Thank you."

While the old man left to find a ladder, several of us began to toss questions in Holmes's direction, but he simply shook his head with a smile. At times like this, he was like a magician, and the trick was the thing. When Linkous returned, Holmes said, "I apologize – I should have requested the ladder before we came upstairs."

"No worries, sir," said the man, a note of enthusiasm in his voice.

"Please lean it there," instructed Holmes. "Against the north wall. Yes, there in the center. Thank you."

Then he walked over, mounted the ladder, and climbed the four feet or so until he could reach his hand back into the recess of the picture rail. We shouldn't have been surprised when he brought forth a small cardboard box – but we were.

"Is that it?" asked Hutton, stepping forward. "Is that the object I'm supposed to bring to Harrell to get the inheritance? Is it the key?"

Instead of replying, Holmes returned to the floor and handed the box to Hutton, who scrabbled to open it. There was no difficulty – it was just a couple of inches square, a box of plain grayish color, and an inch deep, much like something that might contain cheap jewelry.

The lid came off and Hutton reached in – pulling forth not a key, but instead a small folded piece of paper. He opened it and, with a groan, handed it to Holmes.

"It's just another riddle!"

"Not to worry," said Barker. "Holmes has an understanding of how to read them now."

And apparently Holmes did, for after just a moment he simply said, "Come with me."

As he led us from the room, he handed me the note, which simply read:

dbjfpavegyczmigcvigdqcveghkqeegkuqqsg

Without even wasting time to lament our incomprehension, we followed Holmes back downstairs, this time to the kitchen, where he turned on the electric lights and then walked directly to the stove. It was a handsome thing, resting on top of four sculpted legs. On the left side were two stacked ovens, and on the right a flat panel with three pot-sized burners – the latest electric model, and without a doubt costing a pretty penny. Jonah Hutton had certainly been willing to spend a bit to have nice things.

Kneeling on the left side, Holmes felt around in the space by the back leg, reaching up and underneath the oven compartments, and taking a minute to work loose another small box, identical to the first. He rose and handed this to Hutton as well. It was almost no surprise when Hutton simply said with boyish dismay, "Another riddle!"

Holmes, far from being frustrated, simply smiled as he matched wits with the dead man. After taking a moment to sort out the coded message, he passed it to me:

ulwqjtgpvzqopbtlhzginxt

"Is that the cellar?" Holmes asked, nodding toward a closed and unassuming white-painted door. When this was confirmed, he immediately stepped across, pulled open the door, felt around until he located an electric light switch, and then disappeared down the stairs. Of course we followed, and I reached the bottom and oriented myself in time to see Holmes in a dark corner, setting aside an old coal scuttle to reveal yet another small box. He stood and handed it to Hutton who, upon opening it and finding yet another folded clue, handed it right back to

Holmes. After just a moment of consideration, he simply stated, "Back upstairs," and away we went, returning to the front room.

Holmes handed me the small slip of paper, which read:

hoqkvoqloyqlmpjbncybuqyxnixlnrobhlwofbeIkkgccinoqjcku

Then, in just seconds, Holmes had liberated the next clue – this time a folded sheet, no box, placed in one of the volumes of Gibbons' *The History of the Decline and Fall of the Roman Empire*, recognizable by the distinctive decorations upon the books' spines. In reading it – now with apparent ease – the smile faded from Holmes's features for just a moment. Then, he seemed to reach some sort of understanding of the dead man's challenge. With a nod of satisfaction, he looked to Mr. Linkous.

"Do you have a hammer and chisel? A small one? Or if no chisel, then perhaps a screwdriver?"

"We have that."

"Good. Please get them, and meet us back upstairs in the master bedroom." And then, with no explanation, he charged back the way we'd already traveled.

By the time Linkous arrived with a hammer and screwdriver, Holmes had returned to the ladder, at the spot where he'd found the first clue. But he had climbed higher this time, his feet on the top rung, right to the ceiling, turning his head sideways and trying to see into the crevice over the picture rail. When Linkous handed him the tools, he reached up and awkwardly started to use the screwdriver as a chisel, pushing it into the darkened space over the picture rail and tapping it gently with the hammer to break up the plaster.

He only gave four taps before handing the tools back to the former butler. Then he reached into the hole, turned his hand from side to side, working something loose, and pulled forth another small box – this time covered with plaster dust. He blew on it, climbed down from the ladder, turned to Danforth Hutton, and placed the box into his hand.

Without a word, the young man opened the box and turned it up, dropping a small key with a paper tag onto his other palm. He dropped the box and picked up the key, holding it close to his eyes to read aloud, "*Capital and Counties Bank, Oxford Street Branch.*" He then looked up at Holmes. "This must be it – this will open a box at the bank, where I'll find what my Uncle left me."

"Something that he left you, at any rate," added Holmes, "in addition to the inheritance that you'll receive by solving the riddle and notifying your uncle's attorney – fulfilling the requirements of the will, even if you have to do so by speaking to him through his prison bars."

"Prison?" squeaked Dunwoody. "I wasn't involved! I didn't do anything wrong!"

"Well done, Holmes," growled Barker. "Very workmanlike."

Holmes nodded in acknowledgement, while everyone else started to speak. Two voices rose more clearly than the others: Hutton saying that he couldn't take credit for solving the riddle, and Mrs. Linkous, demanding that some explanation be given as to how Holmes could read those "foolish notes".

Holmes raised a hand, and the voices diminished and then ceased. "If we return to the front room, I'll explain."

When we had done so, Holmes resumed speaking.

"I knew that the secret to unlocking the clue was in understanding the dead man – how his mind worked. It was no typical code, so it had to be something specifically associated with him. I'd asked Mr. Hutton if his uncle had any specific words or phrases he used, but apparently there weren't any. It was only when we reached this house, and saw the manifestation of the dead man's somewhat negative attitude, in the form of all the framed mottos, that I understood how to solve the code."

He pointed to the mantel, where the credo was painted over the fireplace.

"*Two steps forward, three steps back,*'" Holmes recited. "What seems to be just another clichéd phrase was actually the key. One can spot its importance when seeing that he chose to place it there, in the most prominent spot. And it *sounds* like instructions to solving a cypher.

"I just thought that it reflected his overall attitude toward life," explained Hutton. "That all forward progress is always negated by inevitably going backward."

"No doubt – but it was also the clue to solving the messages. As soon as I saw this phrase, I realized that it could apply to *letters* – specifically in the coded messages. The first letter in the first message is *H*, which is shifted *two steps forward* from *F*. The next letter, *F*, is backed up three spaces from *I*. The third, *T*, is two steps forward from – "

"*R!*" cried Hutton, and Holmes nodded.

"And *P is* three back from – ?"

"Hmm . . . *S!*"

"Correct. Now, without working out the rest of the message letter-by-letter, which you can do on your own if you don't believe me, the first message from the will spelled '*first floor back bedroom north wall picture rail center*'. When I realized that, there was nothing to do but go upstairs and see what we'd find. Disappointingly, we found another message which, when decoded, said '*behind the back left leg of the kitchen stove*'.

"As you saw, we found another message there – just as expected – directing us to '*southwest corner of cellar*', and from there to a bookshelf in the front room, and even a certain book: '*front room bookshelf west wall volume four decline fall romans*'. But then I was dismayed to see that the treasure hunt was suddenly stalled." He pulled out the sheet which he'd found in the book. "Would anyone care to decode the message that I pulled from the book?"

Hutton eagerly reached out his hand, as if to claim it before anyone else might, but in truth, no one was reaching for it, happy to let the lad work it out for himself, in some small way earning the right to claim that he had also solved the riddle of his inheritance.

I looked over his shoulder to see the following –

voaxixkkkqkpplvqjxvbcpaagixbfbgmgovekkm

– just as he stated, "It says, '*try again it is not that easy delve deeper think*'."

"And," explained Holmes, "that's when I remembered the nature of the clues we were solving – *Two steps forward, three steps back.* We had followed the clues to specific places, but the last, in the book, said to '*try again*' and to '*delve deeper*'. I was at a loss – until I remembered Jonah Hutton's philosophy – *three steps back.* And three steps back took us to where we'd been before. One step back from the book clue was the cellar. Two steps back was the stove in the kitchen. And three steps back was the bedroom – and specifically the space above the picture rail, where we were to '*delve deeper*'. Clearly the first clue had rested in front of the final clue – or rather, in front of the key, which was the item to be found and given to Mr. Harrell to fulfill the requirements of the will."

Barker's agents, who had been watching Harrell, stayed on his trail as he took a cab to Victoria Station. He wasn't fleeing the country – not yet – as he had to stay in London long enough to confirm that Danforth Hutton hadn't solved the riddle by the following Monday so that he could lay claim to Jonah Hutton's estate. But Harrell did visit the station to purchase railway tickets on the boat train to France so that he could leave as soon as possible.

A thorough investigation showed that Harrell hadn't actually stolen anything from Jonah Hutton's estate – either before or after the man had died – but he had certainly taken advantage of his position. Although recommending that Hutton not invest in a bicycle factory – this fact was confirmed – he himself had done so, and had made a financial killing. He was charged with changing and registering the false will, although events didn't proceed to the point where he actually benefitted from his actions. And his legal career – should he have needed to resume it after his unexpected reduction in ill-gotten income – was finished.

An examination of the funds that Harrell had managed, and hoped to acquire through his chicanery, showed that Hutton was indeed very wealthy by way of his inheritance. But that turned out to be just a fraction of the estate, as the key to a lockbox at the Capital and Counties bank revealed an incredible second fortune in the form of bonds, stock certificates, and jewels that old Jonah Hutton had purchased on his own over the years with money earned on investments from what he'd inherited from his own father.

In a letter contained in the box, the late uncle explained that he had always felt that his younger brother, Danforth's father, had been unfairly excluded from their parents' inheritance, and so he'd kept a secret separate fortune hidden away for his brother, and – when his brother suddenly and unexpectedly perished – for his nephew. But he wanted to make Danforth earn it by displaying cleverness, and also by showing an understanding of his uncle. After the fact, Danforth Hutton recalled that his uncle had quoted that one specific phrase – "*Two steps forward, three steps back*" – much more often than others, giving it special significance.

Fortunately, while Danforth Hutton did not inherit his father's technical skills, he also did not inherit his uncle's generally dark-turned frame of mind. The young man had a pleasant disposition and a bright attitude, and it was no surprise to either Holmes or me that within a few years, he had achieved a great deal of success in his literary endeavors. During that same period, he relocated to his late uncle's Mayfair house, which became a center of literary culture throughout the next couple of decades.

"Jonah Hutton didn't strictly follow his own motto," I said. "There were more than two steps forward – the clue in the will to the bedroom. The bedroom to the kitchen, the kitchen to the cellar, the cellar to the bookshelf."

"That's true," said Holmes, "but I think that we must give a little leeway to Mr. Hutton's arrangement – for if there were only two clues for progressing forward – from the will clue to the bedroom, and then the bedroom to the kitchen – how would one go back *three* clues? The kitchen to the bedroom, and the bedroom to the will, and then – to *where*? No, he had to build in enough clues to have a place to return and find the key."

In later years, Sherlock Holmes would reference this little case on other occasions, always having a warm feeling for it. "Once I understood the nature of Jonah Hutton," he explained as we walked back to Baker Street from Mayfair that summer afternoon, "it really wasn't complicated at all – rather like something that was devised by a certain turncoat Anzac major in Malta, back in '77, when he was being treated for a gunshot. I had a much more difficult time with that one . . . ."

He then dived deeply into explanations of symmetry and asymmetry, rule-based calculations, keys and substitutions, double and triple authentications, and other phrases and terms that went over my head. My hopes for a simple recounting of one his past cases soon nudged my mind wandering toward what refreshments we might find upon our return to 221b. Fortunately, Mrs. Hudson did not disappoint . . . .

The Adventure of the Amnesiac

by Dan Rowley and Don Baxter

"Holmes, if you're free, would you care to accompany me? Should this matter prove to be of interest, I know you would prefer to be involved from the outset."

My friend looked up from the telegram I had just handed him. "Quite amusing, employing my own words against me. Shall I retrieve the service revolver?"

I laughed. "I am sorry. I couldn't resist, because it's normally you the police want to consult. But in all seriousness, I would be delighted if you would come along."

"Then I indeed shall. Let us go down and hail a cab."

We immediately found a hansom in front of our Baker Street abode and, having instructed the driver to take us to Scotland Yard, settled ourselves. Holmes read the telegram aloud: "'*Dr. Watson. Man found unconscious in the Strand. Doesn't know who he is. Please come to the Yard to assist. Knox.*' Could you please explain the background to this? It is clear you know Knox, whoever he is, but why does he seek your help?"

"It goes back several years ago, when we thought you had perished at the Reichenbach Falls along with that fiend, Moriarity. Knox is Wallace John Knox, an acquaintance from when I worked in surgery at Barts. He's now a police surgeon at the Yard. While you were gone, the police had a curious case of robbery. An elderly lady was knocked down and her purse purloined. The only witness was a solicitor, who happened to be nearby. Unfortunately, he had severe aphasia."

"The condition where one forgets how to speak or write English?"

"Correct. The police were baffled about how to get information from the witness. Knox is an excellent police surgeon, and he mostly assists in the investigation of violent crimes such as murder. He is well-versed in examining victims's wounds, and in fact has attended some rather gruesome autopsies. Although he isn't so familiar with nervous issues, he and I had met periodically to catch up, and he was aware of my 'hobby' (as you refer to it) of keeping up with current developments in the treatment of nervous disorders that affect the brain. He overhead the police discussing the matter, and suggested they call me in."

"And did you resolve the case?"

"After some probing, I determined the solicitor wanted a pen and paper. I procured them, and he proceeded to write in Latin. My knowledge of that language was inadequate to make it out, but the police brought in another member of the legal profession who was able to decipher the message. The scoundrel was apprehended and convicted."

"Capital, Watson. Soon you will not need me and can create melodramas from your own adventures."

I ignored the jibe, as we had arrived at our destination. Alighting from the hansom, we made inquiries and were soon met by Doctor Knox, a tall, thin Scot about my age with sharp features, striking blue eyes, and a receding hairline. I started to introduce Holmes but Knox exclaimed, "Na neit. Wha' does no know him?" Knox's accent was still very thick, but of course Holmes, with his keen ear for dialects, understood perfectly. To spare the reader, I shall render Knox's speech in the Queen's English.

Holmes nodded graciously. "You have quite the combination of Scottish names, sir. I'm not sure I ever met someone named after both William Wallace and John Knox."

"Yes, indeed. I'm named after my grandfather, and my father was quite proud of our heritage. Watson, so good to see you again. I trust you still dabble in the nervous disorder field."

"Of course. I was reading just the other day some summaries of developments on the Continent. Apparently that Viennese fellow Freud, who studied with the renowned Charcot in Paris, wrote a piece on aphasia a few years ago. I wish it was translated. as it likely could have assisted us in our old case." Jean-Martin Charcot had established the first neurology clinic at the Pitie-Salpetriere, and had become quite famous in the medical community.

"That's excellent. We must discuss it at some point. But come, allow me to take you to Inspector Lestrade, who is handling this unusual case."

We followed Knox down a corridor until we came to Lestrade's office. He, like Holmes, never seemed to change. His sallow complexion, dark eyes, and rat-like face were almost as familiar to me as the countenance of my friend. Upon our appearance in the doorway, he immediately rose to shake our hands. "Doctor Watson, so good of you to come. And, Mister Holmes, I was hoping you would be here as well."

"Thank you, Lestrade," Holmes replied. "Can you give us a bit of detail concerning your amnesiac?"

"Certainly. He was found this morning a little after two near the Ritz by a patrolling constable. He was wearing a shirt and trousers along with dress shoes, but had no coat or tie. The clothing was dirty and disheveled. There is a large wound on the left side of his head that was still bleeding slightly, but now has been treated and bandaged by Knox. He appears to be in his mid-fifties with a medium frame, grey hair, a rather round face, and no facial hair. He was unconscious when found, and just awoke a little while ago. He says he doesn't know who he is and cannot recall how he was wounded or came to be lying on the Strand."

"Why was he brought here rather than to a hospital?"

"When the constable searched him, he discovered a woman's diamond bracelet in the pocket of his trousers. The constable thought there might be some crime involved, so decided to have him brought to the small infirmary we have here at the Yard. I likely would have had him taken to a hospital and placed under guard, but felt it better, once he was here, to not move him again for fear of harming him further. Now that he's awake, Doctor Knox and I agree we should take him to a hospital."

"Quite sensible. Might Watson and I see him before that's done?"

"Certainly. Follow me."

We left the office and took a staircase down several floors. We came to a small room with a cot and some basic medical supplies. A man was lying on the cot, and was as Lestrade had described. Holmes nodded for me to approach him.

"Good morning, sir. I am a doctor, a colleague of Doctor Knox. Might I ask you a few questions?" The man nodded, so I proceeded. "Do you remember your name?"

"N-n-no."

"No need to be afraid. We are here to help you. And you don't recall how you were injured or came to be found in the street in a state of partial undress?"

"No. I just don't understand what is happening. Why am I with the police?"

"It is for your own safety. Can you describe how you feel."

"This is all so confusing. I feel nauseous and a bit dizzy. I should like to go to sleep, but may I first have another glass of water?"

While Knox went to fetch the water, Holmes came over to the man and smiled reassuringly. "Please relax, sir. I am consulting with the police. I merely want to look you over a bit." Holmes proceeded to examine the man from head to toe with his usual exact and searching scrutiny. When Knox had returned and given the man his water, the four of us returned to Lestrade's office.

The inspector spoke first. "Well, Knox, what do you make of it?"

"He has all the classic symptoms of a concussion: Confusion, dizziness, sleepiness, nausea. Likely caused by the blow to his head. What say you, Watson?"

"There seem to be a number of unresolved points here. How did he receive the wound? Why was he dressed in such a manner? How did his clothes become dirty? Why was he found on the Strand? Why did he have a woman's expensive bracelet in his pocket?"

Holmes stepped in. "All excellent questions. I believe that the first step is to ascertain who he is. Did anyone else notice the monogram on his shirt cuff. It was covered with grime, but I believe it read '*JER*'. Lestrade, the shirt appeared to be custom made. I suggest you send some officers to the various tailors in Jermyn Street and consult their records to ascertain who purchased a shirt with that monogram."

"Excellent suggestion, Mister Holmes. We'll start immediately. As always, we appreciate your assistance."

"That's all Watson and I can contribute for the moment. This matter has some items of interest. If you don't mind, I would be willing to continue once you determine the man's identity."

"Certainly. Knox, go see to the transfer to the hospital. I'll stop by Baker Street once we have an answer."

We said our goodbyes and returned home. We decided to spend our our time waiting for Lestrade by engaging in productive activities, me reading a journal and Holmes performing some odiferous experiment with his chemical apparatus. It was a bit after one o'clock when Mrs. Hudson brought Lestrade up to our sitting room. He didn't bother to remove his overcoat, but instead delivered his news. "Mister Holmes, your idea bore fruit. We tracked down the tailor who made the shirt. Our mystery man is Jonathan Edward Roberval. He manages an import-export business. He has a townhouse in Mayfair, and I'm on my way there now. I have an officer there waiting for me. If you and the Doctor would care to join me, I have a cab waiting downstairs."

"By all means, Lestrade. Watson, this time I shall ask you to come along."

We donned our coats and hats, went downstairs, and climbed into the cab. Shortly we pulled up in front of a stately Georgian townhouse with red brick and white trim. We climbed the stoop and rang the bell. The door was opened by a cadaverous man in his sixties with snow white hair, glasses perched on the end of his long nose, and a deferential demeanor. We introduced ourselves. He said he was Morgan, the butler, and that he was expecting us, as the officer Lestrade had sent had informed him we were coming. Morgan also said the officer had briefly explained the circumstances that had prompted our visit. He led us to the study at the back of the ground floor, a book-lined room paneled in oak with heavy red leather furniture, a large desk, and a fireplace with a glowing coal fire already lit.

We sat down by the fireplace, and, after Morgan anxiously asked after his master's condition, Holmes began, "Lestrade, if you don't mind, I would like to ask Morgan a few questions."

"Go right ahead."

"Could you describe for us the members of the household and the normal daily routine?"

"Since Master Jonathan's wife passed away, he lives a rather solitary existence. There are three servants: Myself, the cook, and a house maid. None of us live here. The cook arrives early to prepare breakfast. The maid and I came a bit later. The maid leaves at about six, and the cook and I leave after the evening meal if Master Jonathan dines in. While the Master is dining, I come into the study to prepare a drink for him, normally a very peaty scotch whisky, his favorite. He likes to sit in here after the meal by the fire, read, and sip his drink."

"Was that routine followed last night?"

"Not quite. We had guests for dinner, but otherwise it was the same."

"Who were the guests?"

"Master Jonathan's niece, Edith Roberval, the daughter of the Master's younger brother. She lives in Manchester, and came down to London to visit a friend. She wanted him to meet her fiancé, a man by the name of William Fawcett. They were here, along with the Master's nephew, Samuel Lawrence. We also had the Master's business partner, Henry Compton, and his wife, Isabell."

"Did you stay until they all left?"

"Yes. They retired to the drawing room for sherry after the meal. I stayed there to serve them. Mister Lawrence left first, at around nine. The Comptons left shortly after, and then Miss Edith and Mister Fawcett left at about half-past-the-hour. I checked on the cook, who was just finished stacking dishes for the maid to clean in the morning, so we left together."

"Was the door locked?"

"I checked the back door, and it was. Master Jonathan normally locks the front door behind me before retiring to his bedroom."

"Was there anything unusual?"

"I don't know if you would call it unusual, but normally the Master is pleasant and polite with us. He seemed a bit out of sorts, complaining that the roast was over done and telling me to have a word with the cook. I suspect it might have been because he had a head cold coming on." Holmes then asked Morgan to describe what Roberval had been wearing that evening, and it matched exactly what we had seen at the Yard, minus his jacket and tie.

"Morgan, you are an excellent reporter – to the point, along with good recall. Lestrade, do you have the bracelet? Good, please show it to Morgan."

After Morgan examined the bracelet found in Roberval's pocket, he looked at Holmes. "Indeed, I do recognize it, as it belonged to the Master's late wife. I believe it was a wedding present from him, and it had great sentimental value."

"I see. Where is it normally kept?"

"In the safe behind that picture over there. May I show it to you?"

At a nod from Holmes, Morgan went over to a Rembrandt reproduction hanging behind the desk. He swung the picture out on its hinges, and exclaimed, "Why, the door is ajar!"

Holmes and Lestrade leapt to their feet, followed by me. Before Morgan could touch the safe, Lestrade used a handkerchief to slowly open the safe door. Peering inside, he stated the safe was empty. Holmes turned to Morgan. "What normally was kept in there?

"I believe a rather large quantity of jewels and some bonds."

"Who knows the combination?"

"Only the Master, but I think he made a notation of it in a small book he carries in his jacket breast pocket, because he could be a bit forgetful at times."

"Thank you, Morgan. That will be all for now." The butler solemnly bowed and left the three of us alone. Holmes was the first to speak. "Lestrade, I think it would be prudent to have the dinner guests come here for some questioning. Perhaps one or more of them can shed some light on this affair."

Lestrade agreed and left to make the arrangements. Holmes availed himself to make a thorough inspection of the room. He looked at everything, at times stopping to peer at particular objects for several minutes. I couldn't fathom why he chose those in this way, but was confident his powerful intellect was collecting the information he wanted.

A while later, Lestrade returned to inform us that the nephew had arrived first. Then he brought in a young man in his twenties with reddish hair and mustache, a conservative black suit and tie, highly polished shoes, and a waist coat with a watch chain. He introduced himself as Samuel Lawrence, the son of Roberval's younger sister. He sat down where we indicated, and Lestrade commenced to explain to him how his uncle was found, his condition and current location, and the missing jewels.

"Good Heavens, I hope this has nothing to do with Uncle's business problems."

Holmes spoke up. "What do you mean?"

"Well, I don't know the precise details, but I overheard Uncle and Compton, his partner, arguing about money here in the study last night before we went into the drawing room for drinks. I had come back to ask Uncle about some potential investments we had been discussing with Edith's fiancé, but decided to do it another time."

"I see. Do you handle investments?"

"No. I'm in commercial banking at National Westminster. Fawcett, Edith's beau, works at a brokerage house."

"Did you notice anything at all unusual last night?"

"Uncle seemed a bit distracted. Took old Morgan to task over some minor things. I don't know if it was because of an oncoming cold, or the argument with Compton."

"Did you know of the contents of the safe in this room?"

"Not completely. I knew some of my Aunt's jewelry was in there. Uncle had a sentimental streak, and often talked about how it reminded him of her. I suppose everyone at dinner had heard him speak about it, with the possible exception of Fawcett."

"Morgan has told us you were the first to leave at about nine. Do you mind telling us what you did the rest of the evening."

"I went to my club – the City of London Club. Played whist there with friends until about midnight. Then shared a cab with one of those friends to my flat. Went to bed and fell right to sleep."

"I have no further questions. Lestrade, Watson? No, then that will be all for now, Mister Lawrence. Thank you for your time."

When he had left the room, Lestrade turned to us. "Well, there you have it. Clear as day."

"How so, Lestrade."

"Roberval was having money problems. He decided to steal his own jewels and sell them to a fence. They probably were insured, so he likely planned on collecting twice. He went out to meet the fence who double-crossed him, struck him on the head, and made away with the jewels."

"Why was the bracelet still in Roberval's pocket?"

"Must have had second thoughts, and couldn't bear to part with it."

"Why didn't Roberval have a coat or tie?"

"The fence must have stolen them. Do you still want to speak to the others?"

"Yes, and do you mind if I send one of your constables on an errand?"

"Of course not. Let me fetch one, and also see who else has arrived. I wouldn't normally bother with the rest of them, but I learned long ago to allow you to pursue what you call your 'methods'."

As Lestrade left, Holmes went over to the desk, obtained a pen and paper, and began writing. When the constable entered, Holmes placed the paper in an envelope, wrote on the outside, handed it to the constable, and held a murmured conversation. The constable nodded and, as he went out the door, Lestrade returned with a plump woman in her forties. She had graying brown hair, a small nose, alert brown eyes, and was dressed rather fashionably. Lestrade introduced us to Isabell Compton, the wife of Roberval's partner. She settled herself.

"I am terribly sorry Henry cannot come quite yet. He's busy at the office, but I'm confident he will be here later. The inspector explained what happened to poor Jonathan. How may I be of assistance?"

Holmes began the questioning after Lestrade inclined his head. "Did you see or hear anything out of the ordinary last evening?"

"Well . . . ."

"Please, Madame, anything, however trivial, could be of help to us."

"I don't care to gossip, but when we arrived, Henry went back to this study to talk to Jonathan, apparently about some urgent business matter. I took off my wrap and handed it to Morgan. As I approached the drawing room, it sounded like Edith and her fiancé were having some sort of disagreement. I didn't want to intrude, so I stood in the hall until they were finished. I couldn't help but overhear."

"Naturally. What did the disagreement concern?"

"I wasn't listening, but I believe that Edith was asking why they had to postpone their engagement party. Fawcett, the fiancé, said something about a problem at his office – misplaced funds, and an investigation. Young Lawrence had come in but didn't see me. He went back toward the study, but then returned rather quickly, so he and I entered together. I must say, I was surprised Lawrence was able to tear himself away from the tables long enough to attend."

"You do not approve of him."

"Let us just say that, if he were my nephew, I would take appropriate measures."

"I see. Anything else of note during dinner last night?"

"No. It was a pleasant meal. Henry and I left a bit after nine."

"You went home?"

"Yes. We sat together for a while. Henry was reading some business papers, and I was doing some crocheting. I went to bed a bit after half-past-ten."

"What time did Mister Compton retire?"

"I wouldn't know. He has trouble sleeping, so we use separate bedrooms."

"I have nothing else for now. Thank you for your time."

After she had left the room, Lestrade snorted. "Doesn't like to gossip! Then why did she stand outside the drawing room listening in to that couple?"

"There are times, Lestrade, when a gossip can prove useful. Is anyone else here yet?"

"The niece, Edith, and Fawcett are here. Do you want to see them together?"

"I believe separately would be best. Let us start with the niece."

Lestrade went out and returned with a rather plain-looking young woman about twenty years old, dressed in a grey frock without adornment. She nervously looked at us, and then took the chair across from Holmes. She was twisting a handkerchief in her hands and avoided looking at us.

Holmes attempted to calm her. "No need to be nervous, Miss. We have just a few simple questions, and then you may go. I take it you know what has happened to your uncle?"

"How terrible! I cannot stand the thought of it. He was always so kind to me and Samuel. At times, he's even loaned Samuel money."

"Did you notice anything unusual during dinner?"

"We had a pleasant meal. Uncle was a bit distracted, but it sounded as if he was beginning to have a cold. After the meal, we all went to the drawing room. Uncle seemed to perk up a bit. Samuel left at about nine. He was in a good mood. He made a jest with Morgan about knowing the way out. The Comptons left a little after. She came over and congratulated me again. He told Uncle he would see him in the morning, then went up to William, shook his hand, and said something about William being a lucky chap. William and I remained for a while, until Uncle indicated he wished to retire to the study. I wasn't surprised, as he is quite a creature of habit. To the study after his meal, then in bed no later than eleven or shortly after. We left, hailed a cab, and William dropped me off at a friend's flat, where I am staying while here in London.'"

"What did you do then."

"My friend and I visited for a bit, but she was tired and went to bed. I stayed up to write some letters, then went to bed. It was about midnight because I heard the clock in the sitting room chiming."

Holmes sat for a minute, deep in thought. I was accustomed to this behavior, but Edith seemed flustered. I realized Holmes was done, so I escorted her to the hallway and assured her this was merely normal behavior by my friend. We came upon a tall, robust man in his mid-twenties. He had brown hair, a luxuriant mustache, large ears, and soft grey eyes. He introduced himself as William Fawcett. I asked to be excused for a moment and went back to the study, where Holmes and Lestrade were discussing the matter of the ink stain shaped like Germany, a case where Holmes had assisted the Yard the previous year. When I informed them of Fawcett's presence, they indicated I should fetch him. I went into the hall and brought him to the chair where his fiancée had been seated. Unlike her, he showed not a trace of nervousness.

"What, ho! I trust this will not take too long. Must be getting back to the office."

"What business are you in, if I may ask?" questioned Holmes.

"So you are the celebrated Sherlock Holmes. This doesn't seem to the type of thing in which you would normally be involved. To answer your question, I work in a brokerage house. Learning the ropes of stocks and bonds, you know."

"Is there a specific reason you have to be back so quickly?"

"Er, um, no. Just the normal press of business."

"Did anything unusual occur while you were here yesterday?"

"Can't really say. First time I ever met any of them. This is the first opportunity Edith has had to come down to London since we became engaged. I met her while doing a stint in a branch office in Manchester, you see, and came back to the main digs here about six months ago. It's easier for me to take the train up there to visit her than it is for her to come down here, as she has an office job in a factory – modern girl, you see – and often has to work on the weekends. Low man – or I should say *woman* – on the totem pole, you know. During those visits, Edith has regaled me countless times about all of them, so in a sense I feel as if I know them. When the old *pater* said he wanted to retire, I realized he was off to the study for his nightly libation. But 'unusual' – no."

"I understand you dropped Miss Roberval at her friend's flat. What did you do after that?"

"I met a few chaps from the office for a nightcap. We had arranged it that afternoon. We went to a pub called The Bull and Bear. I left a bit before half-past-ten, went home, and slept the sleep of the just, you know."

"Fine. We have nothing further. Thank you for your time."

"Cheerio. Cannot wait to tell the fellows I have met you. Best of luck."

When he had departed, Lestrade glared at the closed door. "Pompous popinjay, if ever I saw one. Not a bit of useful information."

Before Holmes or I could respond, there was a light knock at the door. I went to open it, and Morgan informed us that Henry Compton had arrived. In response to Holmes's directive, Morgan ushered in a short, plump man in his mid-forties. His face was red and shining with perspiration, which he paused to wipe with a pocket handkerchief. His eyes bulged behind a pair of thick spectacles.

"Oh my, oh dear. Poor Jonathan. Isabell stopped by the office on her way home to tell me what happened. The woman cannot bear to hold back any news once she as it. You must be Sherlock Holmes. Pleased to meet you. And you are the inspector she mentioned. As the last man here, you have to be Doctor Watson. I must say, I wish we had met under better circumstances. I quite enjoy the write-ups of your escapades."

Holmes decided to break in on the deluge of words. "Perhaps we can discuss that at another time. Did you notice anything odd last night?"

"Well, Isabell told me about Edith and Fawcett having words. Other than that, no."

"No other arguments or disputes?"

"Not that I know of."

"Had Samuel Lawrence asked his uncle lately for money?"

"I know he had in the past, but don't know anything recent."

"Do you know what Lawrence needed the money for?"

"I don't recall that Jonathan ever mentioned it."

"I understand from your wife that you returned home after leaving here, and that she went to bed but you stayed up reading business papers. What was the nature of those papers?"

"Routine documentation related to some shipments we are due to receive shortly."

"What time did you go to bed?"

"I cannot say for sure, but I would say shortly after midnight."

Holmes again fell into a deep reverie. The inspector and I took Compton out into the hall and said we would contact him if we needed further assistance. Lestrade went off to tend to other business and said he would return in an hour or so.

Morgan approached me and inquired whether Holmes and I would like anything to eat. While my friend often neglected food or drink when in the throes of a case, I took it upon myself to ask Morgan for some cold meat and cheese, bread, and perhaps a light wine. He nodded, solemnly as always, and went to obtain it.

I returned to study and Holmes was still deep in thought. While I was gone, he had taken the liberty of lighting his favorite pipe, sitting next to the fireplace and puffing away. In a bit, Morgan returned with the food. I began helping myself, when Holmes finally spoke up.

"I suppose you will insist on my partaking of this repast. Very well." As he placed some meager scraps on his plate, a constable entered and handed him an envelope. Holmes opened it and read the contents. A slight smile passed his lips as he said, "Watson, how does all this appear to you?"

"To begin with, I have some doubts about the concussion theory."

"Yes, I noticed your hesitation to reply when asked at the Yard. I share your reservations. Let us pass that by for the moment. What else troubles you?"

"If we turn to motive, it seems everyone involved had a motive for financial gain."

"Excellent. Your ability to listen carefully has manifestly improved. Please elaborate."

Basking in his praise, I continued. "If the import-export business is in financial difficulty, Lestrade has correctly pointed out that provides a motive for Roberval. But the same could be said of Henry Compton, and perhaps of his wife as well.

"As to Lawrence, his gambling problems could be financially pressing. And the mysterious affair at Fawcett's brokerage house, with presumably missing funds, could act in the same way."

"I know how you feel about women, Watson, but we must not be overly chivalrous."

"You refer, of course, to Miss Roberval. I suppose she might have stolen the jewels to protect her fiancé, especially as it might affect their engagement, at least according to that gossip Isabell Compton, whose own motive could have colored her account.

"But where I remain perplexed is opportunity. Morgan confirmed that Roberval was still in the same clothes he wore last evening, down to the shoes. If, as Miss Roberval told us, Roberval retired by eleven or shortly thereafter, and if Lestrade's theory is incorrect and Roberval didn't leave here to meet a fence, that suggests the culprit returned some time before eleven or so. The culprit must have rendered Roberval unconscious (whether by striking him or otherwise), stole the jewels, and moved him to the Strand. That lets out Lawrence, who was at his club until midnight with companions, a fact that can be easily confirmed. Fawcett left his friends a bit before half-past-ten, which is tight but possible. The Comptons were together until half-past-ten or a little after, so it is also just possible for either of them, or they are in it together and covering for what one of them did earlier then half-past-ten. The only one who had the largest increment of unaccounted time is Miss Roberval, but – "

Just then, Inspector Lestrade entered the room. He smirked and said, "Well, Mister Holmes, do you have a solution for me?"

"I believe I do, Lestrade. Have a seat and allow me to explain.

"The first point is the matter of Roberval's concussion. Both Watson and I had doubts about that as an explanation of his amnesia. I'll set that aside for the moment and instead focus first on motive and opportunity. As you correctly pointed out, if Roberval was having financial difficulties, that gave him a motive to fence his jewels and perhaps make an insurance

252

claim. But that also would provide a motive for both of the Comptons. Lawrence may have a gambling problem, and possibly Fawcett is in some sort of trouble at his brokerage house over funds, if Isabell Compton's account is to be trusted. That might lead either of them to purloin the jewels, as well as Miss Roberval to protect her fiancé. It's probably common knowledge that everyone knew about the jewels, and that Roberval kept a pocket diary with the combination of the safe. That would seem to also include Fawcett, as he told us Miss Roberval had shared with him about all her uncle's habits.

"Lestrade, your assumption is that Roberval left here to meet his fence, retained the bracelet for sentimental reasons, and was double-crossed, struck down, and robbed. He was found at about two in the morning. Because that portion of the Strand is heavily patrolled, your theory rests on the assumptions that the crime occurred shortly before two and that it took place in the Strand. Let us examine both assumptions.

"Roberval was found in clothing that would support your theory that he left here to meet someone. Watson correctly observed that, if Roberval normally went to bed by eleven or so, then of the five dinner guests, the Comptons and Fawcett could have come here before eleven to commit the crime, but that would be a very tight time frame for any of them. Miss Roberval could have had more time.

"Let us examine a different scenario. What if the crime began in this very room at a time substantially before eleven?"

Lestrade objected. "I'm not following you."

"Your theory is premised on the notion that Roberval was conscious when he was struck. It's true he had signs of a concussion – memory loss, confusion, nausea, dizziness, and sleepiness. There were other signs as well. While we were there at the Yard this morning, he asked for 'another' drink of water, which indicates his mouth was dry. I noticed that he was having some trouble breathing and that his pupils were extremely small. I'm confident Watson noticed these symptoms as well, because he didn't agree with the concussion diagnosis. These three, added to the others, mean Roberval may have been subjected to a dose of opium."

"But how on earth could Knox have missed that."

"As you know, his primary duties are in connection with the victims of violent, mostly deadly, crimes. I would assume he hasn't had extensive experience, if any, with partakers of opium, especially while they're under the influence. Opium is easy to obtain in the form of laudanum. Our culprit may have distilled it a bit by boiling off some or all of the alcohol in the solution."

"How could the culprit be sure Roberval would end up with amnesia?" I asked.

"An excellent question. He could not. As will be clear from my explanation, he would know that Roberval would have a blackout period during which he wouldn't remember anything. The fact that Roberval was in such a stupor that he couldn't remember who he was proved an added bonus for our criminal. It meant Roberval couldn't even deny the inspector's theory.

"Now let us reconstruct the crime with this new information. The culprit knows Roberval's routine, including the fact that he had a whisky prepared in the study for him by Morgan while the guests were dining. Even Fawcett knew that, as he himself referred to it while talking to us The culprit found an opportunity to add opium to the whisky after the meal. The strong peat flavor, which Morgan mentioned, and the fact that Roberval was coming down with a cold masked the flavor of the opium. When I inspected this room, I noticed that the glass was luckily still sitting next to the chair by the fireplace. In the confusion over Roberval's disappearance, apparently it wasn't taken away and cleaned. When I smelled the glass, I could detect the vinegar-like aroma associated with opium. It was faint, but as you know I have trained my sense of smell.

"All the guests, including the culprit, left, as did Morgan and the other servants. I suggest that Roberval went to his bedroom, removed his jacket and tie, and probably donned a smoking jacket. He then settled down in the study, consumed his drink, and blacked out, let us say by ten or so. Some time after midnight, the culprit returned, perhaps through the front door because Roberval hadn't yet locked it, or perhaps he – I'll use the male pronoun only for convenience – had purloined a key that evening. Assured that Roberval was unconscious, the culprit removed the smoking jacket and went upstairs to hang it up so that the police wouldn't realize Roberval was wearing it, which would suggest the he hadn't left the house. The culprit then found the pocket notebook in the bedroom with the combination, came back down, opened the safe, and removed the jewels. He then placed the bracelet in Roberval's pocket and struck him over the head. I believe that poker by the fireplace is suspiciously clean for a tool used to stir coals. Lestrade, you should be able to determine if there is any residue of blood on it. There also may be some specks on the chair, which the red leather makes it difficult to detect.

"You will recall that the monogram on Roberval's shirt was almost obscured by grime. I have made a study of various materials of that nature, and it clearly was coal dust, which could be obtained from that scuttle there by the fireplace, but hardly on the Strand where Roberval was discovered.

"I assume the culprit procured a cab, told the driver his companion was drunk, and pretended to help him into the cab. Again, you should be able to track down the driver. The culprit left Roberval in the shadows on the Strand, where he was discovered on the next round of the constable."

"That's all well and good, Mister Holmes, but all that tells us is that any one of the five guests could have done it, because no one has a solid alibi for the time you posit."

"Ah, you see Lestrade, there are clues as to the identity of the culprit. Only one person had a solid alibi up until midnight. Only one person was so anxious to tell us about Roberval's financial problems that he didn't even wait for a question about it. Only one person left alone and made a point of telling Morgan he knew the way out – which is when he slipped down the hall to drug the drink while the others were together. And only one person has been to the British Library doing research on laudanum and opium. I had your officer send an inquiry there to a clerk for whom I once performed a service to recover a stolen Chaucer manuscript. Here is the reply."

He handed over a piece a paper, and Lestrade quickly scanned it. "Lawrence. So his gambling led him to concoct this elaborate scheme. He clearly wanted us to suspect his uncle, but as always he didn't count on you being involved."

"He may have had one additional motive: I suspect he was being blackmailed. If his employer had learned he was gambling, he would have been cashiered immediately."

"Blackmailed by who?"

"It's obvious that Isabell Compton tells everyone everything she knows. She told us about Lawrence's gambling. Her husband knew about the other indiscretions she shared, but professed to know nothing about Lawrence's love of the tables or even that he had asked his uncle for money lately, which is likely why Lawrence went to the study last evening. Compton needed money, and may have been blackmailing Lawrence. In any event, it's worth following it up."

"I certainly will, Mister Holmes. If you will excuse me, I have much to attend to."

After he left, I smiled at my friend. "Holmes, that was brilliant."

"It had some interest. I'm grateful you asked me to accompany you."

The Adventure of the
Murderous Clown
by Tracy J. Revels

"Holmes," I observed, "you are not human."

I uttered these words for the simple reason that my friend, Mr. Sherlock Holmes, was incapable of taking an aimless yet restorative holiday. It was a lovely Midsummer's Eve, and all the flowers were in bloom, making the Lake District even more charming than its usual wont. We had taken a small cottage for a week, with no plans beyond long walks in the fresh air and pleasant conversation on topics unrelated to murder and mayhem. Excessive work – including two cases that would result in villains swinging from the gallows – had taken a mental, physical, and (I feared) spiritual toll on my friend. He was restless, lean-faced, hollow-eyed, and expressing somewhat morbid thoughts on the possibility of the soul being finite and the pursuit of true justice futile. I had prescribed this short holiday as his physician. But, as usual, Holmes was the worst of patients.

"I have merely observed that the quantity of foxglove and rhododendron blooming in this particular churchyard would be quite useful to any vicar in a homicidal mood," Holmes said. "Or practical to his lady, if she had wearied of being tied to an impoverished prelate. Judging by the disrepair in the sanctuary, the congregants are not wealthy, nor does there appear to be a generous noble patron for the parish. If you observe the state of the cobblestones, you will deduce – "

"Holmes, I positively order you to stop! You must give your body and your brain some rest!"

My friend favored me with a look of utter contempt. "I suppose you will suggest a trip to the circus next."

I couldn't resist a chuckle. Just that morning, we had been awakened by the sound of a circus making its way down the path before our rented house. A calliope piped out polkas and patriotic airs, while the residents of large, caged wagons protested their confinement with roars and shrieks. A herd of elephants marched along, single file, and one left quite the odoriferous present steaming at our gate. High-spirited horses dressed in velvet blankets and ostrich plumes pranced behind the pachyderms, each with a trained dog mounted on his back. Amid the carts and conveyances were clowns, acrobats, and assorted human curiosities, including a towering woman in a sparkling gown whose beard would have made

Methuselah envious. From flyers left behind in our hedges, we learned that the Cavalier Circus would be setting up in a meadow near Castle Cignet, a ruined tower with a tiny hamlet in its shadow, just two miles from our residence.

"It wouldn't harm you to spend an afternoon eating roasted nuts and watching jugglers and trained monkeys," I said. "If you don't learn to relax," I continued, "you will not live to – "

Holmes threw up a hand, silencing me. I realized a moment later that his refined hearing had picked up the sound of a galloping horse. A lathered bay mare appeared at the crest of the little hill near us, bearing a youthful rider. We moved toward the churchyard gate, and the boy – who, much to my astonishment, was riding without a saddle or bridle – drew his steed up short with a yank on its mane.

"Sirs – did you see a dogcart go by? Just now?"

We exchanged a glance. We had been in the little churchyard for almost two hours, as Holmes jotted down intriguing epigraphs from ancient tombstones, and had seen no one pass, either on foot or in a conveyance, and told the lad as much.

"He must have gone the other way at the crossroads. I've lost him and – I can't go back! I must find a doctor for my mother! She's been shot!"

"I'm a doctor," I offered. "Where is your mother?"

"A half-mile down the lane, in the yellow house. Please hurry sir! Please! And I swear, I'll catch him! I'll catch that murderous clown!"

"I'll need my bag – it shouldn't take a moment," I said to Holmes, as we both began to run, while the youth kicked his heels against the horse and propelled him onward. We were almost to the gate of our rented cottage when Holmes skidded to a stop.

"Watson . . . did the boy say *clown*?"

Some ten minutes later, we came upon a doleful scene. The yellow house – two stories, neat, and with an air of modest prosperity – sat at the end of a graveled drive. The lawn was well-groomed, and even as we hurried toward the doorway, Holmes observed the owner had several children of different ages, based upon the toys strewn about the grass. The front door was open. A frightful wailing emerged from within, and we dashed inside. I shall never forget the horror I felt as we stepped into the foyer.

A lady lay upon her back, her arms spread wide, a pool of blood formed about her head like a scarlet halo. She had been shot in the mouth, and her face was distorted and blackened, as if the pistol had been within inches of her skin when discharged. Death, mercifully, had been instantaneous.

There was no sign of another adult, but through an open doorway, at the front of the house, I could see two children. One appeared to be a lad much smaller than the fellow on horseback, and the other a toddling girl, who was inconsolable. The boy backed away, pulling his sister to him, then grabbed a hobbyhorse, waving it above his head like a weapon.

"We are friends," Holmes said, holding his hands up, palms open. "We have come to help you. Your brother has gone for another doctor, and the police."

"Did he catch the man in the clown suit?" the young boy asked, without lowering his toy.

"I fear not," Holmes said. "But my friend and I will find that individual. It is he who has done this to your mother?"

The little boy nodded. Seeing there was nothing I could do for the poor lady, I rose and joined Holmes in the parlor, carefully pulling the sliding door closed, so that the youngsters were no longer looking at their mother's corpse. The boy at last dropped his improvised weapon and spoke to his sister.

"They will help us, Becky. See – that man has a bag. He is a doctor, just like Father."

It required all my knowledge, and Holmes's gentle way with children, to persuade the trembling little lass to swallow a spoonful of a sedative. She began to nod, and we placed her on the sofa. The boy sat beside her, one hand combing her chestnut brown locks.

"Thank you, sir. Becky is prone to fits. I was afraid she would have another." The boy rubbed away a tear. "I'm Henry Donner. My sister is Rebecca. You said you saw Eddie on the road?"

Holmes deftly introduced us, and assured Master Henry that his brother would soon be back with more help. He asked if there were servants about, or other children in the house.

"Just Abbie, and she is a baby. The servants all left to go to see the circus. Mother said we would go tomorrow, when Father comes back home to go with us. She said we . . . we would have a grand day here together, just us, and we did. All morning, we played, and Mother was about to go to the kitchen, to make us some sandwiches, when . . . ."

The poor lad's courage failed him, and he began to wail. Holmes didn't press the child for more information, but allowed him to cry, holding the child curled against his waistcoat. We sat in silence until at last, exhausted, young Henry fell asleep and could be placed beside his sister. We tiptoed back into the foyer, speaking in whispers as Holmes examined the body.

"At least she didn't suffer," he said, "though I fear her offspring will be unable to forget this horrible event. They clearly witnessed the murder."

Holmes rose and walked through the open doorway. "Mrs. Donner had no fear of whoever was on the threshold. There is no sign of struggle. She was taken unaware. Hello, what is this?"

I followed his gesture. A white wicker basket, filled with daisies, was overturned on the ground beside the step.

"Holmes, what could this mean?"

"It is too soon to speculate," my friend said. "Fortunately, we shall soon have some answers, for I see a cart turning onto the drive."

"She was a beautiful woman," Inspector Harold Lawrence told us. He was staring down at a photograph of the late Mrs. Celeste Donner dressed in her bridal finery. "She had a kind and gentle heart. She was a loving wife and doting mother. She didn't deserve the wickedness of the past to rise from the pit and claim her."

We were seated in the parlor, perhaps an hour after the arrival of Lawrence and a local medical man, along with a pair of the doctor's servants. The physician confirmed the cause of the lady's death, and he and his men gently carried the poor woman away, saying that they would alert any of the family's staff they might encounter, and send a telegram to the village of Rosthwaite, where Doctor Donner had his surgery. Meanwhile, there was little we could do except stay in the house for the safety of the children. Master Eddie, who was fourteen, had given us a clear statement, speaking with a firmness that belied his youth and the great tragedy he had just experienced. According to his testimony, at eleven that morning Mrs. Donner had settled with her children in the parlor, after putting the baby to sleep in the nursery. Everyone was hot from playing on the lawn, and she urged them to rest and cool themselves before she prepared their luncheon. She was just rising from watching her boys play checkers when there was a knock at the door.

"'Who could that be?' she said, and then she opened it. I heard Mother laugh. She sounded so jolly that we turned to look. She had her hands together and I heard her say, 'Oh, how rare! Are those truly for me?' And then, not a heartbeat later, I saw an arm thrust in through the door, and a pistol, and Mother gave a cry. There was a loud bang, and she fell backward. And that was when . . . Sirs, I swear to you, it was a clown! A tall clown, in a yellow-and-orange suit, his face all painted white, a great red rubber nose tied to his face with a string. He had a wild wig – it was bright blue and curly – and a silly straw hat perched atop it. He took one step inside, looked down at Mother, then turned and looked at us. Before I could make a sound, he whirled around and darted off. I ran up, saw Mother was no more, and gave chase. He was driving a dogcart, pulled by a white horse with brown spots on his rump. I knew I would never catch him on foot, so I ran for the stable and mounted Blackjack, but the murderer beat me to the crossroads, and I didn't know which way he went."

Holmes assured the boy he had done well, and bravely, before sending him upstairs to comfort the other children. Now our attention turned to the inspector, a handsome man of some fifty or so years, with a dark beard and piercing grey eyes.

"What do you mean?" Holmes asked. "About Mrs. Donner's past?"

The man rose and motioned for us to follow him deeper into the house. It was a well-appointed dwelling, with a pleasant, modest air that bespoke a comfortable family not given to pretension. We glanced inside the doctor's study, which was filled with books and an examination table, as well as chemical apparatus.

"Donner sees a few local patients here, but his primary practice is in Rosthwaite. He has a large office and a surgery there, and often spends the night away from home. I have spoken with him more than once about it, warned him that he did wrong to leave his lady and children unguarded. Look here, and perhaps you will understand my concern."

The inspector next opened the door to a room that was the lady's private chamber, clearly her suite for artistic endeavors. It was bright and airy, thanks to the windows that looked out onto the lawn. An easel was set up, bearing a half-completed painting. Much to my astonishment, the face on the canvas wore the makeup and grinning features of a clown. Lawrence drew our attention to a large, framed illustration on the wall, a colorful broadside advertising *"Richland's Circus: The Wonder of the Age!"*.

"Are you familiar with the tragedy?" he asked.

"Yes," Holmes said. "Though only through reading of it. What was the year – '55?"

"I believe it was 1859," the inspector said, elaborating when he spotted the look of confusion on my face. "Richland's Circus was one of the most successful in England, and had just returned from a triumphant Continental tour. At a performance in Coventry, a fire broke out in the grandstand. As the alarm was raised, the blaze leapt onto the tent. All was confusion, a great stampede of people fleeing. Twenty patrons were killed, among them at least five children, trampled in the rush or lost amid the flames. Many animals expired, and some eighteen performers died or were maimed. Blame was laid upon two boys who tossed cigarettes into the straw beneath the seating, but many people held that Colonel Arthur Richland, the owner of the circus, was responsible. At the time, Celeste was only a child. Rather than face the boos and hisses of the irate crowds, her father, Old Richland, sold everything he had and moved here, to this house, and lived in retirement."

"I don't understand," I said. "How does this affect the lady?"

"Shortly before Mrs. Donner's marriage, her father was found murdered, in the very room that is now her husband's study. His staff was at church and his daughter was visiting friends, so the old man was quite alone. He was found slumped over his desk, with a great wad of bank notes in his hand and an ornate dagger through his throat. My predecessor worked for many years on that case, but was never able to bring it to a conclusion."

"The obvious one being," Holmes said, "that someone in his troupe blamed him for the disaster. He agreed to meet with that person or persons, in hopes of buying their forgiveness. Vengeance, however, was the preferred reward."

Lawrence nodded rapidly. "Inspector Clive said the same thing – and a circus was at Castle Cignet when old Richland was murdered. Clive knew many of Richland's company had moved along to other outfits, but he was never able to build a case against any former employee. And now . . . now that villain isn't satisfied and has taken out his wrath on the next generation. I fear for Celeste's innocent children!"

Holmes made a circuit of the room, studying the paintings on the walls. They were clearly the work of the same untutored artist, depicting not only clowns but jugglers, tightrope walkers, and lion tamers.

"What can you tell me of the Donner marriage," Holmes said. "Was it a happy one?"

The question hung in the air. I looked up from my perusal of some trinkets. The inspector's handsome face had gone bloody with strong emotion.

"It isn't proper for me to speak of that."

"Shall I read discomfort with the truth in your silence?" Holmes asked. The man put a hand to his mouth, for a moment biting on his knuckles. Then he seemed to come to some hard resolution, lifting his head and stiffening his spine.

"I know of no discord – I only know that Edgar Donner is a foul wretch unworthy of her! There, I have said it! If you must know, Celeste was my sweetheart many years ago, and would have married me, if not for her father's objections. Circus folk have no fondness for the police, and he steered her toward Edgar's attentions, because Edgar is a physician. And what has Edgar done with his life since marrying Celeste? Almost nothing! It is Celeste's inheritance that keeps them, not his pitiful earnings. He stays away from home because he prefers the company of low women. I have been in Rosthwaite on many evenings, and seen him in the pubs, entertaining females who aren't fit to lace Celeste's boots!"

At that moment, we heard a door opening, and the rush of footsteps in the hallway. Lawrence strode past me, intercepting the newcomer as she was hanging a bonnet on a hat stand.

"Alice, thank God!" the inspector breathed. He introduced the young woman as Alice Jones, the Donner's governess. She was an attractive girl, rather tall and not quite thirty, with butter-colored hair and bright blue eyes. Her face was raw and chapped, and she gasped for breath. Clearly, she had run all the way up the road, for her dress was dirty at the hem, her boots caked with mud. "The children need you," the inspector insisted.

"Just one moment, Miss Jones," Holmes said. "Were you at the circus with the rest of the staff?"

"No," she answered, feverishly tugging at her gloves and dropping them into a basket beside the stand. "I care nothing for such foolish exhibitions. I was just coming back from window shopping in the village when I saw Doctor Smith and he said – it is too horrible! Murder! Oh God, I must go to the little ones. I know they are terrified."

Lawrence motioned for her to ascend the stairs. Holmes watched her go before turning back to our companion.

"I am loathe to leave a young lady unguarded with a vicious killer on the loose. Surely Smith's telegram will retrieve the father of the house in a timely manner. Inspector, if you will trust me to handle an aspect of this investigation, I believe we may make significant progress."

"You are asking me to stay here?"

"The sooner questions are put to Dr. Donner, the better. And he may be more honest if you conduct the interview alone."

A savage smile twisted the man's lips. "I see your point. Yes, please – your reputation proceeds you, Mr. Holmes. I will wait for Donner and see if Miss Jones has anything to add. She may have observed something of value."

He climbed the steps in the lady's wake. I started for the door, assuming our next destination would be the circus at Castle Cignet. I was several steps down the drive before I realized I was alone. I trotted back to find Holmes returning the lady's hat to the curved wooden holder.

"A lovely chapeau, perfect for summer," he said, with a wink. "You have been married, yet know nothing about fashion? For shame, Watson. You should have been a more observant husband."

Much to my astonishment, Holmes didn't go to the circus grounds, but instead chose to wander about the handful of shops surrounding Castle

Cignet. I soon garnered that it was a place catering to tourists and idlers. The stores sold supplies for anglers, along with stout boots and sturdy walking sticks for those wandering amid the lovely, rolling hills. Holmes gave a short sigh of appreciation and pointed toward a little theatrical venue, with advertisements for a variety of amusements pasted to its walls and windows. Within minutes, we were being ushered into the manager's office. The fellow – Augustus T. Philomean according to his ornate nameplate – greeted my friend with a flourish.

"Your name isn't unknown to us! Indeed, even in this little corner of England, the flame of fame for the great detective burns bright! Pray, sir, how can I help you? Can I convince you to give some lectures on your adventures? You would draw quite the crowd, even in the slowest of seasons, I assure you."

"My blushes, sir," Holmes said, with a short bow. "I fear I have nothing so dramatic in mind. I am merely here to ask you a question: Did you once have, among your costumes, a suit for a clown? One that is yellow-and-orange in color, accessorized by a blue wig, straw hat, and rubber nose."

The sudden change in the blustering man was greater than anything ever achieved on a melodrama's stage. He went white and dropped roughly into his chair.

"Sir . . . you must be clairvoyant! To know it was gone! Can you tell me who stole it? While the costume itself wasn't valuable, its theft caused some embarrassment, and I would very much like to get my fists on the miscreant who made off with it!"

"When did it vanish?" Holmes asked.

"It was three weeks ago. We were giving a series of pantomimes. One night, right in the middle of the show, a cry of fire rang out. Well, you can imagine the chaos, especially as the audience was filled with women and children! The patrons and the actors all ran out into the street, and it took us half-an-hour to determine it had been a false alarm. We coaxed those who had remained back inside, but when Alex Randall, who played the clown in the final act, went to his dressing room, he found that his entire outfit had disappeared! We fortunately had another suit, but it was far too short and uncomfortably tight, and what was supposed to be a dramatic scene was transformed into a comedy of errors when Randall split his pants. I assure you it wasn't amusing at all."

"Forgive my friend," Holmes said, elbowing me to stop my chuckles. "I am certain it was humiliating to your company. Did you report the theft?"

"It was hardly a matter worth bothering Inspector Lawrence over. Still, the thief made off with everything – the paint, the wig, the nose – all

263

except the shoes. I would very much like the satisfaction of giving that villain a good thrashing."

"Watson, are you as footsore as I am?" Holmes asked, as we emerged from the little theater. "If so, let us hire a horse and vehicle and enjoy the countryside in comfort."

"We aren't going to the circus?"

"I have little interest in ringmasters or tightrope walkers today," Holmes replied. "And I feel more akin to the tiger than his trainer. Let us see if we can find transportation."

But in this, Sherlock Holmes was to be disappointed, for the proprietor of the livery stable gave us a sharp look and shook his head. My friend leaned on his cane.

"You don't have a horse and trap to let? I see several likely candidates in these stables."

"Not to you gents. Not today."

Holmes frowned. "May I ask what motivates your sharpness, sir? I assure you that I have funds for the hire, and will pay you handsomely, even for your poorest nag."

The man looked up with a surly expression. "I'll wait 'til Dolley comes home with her dogcart before I lease another horse to any stranger, especially two toffs from London! I rented Dolley a week ago, and she's been due back for five days. Have I seen her? No! I should never have rented to such a short, ill-kempt man as he was. I sensed something queer about him, but the ready silver turned my head, and I regret it. Dolley was my best mare, and now I have lost her."

"Can you describe the man?"

"Red hair and great ginger beard, dark glasses, all bundled in a coat when I was drenched in sweat that afternoon. Disgusting warts upon his brow. He gave his name as Jake Thomas, but I know nothing more about him."

"You shall hardly earn a living if you refuse to hire to tourists," Holmes said with a sneer. "But we shall watch for Dolley. Have you offered a reward for her? Only five pounds? She mustn't be as valuable to you as – Very well, we know when we aren't welcome. Come along, Watson."

"Let us see if we can find more accommodating individuals," Holmes said, as we walked away from the stable. "This little shop looks promising."

I shook my head in bafflement as Holmes walked inside. The business was a curious mix of merchandise, from books and tin toys to ladies' fans and ceramic curios. Hand-tinted prints of Castle Cignet hung along the walls, and numerous shelves were lined with plates bearing images of local landmarks. The air smelled sweet, and I realized that the back of the store was covered in flowers. A plump little lady, apple-cheeked and snowy-haired, with an apron around her waist, stood behind a counter.

"Good afternoon, gentlemen. Can I assist you in any way?"

Holmes could radiate charm when he chose. Never had he been more ingratiating.

"Yes, Madame – I am in hopes of proposing marriage to a very special lady this evening. Her favorite flower is the humble daisy. A bouquet of them, in a lovely wicker basket, should guarantee my success. Can you help me in my quest?"

Five minutes later, we were walking back toward the churchyard, Holmes swinging the basket and its contents rather carelessly.

"How dastardly of that unknown French lady in the widow's weeds to have purchased all the daisies in stock," Holmes grumbled. "My dear Irene shall never agree to be my wife when I present her with these much inferior roses!"

"I think you may be in error this time."

"I am never in error about *The Woman*."

"I meant, about the French lady in the veil, that the proprietress described. Clearly, you suspect her of being the murderous clown, as well as the ginger bearded man at the stable – but she cannot be he."

"And why not?"

"The flowers we saw in the basket weren't wilted. They appeared to be fresh. Yet the shopkeeper said the last of the daisies were sold a week ago."

"Watson, did you ever bring flowers to your spouse?"

"Of course I did. I am the soul of romance!"

"But not of observation. If properly watered and attended, daisies will remain lovely for well over a week. Perhaps such endurance wasn't the origin of the saying 'as fresh as a daisy', but it certainly fits."

"There is another obstacle," I countered. "The individual's height. The lady was described as quite tall, but man as very short. Did you notice the stable owner's gesture, where he held his hand as he described the fellow? The man must have been unusually small in stature."

Holmes smiled. "Of all the tricks of disguise, altering height is among the most difficult, especially for a man. I have some experience in that regard. However – Ah! We have reached the crossroads, and I perceive a farmer's wagon approaching. Let us see if this gentleman might be useful to our quest."

The rather strange afternoon continued with a jarring, rough ride in the back of the farmer's cart, while a flea-bitten, sad-eyed hound sat between us. The driver was frustratingly taciturn, answering every question with a grunt, until Holmes mentioned the subject of farmsteads to let.

"Right down that path is an old cottage and a barn. No one lives there, roof's fallen in, pasture is poor."

"Why, it sounds like a perfect spot for my retirement. We shall disembark and view it."

The farmer gave us a hard, silent look that eloquently expressed his contempt for city dwellers, and Holmes led the way toward the tumbledown house at a brisk pace. He directed my attention to ruts in the dirt, as well as the tracks of hooves.

"One shoe appears loose. Let us hope we aren't too late to help poor Dolley."

"Good Heavens! How did you know a hideout would be here?"

"Because the evidence suggests it. Think, Watson – does it stand to reason that some three decades after the tragedy at the Richland Circus, a murderer would come, in a clown costume, to slay a woman who had been a mere child at the time? Or that, if such was his goal, he wouldn't have likewise killed her offspring while he had the chance, and thus completed his mission of revenge? No, our killer knew exactly when Mrs. Donner would be alone, the very hour when the lady's staff and spouse would be away. Therefore, our villain is a local, familiar with the family and its routines, as well as the timing of circus's arrival, an event which could be used to cast suspicion on others."

We reached the dwelling. The cottage door was off its hinges, and a quick perusal confirmed that the interior hadn't been entered except, perhaps, by wandering wildlife. Holmes continued his discussion as we moved to inspect the barn.

"A clown suit and makeup aren't as simple to remove as a cloak or wig or spectacles. I must confess, it is a cunning disguise, for when we see a clown, we see an *idea*, not a human being. Let us imagine the scenario from the killer's perspective. He must dress and paint his face, and he must have somewhere to hide the horse and cart that he will use for his escape. What better place than an abandoned property where – Hello, girl! Your master will be most grateful for your discovery."

A white mare with brown spots on her rump stood in a stall. Nearby was the dogcart, and beside it a crumpled pile of brightly colored fabric. I lifted the suit from the straw, finding a hat, blue wig, and rubber false nose beneath it.

"Here is the clown's vanity," Holmes said, gesturing toward a bucket of water, several greasy towels, and a broken mirror propped against a wall. "It was essential that his face be covered adequately, but also that the makeup – I see the kit tossed to that corner – be spotlessly removed. I can speak to the difficulty of doing such in a well-lit green room. If the crime weren't so hideous, so unthinkable, I might profess an admiration for the killer's ingenuity." Holmes turned and walked to the horse, which eagerly thrust its nose toward the basket of roses. "Let us reward our equine friend by finding him some fresh water, untainted by greasepaint, and return to the Donner household."

"Surely Mr. Donner is home by now."

"I hope so. I have several inquiries to put before him."

We reached the yellow house just at four, and I was relieved to see the family's staff had been summoned back to their duties. A stable lad took charge of the horse and vehicle, with Holmes insisting that the spirited little mare receive a double bag of oats and a careful brushing, for she appeared neglected and malnourished. Holmes leaned down and whispered to me.

"The middle window on the upper floor. Look quickly."

I raised my head but saw only a curtain being snatched closed. Holmes led the way through the door, and a butler – grim-faced and red-eyed from weeping – guided us to the doctor's study, where Inspector Lawrence waited with the widower. Donner was clearly agitated, his voice loud and rough as we entered.

"I think you are a cold and cruel man, to accuse me of killing my wife! I have a dozen witnesses – among them, Joe Farleigh, who I believe is your cousin – who will testify that I have been in Rosthwaite since eight this morning. I can give you the list of my patients, and I was performing a tonsillectomy when the terrible news was brought to me. I would like to see your hand hold steady when such a – Who are these men? What is this!"

The last cry was uttered as Holmes slammed the basket, now laden with the clown suit and wig, onto Donner's desk. Lawrence gasped, eagerly pulling the gaudy costume free.

"My God! Is it the murderer's attire?"

"I have every reason to believe it is. Doctor Donner, my name is Sherlock Holmes, and this is my associate, Doctor John Watson. I believe you have heard of us. These are the relics of the individual who murdered your wife."

"I . . . I have never seen these things." Donner looked to the policeman in a panic. "Lawrence, I swear, I have never laid eyes on them."

267

"I don't believe you!" the local inspector snapped. Holmes put a hand on his arm.

"Hold your outrage, for our physician may speak a literal truth. He may never have viewed this disguise. However, if you can collect a warrant, I suspect you may find another disguise – either here, or more likely, in his surgery at Rosthwaite – a large coat, a ginger wig and beard, as well as putty and makeup to feign the shape of hideous warts."

"You lie!" the man shouted, springing to his feet. Holmes and I exchanged a quick glance. The top of Donner's head would barely have met my chin. He was an exceptionally short individual.

"Love," Holmes said cooly, "is a wonderful, yet terrible thing. For it, a beast of a man may be tamed . . . or the most delicate of females may lose her sanity and her soul. Tell me, Donner, what did you promise your *inamorata*? Was it marriage within a year? A new home, extensive travels abroad? And what did you intend to do with your children? Would you send them away to school? To other relations – or was there a dollop of poison waiting in their innocent cups?"

Donner's face was ashen. He stumbled and fell sideways into his chair. His jaw worked, but no sound emerged. Holmes folded his arms.

"In my experience, any man who regularly betrays his wife also has no compunction about murdering her, for she has become an inconvenience to him. If she holds the key to wealth, there is even less reason to stay the murderous blow." Holmes nodded toward the bundle of fabric. "Such a man may also be depraved and cruel enough to convince his lover to do the deadly business while he cowers within the safety of an alibi."

"But who – ?" Lawrence began. Holmes snapped an answer before the question was complete.

"The governess, Miss Jones. A lovely young woman who meets all the qualifications for our assassin: Intimate knowledge of the family and its routines, an awareness of how a circus figured into Mrs. Donner's past, and the lady's fondness for clowns. Miss Jones knew that her victim wouldn't scream – As many women might! – if she found a clown, bearing a basket of daisies standing upon her doorstep. Miss Jones also knew that with her unusual height, in such attire she would be perceived as a man, for who thinks of a woman in that role? Even 'female' clowns in gaudy dresses are always portrayed by men. She knew there was a chance the children might see her, so she made certain to appear as something they only describe, but not identify. The basket and flowers not only were alluring to Mrs. Donner, but provided a hiding place for the gun. Miss Jones was careful to purchase the flowers ahead of time, in the guise of a

French widow, her face covered by a veil. I presume Miss Jones came highly recommended for her command of languages, *non*?"

"Please," Donner murmured. "This cannot be true. I thought she was a good woman! Lawrence, you must believe me – I knew nothing of this! Nothing!"

The inspector looked from the physician to my friend. Holmes's gaze had never been colder.

"Mr. Holmes, perhaps – "

"Miss Jones could don widow's weeds and a veil to purchase the basket and flowers anonymously. She could steal the clown's attire from the theater by the simple expedient of emptying the dressing rooms with a shriek of '*Fire!*' It was a performance for the young folks. Someone at the box office will recall her attending with Mrs. Donner and the children. But there was one aspect of the preparation she couldn't accomplish. For that, she required her lover's assistance."

"Lawrence, I swear – none of this is true! I loved my wife!" Donner shouted. Holmes held out one hand, silencing him.

"Miss Jones feared to acquire the horse and cart. It is, one admits, rather a job for a man. Therefore, the role you had to play, Doctor, was that of a stranger hiring a horse and dogcart, once you had located a suitably deserted barn to hide them. Perhaps you did so a week ago to allow Miss Jones some time to practice her driving – we will need to interview the staff as to when the governess took 'long walks' by herself. As the mare wasn't entirely starved, I also suspect you also saw to the horse's care in the mornings or evening, when you were in transit to your surgery. Today, you left early, and made sure to have a full schedule of patients, to establish an alibi. Miss Jones, meanwhile, had been given a day off with the rest of the staff. She struck out on a hearty constitutional, made her way to the barn, donned her attire, and returned to the house to murder your poor wife. She hoped that if anyone should see her on the road, they would recall the circus was in town, and think no more of it."

"And Eddie nearly caught her," Lawrence said.

"She had surely not planned on that possibility. It was only good fortune that she outpaced him, and he chose the wrong fork in the road."

"You . . . you can prove nothing against Miss Jones," Donner muttered. "This is wild nonsense! There are no witnesses except . . . mere children. No jury would believe it."

"Something I have noted in my years of studying crime," Holmes continued dryly, with the air of a rather bored professor, "is that a criminal usually manages to leave some trace of himself in the place where he commits his misdeed. Inspector Lawrence, within this handkerchief are several unusual blue fibers, which I think you will find are a perfect match for the bright cerulean clown wig. I retrieved them from Miss Jones's hat, which I noticed is still hanging in the hall. You will no doubt find more blue fibers within that piece of headgear, for Miss Jones's lengthy tresses came undone while she was wearing the wig, capturing fibers and later mingling real and artificial hairs in the lining of her bonnet. You will also note the lady's glove, which I took the privilege of confiscating from a hallway basket where it was flung. Observe the powder stains upon it. Unless Miss Jones enjoys target practice, I can think of no reason why powder residue should be there, unless she wore this glove while committing the crime. You might also examine her face – greasepaint can be an irritant to such a peaches-and-cream complexion as hers, and I couldn't help but see how raw and rough her skin appeared when she returned, breathless, to this home. The hem of her frock was also dirty, and I suspect her boots still carry mud, straw, and manure from the barn. In fact, there is only one more question remaining, which is – "

"Holmes!" Lawrence shouted. The door behind my friend had opened, and Miss Jones stood in the threshold. She had clearly heard every word my friend had spoken, for her lips quivered, tears streamed down her face, and she held a pistol in her right hand. I grabbed Holmes's arm, snatching him back, but the lady turned toward the desk, aiming her weapon at Donner.

"Tell these men the truth," she said. "Tell them what you told me . . . How easy it would be. How we could place the blame for Celeste's murder on some shadow of her past. Tell them how you lured me, with the promise that the children loved me, and would accept me as their stepmother. Tell them, Edgar!"

The man slumped down in his chair. He shook his head frantically.

"You are . . . *insane*. I never said those things or did anything to hurt Celeste."

"Tell the truth, please," girl whispered, her voice wavering. "Did you ever love me?"

Donner huffed. "No, you stupid wench. *Never*."

The explosion was deafening in the chamber. Donner kicked back in reaction, falling from his chair, blood spurting from his shoulder. Holmes gave a warning cry, but before he could pounce, the poor woman reversed the gun's muzzle, pressing it to her temple. The second shot was muffled and instantly fatal, and the governess collapsed in a pile of skirts. The butler and a maid flew to the door, but Holmes waved them off, ordering them to see to the children. With Lawrence's help, I levered Donner onto his own examination table, and began the process of probing the wound and assessing the damage. I quickly determined that his life wasn't endangered, and injected morphine as a prelude to removing the bullet.

When I finished my task, I found Holmes still kneeling by the dead girl's side.

"Holmes," I said, as gently as I could, "what was your final question?"

"Only this: How did the lady acquire the gun?" He gestured clumsily toward the nearest wall, where several military commendations were framed. "This is an army revolver, and I see that Donner served with distinction in the colonies. The riddle is solved."

Holmes was clearly in no mood to continue our holiday. He returned to our cottage in a black study, and the next morning I judged that it would be better to return to London. We journeyed to the train station at Castle Cignet, and I waited with our bags while Holmes attended to the tickets.

"Doctor Watson?"

I turned, startled at the soft voice that had spoken my name. Master Eddie Donner stood beside me. He was very properly dressed, with a black armband around his jacket. He snatched off his cap and dipped his head.

"I wished to offer my thanks, sir – to you and Mr. Holmes. Inspector Lawrence sat down with me last night, and explained what had happened to Mother and Miss Jones, and why he and his men were taking Father off to jail. The inspector has sent word to our great-aunt to come and care for us, and she will be here by this afternoon." The lad swallowed tightly. "Sir, do . . . do you think Father will hang?"

I glanced sideways. Holmes was still waiting at the window. I sought to answer the question as he would.

"You must trust the Queen's Justice. It is fair and right and can be merciful."

Eddie nodded solemnly. "We would never have known, if not for you and Mr. Holmes. I think the inspector would have blamed someone from the circus, and the mystery would have been much the same as with our grandfather." He coughed, then forced himself to speak. I could tell how much the words pained him to utter. "Sir . . . please be honest with me. Is my father a wicked man?"

Holmes was just now collecting the tickets. I leaned forward and put my hand on Eddie's shoulder.

"Only God can know your father's heart. And for now, you must be the protector and guide for your brother and sisters. They will need you to be strong and kind – just as your mother was."

A slight smile tugged at the boy's lips. "Mother loved us so much, and she never said a hard word to Father. I don't understand how this could happen . . . but maybe, when I am older, I will understand it? Are these things clearer, when we are grown?"

In truth, I didn't know how to answer, but I suspect that I nodded, for the lad seemed relieved, and returned his cap to his head.

"Will you give Mr. Holmes my thanks? As terrible as it is to know the truth, sir, I think being ignorant would have been harder on us."

I assured him I would express his gratitude, and he walked away. Not ten seconds later, Holmes joined me, and I relayed the conversation. My friend studied the tickets in his hands.

"I considered not revealing what I knew. When I realized who was involved – was certain that the father was implicated with the governess – there was a moment when I asked myself: Would it be better for the children to be unaware? But I couldn't . . . I feared for their safety. They couldn't be left in the care of vicious killers. Truth prevails, Watson, but at what cost?" He flung the tickets onto the bench beside me. "Sometimes I wish our Creator had made me dull or incompetent, or even stupid."

"Holmes," I said, as I retrieved the tickets, "your gifts aren't a random offering from Heaven. You are a vain man, I know, but you have just cause to be. I will give you the same advice I gave the lad: You must accept what is, serve and protect those who are weaker, and wait for God, in his good time, to reveal the plan behind your singular powers. You were never promised ease or delight in your work, only purpose."

Silence hung like a heavy curtain between us. I looked up to find my friend staring off into the distance. Emotion was a foreign thing to Sherlock Holmes, but for just an instant, I thought his eyes were glistening, and I detected a slight wobble in the set of his chin.

"Watson," he said softly, "your original diagnosis was a sound one, which I ignore at my peril. I confess I haven't followed your prescribed treatment as I should. Give me the tickets and I will exchange them. How would a few restful days in the Scottish Highlands sound?"

The Killing of
Lady Grace Everley
by Paul Nash

F ew Englishmen will, I think, be able to read the title which I have given to this memoir without recalling the events it describes, and wondering at the use of the word "killing" for a death which was generally believed, at the time, to have been accidental. The reader will readily understand that I hesitate to bring the details of Holmes's involvement with the case before the public. There was hardly a better-known name in all England, or indeed the civilized world, than that of Lady Grace Everley. Her youth, beauty and sudden death seemed to mark a generation and are spoken of still today. (I am writing this in the year 1923, more than twenty-five years after the events I am about to describe.)

The case involved two of the foremost families of the land. But there are other reasons, which the reader will come to understand, why I hesitate even now to commit the story to paper. No account of the cases undertaken by Holmes would be complete without it, however, and, though it could hardly be called a triumph for Holmes's powers of deductive reasoning, he did identify the killers, albeit without any hope of bringing them to justice. I have placed this story under an embargo of fifty years, to protect the reputations of those involved. [1] Even at that distance of time it is unlikely that Lady Grace's name and the events of August 1897 will have been entirely forgotten. But it may help the reader if I summarise the story at the outset.

The most opulent and fashionable marriage of the year 1881 was that of Lady Grace, only daughter of the Sixth Earl of Everley, to Henry, Viscount Penarth, eldest son of the Duke and Duchess of Lowther and heir to the great Pennington estate. The wedding fascinated the public and seemed to be pictured and described in every newspaper and magazine across Europe and America. The youth and beauty of the bride, the wealth and prospects of the groom, the splendour of the ceremony and the ostentation of the ring were all remarked upon in the public prints. Lady Grace was immediately the darling of the common man, and behaved, in some respects, quite unlike a member of the aristocracy. She spoke often to journalists – who were more than happy to use her words and stories – and made many appearances in support of charitable and public works. Indeed, she seemed to relish the fame which marriage had brought her, and courted the gentlemen of the press almost as assiduously as she had once,

273

it seemed, been courted by Viscount Penarth. What she did not relish, it soon emerged, was the Viscount. There was talk of "another woman", and of a growing coldness and indifference upon his Lordship's part. The press, as ever, were keen to hear of the Lady's troubles and to report them to the eager ears and eyes of her followers.

She bore Penarth two sons, the first with almost indecent speed after their wedding. But within four years, the papers were reporting that the marriage was over in all but name. Throughout this period, Penarth and his parents maintained an outward dignity and wouldn't speak directly to the reporters who pursued them whenever they were in town, and who went so far, on occasion, as to invade the grounds at Pennington. However, stories appeared in the papers about Penarth's dissatisfaction with his wife, stories emanating indirectly from his Lordship, through friends and noble relations who had spoken with journalists. Penarth too, it appeared, believed his spouse hadn't been faithful to him or fully committed to their marriage.

For some years this unhappy state continued. The Parnell divorce scandal of 1890 did nothing to encourage the couple to seek a formal dissolution of their union, and neither was willing to admit fault. However, in 1894, knowing that her son wished to marry a lady with whom he had a long-standing connection, the Duchess of Lowther engineered a divorce on the grounds of Lady Grace's infidelity, which the Lady did not contest. A young Major in the Guards was named as co-respondent, but it was widely rumoured that he was a willing pawn in the Duchess's game and had not, in fact, been the Lady's lover.

After the divorce, Lady Grace made some seemingly half-hearted attempts to escape her former life of fame. However, the public affection for her, and the interest of journalists, could not easily be quelled, and hardly a week went by without her name and face appearing in one newspaper or another. The appearance of photographs in the papers at this period, printed directly and not reproduced from wood-engravings as heretofore, made her face and figure all the more familiar to the public and, it was said, many of those who couldn't read would yet recognize the word *"Grace"* and associate it with her countenance, so that they would spend their pennies on magazines and papers on the strength of her name and portrait alone. Lestrade told us that when they arrested Hurst, the Limehouse killer, in ninety-three, they found the walls of his room covered with pictures of Lady Grace, cut carefully from the pages of *The Illustrated London News*, though Hurst could neither read nor write and signed his name with a crude mark.

It was into this atmosphere of fascination and devotion that the shocking news of Lady Grace's death intruded in August 1897. The grief of the common man could hardly have been greater had our beloved sovereign herself passed away. Indeed, similar images of sorrow weren't seen in London until the death of Victoria four years later. The details of Lady Grace's death were quickly published. She and a young Indian gentleman, Edward Singh, had been racing along Whitehall together in a four-wheeler in an attempt to elude journalists who were pursuing them in four or five hansom cabs. At the end of the road, the four-wheeler passed into Trafalgar Square and the driver attempted to turn into the Strand, but took the corner too quickly so that the cab overturned into the square and collided with the pedestal of a fountain. Lady Grace died instantly of a broken neck and Singh shortly afterwards of internal bleeding. The driver of the clarence cab, and his horse, also died in the collision.

At first the crash was regarded as a mere accident. But then rumours began to circulate about the driver, a man named Wilfred Davie. He had been employed as an ostler by Edward Singh's father, the wealthy merchant Sir William Singh, but had formerly been in service with the Duchess of Lowther. Davie was said to have been intoxicated with strong liquor on the day of the crash, and many blamed him for the loss of the young noblewoman. Then it was pointed out that he would hardly have been driving with such fury had the reporters from several daily newspapers not been pursuing Lady Grace and her companion on the scent of a story, and therefore the journalists were to blame. This was a notion which did not, for obvious reasons, find favour in the columns of the newspapers. What they delighted in reporting, however, were rumours of a secret engagement between Lady Grace and Edward Singh, a story both romantic and shocking. The suggestion that a high-born Englishwoman might wish to marry a handsome Indian was, in some quarters, regarded with the greatest scorn. But the rumours persisted and the common man and woman found the idea intoxicating.

Sherlock Holmes showed little interest in the life and death of Lady Grace until one afternoon in the high summer of 1898, almost a year after the accident in which she had died, when there was a sharp ring upon the doorbell. After a few moments the page brought up the card of Sir William Singh and, in a few moments more, the Indian plutocrat stood before us. He was a short man, rather stout, with thick, dark hair and immaculate dress. A diamond pin glittered in his tie and his small hands were heavy with rings. He had only one attendant, a fair-haired Englishman even smaller than himself who Singh introduced as his secretary, Fanning.

"My dear Mr. Holmes," said Singh, shaking the detective's hand is if they were old friends. "I hope you will forgive this intrusion. You are, I think, the only man in the world who can help me."

"Really?" said Holmes.

"You were recommended to me by Sir James Mann-Ingleby. He told me how you had solved the case of his missing heir, and terrier, when the official detectives had given up the chase."

"It was a trifling matter," said Holmes, "but I was pleased to bring it to a satisfactory conclusion."

"You know my name, of course?" asked Singh. Holmes, who knew with perfect certainty the name of our visitor, and a great deal more about him besides, shook his head with a look of sadness.

"It seems familiar," said he, "though I regret I cannot quite – "

"No matter," said Singh with a great show of good cheer. "You have no doubt heard of Lady Grace Everley?" Holmes nodded. "Good. Her most unfortunate accident last year also robbed me of my eldest son, you know, and I have come to believe that the collision in which they died was not, after all, an accident."

"I see," said Holmes. "Do you have any evidence for that belief?"

"Nothing solid, sir. Only rumours and suspicions. The police say they have investigated the business and are satisfied that the carriage and driver weren't interfered with. But I am not so easily satisfied, Mr. Holmes, and want you to find the evidence I need to oblige them to re-open the case. I am quite convinced that my son and his fiancée were murdered."

"Fiancée, you say? The two were betrothed then?"

"Yes, sir, upon my oath, though they hadn't made any public announcement of the match. But I knew and, what is more, the Lady's sons knew. They had told Viscount Penarth and he had told the Duke and Duchess of Lowther."

"Am I to take it, then, that you believe the Duke and Duchess responsible for your son's death, and that of their former daughter-in-law."

"They told me you were clever, sir, and thank God you have understood my meaning at once. It is my belief that the Duke and Duchess, especially the Duchess, were behind the carriage accident. Think of the scandal, sir, the shame which they already perceived to have been brought upon their son's name and family by the divorce of ninety-four. How much deeper would have grown their sense of offended dignity when the engagement was announced between the woman who had humiliated Penarth and the son of a humble merchant from one of Her Majesty's colonial outposts. Grace was a talkative woman, Mr. Holmes, forever speaking to reporters about her former husband and his parents and, as they saw it, bringing ignominy on the Lowther name. They wanted to silence her before she could say any more and contrived her death."

"I see. Pray, how did they engineer an accident in so public a place as Trafalgar Square?"

"That is for you to find out," said Singh. "Perhaps the carriage was tampered with. Perhaps the driver, Mr. Davie, was bribed, or drugged, or simply ordered to crash by the Duchess – he had been her loyal servant, after all. Perhaps one or more of the journalists in pursuit, or the cab-drivers, had been paid to arrange a crash. Perhaps some other method, or combination of methods, was employed. As I say, Mr. Holmes, the details are for you to ascertain. If you can produce the evidence, sir, you will not find me ungenerous."

"I will expect the same remuneration for my efforts, Mr. Singh, whatever the outcome of my investigation."

"Then you will take my case?"

"Well," said Holmes, "I will see what may be done. But I warn you that the work will not be easy, and the chances of success only indifferent. Where great families are involved, there is great difficulty, and no small expense."

"I will write you a cheque for five-hundred pounds this minute. Fanning, my cheque-book."

We watched, I in amazement, Holmes in amusement, as the little man made a great play of opening his cheque-book and laying it upon the desk, taking out a gold pen and writing, in an ornate hand, a draft for the sum he had mentioned, made out to "*S. Holmes, Esq.*". He tore out the cheque, blotted it and handed it over.

"Thank you," said Holmes, placing the cheque between the pages of his pocket-book.

"There is a like sum for you, and more, upon the conclusion of your investigation," said Singh.

Holmes nodded. "There are a few trifling questions I would like to ask before I begin," he said.

"Of course."

"Do you have any concrete evidence of the engagement between your son and Lady Grace?"

"Only my word."

"No letters, or anything of that sort?"

"I am afraid not."

"Do you know anything of this man Davie, who was driving the four-wheeler?"

"He was in my employ for a year or more before he died. But I have a great many staff and servants, and cannot be expected to know them all. I can tell you that Davie was recommended to me in ninety-six by Lady Grace, who had first encountered him when he was among the Duchess's staff. I gave him a job as a groom and driver. But Grace knew him much better than I, and I think she trusted him completely. I am afraid I do not share her confidence, and believe him to have been, all the while, a loyal servant of the Duchess. It has even been suggested to me that he was a spy, sending regular reports of Lady Grace's movements and liaisons back to the Duchess, so that she might put about rumours and blacken the Lady's name. That may, or may not, be the case. I know that he had the reputation of an excellent horseman, and was a fit, strong man, so that Lady Grace felt always protected in his company. More I do not know."

"Pray, what was your son's opinion of Mr. Davie?"

"He too regarded him as a faithful servant. He was an unworldly, trusting boy, Mr. Holmes, and had no reason to suspect him."

"I see. I do have several other cases on hand at the moment, but I will see what might be done, and hope to have something for you soon."

"How soon?"

"Shall we say this time next week?"

"Monday morning would suit me better."

"But not me. Please be so kind as to call upon me on Wednesday afternoon, at three, and I will give you my report."

Holmes wasn't exaggerating his heavy load. I was aware of at least four cases he had on hand at that moment – the mystery of the Two Coptic Patriarchs, the adventure of Hilton Cubitt and the Dancing Men (of which I have already published an imperfect account), the case of the Seven Black Cats (which I hope to document one day), and a case of which I never learned the full details, referred to by Holmes only as that "abominable Sarah Thomas business". [2]

Over the next few days, Holmes took me into his confidence only so far as to ask me to accompany him to a house in Pimlico where he hoped, but failed, to find one of the Seven Black Cats. However, it was clear that he was very busy. On three separate occasions he went out in disguise, twice as a Cockney groom, and once, rather to my surprise, as a uniformed police constable. He had a number of visitors too, including a particularly handsome young woman of the middle class who spoke no more than a few words to him, but handed over a manilla envelope stuffed with manuscripts. In quiet moments he took out and examined the drawing of the dancing men which had been given to him by Hilton Cubitt.

On Sunday evening, after a day spent reading the London papers of the previous week, which we had both neglected while occupied with other matters, we were disturbed by a loud ring at the doorbell. Our page wasn't on duty at that hour so it was a stone-faced Mrs. Hudson who brought up the card of Sir Nicholas Wedgwood of Carlton House Terrace. The gentleman himself was soon in our presence. He was a tall man of around fifty, with a slight stoop and a face that looked as if it had never known laughter. He shook Holmes's hand with cold dignity.

"Who is this person?" asked our visitor, indicating me.

"You are clearly not a reader of *The Strand*," replied my friend, "or you would know that this gentleman is my friend and chronicler, Dr. John Watson. You may speak before him as you would before me. Pray, how can I help you?"

"I am secretary to his Grace the Duke of Lowther," said our visitor. "It has come to the Duke's attention that you have been making certain enquiries about his household. I am here to advise you to cease those enquiries at once."

"Are you? Well, well, I am impressed that the Duke should know that I have been looking into his affairs. Usually, when a man is dogged by Sherlock Holmes, he sees and hears nothing of his pursuer. Pray, tell me how his Lordship came to know of my interest?"

"That is simple enough. That scoundrel William Singh has told his Grace, to his face, that he has commissioned you to find evidence against him."

"Well, that explains all," said Holmes.

"If you persist in your enquiries, Mr. Holmes, it will mean only difficulty and danger for you. There can be no safety, no comfort, for he who opposes the Duke. Give it up, sir, give it up at once."

"You surprise me, Mr. Wedgwood. It is usually the hardest crooks, or their agents, who stand upon my hearthrug and issue such threats. But here you are, a messenger of one of the highest in the land, and, supposedly, a gentleman yourself, threatening Sherlock Holmes, like a common criminal. Let me assure you, Mr. Wedgwood, that I have heard many such warnings. Yet, here I stand, while the men who threatened me lie beneath the soil or linger in Her Majesty's prisons. If they couldn't cow me, is it likely that you will do so?"

"You would be wise to heed my warning."

"And you would be wise to heed mine: Return to your master, and your mistress, and tell them that Sherlock Holmes will not be warned off. If they have secrets, let them tremble. If they are guilty, let them prepare to be punished."

"You must not believe William Singh," said our visitor emphatically. "He is a crooked man, and a man half-mad with grief at the death of his son. He has stirred up a great deal of trouble for her Grace, and if you help him, you will be aiding an alien against the finest family in England."

"Not the finest, surely?"

Wedgwood cleared his throat. "I should have said one of the finest families."

"Well, that rather depends upon one's definition of fineness," said Holmes. "I am sure you are a very busy man, Mr. Wedgwood, and have other duties to attend to, and perhaps other innocent gentlemen to threaten. I too, in my modest way, have much to do and must be about my business. I bid you good day."

"Do not forget my words," said Wedgwood.

"And do you remember mine," replied Holmes, "and be sure to transmit them to their Graces."

The secretary bowed stiffly and withdrew. The encounter seemed to put Holmes in one of his most light-hearted moods. He hummed to himself for the rest of the evening, as he carefully clipped certain columns from the papers for insertion into his scrapbooks. Before retiring he remarked, "Well, Watson. If the Duke and Duchess have set their bulldog on me, I must be on the right trail indeed, or, at least, upon a trail they do not care to have followed. Let us see what tomorrow may bring."

He was not to be disappointed. The next morning, while we sat at breakfast, a strangely-shaped packet was delivered.

"Posted in the Whitechapel Road," Holmes remarked, looking at the postmark. "Addressed in pencil in a chaotic hand. Hmm. What is this? How very singular!"

He had slit the paper wrapping with the butter-knife and drawn out a long, thin cardboard box. It was a little over a foot in length, but very narrow and shallow. It was just the sort of box in which the conductor of an orchestra might have stored his favourite baton. Holmes removed the lid and we peered inside. Resting upon a bed of cotton-wool was a most curious object. It was a smooth shaft of wood, nearly a foot long and very fine and delicate. At one end was a small tuft of blue-green feathers and the other was sharpened to a point. Holmes lifted the object and examined it with his glass. Lying beneath it on the cotton wool was a small, rough piece of folded paper. Holmes put the shaft aside and unfolded the paper. It bore a message, crudely-written with the same pencil used to address the envelope, which ran in this way:

Mr. Homes

If you wants to no what appened to Lady Grace, look no furver than the inclosd. I was there wery soon after she died, and pluckd this from the haunch of the pour horse.

A frend to her Ladyship

"What is that?" I asked, indicating the wooden shaft.

"If I am not mistaken," said Holmes, "it is a dart, of the sort fired from a blow-pipe."

"Like those we saw in the Jonathan Small case? But this is much longer."

"I believe this to be one of those used by the Dayaks of central Borneo. The darts are dipped in poison extracted from a frog, and can kill or paralyse a large animal within a few seconds. But this one," he picked it up again and examined the point, "has not been poisoned. However, we might easily imagine the effect of the point alone, if fired into the flesh of a horse already in a state of excitement. Could this have been the cause of the accident?"

"It seems possible," I said.

"Yet there are many objections. And there is something else in this box."

"You mean the cotton wool?"

"No. I mean the odour."

He held the open box out to me and I sniffed gingerly at it. There was a tangible scent, which I couldn't place. It was a pleasant, sweet, and earthy smell.

"What is it?"

"Ambergrease,"[3] said Holmes. "Now, what common 'friend' to her Ladyship, who writes such a poor letter, would have knowledge of such a perfume? Could the box have come from a perfumier? It is perfectly anonymous . . . ." He placed the box, and its singular enclosures, upon the breakfast table and relapsed into thought.

He sat like this for the better part of an hour, then rose without a word, donned his summer coat, and left our rooms. He didn't return until after dinner. His face was troubled, and when I asked where he had been he replied only that he had spent much of the day reading in the Library at the British Museum. At breakfast the next morning his mood hadn't improved, and he said no more than a few words to me while we ate. However, when our meal was over and Mrs. Hudson had cleared away the things, he looked across at me and smiled.

"Do you have time for a turn round the Park?" he asked.

"Certainly."

It was a lovely summer morning as we strolled along Baker Street towards the Clarence Gate. By the time we entered Regent's Park, Holmes had still said nothing to me of the cases that were clearly occupying his mind, so that I suspected he saw nothing of the flowers and trees that we passed on our way. I knew it was usually futile to attempt to draw him out at such times. Nevertheless, I was growing impatient, and knew Holmes well enough to guess that he hadn't brought me out into the fresh air to pass an hour or two in silence. As yet, I was ignorant even of which case was occupying his mind so fully. As we rounded a corner by a pretty fountain I asked him a question. The resulting conversation was one of the most startling I had ever shared with Holmes.

"Is it," I ventured, "this Grace Everley business which is troubling you?"

"Why no," said Holmes. "I have solved that case."

"Solved it?"

"Yes. Tomorrow afternoon I shall report my findings to Singh and the case will be closed. As far as I am concerned, anyway."

"But what have you found? Was the Lady murdered?"

"She was," said Holmes simply.

"Who killed her?"

"I will tell you that presently. First it would help me very much if you would allow me to rehearse the facts I have uncovered, before my interview with my client."

"I am all attention," I said.

Holmes reached into his breast pocket and took out his notebook. He extracted the cheque which Sir William Singh had written for him and offered it to me.

"What shall I do with it?" I asked.

"Put it to your nose."

I did so, and immediately saw the point my friend was trying to make. There was a faint, but unmistakable, odour of ambergrease.

"That dart was all wrong," said Holmes. "Such a delicate shaft would surely have broken, or at least been damaged, had it been fired at the haunch of a running horse which spilled upon the pavement, and then been plucked from the horse's body by a passing Cockney! In any case, the note sent with it was a transparent fake, written by an educated right-handed man using his left hand, and in such curious language. What true Cockney would spell out '*haunch*' and '*horse*' while writing ' *'appened*'? And '*wery soon*' is pure Sam Weller. The writer of that note had more familiarity with the works of Mr. Charles Dickens than with the working men of London. The scent of ambergrease quite closes the matter. That dart was sent by Singh, or rather by his secretary, Fanning. It was in his pocket that the chequebook was stored and impregnated with that refined odour. Sending the dart was an imaginative attempt to provide me with the evidence Singh craves to put pressure on the police to re-open the case. So much is clear.

"I have made some researches into the life and death of Lady Grace, and regret to say that I found much to repel a rational and moral intellect. Neither are the Duke and Duchess of Lowther guiltless. Indeed, I find it hard to decide whether I care less for the Lowthers, for their feckless and foolish son, for the devious and corrupt Sir William Singh, or for the Lady at the centre of our story. I shall not go into detail. It will suffice to say that the marriage between Viscount Penarth and Lady Grace was arranged by the Duchess against the will of her son, who wished to marry another lady. For her part, Grace Everley had such small intellect and so little of nobility in her nature that it was inevitable the match should fail. She had the appearance of a lady, a certain beauty and an easy way with the common man.

"But all that was surface. Long before their troubles became common knowledge, both parties had abandoned the marriage-bed and sought succour elsewhere. You may remember the young woman who visited me last week?" I nodded. "She was once a confidential servant to Lady Grace, and provided me ample evidence of her mistress's liaisons. Often a carriage would arrive at Grace's house, or even at Pennington, with the Lady on board. She would smile and wave as she drove past the reporters who had gathered at the gate, and the servants positioned there to keep the common people out – and all the while the Lady's lover would be crouching at her feet, with a travelling blanket thrown over him."

"Surely not," said I. Holmes made no reply, but pressed on with his discourse.

"It will not surprise you to hear that the driver of that carriage was invariably Wilfred Davie. I have evidence that if Grace couldn't find a lover among her usual set . . . Well, I will say no more. The Duke and Duchess soon came to understand the nature of their daughter-in-law, and bitterly regretted arranging a match with their son. They did everything they could to control her, to silence her and ultimately to free Viscount Penarth and his children from her influence."

"Was it they, then, who arranged the crash?"

"No. Perhaps, if matters had continued, if the engagement with Edward Singh had been announced, they might have been moved to dispose of the Lady. I think them quite capable of such an act. But they had no need. Lady Grace was hunted by a more ruthless and relentless enemy even than the Duchess of Lowther."

"Then who murdered her?" asked, in some impatience.

"You," said Holmes.

"*Me?*" I asked, quite astounded.

"No, not *you*, Watson. *You*."

I looked round. We were alone by a beautiful lawn in the Park. About twenty yards away a boy was playing with a hoop. A little further off, a nanny rested with her perambulator beneath a tree. I dropped my voice and moved closer to Holmes.

"Who do you mean?"

"I mean, *you*," said Holmes, "the reader."

"What?"

"The reader. *You*. The person who is reading Watson's account of this case. You murdered Lady Grace Everley."

I could say nothing. Though I had, through all my sense of shock and outrage, a sense of what my friend meant, my mind rebelled against it.

"You will write this case up," continued Holmes, "and publish it in *The Strand* or some similar organ. Perhaps it will appear in a book, in a collection of lurid tales. It will be read by the same foolish seeker of sensation, with the same thoughtless appetite for stories of the highest and lowest in the land, who is directly responsible for the death of Lady Grace. What happened in Trafalgar Square was, in one sense, an accident. It wasn't engineered by the Duchess of Lowther, or by any other malignant individual. You might say that Davie was responsible, because he was drunk and driving carelessly. You might blame the journalists, who were pursuing the Lady with reckless haste. But I blame the person who commissioned those journalists to make their pursuit. The reporters wouldn't have been on her trail, and Davie wouldn't have been fleeing, hadn't hundreds of thousands of people been willing to pay, and pay, and pay again for reports and photographs of the woman they, most unwisely, adored. It is, in the end, those people who are guilty of her murder."

"You are too hard," I said. "All the world loved Lady Grace. They wouldn't have wished her harm, not for anything. They couldn't have murdered her."

"In one sense you are right," said Holmes. "Murder is the wrong word, for murder must be wilful. If a great, strong man takes his wife in his arms and crushes her with loving embraces he isn't guilty of murder. Yet he killed the woman just the same. He is guilty of acting without thought, without intelligence, without restraint, without wisdom, without sympathy. He is a selfish lover, who cares not for the object of his love, only for his own sensations."

Holmes paused for a moment. "I cannot imagine William Singh will be entirely satisfied with my report," said he. "The murderer – or killer, I should say – will never be brought to justice, and I doubt that he or she will learn anything by the experience of having destroyed the object of their devotion. They will lament as if they have lost a child, and will relish that lamentation. Then they will seek pleasure elsewhere, in knowledge of some other famous life, some vacuum with a pretty face, some fool of rank or charming knave."

"Those readers," I said, "who you feign to despise, have made your name a household word."

"I regret that it has been necessary for me to become known to the public in order to pursue my calling. I would much have preferred an anonymous life. But if I am to gain clients, and to have a reputation which is, in itself, useful to me in influencing justice, then I must be celebrated, and you, my dear Watson, have played your part in that, for which I thank you. I cannot, however, congratulate you. Your accounts of my work might have been scientific. They might have been studies of a criminal investigator at work, the first essays in a new genre, that of the science of deduction. But you have chosen to write for the popular papers, sensational stories with shocking revelations and dramatic crises where, in truth, there have been none."

"But that has made your name!" I said, with some feeling. "And that is what my readers want."

"Quite so. Sensation and shock is what the reader demands, and you will no doubt supply it in good measure when you compose your account of this case. If I cannot blame those journalists for pursuing Lady Grace, then I cannot find fault with you for satisfying a popular demand. But I can, and do, criticise those who buy and read your stories. Let them seek something higher, something of true worth, something to make them think, rather than tell them what to think."

We returned to Baker Street in silence. I had been stung by my friend's words. Yet, I had to admit, there was some truth in what he had said and I made a promise to myself to attempt, as far as I could, to raise the quality of my writing and to represent the work of Sherlock Holmes as truthfully and scientifically as I could. It might sometimes be difficult to keep the interest of the reader, and there would needs be compromises, concealments, and embellishments in the interest of narrative. But I felt sure I could do better, and earn from Holmes a little of the respect I hoped the products of my pen would deserve. It was, at least, something to which I might aspire.

Despite the great public interest in the Grace Everley case, I naturally felt I couldn't, at that time, publish the story of Holmes's brief involvement with it. Later, I wondered if I had been right to hold back. Perhaps the arrow of Holmes's words might have found its mark and perhaps, despite his doubts, my readers might have learned a lesson. Yet would Smith, [4] or any editor, have been willing to publish a story in which one of the most respected thinkers of the age openly criticised every potential reader? I doubt it.

Holmes was perfectly right in his prediction of Sir William Singh's reaction. When he told the Indian what he had told me, he was met at first with a similar silence. Then Singh made a gesture to Fanning, who stood at his elbow, and again produced his chequebook. A draft for another five-hundred pounds was written, blotted and handed to Holmes.

"I promised you such a payment," said Singh. "And a gentleman keeps his promises. However, I confess I am disappointed in you, sir. I had hoped for more. Indeed, I am fairly convinced that Mann-Ingleby misrepresented your powers to me. You have found nothing to help me in my cause."

"Perhaps," said the detective, "your cause is a lost one."

"I shall never accept that. I am right, Mr. Holmes, and you are wrong. Come, Fanning, we will see if we cannot find a more intelligent investigator to uncover the truth."

"I wish you," said Holmes, "every possible success."

NOTES

1. Watson was, at this date, evidently intending to allow publication of this story after 1973. However, it remained with the other manuscripts in a trunk at the National Westminster Bank and was not read until 2010, when it was still considered unsuitable for the public. Recent events have, however, removed any bar to publication.
2. Among the cases mentioned, only that of "The Seven Black Cats" is described in the papers found in 2010.
3. Watson uses the antiquated variant spelling, rather than the more correct "ambergris", and I have retained his usage.
4. This must be a reference to Herbert Greenough Smith (1855–1935), editor of *The Strand* between 1891 and 1930.

The Box
by Robert Stapleton

I well recall that sunny morning in early October when my friend Mr. Sherlock Holmes and I decided to take a stroll in Regent's Park, which was conveniently situated not far from our Baker Street rooms. Since neither of us had any pressing engagements at that moment, we were at liberty to enjoy this little piece of greenery in central London, a pleasure in which we often indulged whenever possible. It gave us space to think and talk.

That day, we found ourselves wandering through an area close to the canal which ran along the northern boundary. As usual, the sounds and sights of that waterway were largely hidden from us by the cutting through which the canal and its water traffic ran.

But Holmes was attracted toward something else. I can always tell the signs – the pricking of the ears and the sparkle in the eye.

He guided our footsteps toward a gaggle of people gathered around a bush, off to our right, almost hidden among the shrubbery. Most of the bystanders were unknown to us, except in passing, but we both recognized one figure in particular.

"Good morning, Lestrade," said Holmes.

"Oh, Mr. Holmes," said the Scotland Yard police inspector. "Doctor. It is really fortunate that you were both passing at this moment."

"Indeed?"

"A member of the public reported that he had discovered a box – a heavy box – and he wondered if it contained anything valuable."

"May we see it?"

"Certainly. There it is, lying almost hidden beneath this laurel bush."

Holmes stooped to examine the box.

"Quite a substantial strong-box if ever I saw one," said Holmes.

"Be careful, Mr. Holmes. It is very heavy."

"Hmm. But its dimensions are interesting. It measures just over three-feet-square, and approximately two-and-a-half feet in height. Constructed of some kind of hard wood, with heavy iron bars holding the entire structure in a rigid embrace, and locked as well. What do you make of it, Watson?"

I bent down beside him and began to examine the structure in detail.

"It is as you say, and appears to be painted, or stained, giving the appearance of an intense black color. It was easy to hide away down here among the shadows. Perhaps it was just by chance that somebody managed to spot it."

Holmes nodded his agreement. "And?"

I looked more closely. "It also carries handles made of thick rope – one on each side."

"But those handles are not the originals," opined Holmes. "The box is rather older."

I tried to lift the box, but soon gave up the attempt.

"It is extremely heavy, presumably because of those iron bars securing it."

"Possibly," he said with a note of doubt in his voice.

"Well, Mr. Holmes?" said Lestrade. "What do you make of it?"

"I haven't yet made up my mind," said Holmes. "Do I have your permission, Inspector, to open the box?"

"If you can," replied the policeman. "We have no key for the lock, so if you can open it, we might be able to find out to whom it belongs."

Holmes reached into the inside pocket of his coat and brought out his pick-lock.

"Do you carry that thing everywhere you go?" Lestrade asked with a chuckle.

"You never know when it might come in handy," replied Holmes. "Like today."

Holmes began by sniffing the lock. "It's been freshly oiled," he told us. "Interesting. The oil isn't from any whale or seal, and is probably mineral oil of some kind. That, together with the rope handles, might suggest that the man who owned the box was a sailor. Or possibly, based on this type of oil, a marine engineer."

For the next couple of minutes Holmes applied himself to unfastening the lock, which he finally accomplished with a smile of satisfaction.

Lestrade raised the lid and reached inside, withdrawing a bundle: An oil-cloth wrapped around a large iron key.

"Is that all?" I inquired.

"That's it, Dr. Watson," said the policeman.

"I see the inside is painted as black as the outside," said Holmes. "Odd."

Lestrade handed the key and cloth over to Holmes, to make of it whatever he could.

Holmes sniffed at the cloth. "This is a very different oil from that used by our sailor friend on the lock. More an industrial concoction."

"How can you tell that?" asked Lestrade.

"I might refer you to my monograph on the subject," said Holmes, turning his attention next to the key.

"I wonder what it fits," commented Lestrade.

By way of an answer, Holmes fitted it into the lock of the box, and turned the key. The mechanism turned with a click.

"Well, I'll be a monkey's uncle!" declared Lestrade. "So we have the key which fits the lock mechanism which was itself locked inside the box. Here is a strange mystery!"

"No mystery at all," declared Holmes. "Clearly, there has to be another key somewhere which fits the same lock."

"But where is it?"

"Precisely the question that, when answered, will lead us to the solution of this mystery."

"In that case," said Lestrade, "I hope that you might be willing to undertake the investigation for us,"

A smile stole across my friend's face. "Very well, Inspector. If I have your permission to keep this box, then I shall instigate my own inquiry. All I ask is that a couple of your constables carry it around to Baker Street for me."

Mrs. Hudson wasn't best pleased at having such an unusually heavy article brought into her home.

"And where exactly do you intend to store that object, Mr. Holmes?" she demanded, her arms akimbo.

"Upstairs in our rooms," he replied.

"Oh no, you don't!" she retorted. "That thing will just add one more weight to the floorboards. The way you live your lives up there, I completely expect those boards to give way any day and deposit all of your disreputable objects all over my kitchen!"

"Disreputable?" demanded Holmes.

"I have cleaned and tidied those rooms of yours enough times to know exactly what you have up there. I have a right to describe some of them in that manner."

"But this is part of my current investigation," objected Holmes.

"Then you can leave the box down here. But at the very least, take it to the far end of the scullery. Then there's a chance I might not stumble over it quite so often if it remains out of my way."

The two constables smiled at the thought that they wouldn't have to carry the box upstairs to the rooms I shared with Holmes.

"Very well," said Holmes. "But then I need to examine it properly."

"In that case, at the very least you could clean the thing up. Look, there's a smear of blood along part of the lid."

"That is very observant of you, Mrs. Hudson," I said with some surprise.

290

"I hope that blood doesn't belong to either of you," she replied.

"I can assure you it does not," replied Holmes.

Mrs. Hudson gave a grunt, turned, and left for the kitchen, intent upon more important business: Namely, the preparation of our midday meal.

After the constables had wrestled the unwieldy thing to the scullery and departed, Holmes turned to me. "We have already noted the external dimensions, Watson, and somewhat odd they appear to be."

He opened the box again and began to note down the inside dimensions.

"These are revealing," commented Holmes. "The inside is significantly smaller than the outside. and yet, there doesn't appear to be any false bottom or receptacle into which anything could be placed or kept. The weight seems to exist in the structure of the box itself – the wood, together with the iron bars which keep the thing secured. But there has to be more to it than just that, for it's far too heavy."

Holmes used the key to re-secure the lock, slipped it into his pocket, and together we went upstairs.

Over our pot roast, we considered the matter.

"It seems to me," said Holmes, "that somebody must be missing that box, and would be very glad to have it back again."

"Perhaps it was stolen," I suggested.

"Most probably."

"And then hidden not far from the side of canal, ready for somebody to collect it."

"Logical thinking," said Holmes. "But what is there about that box which makes it such a prize for this particular thief?"

"The key seems to be the only thing of any value."

"Perhaps. However, certain things suggest themselves."

"Then what is to be our next step?"

"We need to find the man who constructed that box. He ought not to be difficult to locate, for it is unique. Someone who is a locksmith, and who is also capable of carrying out such wood and iron work. Again, there are a few suggestions."

Holmes jumped up from his meal and began to rummage through his filing system. Within a couple of minutes, he stood back with a cry of delight.

"A-ha! Harringcote. Now there is indeed a name I haven't come across for many years."

"What made you think of him?"

"Take a look at the key. What do you see?"

"Just a large iron key."

"On the inside of the handle. Do you not see a small inscribed *H H H*?"

"Oh, yes. Indeed, there it is."

"And there you are. As ever is the case, you see, but you do not observe."

"*Touché.*"

He nodded, but said nothing in reply.

"Perhaps we ought to call upon this Harringcote at our earliest opportunity," I suggested.

"Or second, perhaps," said Holmes. "First, we need to enter a notice in the personal columns, publicising the fact that we are now in possession of a heavy box of this description, and inviting anyone who is missing said item to contact us here."

I am not sure exactly what I expected to find at the premises of the locksmith, but it certainly failed to match the workshop of the Harringcote Brothers and Nephew. They seemed to be involved in far more than merely supplying locking mechanisms, and were more like a general ironmongers' workshop. But this fact hardly stopped Holmes from marching straight in and making his approach to the management.

A man in brown overalls stepped forward to greet his visitors.

"My name is Morgan Harringcote," said the man, in an affable manner. "How may I assist you, gentlemen?"

"A brother or the nephew?" replied Holmes.

"Definitely one of the brothers."

"My name is Sherlock Holmes," replied my companion, "and this is Dr. John Watson. We're working on behalf of Scotland Yard, searching for the owner of a heavy box which has been discovered close to the Regent's Canal."

"And you think we might have some knowledge of this box?"

Holmes handed the man the iron key. "This carries an inscription which might well link it to your firm, Mr. Harringcote. It is the very key which fits the box, but it was discovered inside the locked box."

"In that case, how did you manage to open the box, Mr. Holmes?"

"Believe me, Mr. Harringcote," said Holmes, "I have my methods."

"Obviously."

Harringcote examined the key, and then displayed an expression of astonishment.

"Well, Mr. Harringcote? It is one of your firm's pieces of work. Is that not so?"

"It is, indeed," replied Harringcote. "But it isn't the work of anyone working here today. It must be at least a dozen years old. Allow me to consult our books."

A few minutes later, the man returned to the workshop, carrying a heavy tome which he spread out across the countertop.

"Here we are, Mr. Holmes," he said. "This is definitely the work of my grandfather. And he died some eight years ago."

"What exactly is the work he was engaged in?"

"The construction of two identical wooden boxes, strengthened with iron bars."

"*Two?*" I was amazed.

"Of course," Holmes chided me. "Remember, we have already concluded that there are two keys, so it is logical that they came with two boxes."

"Perhaps," said Harringcote, "but according to these records, the locks themselves were to be different."

At this news, Holmes appeared perplexed. Had he been wrong after all?

"The waters are becoming ever deeper, eh, Watson?"

"Certainly."

"Mr. Harringcote," said Holmes, "can you tell me who it was who commissioned the construction of these two boxes?"

"It seems to have been ordered by a lady, name not given, on behalf of Mr. Joel Saul-Bakerson."

"And can you tell us anything else about these two people? Do your records give an address?"

"No. At least not after all this time."

"Not even for delivery?"

"It seems they were both collected."

"So, we hit a brick wall," mused Holmes.

"That is the way it seems, Mr. Holmes."

All the way back to Baker Street, without paying attention to anything or anyone else around him, Holmes continued muttering to himself.

Finally, he turned to me.

"Watson, I suspect that the box was being carried on the canal and set ashore. We must scour the canal for any sign of the box's destination."

"I'm happy to help in any way I can. You know that."

"Splendid. In that case, first thing tomorrow morning, we must divide our efforts. We can begin at where the canal passes King's Cross. You travel in a westward direction along the canal towpath, and ask if anyone has been asked to collect and move a heavy box. You have plenty of scope

293

– all the way to Little Venice, and where Regents Canal meets the Grand Union Canal. You may not have time to investigate the entire length. I, on the other hand, shall go in the opposite direction, toward Limehouse and the docklands. I'm acquainted with a certain bargee who works in that area and who is usually a fount of information. I shall see what he has for me on this issue.

The following day, by the time I was ready to set about my allotted task, Holmes had already left, to wend his way along the eastern stretch of the canal.

In my turn, I watched the traffic of horse-drawn barges loaded with their cargoes of coal, wood, and other heavy items. I joined one of these bargees whom I knew as he led his horse along the towpath, towing a load of some fifty tons of coal, or so he told me. And we fell into conversation. I told him about a heavy box that had been discovered, and our search for its owner.

Each time we stopped for any reason, the man put the word around about the box.

"Let's see what information that dredges up," he told me.

It soon became evident that news of any kind spreads with amazing rapidity along the canal.

We reached Maida Hill Tunnel, where the absence of a towpath meant that the horse had to be untied from the barge.

I politely declined the invitation to help man-handle the barge through the tunnel, and instead fell into conversation with a man standing on the towpath who was watching me with particular interest.

"Are you the bloke who wants a box moving?" he said.

"No," I replied. "But somebody else did. Only a couple of days ago. I believe that possibly a barge was hired to move a heavy box from one place to another. I'm looking to find out who did the hiring, and where it was to be taken."

"Well, I can't help you there," said the man on the towpath, "but I can tell you one thing for sure."

"What's that?"

"What's it worth?"

"That depends how good you information turns out to be," I said, and waited to hear what he had to tell me.

"Some toff came along here, just like you did, and said he had a box that he needed shifting – a particularly heavy box."

The man chuckled.

"And I'm the poor fool who agreed to take on that job for him."

"From where to where?"

"He didn't say, but I understood I was to pick it up from somewhere in Regents Park, where it borders the canal, and then take it somewhere along the Grand Union. He said he would meet me close to the park and show me exactly where it was hidden."

"Hidden?"

"That's the very word he used. Anyhow, this bloke never turned up, did he? And now I reckon he owes me for the loss of a full day's wage."

"Is that all you have to tell me?"

"Better than nothing, isn't it?"

I handed him a couple of sovereigns.

After making further inquiries, I had to give up my quest by mid-afternoon and return to the place where I expected to meet Holmes. He was there already, looking as pleased as Punch.

"I may not have found out who was going to transport that box," he began, "but my bargee friend managed to put me in touch with an old man who used to work with the Harringcote firm a number of years ago. He remembered working there when the firm was putting together those two boxes. He knows there was something particularly unusual about one of them. It carried a secret. He didn't know exactly what that was, but what he did tell me seemed only to confirm my own initial suspicions about the box."

"And what exactly are those?"

"That will have to emerge in its own time. But how about you? How did you fare?"

With a great deal of pride, I informed Holmes of my investigations and the discovery I had made during the morning. I told him that indeed a man had hired one of the barges in order to transport a heavy box to some destination, undisclosed, westward along the Grand Union Canal. Sadly, I had little more to relate. Still, Holmes appeared pleased with my success, though perhaps a little disappointed that I hadn't delved more deeply in my questioning.

The moment we entered through the front door of 221b, Holmes and I were confronted by a Mrs. Hudson with a face looking like thunder, evidently with something of great moment on her mind.

"Mr. Holmes," she cried, thus breaking his concentration, "I allowed you to leave that awful box down here out of sheer self-preservation, but I had no idea you were going to turn my scullery into an extension of your sitting room."

"How do you mean?" he asked.

"I have a visitor waiting to talk to you, but she refuses to go upstairs. She says that she has come here in response to your advertisement in the newspaper. She claims that the box in the scullery belongs to her, and she has come to collect it."

"We wish her well with that," I said with a chuckle. "If she can lift it at all, then I'm sure she could take it with her."

Holmes gave me a dark look and turned back to Mrs. Hudson.

"Where is this lady now?"

Our landlady led us through to the kitchen, where we found a woman of about thirty years of age sitting at the kitchen table, drinking a steaming cup of tea.

She stood up as we entered.

"My name is Sherlock Holmes. I'm the one who put that advertisement into the newspapers about the box."

"And I'm convinced that it is the very box which was stolen from my home just two nights ago."

"And who exactly are you?"

"Forgive me for not introducing myself properly," she said. "My name is Charlotte Couperson. And that box belongs to my husband, Jack."

"Ah, yes," mused Holmes. "Then you've examined the box?"

"Indeed, I have."

"And you're certain that it is, without doubt, your husband's property?"

"Yes, I'm certain of that."

"Then I need to ask you a few questions about it."

"Why you?"

"Because I'm a consulting detective, working with Scotland Yard. Now, kindly sit down."

Charlotte Couperson complied.

"Now," began Holmes, "your husband is away from home at the moment because he works at sea."

"Correct."

"Working as a ship's engineer."

"How do you know that?"

"Mere deduction, Madam. The oil on the lock seemed likely to be associated with a ship's engine room. You're in the habit of keeping that box somewhere close to you," continued Holmes. "At home, no doubt."

"True, Mr. Holmes. At least when I'm in residence there."

"But the other night, someone broke into your home and removed it."

"I happened to be out. Staying with a friend for the night. I had imagined I'd locked the house securely before I left, but it seems that I was mistaken. Who would do such a terrible thing?"

Holmes steepled his finger as he sank deep into thought.

"Would you please tell us more about who you are, and something of the history of this box?"

She debated with herself regarding the need to answer these questions, but after all, we did have the box that she wanted. "Very well. My husband, Jack, is the grandson of a rich merchant, now deceased, by the name of Joel Saul-Bakerson."

"Through his mother's side, no doubt."

"You seem to know a lot about our family already, Mr. Holmes."

"No, I assure you, it is all deduced from the different names," said Holmes. "Kindly tell us more."

"We were told that the box has something to do with an inheritance. Keeping it safe is extremely important – more important than you can ever imagine. If Jack returns home to find his box missing, there will be a terrible row. There is no knowing what he might do."

The poor woman burst into a flood of tears.

After a few minutes, she calmed down again, sufficiently for Holmes to continue his questioning.

"Please tell me what you know about the Saul-Bakerson family."

"They are wealthy merchants, dealing with the import and export of materials from all over the world. They're very wealthy. Or at least, old Mr. Saul-Bakerson was. As far as I can understand it, the final inheritance issue was left in abeyance after the old man's death, to be resolved ten years later."

"How unusual. And when it that due to take place?"

"I believe it will be within the next few months – sometime this year, certainly. But I have no idea exactly when. Jack will certainly know."

Holmes excused himself and was absent from our presence for a few moments, before returning with a hefty leather-bound book – a detailed map of London. This he laid on the table and opened it to reveal the central and western parts of the city in great detail.

"Now, Mrs. Couperson," he said, without lifting has head from the book, "where exactly is that family home of the Saul-Bakersons?"

She shrugged. "A place called Withybank Hall," she replied. "Somewhere to the west of here. I've never been there myself."

Holmes used his finger to trace the line of the Regents Canal, as far as its junction with the Grand Union Canal, and then along the length of that waterway until he stopped with a sharp exclamation.

"As I expected: Withybank Hall lies within easy reach of the watercourse, and appears to have ready access from the main road."

He looked up at me. "Watson, I think that you and I should call upon that household at our earliest convenience."

"Perhaps in the morning."

"Bright and early."

"Again?"

"But what about the box?" demanded our visitor, as she stood up in alarm.

"I imagine," replied Holmes, with a reassuring smile, "that Mrs. Hudson's scullery has to be about the most secure of all places in London as a place to shelter something of great value. And it's of such weight that moving it would be bound to draw our attention. No, I think it's safe where it lies. You can leave it with us for now."

She didn't like that, but she soon departed.

Later, I asked Holmes once again about the key that had been discovered inside the box.

"The lady clearly had no idea it was in there, so I didn't feel it was my place to introduce the subject. No doubt its importance, or otherwise, will emerge in the course of our investigations."

During the darkest hours of that following night, the entire household was awakened by a rumpus coming from downstairs. A bumping and thumping sound echoed through the building, together with loud and angry voices. I leapt out of my bed and clambered downstairs, only to discover Mrs. Hudson using a yard-brush to beat an intruder across the back of the head as he disappeared rapidly through the front door and into the night.

"Dr. Watson," she said as she saw me approach, "I had those two roughs on the run, didn't I?"

"You certainly did," I agreed, having only seen one of them.

"Mr. Holmes warned me that something like this might happen."

"That's right," said Holmes, as he stepped out of the shadows. He was fully dressed and was carrying his revolver. "After we've been spreading the word around town that a box has been discovered, I imagined that half the villains in London would be lining up for the chance to get their hands on it."

"But there is nothing in it to attract anyone's interest."

"That is questionable. And because its contents remain a mystery is even more reason why someone might want to get his hands on it."

"But Mrs. Hudson has been very careful to keep the box safe."

"Indeed, but perhaps we'd better remain on guard for the rest of the night in case they come back again. I think that now they'll keep away from here – but you never know."

The following morning, having given up any idea of further sleep and keen to bring this whole business to a conclusion, I accompanied Holmes

298

on a cab ride beyond the western boundary of our great metropolis and into the fresh morning air of the countryside.

Mid-morning found us at the end of a long, gravel-surfaced drive, in front of a flight of steps leading up to a substantial wooden front door.

We climbed the steps and I pulled on the doorbell. A man, obviously the butler, appeared at the door and examined the cards we offered him.

"Ah, yes," he said in a matter-of-fact tone. "You are expected. Kindly step inside."

The entrance hall was decorated with various kinds of marble, and was clearly intended to convey an immediate impression of grandeur, opulence, and of status to any visitor. Clearly the home of an affluent family – descendants of a successful businessman.

"Would you please step this way, gentlemen," said the butler, as he led us into a reception room to one side of the main entrance hall. "Mr. Albert and Mr. George will be with you shortly."

Holmes had already turned his attention to studying the photographs and paintings displayed on the walls of this room, while I looked out of the window at the garden and buildings beyond the main house.

The door opened again and two tall figures appeared in the entrance. One had mutton-chop whiskers, while the other was clean-shaven. Both gave the impression of being in their fifties, but the one with the whiskers appeared to be the senior of the two.

"Mr. Sherlock Holmes," said the whiskered man. "Yes, we received your wire late last night to let us know you would be visiting us this morning, but you gave no indication of the reason for your visit."

"Thank you for being willing to welcome us this morning," said Holmes.

"You gave us little choice," said the second man.

"This is my friend and colleague, Dr. John Watson. We are working in consultation with Scotland Yard."

"And we are the Saul-Bakerson brothers," said the man who had been first to speak. "I'm Albert, and this is my brother, George."

The other man inclined his head serenely.

"But if you're here on police business," said Albert, "then perhaps we had better retire to a more comfortable environment, where we can discuss the matter more fully."

We followed the two brothers along a corridor lined with vases and cabinets of porcelain until we reached a richly decorated sitting room. When we were settled into the easy chairs standing around the room, all attention returned to Holmes.

"We're here in search of the ownership of a wooden box which was discovered in some bushes beside Regent's Canal," said Holmes.

"Oh," said George. "We wouldn't know anything about that, would we, Albert?"

"A box, you say?" added Albert, shaking his head. "How large?"

"About three-feet-square and two-and-a-half-feet high. Constructed of wood and reinforced with iron bars. Very heavy. It was stolen during the night from where it was kept by intruders, who were forced to leave it ready for retrieval later in the day. Unfortunately for the thief, or thieves, the box was discovered before such a thing could happen."

"And what do you imagine we might have had to do with this incident?" demanded Albert.

"You are both businessmen," said Holmes, "and yet you have both been engaged in heavy manual labour in the recent past. I have no proof of your involvement in this burglary, but the signs are there. You, Albert, have sustained a cut to your hand, which is fairly new. Blood was discovered on the lid of the box. My colleague here could examine it for you and apply a suitable dressing."

The two brothers looked at each other. "We are admitting nothing," said Albert.

"Naturally," returned Holmes. "The information I need concerns your father, the late Joel Saul-Bakerson."

"What do you wish to know?"

"I'm interested in the nature of your inheritance."

"The old man died ten years ago, Mr. Holmes," said George. "The will was read at the time."

"But the will carried an important clause," said Holmes. "Delaying its full disclosure for those ten years."

"You have obviously been talking to that Couperson woman," said George, with a sneer.

"But she is your family."

"Only by marriage," said Albert.

"Fleur, our nephew Jack's mother, was our sister," George explained. "Sadly, she is no longer with us."

"She married a man named Frank Couperson," said Holmes.

"Originally," said Albert, "our father's will included provision for only the two of us – the two men. But Fleur discovered this and, more than a dozen years ago, she set about persuading the old man to include her in his provision as well."

"And did he?"

"We don't know," admitted George. "That's what the ten-year delay is all about. At the right time, all will be revealed. Apparently."

"And why did you try to steal the box?"

300

The two brothers again looked at each other, as if acknowledging that they were found out, and then Albert stated, "Yes, we took it. We had no idea what was in it, you see, but we knew that Jack's mother, or perhaps our grandfather, had given it to him for safe-keeping. We felt we needed to try to prevent the full revelation from emerging. We imagined that we would lose out in the end. It took us such a long time to discover where the box was located, and when Jack would be away from home."

"You were impatient," said Holmes.

"A fault possessed by many."

"Tell us about the keys," said Holmes, with a sardonic smile.

The two brothers looked at one another in silence for a moment.

"You are well informed, Mr. Holmes," said Albert.

"Mostly arrived at by sheer deduction, I can assure you."

"I think you had better come outside with us," said George. "Only then can we properly explain about those keys, and the mystery which surrounds them."

A few minutes later, we were standing together outside in the garden, behind the main house, close to a small, single-story whitewashed building with a heavy wooden door.

"This," said Albert Saul-Bakerson proudly, "is the mausoleum that houses the body of our father. In there, so we are told, also lies the sum of our inheritance. The only problem is that we are denied access to the building until the tenth anniversary of his death – an event scheduled to take place in only a week from now."

"And the only access to the building is through that door," continued his brother George. "But there is a problem."

"Indeed," said Albert. "You will notice, Mr. Holmes, that there are *two* keyholes in the door."

"Yes, so I see."

George became extremely serious at this point. "The truth is that we, my brother and I, have been left but a single key. But it doesn't fit either of those keyholes. We have tried. And the mystery deepens when we consider the fact that, as we have been led to believe, both of those keys are required in order to turn the lock in the door. But we have neither of those in our possession."

"Strange," said I.

"Singular," commented Holmes. "And that was why you decided to steal Jack's box."

"After all this time, the box seemed the only possible location for the keys – or at least, one of them. Though in truth, we still have no idea what really rests within that box."

"Why could you not just wait?"

"As you said, Mr. Holmes," admitted George. "Sheer impatience."

"And the fact that we are growing older every day," added Albert. "After all, our sister Fleur passed away a few years ago, and how much longer do we each have left to enjoy life?"

Holmes drew closer to me. "Take them away from here," he said softly, "and keep them busy for a few minutes."

"I think I need to take a look at that scratch you sustained recently," I said to Albert. "I have my medical bag with me. Or my emergency kit, at any rate. After all, what is a physician without his equipment?"

Fortunately, both brothers joined me – apparently George followed Albert as a matter of routine, instead of staying to observe Holmes. As the brothers and I went indoors, I looked back and noticed Holmes remove from his pocket the large iron key he had found in Jack Couperson's box and slip it into one of the keyholes in the mausoleum door. He gave a satisfied nod and returned the key to his coat pocket.

Just moments later, Holmes joined us inside and, with Holmes's announcement that we had concluded our business at Withybeck Hall, we returned to London.

Back in Baker Street, we continued our daily round of events, and the demands of other clients.

And waited.

Occasionally over the following week, a somewhat-bothered and flustered Charlotte Couperson would turn up at the door and ask to see the box. It was always there, intact, and with the key once again safely locked back in place.

Then, one day not long before the tenth anniversary of Joel Saul-Bakerson's death, we heard heavy footsteps on the stairs outside our rooms. A fist hammered upon the door, which was then opened from the outside to reveal a thickset man with a ruddy complexion and a look of anger in his eyes.

"Ah," declared Holmes. "Mr. Jack Couperson, I presume."

"My wife has told you all about me, then," our visitor thundered.

"You have come to collect your box."

"Do you have it safe?"

"We do. But why don't you come inside. I should like to know the story of how you happened to be in possession of that box. Now, sit down here and tell us your tale."

At first, the man was inclined to remain angry, but when he saw no purpose, he calmed down and settled amicably in the basket chair we generally reserved for visitors.

"As you hear from my wife," said the man when he was settled, "my mother was the daughter of a wealthy businessman, by the name of Saul-Bakerson."

"Indeed."

"She married a man called Frank Couperson, and the couple had a single child: Myself. Something like a dozen or more years ago now, the old man made a will which benefitted his two sons, but failed to provide for my mother. She felt that such treatment was extremely unfair. During the following couple of years, my mother took a great deal of trouble to cultivate a better friendship with her father. Even though she was married and had a husband and child, she also looked after him with the greatest of care. She was hoping that he would alter his will to include her, but in the end, he still decided that he would make other arrangements instead. The will was divided into two parts. The first part gave the estate and the business over to the two sons, as originally planned. For the second part, my mother arranged, with her father's permission, to divide his remaining property, sealed in two wooden boxes, heavy and so reinforced internally as to be practically immovable, and to be opened on the tenth anniversary of his death. With this involvement of my mother, the old man had all of this organized before he died."

"And when your mother died, she bequeathed her box, together with whatever it contained, to you."

"I have no idea what the box contains," explained Couperson, "or how much it is worth. But I've come back home now, just in time for the opening of the box. That is due to take place tomorrow, at Withybank Hall."

"Tomorrow," repeated Holmes. "So, the whole thing is about to come together,"

"I only hope it will be worth this long wait."

"I can only suggest, Mr. Couperson, that you come here at first light tomorrow morning to pick up your box – Now, now, it will be safer here than if you tried to take it back home. – and we shall travel together to Withybank Hall."

"Another early morning," I muttered after Couperson has departed.

"But I think we are about to find it immensely worthwhile."

The next morning arrived, dry and bright, to find us all ready to depart. I was amazed to see how effortlessly Jack Couperson was able to lift the black box and take it out to the waiting vehicle. I pitied the poor old horse hired by Couperson who would be pulling the weight of the box, as well as the Coupersons, Holmes, and me. I hoped he would enjoy an extra helping of oats as a due reward for his hard work.

We arrived at Withybank Hall, only to be directed by the butler who met us a week earlier that the two brothers were 'round at the back of the house, at the Mausoleum, and that we should join them there. Couperson directed the carriage in that direction, and in a few moments, we arrived, stepping down to join his two uncles, hairy Albert and clean-shaven George Saul-Bakerson.

"This is the entire family," Albert explained, explaining why there were no other relatives. "Neither of us ever married. We were so involved in the business that we never ever felt the time was right to enter into any such arrangements. And now it is too late."

All seemed to be ready.

Dark looks were being traded between the Saul-Bakerson brothers and the Coupersons. Although neither had met Charlotte, they were well aware of who she was.

Jack stood guard over the heavy box that he had brought.

As the clock which was situated above the stables rang out the hour of ten, another figure appeared. The man was every inch a solicitor. He acknowledged us with a reverential nod.

"My name is Richard Butterworth," he announced. "Our firm was selected by Mr. Joel Saul-Bakerson to deal with his will. As you will all no doubt be aware, the will was divided into two parts. The first part was dealt with at the time of his demise. The second part instructed us all to be gathered here today. At the tenth hour, of the tenth day, of the tenth month, in the tenth year after his death."

"He enjoyed these pointless gestures," muttered George Saul-Bakerson.

"Quite," retorted Butterworth. "But now we come to the completion of the will. Mr. Jack Couperson was entrusted with the care of a box."

Jack indicated the box at his feet.

"For all these years," continued the solicitor, "my firm has kept this key."

He removed from his coat pocket an iron key, which he held up for all to see.

It seemed to me to resemble exactly the key that we had found in the heavy box, and had been carefully returned to its place without anyone's knowledge.

"I'm instructed to use this key to open the box which was entrusted to Mr. Couperson."

Butterworth crouched down, fitted the key into the lock, and turned it until a satisfying clunk indicated that the lock had been opened.

On lifting the lid, the solicitor reached in and lifted out the other key, rewrapped in its oil-cloth.

"These two keys," said Butterworth, "and are to be used to open the door of the mausoleum. Mr. Couperson, would you please take your key and insert it into the right-hand keyhole, while I do the same for the other one."

The two men turned the keys at exactly the same moment, and the sound of a heavy locking mechanism issued from the door. They looked at each other, and then the lawyer pushed the door open. This required some effort, but Butterworth refused to allow anyone else to help him in this matter.

Then the door stood fully open, for the first time for some ten years or so.

"Misters Saul-Bakerson," said Butterworth, "I asked that you bring some lights,, if you please."

The brothers nodded and stepped to one side, retrieving a set of lanterns, which they lit. The, with the attorney in the lead, we all stepped inside, looking around at the illuminated surroundings. A musty smell filled the air, the odor of something old.

On a plinth at the far end of the burial chamber stood a pair of caskets containing the bodies of the long-deceased Joel Saul-Bakerson and his late wife. On the floor before the former's coffin stood a wooden box, the same size and appearance as the one outside which belonged to Jack Couperson.

We waited expectantly for something to happen.

Butterworth looked around. "Now," he said, "who has the key for this box?"

"That must be the one in our possession," said George Saul-Bakerson as he looked to his brother.

The older brother gave a smile and drew from his jacket pocket a key which looked rather different from the other two, and which we knew fitted a different lock: This one.

Albert stepped forward and fitted the key into the lock. It slipped in without much effort and turned with only slightly more effort.

It was Butterworth who then stepped forward and lifted the lid, pushing his hand into the interior. A moment later he withdrew a small sheet of paper.

This he studied carefully, while everyone else watched on.

"It is Mr. Saul-Bakerson's final word," said the solicitor. "It says that his two sons already have their inheritance. They have possession of the house and the estate, the deeds of which are held in a safety deposit box at our offices."

The two brothers stared at each other for a moment.

"Is that it?" demanded George. "We've been waiting patiently for the last ten years, and this is all we receive?"

"This is all Fleur's doing!" said Albert bitterly. "Our sister was always resentful that she wouldn't have a fair share in the family's inheritance. This is how she has secured her revenge. Even from beyond her grave. And his."

"The old skinflint," added George. "What happened to all his other riches?"

"The note adds that his grandson, Jack, is to inherit this box, along with the first, and all that is in them."

"But there's nothing else in them."

"Huh!" exclaimed George angrily. "Well, as far as I'm concerned, he's welcome to them."

With that, the two brothers turned on their heels and headed for the house, leaving their visitors alone.

We all turned to Sherlock Holmes.

"What just happened, Mr. Holmes?" demanded Jack Couperson, with a note of bitterness in his voice.

"Your mother was a very clever woman," said Holmes. "When her father had this mausoleum built, she arranged, with his secret permission, to have the double lock fitted to the door, and then the two boxes constructed with different locks."

"But why?"

"When the original will left all the old man's possessions to the two brothers, Fleur decided to make her own arrangements so she could provide for her son. And that provision lay in the boxes."

"But there is nothing in the boxes," he exclaimed. "They're quite empty."

"Really?"

"Is there perhaps more to the boxes than we imagined?" I demanded.

"Watson, has it taken you all this time to realize that?"

Holmes turned to Jack. "Now," he said, pointing to the box on the mausoleum floor, "open the lid and scrape away the paint from the bottom of the compartment."

The owner of the box did as he was instructed.

"Mr. Holmes," he said, gazing inside, "is this what it appears to be?"

"The dimensions of the box, together with its unusual weight, make it the only logical conclusion: Ingots of gold lining the bottom and sides of the box – and the other box as well. This is your inheritance, Mr. Couperson."

"How amazing!" he cried. "For the first time in my life, my wife and I are rich."

"Now," said Holmes, "perhaps it's time to celebrate. Well, congratulations to you both. But you're going to need some help to realize the value of that gold, and you'll probably need somebody to disassemble the boxes for you. I might suggest the workshop of the Harringcote Brothers who built them."

"Then you'll need a decent broker," said I, "to help trade the gold at a decent rate."

"And then a good bank manager," added Butterworth. "I can suggest a few."

"We all wish you a comfortable and secure future together," concluded Holmes to the couple he and I walked away to find transport back home.

"Tell me," I said later that day, as we sat together in our rooms in Baker Street, "when exactly did you begin to think the bottom of the boxes were in fact lined gold ingots?"

"Oh, almost at once," he told me. "You need to have a broad imagination in such a case as this. The unusual weight, the circumstances of their construction, and the question of a delayed inheritance – it was all quite suggestive."

"Obviously. But how is it that I missed all the signs?"

"I have told you before," he said with a thinly disguised smile, "you see, but you so often fail to observe."

"Well, today I have both seen and observed that Jack Couperson and his wife are happy, and that they can look forward to a golden future together."

My companion nodded. "That, Watson, is something with which I can wholeheartedly agree. But it's up to them to grasp the opportunities and decide where exactly they are going to go in life."

A Puzzle in Porphyry
by DJ Tyrer

The late-morning sun was streaming in through the windows of 221b Baker Street as my friend, Sherlock Holmes, and I relaxed in our respective armchairs. I was attempting to familiarise myself with the contents of the latest issue of *The Lancet*, despite the lethargy the warm sunlight inspired in me, while Holmes was busy reading his way through a pile of newspapers and puffing on his pipe. Those papers he was done with he tossed aside, leaving sheets scattered randomly across the floor.

Pausing to regard the mess, it never ceased to bemuse me that someone of such a methodical mind could leave such chaos in his wake.

Hearing the tread of Mrs. Hudson upon the stair, I realised that a tray of tea was on its way and tucked *The Lancet* down the side of my chair before asking Holmes what news there was.

He tossed *The Times* aside and said, "Much the usual, Watson: More rumblings of war, disputes between the monarchies of Europe, a political brouhaha amongst our American cousins, criticism of that so-called 'Merchant of Death', Zaharoff. The retrial of poor Captain Dreyfus has begun, and sundry other of the daily consternations that threaten to disrupt our peace."

Just as he finished speaking, Mrs. Hudson entered with a tray and gave a shriek as her foot slipped on one of the discarded sheets of news and she stumbled, desperately trying to keep ahold of the tray.

Before I could move to help her, Holmes sprang from his seat and caught her in his arms as if about to spin her away in a dance. There was a crash as one of the delicate tea cups fell from the tray and smashed upon the floor.

As my friend helped right our landlady, I got down onto my knees and collected as much of the broken cup as I could spy and placed the fragments upon the tea-wetted tray.

"I shall return shortly," Mrs. Hudson said in an aggrieved tone, "and I expect those papers to be tidied up."

Holmes smiled and said, "For you, Mrs. Hudson, anything," before setting to work gathering them up.

He was just finished with the chore when Mrs. Hudson returned and gave a satisfied nod at the slightly tidier room.

"You're very lucky these hadn't arrived when I brought the last tray up, Mr. Holmes," she said as she laid the tray on the table between us. The morning's post stood in a toast rack upon it.

"Indeed," said Holmes, "it would have been a trifle messy. Thank you so much, Mrs. Hudson."

She rolled her eyes as she departed, but Holmes was already busy shuffling the letters.

"Shall I pour?" I asked, and my friend gave a slight nod.

Then, as I set the teapot back down on the tray, he held one of the letters up.

"A missive from Professor Xavier Woodridge," he told me in that almost-theatrical manner he liked to adopt when showing off his deductive powers.

I scoffed at the pronouncement. "The man's name is on the return address."

"No." He handed me the letter. "There is none."

It was true. Then, he added, "The letter concerns a break-in."

"How can you know that?" said I, tearing it open and seeing that, indeed, the letter was from a Professor Xavier Woodridge and, as Holmes had said, was something to do with a break-in at his house. The man's name, I was certain, was not one that Holmes had ever mentioned, nor one which had ever been mentioned to him in my company, and as to the nature of the contents, I could see no way in which he could know it.

Holmes chuckled. "My means is quite elementary. Note the postmark: Shoeburyness in Essex. Professor Xavier Woodridge lives in Prittlewell, near to Shoeburyness, allowing me to make the assumption that it was he who had sent the letter, as it was unlikely another person from that district would be writing to me at this precise moment."

I shook my head. "I don't understand how you could possibly know he would be writing to you, nor why."

Seizing up a newspaper from the pile he hadn't long ago gathered together, Holmes flapped it at me.

"In here. There was a brief mention of the Professor's unfortunate encounter with an intruder at his home – it says he was left shaken and his assistant mildly hurt – which gives his place of residence as Prittlewell in Essex. Although I know nothing of Professor Woodridge, when I saw the postmark, it seemed most likely that a man who had suffered some sort of encounter of a criminal nature would write to me for assistance and that the odds of another person in the district choosing to write for help on some other matter were remote. Therefore, the letter writer would be he, or someone on his behalf, concerning the break-in.

"Of course, I knew where Prittlewell lies thanks to the infamous murder that occurred there. You will recall, of course, the so-called 'Southend Mystery', upon which I consulted?"

"Yes."

"It began with that killing, the resort and its pier being located, as the town's name suggests, in the south of Prittlewell parish. Hence the geography sticks with me, yet."

I snorted. "Nothing but a cheap parlour trick."

Holmes laughed. "One day, when you have mastered all my secrets, Watson, then you may call my methods cheap – but not yet."

I had to chuckle myself, but then grew serious and asked if I should read the letter.

"Please, do. The article was woefully brief, and I should like to learn if any more details are provided."

I did so, pausing for a moment only when Holmes let out a soft interjection at the reference to two burglary attempts, something that his article had obviously not mentioned.

> *Brookside Cottage*
> *Prittlewell, Essex*
> *9th August*
>
> *Dear Mr. Sherlock Holmes,*
>
> *I require your assistance, for I fear that I cannot reveal the whole truth pertaining to the two recent burglary attempts here at my home to the police. I have recently come into possession of an object, an ancient sarcophagus lid made of imperial porphyry, in somewhat less-than-ideal circumstances. It is this object in which I believe the thief was interested.*
>
> *The first attempt was almost without incident, for I heard a noise downstairs and called out for my assistant, Frederick, who immediately investigated and found a window had been forced, but nothing taken. The second one very nearly cost me my loyal friend's life and proceeded as follows: I woke in need of water to wet my lips in this awfully hot and stuffy weather. Going downstairs, I heard a scraping sound, as if two bricks were being rubbed together. I entered the room where the sarcophagus lid was and saw movement in the darkness. I was certain it was poor Frederick and so called out, but alas! it was not he, but an intruder. A brief struggle followed and*

*there was a loud crashing sound as the lid was knocked to the
floor and broken. Then, they were gone. Poor Frederick had
been struck and injured by the intruder and remains unwell.*

*The police were summoned, of course, but their
investigation was perfunctory and I dared not tell them what
I really thought, lest Frederick should find himself in trouble.
I am now worried that the intruder might return for a third
time and, having heard of your investigative skill and your
circumspection, I implore you to help me. I am certain I can
match whatever reasonable fee you may request.*

*If you are willing to help me, I would suggest you take on
the guise of an amateur historian interested in my researches
into the Roman period, for I have entertained numerous guests
of the sort, and another such will be unlikely to arouse
suspicion.*

Yours faithfully,

Xavier Woodridge (Prof.)

"Interesting," said Holmes as I finished reading it. "A prior break-in
that went unreported and an unwillingness to involve the police. Professor
Woodridge has his secrets, it seems."

My friend gestured to a side table. "Pass me the pen and paper, please,
and I shall compose a brief reply. A pair of historians will be paying him
a visit tomorrow."

We boarded the train at Liverpool Street and undertook our journey
through the fields of Essex to the quaint railway station at Prittlewell. We
were dressed for the countryside in tweed. My friend spent the journey
with a volume of Gibbon's *Decline and Fall* in his hands, whether merely
to complete his disguise or as a refresher on the key points of Roman
history, I wasn't sure.

At the station, we approached a porter and asked for directions to
Brookside Cottage and Professor Woodridge.

The porter scratched his nose. "Queer fellow, keeps to himself?"

"A historian," said I.

"Aye, as you say. If you follow the lane from the station and, then,
turn right, his house is the one out on its own with the brook at its back. If
your feet get wet," he added with a chuckle, "you've gone too far."

"Thank you," said Holmes. "And The Blue Boar? I telegraphed to
arrange a room."

311

"When you reach the end of the lane, rather than turning off, you keep going straight along East Street, past the church, 'til you get to the crossroads, and there it is."

Holmes thanked him again and pressed a shilling upon him for his assistance.

From the station, it was no more than a ten-minute walk to the rather-picturesque Blue Boar public house, where rooms awaited us. We paused in the bar for a light lunch of sandwiches and a revivifying libation before setting out for the professor's house.

Brookside Cottage wasn't difficult to locate. Following the railway porter's directions, it took us possibly twenty minutes to reach it from The Blue Boar. On our left, as we followed the unpaved lane, we could see, above the treetops, the roof of Prittlewell Priory. As described, the house lay beside the brook that gave it its name.

There was no bell, so I rapped smartly upon the front door with my cane.

Barely had I done so, our approach no doubt noticed from within, the door opened to reveal a tall and lean young man in his shirtsleeves. A bandage was wrapped about his brow. Recalling the professor's letter, I realised this must be his assistant, injured by the intruder.

"Yes?" he asked, his tone a little brusque, but not unfriendly. I suspected the lingering effects of his wound had left him a little out-of-sorts.

"Mr. Holmes and Mr. Watson," said Holmes. "We wrote to Professor Woodridge to say we were coming. He invited us to see his latest acquisition."

"Oh, yes, your letter arrived this morning. It is a trifle inconvenient, but . . . No, no, come in."

I glanced his Holmes, but his expression was sphinx-like.

He led us through into a small front room and introduced us to the professor, a rather short and frail-looking elderly individual with a shock of white hair that was receding from his brow and a pair of equally-wild mutton-chop whiskers upon his cheeks.

The professor didn't rise, but directed us to sit without formality.

"Frederick," he said to his assistant, "would you be so good as to get our guests some tea?"

As soon as the young man was gone, Professor Woodridge's genial and somewhat-vague expression was replaced by a sharp-eyed seriousness. To see the transformation was quite a surprise.

"I don't want Frederick to know why you are here," he said. "I don't want him to worry."

"I quite understand," said Holmes, although I wasn't entirely certain I did.

With a glance towards the door, the professor added, "I'll send Frederick away on a pretence. Then we shall be able to talk freely."

The young man returned shortly with a tray upon which there was a simple teapot, three chipped tea cups, and a battered tin that proved to contain biscuits.

Having thanked him, the professor said, "Oh, I just remembered that I need some items from town. Would you be so good as to walk into Southend and purchase them for me, like a good lad? I hate to ask when you are still suffering, but –"

"I'm fine," said Frederick in a world-weary tone. Clearly, his employer made overmuch of his injuries.

"Very good, very good. Now, where did I put that list . . . Oh, yes! Here it is."

He gave Frederick the list and the young man departed, allowing us to speak frankly.

The professor sighed. "It is my fault he is injured."

"Tell us everything, from the very beginning," said Holmes.

"I am a professor of history," said Woodridge, "although I am living in quiet semi-retirement. My area of speciality is the Roman Empire and, recently, I came into possession of a particularly fine item, the sarcophagus lid that I mentioned in my letter to you."

For a brief moment, a look of rapture crossed his features, then he said, "It is made of imperial porphyry, a stone reserved for the use of the emperor and those closest to him. On the edge, as you will see when I show it to you, is engraved *Spos. Imp.*, which I believe means that this lid was taken from the tomb of Emperor Sponsian, an emperor previously known to history only through a few coins and whose very existence has sometimes been doubted. If so, it will be one of the greatest historical finds of all time."

He began to veer into a rambling account of the putative emperor and his theories upon his reign, from which Holmes was finally able to steer him back onto the topic of our visit.

"I am sorry," said the professor. "Whenever I start thinking about Sponsian and the fact that I might be able to prove his existence, I'm afraid I get quite carried away . . . Now, where was I?"

"If it is from his tomb," said I, "it would be the greatest find of all time."

"Oh, yes. And, if not, it remains a very fine and valuable piece, even after becoming broken."

"And that is why you think someone is trying to steal it?" I prompted.

313

"Precisely. To any collector, it is practically priceless."

"How did you come into possession of it?" asked Holmes.

"It wasn't long ago. I was on my last tour of Greece and Turkey, when I received word that this rarity had come into the hands of an antiquities dealer in Istanbul whom I had used before. I wasn't the only one interested in it. There were the usual sorts attracted to it because of national chauvinism, or simply because the stone it was made of was valuable. There was a Greek businessman, Zarkoff or Zhukov or something similar, and a Turk named Berat Kemal, as well as a rival historian of mine, Herr Doktor Schlosser."

He began to talk of his attempts to purchase the sarcophagus lid and the difficulties of dealing with unscrupulous dealers and the Turkish authorities, until Holmes managed to guide him back to the actual question of who might be attempting to steal it.

"Oh, I have little doubt that Schlosser is the one behind these break-ins," he declared, "keen to steal my thunder."

"Really?" asked Holmes. "In which case, why not name him to the police?"

"Well, you see," the professor said, twisting his hands together, "the sarcophagus lid wasn't declared to the Ottoman authorities, and Frederick arranged for it to leave the country without the officers of the Sultan knowing. Thanks to his careful planning, we pre-empted the other bidders and got it away from Istanbul for London. If anyone were to look too closely at events, my dear friend could find himself in trouble."

Holmes gave a nod of understanding, and I wondered what his thoughts were on the object's dubious acquisition.

"And," Holmes prompted, "what brings it, and you, to Prittlewell." He affected to look about. "It isn't the British Museum."

Woodridge chuckled. "No. I was looking for peace and quiet, Mr. Holmes, and we have that in abundance here, despite its relative closeness to the capital. In a word, it is ideal for me, as I, or more often Frederick, can go into London to the Museum or Library for research, yet I can pursue my studies without the noise and distractions that infest the city. In addition, I had long planned to carry out a survey of this district, for I believe there are any number of unknown Roman sites hidden beneath the fields of south Essex."

"I see."

The professor set down his teacup and pushed himself up from his seat with a groan.

"Now," he said, "let me show you."

We followed Professor Woodridge into the rear room of the cottage. The richly-coloured rectangle of purplish stone rested on a sturdy table. Its subtle dappling was broken into three large and five smaller pieces that had been laid out like a jigsaw. The angled top was smooth, but each corner had a sort of cherub or cupid carved on it, which held coiling parchment that extended along the edges of the lid and was finely carved. It was upon one edge that the Latin letters that so excited the professor had been carved.

"Of course," said Woodridge, wistfully, "it was even more splendid to see when it was whole."

Holmes walked around it, leaning in to look at it closely, and lifted one of the smaller chunks in his hands, holding it for a time as he gazed at it thoughtfully.

"Was anything else out of place or anything missing after you interrupted the intruder?"

Woodridge shook his head. "No, everything was as it should be, save the lid, which was shattered upon the floor."

"So, they weren't after your research or your valuables?"

"No, not at all. It was that Schlosser, I tell you."

Holmes gave a nod and asked him to go over the events of the night it was broken.

"As I said in my letter, I woke in need of a drink. It was hot." He produced a kerchief and dabbed at his brow. "As it is now. Coming downstairs, I was surprised to hear a scraping sound and came in here to investigate. There was movement in the darkness. I thought it was Frederick and spoke his name, but it wasn't. I didn't get a proper look at the figure, for they barged into me. I then tried to seize hold of them, but alas – " He gestured at his frail frame. "I am old. We struggled and there was a loud crash. I managed to light a lamp and saw they were gone and the lid was shattered upon the floor, having been knocked from the table."

"And Frederick?"

"He had encountered them first and been struck a blow on the brow that had left him stunned and bloodied."

"Terrible," said Holmes. "How did they enter? Was it through the window that had been forced the day before?"

"Yes, it had been forced again. It was the one beside the kitchen door. Frederick was in the kitchen when he was struck."

"And you never saw the intruder?" said Holmes, heading for the kitchen, the professor and I trailing after him.

"Not clearly. It was a man, tall, but I can say no more than that. It all happened so swiftly, you see."

Holmes looked at the kitchen window, the lock of which had been repaired and the sill damaged.

"I take it that Herr Doktor Schlosser is not fit and tall?"

315

"No. I would assume it was some hired thug of his."

"Have you seen anyone suspicious in the vicinity?" Holmes asked as we returned to look at the lid. He paused to check the door frame. "Perhaps observing you from a distance?"

"No, no, I don't think so."

"Have you heard of any foreigners – "

Holmes fell suddenly silent. There had been a noise by the half-open window, as if of a footfall.

He gestured to me, for I was standing nearest to the window, and I stepped over to it and threw it fully up.

"Nobody." I leaned out to see if anyone were pressed against the wall of the cottage, but there was none. All I could see was the slope of grass to the ditch that held the brook.

There was another sound, the front door, and we heard Frederick call out that he was back. Holmes and I exchanged a look, but didn't speak.

The professor went out to his assistant for a few minutes, then returned.

Holmes pulled out his pocket watch with exaggerated casualness, in case Frederick were spying upon us, and said, "It's getting late and we need to be going, sir. We shall doubtless call upon you again tomorrow before we leave for London."

Professor Woodridge blinked, then seemed to understand and nodded, bidding us *adieu*. Frederick wished us a good night, too.

We left the cottage and began our stroll back towards The Blue Boar.

Having waited until we were some distance away from Brookside Cottage and, having looked about to ensure nobody was in our vicinity to listen in to our conversation, Holmes said, "What do you make of all that?"

"I cannot say I'm surprised the professor is concerned if he was involved in dubious dealings to obtain that sarcophagus lid and bring it here."

Holmes shook his head and said, "What more?"

"Were we spied upon?" I said. "I didn't see anyone, not even a rabbit."

"Not that," said Holmes, "although that is another question to ask."

"Then what?"

"Did you not consider the lid itself?"

"It was certainly a splendid thing, even broken," I offered.

"Not only splendid, but large and heavy when complete."

It took me a moment to grasp his meaning.

"Yes," he said, "Woodridge would have us believe – and, I have no doubt, he himself believes – that someone broke into his home to steal the lid away. Such a task would be impossible to achieve in stealth, even for

316

the two of us working together. But for a lone thief? No, theft is quite an impossibility."

"Maybe they after something else instead?" I suggested.

"No, you heard the man – nothing else was touched. Yet, the lid fell from the table."

"So?"

"The lid wasn't light and the table, as you saw, wasn't flimsy. A jolt during a scuffle wasn't going to send it flying off. We can be certain that the intruder was interfering with it, had moved it, for it to be knocked so. Which raises a fresh question."

"I don't follow."

"We know that one man alone wasn't capable of stealing it and only an utter fool, unfamiliar with the object, would've thought so, and someone unfamiliar with it would have no cause to steal it. Therefore, we can rule out it being moved during an attempt to remove it. We also know that the intruder showed no interest in the professor's research, which doubtless included sketches and notes about it. Thus, this interest cannot have been in the general appearance and dimensions of the lid. Nor can his presence have been due to an interest in the carving of this Sponsian's truncated name upon the lid, the cupids, or anything else about its design, for that would all have been visible without the lid being moved."

"So, you're saying . . . What? That there is something about the underside of the lid?"

Holmes nodded. "Yes, that would be my conclusion. The intruder was attempting to lift the lid – doubtless this was the sound that the professor heard. He described the sound as like two bricks rubbing against one another and the table has a slate top. I would hazard that there is a marking of some kind, or the intruder suspected there was some such marking, upon the underside of the lid, or perhaps, some hidden compartment."

"Which," said I, "would imply that, whatever his interest in the lid, it isn't to do with its value or its historical importance – ruling out this Schlosser with whom he seems obsessed, and probably the Greek and Turk he mentioned."

"Yes. It would seem there is more than greed or an obsession with history behind the break-ins."

We were nearing The Blue Boar.

"Did you notice anything else amiss?"

I shook my head. "No, what?"

"The window was forced from the *inside*," said Holmes. Then he stepped inside the public house.

Holmes asked for some cold beef in our upstairs sitting room and we ascended to it.

Once we were inside, I felt able to ask him what he meant.

"Exactly what I said. The window was forced open from the *inside*. The first break-in was no break-in, nor the second."

"You mean . . . Frederick?"

"I would assume so."

"His return was suspiciously close to us hearing a sound at the window."

"He may have been suspicious of us," said Holmes.

"Ah, but he was struck by the intruder," I reminded him.

"I think not."

"No."

"No?"

"If we assume that it was Frederick whom the professor heard, and not an intruder who was interfering with the lid, then we have no reason to suppose there was anyone else present. Therefore, he cannot have been struck by another."

"He struck himself?"

"Yes. The kitchen door frame has dried blood on it. The professor doubtless either didn't notice it or assumed it was a splash from when Frederick was struck, but I believe it shows where he wounded himself. Remember, the supposed blow was to the brow. It would be easy for anyone to smack their head against a frame like that."

"But why?"

"That I cannot say, yet. Perhaps his ensuring the professor got the lid to Britain was for his own benefit, but why not make his move before now? And why the subterfuge when, surely, there must have been times when he might have examined the underside of the lid without risking discovery. Certainly, as we have established, it isn't about stealing the lid for profit or academic glory."

"Yes," said I, "it is odd. It's as if he were suddenly in a hurry. But for what reason?"

"If we can establish that," Holmes said, just as there was a knock on the door and our beef was delivered, "we will doubtless know the answer to the entire riddle."

That evening, we descended to the bar to enjoy a drink and observe the locals at rest.

"Look," said Holmes, softly, nodding across the bar, "it's Frederick. And who is that he's speaking to? He doesn't look like a local."

318

The professor's assistant was bent close in conversation with a large, dark-skinned fellow dressed in rough trousers and jacket.

"He looks like a Lascar," said I.

"Yes, or a Turk."

Holmes waved the barman over and asked him about the man.

"I'm not sure," he said, "but I think he's a sailor who came ashore at Leigh. He's been in here twice before in the last week. Why, yes, he does seem to know Frederick there. Each night he's been in, they've chatted."

Holmes thanked him and he went on to serve someone down the bar.

Holmes leaned close to me and said, "I think we may have the reason for his sudden haste in trying to find whatever it is he's looking for."

"His co-conspirator?" I asked. "Or do you think he has been bribed or threatened?"

Holmes glanced their way again. "He doesn't look happy talking to him, does he?"

We looked away, for the swarthy man had turned his head in our direction.

"He's going," I told Holmes.

"Let's follow him."

We stepped away from the bar and headed for the exit, but a large man with quivering jowls stepped in our way and blocked us, causing us to bump against him.

"You looking for trouble?" he demanded.

"Certainly not, sir," said Holmes in a quavering voice quite unlike his usual one, "I'm a historian."

"You'll be history, if you don't watch where you're going," the man said, shoving him in the chest.

"My apologies," quivered Holmes, and we slunk back to the bar as if defeated.

Holmes called the barman over and asked for fresh drinks. "It seems someone didn't wish us to follow."

He thanked the barman and asked him who the man who's accosted us was.

"Oh, his name's Bill Wragg. You were wise not to let him rile you, sir, for he isn't just bluster."

"Indeed," said Holmes and he took a sip of his beer.

The next morning, as we were heading out to see the professor again, the barman waved us over and said, "I had a quiet word with Bill Wragg last night. He was far enough along that he gave no thought to blathering, and he told me he was given two shillings by that dark gentleman you enquired after, the sailor, to accost you. He didn't know why. I'm sorry for the incident, sir."

"Think nothing of it," said Holmes with a smile. "It merely adds to the ambience of the country hostelry."

We walked back to the cottage, the air heavy with the summer heat and, once again, I rapped upon the door with my cane.

Frederick answered the door and let us in. His head was no longer bandaged and the cut was healing. A quick glance was enough to tell me that it was nowhere near the serious wound it had been implied to be.

Professor Woodridge greeted us cordially.

"We'll be returning to London this afternoon," said Holmes, making certain that Frederick was within earshot, "so we wished to take one last look at your prize. It really is most splendid."

"Excellent, excellent." The professor led us through to it.

Holmes picked up each piece in turn – I had to assist him with the larger sections, which were still quite heavy – and examined them meticulously.

"Whatever are you doing?" asked the professor, but Holmes held a finger to his lips to silence him.

Then, when we heard the front door open and close, Holmes said, "Watson, check if he's gone."

"He has," I said, returning a moment later, "I could see him going down the lane."

"Good." He turned to the professor. "Unfortunately, I suspect that Frederick has got himself caught up with whatever villainy is going on."

"No, no! I won't believe it!"

"You must," said I. "It may be that he is being coerced in some way, but he is involved."

"It will be easy to be certain," said Holmes. "You see, I wish to practice a small deception upon him which shall, if he is involved, cause him and his compatriots to reveal their hand and allow us to catch them in the act."

"I very much doubt you are right," said Woodridge, "but if it will prove his innocence, I shall play along. What do you plan to do, Mr. Holmes?"

"I – A-ha!" Holmes held up two of the smaller fragments of the sarcophagus lid, which fitted together like puzzle pieces, and showed the underside to the professor. "Have you seen these letters before?"

He showed the underside of the lid to the professor. There were capital letters carved into it. They didn't form words.

"Roman numerals," I exclaimed.

"Correct, I believe. Well, Professor?"

"Yes. Initially, I took them for a date, but they made no sense. My best guess is that they were some sort of maker's mark."

"You're wrong," said Holmes. He considered them for a moment. "Yes, that's it. They're longitude and latitude."

"But surely," said I, "longitude and latitude didn't exist in Roman times."

"Precisely. These scrapings aren't Roman. See?" He held one of the pieces towards us. "The patina that covers the rest of the surface is missing. These marks are relatively fresh."

"By Jove! He's right," cried the professor, smacking his brow. "But whatever can it mean?"

"I have one or two thoughts on the subject, but nothing quite certain yet. However, I think we can safely say it explains why someone is interested in this, and in particular, its underside."

Holmes gave a quick summary of how he had deduced that interest, causing the professor to exclaim at it, impressed.

"So," said Holmes, "I think we can exclude Herr Doktor Schlosser from our suspicions. Most likely it was one of the others who wished to obtain the lid, and I have a thought in that direction, too."

"Who?" I asked, but Holmes refused to answer.

"We likely shall know tonight. Now," he said to Professor Woodridge, "to that deception I mentioned. You will tell Frederick that I was acting on behalf of a wealthy benefactor of the British Museum and, having inspected the lid, have gone back to London to confirm its authenticity and that you expect me to return tomorrow or the day after with payment for it, and that it will go on display in the museum."

I gave a laugh. "I see. He must act tonight to get the coordinates. He cannot delay!"

"Yes, and we shall have returned in secret to catch him."

He looked at the professor. "Can you do that?"

Woodridge nodded. "I can."

We left before Frederick returned and headed back to The Blue Boar to collect our bags. We were almost there when Holmes said, "Ahoy, Watson – our friend," and pointed to the bulky form of Bill Wragg, who was progressing towards us. Even sober and in daylight, he was a hulk of a man.

"That Lascar is getting his two shillings' worth," said I.

"Or he's paid him more," replied Holmes as we neared him.

"You still here?" Wragg sneered.

Holmes looked down at himself as if in surprise. "Why, yes, it seems so."

"Funny." The man spat. "Take some friendly advice: Leave. Get out of Prittlewell and back to London."

It was all I could do to restrain myself from striking the vulgar man with my cane, but Holmes was always the better actor and cowered before him.

With a quaver in his voice, Holmes said, "We are! We are!"

"It's true," I said. "We're on our way to collect our bags, and then we catch the train home."

"Good. Don't let me catch you around here again."

I trailed after Holmes as he scurried away, as if in terror of the big man, and followed him into The Blue Boar, where he made a point of loudly telling the barman we were returning to London.

"If Frederick and his friend were in any doubt," said he as we walked back up East Street towards the station, "this should assuage them. Still, let's hope someone sees us board the train."

"And nobody sees us return later."

We only went as far as was necessary to find a busy telegraph office.

"We don't want to stand out," said Holmes as we queued.

"Who are you going to contact? Lestrade?"

"Istanbul," he said, to my surprise.

"Really?"

"Yes. I know a police officer there who can be trusted. He has helped on a case or two before. The longitude and latitude we found is somewhere in Asia Minor, so I'll let him have the information and he can see what he can find."

We spent the rest of the day at the station, enjoying some refreshing cups of tea and hearty sandwiches, before returning to Prittlewell on the evening train.

Our plan was simple: Frederick would head to The Blue Boar for a drink as usual – of this we were sure – as he wouldn't wish to arouse any suspicion in his mentor. We would enter Brookside Cottage and take up a position of concealment, and then, when he moved to examine the sarcophagus lid, we would catch him.

Simple. Only we hadn't bet on Bill Wragg to derail it. His home must have been near to the station, for he was East Street as we reached the top of the lane from the station, I spotted him, clearly heading for The Blue Boar.

"Wragg!" I hissed at Holmes and we moved to take cover in the shadow of the hedge, hoping he would pass by without noticing us, only for him to look around and see us.

He peered into the shadows for a moment, then snarled.

"You again!" he cried, heading for us.

"I think," said Holmes, no longer putting on his quivering-academic act, "this has become personal for him."

He readied his cane and, as Wragg swung a fist at him, moved his body aside and gave the man a smart blow on the side of his head.

Wragg stumbled and almost fell to his knees, but bellowed and turned, fists ready.

I didn't wait, but swung my own cane at the back of his knee, causing him to fall onto his hands and knees with a cry of pain.

Holmes provided another blow to the head that rendered him unconscious.

"His belt, Watson."

We bound him and I stuffed his handkerchief into his mouth as a gag. Then we laid him in a ditch a little distance down the lane to Brookside Cottage where he wouldn't be seen.

"We mustn't forget to come and release him later," said Holmes, and I was almost certain he was grinning as he spoke. "Poor fellow will have an awful headache when he comes to."

We delayed no longer, but went to the cottage and knocked on the back door. The professor let us in, confirming that his assistant had gone to The Blue Boar as usual.

He showed us an alcove where we could hide, out of sight of both window and door, but with a view of the lid.

"Promise me you won't hurt the lad," he said.

"We won't," said Holmes, although, once the old man was gone, he asked me, "Watson, do you have your revolver on you?"

"Of course."

"Good. Only use it if absolutely necessary."

Then, we waited.

I'm not sure if I dozed off while squashed into that alcove with Holmes, but I started at a sudden sound.

"Someone's forcing the window," Holmes whispered in my ear.

We heard the window slide up and the noises of someone clambering through it, then the sound of the pieces of porphyry being handled.

"Stop there!" cried Holmes, stepping out from the alcove, cane in hand.

I was behind him in a moment, my revolver aimed at the figure.

It wasn't Frederick.

The shadow threw a piece of the lid at Holmes, who gave a pained cry as it struck him, and then leapt for the window and threw himself out.

I fired, but my shot was wild and struck the wall.

I ran to the window.

"Stop, or I'll shoot!"

The dark figure kept running and I fired again, but must have missed for he didn't lose a stride. From elsewhere in the cottage, I heard the professor shouting something in alarm.

I fumbled my way out through the window, wishing age and my old war wound didn't make me clumsy and slow, and began to run after the figure. Behind me, I thought I heard Holmes cry something and then the sounds of him following after me.

It was useless to fire again in the deep darkness of the country night. All I could do was try and catch up with the figure before he vanished into the black, something I didn't hold out much hope of achieving as I chased him across uneven ground and was forced to push through a hedge.

There was sudden cry and a splash and I halted in surprise as the shadow had vanished from my line of sight. Then, I looked down and was grateful that I had stopped so, for I was standing at the very lip of the broad ditch that held the brook that gave Prittlewell its name. The path had turned and cut across our path. In the water, stunned, was the man I'd been chasing.

I pointed my revolver at him and told him not to move.

"I shan't miss this time," said I.

He groaned and held up his hands in surrender.

Holmes reached us, then, and had a lantern with him that he shone down into the ditch to reveal our quarry to be the Lascar or Turk we had seen speaking with Frederick, now sodden and muddy.

"Well done, Watson," said Holmes, laughing. "Well done."

Leaving Holmes to watch over our prisoner, I went to The Blue Boar to bring back Frederick on some vague pretext. He was surprised to see me, but didn't object. Having told him to wait outside, I asked the barman to send someone to Southend to fetch the police, telling him only that a burglary had been foiled at Brookside Cottage and arrest needed to be made.

As soon as we arrived back at the cottage, Frederick admitted what little he knew immediately upon seeing we had the man bound and in our custody.

It transpired that the man had, through a mixture of blackmail and threats, turned the young secretary into his accomplice in obtaining the coordinates marked onto the underside of the lid. Frederick proved a failure in lifting the lid and obtaining them, and as far as they knew, it was about to go into the possession of the British Museum, where access would likely prove impossible. The man had been forced to intervene himself.

The man was, Frederick informed us, a Turk, although he wasn't sure for whom he was working, or the relevance of the coordinates.

"We'll know for certain soon, I should think," said Holmes. "Perhaps even tomorrow. I telegraphed my contact in Turkey, and they will be searching the site."

The Turk groaned.

"I suspect I know what they shall find," Holmes continued. "When Professor Woodridge described his acquisition, he mentioned a Greek businessman whose name he thought was something like Zarkoff or Zhukov. I believe the man was *Zaharoff*, the so-called 'Merchant of Death', whose name has recently been in the newspapers again. The longitude and latitude likely refer to where a payment had been left for him in return for weapons provided to some group opposed to the Sultan's rule."

He looked hard at the Turk. "Am I right?"

The man didn't reply, but squirmed against his bonds. Within a few days, we would learn that Holmes was indeed correct, and that the payment had been in return for arms sold to an Armenian group fighting for their independence.

"It really was a quite cunning plan," said Holmes, "and, one I suspect has probably been used many times before. Some antiquity is found and the location marked upon it. Then it's sold cheaply to Zaharoff, who learns where to collect his payment, as well as obtaining an artifact he can sell for a profit. Almost undetectable and, even if someone like the professor notices the markings, their true nature will remain meaningless to them, for, as you said Watson, the Romans didn't have longitude and latitude.

"Unfortunately, this time the location was marked upon an object of exceptional value, both real and historical, and Zaharoff lost out. So he sent his thug here to discover the coordinates."

Holmes picked up one of the pieces of porphyry and said, "The puzzle is solved."

The Turk snarled, straining at his bonds.

"You know too much, Englishman!" he cried. "My master will not look kindly upon being thwarted. He shall have his revenge upon you!"

Holmes scoffed at that. "I have thwarted any number of dangerous criminals, sir, and I fear revenge from none of them. Zaharoff is no different."

"You shall see!" spat the Turk.

"Perhaps," said Holmes.

"I should probably go and untie Bill Wragg," I said.

"Perhaps," repeated Holmes, and then, he laughed.

The police arrested the Turk, who was tried and jailed for his crime. Holmes received a telegram to say that the money had been recovered and the cell of Armenian fighters arrested. Zaharoff, however, could not be linked to any of this, so he went unpunished.

I never heard another thing about Emperor Sponsian, but Zaharoff wasn't absent from the news, remaining involved in war-mongering and accused more than once of criminality.

"He seems untouchable," I told Holmes.

"Such is too often the way with such men," said Holmes. "But those who believe themselves to be so often make a mistake sooner or later and bring about their own downfall. It will delight me," he added, "to be the one to detect that mistake."

The Adventure of the
Fearful Printer
by Arthur Hall

As Holmes and I returned from a pleasant walk in Regent's Park one fine early autumn morning, I felt my fingers automatically tighten on my service revolver in my pocket.

"We are being observed," I told him in a low voice. "from the corner opposite."

"If you mean the gentleman in the crumpled morning coat, he has been following us since we passed that rather splendid oak that you were so taken with."

I looked out of the corner of my eyes, without turning my head. "He appears rather distressed."

"Indeed he does. I imagine he has been toiling under the indecision of whether or not to consult us, since he recognised us in the park. But we are nearing our lodgings now, as you see. Perhaps you would care to approach the fellow, and possibly help him put an end to his torment? If you conclude that we can be of any assistance, pray invite him to join us in our sitting room. I will ask Mrs. Hudson to bring us tea."

"But surely you're in the midst of the Alladyne case?"

"That was yesterday," he smiled. "I spent much of last night attending to it while you slept. The letter that you saw me post on the way to the park contains my evidence which will certainly exonerate Mr. Fountain."

"Very well," I acknowledged, somewhat surprised. "I'll see what this fellow has to say."

Holmes entered 221 as I turned away and crossed the road, avoiding a landau passing at what seemed a quite unnecessary speed. Our follower, loitering nearby, looked away, attempting to give an impression of disinterest, and I was able to see that he was probably in his mid-fifties, stocky and of medium height, with a rather prominent nose. I addressed him and saw that he was in an embarrassed state, but after a few moments of conversation was able to convince him that Holmes was accustomed to hearing all sorts of extraordinary accounts, many of which would form the basis of subsequent enquiries. Red-faced, he agreed to accompany me.

"Ha! Who have we here?" Holmes asked as we entered our sitting room.

"This is Mr. Julius Braddock," I explained, "who is considerably worried regarding his recent experiences."

327

"Then let us discuss them, and see how we may help."

I relieved our visitor of his coat and hat and hung them up with my own. Holmes indicated the basket chair to him and we were all settled by the time our good landlady appeared with tea.

I poured for us after she withdrew. Mr. Braddock accepted his cup with thanks but left it on a side-table untouched, and I saw from his anxious expression that something stronger was needed.

"I agree," Holmes said as he replaced his empty cup. "Our client is in need of a restorative. Pray pour him a brandy, and we'll allow him a little time to recover himself."

Feeling, as often before, that Holmes was sometimes able to read my thoughts, I took up the crystal decanter and complied. Mr. Braddock took the harsh spirit in a single swallow and his face contorted momentarily as it reached his stomach. He was still for a moment before he also drained his teacup and sat back in his chair showing signs of exhaustion.

"You are in a highly agitated state," Holmes said in a kindly tone. "You must take your time, to recover at your own pace. When you are ready, put your thoughts in order and explain your difficulty to us. You have my word that we will do all within our power to help."

"Thank you," our client gasped. He closed his eyes and dabbed with a handkerchief at the sheen of sweat on his reddened face. A few minutes passed in silence, except for the sounds of activity that reached us from Baker Street, and then he gathered himself and sat up straight in his chair. His voice was now steady, but tinged with fear.

"Gentlemen, I cannot apologise enough for the inconvenience that I have caused. I fear that my experiences of late have drained my energy, for they defy my understanding."

I noticed that the trembling of his limbs had decreased somewhat, and his breathing had become regular.

Holmes nodded. "I see that you are calmer now. Your printing concern is, I see, doing well, but I cannot tell if you are recently widowed or have been abandoned."

Mr. Braddock became very still, staring at my friend fixedly. When he spoke, his voice was full of wonder.

"How could you know those things, sir? We have not been previously acquainted, have we?"

"Not at all, but the ink stains upon your hands are fresh, and not from such a fluid that would be used in writing letters. Also, if you will forgive me for saying, it would be a poor wife indeed who allowed her husband to set out with a collar so creased, not to mention your morning coat."

Our client sighed deeply. "Yes, I must apologise for my appearance. It is true that Madeleine has left me after only two months of marriage,

328

and I know not why. I believed we had settled what differences we had, yet I returned from work to an empty house one evening and have not seen her since. I am becoming accustomed to finding for myself again."

"How long ago was this?"

"One week to the day."

"There are no children concerned, of course?" I ventured.

Mr. Braddock laughed shortly. "I am a little too old for that, sir. In any case, my wife mentioned several times that she wished for none. I do have a son, however, from my previous marriage to Anna. She passed on some years ago, and Benjamin died six months ago in South Africa."

We expressed our condolences.

"Forgive my digression," he said then, "for it is not concerning those happenings that I am seeking your assistance."

"Then pray elaborate," Holmes said.

"The fact is sirs – " An uncertain look crossed our client's face. " – that I am afraid you will find my account difficult to believe."

"Many of my past enquiries have seemed so, at first."

"You may consider this to be different. Since my wife left, I have been followed by a woman on my return from work in the early evening. She appears for a little while as I walk along Kensington High Street, and then disappears."

"Is there more?" Holmes asked when it was apparent that Mr. Braddock had ceased to speak.

"Indeed there is. I quickly realised that she is Miss Eleanor Ferrell, Madeleine's younger sister. I should explain that I wooed her before meeting my wife, after which we began to quarrel. This caused such strife that I was obliged to break off our engagement, and I found that I had unconsciously transferred my affections."

"And you believe that these appearances are meant as some sort of revenge?" Holmes's tone was tinged with disapproval. I surmised that he had begun to consider our client as something of a cad.

"This seemed likely, since our relationship was a stormy one. Eleanor several times threatened to kill me if I betrayed her."

My friend and I glanced at each other, appalled.

"Have you confronted her, as she followed? It would have taken no more than to turn and retrace your steps, surely."

"I did so once, but she was nowhere to be seen."

"And the next time?"

Mr. Braddock avoided our eyes. "I did nothing. I confess to being afraid."

"Good Heavens, man – !" I began, until Holmes silenced me with a gesture.

"Why were you afraid?"

Our client raised his head, and I saw that there was indeed terror in his recollection.

"Because Miss Ferrell killed herself, shortly before my marriage."

Holmes was quick to respond. "You must abandon any notions you may have regarding ghosts or vengeful spirits. Long experience has revealed that the dead never return."

"But I attended her funeral, and have seen her since."

"Could it be," I intervened, "that you blame yourself for her death, and that the events you describe are imaginary?"

He shook his head. "I consulted a physician, the one that my wife and I both used on her recommendation, and that was his conclusion also. But she is real, I tell you. I am not mistaken."

"While she pursues you," Holmes said after a moment, "can you hear her footfalls?"

"I can, since on one occasion she hurried to follow me more closely. I heard them distinctly."

"Then surely that suggests to you that she is no phantom? After hearing your physician's advice, did you do anything more before today?"

The look of shame returned to our client's face. "Knowing that it couldn't be done lawfully, I engaged two body-snatchers to open Eleanor's grave. It was done in the early hours, and we weren't disturbed."

Again there came a short silence, which Holmes quickly ended.

"And the result?"

"The coffin contained nothing but stones."

Holmes rested his chin on his steepled fingers, thinking.

"Mr. Braddock, has this woman who follows you become a threat in any way? Has she repeated her intention to kill you?"

"She hasn't spoken at all."

"Have you disclosed these incidents to the official force?"

"I cannot, for no crime has been committed."

"Quite. I was on the point of recommending that you consult either a priest or another physician, but there are aspects of this which don't sit well. Give your details, even the smallest, of this affair to Doctor Watson and then leave us. Expect to hear from us within a week."

At that, my friend walked away to gaze from the window. When I had completed my notes, Mr. Braddock left with an unanswered word of thanks.

"He hasn't, at least, been pursued here today," Holmes said as he turned from his observations and resumed his seat. "What did you make of him?"

"His anxiety, at least, was genuine. The man was terrified."

"Quite so. Clearly Mr. Braddock is being persecuted, although he appears to be doubtful as to the reason. I trust that you didn't fail to obtain from him a more exact description of the place where this so-called apparition appears?"

I retrieved my notebook. "He specified that the woman begins to follow him near the stables situated on the second corner of Kensington High Street, and ceases her pursuit after about one-hundred yards. That is to say, close to the almshouses."

"Always there, without exception?"

"He was specific on that point."

"That is significant in itself. Doubtless Mrs. Hudson will be serving our luncheon soon. After that, I suggest we spend an unhurried hour of conversation, then a wander along Kensington High Street would seem to be in order."

"I will be glad to accompany you. My recent bout of influenza has now subsided, and I am at your disposal."

The warmth of his smile was not lost upon me. "I was certain of it, old friend."

When Mr. Braddock appeared, walking cautiously and often pausing to glance behind, darkness was almost complete. Between the pools of light cast by the newly-lit lamps were areas of deep shadow, so that he and other passers-by were alternately visible and partially concealed. We had identified the section of Kensington High Street that he had described sometime earlier, and found concealment in the deep doorway of a chemist's shop on the opposite pavement.

"He is passing the stables now," Holmes whispered, although we stood far enough away to make the precaution unnecessary. "Note that he walks this way always at the same time, enabling his tormentors to make their plans."

"They must therefore enjoy a certain familiarity with his habits."

"Precisely."

The slow-moving crowd was thinning, as cabs were engaged and those continuing on foot passed out of our sight.

"Holmes, look!"

"I see her."

As our client passed a narrow alley, a tall woman emerged. She wore a bonnet and a long dark coat, and her face was covered by a veil that made her expression difficult to see. After standing and watching for a moment or two, she began taking long strides in pursuit. Mr. Braddock looked over his shoulder and quickened his pace. We stepped from our hiding place and approached her, and only then did I become aware of the two burly men, also darkly-dressed, who sauntered along in her wake.

They came to an immediate halt, barring our way as they realised our intention. I saw that Holmes had gripped his stick in readiness.

"You don't want to do business with her, gentlemen," the tallest of them advised us. "She isn't a lady of the night."

"That was not our intention," I replied, a little outraged.

"Do you know her, then?"

"We merely wished to ask her a question or two," Holmes said.

The man who had not yet spoken called out, and the woman turned and retraced her steps. Mr. Braddock, now further along the street, had hailed a hansom and departed.

"Oh, I wouldn't advise asking questions, really I wouldn't." The tall man advanced towards us and the other joined him. Now that they were closer, I could see that they had the appearance of prize-fighters. I sensed the tension in Holmes as he prepared to defend himself, but I drew my service revolver and they halted at once.

"Be assured that I will not hesitate to fire if you attack."

They stood still for an instant. Then the second man glanced to ensure that the woman had gone. He said something to the tall one, who nodded.

"All right," he looked at my weapon and retreated, "but you shouldn't be interfering in things that are none of your business. See?"

They backed away from us, then turned and made off at a quick pace.

"I should have anticipated," Holmes said, "that some arrangement would have been made to prevent Mr. Braddock from accosting the woman if he had a mind to. Those two are quite far off now, so let us see where she has gone."

We approached the alley and entered into its deeper darkness. I saw that we were in a network of poorly lit narrow streets, deserted and silent except for the scuttling of rats or cats near the piles of rubbish and the faint cries of a distressed infant.

Holmes had been listening intently. "There is no movement here, at least none nearby," he concluded. "Either she has taken refuge in a house, or engaged a cab. I think there is nothing to be learned here, so we may as well return to Baker Street and a rather belated dinner."

We interrupted out journey once, for Holmes to dispatch a telegram.

"To Lestrade?" I asked him on his return from the Post Office.

He settled back into his seat and signalled for our driver to continue, before shaking his head. "To Mr. Braddock."

"You enquired as to whether he returned home safely?"

"Not at all. After our disappointing escapade this evening, I decided upon a different approach. I asked him for the name and address of his physician, which he neglected to leave with us and you neglected to request."

I realised at once that I had indeed omitted it from my notes, but ignored both the criticism and the momentary stony glance.

"So you believe this physician may have additional information regarding our client's situation, or his wife?" I ventured. Then after a moment's thought. "Or have you reason to suppose that he is involved in some way?"

"That is a possibility. Unless there is another person, as yet unknown to us, behind this apparently purposeless affair, we have to choose between the woman and those two roughs who we encountered earlier. I don't consider this likely. My suspicions were aroused when Mr. Braddock indicated that his physician quickly attributed the sightings of this woman to imagination, rather than the far more likely explanation of an actual presence. Other than simply repeating tonight's observation, I see no other way to progress."

We both received disapproving looks from Mrs. Hudson on our return to our lodgings, but I was pleased to discover our dinner to be hot and not over-cooked, despite our delay in consuming it.

Holmes decided to conduct one of his violin recitals immediately after our plates had been cleared away, wearing a deeply thoughtful expression as he entertained me with one of his own compositions. When we finally settled ourselves in our armchairs, I was about to open a conversation regarding an item I had read in *The Evening News* when I was interrupted by the chimes of the doorbell.

"A new client, perhaps?"

"No. I heard no cab come to rest near our front door, so unless someone has arrived on foot, it is the telegraph boy on his bicycle."

And so it proved to be. Moments later, after our landlady had delivered the yellow envelope and withdrawn, Holmes tore it open and extracted the contents.

"Mr. Braddock tells us that his physician, and that of his wife, is Doctor Luca Belasco. Do you know of him?"

I thought for a moment, then shook my head. "The name is unfamiliar to me."

He nodded. "He practices in the Old Kent Road, it seems." Lowering the form, he turned to me. "Well, we'll see what can be learned there in the morning. As for now, what do you say to a brandy before retiring?"

It had been some time since I had found myself in this southeast district of the capital. Holmes said little during the journey, and so my attention had been captured by our passing surroundings. I saw the glint of pale sunshine on the Surrey Canal, followed soon after by the stark countenance of the Metropolitan Gas Works, and knew that we couldn't now be far from our destination.

The thoroughfare now boasted many more buildings than I remembered. Between the numerous coaching inns that had long been present, various industries were now represented. Some of the structures were already blackened by smoke and soot, doubtless from the tall chimneys that poured forth continuously.

Holmes rapped on the coachwork with his stick. "Stop here, Driver, if you please."

We alighted and he paid our fare. The hansom rattled off as we confronted a Georgian-style building which appeared to be in need of some repair. It struck me as strange that the waiting room was empty, as that of my own former practice never was for very long, and that the young woman who received us wore no nurse's uniform. She listened to my friend's request and left us to see if the doctor was free.

Moments later she returned with a white-coated man of average height. He was olive-skinned, Italian or Greek I surmised, holding Holmes's card and wearing an expression that could have been amusement. His voice was smooth, his English perfect, and he spoke with an accent I couldn't identify.

"Gentlemen, I have heard of you, of course, but I am surprised that a consulting detective should have reason to visit my practice."

"We are merely here to obtain information," answered Holmes, "if you would be kind enough to supply it, and it doesn't break any confidentiality between you and your patient."

"That must always be a consideration, of course, but if you would care to step into my office, there may be some assistance I can provide to you."

We followed him into a room where a large desk stood surrounded by several straight-backed chairs. At his invitation we sat and faced him. His smile, I noticed, never varied, so that I was reminded of a ventriloquist's dummy.

He placed his hands upon the desk before him. "Now, gentlemen, about which of my patients do you wish to enquire?"

"It is my current client, Mr. Julius Braddock."

"Ah. I suspect that he may have consulted you about his visions of his wife's deceased sister. The poor man is quite obsessed and in a considerably excited state."

"As he was during his visit to us. He is adamant that his sister-in-law still lives. I have assured him that the dead do not return to haunt the living. Is it true that you suggested that his sightings are nothing more than imagination?"

Doctor Belasco nodded. "His condition isn't that unusual. I have had many such patients before. They are convinced that they are seeing something or someone that cannot possibly exist. Often, this is a temporary condition resulting from severe shock of some sort. When next I see Mr. Braddock, I intend to define the cause specifically. Having identified it, I will then decide how to treat it."

"What would you say," Holmes said, "if I told you that his 'visions' are nothing of the sort. They are real."

"How would you know this?" the physician asked after a moment.

"Last night, Watson and I followed our client. We saw the woman appear and pursue him. She was as real as you or I."

The smile narrowed and confusion crept into his eyes momentarily. "Then Mr. Braddock has represented his ailment to me inaccurately," he said thoughtfully. "I must start again at the beginning and question him further."

"I am curious," I said, "as to where you learned your techniques. Illnesses of the mind, such as you attributed to our client, are very much a new field of study."

"Indeed. The knowledge that I gained at the University of Milan was most enlightening, but since then I have broadened and varied the methods since. I – "

The inner door opened, interrupting him. A heavily-built man, similarly white-coated, entered. His eyes widened in surprise as he saw us, but he said nothing and left after whispering briefly to Doctor Belasco.

"Were the theories of Freud among your sources of study?" I persisted.

"Of necessity, yes. I should explain that my practice is a private one, accepting only patients suffering from ailments familiar to me. This specialization is why you have probably not heard of me as being prominent in the medical profession." He glanced up to the clock that ticked loudly on the wall behind us. "But now I regret to have to end our discussion, gentlemen. My next appointment in imminent. I hope I have thrown some light upon your difficulties."

"You have indeed enlightened us," Holmes agreed as we left.

Owing to the energy displayed by the horse, the hansom that conveyed us back to Baker Street seemed to cover the distance in less time than that we had taken earlier. Holmes was clearly excited by the prospect of the conclusion of the investigation, and I knew why.

"I trust you recognised Doctor Belasco's assistant," I stated, "if that is what he is?"

"I could hardly have failed to, any more than he could have failed to identify us. A rough, or a prize-fighter, retains his appearance no matter how he chooses to present himself."

"But what of Doctor Belasco? He doesn't strike me as a genuine practitioner."

"Nor I. I will consult my index regarding his career, and then I think a visit to the Yard is indicated. After luncheon, I think I'll have to leave you for an hour or so."

We arrived back at Baker Street in time for Holmes to spend some little time searching his index before Mrs. Hudson served roast chicken. He barely touched his before resuming his task, finally replacing the last volume as he shook his head.

"There is no mention there. Possibly he has used other names, or disguises." He put on his hat and coat and called back to me as he descended the stairs. "I won't be long."

He was as good as his word. I hardly had time to peruse the mid-day edition of *The Standard* before he returned. He entered the room with a flourish, and I knew at once from his expression that he had met with some success. He divested himself of his outer garments and threw himself into his armchair.

"You have learned something of this questionable doctor, I see."

"Indeed." He reached for his clay pipe, and then decided against it. "As I suspected, our doctor isn't a doctor at all. Lestrade wasn't at the Yard, but I was fortunate enough to encounter MacDonald, who knew at once our adversary from my description. It seems that Doctor Belasco has passed himself off as a schoolmaster, a solicitor, and a university lecturer in the course of his various swindles, as well as an assay expert in South Africa. MacDonald produced an old telegram from Inspector Van Raat of the Pretoria Police Division, containing a warning that Belasco had left the country for England, and much information regarding his previous activities."

"I am surprised that he hasn't crossed your path before."

"As was I, until MacDonald explained that his recent crimes have been confined to Scotland and the north. I would wager that Belasco will bring his attempt to defraud our client to a premature end, since he now realises that we are but one step behind him. Were we to return to the premises on the Old Kent Road, I wouldn't be at all surprised to discover that they are now deserted."

I leaned towards him in my chair, as I realised what he had implied. "You now know the purpose of this affair, then?"

"Some of it, I think. It wasn't difficult to deduce, once I added this new information to our own. Also I dispatched several telegrams on leaving here, and returned to the office for the replies on leaving the Yard."

"I confess to being confounded as to the reason of our client's torment."

"That is quite a simple matter. We have discovered no motive from Mr. Braddock's disclosures because he himself is unaware of it. My enquiries have revealed that his son, Benjamin, had considerable interests in a South African gold mine. When he died, his shares were sold by his advisers and a telegram sent to Mr. Braddock to inform him that he and his wife were sole beneficiaries. As it happened, the message was received by the wife while our client was engaged in his employment, and she promptly left their home, taking it with her."

"Leaving Mr. Braddock in ignorance of his good fortune."

"Quite so. Mrs. Braddock's intention was of course to keep the entire amount for herself and disappear."

I nodded. "He has my sympathy – but where does Doctor Belasco come into this?"

"As to that, I am as yet uncertain. However, I have discovered that our client's previous doctor, before his wife recommended Belasco, was Doctor Ephraim Simmonds. Unless I am mistaken, I have heard you mention him on several occasions. Is he an acquaintance?"

"We have been opponents at my club in one or two games of billiards."

"Excellent. Do you believe he would disclose information concerning Mr. Braddock's health?"

I considered for a few moments. "If I stress that the reason for my enquiry is urgent, perhaps he would be willing to confide somewhat in me as a fellow member of his profession."

"Capital!" He hesitated, and I realised that it was because he had heard Mrs. Hudson on the stairs. "But now the early dinner that I requested is at hand. I suggest a brisk walk afterwards, during which you can dispatch a telegram from the nearest office."

Both our dinner and the walk were over quickly. On our return, Holmes was absent for a while, and then began one of his chemical experiments while I read a recent report concerning a minor measles epidemic in the West Country. We were both surprised when our landlady appeared with Doctor Simmonds' reply within the hour. I had expected him to suggest a meeting at our club, but as it was he replied in medical terms which would have been incomprehensible to all except those of our calling.

Holmes replaced a test-tube in the rack. "What does he say?"

"His reply is as obscure as a secret code."

"Yes, yes, but what is it's meaning?"

"Simply that he warned Mr. Braddock numerous times against over-exertion. The fellow has a heart that is unlikely to withstand a severe shock."

"Such as encountering his former fiancée, when he knows that she isn't only deceased but apparently risen from her rest. It seems that his death is required by his tormentors, as well as the considerable sum from his son's estate."

"To prevent a claim, do you think, should he discover his wife's treachery?"

"That is most likely." He consulted his pocket watch. "But now I see that a hansom has just delivered its passenger almost opposite. Kindly get our hats and coats, and if we are quick we will catch it."

"Where are we going?" I asked as I rose from my chair.

"To observe Mr. Braddock return from his work again, of course. If they fail to induce his demise tonight, I am wondering what action they will take."

"You indicated that Doctor Belasco, if indeed he is behind this, will be obliged to bring an end to this soon."

"As he will, I am certain."

Kensington High Street was darker than before. One of the street lamps had either failed to ignite or gone out, so that the hurrying folk appeared half-shadowed as they returned to their homes. From our place of concealment we saw a brougham speed by, one or two pedestrians glancing at it momentarily.

Holmes had dispatched a further telegram during our journey, explaining that he had promised to inform Inspector MacDonald of any developments. If it had been received or acted upon I couldn't tell, for there was no sign of the official force here.

"There," Holmes said, indicating a figure walking briskly towards us from our left.

Mr. Braddock scurried past the entrance to the alley where the woman had appeared before, and had gained perhaps ten yards before she reappeared. He turned warily, and was about to increase his pace when a shout from Holmes bade him stand still.

We approached and the woman, seeing us, turned to retreat. Behind her stood the two burly men who had confronted us previously, but were now quickly restrained by four constables and Inspector MacDonald, who emerged from a nearby shop.

"Are these the two, Mr. Holmes?" He held his bony physique at its full height as he addressed my friend.

"They are indeed, Inspector. I shall be surprised if they aren't already sought by the Yard. But," he confronted the woman, no longer an apparition but now quite clearly afraid, "it is this young lady who interests me."

He gestured to Mr. Braddock, who then approached cautiously. When he drew near enough, Holmes removed the woman's dark wig and veil with a swift movement.

Our client appeared shocked, his mouth gaping. "Madeleine! How could you do this to me?"

"It was Belasco," she stammered. "He made me do it."

"I think not," Inspector MacDonald said then. "Down at the Yard, we have a long history of your crimes together, and with your sister,."

At that moment there was some confusion, as another figure appeared from the alley and, after a quick glance at us, ran headlong in the opposite direction.

"Quickly!" I shouted. "Or he will escape."

"It has been allowed for, Doctor," the official detective said calmly with a wry smile.

His meaning became clear moments later when another tall and thick-set constable appeared from the shadows. He held the man we knew as Doctor Belasco by the scruff of his neck. As a prisoner he was no longer smiling, and his eyes were full of desperation.

"We are aware," Holmes said to Madeleine Braddock, "of the practice of your sister and yourself of marrying rich men before absconding with their wealth. Doubtless *Mr.* Belasco here has connections in the financial world and elsewhere that enabled you to seek out such fortunate individuals. On this occasion, however, I would speculate that an irregularity occurred."

"Say nothing, Madeleine!" Belasco cried. "Or it is all up with us!"

The constable increased his restraint and said something in a low voice. Belasco fell silent.

"My sister began to care for Julius," she murmured.

"And so," Holmes continued, "she resented it greatly when Mr. Braddock transferred his affections to you. Belasco will have realised at once the threat she now represented to the scheme to defraud your husband, but it was saved, was it not, by her convenient suicide."

"Eleanor took her own life. It was a terrible thing to happen."

"Yet you didn't object to the removal of her body from its resting place, to make it appear that she still lived."

She said nothing, her eyes downcast.

Holmes was undeterred. "Who decided then that you should resurrect her by altering your appearance so that Mr. Braddock would, from a distance, be deceived? Who decided to ensure that he could never contest the ownership of the inherited proceeds from the South African gold shares by creating a state of fear and confusion calculated to be fatal because of his ailing heart?"

She became immediately excited, pointing at Belasco and sobbing, "It was him! I swear it was him!"

"Your tone is sincere, but it doesn't answer the remaining question."

I saw Inspector MacDonald glance towards them with renewed interest. "What is that, Mr. Holmes? Clearly, I have missed something here."

"Only if, like myself, you disbelieve coincidences, Inspector. The question is, who murdered Eleanor Ferrell?"

The prize-fighters looked at each other anxiously, and Mrs. Braddock stood agape.

"Not I!" cried Belasco. "I have killed no one."

"But you are guilty of an indirect attempt, at least," the inspector reminded him.

"How did your sister die?" Holmes asked Mrs. Braddock.

She appeared confused by the question, but then: "I was informed that she took a fatal dose of arsenic."

"Did she ever threaten such an action – perhaps when it became clear that you had replaced her in Mr. Braddock's affections?"

"Never. I couldn't believe that she had done this. It was so unlike her."

Holmes nodded. "Was the poison readily available to her, perhaps kept to destroy an infestation of rats?"

"No." She shook her head. "I hadn't known her to possess any, nor of any vermin in her house."

"This is futile," Mr. Braddock interrupted, breathing in short gasps. "It is obvious, surely, that Belasco killed her to safeguard his intention to rob me."

"I have said before now that there nothing as misleading as an obvious fact," said Holmes. "It seemed to me prudent to establish that the 'suicide' of Miss Eleanor Ferrell was as it had been told to us. Therefore, soon after beginning my enquiries, I consulted the pharmacies in the area as to the identities of any recent purchasers of arsenic. The fellow at the fourth that I approached proved to be most helpful. His description of *you*, Mr. Braddock, was quite accurate. I confess to feeling somewhat aggrieved when a client turns out to be the villain of the piece, but of your reason I am unaware."

Mr. Braddock's face showed momentary shock and fear at this sudden exposure, before he turned quickly to flee. The sight of my service revolver, aimed at his heart, halted his escape, and his expression became one of resignation.

"I see that I, too, am finished," he said between laboured breaths. "It is true that I poisoned Eleanor. That is why it was so terrifying when I thought she had returned. I am a superstitious man by nature, and I feared her retribution."

"But why," Holmes asked, "did you find it necessary to resort to murder?"

Our client bowed his head, his shame now apparent. "Eleanor realised that she had become a woman spurned, and it didn't sit well with her. During our courtship, she accidentally discovered some papers which implicated me in the death of my first wife, Anna. She made no further mention of them, but I couldn't risk her revenging herself upon me by blackmail. I engaged you, Mr. Holmes, to rid me of the resurrected Eleanor, for it was clear that harm was meant to me, were she living or dead."

At this, and a sign from Inspector MacDonald, one of the constables produced a pair of police handcuffs and restrained our former client.

The passers-by were fewer now, and several hansoms waited nearby in the hope of further fares. The meagre lighting lent an almost spectral glow to the street, and I saw that the moon had emerged from behind a bank of cloud.

"Well, gentlemen," Holmes addressed them all. "That would appear to account for everything. But now I feel that it has become a little chilly, so Watson and I will return to Baker Street to indulge ourselves in a welcome glass of brandy. I will see you at the Yard in the morning, Inspector Mac, to furnish you with a more complete report."

The Prophecies of the
Brahan Seer
by Paul D. Gilbert

It is a well-documented fact, that when not actively involved in an intriguing case, both my good friend Sherlock Holmes and I have been prone to keep the most Bohemian of hours. Not least, of course, in the middle of a harsh and bitterly cold January.

The transient pleasures and merriment of the Christmas period had already faded into a distant memory, and when I woke up one morning to find that my small fire had long-since expired, my first instinct was to return once more to the warm security of my bedding. I was finally lured from my sanctuary, however, by the delicious aromas that were wafting up from Mrs. Hudson's kitchen and the thought that our sitting room fire would in all probability be fully ablaze by this late hour.

I dressed hurriedly and rushed downstairs to find that both of these enticements were exactly as I had hoped they would be. Our landlady was still complaining that there was very little point in her planning our breakfasts, for they invariably became lunch, and Holmes was laughing at my rushed toilet and my consequential dishevelled appearance.

"My dear fellow, we really must find you some form of gainful employment. Otherwise, I fear that you are likely to become something of a recluse." Holmes smiled while pointing towards the clock on the mantelpiece.

I was embarrassed to see that there weren't many minutes before midday, and I stole a glance through the window before sidling over to the fire. It seemed strange to note that something as white and pure as virgin snow could appear to be so bleak and gloomy within the confines of a grey city thoroughfare. The empty and barren streets were as deserted and bereft of movement as I had ever seen them, and the eerie silence was almost surreal.

By the time that I had managed to thaw out my hands by the cheery flames, Mrs. Hudson had returned with a pair of steaming tureen dishes, and I hurried over to the table to discover the nature of their hidden delights. Holmes sat opposite to me with his arms crossed and a look of bewilderment on his face as he marvelled at the amounts of devilled kidneys and curried eggs that I had been able to maneuver on to my plate.

"You seem to be able to defy all of the laws of physics, dear Doctor." He smiled again, and my embarrassment was only tempered by my hunger and the need for internal warmth.

"You appear to be of a more affable disposition than I might have expected, considering that you have been so confined by the weather and bereft of mental stimulation for so long." I paused between mouthfuls before pouring out my first cup of coffee, all the while observing my friend's inability at suppressing his excitement. "I presume that you have received a letter?" I speculated while holding out my hand.

"Oh, Watson, perhaps I am not as much of an enigma as I have always thought myself to be," Holmes said with feigned disappointment while reaching into the pocket of his favoured purple dressing gown.

I opened up the envelope with almost as much excitement as I had displayed upon lifting the lids on Mrs. Hudson's tureens. However, I was somewhat mystified by the unusual Coat of Arms that crested the top of the enclosure. This fact had not been lost upon my friend.

"I can understand your confusion, for this is no ordinary set of arms. Nonetheless, good old *Burke's Peerage* has already come to our rescue, and you will doubtless now agree that our time is best spent when not hiding beneath one's bedding."

"You have more than made your point," I exclaimed, now thoroughly ashamed by my tardy behaviour, and not a little embarrassed by the huge amount of food that still remained upon my plate. "Now, could you please elaborate upon this unique Coat of Arms?"

"They belong to the ancient and noble house of Seaford, and more specifically its current Earl, Tyrell Humberton MacKay, from whom we have received this heartfelt cry for help." Holmes motioned that I should now read from the contents of the envelope.

The letter was, in fact, a long and rambling affair, as one might have expected from a gentleman of a certain age and with far too much time on his hands. Nevertheless, once the reader dispensed with the lengthy preambles, it wasn't hard to perceive the sense of urgency and mortal dread that the author had been attempting to convey.

In brief then, due to his great age and the harsh weather that threatened his smooth passage from the North and indeed his well-being, the Earl would dispatch his trusted servant and confidant, Kenneth McCoist, to explain matters in person and in more detail than a letter ever could. I glanced at the time referred to in the letter and then to our clock.

"Good Heavens!" I exclaimed in a blind state of panic that had clearly reignited my friend's amusement. "Unless McCoist's train has been inordinately delayed by the weather, he could be arriving here at any minute!"

"Quickly, Watson! I shall arrange the removal of our breakfast things while you make amends to your toilet with all speed!" I ran up the stairs while Holmes called down to Mrs. Hudson, his tried-and-trusted method of dealing with a crowded and chaotic table.

Our landlady's heartfelt and fulsome complaints echoed right up to my room and, once I had put my grooming to rights and grabbed hold of my notebook, I descended the stairs with much relief, for the poor woman was now being summoned to the front door to bring up our guest. Only grudgingly did she show McCoist into our sitting room, and she glared at Holmes as she closed our door behind her.

Holmes jumped up at once and greeted this fearless and devoted servant with a strong handshake and an invitation to share of our roaring fire. Another vibrant call down the stairs would soon realise a reluctantly produced coffee tray and, once our visitor's first cup had been poured and Mrs. Hudson had grumbled her way from our room yet again, Holmes invited our guest to explain the reason behind his perilous journey.

"I perceive that you have only recently ingratiated yourself into the privileged position of being the Earl's esteemed confidant," Holmes stated provocatively.

I will not tire my readers by repeating McCoist's dialogue verbatim, for his Highland accent was strong and colloquial, and therefore to do so would slow my narrative's flow. Suffice it to say that McCoist's reaction to Holmes's statement was no different to that of the countless others who had sat in that chair before him, and I will interpret his words as best I can.

"The Earl spoke most highly of your abilities, Mr. Holmes," McCoist exclaimed with a smile, "and although I cannot fathom how you came to your conclusion, I simply cannot deny its validity."

"The muscular development of your hands and wrists show me that the majority of your working life has been spent in doing physical labour, and even through the bulk of your heavy outer garments, I can still make out the defined shoulders and upper arms of an artisan. The gunpowder marks that will forever stain your fingers tell me that you were once a gamekeeper, and the ruddiness of your complexion tells me that your promotion has only been a recent one, for you haven't yet attained the pale pallor of a man who rarely ventures outdoors." The fact that Holmes had not presented this explanation with his customary dramatic panache told me that his instincts were predicting a tale of great gravitas and mystery.

"You are correct on every count, Mr. Holmes." McCoist confirmed. "The Earl had always taken a keen interest in the welfare of his grounds, and he took as much pride in their maintenance and presentation as I had always done. Furthermore, he had always been a very able and enthusiastic angler and hunter, and he sought my advice on all associated matters.

"Therefore, it was only natural that we should spend much time in each other's company, and slowly he began to trust my counsel on many other matters too."

"Your statement makes reference to everything in the past." I pointed out while looking away from my notebook for an instant. I noticed my friend smiling to himself as he lit a cigarette.

"Sadly that is so, Doctor Watson, for age hasn't dealt kindly with my master, and his poor health began to limit the amount of time that he was allowed to spend outdoors, before prohibiting it altogether."

"I understand," I observed, "and that is a sorry eventuality indeed."

"I am glad to report that the Earl's interest in his grounds remains undiminished, although only from a distance nowadays, and in both Jessica Renfrew and myself he is blessed with two stalwarts who will always give him the best and most considered advice."

"Who, pray, is Jessica Renfrew?" Holmes asked with a smile.

"Miss Renfrew is his trusted and highly valued housekeeper of long standing, who also happens to be, without a doubt, the most knowledgeable and intelligent woman that you are ever likely to encounter," McCoist replied with a great sense of pride in his voice, although Holmes seemed to be uncomfortable with such a description.

"So with two such stalwarts at his disposal, it must be a dilemma of seismic proportions that would compel the Earl to seek my advice." Holmes invited McCoist to explain the problem with an impatient wave of his arms and this unnecessarily sarcastic remark.

McCoist shifted uncomfortably in his seat before beginning his tale.

"Indeed it is, Mr. Holmes, and one, I might add, that has left the old fellow in a state of mortal dread!"

This statement had been used on more than one occasion within the confines of our sitting room, and if McCoist had been expecting an equally dramatic reaction from my friend, then he was to be left sadly disappointed. Holmes merely lit a cigarette and glanced at our guest with an impassive air of indifference.

"Mr. McCoist, you have endured a long and arduous journey in order to set your employer's case before me. I sincerely hope that it doesn't prove to be a fruitless one."

McCoist leaned forward in his chair with a steely intent that this shouldn't prove to be the case.

"I wonder if either of you gentlemen have ever heard of the 'Brahan Seer', also known as Kenneth MacKay, or by his Scottish Gaelic name: *Coinneach Odhar*?"

Holmes and I exchanged glances of a shared ignorance of these titles, and our guest lost little time in enlightening us.

"Despite possessing a shared surname, the seer bore no family connection to the Earldom. Nevertheless, he was employed as a labourer on the Brahan estate, which was the seat of the Seaford chieftains in the second half of the seventeenth century. According to legend, he was born at Baile-na-Cille, in the Parish of Uig and Island of Lewis in the early part of that century. He lived at Loch Ussie, near to Dingwall in Ross-shire, and very close to the Brahan estate itself.

"Without praying upon your impatience and indulgence too much, I will *précis* the remainder of the legend by merely stating that the seer received his great gift courtesy of his mother's graveyard encounter with the lost ghost of a Danish princess, who bestowed it upon him in exchange for her safe return to her grave. Odhar was then sent a stone with a small round hole in its centre, through which he could see his visions."

Sherlock Holmes, who generally speaking held no truck with such tales, stubbed out his cigarette impatiently and growled at our guest.

"Really Mr. McCoist, you could have saved yourself the journey and merely referred me to a book of fairy tales!"

McCoist smiled ironically at Holmes's brief outburst before lighting an old brier pipe.

"Knowing your reputation for pragmatism, Mr. Holmes, I was expecting this reaction, or something of the sort. It is easy to take a cynical view of something that you have neither experienced nor heard of oneself. Nonetheless, that doesn't detract from the reality of the facts." McCoist suddenly reached into a battered old leather attaché case, which I had not noticed, and produced a wad of well-thumbed papers. He brandished these in front of him defiantly, as if they were a weapon of enlightenment.

"I have in my hands actual proof of the gifts and powers that were bestowed upon the Seer of Brahan!" McCoist's lively green eyes positively ignited with excitement and inspiration as he threw the papers down to the floor.

"If you will allow me to continue for a wee while longer, I am certain that I can convince you of how sorely the Earl needs your aid."

Clearly moved by our guest's great passion and conviction, Holmes smiled warmly at him as he bade him to state his case.

McCoist gathered up his papers and immediately explained to us how the Seer's great powers had led to his own awful and most-untimely death.

"At the time of Odhar's employ upon the Seaford estate, the wife of the Earl had accrued a reputation as being amongst the ugliest women in all of Scotland! Her husband was taking an extended trip to Paris, and the Lady Isabella asked Coinneach Odhar to impart any news he might have of her husband's well-being. After some hesitance and deliberation, the

346

seer told her that the Earl was in good health, but he steadfastly refused to elaborate any further.

"This response so enraged Isabella that she went so far as to threaten Odhar with death should he not divulge his secret. Faced with such a choice, Odhar felt obliged to tell her that the Earl's time in Paris had been spent in the company of a young woman whose beauty was legendary, and far exceeded her own. He then foretold the end of the Seaford line by correctly predicting that the last of the direct line would be deaf and dumb, and would go on to produce four sickly sons who would all die prematurely.

"For his pains, Odhar was promptly seized and then hurled into a barrel of boiling tar, while the lady of the house looked on and smiled maliciously at the poor man's suffering and slow, lingering death."

"A vengeful woman indeed," I said, whistling. "Yet the Seaford line did continue, as attested to by the existence of your employer."

"Yes, Doctor, but only by virtue of a distant relative, and a productive marriage almost a hundred years after the events that I have just described to you. The pure MacKay line died out at the time, and in the manner that Coinneach Odhar had prophesied!" McCoist confirmed emphatically.

"I fail to see how the tragic fate of this legendary prophet has any bearing upon the current Earl and his apparent plight," Holmes observed with an air of cynical nonchalance.

"I only mentioned the tale of Odhar's final prediction and his tragic end as a means to emphasise the authenticity of his gift of second sight. However, it is the matter of the Three Lost Prophecies that I have come to present to you today. These scrolls were discovered by mere chance, deep within the wine cellars of Brahan Castle, just a few days past. At the request of the Earl and in preparation for an auction, Miss Renfrew was conducting an inventory of every bottle that had been laid down there.

"As you might imagine, the Earl rarely socialises nowadays, and he barely takes a single glass of wine with his evening meals. The Brahan cellar and its treasures has achieved an almost legendary reputation down the years, and so an auction seemed to be an excellent idea. However, since the discovery of the three lost scrolls, relating the prophecies, my poor master has barely given the auction a moment's thought, nor consideration, so profoundly have their contents affected him."

McCoist produced a few sheets of paper from his inside pocket and Holmes leaned forward to feign at least a little interest.

"The original papers were deemed as too fragile to travel, so Miss Renfrew and I have put together this replica as best we could." McCoist handed them over to my friend, who passed them on to me after he had briefly scanned them.

"It seems that Miss Renfrew is of a strong and forthright nature," Holmes observed.

"You are so convinced that this is a female hand?" I asked, and I noted a brief and knowing smile upon our guest's face.

"That is Miss Renfrew to a tee," McCoist confirmed admiringly.

I began to read from the summary of the first prophecy.

"'*One day ships will sail around the back of Tomnahurich Hill*'," I stated, and McCoist explained its significance.

"Gentlemen, at the time of the predication, such an occurrence would have seemed both illogical and absurd, which probably explains why it never saw the light of day until now. However, in the year of 1822, Thomas Telford completed the construction of the Caledonian Canal, and the prophecy was fulfilled! The canal actually forks off from the River Ness and then, via Inverness, heads northeast '*round the back of Tomnahurich*', and into the Moray Firth."

"Are you certain of the scroll's authenticity?" I asked.

"The ink and hand are identical to those upon the better known prophecies," McCoist confirmed, and I began to read from the second part, the contents of which were so dramatic and outlandish that I have reproduced it here extant:

> *There will come a time when great, black, bridleless horses, belching forth fire and steam, will be seen drawing long lines of carriages back and forth through the Glens.*

McCoist almost finished my sentence for me, such had been his state of excitement.

"You must see, gentlemen, that as far back as the seventeenth century, Odhar was foreseeing the coming of the Highland railways, which, as you know, have only recently been completed!"

"That is certainly one way of interpreting so bizarre a line of prose." Holmes persisted with his scepticism, although he couldn't disguise a touch of intrigue that was now creeping into his tone.

"Odhar even predicted the awful Battle of Culloden, but it is the third of the lost and forgotten prophecies that has brought me here today, as you have already doubtless surmised."

"I would have hoped that there was more cause for your perilous journey than the few lines of fable that we have just heard. Perhaps you could read on, Doctor?" Holmes suggested, and I nodded my assent.

"'*During the course of a terrible conflict that will engulf a far off and distant land, the last of his line will meet with a terrible and untimely death on the very day of the anniversary of his birth*'," I read breathlessly. "The war with the Boers has only recently begun, and threatens to become a far more intense conflict than was originally supposed!" I pointed out somewhat superfluously, for the troubles in South Africa had been dominating every front page for months.

"I suppose that the Earl's birthday is imminent, and that he is taking this threat to his life in a more than serious light?" Holmes conjectured.

"He is indeed, Mr. Holmes and who could blame him? After all, each and every one of the seer's other prophecies have been fully validated and, being with neither offspring nor heir, he is the last of his line. To put his feelings on the matter into perspective, I would tell you that his birthday is regularly celebrated with a huge ball within the castle grounds, to which all members of his considerable staff, together with all who live within the surrounding area, are invited. This year, however, no invitations have been sent out, and the great halls are silent and shrouded in a dark cloak of foreboding and despair."

Holmes stroked his prominent chin slowly, lost in deep thought.

"How many days is it until the Earl's birthday?" Holmes asked.

"It is three days hence." McCoist replied expectantly.

"I suppose he feels that my presence will in some way ward off the evil that threatens him?"

"He has implicit trust that this will prove to be the case. Naturally, if Doctor Watson were to accompany you – Well, then so much the better."

"I should be honoured!" I confirmed, and our guest and I then turned towards Holmes to see if there was any indication of a similarly positive response being forthcoming

"I do have other matters that will keep me engaged in London for a while," Holmes began in his typically inscrutable manner, "but if you will arrange transport for us from the local station, I will wire you with our arrival time, after due consultation with Watson's ever-reliable *Bradshaw*."

McCoist sank back into his seat with a deep sigh and his relief was palpable.

"I can assure you, Mr. Holmes, that there will be a carriage with four awaiting you at the station, whatever time of the day or night that you deem necessary. You may also rely upon the fulfilment of whatever professional fees that you see fit to charge."

"My professional fees are set at a fixed rate, apart from those occasions when I waive them altogether. This will not be the case this time, however, for we shall be attending at considerable expense and great inconvenience, and I cannot yet even be certain that there is a case for me to investigate."

"Ah, so you are not yet convinced of the validity of the prophecies of the Seer of Brahan? Perhaps once you have arrived upon the very rail line that Odhar foresaw all those centuries ago, or seen the Caledonian Canal that he predicted, you might feel differently. In any event, you will doubtless be consoled to know that you are bringing much comfort and assurance to a frail old man."

"For that, at least, I shall undertake your mission." Holmes smiled with a reassuring nod of his head before indicating that it was now time for me to show the gamekeeper to the door.

Before I took our guest down the stairs and towards the harsh conditions that still prevailed outside, he turned towards the centre of our room once more.

"Gentlemen, we shall look forward to welcoming you to the Highlands, and shall be eternally grateful for your agreeing to such an undertaking." There was something very agreeable about the man's manner, and the flavour of his northwestern vocal lilt, and I was resolved to do my very best by him and his employer.

I raced back up the stairs to lay my hand upon my *Bradshaw* before Holmes had had the time to change his mind. Before I began to rummage through those well-thumbed pages, I asked him about something that he had said earlier.

"Would you mind explaining to me what those 'other matters' that shall keep you engaged actually are?" I enquired, for there had been nothing afoot for several days now.

Holmes strolled from the bureau and turned towards me, once he had taken to his chair.

"Watson, I never like to begin a venture until I am fully prepared. Therefore, I shall use the time still available to us in awaiting a reply from my brother to this wire." Holmes smiled.

I should point out that Mycroft Holmes had always maintained a very keen interest in both the affairs and culture of Britain's most northerly part of the union, perhaps born of Her Majesty's love of the place and her frequent visits to Balmoral. Therefore, I was in little doubt that Holmes had asked his brother for any information that he might possess pertaining to the Earl of Brahan, and even the legend of the seer.

Holmes did not deny it, and as I anticipated an indeterminate wait for a reply, I decided to dive into my *Bradshaw* without delay. A number of fishing treks of mine to the lochs and glens of the region meant that the logistics of our journey from London to Inverness didn't present me with any problems, save perhaps for the unpredictable effects of the weather.

Nevertheless, the arduous trip beyond this familiar territory was a different matter altogether. Fortunately, the recently completed Inverness and Ross-shire line afforded me a number of options and, once I discovered that the station of Conon Bridge was barely two miles East of Brahan Castle itself, the matter was virtually decided.

The timings now became all important, but when I broached the subject to my friend, he merely waved me away with a long languid sweep of his arm, and I knew that that the responsibility rested upon my own willing shoulders. Holmes was now well into his pipes, and since there was nothing else to do nor discuss until the arrival of Mycroft's reply, I went upstairs to stoke up my fire and ensure that my windows were securely shut. As I drifted off into slumber, I sincerely hoped that we would hear from Mycroft before the time of our departure.

Breakfast came and went on the following morning, but there was still no sign of our eagerly awaited reply. Still, our plans for departure proceeded, and my final task was to ensure that my army revolver was in prime condition and stowed away securely. Rather concerningly, Holmes had been most insistent on that, and it seemed to me that he was taking the seer's warning from the grave somewhat more seriously than he had hitherto been willing to admit.

Finally our cab arrived at the appointed time, and it was only as we climbed slowly and reluctantly aboard that the long-awaited wire was thrust into Holmes's eager hand by a breathless delivery boy. We sank back into our seats in a state of great relief and Holmes read the contents of his brother's correspondence in a frustrating and inscrutable silence. I knew from past experience that any attempt of mine to extract information from my friend, before he felt ready to impart it, would prove to be a futile waste of time. We concluded our journey to the terminal at Euston in silence, and it was only once we were safely aboard our train that Holmes finally seemed to relax.

He lit a cigarette and began to gaze through the window at the ever-changing and dramatic landscapes, once we were clear of the sprawling suburbs north of London. It was only now that the true devastation of the recent snowfall was evident, and the endless deep drifts inevitably worsened the further north we travelled.

Holmes suddenly turned to me and addressed me with a rather challenging smile and tone.

"So, Watson, what are we to make of this Scottish business?"

"Well, I must confess to being just a little surprised at your acceptance of such an *outré* commission. After all, have you not so often propounded that your consultancy should remain forever rooted within the realms of proven and logical facts, and not mere flights of fancy?"

"Bravo! You are correct, of course, but my brother is also of the opinion that there is something of the uncanny about the accuracy of

Odhar's predications that might beggar further investigation. According to Mycroft, McCoist barely scratched the surface when he highlighted some of those prophecies, for there were many, and all of them of proven accuracy.

"Besides, there is a frail old man, the last descendent of an ancient and noble line, who is in fear of his life, and he has requested our aid in his time of need. Are we to ignore this plea and bear the guilt should his untimely demise come to pass?"

"No, of course we should not," I confirmed emphatically and, as our journey continued, I became all the more determined to aid Holmes and the Earl in any manner that I could.

Despite the terrible blizzards that had been bombarding us throughout the month, it was comforting to note that the snow had remained soft, and therefore caused no real impediment to the progress of our train. Nevertheless, as we travelled ever northward, the depth of the drifts were accumulated into threatening mounds that left me dreading the final stages of our journey.

By the time that we had reached Crewe, I found myself in urgent need of the buffet car, and to my pleasant surprise, Holmes agreed to join me. We enjoyed a pleasant-enough meal together and, over our coffee and cigars, I noticed Holmes gazing through the window at the frozen landscape with a steely intent.

"It must be difficult for you to embark on a new case that is lacking both a confounding mystery to solve and a series of impenetrable clues to unravel." I proposed.

"It is certainly unusual, but not unique. You might recall, for example, the affair of the Copper Beeches, whereby we merely followed a series of events that unfolded before us to their natural conclusion. On this occasion, we aren't coming to the aid of a perplexed young governess, but our mission is no less righteous merely because our client is an elderly Earl. Indeed, if we can put at ease the mind of the last of an ancient and noble line, we will be fulfilling a great service to his house."

"So you see this more of a matter of appeasement rather than protection, with no consideration for any potential threat to the Earl's life?"

"I do, although it would be foolish of me not to give due consideration to my brother's words, and we should, at all times, maintain our vigilance. See, Watson – the weather is closing in and growing ever more threatening." Holmes returned his attention to the view from our window, and I began to fear for the hazards that threatened the final leg of our journey.

We finally reached Inverness without any real inconvenience, although we soon found out that our connection to Conon Bridge was held up by a snowdrift close to Dingwall. Holmes immediately sent a wire to McCoist, informing him of our delay, although our main concern was that we wouldn't reach Brahan before the Earl's birthday.

"Should we not, Watson, this entire journey will prove to be a complete waste of time," Holmes complained, although this much was obvious even to me.

Mercifully, our train appeared in a shorter time than had been predicted, and we were soon making a slow progress towards our final destination. The landscape that we passed through, normally so stark and undulating, had been smoothed and levelled by the snow, although it was no less the spectacular because of this. The eighteen-mile trek felt all the longer each time the track was forced upwards by every incline, and occasionally it felt as if the engine would surely stall, so great had been the strain upon it.

Finally, as we neared the picturesque village of Muir of Ord, I knew that we were fast approaching our journey's end. Our engine built up a decent head of steam just then, for the track was flat and true and the views of the Black Isle, from this vantage point, were both awe inspiring and compulsive.

As we pulled into the tiny station at Conon, Holmes emitted a sigh of relief as he checked his pocket watch, for he noted that we still had thirty-six hours before the dawn of the day of the Earl of Brahan's birth. McCoist proved to be as good as his word, for a very fine carriage drawn by four was awaiting our arrival. Although its size and stately apparel sat rather incongruously against the background of that pretty little station, its was nonetheless a welcome sight for us, as a smaller vehicle would surely have struggled through the drifts that blighted the two miles to the castle.

The driver and footman were clearly as glad to see us as we were them. Undoubtedly it must surely have been a long cold wait, and both men seemed in need of some warmth, and perhaps a small measure of whisky. Not unmindful of this, Holmes generously produced his flask and passed it over to both men who received this bounty with great enthusiasm and gratitude. The appreciative servants helped us with our overnight bags and, once we were aboard, the staunch vehicle moved off with a sense of determined endeavour.

The road took a most convoluted route, as it was forced to by the undulating terrain and the rise and fall of the hills and crags that would otherwise have blighted our way. The courageous beasts had pulled us over a mile from the station before we began to catch our first glimpses of the distant castle. Each sharp bend in the road either obscured our view or afforded us a better one as we drew ever closer. Finally the monolithic pile of dark grey stone reared up before us, although it was only impressive by virtue of its size and solidity, rather than any great architectural achievement.

The building was a simple construction of two great wings, and the only features of note were a single round tower and some enormous chimneys that were pumping out generous amounts of welcoming dark-grey smoke, which promised some well needed warmth. We weren't to be disappointed, and McCoist was standing on the long flight of front steps to greet us. His relief at observing our safe arrival was unmistakable, and he grasped us with a strong appreciative hand as he instructed the servants in making us comfortable. Our bags were taken to our rooms and McCoist showed us into a large, empty drawing room where the roaring fire enwrapped us with a warm and embracing glow.

McCoist then presented us with a large crystal decanter, which we were assured contained one of the finest single malt whiskys that the local distilleries had ever produced. We cradled our large dimpled tumblers in great anticipation as they were being filled, and our hopes of an internal glow and immense flavour were soon fulfilled. Holmes, however, didn't linger upon this divine moment for very long.

"Time is at a premium, Mr. McCoist, and I will require a plan of the house, and perhaps a tour of its most notable aspects before too long. Will the Earl be joining us shortly?"

Holmes's question soon became redundant, for a moment later the heavy oak doors were opened once again, and two of the most striking individuals that one could possibly imagine strode into the room. The woman was distinguished, not only by her height, which was well above the average for a woman, but her slim, upright figure and her sleek tied-back hair gave her an unmistakable air of authority. Her somewhat-pale complexion made her difficult to age at a glance, but she was certainly not unattractive. This undoubtedly was the very same Jessica Renfrew who McCoist seemed to hold in such high regard.

She guided her elderly companion towards us, and then completed the formal introductions with a clipped and impassive phrasing. The Earl himself, despite his great age and frail stooped posture, commanded our respect and esteem by virtue of his broad shoulders and his strong booming voice. His long white hair cascaded down his back, and dropped on to the shoulders of his heavy dark brown plaid dressing gown, undoubtedly fashioned from the tartan of his clan. His eyes sparkled when he spoke, even more so when he saw the golden liquid glimmering in our glasses. Without a word, Miss Renfrew poured him out a glass which he took enthusiastically from her as he sat down between us.

"So, Mister Holmes, Doctor, you have graciously come all this way to protect the life of an undeserving old man. Obviously I will recompense you most generously. However, I suspect that any financial reward is far from being your primary motivation. For you and other enigmas like you, it is the challenge that compels your actions above all else. Well, I can tell you that on this occasion, your thirst for stimulation will be more than satiated by the end of it." The Earl smiled as he raised his glass.

"I perceive that you are a student of the writings of my friend and chronicler, Doctor Watson," said Holmes. "He does convey, with a small degree of accuracy, features of my nature which are inexplicably of interest to his readers. However, I should tell you from the off that I do not necessarily share your enthusiasm for the prophecies of Coinneach Odhar. After all, there are certain aspects of his predictions that might be left open to a different interpretation or even be put down to a fortunate coincidence. Nevertheless, you seem to be convinced of this threat from the distant past, and I will endeavour to pacify your fear – at least until the passing of your date of birth."

"That is all that I could reasonably ask of you, Mister Holmes, and for that, you shall have my eternal gratitude. What steps or measures do you intend to take?" McCoist asked this with an air of relief which hadn't been apparent previously.

"This really is most excellent," Holmes remarked as he sipped luxuriantly from his glass, caressing the crystal object as he did so.

"Ah, so you possess a decent palate, although you have yet to answer my question. I assure you, Mister Holmes, that my staff and I are willing to take whatever measures, regardless of their inconvenience, that you might deem to be necessary."

Holmes drained his glass before suddenly jumping up to his feet.

"Miss Renfrew, if you would be good enough to take me on a tour of the upper bedchambers?" Holmes suggested, rather surprisingly. "More especially those rooms adjacent to and closest to that of the Earl's, while Mr. McCoist might draw up a plan of the layout of this wing of the house. Afterwards, we might be able to put our plans into action – perhaps after a light supper?"

The Earl clapped his large hands resoundingly.

"Of course, of course! My entire household shall be at your disposal, Mister Holmes!"

Initially I had been a little confused by the Earl's unusually relaxed demeanour. McCoist had made it abundantly clear that his master had been in mortal dread of his life and that he was prepared to take any or all steps necessary to preserve it. Yet here he was – sipping whisky with us and apparently at ease with the idea of such upheaval invading his household.

Then, however, I began to notice certain traits and aspects of his behaviour that belied my initial impression. The Earl was smoking a very strong brand of Turkish cigarettes in copious amounts, and he was drawing the smoke down as if every inhalation was to be his last. Furthermore, each of his fingers were strumming incessantly upon the arms of his chair while his eyes could be seem darting continuously from side to side without actually focusing on any particular object. Clearly, he had no intention of betraying his true fears and feelings to anyone present, although his dread of Odhar's dark portents coming to fruition were evident.

Obviously I was most welcome to the idea of some supper, but I was also mindful of the fact that we had very little time in which to make our preparations. Therefore, Holmes and I made short work of a plateful of very fine local venison before following Miss Renfrew to the upper floor. We were briefly shown the location of our own rooms before entering the Earl's vast bed chamber.

Holmes ensured that the windows were securely fastened and that the shutters were tightly shut before testing the book shelves and walls for any indications of a false means of entry, a not-uncommon facility in a grand and ancient building. We were glad to note that the rooms on either side of the Earl's were occupied by Miss Renfrew on the one side and McCoist on the other. Holmes and I had been given the guest rooms adjacent to those.

The remainder of the rooms lay vacant, but we checked the doors and windows of each one to ensure that they were locked and secure before returning to the drawing room. McCoist led us around the ground floor, while explaining that he would station a number of footmen and other servants at each of the more vulnerable positions during the twenty-four hours of the Earl's birthday. The enormous front doors seemed to be impenetrable, but the large glass doors that led from the ballroom to the terrace outside, somewhat less so. Therefore, this room, together with the dining room, which had a similar outlook, would be manned by armed footmen at all times going forward.

Holmes seemed satisfied with these arrangements, and I began to wonder why our presence was even necessary at all. Upon completing these rounds, we all convened once more in the drawing room before turning in for the night. We knew that the following night would prove to be a restless one, and that we should take advantage of any sleep that we could manage.

Nevertheless, and before retiring to our rooms, Holmes asked Miss Renfrew to produce the manuscripts that alluded to our host's untimely demise. There was something almost challenging in his tone, which surprised me at the time, and he was staring at her with an intense curiosity.

McCoist had been most enthusiastic when describing her knowledge and capabilities, and yet she had been unusually silent since our arrival.

"Of course, Mister Holmes, although I fail to see what further information you expect to learn from them."

"We shall see, if you would be so kind as to oblige me." Holmes smiled and the woman left the room without another word.

She returned in no time at all, and Holmes began to examine those sheets with his glass most intently.

"It is strange, is it not, that such ancient and important documents should resurface in a rack of wine? How do you suppose they came to be there and discovered after so long a period? It seems almost beyond the realms of coincidence that they should come to light again at such a portentous time."

"Indeed it does, but unfortunately I cannot offer you a satisfactory explanation. As Mister McCoist has doubtless told you, since my arrival at Brahan I have taken a most keen interest in the history of both the castle and the noble family that have resided here for so long. However, it has been the prophecies of Odhar the Seer that have most occupied my attention, and I can tell you, beyond all doubt, that the prophecy pertaining to my poor master is absolutely genuine." The woman had an unusually deep resonance to her voice, and she spoke with a resounding air of confidence.

This didn't seem to impress my friend unduly, for he barely offered Miss Renfrew a single glance, nor acknowledgement as he continued with his examination of the papers with his glass. He merely grunted a couple of times to himself and smiled as if a secret thought had suddenly occurred to him, but one that would remain his own – for the time being at least.

"May I borrow these and take them with me to my room overnight?" Holmes asked without bothering to look away from the papers.

"By all means," Miss Renfrew replied with a doubtful and condescending air, "if you think that would be of any use."

Holmes gathered the manuscripts together as we all rose to go to our respective rooms, and I was gratified to note that the numerous servants had been busy stoking up the fires, rather than allowing them to die out overnight. The room we were leaving had been gloriously warm, and as I glanced out of the ice-rimmed windows, I realised how miraculous and costly that achievement must have been.

As I arrived at my room, a young maid was closing my door and leaving with an empty scuttle, a sight that left me feeling certain of a comfortable night. Holmes had been so preoccupied he hardly acknowledged me as I wished him a good night, and I was left wondering as to his discoveries within those ancient texts.

In a sense I was dreading the morning, for it would dawn on the day of the Earl's birthday. I changed for bed and, with that thought now uppermost, I moved over and opened my large sash window where I lit a cigarette. To my astonishment, I observed the beginning of yet another substantial snowfall, and the large torches outside, which lined the long driveway and the gardens, revealed flakes of an unusual size and density. I shuddered at the thought of a further accumulation, and it suddenly occurred to me, albeit somewhat prematurely, that such a snow fall might even prohibit our immediate departure upon the completion of our mission.

At that moment, as if to compound my incertitude, a strong northerly wind seemed to spring up from the surrounding glens and lochs, with its sharp talons intent on disrupting and then dispersing the steady descent of the icy flakes into a silent storm. The violent gusts prevented the flakes from reaching the ground immediately and as they pursued their random course, my mind was drawn towards the notion of a thousand lost spirits searching in vain for their final resting place. With a shudder, I closed the window hurriedly and pulled my dressing gown around me as I clambered into bed, grateful for the defiant flames from my fire.

My sleep that night proved to be a fitful and restless affair, and my troubled mind had been grappling with endless images of the risen dead and an insurmountable mountain of snow. Naturally, the sound of the breakfast gong on the following morning was a welcome one indeed, even though food was not uppermost in my thoughts on this occasion. My bedroom had become synonymous with my ghastly visions, and I felt the need to vacate it without delay.

The vast dining room was surprisingly empty, save for a brace of bored house maids, a rich array of serving dishes on the oak sideboard, and my friend Sherlock Holmes, who was engaged with his usual breakfast staple of a cup of coffee and a cigarette. He glanced up at me with a faint smile and, when I joined him at the table with nothing more substantial than a single boiled egg on my tray, he barely expressed his surprise.

"Oh, Watson, despite my grave doubts as to the gifts that Odhar the seer might have possessed, this morning certainly has a portentous air to it that is both inescapable and inexplicable. The elements seem to have unleashed their harshest form of munition upon us, and no access or departure will be possible from the castle for many a day, I would wager. Potentially, of course, this fact makes our task somewhat easier than it might have been. Nevertheless, I would strongly advise you to have your army revolver ready and by your side at all times."

By way of reassuring both Holmes and myself, I patted my jacket pocket with a smile of self-satisfaction, although the presence of my gun did very little in alleviating the unease and uncertainty that seemed to be gripping the entire household.

The sparsity of the dining room was soon explained to us by one of the maids. For many years, the Earl had acquired the habit of taking his first meal of the day in his bedroom with a newspaper, and either Miss Renfrew or Mister McCoist for company. Today it was Miss Renfrew who had been sitting by his side, while McCoist was busy going about the house and ensuring that the footmen were all in their prearranged positions. We had been assured that nothing could get through this cordon of security, and of course the weather would be prohibitive of any intruders attempting to approach the castle.

Holmes, it seemed, was not so easily convinced of this, and his wiry frame was contorting in tension as he sat upon his chair. He drained his cup violently and lit another cigarette as he rose to examine the terrain outside the dining room door. He grunted his disapproval, and then raced upstairs to fetch his hat and coat without affording me a single word of explanation. As a matter of fact, he didn't offer me another word until he had completed a full circumnavigation of the castle grounds. Even then, it was simply to inform me that he hadn't discovered even a single trace in the deep-laying snow, and that he was now going off in search of McCoist, who was doubtless on his rounds.

It was only then, when Holmes was out of sight and I found myself alone in that vast empty dining room, that I heard the first sounds of commotion echoing down from the upper floor. Evidently Holmes had heard it also, for he came back to fetch me before racing up the stairs at a speed that I could never even hope to match.

"Quickly, Watson! The moment has finally arrived!"

I joined him upon the upper landing a few moments later and found that he was already outside the Earl's bedroom door with his ear pressed hard against the thick solid wood. Evidently nothing had been heard from within, and Holmes pulled away from his inspection in disgust. The cry of one of the maids brought Holmes and me further down the corridor until we arrived at the door to McCoist's bedroom.

Then we saw it!

The heavy door had been so well fitted and hung that the smell of various smouldering materials reached our nostrils long before the first fingers of grey heavy smoke began to force their way through the tiny gap at the base of the door. No cry could be heard from its occupant, which told me that the smoke had already rendered the person inside unconscious. Evidently, McCoist hadn't been on his rounds after all, for the sound of us crashing upon his door with all of the force that we could muster seemed to be slowly arousing him.

Holmes called a halt to this while he examined the keyhole, and as he stood up again he gravely informed us that someone had deliberately locked the door and jammed it before actually taking the key away with them. This had been no inadvertent misadventure, and Holmes and I, together with a burly footman, redoubled our efforts at bringing the door down before it was too late. A cry went up from behind the door followed by the sound of crashing glass.

"He is clearing the smoke through the broken window, but we need to reach him before the flames do. Is there a ladder in the house that will reach that height?" Holmes asked of the footman with not a little urgency.

"I have just the thing, Mr. Holmes."

"Then meet us outside below the window as quickly as you can!" Holmes commanded, for there was still little sign of the door capitulating.

The footman joined us below McCoist's shattered window in very short order and, as we began to raise the ladder into position, we realised that the most difficult aspect of this entire operation would be preventing the ladder from sinking too deeply into the drifts of snow. The footman ran off to fetch a large flat block of wood from the workshop, and before long the ladder was sitting upon a more solid and stable footing.

Despite my entreaties to the contrary, Holmes insisted upon being the first to climb up, and we all did our level best to keep the steps as secure as possible as he did so. My friend seemed to be oblivious to the potential dangers of his actions, and he proceeded to climb as if he was ascending the steps to our Baker Street sitting room. All the while, we looked out for signs of McCoist at the window, but when there were none. It seemed more and more likely that he had succumbed to the effects of the smoke and fumes. By now the orange flames had begun to lick around the edges of the window frames, and Holmes forbade anyone else from joining him in the climb. A moment later, my friend raised himself over the sill and climbed into the Halls of Hades!

As one might expect, and in complete defiance of Holmes's last instruction, I began to scramble up the ladder with all speed. I had no idea as to what condition I would find either man, so as I climbed, I instructed the footman to gather together as many of his colleagues as he might and then to bring all due force to bear upon that fortress-like bedroom door. This he did with a vocal enthusiasm and great determination.

By the time that I had made good my ascent and fallen through the open window, Holmes had already managed to smother the flames with a large set of heavily lined drapes that had once adorned the windows. My friend didn't seem to be any the worse for wear, and he was on the floor cradling McCoist's head in his arms while gently reviving him.

As the situation was clearly more under control than I could possibly have hoped for, I fully expected a chastisement to follow from my friend for my having openly defied him. Mercifully, the opposite proved to be the case.

"Ah, Watson," Holmes exclaimed, "good of you to have joined us. Our friend McCoist is clearly not out of the woods just yet, and your medical bag and highly skilled hand is sorely needed." He said this with a sincerity that certainly gladdened my heart and made me all the more determined to do some good.

All the while, the footman and several of his colleagues had been labouring against all of the skills that the local carpenters must surely have mustered and slowly that Herculean and ancient wood began to succumb to the combined brute force of those determined servants. Slivers of wood became chunks, the resolute lock finally fell out and dropped to the floor and a moment later the door was hanging dejectedly ajar.

I lost no time in grabbing my bag from my room and I relieved Holmes of his duties immediately upon my return. Obviously, there were a countless number of questions reverberating around my head, not least of all why the fire had occurred in McCoist's room and not in that of the Earl. For now, however, my duties lay with the welfare of the man lying on the floor beside me and the battle that he was fighting for his life.

Needless to say, my task had been made all the easier by virtue of McCoist remaining conscious, aided by the constant stream of fresh cold air that was rushing in through the shattered window. I dispatched two young maids to the kitchen with my instructions, and in a short while they had both returned, one bearing a large urn of sweet tea, which I began to administer in copious amounts without a moment's delay, while the other had prepared a large steaming bowl of thyme-infused water for my patient to inhale.

To my great relief, McCoist responded positively to both treatments, and in a short while his breathing had settled into a stable rhythm while his deep rattling cough began to lighten and abate. Once I became certain that I could allow him to sleep without fear, I had two footmen remove him to a spare bedroom, where he was put to bed with instructions that a maid should remain by his side at all times.

I could now turn my attention towards the other matter at hand, and immediately became aware that my friend was nowhere to be found. Evidently I had been engaged with my patient for a lengthier period of time than I had been aware, for during that hour or so, Holmes had managed to conduct a thorough search of the entire wing of the house, both inside and out, and had already come to the conclusion that the object of this hunt was none other than Miss Renfrew, who had disappeared without a trace.

This much I had learned from two of the senior footmen, although neither of them could tell me what had since become of my friend. I was standing in the corridor, just outside McCoist's old room, when I had been greatly surprised by a familiar voice summoning me from within. This seemed to be inexplicable to me, for the room had been quite empty when I had left it previously and no one had passed me since.

I ventured hesitantly through the shattered doorway, there to be confronted by my friend, clearly amused by the look of bewilderment upon my face.

"Watson, you look as if you had just seen a ghost, but I can assure you that I am undoubtedly made of nothing less than flesh and blood. Now, apply my old maxim, and I'm certain that you will undoubtedly save us the wasteful and time consuming list of questions and answers that you are so prone to ask." Holmes smiled, but with a decidedly challenging tone to his voice.

I tried to eliminate the impossible from my reasoning, but found it considerably harder to discern an improbable truth. Then it occurred to me that simply because there had been no secret exit and passageway leading from the Earl's chamber, we shouldn't have assumed that such a device did not exist elsewhere in the old castle building. Indeed, by what other means could Miss Renfrew have executed her escape and disappearance? Furthermore, it would also explain Holmes's sudden and inexplicable reappearance in McCoist's bedroom. I felt confident enough in my theory to risk airing it to my friend.

"That is a most excellent piece of reasoning," Holmes exclaimed with a smile that did much to relieve my anxiety, "and I truly congratulate you. Come and see this remarkable mechanism." He beckoned me to follow him into the room and he led me over to a heavy oak bookcase that sat close to the fireplace.

He removed a leather bound edition of *The Annals of Imperial Rome* by Tacitus with a slow but nonetheless dramatic flourish. This ancient tome had left a huge gap in the collection, into which Holmes inserted his left hand right up to the wrist. Evidently he had triggered a geared apparatus of some sort, for a moment later and with a quiet growl that belied its size, a large panel to the right of the fireplace began to slide smoothly and effortlessly one side! This feat of engineering filled me with wonder, but it did not prevent me from asking Holmes why he had selected that particular volume.

"That will become self-explanatory once you have examined the spelling more closely," he advised, and sure enough I soon realised that *Tacitus* had been spelled with a *double cee*!

"Are you up for a journey into the unknown?" he asked.

"Well, of course I am!" I confirmed emphatically while producing my revolver from my jacket pocket. Holmes grabbed an oil lamp from one of the side tables, and a moment later we stepped through the fireplace and into the dank, dark passageway that lay beyond.

Before proceeding any further, however, I put a fairly obvious question to my friend.

"Would you mind explaining to me exactly why we are taking such an potentially hazardous step?" Holmes replied without even a hint of impatience nor irritation.

"As you know, since the incident in McCoist's bedroom, I have conducted a thorough search around the exterior of the castle for any traces in the snow, which the conditions have made all-the-easier for the trained observer to detect. Naturally our own boot marks have been easy enough for me to identify, and those of the footmen only slightly less so. However, the absence of any others has led me to draw the indisputable conclusion that nobody else has ventured outside of the castle since the last fall of snow. Therefore, as a result of a fruitless search of every room in the building, we now know that Miss Renfrew must have taken refuge in these passages," Holmes concluded emphatically, "simply because she can be nowhere else!"

There was no denying the logic behind my friend's reasoning, and I realised that now was not the time to ask him for the motives behind the housekeeper's bizarre actions. Therefore, I blindly followed him across that ancient and mysterious threshold.

The darkness was complete and all embracing, so the oil lamp that Holmes was holding before him became a beacon of light and hope without which we would surely have floundered. The stone slabs which ran through the entire network of passages were impossibly smooth and damp, made all the more so by the constant stream of water that was seeping from the leaking old piping and guttering that ran through the entire building. Consequently and by necessity, our progress was slow and tentative, and even Holmes was moving with an uncharacteristic caution.

Nevertheless, based upon our starting point, Holmes was convinced that we were moving towards the location of the cellar. Naturally I followed him in very close attendance, for I realised that any misstep would undoubtedly result in an unpleasant fall. The seepages, which had stained and damaged every surface, had evidently been occurring over a period of many years, for their constancy had even resulted in the formation of small stalagmites here and there. This was indeed a dreadful place.

We continued with our slow and cautious progress for an indeterminable length of time, when Holmes suddenly stopped and produced a small compass from one of his inside pockets. He examined this minutely under the light from his lamp, before dropping his voice to a whisper.

"If my calculations are correct, we will soon reach the cellar. Therefore, we must lighten our step. These halls resound with every echo that we create, and our quarry will surely be alerted to our approach. Although there is no escape for Miss Renfrew, it will make our task of apprehending her considerably harder, should she be alert to our presence. After all, she has a far greater knowledge of the twists and turns of this labyrinth than we could hope to obtain, and our search could stretch to days rather than hours."

I acknowledged my appreciation of this fact with an emphatic nod and I began to lift and lower my feet with far greater care. We continued in the aforementioned manner until Holmes suddenly halted in his tracks and gripped my shoulder in a painful and vise-like grasp.

My friend pointed ahead towards a sudden turn in the tunnel's direction, some way in the distance. I followed the line that Holmes's finger had indicated and soon made out the object of his urgent attention. There was no mistaking the glow from an oil lamp, for it was identical to the one being emitted by our own. To our horror, however, it appeared to be moving away from us!

"We must quicken our gait," Holmes keenly advised, "although maintaining our silence all the while."

Unfortunately, the glow ahead of us was keeping step with our own and, after a few minutes of a fruitless and frustrating pursuit, my friend threw caution to the wind and quickened his pace, with no regard for the clatter that he was now creating. We were now clearly gaining ground on our quarry, and a loud cry of frustration, that echoed back to us, told much of the desperation of the be leagued Miss Renfrew.

When we finally arrived at the door to the cellar, the silence from behind it put us on a state of vigilance, for it was now harder to discern her exact location within the room. Yet Holmes still demanded great caution, for he knew only too well how inevitable defeat can very often induce a final and desperate action. We already knew how capable she was of one unholy act, and therefore another would not be beyond her. Holmes slowly turned the door's handle, and we were greeted with a blood curdling cry that brought to mind those that I had once heard from within the halls of an asylum. I cocked my revolver and followed my friend's footsteps into the cellar.

Those grey and ancient walls echoed our every movement, and the sobbing of Miss Renfrew was amplified to a frenetic level. I returned my gun to safety and replaced it into my pocket, for no threat now remained within the sorry soul who was sat before us upon a case of very old Madeira. She barely looked up to acknowledge our arrival, and offered no resistance when we each grasped one of her elbows to guide her gingerly from the room. She was now icy cold to the touch, and her constant and violent shivering caused me to remove my jacket and place it upon her slim and quivering shoulders.

Slowly we finally made our way back to the main part of the house through the creaky old cellar door, where Holmes closed off the entry to the hidden passageway. By the time that we had reached the drawing room, I was pleased to note that McCoist had recovered sufficiently enough to join us there, together with our noble host and two trusted servants. It was soon agreed that the weather made it impossible to send for the local authorities, and we all looked towards my friend for an explanation for these extraordinary events.

A maid poured out glasses of the malt, and Holmes lit a cigarette with a piece of fire debris that he had grasped at the end of the tongs. Miss Renfrew was clearly in no condition to explain the motives behind her actions, and so it was left to Holmes to piece together, as best he could, the chain of the dramatic events that had ensued and their cause. Understandably, it was McCoist who appeared to be the most eager for an explanation. His experience had left him weak, breathless, and most-grey of pallor, but he insisted on remaining with us throughout. He sat there shaking his head in bewilderment.

"Miss Renfrew, I simply cannot understand why you would attempt to do such a dreadful thing," McCoist stated softly. "After all, we have always worked together as friends, with the welfare of the Earl as our mutual aim and responsibility, "

The tormented woman simply sat there impassively, with neither a sound nor movement in acknowledgement of her colleague's words.

"It would seem that Miss Renfrew is neither aware nor conscious of the peril in which her actions had placed you," Holmes responded. "However, we should also not lose sight of the fact that the evidence, which certainly indicates her guilt, is at best circumstantial. There are others present who might have had knowledge of the hidden passageways and her disappearance, while undoubtedly suspicious, is by no means proof of her supposed actions."

"Oh, come along!" I protested. "Who else is there who had both the opportunity and the knowledge to perpetrate such a deed? Besides, everyone else can account for their positions and actions at the time of the fire's inception, and her subsequent actions were not exactly indicative of innocence."

Holmes touched his lips with a forefinger.

"Calm yourself. You know my method well enough to realise that mere emotion is, without exception, an insufficient testimony. In this case, our conclusions can only be corroborated with a motive, and for that we have my brother Mycroft to thank."

"The telegram!" I exclaimed. "Of course!"

""Despite the undoubted intelligence that Miss Renfrew has in abundance, her arrogance has also led to her to the erroneous conclusion that she has rights of exclusivity to the knowledge that she possesses. To understand the motives for her actions, we must return to our first meeting with Mr. McCoist back in Baker Street, and the tale of the unfortunate demise of the Seer of Brahan.

"You might recall how the tragic Odhar was ruthlessly flung into a vat of smelting tar, merely for carrying out the task for which he had been commissioned by the Earl's wife, Isabella. Obviously she had not been best-pleased with the news that Odhar had imparted, not least because of the apparent beauty of the Earl's Parisian paramour and her own near-legendary ugliness. Goodness knows what she would have made of the more clandestine nature of the consequence of the Earl's affair."

At this point, it became obvious that Holmes's line of reasoning was beginning to resonate with Miss Renfrew, for she shifted erratically in her seat, clearly in a state of great agitation. The reason for this would soon become apparent.

"You see, this affair did have a consequence of a tangible nature, and the resulting progeny presented the Earl with a dilemma of seismic potential. To his credit, he did refuse to disown the woman and her child, but to present the product of an illicit affair as his own would have created a scandal that even an Earl of his standing would have found hard to endure.

"His solution was a simple one, but at the same time, one that was acceptable to all concerned parties. The woman in Paris had no real interest in the boy, and so it was agreed that the Earl would seek the child's adoption somewhere closer to home, so that he could oversee the boy's progress. A young family who farmed on his estate were found to be agreeable to the scheme, albeit for a substantial recompense, and thus the Earl's illegitimate son grew up to be a happy and robust young man, under his father's discreet but ever-watchful eye. By now, I trust, you should have no great trouble in deducing the surname of the young couple who agreed to the adoption." Holmes leaned back in his chair, downed his glass of malt with an air of satisfaction, and slowly lit his pipe.

There had been little doubt in my mind that Miss Renfrew was indeed a most troubled soul, and her reaction to my friend's revelations almost led to her going into convulsion.

"I am the true heir to this estate!" she proclaimed with a wild shriek, as if any of us were now in doubt as to the reason for her grotesque behaviour. Nevertheless, there still remained the matter of why McCoist had been the object of her attack and not the Earl.

I put this to Holmes, once two maids had been summoned to comfort and subdue the poor anguished woman.

"As is the case with many scholars, Miss Renfrew, the last in line of an ancestry that goes all the way back to that fortunate young couple, possesses an almost limitless pool of patience. Therefore, she was quite content to let nature run its course and await the Earl's passing before bringing her evidence to the attention of the estate's attorneys of probate. However, when McCoist summoned us to the Earl's aid, she mistakenly assumed that he suspected her of some malevolent act against his noble master.

"As we now know, however, McCoist was acting out of genuine concern, due primarily to the accuracy of Odhar's other prophecies, and that nothing could have been further from the truth. In a way, our arrival here almost did more harm than good, and I should be glad to pass this matter over to the local officials just as soon as they are able to reach us."

For a moment we had all been stunned into silence, and only the gentle sobbing of Miss Renfrew broke through that fine veil. Suddenly Holmes left his seat and raced to the window in a state of great excitement.

"Do you hear that, Watson?" My friend beckoned me over to the window, and sure enough the sound of dripping water from the thawing snow was unmistakable.

"It is the sound of our salvation, for surely the surrounding roads will be more passable than they would have been a few hours ago. If my memory serves me well, we have enough time to make the next train to Inverness from Colon Bridge – that it is if your noble steeds are available to us once again?" Holmes proposed.

"Indeed they are, Mr. Holmes," the Earl affirmed, but with a little disappointment. "I had hoped to extend some further Scottish hospitality to you in appreciation of your services. Then again, perhaps a cheque might suffice?"

McCoist gave the order for the carriage to be brought around, and while we awaited our ride, the Earl hurriedly scrawled a figure and signature on to a cheque before he thrust a plain brown envelope into Holmes's reluctant hand with a reticent smile. It was arranged that the driver and footman would summon the authorities to take Miss Renfrew into their care and custody while they were in town, and a few moments later Holmes and I were being borne away from the noble house of Brahan through worn and slushy snow.

Unfortunately, the journey south from Inverness went a little less smoothly than that from Colon to Inverness. The snow had been considerably slower to thaw the further we travelled, and numerous delays along the route led to us arriving at Baker Street in the dead of night, cold, damp, and bedraggled. Our poor landlady was not unmindful of our tardy and unannounced arrival, but she had been good enough to provide us with a hot pot of tea before she returned to her bed. As she left the room, she indicated a wire that had arrived during our extensive travels, and a message from the north had evidently overtaken our trains.

Before opening his brown envelope and the wire, Holmes poured out a generous measure of cognac for us both and he shook up the dying embers of the fire with the poker.

"It would seem that the Seer of Brahan did finally miss his mark," I pronounced with a smile, "with the last of his three lost prophecies, for the Earl has certainly survived his birthday."

"No doubt you recall the time of day when we finally quit the castle?" After I nodded my confirmation, Holmes continued by reading from the wire.

"It seems that the Seer did indeed have the gift, for the Earl's ancient and battered heart finally gave out barely ten minutes before the stroke of midnight!"

The Clockmaker's Fate
by Mike and Arianna Fox

It was upon a tempestuous morning in the autumn of the turn of the new century, when the wind howled its grievances and the rain joined with wearisome cries, in which began the most remarkable link in a singular chain of events which I will now lay before you. It is another one of those tales which present alluring features not so much from the magnificent deductive powers of my friend Mr. Sherlock Holmes, but more so from the elements of suspense and intrigue for which I must confess that he would admonish me for including.

The ghoulish gale and hopelessly violent downpour only but reflected the moods of the dwellers, for Sherlock Holmes stood staring dismally out the window, his violin dangling limply from his sinewy hand. As for myself, I was attempting to divert my mind from the gloom by reading the recent newspapers. I had been at the task for over an hour when at last with an effort Holmes pulled himself taller, and for a moment I dared to hope that the wretched melancholy droning would be replaced by the undertaking of some new study or some intricate chemical analysis, when instead he reached for the customary location in which his pistol and Boxer cartridges were stored.

I have mentioned upon a previous instance that it was a habit of my friend, in one of his eccentric humors, to adorn the opposite wall with bullet-pocks of Her Majesty's Royal Monogram, and I find no difficulty in recapitulating to you that I do not believe our chambers to be in any way improved by this attempt at ornamentation.

Finding that the items were absent upon this occasion, however, Holmes turned to me with a sardonic smile.

"I observe that you have confiscated my pistol, Watson," said he. "There returns the vein of pawky humor which I have pointed out to you, except that it now reveals itself through a rather more evident and obnoxious channel."

"When you consider that my check-book remains locked in your drawer," I countered evenly, "perhaps you will find it perfectly just. I have not acted without good reason, however, for we are once again receiving complaints from our gracious landlady, and I too have some small scruples as to the damaging of her property, as well as the noise which it emits."

"Ha! A most reasonable request. I would gladly abstain from turning to an avenue so dramatic if I had a problem on hand which presented any features even vaguely fascinating. At present, however, there are none. Thus, I return to the vices which try your patience so severely."

"Oh, come," said I. "There are countless cases which present features of interest, if only you search for them. Allow me to show you an example which, I hope, should suffice as ample proof of this."

I picked up an edition of *The Times* from the pile of papers which it had been crowning and, after mumbling a few various possibilities, read aloud one story which caught my eye.

Proprietor Dead by Horrific Bomb-Blast

On Tuesday afternoon, the well-respected businessmen Mr. Stephan Fenwick perished in a massive explosion in his house at Clapham. It was reported to the police by a neighbor, who witnessed the event from outside upon returning homeward from a social visit. She claimed to smell something akin to burning metal, and she feared to venture inside, lest another explosion take place.

Upon their arrival, the official forces found the cadaver of Mr. Fenwick lying upon his back with multiple fatal injuries from the blast. Scotland Yard has sent out their smartest and most tenacious men, Inspectors Lestrade and Bradstreet of B Division, who are now hot upon the scent and attempting to identify a motive.

"You deceive yourself, Watson," Holmes said, fixing me with a keen eye, "in thinking that solely because it is an event of an *outré* and sensational nature which strikes the attention of the ordinary reader, it is a problem which presents any interest to me. *The Times* says a motive is being identified. I say the motive is obvious. It appears that the press and I, as is the custom, have our little differences of opinion."

"How can you deduce a motive from an article which objectively gives so little explanation?"

"Because, my dear fellow, this article which you have done the kindness of reading aloud was not my sole source of information. Any man who concerns himself with current events knows Mr. Stephan Fenwick for his rising fame and iron ambition. Surely you know him too, as you are more an avid paper-reader than I. Indeed, I also happen to understand that he has both a vengeful son and a wronged lover."

"Yes, I recall the notorious scandal which took place some years ago involving his wife and some past lover."

"Observe, then, the following events which prove themselves to be most probable: Fenwick, who has begun already to amass a considerable fortune, has a Will and Testament drawn up. The son, who is in the gunpowder business, works in league with his mother to devise a plan. Here we have at our finger-tips the motive and the suspects, and now I say without guilt of exaggeration that I have done a better day's work in my little armchair than did our worthy Scotland Yarders at the site of the crime."

Sherlock Holmes, being a man of brilliant mind and immense faculty, is a difficult man with whom to argue. I found myself presenting the weapon and cartridges to him against my will and resigning myself to silence, though there was something in that story of the explosion which persisted in intriguing me for reasons I could not yet name. Perhaps it was my medical experience, or possibly it was my writer's imagination which was piqued by the dramatic method of murder which the unfortunate proprietor's son had chosen. In either case, it was certainly unpleasant enough to leave a mark upon my mind for the remainder of the day.

Holmes and I were taking coffee upon the next sunny morning when, upon my opening the morning paper to see if anything of interest had made its way into the public news, the top heading sent a chill to my heart.

"Holmes," I said, "there has been another explosion."

"Indeed," said my friend gravely, glancing down at a telegram which lay beside his barely eaten plate of scrambled eggs. "The good Inspector Lestrade has already sent me the closest thing to an entreaty for assistance his dignity will allow."

The telegram was succinct. It read:

> Second explosion this week. Of chemical interest to you as well as criminal. Would be much obliged if you came down. 112 Stockwell Road.
>
> Lestrade

"Will you go?" I asked, replacing the telegram upon the table.

"Of course I shall. The matter begins to grow a more fascinating and sinister light."

"This article states that the deceased, another proprietor named Mr. Samuel Walker, perished from his injuries at the young age of twenty-five, that he had no family left alive, and that he had not married. The man was perfectly alone in the world. This doesn't seem to substantiate your theory that the previous victim was murdered for his inheritance."

"Indeed," said Holmes thoughtfully, and I could see quite clearly the mechanism of intense thought. "I suppose it puts me quite in error." Despite the shameful implication of his words, there manifested a good-humored glint in his sharp gray eyes which betrayed his gratification. "I have previously told you, my dear Watson, that the event of my making a blunder is a more common occurrence than your loyal readers should ever imagine. Well, then, let us depart for Stockwell Road and see whether we can make up for yesterday's lost time."

Within some minutes, we had abandoned our cold breakfast and were well on our way to the location of the crime. The hansom rattled along the cobble-stoned streets, and I could hear the splashing of wheels in puddles caused by the tempest of the day before. Holmes sat with his head sunk upon his breast in profound thought and, not wishing to disturb him, I remained silent. My mind began to wander to the dreadful explosive events which occurred in rapid succession and how they could possibly be related. I knew, too, that the case couldn't be a simple one if Holmes was as pensive as I.

At length we arrived, where Inspector Lestrade was awaiting us beside a row of constables. Though his welcome was congenial enough, his sallow, ferret-like face was twisted into a cringe as if to warn us of the sight we were about to behold.

"I see that you received my telegram, Mr. Holmes," said he, after greeting us both. "It's a thick business, and unpleasant too. You might wish to cover your mouth when you enter. This way if you please, gentlemen."

Upon entering the house, I could see the tall, stout form of Inspector Bradstreet approaching us, two eager green eyes peeking out from under his peaked cap.

"Mr. Holmes, Dr. Watson, how are you?" He shook us warmly by the hand and led us to the room in which the blast had occurred. Shaking his head, he added, "I have seen few things that are quite so horrible as this."

I was struck immediately with a metallic scent, but the appearance of the room didn't take long in arresting the attention directly after the odor.

It was a terrible sight to behold. The rubble of an abode which once housed a wealthy, rising debutant now but housed what remained of his corpse, the very sepulcher of fleeting fame and greatness. What was once a green and ornately dressed wall had been destroyed, shattered glass from once-hanging portraits littered the floor in a dangerous array, and the scattered tumbledown furniture was irreparable. Nothing, however, was so starkly disturbing in nature as the body of Mr. Samuel Walker, who lay in a contorted position upon the damaged floor.

He was an athletic, well-built man with a burned and contorted face that must once have been as hard and resolute as granite, the very picture of a man who was in the prime of life – until life itself had been swept out from under him. The blast of the explosion told a tragic story upon his features, with various jagged scratches mottling over his already-dreadfully burnt skin, a small remainder of black suit that wasn't horribly ripped or missing, and a light, powdery ash scattered about his person. The combined sight was enough for the three of us to spend a moment gazing down in sober silence.

Within an instant, however, Holmes had returned to the keen, alert nature which was characteristic of him. He squatted down and glanced minutely at every aspect of the man, examining the wounds and the small, nigh-imperceptible glass shards which stuck out in various locations. One of these small shards, which was lying on the carpet beside Walker, he picked up, thrust into an envelope, and carefully placed in his coat pocket before continuing his investigation.

The next objects of his attentions were scattered splinters of wood and strange metal pieces which lay about the room in a disordered array. He picked some of these up, then lay flat upon his face to examine the carpet with his powerful convex lens and crawl round the vicinity. Removing a rather large piece of wood which was covering the opposite wall, he uttered an ejaculation of mixed surprise and delight. I craned my neck to observe the contents to which he directed his satisfaction. They appeared to be three metal Roman numerals, about three-quarters-of-an inch tall, akin to those used for clock-faces. Holmes methodically placed these in their individual envelopes and then into his pockets.

The dual elements of thrilling suspense and trying impatience hung in the air for several more minutes until at last Holmes stood and turned to face us.

"Had the man any servants or maids?" he asked the inspectors.

"No, sir," answered Bradstreet. "I made certain of it."

Holmes thanked him, returned to his previous actions as if we weren't present and began to examine a fallen table, beside which lay a small piece of note-paper which was singed at the corners, but otherwise in fair condition. I could not, however, catch a glimpse of the words before Holmes slipped it into his trouser-pocket. I could see the gleam in my friend's eye when he turned back to us, as if he had picked up a scent and was quite unwilling to let it vanish from his cold, firm grasp.

"The matter proves more interesting with each new development," said he. "I've seen all that I wish to see, and I have here some trinkets to serve as mementos. You are right, Lestrade: This is indeed interesting chemically as well as criminally. Good day."

"Mr. Holmes," said Bradstreet in an astonished tone, "what about the case? Do you see any clue which could lead us to the suspect? Surely there is some vital link to the chain which we are missing."

"Even a motive would suffice," Lestrade added drily.

"All shall come in due time," Holmes said cheerily. "Come along, Watson. The answers lie at the bottom of a test-tube."

I had hoped that Holmes would prove a trifle more communicative upon the ride back to Baker Street, for there were many facts about the case which puzzled me greatly. I wished to inquire how the two business owners were connected, but there was something in his manner which told me that the intrusion upon his thoughts wouldn't be a welcome one. When we returned to Baker Street, he immediately delved into experimentation, not deigning to open his mouth even once as he set to work with brows firmly knitted.

The room began very quickly to reek of chemicals, and I occasionally had to pause my studies to throw open the window and let in the fresh, unsullied London air. From the corner of my eye, I saw Holmes working tirelessly upon the substances which he'd found in Walker's house, probing and testing them as he alternated between flaming Bunsen burners and boiling retorts. He appeared perfectly immune to the effects of his malodorous experiments, and it was approximately one o'clock in the afternoon by the time he had finished. Without a word of warning, he took his hat and coat and departed, leaving me more curious than ever about the events which were transpiring outside of the realm of my knowledge.

It wasn't long, however, before he returned, and at last I summoned up the courage to ask if he'd discovered anything of interest.

Holmes shrugged his shoulders. "I made a few significant inquiries about a certain worthy clockmaker," he answered, "and I wired to Lestrade to meet us at six o'clock. But my dear fellow, I fear that I have quite sorely tested your patience. I have a theory which I shall communicate shortly to the good inspector, and I shouldn't be sorry to hear your thoughts when I have finished."

"I am all attention," said I.

"Let us get the obvious points out of the way. First, I tested the chemical compound which left traces upon various shattered splinters of glass. It is lead azide, made specifically for the purpose of transportation and stability. It is really an ingenious and carefully prepared method, and something I may perhaps replicate when my leisure time returns to me and the opportunity presents itself.

"After my experimentation reached its conclusion, I went to visit an acquaintance of mine to ascertain which chemist sold it, but his shop was closed due to unexpected circumstances. I shall revisit it tomorrow. I then diverted my attentions to the other object of my excursion.

"As you may possibly have observed, I found at the site of the explosion three fascinating pieces of evidence which deserved attention: Roman numerals of the clock-face variety – namely the numbers three, four, and five. They were, however, rather small in comparison to those of the average wall-clock – I measured them each at three-quarters-of-an-inch – which gave me sufficient data from which to draw when making my inquiries. Clearly the presence of these numbers, as well my discovery of metal pieces which are used for clocks, told me all which I needed to know. I suspected that a clockmaker was somehow involved, though in what way I remain uncertain.

"This development led me to visit two local clock-shops of some repute, the first being D'Angelo's Clock Shop in Regent Street. It yielded no very desirable results, as all the clocks which I observed through the window-pane were of ordinary size, and their numbers also.

"Upon my journey homeward, however, I discovered another clock-shop whose name I had heard in recent circulation: Credge's Clock Emporium of Oxford Circus. In looking through the window, I observed that the clocks hung upon the wall were smaller. From a glance, I knew that the numbers matched my previous measurements, and that I had hit upon something of value. I then hastened here, for I should not dream of venturing into any location with such a keen element of suspicion without my Boswell by my side."

"I would be glad to accompany you."

"Good old Watson! Your loyalty never wavers. Well, then, I believe we have a Mr. Alistair Credge to interview, so if you'll get your hat, we shall be off in a moment. As the day comes to a close, it is my belief that no time should be wasted."

We took a cab to Oxford Circus and were off in a flash. We arrived at the clock emporium just as a middle-sized, broad-shouldered man was beginning to pack up his personal items for the day. He was dressed in a black frock-coat, a modest brown waistcoat, a golden Albert chain, and brown tweed trousers. He had a short, respectable stubbly beard and keen, perceptive blue eyes which shone from a well-chiseled face. He glanced furtively at us with the look of one who does not welcome customers so near to the closing time of his shop, but he soon mastered himself and set down his portmanteau.

"Good afternoon, gentlemen," said he. "What can I do for you?"

"We simply wished to have a look round," Holmes said in his kind, genial way, utilizing with perfect cadence the tone of voice which he used when he wished to extract information out of even the toughest of men. "I have been referred to you by a customer of yours who would proclaim your emporium to the London masses as though it were the only one in the world."

After some consideration and what appeared to me to be intense scrutiny of us, his countenance changed fantastically to that of a welcoming merchant.

"I'm glad to hear that I have some small reputation," said he, modestly, "and more importantly, that my reputation is a good one."

Holmes had opened his mouth to reply when, behind the desk, the back door opened and in came two identical-looking lads, approximately twelve or thirteen years of age. Both carried small parcels in their hands which were wrapped in brown paper, and while one brother patiently waited for the conversation to subside, the other fidgeted with his, as though he had an infinite quantity of tasks to accomplish after this one.

"I'm going out to deliver the next clock on the list, sir," the latter said in a light, airy voice.

"Very well, Reggie," the clockmaker said in a suddenly pointed tone. "I am with clients at present, but please do not wait for my permission to carry out your duties."

"Yes, sir," said the lad, and the twins and their packages were off in an instant.

"I apologize for the interruption," said Credge, donning once again his pleasant, cordial smile. "What were you gentlemen saying?"

"It is of no consequence," Holmes returned. "It is to be our dear brother's birthday next week, you see, and he is an avid admirer of all things mechanical. We don't know quite what we're looking for just yet, but we should like to look round the place all the same."

"By all means, gentlemen," the clockmaker said with a wave of his hand. "I am closing the shop in quarter-of-an-hour, however, so I would advise you to be quick about your selection."

Holmes and I meandered about, taking in whatever information was available to us, though I supposed that Holmes found more of practical use than I did. As for myself, I could not but notice the quaintness of the shop, with clocks hung nearly upon every available spot on the walls – some old, others new, and all expertly made – and I delighted in the soothing atmosphere which resulted from the quiet but constant ticking which emanated from all sides. In addition to the clocks of various shapes and sizes, there were pocket watches gleaming in the window-light, and there lay also small time-pieces lined neatly upon a mantelpiece, present only to show the handiwork of their creator. Indeed, it wasn't difficult to pretend to admire them for the purpose of finding a gift sufficient for our non-existent brother.

After I examined the clocks and took a couple in my hands to inspect them more closely, I could see that Holmes's attentions were no longer directed at the clocks but at Credge. As I joined him at the desk and glanced round at the various bric-a-brac which cluttered the clockmaker's working-space, I observed a blotting-pad situated between a quill pen and a ledger.

"Your work is quite impressive, Mr. Credge," Holmes said heartily. "You ought to take great pride in it."

"Thank you, sir," returned the clockmaker with a humble bow. "As a matter of fact, I do take pride in my work. I labor all the day and oftentimes the night to ensure the satisfaction of my customers."

"Very well. I think this, then, shall prove to be the perfect gift." As he said this he hefted up a small wooden clock with a gilded circle round the face, and laying some coins upon the counter, paid readily for it.

The clockmaker thanked us for our business and wished us a good evening as we departed, and when returning to Baker Street I found myself astonished at the fact that Holmes was already beginning to disassemble with great alacrity the new item which he had purchased.

"I assume," said I, "that you are looking for similarities between the pieces of the clock and the bomb, for a clockmaker would use the same manufacturer for his clocks as for his other works of machinery if he could help it."

"Excellent, my dear fellow! You are indeed making rapid strides in the art of detection. Yes, additional evidence is always advantageous, and I want to be certain before alerting Lestrade of our suspicions."

I confess that I felt a trifle of pride swelling in my chest at the notion.

"Were you successful?" I asked.

"Yes, I rather think I have hit upon it. The golden metal pieces which I found in the rubble of the explosion are positively the same parts. Well, then, there remains only one thing to be done."

"And what is that?"

"To await friend Lestrade's arrival. I have called him down to alert him of our findings and give Scotland Yard something to go on. It seems to have been a simple case after all, Watson, just as I had remarked to you from the first. It is all so painfully obvious. And yet – and yet – "

"What is the matter?"

"Well, I must admit that there is something about it which leaves me uneasy in my mind."

"Yes, it seems to me that everything we have found is a trifle too convenient."

"Precisely so. The mechanical parts are the only factor to really tell us that Credge is involved. But we can save the rest of our hypotheses for

Lestrade. If I'm not much mistaken, that is the heavy thump of his boots. Ah, yes, that is certainly his knock. Come in!"

Lestrade entered looking, as I thought, rather more careworn than usual. His brown eyes sagged, his face was pale, and his frame wasn't as rigid as that of a policeman ought to be.

"How do you do?" Holmes asked genially. "Pray seat yourself and take a cigar."

"Thank you, Mr. Holmes. I must confess that I am a trifle out of my depths. The first victim was easy enough to understand, for he had many enemies, but Walker had none. He seemed an exceptionally amiable fellow, and much revered by his acquaintances. It all seems to me to be so very unclear, and apart from the fact that both victims were business owners, I find the connection a weak one."

"Humility suits you, Lestrade," said Holmes with a twinkle of a smile in his eyes. "I advise you not to lose sight of it. Now, onto the matters at hand: I have something of importance which will undoubtedly aid you in your search."

Presently he took from his pocket the envelopes of glass and the metal clock numbers.

"I would recommend that you take all facts into account, and do not immediately come to rapid conclusions. However, these items which I took from the site of the explosion contain traces of a man who was certainly involved in the business, likely in the construction of the explosive device."

Lestrade glared peculiarly at my companion as he reluctantly accepted the objects. "This is evidence, you know, Mr. Holmes. We've let you do a great deal of snooping about, but I'm afraid I must set the limit at absconding with important items from the site of the crime."

"I don't suppose Scotland Yard owns a first-class, up-to-date chemistry set," Holmes said good-naturedly, "or if you do, you don't seem to utilize it. I required the glass shards to analyze the traces of the chemical used in the explosion, and now I have no further use for them. As for these metal numbers, they are the kind used in clocks, and I have already located for you a fine suspect."

Placing the evidence in his pocket, the inspector only shook his head as though he had a great deal more to say than propriety would allow him.

"I recommend, then," Holmes continued, "that you seek out this man, Mr. Alistair Credge. I have done as much research as half-an-hour's time permitted me, and I have discovered that he was previously convicted and imprisoned for robbery of a large scale, as well as another attempted robbery. The two businessmen who perished in the blasts were Mr. Stephan Fenwick and Mr. Samuel Walker, two men to whom Credge had previously applied for work after his freedom was granted to him – and more gravely still, two men who rejected him on account of being an ex-convict. Though I hesitate to place my theory in one avenue, I can at the very least give you a starting-point for your investigations."

"By Jove!" cried Lestrade. "If he's our man, I'll be on him in a flash!" "I shall head down to the Yard and secure a warrant at once." With no other words, he bolted out of our sitting room shortly before we heard stamping of his boots on the stairs and the whistle for a cab.

Sherlock Holmes chuckled softly to himself. "You know quite well, Watson, that if there is one thing for which I can credit our friend Lestrade, it is his remarkable tenacity. Indeed, I confess that it astounds me how he retains all his energies even after all these years."

"It astounds me also," said I, still gazing at the open door.

The next day, London felt as though it had at last, for the one moment in all its glorious history, come to a lull. The air was dry but too brisk for a walk, and through the window I could see few people treading upon the cobble-stoned streets. Apart from the occasional wheels of a hansom or clicking of horses' hooves, there was little to be heard. Most loathsome, however, was the sheer lack of activity. Perhaps my friend's penchant for constant stimulation had somehow carried over into my habits, for I found myself seated alone in our Baker Street sitting room with the burning regret that I didn't follow my friend earlier that morning.

He had conveyed his level of displeasure about the case, telling me that he was going out to make inquiries and clarify one or two points, for although he had given Lestrade the clue which he possessed, there was still something which disquieted his mind. At the time I had wished to remain at home, but I now found that it was a foolish decision. All the afternoon I lingered in there, oscillating between a treatise upon biology and a novel.

At four-thirty, my monotonous routine was broken by a ring at the front door. I knew that it wasn't Holmes, for he would have let himself in. Thus, I couldn't but feel a slight thrill of intrigue as to whom our late visitor would be. I waited at the door until, rather disappointingly, Mrs. Hudson entered with a parcel. She handed it to me with an indifferent shrug.

"This is for me?" I asked, thoroughly surprised at having received any such item. Holmes was always the recipient of varied and often questionable correspondence which included a good deal of boxes and packages sent from admirers and enemies alike, but I seldom received anything, save the occasional letter from an old army acquaintance or past fellow-student who desired my advice on some medical matter.

"I haven't the faintest as to whom it is meant for, Doctor," said she in her kindly, good-humored way. "There is no inscription save the address."

"Thank you, Mrs. Hudson."

As she left, I took the package into my hands and glanced at the singular label which contained no name, but only the following:

221b Baker Street
A gift from an admirer
Precious Materials – Handle with caution!

The last instruction was written in a heavy hand with a slant of importance. With a mixture of trepidation and curiosity I tore the paper and opened the wooden box. Inside it lay the most beautiful cuckoo-clock I had laid my eyes upon. The wooden carvings were perfectly intricate and depicted some of the various beauties of Nature, with carved leaves and roses situated upon the top of the clock, and spiraling flourishes lining the sides. The ornamentation was truly magnificent, and I couldn't but admire the beautiful craftsmanship of its creator. There was something about it, however, which made me wonder if it were a specimen of Credge's Clock Emporium, and if it were, what purpose it served.

I examined the back of it and the front again, and turning to glance at the time-piece which Holmes had bought the day before, I noticed that it was assembled once more and excellently adorned his mantelpiece, perched directly above the hanging Persian slipper which contained his tobacco. If he were to have a new clock, thought I, why should I not also? I placed the item on the wall near my desk and set myself to pinning it there for the next quarter-of-an-hour. It was an enjoyable task which aided me in forgetting the monotony of the day, and I was glad for the opportunity to do something of practical use. At last I had succeeded in placing it in my desired location and, winding the hands upon the face in accordance with my pocket watch, I set the pendulum in motion. It worked exceptionally, and I could hear the gentle ticking of the second-hand lulling me into a reverie.

By the time I had finished it was only three minutes until the five-o'clock chime, and with a cigarette in my hand and a feeling of relaxation in my heart, I awaited the introduction of the little cuckoo-bird remarking the time in its sonorous tones. I stood gazing at the complex designs and pleasing patterns, eventually watching the minute-hand turn to four fifty-eight, then four fifty-nine, and then –

Before I knew what transpired, I heard the front door burst open, steps booming on the stair like a barrage of cannons, and none other than Sherlock Holmes himself shoving his way inside the sitting room with his face covered in light gray soot and ash and an expression of haggard, unrestrained anxiety which I seldom saw grace his customarily austere features. He looked round in a frenzy, then, clapping his eyes upon the clock which I had just placed upon the wall, he lunged forward and grasped the pendulum, holding it in place and preventing it from swinging.

"Holmes!" I cried. "What on earth are you doing?"

"It's the clock," he gasped. He heaved several more breaths before glancing at me and whispering in a voice barely audible, "Had I not stopped it, you would have been blown to bits in a matter of seconds."

I stared awestruck at the man, completely baffled by this turn of events.

"Quick – get a piece of twine," he said, returning at once to his calculating and authoritative tone.

I did as commanded.

"Thank you. We are now going to incapacitate this clock. I would remove the pendulum, but there is always the chance of a secondary charge, and I have only a suspicion as to where the mechanism is." He carefully tied the twine round both the weights and the dual chains, breathing a sigh of immense relief once they were secured. "Now, one final test and all shall be quite cleared up."

With a firm steady hand, he opened ever so slowly the small door which revealed the cuckoo-bird and closed it again with the look of a man who wishes his theory was not the correct one.

"Ah! it is just as I thought. We must get this out of sight at once. The Regent's Park boating lake is only minutes away. If you would be so good as to hold the chains and weights as tightly as you can – Just so! – I shall pick up this clock, and when we arrive you shall see how close a shave we have had."

It was certainly an awkward way of walking, for our pace was quick, yet Holmes warned me upon multiple occasions to maintain my grip with steady hands. We passed buildings like this for some minutes until we stopped at the edge of the lake. Holmes heaved the clock into the lake, and I witnessed my beautifully constructed time-piece slowly sink, the water bubbling to signify its descent to its slow death. Within seconds, the ground shook and water sprang into the air as a massive blast overtook our senses, and various pieces of the clock littered the ground.

"Holmes," I said in amazement, "how did you know that the clock was the explosive device?"

"I have had just a little first-hand experience," said he, rubbing off the soot from his jacket, which I then realized was the standard blue pea-jacket of a mariner. It wasn't until then that I observed that his cap, too, was sailorly in nature, and the remains of what must have been an excellent disguise were scattered about his person.

"That I can perceive. Where were you?"

"It's a fine enough story," said he as we began our journey back to our lodgings at a more leisurely pace, "with supple action for which your readers would ardently clamor, no doubt. I went to the clockmaker's shop under the guise of an anonymous sailor to make further inquiries. As of now, he has not yet been arrested. By the greatest luck, arrived in time to see both of Credge's delivery lads discussing their next locations before setting out from the shop with parcels in hand. I heard mention of two addresses, but to my confessed surprise, our dear old lodgings of 221b Baker Street were the second. I was then faced with the grievous fact that I must choose which boy to follow, but I knew that I could find my way back to Baker Street with less difficulty than the former address.

"My suspicions were already aroused when I observed his slow, meticulous pace, as though he didn't wish to – or was told not to – run for fear of upsetting the contents. It was, of course, only a suspicion, and it was possible that the clocks were simply delicate due to fragile parts. Even so, I desired to see it through to the fullest, and I dogged him without his ever having had the notion that he was being pursued.

"As time passed, the boy began little by little to grow a more anxious attitude as if he had lost his bearings, and turning around abruptly, he caught sight of me. It was too late to conceal myself, so I waited with interest to watch his next actions. As if forgetting all his meticulous training, he turned round and bolted in a useless attempt at escaping my grasp. I followed after him for a great distance, where I must confess his speed and determination were admittedly quite admirable, until we had reached a deserted alley, where in looking back to gauge how far away I was, he stumbled on a rock and fell to the cobble-stones. The parcel which he held in his hands hit the ground first, and an explosion much like the one you saw here occurred in that vile alley."

"And the boy?" I asked, in an undertone of dread.

My friend said nothing, but only shook his head somberly.

"I am glad, at the very least, that you don't appear much injured."

"I should direct the same statement towards you. After the explosion, I would certainly have stayed at the scene, if not for the fact that I knew Baker Street could very possibly have been the next target. I took no risks, and now we are both the more fortunate for my haste. I have reason to believe that this was the last attempt at revenge desired to bring ruin to our establishment for meddling in affairs which aren't ours. Did the label possess an intended recipient?"

"No," I answered. "It had only our address."

"It likely didn't matter, then, who the intended recipient was, so long as it sent a clear message."

"What message?"

"To stay out of the way," Sherlock Holmes said gravely.

I felt an unwelcome chill crawl over my skin. Clearly we were dealing with a formidable individual who harbored a great capacity for vengeance. I was about to relapse into a pensive silence when, upon arriving at the entrance to our flat, we saw the familiar faces of Inspectors Lestrade and Bradstreet on their way to the same destination, their brows twitching with agitation.

"Any news?" Holmes asked, gaining their attentions before they wasted more time in venturing inside.

"There has been another explosion," Bradstreet reported as he turned to my friend. "It was in an alley not far from – Why, good Heavens, are you all right, Mr. Holmes? You look like you could use a good bath, if you don't mind my saying so."

Holmes's gray eyes glittered ever the brighter for his dark face and ashen clothing. "Undoubtedly I could. The truth, Inspector, is that I have just come from the scene which you describe, and I think our energies could be better spent in conversing with Mr. Alistair Credge once more and asking him some pointed questions."

"Wait just a moment," Lestrade interjected. "You mean to say that you witnessed the blast?"

"Quite so. I shall be glad to answer any official questions which you may put to me later. We have another line of investigation which requires our utmost attention."

"I was already on my way to his shop before I heard the news," replied Lestrade, "for I just secured a warrant for his arrest."

"Then let us go down together. There is not a moment to be spared."

With those words, Holmes and I followed Lestrade and Bradstreet out to the street. We attempted to hail a cab, but no such vehicle presented itself. With a bitter snarl upon Holmes's part, we had no choice but to make our way on foot as quickly as propriety would allow us. I confess that my injured leg ached a trifle with the strain in addition to the contraction caused by the brisk, windy London air, but it was quite worth the pain to know that we were making rapid strides and could, with all the hope which I had in my heart, catch the clockmaker before his next trap took another life.

We arrived at the shop panting and gasping, and when we entered there sat upon a chair one of the twins I had seen earlier, sobbing quietly to himself in the corner.

"Where has Mr. Credge gone?" Holmes demanded.

The lad said nothing but only continued weeping, his eyes fixed upon the floor.

"By refusing to tell us," Lestrade said firmly, attempting to offer what he must have supposed was some assistance in the matter, "you are obstructing the law."

The child remained perfectly motionless, ignoring my companions' firm questions as if his grief had somehow rendered him deaf.

"Come now, boy," said Holmes tersely. "This could be a matter of life or death! We haven't the time for further delays. We must know where your employer has gone."

"Wait a moment," I interjected. "He has just lost his brother. Perhaps we can try a different approach."

I knew well that Holmes had his soothing way with women from whom he wished to extract information, but an emotional child who refused to answer important questions in a situation so tense did little for my friend's limited patience. While I could not grant myself the same natural pacifying quality, I could at the very least attempt to replicate it. Presently I squatted down to the boy's level, waited for the sobs to subside a trifle, and then said, in my gentlest voice, "It's all right. We do not intend to cause any harm to your employer. We only require information that will help us track down the man who is responsible for the death of your brother."

The lad looked up at me with flushed cheeks and red-rimmed eyes, his lips quivering in agitation.

"I give you my word of honor," I added, "that my friends and I shall do everything we can to set things right if only you will tell us where Mr. Credge has gone."

The boy sniffed once before turning his gaze upon Holmes.

"He's gone out the back door," said he, in a congested voice. "Just before you arrived."

There was a semblance of pride which twinkled in Holmes's eye when I chanced to look back at him. Not another moment elapsed, however, before we all dashed out the back of the shop and into the open air. We glanced round for a moment and ascertained in which direction the clockmaker could have gone before I spotted the small brown-and-black speck of Alistair Credge's figure disappearing into the bustling London crowd.

"There he is," I exclaimed.

"After him!" cried Lestrade.

The ensuing events were in such a blur that I confess to a difficulty in writing them as they occurred. It was as if the winged sandals of Hermes were momentarily placed upon our feet. The faces of the crowds merged into one another, and the public were nothing but obstacles through which we had to push, and all the while we yet maintained our man in the center of our vision like the focused view of a target through an army rifle. I have never been a policeman, but I have been a soldier, and from all my combined experience, in addition to serving as Holmes's partner in the detection of crime, gaining on an elusive suspect was nothing new to me. It did not take long, however, to reach him, for he had not observed that we were in pursuit and was still strolling at a leisurely pace. Taking my proximity to him as fresh motivation to lengthen my strides and give one final push of effort, I at last laid a hand upon his shoulder at the entrance of an alley. Holmes and the inspectors came up directly behind me.

"Just a moment, Mr. Credge," Lestrade said. Alistair Credge gave a cry of astonishment as he looked at the four of us with a clear warning written upon our faces. His countenance was plastered over with confusion.

"What in Heaven's name is all this?" he exclaimed.

"We'd like you to come with us," said Bradstreet.

Credge had opened his mouth to further protest when Lestrade interjected, "Resistance is futile, Mr. Credge. We've a warrant for your arrest."

There was a dangerous flash of rebellious indignance in the man's eyes which his past years of criminal activity had afforded him. It very nearly prompted me to draw my revolver from my pocket, but the expression quickly subsided. It was replaced by a look of intense concentration, as if he were working out the mental calculations of each possible result to each response which his lips could utter. It was then that for the first time I perceived the traces of a brilliant, scheming mind behind the businesslike exterior.

"Very well," said he, slowly. "I should, at the very least, like to know what it is of which you have so mistakenly accused me."

"For the murders of Mr. Stephan Fenwick and Mr. Samuel Walker," Lestrade stated, "the attempted murders of two innocent men, and the death of one of your delivery boys."

"What? My delivery boy? Which one? And those massive explosions detailed in the papers? I tell you, I had nothing whatever to do with them! I know nothing about the construction of explosive devices."

"And I tell you that we've plenty of evidence to attest to the contrary. Now, if you'll come with us, we shall discuss the matter in greater detail at the Yard."

"For your own sake, Mr. Credge," Holmes said suavely, "I would advise that you listen to the inspector. Your innocence can be argued at a more convenient location than this cold and cramped alley."

It was then that something dawned upon the clockmaker, and his eyes sparked with recognition as he oscillated glances between Holmes and me. He had, then, noticed Holmes's voice and the sharp gray eye behind his sailorly disguise, in addition to my own appearance, and recognized us as his previous customers. I could see the train of thought beginning to run upon his brain-tracks, and with a resigned smile he said, "You are very clever men. I know not why I am suspected, but clearly you know more about the thing than I do. I shall follow your lead."

"Come along, then," said Lestrade.

From that moment onward, despite his stoic nature, Alexander Credge was complacent and sometimes even genial with us in obeying our wishes. As we rode in a cramped growler to Scotland Yard, the man of tact and diplomacy had gradually replaced the man of crime and delinquency. At first I thought that it was due to the knowledge of his guilt, but there was something in his manner which brought to mind all the cases upon which I had worked where an innocent man didn't attempt to plead his innocence or fabricate a false story, feeling that the Fates were against him, or the evidence too substantial to exonerate him. I couldn't help but wonder, then, what questions Holmes would put to him.

I hadn't long to ponder, for we were at the Yard in less than ten minutes. Upon entering, Bradstreet led us through the building, and then opened the door to Chief Inspector Witherspoon's office. It was neatly ornamented: A desk and two chairs lay imperturbably in the center of the room, with nothing to adorn the former but some note-paper, a blotting-pad, and an unopened parcel. A clock and portraits lined the walls in an attempt at making the room not-entirely a barren one. Witherspoon, a jovial, rotund man who sat behind his desk, greeted us and beckoned to Credge to sit upon one chair while Bradstreet took the other.

"You know, sir," said Credge, glancing at Holmes, "I would likely have presented more indignation at your deception if not for the fact that you were a client of mine."

"And I," said Holmes calmly, "would have presented more indignation at your actions if you had truly been responsible for the deaths of those businessmen."

It was now Lestrade's and Bradstreet's turn to look astonished.

"Mr. Holmes," said the former, "what are you implying? You can't mean that Credge is innocent. Indeed, you were the very man who told us we should suspect him!"

"Suspect him, yes, as we should all players in the intricate chess-game of crime. But to accuse him – that is another matter entirely. I have had the opportunity, between intervals, to conduct further research upon Mr. Credge, and I have reason to believe that not all is as it first appeared, and that he has been used as an unwitting accessory to these tragic incidents."

Credge turned to Holmes in astonishment, his eyes gleaming with the hope of acquittal returning to him as though he was at once determined to grasp onto it with the little tenacity which remained.

"You cannot be serious," ejaculated Bradstreet. "The clock-parts and the numbers were a perfect match to his clock-shop, and Lestrade informed me it was you who mentioned that the victims were employers who had refused his work. His own delivery boys carried the bombs, and one has died. I do not believe in coincidences, Mr. Holmes, and the case of Mr. Credge is no exception."

"It is true," said Holmes, "that the sign of his work in the matter was clear as day, and Watson and I nearly fell victim to an explosive contraption set within one of his hand-made clocks. However – "

"I did not know it," Credge interrupted fervently. "I swear by my sister's grave that I didn't know my clocks were used to – to cause such destruction." There was a break in his voice and a sob which indicated enough genuine despair to convince any man, but Bradstreet shook his head with the cynicism of the trained inspector.

"How in blazes could you have lacked that knowledge? You cannot expect us to believe so ludicrous a story."

"I don't expect you to believe it," said the clockmaker, "but it seems to me that this Mr. Holmes has a greater grasp of the situation than you have, and thus it is my deepest hope that *he* will believe me."

"I assure you that I have considered all factors," said Holmes in a slow, methodical pace. "One's actions tell an infinitely truer story than one's words, and your reformation from a convict to a generous and charitable man who donates twenty-per-cent of your profits to impoverished youth was quite an impressive one. I should, however, wish to hear a trifle of your history as a criminal. I believe that the facts could prove most illuminating."

"Very well, then, Mr. Holmes. I shall make a clean breast of the fact that we had landed ourselves among the wrong sort of crowd, my sister and I, when we were young. She was a brilliant chemist – one of the greatest minds of her generation – and I prided myself on my mechanical inventions. When we turned our minds to crime, it seemed there was nothing which we couldn't accomplish. Not long before my recent incarceration, we even had a great heist planned for Lloyds Bank, not far from your dwelling-place, Mr. Holmes, and all was set to go perfectly. But it was a disaster – an unmitigated disaster.

"I still remember how the stars looked in the sky when I think of that fateful night. There were four of us: I was heading the thing, Wilson and

Gavin were assisting me, and my sister Honoria was established to drive us away in a stolen growler. But at the last moment, one of our men had squealed on us and alerted the authorities, so with bitterness and failure in my heart I got in the carriage, and we were off. We were going as quickly as the horses could take us when she saw a group of street Arabs directly in our way, gazing up at us with beady and innocent eyes, and in turning to avoid them, crashed into the building. Gavin and I made it out all right, but Wilson and my dear sister perished in the blast which ensued.

"That is our tragic tale, Mr. Holmes, and I am sure that you will understand perfectly my reasoning for wishing never again to enter into such a disreputable line of life."

"Your frankness is indeed appreciated," Holmes said, after a moment of pensive silence. "Now, Inspectors, more important than further discussion about our worthy clockmaker is finding the real culprit."

Bradstreet and Lestrade exchanged a glance of confusion, as if they still deemed it impossible that the culprit could be anybody but Credge.

"Our first clue," Holmes continued like a master professor mid-lecture, "lay quite evidently in the note which was left for Mr. Samuel Walker." He then pulled forth the piece of notepaper that I'd seen him pick up near Walker's body. The inspectors made no comment. "The message was the very same which was sent to our lodgings in Baker Street, along with a deadly time-piece: '*a gift from an admirer*'. The writing was undoubtedly a woman's. That information is easily obtained from the rounded style, the rightward slant, the proximity of the letters, and the loops in the *G*, the *O*, and the *A*. This drew my attention to the fact that there was another person involved in the matter, whether it was simply an accomplice or the principal actress in this little drama.

"Now we come to another vital thread of all in this tangled skein: The chemical evidence. Today I met with one Mr. Fink, a local but first-rate chemist with whom I have an excellent rapport. I inquired if he had any singular customers of late, particularly who purchased lead azide, and indeed he had. He informed me also that other agents were purchased, and from the names with which he provided me, I can tell you without a doubt that they were used for the purpose of chemically augmenting the lead azide for the most explosive reaction possible. I must admit that the process was quite brilliantly executed.

"Now, Mr. Credge, I am going to ask you my following question very clearly, and I ask for nothing more than the same clarity in return: Do you know who ordered the clocks? Describe her to me, and pray be precise as to details."

"I do not know her name," Credge said with a despairing glance at each of us. "It was a woman, just as you said, but she was veiled and

388

always spoke in a peculiar hushed, rasping sound, as if she had had some vocal damage."

"Precisely the description given by Mr. Fink," Holmes muttered. "Pray continue."

"It isn't my business to inquire anything personal of my customers, Mr. Holmes, and I'm not a very curious man by nature. I simply appreciate my clients and the living which I earn by their generosity. As for my recent client, she gave no name when I asked for the sake of the package-label, and insisted that her gifts be anonymous. She also curiously begged that I would not put my own label upon the parcels. She had few requests about the cuckoo-clocks save one, which she deemed absolutely vital: That I would use already-built figures of the cuckoo-bird which she handed to me personally in a well-stuffed box.

"'Take great precaution in handling these,' she instructed me in her strange rasping way. 'The eyes contain jewels which are of the utmost value and importance. They are heirlooms from my father, and nothing can happen to upset the birds, for if it causes even the slightest crack in the gems, all is over. I trust that I may confide in you, Mr. Credge?'

"I began to protest against using such a delicate mineral in the wood and how dangerous it was to leave it to chance when she perceived the vacillation in my tone and added, 'Well, I suppose if I cannot convince you to manufacture these items for me, I shall have to find another clockmaker.'

"You must understand, Mr. Holmes, the situation in which I found myself. Money is scarce, and I hadn't any clients for the past four weeks. She was, in truth, the first potential customer who graced my shop in a longer duration of time than I should like to admit. I thought of my declining income, of my two delivery boys who were constantly playing games in the shop on account of their boredom, and of my still-fragile reputation. It was, in conclusion, impossible to refuse nearly any offer I could have gotten. Thus it was that I put a bold face upon the thing and accepted the job.

"It was initially an order of four. I set to work immediately upon the clocks and did what I still would consider my very best work, even if I didn't realize at the time how destructive they were. Then she came back this morning, complimenting me with the pleasure she took in her previous items, and told me very eagerly that she would pay me five pounds if I could make one last clock for her within a matter of hours. It was a handsome sum, but I was uncertain of my own abilities. One of my delivery boys, too, had just returned from another run, and I didn't wish to overwork him. I said as much, to which she offered me twenty-five pounds. I don't wish to appear a greedy man, Mr. Holmes, but when one makes such an appealing offer to a humble clockmaker such as myself, I must regard it as something of a miracle of which I would be a fool not to take advantage."

Sherlock Holmes had been listening languidly to Credge's narrative for some minutes, but presently a flush sprang to his cheeks, and his eyes were once again alight with urgency.

"Wait a moment," he interjected. "You said that it was initially an order of four – with an additional delivery of priority."

At this, Lestrade and Bradstreet exchanged a glance of concern.

"I understand," Holmes continued, "that the first two targets were Mr. Stephan Fenwick and Mr. Samuel Walker, who had refused you employment. The third ended up on our rooms, and the fourth was intercrupted by the unfortunate incident of your delivery-boy – Reggie, I believe, was the twin, for he had a singularly fidgeting way of reacting to unexpected events which his brother didn't share."

"It was Reggie?" Credge interjected, his eyes alight with horror. "How did it happen?"

"He fell carrying one of your parcels," my friend said bitterly. "But there still remains the last fifth clock to answer for. Who was it for?"

"I do not know."

"For Heaven's sake, man, can you not think of one name?" cried Holmes with some heat. "There is a life which might hang in the balance this very second!"

"No, sir, I really cannot," Credge said firmly. "I have a faulty memory, and even then, my client never told me the full names of the recipients, but always an initial and their surname."

"Did you at the very least keep a list of intended recipients?"

"Yes, I do. It's on my desk beside the ledger."

"Then we must see the last name upon the list. We can concern ourselves with the lady client afterwards."

"I'll keep him here until you return," said Chief Inspector Witherspoon genially.

"Bradstreet and I shall be behind you directly, Mr. Holmes," said Lestrade. "We shall just see to a few matters with Mr. Credge before joining you."

Holmes and I, along with a pair of constables, hailed a growler and were off for Oxford Circus directly. It was barely a ten-minute journey at the pace at which we were flying, and we dashed out with great rapidity. Holmes instructed the policemen to maintain a watchful eye upon the exits while he and I would inspect the interior and search for the list. We then darted into Credge's Clock Emporium with one objective clear in our minds.

I was grateful that the shop was empty, for our search was most frantic and devoid of any respect of Credge's privacy. Upon failing to find the list readily available atop the desk which lay in the corner, we inspected all the items upon his modest bookshelf and began to rifle through his drawers. As Holmes and I were opening the last drawer, I heard the door swing open, dainty footsteps patter across the wooden floor, and a feminine but strangely rasping voice utter, "Mr. Credge? Is Mr. Credge here?"

Noticing us as we rose, she curtseyed cordially and asked as she craned her neck round the shop, "Pardon me, gentlemen, but have either of you seen Mister – " It was then that something like realization must have dawned upon her, for she drew in a breath and said nothing for some seconds.

Holmes and I took in the appearance of the newcomer who had come to the desk while we were searching. She was clad in a black dress, her face was covered by an even blacker veil, and her whole appearance was a singularly shrouded one.

I exchanged a glance with my companion. I'm certain that the suspicion of this woman being Credge's elusive client crossed his mind at the same time as – or, indeed, before – it crossed mine.

In a surprising act, however, the woman's voice turned soothing and gentle as she said calmly, "Ah, the famous Mr. Sherlock Holmes, I perceive – and his faithful biographer Dr. Watson. It is an honor. I am, as it happens, quite an admirer of your chemical work. Your test upon hemoglobin to distinguish blood-stains from any other similar red mark was a particular favorite of mine. Well, well, I should have known you were too clever to let that little contraption stop you or your efforts. Goodbye, then, Mr. Holmes."

At the last words which she had growled in a menacing tone, she pulled out a revolver in an instant, and cocking and holding it directly at Holmes's head.

Within an instant of the tense moment, however, I saw the front door swing open, and before I knew what was occurring, I saw the forms of Lestrade and Bradstreet rushing inside. The woman was thrown off her guard for only a moment as she glanced at the unexpected intruders, but a moment was all Holmes required to forcefully wrench the gun from her grasp and pull her forward by her outstretched arm. I consider myself to be a man of steady nerves, but I confess that I nearly started when I heard the unexpected cracking report of the revolver from the sudden action, and especially one so close to Holmes. It was with great relief that I observed that the bullet had firmly lodged itself into the back wall. While I was reacting in this rather dazed manner, the inspectors had lost no time in taking both of the woman's arms and cuffing them behind her back.

Holmes clapped at the inspectors, a smile of exultation gracing his features. "Well done, gentlemen! I couldn't have timed the distraction better myself."

"I see that our intervention has pulled you out of rather a precarious situation," said Lestrade with a chuckle of delight.

"Indeed, but there is no time to lose," Holmes said, returning to his cold and authoritative manner. "We must find that list."

While the inspectors were maintaining a tight grip upon the assailant, Holmes flung open the last drawer and let out an exclamation at finding the object which he sought.

"'*Mr. J. Witherspoon*'," he read aloud, his finger upon the last written name, "at – "

"Why, good Heavens," Bradstreet interrupted, "that's Scotland Yard!"

I glanced at Holmes, and more horror could not have been plainer upon his features than if he had witnessed an apparition. My blood, too, ran cold as I thought of the chief inspector and his constables being in apparent danger.

"What time is it?" Holmes demanded.

"Five-minutes-to-eight."

"Then we must hurry."

We all followed him out the front door and out into the street, where he fixed his eager and alert gaze upon a growler whose coachman was standing upon the pavement, stretching his legs and slowly returning to his vehicle. Holmes had bounded across in a flash and climbed into the driver's seat with an apology and a few brief words that we were officers of the law en route to prevent a disaster. Lestrade and I, shocked but sufficiently comprehending our objective, succeeded in hampering the enraged cabman in his attempt to retake his seat while Bradstreet kept a firm grip upon Miss Credge's arm. When at last the cabman desisted, we beckoned to the policemen to climb inside, and the inspectors followed her in while I seated myself beside Holmes for a better view of the surroundings.

"We are nearly there," I informed the passengers when we turned onto the road and Scotland Yard came in view.

Then it was that an extraordinary thing occurred. Something like an orange light radiated from the building ahead, providing a blinding contrast against the darkness of the night sky, and in less than a second I heard a massive boom emanating from the same location. In an instant, I knew what occurred. Holmes pulled the reins to the side of the road, and we came to a stop. My friend gazed despondently at the source from which now came a multitude of frantic yells and shouts.

"We are too late!" he gasped.

"There may be survivors," I endeavored to assure him. "We cannot know for certain until we see for ourselves."

Holmes nodded his acquiescence and he finished the rest of the drive. Upon our alighting from the growler and running into the building, I observed that the place was in a frenzy, with policemen rushing to and fro in all directions. The room in which the explosion occurred was visible to us at once – for the door was open – with an injured Chief Inspector Witherspoon being carefully escorted by a constable away from the scene while the familiar athletic figure of Alistair Credge lay, still and prostrate, upon the floor. As for his sister, Bradstreet and Lestrade quickly whisked her away to a side-room without her ever having obtained a glance of the horrible scene.

"Thank God for that desk," remarked one constable to another as they passed us by, "or the poor chief might not live to tell the tale."

I saw with no further necessity for elucidation how narrowly the chief had been saved. The clockmaker, however, remained another matter entirely. My companion and I rushed into the room, which still smelt strongly of metal, and I lay my fingers upon the man's carotid artery before shaking my head somberly to Holmes.

He said nothing, but began to pace about the room until eventually the fervor grew so great that it almost concerned my medical instincts. I had seldom seen him so agitated or moved as in that instance, when with a flushed cheek he muttered incomprehensible self-remonstrances. The only words which I could make out were "another life lost" and "my responsibility".

"Dear me," said my friend at length, when he had regained his composure and now stood staring at the prostrate clockmaker. "There are no bounds to the cruel tricks which Fate can play."

Holmes and I were still standing a quarter-of-an-hour later in the bustling building, through which doctors and other emergency officials were now passing when Lestrade came to inform us that they were ready to begin the lady's interrogation, and that he would be grateful if Holmes could assist in shedding more light upon the matter.

"Come along," Holmes said, motioning to me to follow. "Let us have a word with her."

We entered the room after the inspectors, which was quite clear of any blast damage from the adjoining office. The veiled woman sat in a chair in the corner, as still and silent as a statue of granite. The very picture of guilt was read in the clasping and unclasping of her thin gloved hands and her bowed head. When we advanced towards her, she raised her head like one who expects to be executed at a gallows and is willing to take the punishment.

Holmes sat in a chair opposite the woman and fixed her with his keen and analytical eyes.

"I think, Miss Honoria Credge, that your best course of action lies in telling us all. Secrecy seldom does humanity any good, and your case is no exception."

At the mention of her name, she drew in a breath as one who is taken completely by surprise, and I could only imagine the whiteness of her face and the protrusion of her awe-struck eyes behind that black veil. The inspectors and I, too, shared a common look of amazement.

"Yes, I determined it would be simplest to start with the basic facts. After all, you knew who Watson and I were. It is only just to return the surprise. Now, your only hope for clearing your brother's name lies in making a clean breast of it."

It seemed that the woman needed to muster a great deal of courage and strength to utter her next words.

"I don't know what you are talking about," she said in a voice which sounded so thin that I feared she might faint.

"Come now, Miss Credge," said Holmes with some asperity, "you really do not benefit from this mock ignorance. It is evident enough that you are Alistair Credge's sister. It was evident from the moment in which I observed the peculiar R's, T's, E's, and three other distinct letters in your anonymous notes which you share with your brother in his ledger and recipient list. It was even more evident from the fact that you wore a veil to conceal some injury from your most tragic carriage accident, and it was painfully evident when you disguised your voice to your brother with a rasping quality, yet it was perfectly smooth when addressing strangers such as Watson and myself. Additionally, Mr. Credge described his sister as one of the most brilliant chemists of our generation, and only a mind as clever as yours could devise that form of chemical augmentation which would increase the radius of the blast. Must I expound on these superfluous details, or can we simply crack on?"

A long moment of silence passed before, in a determined action, she slowly lifted her veil. The revelation was like Scylla and Charybdis: One half of her face was chiseled wonderfully, and even in her middle age looked as though she must have been a very beautiful woman in the prime of life. The other half, however, was horribly disfigured in what looked to me to be severe trauma from burn injuries. The half of her lip was contorted so that it curled upwards in an eternal smile, but her wide eyes betrayed the fear and agitation which writhed within her.

"Right on all points," she said coldly.

"Your brother," Holmes continued in a softer voice, "for whom you clearly care a great deal, shall be known by all as a murderer unless you take the blame and set this right."

A lone tear ran down the woman's disfigured cheek.

"Then I am prepared to confess," said she. "You are right, Mr. Holmes. I do love my brother. I love him with all the ardor which a sister could possess. In that carriage accident to which you refer, I nearly thought I was dead before I came to. I was in such excruciating pain, but when I perceived that my brother had disappeared from the carriage I realized that my course of action should be the same. I got away before the police came to investigate, but how could I show myself to my brother when I looked like this? I tried what must have been a hundred times to reveal myself to him, but each time the courage flapped off from under me.

"It was a difficult many years, Mr. Holmes. I had no want of funds due to previous successful heists, but I engaged myself in work nevertheless, for it proved a soothing balm to my afflictions. I had also taken this time to improve and eventually perfect my chemical processes, and I do not regret a moment of my studious labor.

"I had begun shortly after the accident to think of ways I could help him without his knowledge, as a guardian angel does his charge. It started off innocently enough. I would sometimes leave money upon the door-step or provide rare clock parts. I watched him nearly every day, but my thoughts soon turned bitter as I realized how few employers were willing to give him a chance at greatness simply because of his previous criminal acts. At last I decided I should exact my revenge upon the men who made his life miserable – from the employers who refused him work, to the chief inspector who incarcerated him, to the man who was meddling in affairs that weren't his own." Here she glanced at Holmes. "I thought of the mechanisms of clocks with which I am already somewhat acquainted and placed gem-encased lead azide inside the eye-sockets of the cuckoo-birds, which I specially prepared so as not to detonate at the faintest motion. It wasn't an easy process, and it took me months to complete. I am proud of my successes, gentlemen, but never in my life should I wish to bring ruin to my dear brother from my actions. I shall do whatever is required of me to save his name."

"You have brought your brother more ruin than you can imagine, Miss Credge," said Holmes quietly. "Your only consolation rests in the actions which lie ahead of you."

With no more words, he stood and beckoned swiftly to me to accompany him in exiting the room. The inspectors walked beside us with Miss Credge in order to convey her to a cell, but as we passed she caught a glimpse of the familiar corpse, with his stubbly beard and the little that remained of his brown waist-coat, and a gleam of recognition dawned upon her scarred features as she attempted in vain to escape the inspectors' grip. Lestrade and Bradstreet were now practically carrying her away as she began to shriek ear-piercingly and demand in incoherent tones to be let into the room. As Holmes and I departed from the station, I could hear the haunting, inconsolable wails of Honoria Credge upon knowing that her brother was the victim of her own contraption.

And so it was that we sat before the fire in our Baker Street sitting room in an attempt at warming not only ourselves but our chilled hearts. Little remains to tell of the following events. Honoria Credge confessed at the Assizes and joined her brother in the grave. The surviving delivery boy, Eddie Brown by name, and his father now manage the old clock emporium, keeping it alive and well in honor of its late owner. From my knowledge, twenty-per-cent of the proceeds are still donated to the young and poor, and Mr. Brown is reported to craft time-pieces almost as excellently as his predecessor.

How ironic, thought I upon that cold and windy autumn night, that Miss Credge had wished with all her heart to help her brother, and yet she unwittingly sent him away to his death. I suppose, when one repeatedly meddles with the lives of others, one invariably hears the ever-repeating, ever-swelling toll of funeral bells until at last they are meant for the meddler.

If there is one thing which I have learned and taken to heart in all my years of viewing both simple and complex crimes, it is that life always sets itself aright and, indeed, just as my friend Sherlock Holmes remarked that very night, there are no bounds to the cruel tricks which Fate can play.

397

The Wages of Loyalty
by Mike Adamson

In our almost twenty-year association, I had seen my friend, Mr. Sherlock Holmes, tackle every conceivable sort of task from the trivial to the monumental, and with consequences from the personal to the global. But I could count on my fingers the number of cases in which Her Majesty's Government had solicited his peculiar talents on matters of international tension.

An evening in the autumn of 1900 found us journeying from Baker Street – where I once more lodged with Holmes since his return in '94 – along Whitehall to the heart of government. But we understood the circumspect nature of the case when our rendezvous was hosted not by the Home Office but, indeed, at the Diogenes Club in Pall Mall. This was almost to be expected when the invitation originated with Holmes's brother, Mycroft.

Now fifty-three years of age, Mycroft had, perhaps, lost something of his considerable bulk for which, as a doctor, I was profoundly grateful. Nevertheless, he remained an imposing fellow whose craggy features and ponderous, precise manner commanded one's attention, informing the beholder of the fierce intellect behind his bright, sharp eyes. I had come to know that should Mycroft be part of a case, it was usually of the most singular nature and importance.

Hurrying from our hansom through October's desultory showers, we entered the Diogenes Club's cheery gaslight. A steward took our coats and showed us silently through that haven of peace to the Stranger's Room, and we found a welcome blaze in the hearth, with whisky and cigars provided. Mycroft sat by the fire in one of three armchairs, and when we had been supplied with refreshment and settled in at his side, Holmes plumed smoke at the fireplace and raised a brow at his brother.

"And how may I assist the Government of Great Britain and her Empire today?" he began with a subtle note of wry humour.

"Why must there be an issue of national urgency?" Mycroft replied, a shrewd smile in place. "Cannot a brother simply seek the company of his blood kin?"

"Because it is invariably a matter of severe import that draws us together. What puzzle can the mind of Mycroft Holmes not solve? Very few indeed. Thus, I deduce that a certain degree of fieldwork is involved, for nothing has yet extracted the senior Holmes from the arms of London."

Mycroft barked a laugh and gave a half-shrug, half-bow. "Pellucid as ever, Sherlock. Quite, quite pellucid." He sat forward and eyed us with a conspiratorial air. "You're perfectly correct. I have a small task for you, and it does indeed involve a degree of journeying."

Holmes sipped his whisky and stretched his long legs towards the fire. "Enlighten me."

I jotted notes in my accustomed way, absorbing the moment and recording only specifics that would guide my reconstruction later. In the firelight, the Holmes brothers conspired with a certain glee, the thrill of a chase that seemed destined never to end.

"Britain maintains a network of agents in foreign countries, friend and foe alike, to keep us up to date with the dealings of our competitors in the world. These men – and women, I hasten to add – are people of the highest calibre, in whom we place an inordinate amount of trust. Very occasionally we have reason to suspect that such trust might be misplaced."

"You have your doubts about an agent," Holmes observed.

"His name is Martin Cayley. He's been with us for several years, and his performance has always been excellent. But his spymasters have begun to suspect he serves more than one agenda. He's always been solid as a rock, but last year he lost a partner, a fellow agent he worked with often. Cayley was watched closely, and to the best of our knowledge, he was fit for service. But after that point – " Mycroft frowned deeply. "Messages whose content remains unknown and for which he cannot account or denies sending. Meetings with people outside the scope of his assignments, for which his explanations, while on the surface reasonable, fail at some deeper level. What some putative second agenda might be, we have no idea, but we cannot ignore the possibility that he has in fact been turned by some foreign power, whether as some consequence of losing his partner or otherwise. If so, Cayley represents a double agent, and he is in a position to damage us severely at some moment opportune for the fortunes of others."

"And you want me to determine the nature of his treachery, if such there be?"

"You have it." Mycroft opened a case and produced a document. "His file for your review – it must not leave this room. Cayley has been active in the east, in the Baltic Provinces – Courland, Livonia, and Estland, uneasy parts of the Russian Empire that chafe under the Czar. Russia keeps a watchful eye on its western annexations, and the Kaiser's German Empire is always interested in its immediate neighbours. Cayley operates through our good friend Denmark, taking on a new identity there to associate with his contacts in Vilnius and Riga before reporting back to us.

He is due home two days from now. A fishing boat out of Esbjerg takes him to the Dogger Bank region, where they rendezvous with one of ours, which brings him back to a landfall at Whitby, in Yorkshire. He passes himself off as a member of the crew to come ashore, and then melts into the background like the professional he is."

Mycroft tossed down the rest of his whisky as Holmes opened the folder and perused the documents. An attached photograph depicted a clean-shaven fellow with bright, clear eyes, a firm jaw, and close-cropped hair, though I assumed he wouldn't look much like this in his guise as a Danish fisherman.

"Then we intercept him in Whitby," Holmes mused in his precise, clipped way. "We carry your authority to direct him to cooperate, and I debrief him on the various points you have raised."

Mycroft proffered another folder. "Your background information."

"Very well, Brother. This task calls for some discretion. The name of Sherlock Holmes must, I think, be left behind this time."

"Along with the deerstalker and Inverness cape. They really are very well known these days, Sherlock."

Holmes finished with the file and returned it, and I kept my silence as he digested the information the second contained. I envied the nigh-photographic memory that allowed him to absorb the facts while leaving the document behind. He had told me, long ago, that it was a trick of memory, a way of filing away the details, and that he employed it only when necessary. Otherwise, his mind would become irretrievably filled with information no longer pertinent.

Taking back the second folder, Mycroft presented us with identity papers – our "warrant cards", as it were. I smiled as I realised that, just for the moment, we were ostensibly employees of the Government – indeed, of the secret intelligence branch of the military.

"You will exercise every caution," Mycroft said with a dull intensity. "Your object is to discover if Martin Cayley has betrayed his oath in any way, shape. or form. If you clear him, we will hear no more of it and proceed as usual. If you find he is being less than candid with us . . . ."

"Return him for closer questioning?" Holmes asked with a blank look.

"Certainly." Mycroft let a long pause go by. "If possible."

No more was said, and it seemed no more need be. In the evening rain, Holmes and I left the Diogenes to find a cab home to Baker Street, and all the way there I pondered what Mycroft had implied. A promising adventure had abruptly taken a darker turn.

* * * * *

"Am I to assume that Mycroft meant what he appeared to mean with his last remark?" I asked after a long silence. The train, originating in Hartlepool, was making its way across the North Yorkshire moors towards the port of Whitby, and Holmes and I shared a first-class compartment, with the privacy it afforded.

"You are correct in your assumption, Watson," Holmes said mildly, folding his newspaper and raising a false eyebrow. We were both attired in the country tweeds of businessmen in the fisheries trade. A mild facial disguise complemented them to erase any immediate overtones of London or our popular selves. "Mycroft has given me the option of eliminating this fellow – not that I appreciate being handed the service's dirty work. I assure you, if I determine that he has a case to answer, I shall ensure that he is delivered to those best qualified to prosecute it. And nothing else."

"I'm relieved to hear it," I murmured.

The moorland heather had faded with the season. The summer's bracken was dying back to reds and russets, and here and there we saw grouse rise from the undergrowth at the shrilling of the train whistle when we passed through tiny, charming villages with their grey stone houses. The skies were heavy in this rainy season, the land already sodden as November approached. We knew the north-country could become a white wilderness with ease. Hopefully, we would be back on our native streets before such weather came visiting – if, indeed, it did in this last year of the nineteenth century.

"You have, of course, absorbed the pertinent details," I commented, more or less for something to say, and at once regretted it as Holmes arched that false brow at me once more. "Yes, you're right," I added. "I'm not entirely happy with the assignment, and talking for the want of hearing my own voice." I smiled thinly. "I shall endeavour to pull myself together."

We had overnighted at a hotel in York before adopting our full disguises for a connection into Stockton. There, we boarded the 10:50 service through the picturesque Esk Valley, following the tumbling river on its way to the sea at the fishing town. Among the greens and russets, sheep made white specks on the slopes, and we passed by quaint farms nestled in the autumn countryside.

We were due into Whitby Town Station at 12:45, and had reservations at the Metropole Hotel, the elegant new building on the busy Westcliff. The only drawback was the necessity of remaining in disguise at all times, other than when in our rooms, but even I had become

401

accustomed to the demands of going *incognito* when the situation demanded it.

I took out my notebook and composed my thoughts to record this moody, atmospheric part of the country, where the turning season seemed so close at hand. It would be Hallowe'en soon, that night for telling stories and playing games – of costumes and masks and old folk ways. Five days later, Guy Fawkes would be burnt in effigy all over England as fireworks and bonfires blended ancient pagan ways with historical politics in a doubled fire-festival – the unspeakably old and the comparatively new going hand in hand into the new century.

This was an eerie time of year to be abroad in dire purpose, and I reminded myself that the town of Whitby has a tradition of occult lore second to none. Ghost stories abound, especially surrounding the seamen's graveyard and the haunted mansion of the old pirate, Browne Bushell. Few places can boast so rich a tradition of the strange, and we were bound for this quaint town, nestled at the mouth of the Esk between tall headlands, with All Hallows' Eve upon us.

This had the makings of a most unusual outing, and in the spirit of the season, I set pencil to paper and, as the train chuffed resolutely on towards the sea, wrote with eloquence of skeletal trees silhouetted against brooding skies.

The Metropole is an impressive five-storey hotel building on the North Promenade. It stands just a few hundred yards from the Whitby Pavilion, the great theatre complex nestled on the slope below the cliffs, while a little further east lies the Royal Crescent with its arc of Georgian houses, long since turned into holiday hotels. It was in one of these that Bram Stoker wrote *Dracula* a few years earlier – a novel I had brought with me to enjoy when the sea wind blustered in the night and waves crashed upon the shore.

We had booked rooms on the second floor and rode the omnibus that met each train at the station to deliver guests to the hotel. We affected a midlands accent of sorts and provided further false names and addresses – a double covering of our tracks – so that when we sat with drinks in the hotel's elegant foyer to eye the tumbling clouds over the North Sea, I had to remind myself who we were supposed to be at this moment and who we would become that night.

The fishing boat in which we were interested was due in on the evening tide after spending a couple of days out. It had sailed to the rich fishing grounds of the Dogger Bank, midway between Whitby and Denmark. The season was almost done, and the shoals would be well-thinned by now, so we could expect the crew to unload only a light cargo.

402

This might be their last profitable run before the winter came on, and indeed, the gloomy skies made one think of cheerful hearths rather than the tossing grey seas eastward.

To Englishmen it is, as I have said, the North Sea, but it is also known as the "German Ocean", a name descending of course out of the Latin. Both names are used interchangeably, but the latter seems to be favoured by our Teutonic friends, which reflects somewhat upon our national characters. To deem a shallow coastal sea an "ocean" seems to neatly summarise the kind of ego at work on the Continent today, while acknowledging the name from Classical antiquity also offers it the respectability of the ancient.

I set all this down under a date of Tuesday, October 30th, 1900, noting a first quarter waxing Moon and an evening high tide due just after ten p.m. Two hours on either side of that time, the boats would come streaming in from the fishing grounds to berth without fear of the mudbanks that so hamper navigation at the mouth of the Esk. The river hasn't been intensively dredged since the last proper ship was built there in 1871. Holmes and I would be on hand with our credentials, both as inspectors from the Board of Agriculture, under which all fisheries were administered, and, for Cayley's eyes only, as agents of Her Majesty.

Until then, we had the comfort of the hotel and could familiarise ourselves with the town. We took a turn upon the North Promenade to view the Pavilion and the Crescent, and to watch gusts of white as waves creamed upon the great twin breakwaters. In the soft light of an autumn afternoon, with the sun often hidden by flurrying clouds, we walked along to the cliff slope overlooking the river, its shores lined with the fisheries wharves and their associated sheds. On these cliffs stand the famous whalebone pillars, erected in 1855 to commemorate Whitby's history as a whaling port, hometown of the great Captain William Scorseby, who penetrated the high latitudes in the 1700's.

On the East Cliff, opposite, rise the towering ruins of Whitby Abbey, another of the ecclesiastical houses ruined by Henry VIII's purge of the monastic system. Now the bare and eroded stone columns and Gothic arches are exposed to the elements, a sad testimony to the turnings of fate. In its shade is the Church of St. Mary, which dates from Norman times, though the parts of the building we glimpsed up on the heights are actually quite new additions.

We wandered the streets, the smell of the sea strong in our nostrils, and took afternoon tea and toasted crumpets at the Magpie Cafe on Pier Street, west of the river. Then we strolled on across Francis Pickernell's 1835 swing bridge to Church Street and Grape Lane, where the young James Cook worked before beginning his voyages. The town fairly reeks of the ages, from its medieval town hall to the quaint shops that sell jewellery made from the locally mined black mineral known as "jet" and the ancient taverns – The Black Horse, The Duke of York, and so many more – and the one-hundred-ninety-nine steps that wind up from the end of Church Street to the sailors' graveyard above.

Topcoats and scarves were the order of the day, for the sea wind was bitingly cold. By midafternoon, we had both had enough of sightseeing and made our way back to the more fashionable Westcliff. After an early meal at the hotel, we settled in for some rest, sure our expedition this evening would call for all our wits and stamina.

The fisheries wharves, also on Pier Street just inland of the breakwaters, were a hive of activity as the catch came in. By the steady glow of a hundred bright gas mantles, brawny dockhands heaved baskets ashore from the broad-waisted open sailing smacks. Crews were exhausted, as one would expect of so hard a profession, even when the sea wasn't being too unkind.

As inspectors, we entered the sheds around eight of the evening and chatted with the receivers – those waiting to sort, weigh, and grade the catch before it went to market. Great, sleepy herring gulls dozed on the bollards, confident of their share of the scraps when the fleet returned, and sure enough, they received the unsalable. Holmes hovered with a clipboard, taking down this and that, speaking in the language of the trade as if he had worked all his life in the processing and distribution of fish.

Before reaching the wharves, we had taken a room on the top floor of a boarding house on Cliff Street, one step higher on the western slope, opposite what we already knew to be Cayley's accommodation. We did so under further aliases, certain we wouldn't be using our reservations at the Metropole this particular night, when surveillance was almost certainly the order of the moment.

The *Myrtle McCoy* was one of the larger boats. With half-decked bow and stern for better seaworthiness, she could go farther and stay out longer. A run to the banks and back could be a two-day journey, with time to cast the nets while the weather remained fair. She was a solid sea boat, well-used and hardy, like her crew, and it seemed none noticed that she came home with six men aboard instead of five. They were, of course, also members of the intelligence service, if only of a peripheral sort.

Martin Cayley – heavily bearded and with hair wild on his collar – was unrecognisable from his photograph, but we knew him easily enough. He was the only member of the boat's crew to bring a single basket ashore on his shoulder, then melt into the press of bodies in the gaslit sheds.

404

Holmes was expecting this move, and we intercepted him where the sliding doors stood open to the street, just fifty yards from the Magpie.

"Cayley," Holmes murmured as he appeared from a shadow beside the door and launched into the expected recognition patter. "*Cordon bleu.*"

The seaman squinted in the streetlights and paused for a long moment as if he expected some trap before grunting a cautious reply. "*Bayleaf.*"

"*Whitstable.*"

"*Sandcastle.*"

The three of us relaxed slightly as they completed the double challenge-and-reply. Holmes allowed a faint smile to come through. "Weston, and this is Harbrook. Your superiors are eager for your report."

"You have credentials, of course – ?" Cayley asked, his expression unreadable.

We flourished the warrants we had been issued, and Holmes tapped a breast pocket. "And a document for your attention. Really, we must insist."

"Good God," he muttered, glancing back at the busy interior of the long shed. "Can it not wait until I have scoured the sea from myself?"

"You have lodgings nearby," Holmes fired in unemotionally, stating rather than asking.

"It's the slack season now. You can always find a room. I have one in Cliff Street and want nothing more than a hot bath and a night's sleep." Cayley shrugged his shoulders, then managed a smile. "When the boats come in on the evening tide, hot baths are drawn all over this town." We stepped into the street, and he spoke softly. "If you're determined to debrief me at once, you'll not have to mind me soaking in water up to my neck in the process."

Holmes acquiesced, and I could see why – it is very difficult for a man to stage an escape while wet through, and deprived of his attire. We accompanied him to his boarding house, one street inland and higher on the cliff slope.

A light had been left burning at the door in anticipation of his return, and we followed him upstairs with nods to a sleepy landlord who looked out of his parlour with a greeting for his tenant. A shilling changed hands and the man promised Cayley a jug of cocoa and a plate of supper.

Holmes and I waited on the upstairs landing as he put a key to his door. From his pocket, Holmes passed him what seemed a blank sheet, and Cayley nodded his acceptance before disappearing into his room for a few minutes.

I knew he was applying a mild citric acid solution from a vial he kept hidden away to activate the chemistry of the invisible ink and read the message it contained. When he emerged, he spread his hands in a gesture of acceptance. "The message is your authorisation in the hand of my supervisor, Colonel Flynn. It contains a recognition code known only to him and to me, so, unless it has been tortured out of him, I must accept you gentlemen at face value." From the shadows at his side, he raised a small pistol and lowered the hammer with his thumb.

There seemed no way for Cayley to evade us, and I was pleased he didn't try. Indeed, he had soon run a bath as hot as he could stand in the shared bathroom along the hall from his lodgings and was relaxing in it when the landlord brought up his supper. By gaslight, he ate ravenously – two thick slices of bread and salted dripping, followed by biscuits and more cocoa. At last, we had his undivided attention, and I took a seat on a polished wood towel box, while Holmes stuffed his pipe and chose to stand.

"Now, Mr. Cayley, you appreciate you are required to answer our questions fully and truthfully."

"Is this an interrogation?" he asked. "Debriefing is one thing. This sounds like an inquiry."

"Let's call it an inquiry, then. We were sent by the highest authority to receive your explanation for certain matters that have raised eyebrows in London."

Cayley stretched. "Very well."

Now Holmes launched into the elements he had memorised from Mycroft's files. "Let us begin with the signals you sent from the telegraph office when you returned from Denmark on 12 March of this year."

"Not *this* again. I made no such signals."

"The operator serving on the day recalled you doing so."

"I was in the office buying postcards. I sent telegrams on other days – often. He was confused."

"When pressed, he couldn't swear to his statement. That seems convenient."

"Perhaps, if you want to view it that way. It is also true."

"What of the man with whom you spoke at length in the front bar of The Black Horse on Church Street? After the signals business, an agent was assigned to watch you during your returns to these shores, and he reported you meeting with the same man three times during May."

"Accidentally – socially. He is a local fellow, a retired fisherman. We swapped sea stories."

"His name?"

"Jeb Mundy."

"No one can find a Jeb Mundy in Whitby, Mr. Cayley. Not then, not now."

"Then he wasn't local. Maybe he came up from Scarborough."

406

"Or maybe he was someone else entirely."

"Very possibly. If so, he went away disappointed, because he got nothing from me but fish stories. Do you have reason to believe otherwise?"

"The agent watching you couldn't get close enough to overhear your conversation, so there is no direct testimony, one way or the other."

"Perhaps it would be better if he had. Then there would be no room for doubt."

"On your return in July, you promptly took the train south to Scarborough and transmitted a coded contact to Colonel Flynn from there. You claimed you felt you were being followed."

"That is right. Someone was sticking too close when I went out the morning after I got back to port, so I put some miles between us. I asked Colonel Flynn to have a guard detail meet me, *incognito*, at York Station for the express down to London. I felt some attempt might be made on my life to prevent me reporting in person."

"Nothing came of it. There was no incident."

"For which I was very glad."

"Or did the request for support merely mask and justify an excursion to a different town that might very well have facilitated a rendezvous with persons unknown while giving the slip to the agent watching you?"

"Has it occurred to you that maybe it was *your* man I spotted? We are trained to evade. I did so and made contact from a secure location."

Holmes shrugged his shoulders and blew a smoke ring. "Look at it from our point of view, Mr. Cayley. Mysterious telegrams that may or may not have been sent. Conversations with a man who cannot be found. A side trip for which we have only your word there was a reason. Individually innocuous. But these events might form a pattern that comfortably describes clandestine meetings for the passing of information."

Cayley stretched in the steaming water. "I have been over this with other agents before. Now, you tell me: Is there any indication as to whom I might have been speaking? Foreign agents? I could more easily do that overseas, out of sight, out of mind. You trust me when I am a thousand miles away, then suspect me on home soil."

Holmes paused for some time, then shook his head slowly. "There are no recorded movements of suspected foreign agents in Britain coinciding with your incidents. That doesn't necessarily mean they did not occur."

"Fair enough. How do you propose to find out?"

"The onus is upon you, Mr. Cayley, to convince us. Produce this Jeb Mundy, for instance."

"That was six months ago. I have no idea where to find him."

"Nor did the barkeeper at The Black Horse, when casually questioned by the agent assigned to you. He was, in fact, a stranger in town."

"There you are, then." Cayley shrugged, creating a roll of the hot suds. "If you mean to investigate every stray conversation an agent ever has, you will find the task impractical. Should you not be asking me about the man who sold me a rail ticket in Copenhagen? Or the cabdriver in Riga? The boy who picks up my laundry in Vilnius? Surely, they are all equally credible foreign agents with whom I could be committing treason."

Holmes had no reply, and Cayley went on. "You know how this chain of reasoning goes. Unless you can attach some concurrent event or circumstance to the events you have chosen, the accusation remains supposition verging on paranoia."

"What would you have us do?" Holmes asked in a whisper. "Forget we were ever uneasy?"

"Unless you can prove some misconduct on my part, your choices are limited to that or removing me from active duty." Cayley reached for a cloth and eased his position in the bath. "Now, gentlemen, unless you have something more, I have been at sea for two days, and I want to get some sleep. Surely, we can take this up again in the morning."

He was quite right, and I had to admit that Cayley had been very convincing in his replies. Holmes hadn't expected to trip him up on facts or details, but meant to judge his manner – *Was he lying?* At this point, Cayley's adamance that he had committed no treason seemed to carry weight.

We retired to our boarding house across the street, climbed to our room, and prepared to spend a long and uncomfortable night. In a chair by the window, I took first watch until three, fighting fatigue to keep the other house in view by the streetlights' golden gleam while mist curled up from the river and lent a Gothic quality to the silent night.

Holmes relieved me at three, and I put my head down, wondering quite how I would write up these affairs – or if, indeed, the matters would be worthy of a narrative at all. I half-expected to be shaken awake to follow Holmes on some desperate dash through the foggy streets as Cayley tried to evade us, and was mildly surprised when morning found us still at our rest.

At this date and latitude, the sun fought through haze in the east around seven, while we passed the time in the boarding house's tiny dining room – a converted front parlour – watching the street for movement opposite as we took bacon and eggs. We seemed to be the only guests at the moment and had privacy for our conversation. But we kept our talk innocuous as eight o'clock went by, and took our leave of the proprietor.

We were loitering upon the street before the front door of the establishment opposite opened and Cayley emerged, markedly different from his appearance the night before. He wore a decent suit of clothes, and his hair and beard were trimmed and washed.

He approached us with a shake of the head and a *tut-tutting* noise. "Weston, Harbrook. Good morning. My, my, you gentlemen look rough. As you are no doubt starting to appreciate, you had no call to watch in case I tried to escape. In fact, if you suspected I was liable to, you should have taken me into custody. That you didn't suggests you have no real evidence and are merely fishing – pardon the pun – in the hopes I would lead you to something. Give myself away, perhaps. Well, where shall we begin today? I must send a coded telegram to Colonel Flynn. That is expected protocol."

"Of course." Holmes gestured along the street. "In your own time."

"The post office will be opening soon. It is my usual routine."

We strolled down to Station Square to find the post office overlooking the harbour. Cayley carefully composed a message, in one of the many codes available to him, informing his superior that he had returned safely and would present himself in London to deliver his report of affairs in the east.

Holmes watched him as we thumbed through racks of sepia postcards, and I bought a couple as souvenirs of the trip. But when we stepped out on the street by the harbour in the early press of foot traffic to the shops, I had to wonder what we were doing here. Holmes caught my eye and knew I was asking if we were achieving anything – or had Mycroft sent us on a total and utter fool's errand?

When we had the privacy of distance from others, Holmes sent Cayley a hard glance from beneath his false brows. "We shall accompany you down to London," he said brusquely. "But that shall be at our discretion. Not today. We have more to consider, and I would rather confine the inquiry to this remote town, isolated by sea and moors."

"Whatever you say," Cayley replied, hooking thumbs in his waistcoat pockets. "The boat will not be going out again right away. We are into the slack time, so there is elbow room for – more questions."

"I have just one at the moment: How do you determine when to return?"

Cayley frowned. "That is an operational detail between me and Colonel Flynn – and so is my mission report."

"The proper answer." Holmes smiled fleetingly. "In general terms, then. Is it prearranged, or determined by changing circumstances?"

After a long pause in which Cayley eyed us with all appropriate suspicion, he replied simply, "The latter."

"Thank you, Mr. Cayley. Now, let us meet at the station buffet at, say, twelve o'clock."

"You want to be sure I do not board the next train and depart." Cayley shook his head. "I suggest you have me arrested. That way you will be certain." He extended his wrists. "Gentlemen, I am no traitor. I shall tender my resignation to Colonel Flynn, as I can clearly not continue to work under these circumstances."

Holmes glanced at me, and I felt some outburst was about to ensue, but he rather took the wind from my sails with the mildness of his response. "You have my apologies, Mr. Cayley. I will ask just one thing: That you allow me a further twenty-four hours in which to consider the matter, at which point we shall journey down to London and each present our findings to our respective commissioning officers."

"Easily done," he replied. "You may find me at my boarding house."

With a justifiable degree of frustration, Cayley turned on his heel and walked north towards the sea, perhaps for the familiarity of its salt and ozone. I turned an eye on Holmes. "Tell me something, Holmes: Have we established one single thing yet?"

"I am certain our Mr. Cayley isn't lying," Holmes replied simply. "This doesn't guarantee he is also telling the whole truth. I shall use the day's grace to address that point, for if he is both guilty and yet has *not* been turned by some foreign interest, we are left with just one option."

"That the interest is domestic," I filled in.

"Your instincts serve you well, Watson." He stuffed his pipe as we waited on a street corner, watching people pass by, and at last gestured at a bench overlooking the harbour. "I must meditate upon matters. Why not take a walk, enjoy the sea air, and we shall meet at the station, as agreed."

I did as he suggested, making my way along Pier Street in Cayley's wake. I didn't see him, but followed the road past the Magpie and the fisheries sheds, past pubs and shops towards the sea. Beyond the bandstand and the lifeboat shed, the west breakwater reaches out over the waves, and in the chill sea wind I walked to the lighthouse at the end.

I have to admit, Bram Stoker couldn't have chosen a more atmospheric place to set his novel. This old town, under the racing grey clouds of the season, can be the very essence of the Gothic and of all things evoking unease. I have read something of the folklore of these parts: A veritable cornucopia of the strange – ghosts, poltergeists, "blackdogs", legends of every stripe, from walled-up nuns to a coach that collects the souls of dead seamen. It is said residents of Henrietta Street, which runs up towards the eastern headland, occasionally still hear the hooves and wheels of a coach that, long ago, failed to stop at the top and plunged over the cliff.

It is enough to give one gooseflesh, and I realised that while sophisticated city folk like Holmes and myself might easily set aside such things as the colour and nonsense of the country, for those who live here, the folklore is their very heritage and not so lightly taken.

I watched boats coming and going, saw a photographer trying his luck for studies across the waters, and soon went in search of a cafe for hot tea and a scone. The wind was making my ears ache, and I was glad to get out of it for a while.

When noon came, I walked into Whitby's small station to find Holmes in the buffet and Cayley about to join him. We swiftly obtained cocoa and ham sandwiches and watched as passengers assembled for the 12:30 service along the Esk Valley to points north. The train arrived, stood to exchange passengers, and eventually departed with a shrill of the whistle and gusts of steam. All the while, Cayley remained entirely calm. He was no more seeking to escape us than it would appear he had told any untruth.

When we finished our lunch, Holmes rose and dabbed his lips with a napkin. "Thank you, Mr. Cayley. You will excuse me now, as I have work of my own to pursue."

When the agent left, I eyed Holmes shrewdly, for I had picked up a note in his voice that told me something had come to pass. "What is it?"

"Your observation that if not foreign, then domestic, has guided my reasoning during the morning, and the time has come to put it to the test. I shall venture to the library for the afternoon and, with a modicum of luck, put substance to the vague suspicions of Mycroft, Colonel Flynn, and others."

As we walked out into Station Square, I turned my collar up against the breeze. "You do feel he's hiding something, then?"

"I do. I could not tell you why, which infuriates me. Intuition is a poor substitute for clear and concise chains of deduction. Allow me to try to place matters upon a more familiar footing, and before dinner, perhaps this strange hunt on which we find ourselves will have taken on a new and more productive character."

"Shall I watch the station for the next service?"

"If you would be so kind, Watson, though it would seem a mere formality. If there is no altercation with Mr. Cayley at that time, come and seek me out at the public library. I shall regale you with my progress."

The next train left at five-minutes-past-three, and I determined to be in the station with plenty of time to spare. I was, however, at a loose end, and sightseeing as All Hallows' Eve came upon us was a chilly business.

411

I had seen preparations for bonfires on both eastern and western cliff areas, and I know how children enjoy this time of year, when ghost stories are told, games played, and sausages cooked over open fires.

Up here in the north, people hollow out large turnips, cut faces into them, and place a candle within to give the semblance of an illuminated face – Jack-o'-lanterns, after the ancient Irish origins of the tradition. Perhaps it was something to do with the Celtic veneration of the human head, whether attached to the shoulders or otherwise. I am told that Americans use pumpkins for the same purpose – a vegetable never seen in these parts.

Clouds came up as noon went by and the afternoon wore on, and it seemed the weather was thickening. I heard a grumble of thunder far off over the moors behind the town, and locals nodded sagely as they considered the sky with their sailors' eyes. Many heads shook, and thick Yorkshire accents framed the sentiment that the evening's festivities might well be rained off.

I was glad to be indoors, going from teashop to coffeehouse, spending a few pennies here, a shilling there. With the summer holiday season a good month past, shopkeepers were grateful for whatever trade they could come by.

At last, I made my way back to the station to buy a newspaper, sit, and watch the platform as the train came in. It stood, carriage doors open, the engine breathing softly to itself. I observed the comings and goings, and when the service finally departed back up the Esk Valley line, I could assure Holmes that our man hadn't been on it.

The West Cliff Station serves a line to Sandsend and Robin Hood's Bay, while the southern link runs to Scarborough via the towering Larpool Viaduct over the Esk, but something deep down assured me our man wasn't on those lines either. He was entirely confident of himself. To run would be a clear admission of guilt, and unless Holmes came up with something, he would walk free in due course. As Cayley had said, he could tender his resignation and, with all probability, leave the service for civilian life.

The stormy sky brought unnatural twilight, and by midafternoon lights glimmered all over the harbour in a purple dusk. The sun would leave us around four in a wash of colours in the west, but the day became gloomy long before then. I hurried north from the station to Pier Street and made my way seven doors past the Magpie to the tall Whitby bathhouse. The baths occupied the lowest level. The top floor was a museum of local history, while between lay the town's library.

I found Holmes in a quiet nook, surrounded with archived copies of the library's subscription collection of our familiar London paper, *The*

Times. Several copies lay open to the financial pages, and when I appeared, Holmes drew me into a seat alongside his reading table. His expression told me much, and I listened carefully as he whispered.

"Your instincts were correct," he began with a razor-thin smile, "and Cayley hasn't told a single lie. The fact remains, however, that this is due to our inability to ask the right questions." He tapped a paper. "A variety of motives is always possible, but it would seem our man is outside the reach of blackmail over family or domestic concerns. He is unmarried, childless, and no casual female companions are noted in his file. As a man of action, it is highly unlikely that he could be influenced by mere threats against his person. Agents are trained to kill without compunction whenever the need arises. Therefore, if he isn't being manipulated by another agency, his actions must be for personal benefit. Therefore: *Money*."

I squinted at the columns of text around me. "He's gaining illicitly?"

"Not in the usual sense, perhaps. I doubt he is blackmailing anyone. But a case exists to be answered. We know the date of each of his returns to England from the Baltic Provinces. There are three previous returns during 1900. Remember, he makes the journey at his own discretion – he sends a message that brings the boat from Whitby to the banks to meet his boat from Denmark. That he completes his obligations to the service doesn't preclude him engaging in extracurricular activities of his own."

"What have you found?"

"In the two weeks following each date of return, there was a minor run or tumble on the London Exchange. In each case, it concerned *Baltic* goods. Timber, grain, pitch, furs, wax, honey, a dozen other commodities. Once might have been coincidental. Twice is pushing the notion – thrice is incontestably a pattern. In each instance, investors positioned in the market made handsome profits, whether from exploiting delays in shipment or windfall gains from some unexpected surplus, which raises the point that for at least *some* investors in this country, the fluctuations were wholly anticipated. How? Because critical information was supplied to them by someone in the perfect position to know."

"Cayley."

"How simple would it be for him to memorise things of value to the financial markets and pass them on, whether by mysterious, coded wires or casual conversations? Assuming he is properly invested or being paid a generous tithe by those his information benefits, he must have accumulated a sizeable retirement fund." Holmes paused. "And the clincher? These events can also be traced into last year, beginning soon after the date at which Cayley's partner was lost overseas."

"Motive? Was he shocked to lose his friend and decided to get what he could for himself before the vagaries of fate sent him to an early grave too?"

"A simple and logical proposal. He had the means and followed through."

I shook my head slowly. "Market trading on the basis of privileged or secret information is widely considered unethical, but to the best of my knowledge, it isn't actually a crime."

"No. But the contract of employment Martin Cayley signed with the government prohibits him from engaging in business, which would provide an Achilles's heel by which an agent could be manipulated by enemies of this country if they so wished. It also prohibits him accepting gifts, emoluments, or any other form of capital advancement other than the stipend he receives from his legitimate employer – to wit, Her Majesty." Holmes folded his hands. "For whatever reason, under whatever justification, Cayley got greedy. No wonder he is ready to retire if he has already put by enough to live comfortably and thus subtract himself from the line of fire for Queen and Country."

"Are you saying he was never agent material? That he wasn't a patriot in the true sense of the word?"

"Not at all. He could be both those things, yet have become disenchanted by seeing the comfort and security amassed by men for whom danger means a gamble on the exchange, not placing their very life in jeopardy – much less doing so on a daily basis." Holmes smiled with a shrug. "Corruption isn't always a wicked or malevolent thing, Watson. Sometimes it is the whisper of regret or resentment, or a justifiable dissatisfaction with one's reimbursement for the sacrifices demanded."

I sighed and shook my head as I cast an eye over the financial news. "The pattern fits, certainly. What do we do? Do we lull him with calm words and turn him over to Mycroft in London tomorrow? Or do we assume he is bright enough to understand his potential jeopardy and expect him to use his skills to vanish here and now – requiring us to have him arrested forthwith?"

"I fear the latter. If I were Cayley, I would be supremely uneasy to have departmental investigators once again following up concerns I had assumed were laid to rest."

"He is a good actor and well able to deceive," I commented and, from windows at our side, glanced at the gloomy sky over the harbour. The unnatural twilight was thickening by the minute. "We'd better make our move, then."

Holmes and I walked out into the sea wind, finding the streets deserted now but for those few on their way to Hallowe'en festivities. We went directly to Whitby Police Station, at the top of Spring Hill Street, where we showed our warrants from London and requisitioned manpower to accomplish the deed. We informed them that our quarry was armed – as were we – and that we didn't expect the local constabulary to place themselves in undue danger, but simply to take custody of the fellow in due course.

A constable and his bewhiskered sergeant walked out with us to Cliff Street, and in the glow of the gas lamps, we retraced our way to Cayley's boarding house. However, a street lad leaning against a grimy brick wall eyed us as we approached. He looked like the kind who make pennies around the fish markets, always ready to earn another copper for a task performed.

He pushed away from the wall, pulled a paper from a pocket, touched his cap brim, and spoke in a Yorkshire accent so thick I had trouble following it. "Evenin', sirs. A gentleman asked me to give you this. It *is* Mr. Holmes, isn't it?"

Holmes paused before plucking the letter from the outstretched hand and unfolding the sheet from the envelope. He scanned it for a moment, then tossed the lad another tuppence, which seemed to please the urchin. He tugged his cap once more and disappeared into the twilight.

"What's the news?" I asked, aware of our audience.

"It seems our man is every bit as perspicacious as you theorised. We have an invitation to meet with him in the abbey grounds at our earliest convenience. He suggests we leave the constabulary at a distance, as he wishes only to talk at this point." Holmes glanced at the dark sky and checked his fob watch. "Nearly four o'clock. No time like the present, gentlemen." He turned to the policemen with a finger raised. "As I said, Mr. Cayley is armed and now, more than ever, is likely to use force. There's nothing for it, I'm afraid: We must tackle him on his own terms. We'll not put you fellows in the firing line, but be ready to help in whatever way you can."

In the gathering dusk, we made our way to the harbour, where the town's lights glittered upon the choppy waters, and crossed the bridge. The cheerful glow of The Customs House Hotel front bar reminded us that everyday life was far from the intrigues of spies. The drinkers who enjoyed the warmth and companionship within would have no thought of the impending drama. We turned into Church Street, hurried its length, took the one-hundred-ninety-nine steps where they diverged at the foot of Henrietta Street, and paced ourselves as we ascended the East Cliff.

Legend has it that you can never count the steps and find the same result twice, and I could believe it – the number is large enough to lose count more than once. As we ascended, we got a view over the harbour to the viaduct and points inland. We saw the gathering end of day where the sun gave rise to a few stray beams between flying clouds, and the purple twilight matched the mood of this All Hallows' Eve. On the East Cliff, a bonfire blazed on the open ground along from the Abbey House, and people in costume were silhouetted against the flames. We heard children's voices, snatches of song and story, as people braved the sea wind that blustered over the cliffs to mark the day before this weather doubtless drove them indoors.

The abbey's Gothic ruins rise over stone walls beyond the Church of St. Mary and its now-disused graveyard, where salt-corroded, pitted stones lean in disarray. The last burial there was nearly forty years earlier, and the cemetery has become an icon of the olden days. We made our way to the old gatehouse to the grounds. Finding the way open for us as a gate creaked in the wind. Holmes and I tugged out our revolvers. The sergeant nodded his understanding and held his man back as we slipped into the gloom of the lawns and towering stonework under the tumbling cloudscape.

Wind moaned through open arches above, playing like a devil's flute across eroded stone. As our eyes accustomed to the dark, we found an obstacle course of pillars and walls. "Careful, Watson," Holmes hissed as we moved from the deepest shadow to the next black patch.

We were about halfway into the maze when a voice called out ahead. "That's far enough, gentlemen! I'll not tell you to drop your weapons. You know I have mine to hand, and that I can see you plainly enough. It would be foolish for you to fire into the darkness, and at this point there is no call. I want only to speak to you."

"What is there to say that you cannot say to our faces?" Holmes called out.

"Much, Mr. Holmes. Oh, yes, I knew you readily enough. Your individual disguises are adequate, but together, Holmes and Watson are an unmistakable pair. Was it Mr. Mycroft Holmes who sent you? I am actually rather flattered." The voice from the darkness paused for a few heartbeats. "The moment you disappeared into the library, I assumed you were thinking about this whole business from a new angle. I knew you had made the connection." Cayley's voice hardened. "It's time to stop playing games."

"Are you confessing?" Holmes asked plaintively, not challenging him, pistol hanging at his side.

"To what? To being a loyal agent of Her Majesty, risking life and limb against all the Germans or the Russians could muster? I'll readily attest to that."

"And what of your lost partner?" Holmes asked softly.

416

No reply was forthcoming for a long moment. "Harold Meecham was a good egg. A good agent who died in a shootout with watchmen in a small town in Livonia. I couldn't save him. And you are right, of course – that was when I asked myself what difference my own death would make if things had happened differently. And I stopped being quite such a do-gooder. I could see a dozen ways to put away the makings of a comfortable retirement, and nobody need ever know how. Only a sense of duty had kept me drawing government pay when I saw fortunes made all around me. Why?" He barked the last in a broken sort of tone. "I ask you, why? If I died, there would be few to even stand at my graveside, and that *galls* a man."

"So you used your east-west shuttling to pass information about the commodities markets," Holmes returned evenly, "knowing full well that it was in contravention of the terms of your employment."

"I hurt nobody," Cayley countered. "Just redirected a few pounds here and there. In the process, I made others wealthy too, and brought trade into this country. I *benefited* Britain!"

I had to admit, he was probably right. But the fact remained that he had disobeyed a key tenet of being an intelligence agent, because once corruption – of any sort – raises its head, a slippery slope awaits. At the bottom lies the status of a double agent in the thrall of some power Hell-bent on taking Britain down a peg or two. And that is intolerable.

"What's to be done, Mr. Holmes?" Cayley's voice challenged.

Holmes rather surprised me with his next words. "What would satisfy you?"

"I want only to disappear. I give you my assurance that I have never acted to the detriment of this country and never shall. But the time has come to part ways, and none will ever hear of Martin Cayley again. Can you turn that blind eye, Mr. Holmes?"

"I think you know I cannot. Your superiors demand greater assurances than a man's word of honour, and they cannot let matters lie. They will doubtless require far more investigation before they are prepared to assert, one way or another, whether your actions have done damage. But quite apart from that, you have broken the law. It is that simple."

"Given the prospect of years in a military prison for breach of contract, you will understand if giving myself up isn't an option." Cayley paused as the wind droned eerily above us and the twilight continued to thicken. Thunder drummed over the moors far away and a tendril of lightning illuminated the towers starkly for an instant. "Last chance, Mr. Holmes."

"For both of us, Cayley," Holmes replied brusquely.

A moment later, I followed him as he dodged into cover behind the stub of a wall. A shot *whanged* deafeningly from the stone in a burst of sparks, and Holmes and I rose together to trigger a few defiant shots into the darkness.

A figure moved among the ruins, and Holmes fired reflexively, then urged me on, and we rushed from one shadow to another. In the last glimmers of twilight, we glimpsed Cayley as he pressed hard through the ruins, a sprinting outline on the lawns beside the abbey. He half-turned, threw back an arm, and sent two more shots our way, but they were wildly inaccurate, and Holmes chanced another round. We heard a cry in the gloom and hurried on but found no body. Had Holmes winged him?

A shape moved again in the darkness. We caught his running image in another flash of lightning and pounded in his wake. He cleared the boundary fence of the abbey grounds and raced on towards the clifftop as we gave all the pursuit of which we were capable. I was vaguely aware of the two policemen following, their lanterns shuttered so as not to make targets of themselves, but Cayley was well ahead when we heaved over the fence.

The roll and rumble of the sea filled our ears. Its salt was in our nostrils, and I became aware of the need for caution. It served no ends for one or both of us to take a tumble here. Cayley could afford no such restraint and pounded through the long grass as if the Devil were behind him.

"*Cayley!*" Holmes roared, "I'll fire! I swear it!" But desperation knows no caution, and as the blurring figure was lost to the darkness, Holmes steadied his aim and fired. A cry came on the wind, short and sharp, then a long, terrible scream that trailed off into nothing.

The policemen reached us, and we stood panting in the bitter wind. As the first raindrops pelted from the swollen sky, Holmes crept to the cliff edge. There was nothing to see but the ghostly white of breaking waves below, and the sergeant shook his head assertively. "I'll not ask my men to crawl around on this cliff in the dark, under a storm, looking for a man who's more'n likely already dead." He raised a hand to forestall objection. "I don't care if he's the most wanted man on Earth – not before first light, and if conditions are unsafe, not even then!"

We could do no more, but Holmes hung back for some time while rain began to patter on our shoulders and lightning snaked through the clouds once more. I knew what he was thinking. *Was Cayley out there, gone to ground, a good enough actor to deliver those cries to convince us that he was now beyond all recrimination?*

I was more than glad to return to the Metropole once we had made our statement at the police station. The hour wasn't yet six of the evening, and we each retired to enjoy a hot bath in our heated rooms, then had a bite to eat sent up for us. In the north, one's main meal is in the middle of the day rather than the evening as it is in the south – a strange thing for a Londoner to get used to.

I met Holmes in the hotel lounge – both out of disguise now, with certain explanations made to the manager. Our warrant cards covered all promptings of curiosity and won us the peace I certainly craved. We smoked and talked for a while, but last night's uncomfortable watch had caught up with me. I excused myself before ten to retire and tucked myself up in bed to read Bram Stoker's wonderful novel as rain drummed at the window. Only once did I pause and wonder if the man we were sent to investigate was lost among the breakers below the East Cliff, or was he still out there in the cold, sodden night, making his way determinedly from one life, one existence, to another?

Morning saw the weather clear, and though conditions were cold and blustery, the police managed to bring together a searching force, contributed to by other towns along the coast. By ten, their report was in: No body had been found on the clifftops, nor had anything been spotted along the surf line. The search would continue in the direction of the prevailing current, but there was little hope of recovering a body that had been pounded in the mill of the waves. Regarding the alternate possibility, the Scarborough Police were given Cayley's description and asked to be on the lookout for anyone entering the town from the north in bedraggled condition.

Holmes and I stood in the biting wind, collars up and clutching our hats as cloud flurried over the abbey ruins. I shook my head. "Well, I don't think he's dead, Holmes. Maybe that's wishful thinking, but I keep remembering that last scream. It was – *theatrical*."

"You may be right. As a consummate professional, Cayley could be expected to have an escape plan laid out in advance and to have put it into operation. People in his pay, transport, and so on. If so, we are left with a conundrum: Does Martin Cayley represent a chink in this nation's armour, vulnerable to probing by foreign powers? Or is he as good as his word and merely withdrawing from the job to enjoy a quiet life? If the latter, he will appear with a new name and identity somewhere, probably in the country – perhaps in Scotland or Ireland – to invest his capital in property, settle down, perhaps find a wife, and live out his days as a gentleman of business and leisure."

"If that is so, I wish him well," I said quietly. "I know he broke the law, but part of me sympathises deeply with his position. He wagered his life for love of his country, and his country repaid him poorly. And I'm not letting my own experience colour my judgement." I was referring to my war wound and the subsequent hard times I found myself in before connecting with a certain co-lodger on Baker Street, so many years before.

"We can but report our conclusions," Holmes went on with a sour air. "That Cayley confessed to wrongdoing before either going to his death or escaping cleanly, and we have no way to know which. After that point, the matter is moot, though I doubt Mycroft and Colonel Flynn will leave it there. They will scour this country using the services of every agent they can spare, and whether Cayley – if indeed he lives – can evade *that* is down to both professionalism and providence."

I sighed into the wind. "This wasn't the usual sort of errand for us."

"Far from it."

"Have we had our fill of the salty northeast?"

"Decidedly."

I nodded back across the harbour at the station. "We can finish up here. There's a half-past-twelve train on the route via Malton that'll have us in York just after three. Then we can catch an express down to King's Cross. We could be home in Baker Street tonight."

Holmes agreed and went to find the senior officer, leaving me on the green stretch above the angry grey sea, wondering at the turns of fate that rule the fortunes of us all.

Death of an Uncommon Man
by Geri Schear

By eight o'clock that Tuesday morning in July 1901, I felt so uncomfortably hot that I had kicked back all the bedclothes. By nine, I admitted defeat. I gave up all notions of sleep, bathed in cold water, then asked Mrs. Hudson for breakfast. She, poor woman, looked as flushed and flustered as I have ever seen. Fanning herself with a dishcloth, she said, "The paper says it's more than ninety-one degrees in Yorkshire, Doctor. It's surely much hotter here in London."

"No wonder I'm so hot," I said.

"Will a cold breakfast suffice? Oh, you're up too, Mr. Holmes?"

Already puffing on a cigarette, Sherlock Holmes sat unhappily at the table opposite me. "What one would give for a decent rainstorm," he said.

A few minutes later, a pair of maids arrived to deliver our breakfast. Holmes and I drank the cold cider at once and refilled our glasses from the pitcher. I ate fairly heartily on the cold chicken, tongue, and other cold meats, as well as some fruit. Holmes made do with sardines on bread, followed by some cold custard.

Before we were quite finished, Mrs. Hudson knocked on the door and entered. "I beg your pardon for interrupting your breakfast," she said, "but there is a gentleman who insists on seeing you, Mr. Holmes. He is very agitated, and I didn't like to send him away. His name is Nicholas Pirowitz. He says it's urgent."

"Pirowitz!" Holmes exclaimed. "Alexander Pirowitz's brother. Show him in, Mrs. Hudson."

"Pirowitz?" I said. "Isn't that that artist you like?"

Before Holmes could reply, the fellow came into the room. From his haggard face and shuffling gait, I thought him at least seventy years of age. I later learned he was at least twenty years younger. His wiry grey hair sprang up like coils of iron reminding me, rather unfortunately, of a spring terrier. His face was pale, the features finely sculpted. His startling blue eyes were accented by the bloodshot whites.

"Do come in and sit down, Mr. Pirowitz," Holmes said. "I see you have suffered a great shock."

"Terrible, terrible. Oh, Mr. Holmes . . . ."

I poured a glass of water and handed it to the man, helping to hold it to his lips, as his hands shook so badly that he couldn't hold it himself.

After some moments, the man managed to calm enough to speak.

"You may have heard of my brother, Mr. Holmes," he began.

"Alexander Pirowitz," Holmes said. "An artist of inestimable talent. I saw his exhibition some eighteen months ago at Royal Academy. But are his injuries severe?"

"You have heard about his terrible event, then? I had hoped the press wouldn't yet have gathered. They are vultures, Mr. Holmes, vultures."

Holmes held up a restraining hand. "I have heard nothing, Mr. Pirowitz," he said. "But the state of your clothing indicates you have travelled some distance this morning, and the blood on the sleeves of your jacket tell of some violent event. Finally, the fact that you have come to see me makes it certain that you are dealing with some calamity. The fact that your opening comment was about your brother suggests that he is in some way involved in this incident."

"You are perfectly correct, Mr. Holmes." With my assistance, our guest sank onto the sofa, still trembling violently. "It is indeed because of my brother that I have come to see you.

"As you say, Alexander is an exceptional artist. However, there are times when the intensity of his emotions overcome him. During these occasions, he has had himself admitted to Colney Hatch."

"The asylum?" I said, not managing to suppress a shudder.

"Yes, Doctor. Because he pays generously for his time there, he is given far greater liberty than the other patients. He is allowed to roam through the grounds, and he is permitted, even encouraged, to paint. He has his own room, and has become a favourite with many of the staff."

"Until this act of violence occurred," Holmes said. "Tell me what happened. Omit no detail, if you please."

"I received a telegram this morning that Alex had been found in the hospital grounds. He had been shot in the abdomen. That is to say . . . the authorities believe the wound was self-inflicted."

"How bad is his injury?" I asked.

Pirowitz released a sob. "He is not expected to survive."

"A tragedy," Holmes said. "A loss to the world. I gather you don't believe your brother shot himself?"

"No, indeed, Mr. Holmes. My brother detests guns. Besides, I spoke to him just two days ago and he told me he was making plans for a new exhibition. He had already planned out some of the paintings. He was very excited about it."

"Who found him, do you know?"

"A man called Findlay. He is the chief porter at the hospital. I gather he was on his way there this morning, cutting through the fields, and found Alex lying unconscious by the fence."

"And the weapon?"

Pirowitz swallowed. "Lying beside him, I am told."

For a moment, Holmes was silent, contemplating what we had heard. At last, he rose and said, "Well, I think we must go to Colney Hatch and see what we can learn."

By the time we reached Colney Hatch, the sun was almost at its zenith. Conveniently, the railway station was attached to the main hospital. We followed Pirowitz through a maze of corridors and up the stairs to what he told us was the infirmary wing. We were greeted by a harried physician who assured Pirowitz that his brother was still clinging to life.

We walked down the ward through an aisle of white-faced men with hollow eyes whose flailing hands clawed at us. Their sobs and screams made me wonder how anyone could endure such a place, and I thanked God that I look after men's bodies and not their minds.

Pirowitz led us to a private room at the end of the ward. Within we found a priest administering last rites to the waxen-faced man who lay in the bed. Pirowitz gasped in despair but calmed when he realised that the patient still breathed. With the ritual complete, the clergyman placed a hand on Pirowitz's arm and said he was available if he wished to talk.

Pirowitz nodded without much interest, all his attention was on the man in the bed. He moved around to the other side of the bed and spoke into the patient's left ear. "Alex?" the poor fellow said. "Alex, it's Nicky."

The patient lay still. His laboured breathing the only thing that made the blood-stained sheets rise and fall. The rhythm hitched slightly suggesting the poor fellow had heard his brother's voice.

"A moment, if you please," Holmes said. He took the wounded man's right hand in his and examined it closely, and then sniffed the artist's fingers. He repeated the action with the other hand. "Watson, your opinion," he said when he had completed his examination.

No doubt I saw precise same things as my friend, but where he was enlightened, I was bewildered.

"Right-handed," I said, starting with the most obvious. "A peculiar burn across his right palm and fingers. From his abdomen, I see he sustained a single gunshot wound at close proximity. The angle is peculiar. Obviously, I cannot be certain, but it looks as if the weapon were fired upwards. Perhaps he was seated?"

"How can you tell all that?" asked our client.

"The right hand is slightly larger and considerably more developed than the left, indicating which hand is prominent," Holmes explained. "In addition, the callouses on the index and middle fingers show that he has spent much time holding a pencil or a paintbrush."

"And the angle of the wound," I explained, "is atypical for a suicide. The entrance wound is low in the abdomen, but the trajectory of the bullet appears to be angled upwards. Obviously, I cannot be certain, it is merely my impression."

"Marvellous," said Pirowitz. "What clever men you are."

"I have no explanation for the burn, however."

The door opened and a nurse entered. We stood silent as she took the patient's blood pressure and pulse. "It won't be long now," she said, looking sadly at the dying man.

"Tell me, Sister," Holmes said, using the title that is traditional for nurses, "Did anyone wash Mr. Pirowitz's hands when he was brought back here"

"No, sir. Poor man was in such pain, we didn't have the heart to bother him too much. I washed his face because he was perspiring so much, and he seemed to find that a comfort, but that and giving him an injection for the pain were all I could do."

"Did anyone see Mr. Alexander Pirowitz before he left the hospital this morning?" he continued.

"Yes, I did," she said. "He was very gay, full of plans for the future, and his 'greatest work ever', he said." Her eyes welled with tears despite her smile. "He even grabbed me around the waist and danced me up and down the ward. I've never seen him in such fine spirits."

"I understand that a weapon was found near him. Do you know what happened to it?"

"I believe it was brought back here. Matron and the senior doctor are meeting with the police inspector in matron's office right now. They probably have it in there."

She directed us to the matron's office and, leaving the dying man in his brother's care, we hurried down a long hallway and up two flights of stairs.

The people in the room started as we entered.

"This is a private meeting," the matron said.

"Excuse us," I replied, undaunted. I am well used to dealing with truculent hospital administrators. "I am Dr. John Watson, and this is my friend, Mr. Sherlock Holmes. We are here at the request of Mr. Pirowitz, the patient's brother."

"Come in and sit down, gentlemen," the doctor said. He was a tall, thin man who exuded that geniality some doctors use to replace competence. He nodded at a burly fellow clad in workman's overalls, and this man immediately brought in two chairs from an anteroom. A uniformed police officer scowled but said nothing. As soon as we were seated, the doctor introduced himself and the others present.

"This is Matron Anderson, and next to her is Sergeant Chadwick from the local constabulary, then our chief porter, Mr. Findlay. I am the senior medical officer, Dr. Burke."

We shook hands and acknowledged each in turn. Other than the porter and the doctor, no one seemed particularly happy to see us. The policeman, in particular, sat with arms folded and his lips pursed. He gave the impression of a man used to being in charge, suddenly being demoted to some menial status. As Holmes later said, we have met happier undertakers.

"This is a police matter," he protested. "Suicide is a crime."

"I think you mean attempted suicide," Holmes said in an amused voice. "One can hardly arrest a dead man."

Findlay tried unsuccessfully to stifle a laugh.

"Who found Mr. Pirowitz?" Holmes continued.

"I did, Mr. Holmes," Findlay said. "I always cut across the fields on my way to the hospital. I saw him from several yards away. At first, I thought he was sleeping, and then I saw the blood."

"What did you do?"

"He's only a slip of a fellow. I couldn't leave him there, so I picked him up and carried him back here. I found the weapon on the ground a foot or more away from him, so I brought that back too."

"Did you see anyone nearby?"

"Not a sinner, Mr. Holmes. Just that poor man."

"Did you hear a shot?"

"Yes, a few minutes before. Perhaps five or ten minutes."

"Did you hear a quick succession of shots before then?"

"Come to think of it, I did. I'd forgotten until you mentioned it. Just a minute or two before that one shot, I heard several coming very fast."

"How did you know that, Mr. Holmes?" the doctor asked.

"Because Mr. Pirowitz's left hand has a burn along the palm. It could only have happened if he grabbed the barrel of the revolver, and then only if the barrel was hot."

"I didn't know guns could get hot," the doctor said.

"They don't, as a rule, but repeated firing can make this happen."

"Well, I don't see how it matters," the policeman sneered.

"Do you not?" Holmes asked in his silkiest tones. "Well, we shall see. May I see the weapon?"

The doctor handed it to him, ignoring the fuming policeman.

"A Colt," Holmes observed. "The so-called Navy revolver of 1850 or '51."

"I thought the Colt was an American weapon," the sergeant said.

"Originally, yes, but it is also manufactured in Colt's London Armory not far from Vauxhall Bridge. I believe there are also Belgian and Russian manufacturers of this model."

Carefully, he cocked back the hammer. "There is blood here," he said.

The policeman looked at the spot that Holmes indicated and nodded his head sagely, as if he had already seen the blood.

"What do you infer from that?" Holmes asked the fellow. Though he kept his face bland, I could hear the irritation in my friend's voice.

"Ah, well," the policeman muttered, "Could have happened at any time."

"This weapon was recently cleaned and oiled. Do you really think an attentive owner would have ignored that stain?"

"Well, perhaps the fellow, Pirowitz, wasn't used to handling guns."

Holmes said nothing, but stared hard at the fellow whose face turned an unbecoming shade of puce.

"Have you determined why Mr. Pirowitz would have shot himself in the abdomen?" Holmes said. "Wouldn't a bullet to the head be more common, not to mention more effective?"

With nothing but silence coming from the policeman, Doctor Burke answered. "Certainly, but it isn't unheard of."

I nodded in agreement. "Some people are oddly squeamish about shooting themselves in the head."

"Perhaps the poor fellow thought he was aiming for the heart," the policeman suggested, "given the upward trajectory of the shot."

Holmes responded with an impatient shake of the head. "As an artist, Pirowitz has studied anatomy extensively. Look at any of his paintings and you will see what I mean. Tell me, Mr. Findlay, was the man conscious when you found him?"

"In something of a delirium," the porter said. "He kept asking for his brother."

"Do we know where the gun came from?"

"Probably the fellow brought it with him for this very purpose," Sergeant Chadwick said. He sat back in his chair and folded his arms, his face as resolute as *QED*.

"In my experience," I said, "it is customary for a patient's belongings to be inspected upon his arrival, just to be sure there were no dangerous items present."

"And so they are," the matron said, with a cold glance at the policeman. "I have the inventory here."

She handed a standard document to Holmes, who scanned it and said, "Nothing other than clothing and other personal items, plus his art supplies. I see a knife was included."

Matron nodded, seeming to have warmed to Holmes by now. "Yes," she said, "but that was taken from him by Sister O'Mara. Mr. Pirowitz said he used it to sharpen his pencils and other drawing implements. Sister said he could do that under supervision. This was standard whenever he was admitted."

"How many times was that, Matron?" I asked.

"This most recent admission was his third in five years."

"Does he usually stay in the same room? The one where he is now?"

"Yes. As well as the door from the ward, it has its own entrance to the outdoors, so he could come and go as he pleased."

"I'm surprised the noise from the ward didn't upset him," Chadwick said, trying to sound compassionate.

"He is deaf in his right ear," Holmes said. "And as that was the ear that faced the ward, the noise probably didn't distress him too much."

"You are worthy of your reputation, Mr. Holmes," the doctor exclaimed.

Holmes waived the compliment aside, though his face flushed with pleasure.

"I should like to examine the area where Mr. Pirowitz was shot. Perhaps Mr. Findlay could show me?"

"I should be happy to," the porter said, "if Matron doesn't object."

"We are happy to accommodate you in any way we can, Mr. Holmes," the woman replied.

"Splendid." At this point, Holmes rose and said, "Would you care to join us, Sergeant Chadwick?"

The policeman sniffed. "I need to return to the station and write my report."

"May I ask how you intend to categorise the shooting?"

"Self-inflicted," the fellow said. His belligerent tone dared Holmes to argue with him.

"That would be an error, one that could have a catastrophic impact on your career, given Mr. Pirowitz's fame. Still, you must do as you see fit, but I would advise you to look at Mr. Pirowitz's hands first."

"His hands? What a foolish notion! What do his hands have to do with anything?"

Holmes merely smiled.

"Come, Mr. Findlay. I will let you know of my findings as soon as I can, Matron."

"Thank you, Mr. Holmes."

Before we left the hospital, Holmes wanted to return to the room where the unfortunate man lay dying. Holmes gave an update to Mr.

Nicholas Pirowitz, then turned his attention to the same nurse who was busily tending to the stricken artist.

"Are you, by chance, Sister O'Mara?" Holmes asked her.

"Yes, sir, Can I help you?"

"I understand you admitted Mr. Pirowitz. I would like to ask you about the knife that Mr. Pirowitz had with him upon his admission. I understand you confiscated it."

She smiled. "I locked it in a cupboard with the rest of Mr. Pirowitz's art supplies. He was happy enough with that, as it's in his own room. He only had to ask for the key, and I would give it to him. Most of his other art materials he kept on the table in his room, or in his case that he took with him when he went out painting."

"You never felt any concerns about letting him have that knife?"

"No, indeed." She frowned. "Despite his occasional periods of sadness, he was as happy as I have ever seen him during these past few days."

"Thank you, Miss O'Mara. You have been very helpful. Ah, what is Mr. Pirowitz's condition?"

"He clings to life, but it shall not be long now."

With these sad words echoing in our hearts, we left the hospital and walked across the yellowing grounds towards the adjoining fields. The blueness of the sky seemed so intense it hurt my eyes to look at it. I wondered how Pirowitz would have rendered it and felt a sadness that he would never paint again.

"Mr. Holmes," Findlay asked as we walked through the shimmering heat, "how did you know Pirowitz was hard of hearing?"

"Watson?" Holmes said.

"When his brother came into the room to see him, he went to the other side of the bed and spoke into the man's right ear. That suggested some hearing difficulties in the left ear."

"How extraordinary!"

"How long have you worked in the hospital, Mr. Findlay?" Holmes said.

"Must be fifteen or sixteen years, now, Mr. Holmes. I were no more'n a nipper when I came here."

"Some might say there are more genial places in which to earn a living."

"True enough, but I suppose you can get used to anything. Over the years, I've come to know the patients, for good or ill. Many aren't mad, you know. Not what we'd call mad. They had families who didn't want them, or they had seizures or what have you. It's a sad place, and no mistake."

428

"It seems strange to me that Pirowitz would come here for a rest."

"Aye, it did to me, and all, but he said it gave him a chance to see people at their most vulnerable. That was the word he used. He sometimes drew the other patients, and he told me once that he used some of those sketches in his paintings."

"How did he get on with the other patients?"

"Well enough. He knew who to stay away from, though we keep the dangerous ones in a separate wing. As far as I know, the other patients liked him well enough. Sometimes he drew pictures for them of trees, or places they remembered, and they enjoyed that."

"What of the staff?"

"He didn't have much to do with most of them. Now and then he'd have a laugh with some of the nurses. In fact, the only one I remember having a problem with him was Tiny."

"Tiny?"

Findlay laughed. "A nickname. His real name is Colin Tyler. He's a giant of a man, six-foot-seven if he's an inch, and nearly as wide. Mean wretch he is, especially to the patients. Mr. Pirowitz didn't like that and scolded him, but Tiny threatened him, too. Then Mr. Pirowitz reported him to Matron. He'd been reported before by some of the nurses, and yours truly had spoken about him, but this time Matron gave him the sack."

"When was this?" Holmes said.

"The last time Mr. Pirowitz stayed here, about a year or two ago."

"I cannot imagine the fellow would hold a grudge for so long. Still, we must not rule out the possibility, not without further information. Where is he now, do you know?"

"He lives in one of the nearby farms. It was his father's, but the old man died not long after Tiny got the sack. Now he runs it with his mum."

Holmes said nothing more, but I could see that he was deep in thought. About ten minutes later, Findlay led us over a stile and followed the fence for about ten minutes, and then stopped under a copse of oak trees.

"Ah, this is the spot, I see," Holmes said. "I must ask you to hang back with Dr. Watson, Findlay."

I was glad to stand under the leafy trees and enjoy the shade. I pitied any poor soul who was still in London being scorched by the heat. Even the ground around us looked parched. The scant grass around the trees had turned yellow, and even the weeds were wilting. Holmes moved carefully through the area, examining the ground and the trees. Findlay and I stood silent and watched. I never fail to feel enthralled watching my friend in action. His movements, though sometimes comical, are always on point and guided by his extraordinary intelligence.

429

"Thanks to this dry spell," Holmes said after several minutes, "there is little enough to see here. What I would give for some mud! I can say, however, that several people have walked here."

"It's close to the stile," Findlay noted, "so a lot of locals come this way."

"Pirowitz was here, by the fence, when he was shot," Holmes observed. "There is evidence of a struggle, you see?"

"Oh my!" Findlay exclaimed. "Then he was murdered."

Holmes said, "I did not say so. We must keep an open mind. A very large man was here, as were two others. I would like to know what they have to say. Also, we mustn't forget the evidence of the trees."

"The trees?" Findlay seemed utterly confused, but I was starting to understand.

"They have numerous bullet holes in them," I said.

"Good, Watson," Holmes said. He straightened up, and I winced as he cracked his back.

"Well, this way, I think."

He led the way along the fence for several minutes, his eyes fixed on the trail only he could see.

"Do you think this Tyler man is the killer?" I asked as we trudged through the wilting grasses.

"You have seen the same things I have, Watson, but you haven't put all the pieces together." He gave me a sardonic smile. "Are you in such a hurry to return to London?"

"Oh, Heavens no," I said.

"Don't worry, Doctor," Findlay said. "Weather will break soon."

After some minutes, we came to a dirt track that wove through the trees. Here, it was much cooler and far more comfortable. Then the trees became sparse, and ahead I spied a small cottage. To my eyes, it looked like a child's painting of a country home, with the little round chimneys, the red door and its brightly polished brasses, and the white lace curtains framing the gleaming windows. The path to the door wound its way through a wonderful display of white roses and a profusion of other plants. Here, even the grass was a rich emerald green. It seemed an oasis of cool and peace in the sweltering day.

Holmes knocked and almost instantly the door opened. A small, tidy woman with a meringue of white curls looked at us quizzically. "May I 'elp you?" she said.

"Good afternoon, Mrs. Tyler," said my friend. "I am Sherlock Holmes. May I have a word with your son, Colin?"

"I'll 'andle this, Mother," a gruff voice said from somewhere behind the old woman.

The man who appeared was a behemoth. He towered over us, at least six-foot-six or -seven, and was almost as wide. Despite the abundance of thick reddish curls on his head and face, the lack of his two front teeth gave him a curiously childish appearance.

"Invite your friends in, Colin," the old woman said.

"But – " the fellow began, but instantly fell silent at his mother's look. "Excuse me," he said. "Please come in, gentlemen."

The sitting room was as orderly as the exterior of the house. We sat on an ancient but well-kept sofa, and Mrs. Tyler served us very welcome tankards of ice-cold ale. Holmes tried to refuse an offer of a salad and cold meats, but our hostess was adamant.

"The food will go bad if we don't eat it soon. Please, you would be doing us such a favour."

We all sat at the table. Findlay and I were happy to partake of the excellent meal on offer. Even Holmes ate a sandwich of tomatoes and cheese. Before long he turned to the business at hand.

"Until recently, Mr. Tyler, I understand you worked at Colney Hatch? I wonder if you know a man by the name of Pirowitz? He was a patient there for some time."

"Oh, aye, I know 'im," he answered in a sneering voice. "Crazy as they come, but given special privileges because 'e were an artist. Some artist."

"Colin!" his mother said sharply.

"Sorry, Mother. Anyway, what's 'e said I've done?"

"Nothing at all, Mr. Tyler. But the poor man was shot early this morning, He's on the brink of death. We wondered if you might have seen anything?"

"I ain't worked at 'ospital for over a year."

"This didn't happen at the hospital. It seems to have occurred about half-a-mile east of here, not far from the stile."

"I know the place you mean. I were there this mornin', as it 'appens. Our old dog wandered off."

"She'd have come back on her own," Mrs. Tyler said.

"She's 'alf-blind," Colin replied, "and old, as I say. Anyways, I went looking for 'er, and found 'er not far from fence. Didn't see Pirowitz though."

"Around what time was this?" I asked.

"Six-ish. A little earlier, perhaps. Maybe closer to 'alf-five."

"And it was light then?"

"Oh, aye. Not broad daylight, mind, but bright enough that I could see."

"Did you hear anything?" Holmes persisted.

"I 'eard yon dog yapping," the big man began. His face creased as he concentrated. "Now you mention it, though, I reckon I 'eard gunfire. Lots of shots coming close together. I think there may've been some shouting, too, but I were too far off to be sure."

"Where were you when you heard this?"

"Nearly 'ome. Dog were yapping, so I couldn't 'ear much over that."

"Thank you, Mr. Tyler," Holmes said. "You have been of inestimable help. One final question, if I may?"

The fellow nodded, looking much more relieved.

"Have you ever seen anyone else about at that hour of the morning? Perhaps some lads?"

"Oh, there's the McEvoy lads. Good boys, but mischievous. Always in some bother over summat or other."

"How old are they?"

"Eight and ten, I'd guess. Do you know, Mother?"

"Youngest just turned eight last week," she said. "Older should turn eleven in a month or two."

"Where do they live?" Holmes said.

"About a mile east from 'ere," Tyler said. "I can show you if you like."

"It's all right," Findlay said, speaking for the first time. "I know the way."

Mrs. Tyler walked us to the door. "Thank you for your hospitality, Ma'am," I said. "We very much appreciate it."

"You boys are welcome any time," she said.

"Tiny – I mean Colin seems very well," Finlay said. "Much happier in himself."

"Oh, he is. That hospital wore him down. Then when his dad got sick it was worse. Now he's home working the farm, he's much happier. He misses his dad, of course. we both do, but in a way it's a relief not to see him suffering."

When we were well away from the Tyler home, Findlay said, "Did you believe him, Mr. Holmes."

"Certainly. You did not?"

"Well, he seems genial enough. More than I'm used to seeing, frankly."

"A mother's influence can have a remarkable effect on even the most passionate of men," I observed.

We trudged through the fields to the point we had left, and then Holmes, following a smaller trail, led us in a more southeasterly direction. We followed him in silence through trees and thick brambles. After about

432

half-an-hour, we arrived at a small, ramshackle farm. This was in marked contrast to the neat and trim Tyler property. Here, fences leaned to the side and the mangy dog who yapped at us looked filthy and half-starved. The mutt ran towards us, growling and snarling. Findlay stepped forward and in a sharp voice ordered, "Down, Mischief!" Immediately the dog fell silent and lay at his feet.

"That's quite a talent you have, Mr. Findlay," Holmes said.

"Poor beast is in a sorry state," I said.

Findlay brought out several slices of cold meat that Mrs. Tyler had given him. "I had a feeling the poor dog would be hungry," he said, and fed it to the ravenous animal. He then filled a neglected bowl with water from the pump and the dog lapped that up too.

"No wonder the dog likes you," I said.

"Old McEvoy lost all interest in the farm when his wife died two years ago. Neglecting the poor animals is bad enough, but his two boys fare no better. It's a downright disgrace, Doctor. Left to fend for themselves, they are, always hungry and running wild. They're good lads, for all that – no thanks to their father."

Our knock at the tired front door went unanswered and Findlay finally just pushed it open. A dishevelled man sat at the table his head resting amid a collection of bottles, snoring loudly. Despite the hour, he still wore his nightshirt and a dressing gown of indeterminate colour. I doubted his hair had seen a comb since Victoria died.

"Mr. McEvoy," Findlay said. The man's snoring hitched then resumed its previous rhythm. Findlay walked into the room and shook the fellow's shoulder.

With a start, McEvoy's eyes snapped open, and he stared at us dully.

Holmes strode into the room and stood before the confused man. To Findlay he said, "Perhaps you could find some coffee for this fellow."

Findlay instantly began to search the cupboards and work on the task.

"Who're you?" McEvoy said in a slurred voice.

"My name is Sherlock Holmes, Mr. McEvoy. This is my friend and colleague, Doctor Watson. I'm investigating the shooting of a patient at the hospital."

"Shooting? I don't know nothing about no shooting," the man said.

"Do you own a gun, Mr. McEvoy?"

"Aye, I'm a farmer."

"May we see it?"

He looked around him in evident confusion. "Lad's'll find it," he said. "Where are those boys?"

"We haven't seen them," Findlay replied over his shoulder.

McEvoy rose unsteadily to his feet and began to call out for his sons. He took down a metal box from a shelf and clumsily managed to open it.

"That's where I keep it," he muttered. "Aye, and bullets too."

"What sort of weapon is it?" Holmes said.

"A Colt. The Colt Navy, they call it. Sean, Davy – Where are you boys?"

"They aren't here, Magnus," Findlay said. He placed a mug of muddy-looking coffee before the old man, and McEvoy sipped it with satisfaction.

"Aren't you worried about your sons, Mr. McEvoy?" I asked.

He looked at me with bleary eyes and said nothing.

Seeing we would get no sense out of the man, we left the cottage, and though the air was now heavy and dark clouds roiled above us, the air felt fresh and clean compared with that inside the cottage.

"What now?" I asked.

"We shall return to the hospital, but I want those boys found."

"I can look for them, Mr. Holmes," Findlay said. "I know them and the area. Mischief will help me, won't you, boy?"

The dog barked in apparent agreement.

"Yes," Holmes said. "That would be very helpful. Please bring them to the hospital when you locate them."

"Do you think they may have seen something?" Findlay said.

"Who can say?" Holmes replied. "I need to question them. Come, Watson."

It took us about half-an-hour to get back to the hospital. By now, the temperature had dropped several degrees, and the wind had picked up, swirling through the trees and the grasses. It would rain by nightfall, I thought. Thank Heavens.

"You know what happened, don't you?" I asked as we trudged through the fields.

"Yes. I was sure from the moment I saw Pirowitz's hands in the hospital. Thanks to our efforts today, I believe I know the rest of the story." Seeing my puzzled look he continued, "A temperamental artist goes out to paint. He brought his equipment with him, so that is in no doubt. He is found a short time later with a wound to the abdomen and a curious burn on his left palm. That is significant, Watson. That is the crux of the matter."

"Oh," I said. "Oh, yes, I see. What a tragedy."

"You have fixed on it at last. Well, we shall reach the hospital in a few minutes. Let us see how Pirowitz is."

Pirowitz was dead. He breathed his last moments just before we entered the room where he lay. His brother sat at the bedside, his eyes red and wet.

"A grievous loss," Holmes said. "Please accept my condolences, Mr. Pirowitz."

"Thank you, Mr. Holmes. Do have any news for me?"

"I do indeed. Let us see if we can meet in Matron's office with the police sergeant and I will update you all at the same time. There is one thing I must do first."

It took almost an hour before we were gathered in the office, most of it spent waiting for the disgruntled sergeant. "I was just sat down to my dinner," he grumbled.

"Now we are all here," Holmes said, unperturbed, "I am happy to tell you conclusively that Alexander Pirowitz did not commit suicide."

"Tosh!" began the policeman, but he was effectively hushed by the matron. The woman seemed utterly captivated by Holmes.

"It is sad that such a remarkable man has died. Before the body was removed, I took the liberty of copying the burn marks on his left hand."

He produced a surprisingly skilled sketch. "Dr. Watson, will you confirm that this is an accurate depiction of those markings?"

"Yes, indeed," I replied.

The matron reached out and studied the drawing very carefully. "It looks as if the poor man reached out and clutched the barrel of the weapon with his left hand."

"Odd," said Doctor Burke. "He was right-handed. I, ah, re-examined him after our earlier meeting, Mr. Holmes. You were quite right about both the burn marks and the distinctions indicating which hand was dominant. I cannot think how I missed it before."

"You were focusing on the gunshot wound," I replied. "Trying to save the man's life."

"Excuse me, Mr. Holmes," said Matron, "but it looks as if there are two parallel burns down his palm, a smaller beside the larger."

"You are perfectly correct, Matron. Yes, the loading lever lies beneath the barrel. If I may have the Colt, Sergeant."

Holmes took the weapon and lay it atop the drawing. "Now," he said, "if we curl up the image to duplicate the hand clutching the weapon, we can see that the burn and the weapon align perfectly."

"Why so it does!" exclaimed Matron. "Genius, Mr. Holmes!"

Sergeant Chadwick interrupted the applause with a sour, "Hold on, hold on – If he was right-handed, as you say, then why did he hold the barrel with his left hand?"

"Watson," Holmes said, as he lit a cigarette.

"He was on his way to paint," I said. "No doubt he was carrying his equipment with his right hand."

"But why grasp the barrel at all?" the doctor asked.

"As Doctor Watson says," Holmes said, "Mr. Pirowitz had gone with the express idea of painting. Two boys, the McEvoy children, had borrowed their father's weapon and were amusing themselves by shooting at a tree. I believe Mr. Pirowitz remonstrated with them, either because he was concerned for their well-being, or because he found their presence distracting. In any case, an altercation ensued, and he tried to grab the weapon."

"And the gun went off," the doctor concluded. "Tragic."

"Did the gun go off by accident, or did one of the boys deliberately pull the trigger?" the policeman asked. However, before Holmes could answer, there came a knock at the door, and Findlay entered, accompanied by two very frightened looking boys.

"Ah, well done, Mr. Findlay," Holmes said.

"Come in, boys," Matron said. "Oh, my, the state of the pair of you. Mr. Findlay, would you please ask June to bring some cocoa for the boys, and a pot of tea for the rest of us. Oh, and perhaps some sandwiches."

With that take-charge attitude so typical of the hospital matron, the porter ran off to do her bidding. In the meantime, the matron took the boys out to a nearby bathroom. When they returned, their faces and hands glowed from what I could only imagine had been a vigorous scrubbing.

A few minutes later, Findlay returned. He held the door open for a young maid who set down a laden tray on the matron's desk. Another maid behind her deposited a second, equally generous tray. Then the two bobbed in curtsey and were dismissed. Holmes asked Findlay to remain.

"Well, boys," began the policeman, standing up and rocking on his feet with all the officialdom of a minion of public service.

"Oh, do sit down, Sergeant," the matron said. "Now, boys, drink your cocoa and have a sandwich. You look like neither of you have had a proper meal in a month of Sundays."

"Thank you, Missus," said the bigger of the two. He elbowed his young sibling. The little lad mumbled something that probably meant "Thank you," but the boy's mouth was too full of chicken sandwich for me to be sure.

Through all this, Holmes waited patiently – or as nearly patient as I've ever seen him.

"Now," he said, when the last of the cocoa was drunk, "tell us what happened today with the gun, and don't lie to me because I know the truth."

436

"Me and Davy borrowed our dad's gun," Sean, the older boy, said. "He's been promising us for ages that he'd teach us to shoot. Last night, he even cleaned and oiled the gun, but then today he said he wasn't up to it. I suppose we got tired waiting."

"So you went down near the stile and practiced shooting at the tree," Holmes said.

The lads' eyes grew wide at this knowledge. "Yes, Mister," said Sean.

"And then the painter arrived."

"That's it. We wasn't doing no harm, 'cept maybe to the tree," Sean said with a sudden grin. "But this geezer tells us to go play somewhere else. We told him we wasn't playing, we was practicing. He said we shouldn't use a gun without an adult to supervise us, and he told us to give him the gun. I had it in my hand and he tried to grab it. And then it went off and shot him. It were an accident. Honest."

For a moment, no one said anything. Then Holmes said, "Now tell us the true story."

"That is the truth," Sean insisted.

"Except it wasn't you who had the gun, was it? It was your brother. Am I right, Davy?"

The little boy started to cry, and his older brother put his arm around him. "Yes, it were Davy, but the rest is true, Mister. Honest."

"I believe you," Holmes said.

"There now, lads," said Mr. Nicholas Pirowitz. "No need to be upset. It was an accident. I see that now. My brother would not want you to be upset."

"Your brother?" said Sean. "Is he the bloke who got hurt? Will you tell him we're sorry, Mister. We should have left when he told us to."

"We will make sure he knows," I replied, as Pirowitz seemed unable to answer.

"Mr. Findlay, will you take the boys home?" Matron said. "And let them take the leftover food with them."

"Boys, I want you to come back here tomorrow. I'll see about getting some clean clothes for you."

"And some grub?" Sean asked, hopefully.

Matron laughed. "Some grub, too."

"You were right, Mr. Holmes," said the sergeant as Findlay led the boys out. "Right in every particular. But how did you know it was the younger boy who had accidentally shot Pirowitz?"

"You remember I mentioned the blood on the hammer? I believed that an unseasoned person had pulled the trigger. The younger lad had an injured finger where he had caught it. Also, though in his state it was admittedly hard to tell, but the boy had blood spatter on his clothes."

"Really remarkable," the sergeant said. "Well, I am happy to let this case rest. Thank you, Mr. Holmes. Doctor, ah . . . Yes. Thank you."

After the policeman left, the matron invited Holmes, Pirowitz, and me to join her for supper. Holmes insisted we had business in the city and Pirowitz had funeral arrangements to attend, so, half-an-hour later, we three sat on the train back to London. As we pulled out from the Colney Hatch station, the heavens released a deluge upon the dry and dusty fields.

About a month later, two pieces of mail arrived for Holmes. The first was a letter from Findlay, saying the matron had all but adopted the McEvoy boys and their dog. There was no change in Mr. McEvoy's condition, alas. The hospital were discussing plans to buy his farm and manage it, but let him stay in the cottage rent free.

I read the letter to Holmes as he requested, but he scarcely seemed to hear me. He was enraptured by the second piece of mail: A large parcel carefully wrapped, and hand delivered. It was from Nicholas Pirowitz.

He opened the parcel with meticulous care and caught his breath upon seeing the contents. "It's a Pirowitz," he said. "One of the last paintings he ever finished, his brother says." He handed me the letter that came with the picture.

"A very generous cheque, too," I said.

"Oh, put it in my drawer. I need to find the perfect place to hang my painting."

The Adventure of the Long Arm
by Alan Dimes

It was, I remember, towards the end of a particularly windy afternoon in late autumn when Holmes received a note from Inspector Lestrade of Scotland Yard. Through the windows of our rooms in Baker Street, one could see the fallen leaves and other items of urban detritus whirling along the darkening thoroughfare, while folk hurried along the pavement, clasping their outer garments to them against the rising cold. For my own part, I would have been perfectly content to remain by our fire, consulting my notebook, and composing the latest addition to my already copious collection of narratives concerning my experiences in the company of my celebrated fellow-lodger. The message from Lestrade, however, specifically requested my presence as well as that of Mr. Sherlock Holmes.

Of late, Holmes had become interested in the history of firearms, and as well as reading as many texts on the subject as he could accumulate. He was also experimenting with gunpowder, mixing it up from charcoal, sulfur, and saltpeter. This didn't make for a particularly pleasing atmosphere, but I was always happy to see him involved in any of his various interests, for while he was concentrated on these pursuits, he was distracted from any lack of cases, and therefore less likely to succumb to the temptation of resorting to any form of chemical stimulus. It was true that he had not used cocaine for many months, but the possibility that he might revert to its consumption was always there, an omnipresent spectre at the feast.

When he had read Lestrade's note, he rose from the seat at the acid-scarred deal table and strode towards the door. He took both our overcoats from their hooks and held mine out at arm's length.

"Come along," he said in a commanding tone. "The good inspector has summoned us both."

I reluctantly set my notebook and pencil to one side and pulled my coat from his bony hand.

"We'll miss dinner," I said somewhat petulantly.

"I'm sure Mrs. Hudson will gladly provide us with something when we return. Who knows – perhaps Lestrade will have a case for us which will be worthy of inclusion in your memoirs. You wouldn't want to miss that on account of your stomach, would you?"

439

I said nothing, but put on my overcoat with a sigh and followed his lithe figure as he eagerly hurried down the stairs and pulled open the front door. Fortunately we didn't have long to wait before the appearance of an empty hansom for hire.

When we arrived at Scotland Yard, the desk sergeant recognised us and informed us that Inspector Lestrade was waiting down in the police mortuary. We descended a set of metal steps and went along the familiar dingy corridor and through a set of double doors into a large room full of long tables whose walls were covered in cold, pale-green tiles.

A single body lay on one of the tables under a voluminous white sheet. Next to it was the familiar face and wiry little form of the Scotland Yarder.

"Good evening, gentlemen," he said. "I'm glad you could come."

"You've asked us here to look at a body?" I said. "Surely you have your own police surgeons for that."

"Of course, Doctor, and one of them will be taking a look at it. But once you've seen it, you'll understand why I've called on you and Mr. Holmes. But I warn you: It isn't a pretty sight."

"We've both seen plenty of the dead," Holmes remarked. "What makes this one so special?"

"See for yourself," said Lestrade, pulling away the sheet. It was a man's body, naked, though perhaps that was to be expected, given where it was. What was unexpected was that the head, hands, and feet had all been removed. Not only the spirit, or the life force, or whatever name one cared to give to the animating principle, was gone, but so too were the indicators of identity that preserved whatever remained of individuality, of personality, leaving only a slab of meat. It was, as Lestrade had indicated, unsettling.

"The only thing we can be sure of," the policeman said with a wry smile, "is his religion."

"Why, because he's circumcised?" said Holmes. "My dear Lestrade, you should know better than that. More than one religion practices circumcision, though I grant you that the balance of probability is against his being a Muslim. There aren't too many of them in London, and the paleness of his skin means he's less likely to be an Arab. And don't forget, some people have it done to their sons on medical grounds."

Holmes took his magnifying glass from the pocket of his Inverness and bent over to examine the organ in question. "I think he was, indeed, a recent convert to the Jewish religion," he said after a few seconds, straightening up, "and that he was engaged to be married. Do you concur, Watson?" he asked, handing me his glass.

440

"I agree with the first part," I said, when I had taken a look, "but I don't see how you arrive at the second."

"The scarring has not fully healed, which means the operation was carried out in the last six to eight weeks."

"That much is certainly correct."

"While the surgical process is perfectly safe, it is still not something most adult males would happily undergo. So he had a strong reason for wanting it performed. What is the strongest reason there could be? Love, the most common factor in religious conversions. He met a woman of the Jewish faith, fell in love with her, and demonstrated the seriousness of his intentions, and his conversion, by having his foreskin removed. At the same time, he would not have done so if he was not assured that she returned his feelings. So I infer that they were engaged, shortly before or shortly after."

"Engaged? How do you know he didn't have it done after they were married?" asked Lestrade.

"Intercourse isn't possible until after it's fully healed. Which, as Watson confirmed, takes about six to eight weeks. Now, while most people are prepared to wait out their engagement, few would be ready to go for that amount of time without being able to consummate their marriage."

"That sounds logical enough," said Lestrade.

"It's a working hypothesis, at least," said Holmes. "Was he found like this, without clothes?"

"Yes."

"That deprives us of one set of clues. Where was he found?"

"Morgan Street, a nasty little back-street in Whitechapel. A nine-year-old girl found him early this morning. Scared the living daylights out of her, poor little thing."

"Let us turn to the rest of his body. What do you make of it, Watson?"

The first thing that met my eye was a series of odd circular wounds that were scattered across the chest, belly, and legs of the victim. They could not be accidental. They must be intentional.

"This man has been tortured," I said.

"Burnt with a cigarette or cigar, " said Holmes. "Nothing else would produce such marks. He worked in the open air, either in short sleeves or with long sleeves rolled up. Though the tan has faded a little due to the time of year, it is still visible, extending from just above the elbow down to the wrists. Whatever labour he was engaged in, it was not hard physical labour. The body is generally fit, but the muscles in his arms are not particularly developed. He spent a lot of time kneeling."

Holmes pointed to the slight but noticeable callosities on the knees.

He pulled out his glass once more, this time looking at the neck, wrists, and ankles.

"At least two people carried out the amputations. The cuts that took off the hands and feet are clean, but the incisions on the neck are ragged. All were probably done with a heavy meat cleaver. A strong man might be able to cut through the wrists and ankles with one blow each. A skillful man might need two, but could still do it cleanly. Whoever cut the neck hacked at it with several blows before the head came off. I hope for this poor devil's sake that wasn't what actually killed him. If his head was in proportion to his body, he must have been about five feet six."

"One thing I don't see is why they cut his feet off," said Lestrade. "I mean, the head and hands I can understand, but you can't identify someone by their feet. Unless – unless he had some sort of deformity or birthmark on one of them. But then, why cut off both?"

"Well," said Holmes, "if you only cut off one, you draw attention to the fact that there may have been something distinctive about it. But I'm not entirely convinced that the purpose of the amputations was the concealment of this man's identity. In fact, I believe I can identify him. Has anything struck you, Watson?"

"I cannot say that it has."

"Let me help. Here we have a man who works in the open air, spends time on his knees, and rolls his sleeves up. That suggest that he is, or rather was, a gardener. He was engaged to be married to a Jewish woman . . . ."

I suddenly grasped who Holmes was describing.

"Good God!" I cried. " Luigi Manoli!"

We had first heard the name some two weeks before, when Hannah Goldman called on us one morning at Baker Street.

She was a petite young woman with a pale face, dominated by a pair of large and beautiful brown eyes. Little wisps of dark wavy hair had escaped from the blue silk shawl that covered her head, which was the only spot of colour in her clothes, the rest being plain black and clearly of poor quality.

The morning was chilly, and when Mrs. Hudson saw the young lady's pallor, she insisted on bringing her a hot bowl of beef broth, which Miss Goldman consumed gratefully. When she had set the bowl aside, Holmes inquired how we might be of service.

"It is my fiancé, Luigi Manoli, Mr. Holmes. We are due to be married soon, but he has vanished."

"How long have you known him, Miss Goldman?"

"About ten months. We have been engaged for three. I first met him when he was walking out with my friend, Sarah Wilkins, but when he saw me, and I saw him, there was an instant attraction, and before too long it had deepened into love."

She lowered her eyes and added, "The first love I have known."

Holmes pressed his hands together before him and said, "And how did Sarah Wilkins react to this development?"

"She was happy for me, happy for both of us. She liked Luigi, of course, but she had not been serious about him. She is my friend. She would not steal him from me, if that is what you were thinking."

As she spoke these words, I saw a hint of a fiery spirit within that slender body and behind that pale face.

"Are there any other young women in his life?"

"No. I have already said – He loves me."

"Then tell us about Luigi," said Holmes. "Does he have any enemies?"

"No, no. He is a good man, a gentle man. He is a gardener for the City of London, he loves to plant things, to watch them grow. He has no hatred in his heart for anyone."

"Was he born in London?"

"No, he came on the boat from Italy, about five years ago."

"From where in Italy, exactly?"

"I don't know. I have never asked. He has never told me anything about his life before he came to England."

"Are you not at least curious?" I interjected.

"Yes, but I am also in love. I know all I need to know – that he is a good man, that he truly loves me, and I him. If he wanted to tell me about his former life, I would listen, but if he does not want to, I will not pry."

Holmes stood.

"Miss Goldman, I am not without sympathy for your plight, but there is little I can do without more data. Do you have a photograph of your fiancée?"

"Yes, yes."

She reached into the pocket of her coat and pulled out a picture.

"Then I suggest you take it to Scotland Yard, or the police station nearest Mr. Manoli's residence, and ask them to deal with the matter."

Hannah Goldman pushed herself up from her chair and said, "So, I will get no help from the great Mr. Sherlock Holmes! I was told that you were willing to help poor people who came to you with their troubles, but it seems that is wrong."

Holmes remained calm.

"I assure you, Miss Goldman, that the wealth or poverty of those who come to consult me is of no importance. It is simply that in your particular case, there is little I can do on the basis of the information you have given

443

me. In such a matter, the official force has more resources than I do. However, I will make a promise: If you leave your address, then should I gain any information at all about your fiancé, I will inform you of the fact. That really is, at the moment, the best I can do."

"Luigi Manoli!" echoed Lestrade. "I remember the name. He's on the missing list. His fiancée came and reported it. Rather pretty, she was. What was her name?"

"Hannah Goldman," I answered. "And yes, she's pretty. Beautiful, even."

I had seen the address on the piece of paper the young woman had handed Holmes. Like Morgan Street where the body was discovered, it was one of the poorest in the East End. If that was all she could afford, then she was doubtless working in one of the worst-paid jobs – as a match girl, perhaps, or as a seamstress in a garment factory. How long would that prettiness, and that spirit, survive the long hours of hard work, the years of poverty, and the childbearing that probably lay in her future? Childbearing, if – when she had recovered from the grief of losing Manoli – she was lucky enough to find another man who loved her. But of that, there could be no guarantee. Two lines from Chaucer floated into my mind:

> *O scatheful harm, condition of poverty,*
> *With thirst, with cold, with hunger so confounded.*

"Well," Lestrade was saying, "she must be told, though it's a task anyone on the Force would avoid if he could. Although thinking about it, we can't, in the absence of clear identifying factors, be one-hundred-per-cent sure that this is Manoli's body, can we?"

"I agree that the evidence isn't conclusive," said Holmes, "but the overwhelming probability is that the body is Manoli's. If it is not, and there is an innocent reason for Manoli's absence, he will return, and in her joy Miss Goldman will forgive the police for any grief you have brought her. If he is still alive, and has vanished because he's with another woman, or has fled after committing a crime, then she is well rid of him, and it is better that she thinks him dead."

"That's certainly one way of looking at it, I suppose," agreed Lestrade. "Well, thank you for coming, Mr. Holmes, Dr. Watson."

"Send us a copy of the Police Surgeon's report."

"Certainly. Good evening, gentlemen."

The solemnity of the experience had made me forget the state of my appetite, but, as Holmes had predicted, when we returned to Baker Street,

Mrs. Hudson had already begun heating up some food in anticipation of our arrival. I gladly fell to it, but Holmes sat with his plate untouched, a faraway look in his keen grey eyes. He remained silent for the next two hours, and I went to bed, leaving him in his accustomed armchair with the smoke from his pipe curling above his head.

As Lestrade had promised, we received a copy of the medical report the following day. In a note at the bottom of the final page, the inspector added that no one else on the list of missing person resembled the description of the body, and he was therefore convinced that it must be Manoli.

The Police Surgeon confirmed that the amount of blood remaining in the body meant that the amputations had been carried out after death. Neither the contents of the stomach nor the blood contained any trace of poison. The surgeon concluded that death might have been caused by strangulation, whether by hand or by ligature, or the throat slit. The ragged state of the neck wounds would serve to conceal either of those methods. Another likely possibility was that the victim had died from a blow to the head.

Holmes summoned Billy, scribbled something on a page torn from one of his notebooks, and told the lad to take it to Scotland Yard. The boy returned in about three-quarters-of-an-hour with another piece of paper on which was written: "*No. 8*".

"*No. 8?*"

"The number of the house in Morgan Street in front of which the little girl found Manoli's corpse. That, Watson, is where we are going this evening. I trust that your old army revolver is in good working order."

"You saw me clean it only the other day."

"So I did. Well, need I add, load it and bring it with you tonight."

With that old familiar thrill of adventure coursing through my being, I joined Holmes as he summoned a cab. When were inside, he yelled to the driver, "Aldgate!"

I gave him a puzzled look.

"Aldgate? But Morgan Street is in Whitechapel, so why Aldgate?"

"As you know, my friend, I keep several rented rooms throughout the metropolis in which I can change both my clothes and my appearance. I keep one in Aldgate because, while it is close enough to the East End to be accessible on foot, it is also too far from there for any of the East End's denizens to see me enter as my own self and leave as someone else. Believe me, if someone suspected that Sherlock Holmes was walking the streets of Whitechapel, and saw me depart in my disguise, my life would not have an hour's purchase."

"But I am with you, and while I'm not as easily recognized as you, it will surely give the game away if I'm at your side."

Holmes gave a little chuckle.

"Really, Watson! What would you suggest?"

"You mean, I am also to be in disguise? But I have no talent for such play-acting. And – you don't intend to have me shave off my moustache?"

"Certainly not. From the many times you have seen me in the guise of someone else, you must have realised that a mere change of clothing is often enough."

"Well, perhaps, but I still say that to be truly effective, the man in disguise must be something of an actor."

"All you need do is remain silent, and leave any talking that may need to be done to me."

Never before had I been in one of Holmes's secret rooms, so I was full of curiosity when we entered an unprepossessing building a street away from the Aldgate pump. Some of the windows were boarded over, and the paint of the front door was almost completely peeled away. Holmes took out a key and turned it in the lock, and as we entered the small hallway, I noticed a distinct, musty smell in the air. As we climbed the somewhat rickety stairs, I saw no sign that the place had any other inhabitants. Whoever owned it was probably glad that there was someone paying some rent, and Holmes was no doubt handing over more than the market price, which would not be difficult. We entered a room on the first floor. Holmes lit a gas lamp, illuminating a chamber that was purely functional, with no sign of any creature comforts. There was a bed, and if for any reason Holmes had to spend a night there, it would just about accommodate his long frame.

Holmes opened a large mahogany wardrobe. Inside was a variety of clothes, hats, and shoes, and on the floor of the cabinet there was a large wooden box full of wigs, false moustaches, and beards, and other less-immediately recognisable elements of disguise.

"We'll set you up first," said Holmes with a smile, and pulled out an off-white shirt that had seen better days, a thoroughly disreputable topcoat, dingy and threadbare, and a pair of brown trousers that were visibly thin at the knee. I divested myself of my respectable outfit and donned those uninviting garments, hoping as I did so that none of them were inhabited by fleas.

"Try on some of the shoes, " said Holmes, as began removing his own clothes. "There should be a pair there that will fit you."

446

At last, we stood facing each other. Holmes was clad in an old sailor's jacket, a pair of faded khaki trousers that must once have belonged to a soldier, and a collarless undershirt. He put a grubby knee-length coat over this ensemble and regarded me.

"You look splendid, Watson."

There was no mirror for me to look at myself in, but I strongly doubted that "splendid" was the *mot juste* for my appearance.

"Now, we just need a few finishing touches."

He rammed a dark curly wig on my head, then glued a pair of side-whiskers to his face and took out two hats, one a dusty bowler which he placed on his own head, the other, a battered cap, he handed to me.

"Left!" cried Holmes when we were once more out in the street. The weather was still somewhat chilly, though the wind had died down. I have never been a frequenter of the East End, and I was worried at first that Holmes had overdone our disguises. But as we made our way through Shoreditch and into Whitechapel, I became aware that many of the passers-by were dressed in clothes that were easily as down-at-heel and mismatched as those we were wearing. Nevertheless, I was happy that I could feel the weight of my old army revolver in the pocket of my shabby coat.

After about twenty minutes' walk we reached our destination in Morgan Street. It was an ill-lit, narrow street along which stretched a line of houses which were, by the area's standards, in reasonably good condition, but were identically dull and monotonous, built merely for use and function. Unlike the main streets along which we had passed, which were full of pedestrians in the middle of the evening, in this back alley there was no one to be seen.

"Now," said Holmes," we need to speak to the inhabitant of No. 8, but I rather suspect he will not open the door to us, not even a crack to see who we are."

"Why not?"

"Because he is in fear for his life. Unless I am much mistaken, he is a fugitive from his own land, and his whereabouts have been the subject of speculation in the European press.'"

"What should we do, then?"

"Observe, Watson, that there is only one light burning in the whole house, on the first floor. That must be where he is. Now, we shall go around to the back of the house, climb over the wall that runs along all the yards in the street, and effect an entry on the ground floor."

So once more, we were breaking the law. I had to trust, from my past experiences with Holmes, that this departure from the straight-and-narrow would have an outcome that would justify our transgression.

Within minutes we were over the wall and standing before a ground floor window. From his shabby coat, my companion drew his glass-cutter and removed a half-circle from the window, next to the handle, then reached inside and turned it. As silently as we could, we crept through the house and up the stairs, and along a short corridor until we saw a light under one of the doors.

Holmes signalled that I should stand by the wall on the right of the door, while he took the left side.

"Count Ridolfi!" he cried. "We have come to help you!"

"So you come for me at last!" came the answer in perfect English, spoken with a recognisably Italian accent. Then there were two loud bursts of gunfire, and the air sang with shattered shards of wood as two bullets ripped through the wooden door.

"I am Sherlock Holmes, and you have surely heard of me. My friend, Doctor Watson, and I mean you no harm. Please allow us to come in."

He pulled off the false side-whiskers and gestured that I should remove the dark curly wig.

"Yes, I have heard of Holmes, but how do I know you are truly he?" the Count responded.

"Have you seen my picture?"

"Yes, but that means nothing."

"Let me open the door."

"Very well, but I warn you, if you or your friend make one false move, I will shoot you without mercy."

Holmes opened the door to reveal a man of about sixty, seated in an old wooden chair, his long legs stretched out before him. His whitening hair was brushed back from his broad, intellectual forehead, and his blue eyes, filled with suspicion, were nevertheless clear and bright. But his complexion was pallid, and his face bore clear signs of illness or stress.

"Are you armed?" he demanded. "Tell me the truth, and remember: There are still four bullets in my gun."

"Yes," said Holmes.

"Then take out your guns, slowly, and drop them on the floor."

We complied.

Count Ridolfi's weapon remained trained on us.

"Now, he said. "Prove you are who you say you are."

"You are Count Giuseppe Ridolfi, former governor of the Italian province of Frascillata. You are a just and honourable man, and you ruled that backward part of the country as well as any man has. But your justice, and your fair dealings, made you a target for the *Vecchia Fratellanza* – in English, 'The Old Brotherhood'."

"Who are they?" I could not help asking.

"Well, Dr. Watson – if that is truly who you are – you have no doubt heard of the *Mafia*, from Sicily – "

"Yes."

" – and perhaps even the *Ndrangheta* of Calabria, and the *Camorra* of Naples."

"No, never."

"The southern part of Italy, along with the island of Sicily, has a long history of brigandage, of secret societies and social unrest. It is not surprising. It is a poor, agricultural area, and its economic weakness and political instability have often been exploited, both by foreign states and by the rest of the country. It is entirely understandable that in the past, before the unification, poor men banded together in their own interest, and that, when they had no access to justice and the law was loaded against them, they broke the law in the cause of justice. That they came together in secrecy, swore oaths of allegiance, and brought vengeance down on those who betrayed them. Inevitably, the original ideals gradually fell away and were replaced by the baser desires of tyranny and greed. And so it was with the *Vecchia Fratellanza*."

"And now," said Holmes, "you are threatened by the *Bracchio Lungo* – 'The Long Arm' – an elite band of assassins, chosen by the council of the Old Brotherhood for their skill in murder. Have you ever known them to employ Englishmen to carry out their work?"

"No, they would never do that. It would be a slur on what they are pleased to call their "honour". Very well, I shall trust you, and I hope it is not the last decision I make in my life."

He laid the revolver in his lap.

"Tell me, Mr. Holmes, how you came to know of this."

"A man was found outside this house. His head, his hands, and his feet had been cut off. Now, although my dealings with them have been few, I have made a study of the practices of these secret societies. I recognised the condition of the dead as a kind of message – a warning to a man pursued by the *Bracchio Lungo* that they know where he is and will soon wreak vengeance on him."

"And this is how they carry out the sentence," said Ridolfi. "The victim is held down and his head beaten to a bloody pulp. Then the head is cut off, along with the hands and feet. The purpose of these mutilations is to send a message – that he who betrays the brotherhood, or leaves it, or stands in its way, is not merely dead, but stripped of all identity, as if he never was. These animals call themselves *Christians*, but this is part of an ancient belief, from centuries before the word of God came to Italy, that if any part of a man's body cannot be found when he is buried, then he cannot attain the afterlife."

"The man who was murdered was Luigi Manoli," I said. "Did you know him?"

The Count passed one of his slender hands before his eyes.

"*Mio Dio!*" he exclaimed. "*Manoli!*"

"Who was he?"

"His father was high up in the Brotherhood, but his mother left him shortly after Luigi was born, and, repelled by his ways, took the boy to the far north of Italy, where she hoped to raise him free from his father's influence. But the older Manoli set the Long Arm upon her, and though it took them seven years, eventually they found Luigi and his mother in the small village near Lake Maggiore, where they had taken refuge. The mother was murdered while the boy was sleeping, and they took him back to Frascillata and handed him over to his father.

"As the son of a member of the high council, he might have risen high in the Brotherhood, but his mother, though long dead, had done her work well, and at the age of twenty he came to me and gave me all the information he thought I needed to bring down the Brotherhood. Though we were able to eliminate many of their cells, it became clear that we had not succeeded in wiping them out completely. It was then that I realised that Luigi was in great danger, and I had him carefully guarded until I could send him to England, where I believed he would be safe."

He cast down his eyes and murmured, "But I see I was wrong. The Long Arm pursued him, even as it pursues me."

He looked up.

"Do you know what some call me in *Frascillata*? They call me *Guiseppe Fortunato* – 'Lucky Giuseppe' – because I survived four of the Brotherhood's assassination attempts."

He smiled bitterly.

"In the first of those attempts, my son died from a bullet that was aimed at me, and in the third my wife was killed by a bomb they planted on our *terrazza*. How then, am I 'Lucky Giuseppe'? It is true, I escaped to London. I changed my appearance, shaving off my beard and moustache. My English is good enough to get by, but I have kept myself to myself and been as inconspicuous as I could. But still they have found me, and I ask myself: What do I have to live for, now that I have lost my family? The only answer I have is that when they finally come for me, I will take as many of them with me as I can."

I was dumbstruck by the sheer tragedy of this narration, but Holmes, as usual, was all business.

"Count Ridolfi, we are here because I know from my studies that the dumping of Manoli's body on your doorstep means that you have three days grace before they come for you. That is why we are here: To stand with you when that moment comes. Are you with me, Watson?"

Stirred as I was by the old count's story, and knowing that I would never leave Holmes's side when he was in danger, I could only answer, "Yes."

"Please leave, gentlemen. I cannot ask you to die on my behalf."

"They will not be expecting three of us to be here instead of only one", said Holmes. "That will give us an advantage."

"They usually operate in cells of six," said the Count, "so they will outnumber us two to one."

"I would also suggest that you turn off the gas light and burn a single candle, so that it will not be so obvious, at least from the street, which room we are occupying."

This was not the first time I had sat in a darkened room with Holmes, my revolver in my hand, awaiting the arrival of a man of violence. Or *men* of violence, in this case.

The crisis came in the early hours of the morning, when the sky was at its darkest and the world at its stillest. All sensible men were long abed. I counted myself a sensible man, yet here I was, awake, with every fibre of my being taut with anticipation of the conflict to come.

From the floor below us we heard the sound of a window being smashed.

"Their entry was somewhat less subtle than yours," the Count said wryly.

There came the sound of doors being slammed one by one, and I realised that the assassins were checking each room. My grip tightened on my revolver as I heard them climbing the stairs. Again, we heard them opening and closing doors, until I realised that the room in which we sat was the only one remaining unchecked. There was no light in the corridor, or they might have noticed the bullet holes in the door. They must have realised that they had reached their goal, but instead of them bursting into the room, guns blazing, there came through the door the sound of low muttering, too low for even the Italian count to make out what they were saying. For long moments nothing happened, and then, finally, the door was kicked open and by the flickering light of the candle I saw three of the ruffians enter.

Holmes and the Count instantly fired, taking two of them down, but I was distracted by a movement at the window. I whirled and saw the other three men in the act of raising their guns to fire at us through the pane. They must have brought some kind of ladder with them. Two bullets whizzed past either side of my head, but I stood my ground and fired off four rounds in rapid succession. I had clearly hit at least one of them, for

451

he fell back with a cry, knocking one of his fellows down to the ground beside him. The last, taking in the situation at a glance, fired off a shot at the Count, who gave a sharp cry as the bullet penetrated his shoulder and fell to the floor.

I discharged my remaining two rounds at the assassin and was gladdened to see him fall back as had his fellows. I then turned to see to the Count. Holmes was on the floor, struggling with the last man, whom he had somehow managed to disarm in the dim light, but they were now fighting for the possession of Holmes's firearm. I turned away from the Count and, seizing my revolver by its barrel, brought the heavy handle down on the would-be assassin's head, knocking him instantly unconscious.

Holmes scrambled to his feet.

"Once more, Watson, I owe you my life."

Holmes's praise was always welcome to me, but at that moment I had more important considerations on my mind.

As he grimaced in pain, I removed the Count's jacket and ripped open his shirt to examine the wound he had sustained. It was serious, but not fatal. The bullet had come out through his upper back, so there was much blood, but less danger of infection. I went down to the kitchen and boiled a kettle of water. In the bathroom I found an old but clean sheet which I ripped into strips. Entering the room once more, I cleaned the wound and bandaged it as best I could.

"You're wasting your time, Doctor, " the Count croaked. "In the end, they got what they wanted. I am dying."

"Nonsense", I retorted. "You'll be in the hospital for some time, true, but there's no reason why you shouldn't recover. You'll have a nasty pair of scars – but that's better than the alternative. I'll send Holmes for an ambulance."

I looked around. The man whose head I had cracked was nowhere to be seen – and where was my fellow lodger?

I later learned that while I had been preparing my makeshift bandages, Holmes had dragged his unconscious assailant down to the ground floor and bound his arms and legs with the sashes of the broken window. He then went into the street and ascertained that all three of the assassins who had climbed to the window were dead, two killed by gunshot and the other by a broken neck, sustained in his fall. The other two men who had come in by the door were likewise gone to meet their maker.

The gunshots had finally aroused the attention of the local constable on his beat, who blew his whistle to summon his nearest colleagues. They were, Holmes told me, at first reluctant to believe that this shabbily-dressed figure could be the renowned detective, but then a policeman with whom he had previously worked arrived on the scene and confirmed his identity. The surviving member of the Long Arm was bundled onto a police cart, and an ambulance summoned.

I have said before that often, when he had come to the conclusion of a demanding case, Holmes might be limp and listless, perhaps staying in his bed for several days. I must say that after the case of the Long Arm I had a somewhat similar reaction. I hadn't seen so much action in many years, nor did I take it lightly that I was responsible for the deaths of three men, however much they may have deserved to die. So it wasn't until some days later that I was ready to discuss it with Holmes.

I need not end this chronicle on such a sad note, for there was at least something of a happy ending. I never learned what became of Hannah Goldman, but Count Ridolfi made a full recovery and returned at last to his native land. Holmes's brother Mycroft had a word in the ear of a certain Gracious Lady, who communicated with her fellow-monarch, King Umberto I of Italy, to suggest that in consideration of his sterling work as Governor of Frascillata, Count Ridolfi should be given a pension and a suite of rooms in the palace, where the Royal Guard would keep him safe from any more attempts on his life.

About the Contributors

The following contributors appear in this volume:
The MX Book of New Sherlock Holmes Stories
Part LI: The True Sherlock Mr. Holmes –
England's Greatest Hero (1897-1901)

Mike Adamson holds a Doctoral degree from Flinders University of South Australia. After early aspirations in art and writing, Mike secured qualifications in both marine biology and archaeology. Mike has been a university educator since 2006, has worked in the replication of convincing ancient fossils, is a passionate photographer, master-level hobbyist, and journalist for international magazines. Short fiction sales include to *Metastellar*, *Strand Magazine*, *Little Blue Marble*, *Abyss*, and *Apex*, *Daily Science Fiction*, *Compelling Science Fiction*, and *Nature Futures*. Mike has placed some two-hundred stories to date, totaling over a million words. Mike has completed his first Sherlock Holmes novel with Belanger Books, and will be appearing in translation in European magazines. You can catch up with his journey at his blog "The View From the Keyboard":
http://mike-adamson.blogspot.com

Donald I. Baxter has practiced medicine for over forty years. He resides in Erie Pennsylvania with his wife and their dog. His family and his friends are for the most part lawyers who have given him the ability to make stuff up just as they do.

Brian Belanger, PSI, is a publisher, narrator, graphic designer, editor, and actor. In 2015 he co-founded Belanger Books publishing company along with his brother, author Derrick Belanger. His illustrations have appeared in *The Essential Sherlock Holmes* series, the *MacDougall Twins with Sherlock Holmes* series, and *Scones and Bones on Baker Street*. Brian has published a number of Sherlock Holmes anthologies and novels through Belanger Books, as well as new editions of August Derleth's classic Solar Pons mysteries. Brian continues to design all of the covers for Belanger Books, and from 2016–2023 he designed the majority of book covers for MX Publishing. In 2019, Brian received his investiture in the PSI as "Sir Ronald Duveen". More recently, he created the logo for the *ACD Society* and designed *The Great Game of Sherlock Holmes* card game. In July 2022, he played Sherlock Holmes onstage in "Yes, Virginia, There is a Sherlock Holmes" and "Sherlock Holmes Goes West". Brian has been narrating Belanger Books audio releases since April 2023.
www.belangerbooks.com and
www.redbubble.com/people/zhahadun and
zhahadun.wixsite.com/221b

Alan Dimes was born in Northwest London and graduated from Sussex University with a BA in English Literature. He has spent most of his working life teaching English. Living in the Czech Republic since 2003, he is now semi-retired and divides his time between Prague and his country cottage. He has also written some fifty stories of horror and fantasy and thirty stories about his husband-and-wife detectives, Peter and Deirdre Creighton, set in the 1930's.

Sir Arthur Conan Doyle (1859-1930) *Holmes Chronicler Emeritus*. If not for him, this anthology would not exist. Author, physician, patriot, sportsman, spiritualist, husband and father, and advocate for the oppressed. He is remembered and honored for the purposes of this collection by being the man who introduced Sherlock Holmes to the world. Through fifty-six Holmes short stories, four novels, and additional Apocryphal entries, Doyle revolutionized mystery stories and also greatly influenced and improved police forensic methods and techniques for the betterment of all. *Steel True Blade Straight.*

Steve Emecz's main field is technology, in which he has been working for about thirty years. Steve is a regular speaker at trade shows, and his tech career has taken him to more than seventy countries. In 2008, MX published its first Sherlock Holmes book, and MX has gone on to become the largest specialist Holmes publisher in the world with over 600 books. MX is a social enterprise and supports three main causes. The first is Undershaw, Sir Arthur Conan Doyle's former home, which is a school for children with special educational needs (SEN) that MX has been partnered with for a dozen or so years and raised over $135,000 for. Steve has been a mentor and Advisory Council member for the World Food Programme's Innovation Accelerator (based in Munich) for several years, and was part of the Nobel Peace Prize winning team in 2020. The third is Happy Life, a children's rescue project in Nairobi, Kenya, where he and his wife, Sharon, spent every Christmas at the rescue centre in Kasarani for a decade. They have written two editions of a short book about the project, *The Happy Life Story*.

Arianna Fox is a triple-published and bestselling author, keynote speaker, actress, professional voiceover talent, award winner, book editor, and public figure whose passion is to motivate, educate, and entertain others through her work. From stories that connect with a modern audience to classically inspired works of literature, one of Arianna's foremost passions has always been writing. An avid Sherlockian and lover of all things Victorian, Arianna disliked reading for years until she read the first few paragraphs of *The Return of Sherlock Holmes* in a bookstore and immediately fell in love with classic literature and the intricate themes woven into its messages. As a whole, Arianna's ultimate goal is to empower others to achieve maximum success and keep their brain-attics well stocked.

Mike Fox is a CEO, entrepreneur, multi-award-winning filmmaker, director, producer, writer, designer, actor, voiceover talent, and all-around versatile creative professional. His professional work is known across the U.S. and has received numerous accolades and awards. As a filmmaker and director, Mike has produced three full-feature films, with over twenty-five Film Festival Awards, including several shorts and many commercials. With a unique flair for suspenseful storytelling, he derives much inspiration from the Sherlock Holmes universe, both of The Canon and adaptations. He was named Alignable's "Business Person of the Year" four years in a row, and has been featured in several news and media outlets, along with a myriad of interviews on podcasts and more. Mike's goal is to impact, empower, and inspire through various forms of media. His professional work is known across the U.S., including having received numerous accolades and awards, including receiving the prestigious Delaware Press Association (DPA) several years in a row. He continues to speak, write, film, and direct to bring quality content to audiences.

Mark A. Gagen BSI is co-founder of Wessex Press, sponsor of the popular *From Gillette to Brett* conferences, and publisher of *The Sherlock Holmes Reference Library* and many other fine Sherlockian titles. A life-long Holmes enthusiast, he is a member of *The Baker Street Irregulars* and *The Illustrious Clients of Indianapolis*. A graphic artist by profession, his work is often seen on the covers of *The Baker Street Journal* and various BSI books.

Paul D. Gilbert was born in 1954 and has lived in and around London all of his life. His wife Jackie is a Holmes expert who keeps him on the straight and narrow! He has two sons, one of whom now lives in Spain. His interests include literature, ancient history, all religions, most sports, and movies. He is currently employed full-time as a funeral director. His books so far include *The Lost Files of Sherlock Holmes* (2007), *The Chronicles of Sherlock Holmes* (2008), *Sherlock Holmes and the Giant Rat of Sumatra* (2010), *The Annals of Sherlock Holmes* (2012), *Sherlock Holmes and the Unholy Trinity* (2015), *Sherlock Holmes: The Four Handed Game* (2017), *The Illumination of Sherlock Holmes* (2019), *The Treasure of the Poison King* (2021), and *Sherlock Holmes: Tales of Darkness* (2023).

John Atkinson Grimshaw (1836-1893) was born in Leeds, England. His amazing paintings, usually featuring twilight or night scenes illuminated by gas-lamps or moonlight, are easily recognizable, and are often used on the covers of books about The Great Detective to set the mood, as shadowy figures move in the distance through misty mysterious settings and over rain-slicked streets.

Arthur Hall was born in Aston, Birmingham, UK, in 1944. He discovered his interest in writing during his schooldays, along with a love of fictional adventure and suspense. His first novel, *Sole Contact*, was an espionage story about an ultra-secret government department known as "Sector Three", and was followed, to date, by three sequels. Other works include seven Sherlock Holmes novels, *The Demon of the Dusk, The One Hundred Percent Society, The Secret Assassin, The Phantom Killer, In Pursuit of the Dead, The Justice Master,* and *The Experience Club* as well as three collections of Holmes *Further Little-Known Cases of Sherlock Holmes, Tales from the Annals of Sherlock* Holmes, *The Additional Investigations of Sherlock Holmes* and *The Hidden Enquiries of Sherlock Holmes.* He has also written other short stories and a modern detective novel. He lives in the West Midlands, United Kingdom.

Paula Hammond has written over sixty fiction and non-fiction books, as well as short stories, comics, poetry, and scripts for educational DVD's. When not glued to the keyboard, she can usually be found prowling round second-hand books shops or hunkered down in a hide, soaking up the joys of the natural world.

Christopher James was born in 1975 in Paisley, Scotland. Educated at Newcastle and UEA, he was a winner of the UK's National Poetry Competition in 2008. He has written three full-length Sherlock Holmes novels, *The Adventure of the Ruby Elephant, The Jeweller of Florence,* and *The Adventure of the Beer Barons,* all published by MX.

Roger Johnson, BSI ("The Pall Mall Gazette"), ASH, PSI, etc, is a member of more Holmesian Societies than he can remember, thanks to his eighteen years as editor of *The Sherlock Holmes Journal* - a responsibility he has recently and gratefully passed over to Dr. Mark Jones. Roger founded and for thirty-two years edited *The Sherlock Holmes Society of London*'s newsletter, *The District Messenger.* For six years, it was edited by his wife Jean Upton, ASH, BSI, and is now in the safe hands of Holly Turner. At its 2025 Annual Dinner, Roger was awarded Honorary Membership of *The Sherlock Holmes Society of London.*

Naching T. Kassa is a wife, mother, and writer. She's created short stories, novellas, poems, and co-created three children. She resides in Eastern Washington State with her husband, Dan Kassa. Naching is a member of *The Horror Writers Association, Mystery Writers of America, The Sound of the Baskervilles, The ACD Society, The Crew of the Barque Lone Star,* and *The Sherlock Holmes Society of London.* She works in Talent

Relations at Crystal Lake Publishing and was a recipient of the 2022 HWA Diversity Grant. You can find her work on Amazon.
https://www.amazon.com/Naching-T-Kassa/e/B005ZGHTI0

Susan Knight's newest Mrs. Hudson novel is *Death in the Harem* (October 2024, MX publishing), in which Sherlock Holmes and Dr. Watson enlist their landlady's help in solving a series of murders at the court of the Sultan of Turkey. Susan has written four previous Mrs. Hudson books, starting with a collection of short stories, *Mrs. Hudson Investigates* (2019). This was followed by the novels, *Mrs. Hudson Goes to Ireland* (2020), *Mrs. Hudson Goes to Paris* (2022) and *Death in the Garden of England* (2023). She has also contributed to many recent MX anthologies of new Sherlock Holmes short stories and enjoys writing as Dr. Watson as much as Mrs. Hudson. Nine of these stories have been included in *The Strange Case of the Pale Boy and Other Mysteries* (MX, 2023), and another story, *The Case of the Reluctant Footman*, has been released on Kindle Unlimited as Volume 7 of its *Discoveries* series (2025). She is the author of two other non-Sherlockian story collections, as well as three novels, a book of non-fiction, and several plays, and has won several prizes for her writing. She lives in Dublin, Ireland.

Steve Lockley is responsible for around 100 short stories and 20 novels, though not all under his own name, including contributions to a couple of Doctor Who anthologies and a novel based on the TV series *Ghost Whisperer*. He has also written several Sherlock Holmes stories, including an appearance in *Encounters of Sherlock Holmes* (Titan Books), and another due to appear in a future issue of *Sherlock Holmes Mystery Magazine*. Steve's work as both writer and editor has been shortlisted several times for British Fantasy Awards. He lives in Swansea and hates writing about himself in the third person.

Bonnie MacBird, BSI is the author of six critically acclaimed Sherlock Holmes novels for HarperCollins. They have been translated into fourteen languages and have been praised by *The London Times*, *Washington Post* , and *The Wall Street Journal*. MacBird read her first Sherlock Holmes story at age ten, and has been a fan since then. She's had a forty-year career in entertainment as a studio story editor, a screenwriter, a multiple Emmy winning documentary film producer, and a screenwriting teacher. She's also acted professionally and directs theatre. She lives in London with her husband, computer scientist Alan Kay, where she continues to write, as well as work in theatre.

David MacGregor is a playwright, screenwriter, and novelist. His plays have been performed from New York to Tasmania, and his work has been published by Dramatic Publishing, Playscripts, and Theatrical Rights Worldwide (TRW). He adapted his dark comedy, *Vino Veritas*, into a feature film, and several of his short plays have also been adapted into films. He is the author of three Sherlock Holmes plays: *Sherlock Holmes and the Adventure of the Elusive Ear*, *Sherlock Holmes and the Adventure of the Fallen Soufflé*, and *Sherlock Holmes and the Adventure of the Ghost Machine*. He adapted all three plays into novels for Orange Pip Books, and the novels have also been translated into Italian by Mondadori Publishing. In addition, he wrote the two-volume nonfiction *Sherlock Holmes: The Hero with a Thousand Faces*, which traces the evolution of the character over three centuries. He teaches writing at Wayne State University in Detroit. His website is: *david-macgregor.com*

David Marcum plays *The Game* with deadly seriousness. He first discovered Sherlock Holmes in 1975 at the age of ten, and since that time, he has collected, read, and chronologicized literally thousands of traditional Holmes pastiches in the form of novels, short stories, radio and television episodes, movies and scripts, comics, fan-fiction, and unpublished manuscripts. He is the author of over one-hundred-thirty Sherlockian pastiches, some published in anthologies and magazines such as *The Best Mystery Stories of the Year 2021* and *The Strand*, and others collected in his own books, *The Papers of Sherlock Holmes, Sherlock Holmes and A Quantity of Debt, Sherlock Holmes – Tangled Skeins, Sherlock Holmes and The Eye of Heka*, and *The Collected Papers of Sherlock Holmes* – seven volumes and more to come. He has won back-to-back first place fiction awards from *The Arthur Conan Doyle Society* (2023 and 2024) and from the Nero Wolfe *Wolfe Pack*. He has edited over 1,200 Holmes adventures and one-hundred books, including dozens of traditional Sherlockian anthologies, such as the ongoing series *The MX Book of New Sherlock Holmes Stories*, which he created in 2015 to promote traditional Canonical Holmes. This collection is now finishing at fifty-two volumes. He was responsible for bringing back August Derleth's Solar Pons for a new generation with his collections of authorized Pons stories, *The Papers of Solar Pons* and *The Further Papers of Solar Pons*. Pons's return was further assisted by his editing of the reissued authorized versions of the original Pons books, and then several volumes of new Pons adventures. He has done the same for the adventures of Dr. Thorndyke, and has plans for similar projects in the future. He has contributed numerous essays to various publications, and is a member of a number of Sherlockian groups and Scions, as well as *The Mystery Writers of America*. His irregular Sherlockian blog, *A Seventeen Step Program*, addresses various topics related to his favorite *Book Friends* (as his son used to call them when he was small), and can be found at *http://17stepprogram.blogspot.com/* He is a licensed Civil Engineer, living in Tennessee with his wife and son. Since the age of nineteen, he has worn a deerstalker as his regular-and-only hat. In 2013, he and his deerstalker were finally able make his first trip-of-a-lifetime Holmes Pilgrimage to England, with return Pilgrimages in 2015, 2016, and 2024, where you may have spotted him. Another Pilgrimage is planned in mid-2025. If you ever run into him and his deerstalker out and about, feel free to say hello!

Paul W. Nash is a librarian, bibliographer, and printing historian. He has worked at the Royal Institute of British Architect's Library in London and the Bodleian Library in Oxford, and is currently editor of *The Journal of the Printing Historical Society*. He writes fiction and composes music as a relaxation.

Sidney Paget (1860-1908), a few of whose illustrations are used within this anthology, was born in London, and like his two older brothers, became a famed illustrator and painter. He completed over three-hundred-and-fifty drawings for the Sherlock Holmes stories that were first published in *The Strand* magazine, defining Holmes's image forever after in the public mind.

Tracy J. Revels, BSI, a Sherlockian from the age of eleven, is a professor of history at Wofford College in Spartanburg, South Carolina. She is a member of *The Survivors of the Gloria Scott* and *The Studious Scarlets Society*, and is a past recipient of the Beacon Society Award. Almost every semester, she teaches a class that covers The Canon, either to college students or to senior citizens. She is also the author of three supernatural Sherlockian pastiches with MX (*Shadowfall, Shadowblood*, and *Shadowwraith*), and most recently, the three-volume pastiche set, *Tales of Light, Tales of Shadow*, and *Tales of Darkness*. She is a regular contributor to her scion's newsletter. She also has some notoriety as an author of very silly skits: For proof, see "The Adventure of the Adversarial Adventuress" and "Occupy Baker Street" on YouTube. When not studying Sherlock, she can be found researching the history of her native state, and has written books on Florida in the Civil War and on the development of Florida's tourism industry.

Dan Rowley practiced law for over forty years in private practice and with a large international corporation. He is retired and lives in Erie, Pennsylvania, with his wife Judy, who puts her artistic eye to his transcription of Watson's manuscripts. He inherited his writing ability and creativity from his children, Jim and Katy, and his love of mysteries from his parents, Jim and Ruth.

Geri Schear is a novelist and short story writer. Her work has been published in literary journals in the U.S. and Ireland. Her first novel, *A Biased Judgement: The Diaries of Sherlock Holmes 1897* was released to critical acclaim in 2014. The sequel, *Sherlock Holmes and the Other Woman* was published in 2015, and *Return to Reichenbach* in 2016. *Great Warrior* was published in 2024. She lives in Kells, Ireland.

Robert V. Stapleton was born and brought up in Leeds, Yorkshire, England, and studied at Durham University. After working in various parts of the country as an Anglican parish priest, he is now retired and lives with his wife in North Yorkshire. As a member of his local writing group, he now has time to develop his other life as a writer of adventure stories. He has published a number of short stories, and he is hoping to have a couple of completed novels published at some time in the future.

William Todd has been a Holmes fan his entire life, and credits *The Hound of the Baskervilles* as the impetus for his love of both reading and writing. He began to delve into fan fiction a few years ago when he decided to take a break from writing his usual Victorian/Gothic horror stories. He was surprised how well-received they were, and has tried to put out a couple of Holmes stories a year since then. When not writing, Mr. Todd is a pathology supervisor at a local hospital in Northwestern Pennsylvania. He is the husband of a terrific lady and father to two great kids, one with special needs, so the benefactor of these anthologies is close to his heart.

DJ Tyrer is the person behind Atlantean Publishing and has had fiction featuring Sherlock Holmes published in volumes from MX Publishing and Belanger Books, and an issue of *Awesome Tales*, and has a forthcoming story in *Sherlock Holmes Mystery Magazine*. DJ's non-Sherlockian mysteries can be found in anthologies such as *Mardi Gras Mysteries* (Mystery and Horror LLC) and *The Trench Coat Chronicles* (Celestial Echo Press), and on *Mystery Tribune*.
DJ Tyrer's website is at *https://djtyrer.blogspot.co.uk/*
DJ's Facebook page is at *https://www.facebook.com/DJTyrerwriter/*
The Atlantean Publishing website is at *https://atlanteanpublishing.wordpress.com/*

Emma West joined Undershaw in April 2021 as the Director of Education with a brief to ensure that qualifications formed the bedrock of our provision, whilst facilitating a positive balance between academia, pastoral care, and well-being. She quickly took on the role of Acting Headteacher from early summer 2021. Under her leadership, Undershaw has embraced its new name, new vision, and consequently we have seen an exponential increase in demand for places. There is a buzz in the air as we invite prospective students and families through the doors. Emma has overseen a strategic review, re-cemented relationships with Local Authorities, and positioned Undershaw at the helm of SEND education in Surrey and beyond. Undershaw has a wide appeal: Our students present to us with mild to moderate learning needs and therefore may have some very recent memories of poor experiences in their previous schools. Emma's background as a senior leader within the independent school sector has meant she is well-versed in brokering relationships between the key stakeholders, our many interdependences, local businesses, families, and staff, and all this while ensuring Undershaw remains relentlessly child-centric in its approach. Emma's energetic smile and boundless enthusiasm for Undershaw is inspiring.

Marcia Wilson is a freelance researcher and illustrator who likes to work in a style compatible for the color blind and visually impaired. She is Canon-centric, and has written many acclaimed stories about Sherlock Holmes and the Scotland Yard inspectors who knew and worked with him. Long unavailable, nine of these novels will be released by MX Publishing in Spring 2025, with more in preparation.

The following contributors appear
in the companion volumes:
The True Sherlock Mr. Holmes –
England's Greatest Hero
Part XLIX – (1880-1888)
Part L – (1889-1896)
Part LII – (1902-1923)

Ian Ableson is an ecologist by training and a writer by choice. When not reading or writing, he can reliably be found scowling at a clipboard while ankle-deep in a marsh somewhere in Michigan. His love for the stories of Arthur Conan Doyle started when his grandfather gave him a copy of *The Original Illustrated Sherlock Holmes* when he was in high school, and he's proud to have been able to contribute to the continuation of the tales of Sherlock Holmes and Dr. Watson.

Mike Adamson *also has a story in Part L*

Tim Newton Anderson is a former senior daily newspaper journalist and PR manager who has recently started writing fiction. In the past six months, he has placed fourteen stories in publications including *Parsec Magazine*, *Tales of the Shadowmen*, *SF Writers Guild*, *Zoetic Press*, *Dark Lane Books*, *Dark Horses Magazine*, *Emanations*, and *Planet Bizarro*.

Hugh Ashton was born in the U.K., and moved to Japan in 1988, where he remained until 2016, living with his wife Yoshiko in the historic city of Kamakura, a little to the south of Yokohama. He and Yoshiko have now moved to Lichfield, a small cathedral city in the Midlands of the U.K., the birthplace of Samuel Johnson, and one-time home of Erasmus Darwin. In the past, he has worked in the technology and financial services industries, which have provided him with material for some of his books set in the 21st century. He currently works as a writer: Novelist, freelance editor, and copywriter, (his work for large Japanese corporations has appeared in international business journals), and journalist, as well as producing industry reports on various aspects of the financial services industry. However, his lifelong interest in Sherlock Holmes has developed into an acclaimed series of adventures featuring the world's most famous detective, written in the style of the originals. In addition to these, he has also published historical and alternate historical novels, short stories, and thrillers. Together with artist Andy Boerger, he has produced the *Sherlock Ferret* series of stories for children, featuring the world's cutest detective.

Deanna Baran lives in a remote part of Texas where cowboys may still be seen in their natural habitat. A librarian and former museum curator, she writes in between cups of tea, playing *Go*, and trading postcards with people around the world.

Derrick Belanger, BSI ("The Board Schools"), PSI ("Albert, the Dove") is an award-winning author, publisher, and educator most noted for his books and lectures on Sherlock Holmes and Sir Arthur Conan Doyle. Derrick is co-owner of the publishing company Belanger Books, which published the first eBook editions of the original Solar Pons books by August Derleth. Derrick's work has been published in *The Baker Street Journal*, *The Sherlock Holmes Journal*, *The Strand Magazine*, and in *The Mysterious Bookshop Presents the Best Mystery Stories of the Year (2023)*. Derrick is a board member of Dr. Watson's Neglected Patients, the Denver-based Scion Society. In January 2020, Mr. Belanger was awarded the Susan Z. Diamond Award in recognition of outstanding efforts to introduce young people to Sherlock Holmes, and in 2024, he won the Arthur Conan Doyle Society Doylean award in fiction for his short story, "The Joyce-Armstrong Confession". Derrick currently resides in Broomfield, Colorado. Find him at:
www.belangerbooks.com

Mike Chinn's first ever Sherlock Holmes fiction was a steampunk mashup of *The Valley of Fear*, entitled *Vallis Timoris* (Fringeworks 2015). Since then he has written about Holmes' archenemy in *The Mammoth Book of the Adventures of Moriarty* (Robinson 2015), appeared in several volumes of *The MX Book of New Sherlock Holmes Stories*, and confronted the retired detective with cross-dimensional magic in the second volume of *Sherlock Holmes and the Occult Detectives* (Belanger Books 2020). He also had a non-Holmes story published in the Lovecraftian anthology *Sherlock & Friends: Eldritch Investigations* (Tule Fog Press, 2024).

Martin Daley was born in Carlisle, Cumbria in 1964. His thirty-year writing career has seen over twenty books and numerous short stories published. Inevitably, Holmes and Watson remain his favourite literary characters, and they continue to inspire his own detective writing. In 2010, Martin created Inspector Cornelius Armstrong, who carries out his police work against the backdrop of Edwardian Carlisle. With the publication of the first *Inspector Armstrong Casebook* (published by MX Publishing), Martin became a member of the Crime Writers' Association. Most recently, he published *The Selected Cases of Sherlock Holmes*. He lives with his wife Wendy, in Kirkcudbrightshire, in Southwest.

Alan Dimes *also has a story in Part L*

Stuart Douglas is an author, editor, and publisher, and the creator of the Lowe and Le Breton Mysteries. He has written four Sherlock Holmes novels for Titan Books, and contributed stories to the anthologies *Encounters of Sherlock Holmes*, *Further Associates of Sherlock Holmes*, and *The MX Book of New Sherlock Holmes Stories*. He runs Obverse Books and lives in Edinburgh with his wife, three children, a dog named after Dusty Springfield and cat named after David Bowie.
Follow him on Bluesky: *@stuartdouglas.bsky.social*
and on Instagram: *@stuartamdouglas*

Brett Fawcett is a humanities and Latin teacher at the Chesterton Academy of St. Isidore in Sherwood Park, Alberta. He lives with his wife and son in Edmonton, where he is a member of The Wisteria Lodgers (The Sherlock Holmes Society of Edmonton). He vividly remembers the first time he finished reading the Sherlock Holmes stories in Grade 6, and has been a student of Holmesian literature and scholarship since then. He is also a frequent author of columns and articles on topics like theology, education, and mental health, as well as the occasional mystery story.

Dick Gillman is an English writer and acrylic artist living in Brittany, France with his wife Alex, Truffle, their Black Labrador, and Jean-Claude, their Breton cat. During his retirement from teaching, he has written over twenty Sherlock Holmes short stories which are published as both e-books and paperbacks. His initial contribution to the superb MX Sherlock Holmes collection, published in October 2015, was entitled "The Man on Westminster Bridge" and had the privilege of being chosen as the anchor story in *The MX Book of New Sherlock Holmes Stories – Part II (1890-1895)*.

John Linwood Grant is a writer and editor who lives in Yorkshire with a pack of lurchers and a beard. He may also have a family. He focuses particularly on dark Victorian and Edwardian fiction, such as his recent novella *A Study in Grey*, which also features Holmes. Current projects include his *Tales of the Last Edwardian* series, about psychic and psychiatric mysteries, and curating a collection of new stories based on the darker side of the British Empire. He has been published in a number of anthologies and magazines, with stories range from madness in early Virginia to questions about the monsters we ourselves might be. He is also co-editor of *Occult Detective Quarterly*. His website *greydogtales.com* explores weird fiction, especially period ones, weird art, and even weirder lurchers.

Arthur Hall *also has stories in Part L*

Paula Hammond *also has stories in Part L*

James R. Hawkins, BSI writes: "I discovered Sherlock Holmes on my fortieth birthday, in Norman, OK. In high school, in Texas, I mainly read Ernest Hemingway and true-life stories set in exotic locations, like Alaska. I was inordinately interested in Eskimos.
I was born in Jacksboro, Texas, in 1944, the only son of Leon and Ruth Hawkins, owners of Hawkins Funeral Home, and little brother to Linda (1939) and Jane Hawkins (1940). My Dad wanted me to take over the funeral home, but I chose a life in music education, which took me to Oklahoma Baptist University in Shawnee, OK, and to the Eastman School of Music in Rochester, NY. With my vocal chops, I landed a place in The US Army Chorus in Washington, DC, during the Vietnam war, (1969-1973). Married in 1966, my wife and I struck out for Los Angeles to work on a doctorate in music at the University of So. California. From there, we moved to Norman, OK, where I was the music director at 1st Baptist Church in Norman before becoming the Youth, Adult, and Senior Adult Music Consultant for the Southern Baptist Convention in Nashville, TN (1985-1992). In 2001, I switched from music to aviation and joined that highly successful company, Southwest Airlines, where I held various positions, settling into the Flight Attendant job, retiring some sixteen years later in 2017. Since then, my life has revolved around Sherlock Holmes and the men and women who are Sherlockians, devotees of the detective "*who never lived, and so, could never die*". In 2018, I wrote about the man who influenced the most in my Holmes and Watson journey, John Bennett Shaw. The website I built for him caught the attention of many of The Baker Street Irregulars, who honored me with membership in their august body and shared with me the same investiture given to Shaw back in 1965, *The Hans Sloane of My Age*."

Stephen Herczeg is an IT Geek, writer, actor, and film-maker based in Canberra Australia. He has been writing for over twenty years and has completed a couple of dodgy novels, sixteen feature-length screenplays, and numerous short stories and scripts. Stephen was very successful in 2017's International Horror Hotel screenplay competition, with his scripts *TITAN* winning the Sci-Fi category and *Dark are the Woods* placing second in the horror category. His collection, *The Curious Cases of Sherlock Holmes*, is now at four volumes. His work has featured in *Sproutlings – A Compendium of Little Fictions* from Hunter Anthologies, the *Hells Bells* Christmas horror anthology published by the Australasian Horror Writers Association, and the *Below the Stairs*, *Trickster's Treats*, *Shades of Santa*, *Behind the Mask*, and *Beyond the Infinite* anthologies from OzHorror.Com, *The Body Horror Book*, *Anemone Enemy*, and *Petrified Punks* from Oscillate Wildly Press, and *Sherlock Holmes In the Realms of H.G. Wells* and *Sherlock Holmes: Adventures Beyond the Canon* from Belanger Books.

Liz Hedgecock grew up in London, England (a train and a tube ride away from Baker Street), did an English degree, and then took forever to start writing. Now Liz travels between the nineteenth and twenty-first centuries, murdering people. To be fair, she does usually clean up after herself. Liz's reimaginings of Sherlock Holmes and her Victorian and contemporary mystery series are available in eBook and paperback. Liz lives in Cheshire with her husband and two sons, and when she's not writing you can usually find her reading, messing about on social media, or cooing over stuff in museums and art galleries. That's her story, anyway, and she's sticking to it.

Paul Hiscock is an author of crime, fantasy, horror, and science fiction tales. His short stories have appeared in a variety of anthologies, and include a seventeenth-century whodunnit, a science fiction western, a clockpunk fairytale, and numerous Sherlock Holmes pastiches. He lives with his family in Kent (England) and spends his days taking care of his two children. You can find out more about Paul's writing at: *www.detectivesanddragons.uk*.

In the year 1998 **Craig Janacek** took his degree of Doctor of Medicine at Vanderbilt University, and proceeded to Stanford to go through the training prescribed for pediatricians in practice. Having completed his studies there, he was duly attached to the University of California, San Francisco as a Professor. The author of over two-hundred medical monographs upon a variety of obscure lesions, his travel-worn and battered tin dispatch-box is crammed with papers, most of which are records of his fictional works. These include several collections of *The Further Adventures of Sherlock Holmes*: *Light in the Darkness*, *The Gathering Gloom*, *The Treasury of Sherlock Holmes*, *The Travels of Sherlock Holmes*, *The Chronicles of Sherlock Holmes*, *The Histories of Sherlock Holmes*, *The Acts of Sherlock Holmes*, and *The Assassination of Sherlock Holmes* – as well as two Dr. Watson novels (*The Isle of Devils* and *The Gate of Gold*), the complete and expanded *Adventures* and *Exploits of Brigadier Gerard* (*Set Europe Shaking* and *A Mighty Shadow*), and two non-Holmes novels (*The Oxford Deception* and *The Anger of Achilles Peterson*). His short stories have been published in several editions of *The MX Book of New Sherlock Holmes Stories, Part I: 1881-1889* (2015), *Part IV: 2016 Annual* (2016), *Part VI: 2017 Annual* (2017), *Part VIII: Eliminate the Impossible* (2017), *Part XI: Some Untold Cases* (2018), *Part XVIII: Whatever Remains Must be the Truth* (2019), *Part XXIII: Some More Untold Cases* (2020), *Part XXV: 2021 Annual* (2021), *Part XXXII: 2022 Annual* (2022), *Part XXXVI: However Improbable . . . .* (2022), and *Part XXXVIII: 2023 Annual* (2023). Other stories have appeared in *Holmes Away From Home: Tales of the Great Hiatus* (2016), *Tales from the Stranger's Room 3* (2017), *Sherlock Holmes: Adventures Beyond the Canon* (2018), *Sherlock Holmes, A Year of Mysteries – 1881* (2021), and *Sherlock Holmes: Stranger than Fiction* (2021). He lives near San Francisco, California with his wife and two children, where he is at work on his next story. Craig Janacek is a *nom-de-plume*.

Steven Philip Jones has written fiction novels for adults and young adults, comic books, graphic novels, radio scripts, non-fiction, and advertising pieces. His Sherlock Holmes pastiches include the novel *The Adventure of the Coal-Tar Derivative* from MX Publishing and the radio dramas "The Adventure of the Petty Curses" and "A Case of Unfinished Business" for Jim French Productions' *Imagination Theatre*. He currently makes his home with his family in northern Utah.

Susan Knight *also has a story in Part LII*

John Lawrence served for thirty-eight years on personal, committee, and leadership staffs in the U.S. House of Representatives. A visiting professor at the University of California's Washington Center since 2013, he is the author of *The Class of '74: Congress After Watergate and the Roots of Partisanship* (Johns-Hopkins, 2018) and *Arc of Power: Inside the Pelosi Speakership 2005-2010* (Kansas, 2022). His collected "history mystery" Sherlock Holmes pastiches have been published in *The Undiscovered Archives of Sherlock Holmes, The Further Undiscovered Archives of Sherlock Holmes*, in numerous volumes of *The MX Book of New Sherlock Holmes Stories*, and in Belanger Books' *After the East Wind Blows*. His novel, *Sherlock Holmes: The Affair at Mayerling Lodge* was published in 2023. He blogs at DOMEocracy (johnalawrence.wordpress.com). He is a graduate of Oberlin College and has a Ph.D. in history from the University of California (Berkeley).

Gordon Linzner is founder and former editor of *Space and Time Magazine*, and author of four published novels and dozens of short stories in *F&SF*, *Twilight Zone*, *Sherlock Holmes Mystery Magazine*, and numerous other magazines and anthologies. He is a full member of the *Horror Writers Association* and a lifetime member of *Science Fiction and Fantasy Writers Association*.

David Marcum *also has stories in Parts XLIX, L, and LII*

J. Lawrence Matthews has contributed fiction to *The New York Times* and *NPR*'s *All Things Considered* and is the author of *One Must Tell the Bees: Abraham Lincoln and the Final Education of Sherlock Holmes* (East Dean Press, 2021). The first novel to bring Sherlock Holmes together with Abraham Lincoln during the American Civil War, *One Must Tell the Bees* was called *"beautifully written and immediately engaging"* in the summer journal of *The Sherlock Holmes Society of London*. Matthews is at work on the sequel, which takes Sherlock Holmes to Tibet in 1891 for Holmes's encounter with the 13th Dalai Lama. He resides in Naples, FL, where his favorite breaks from writing are travel, book club meetings with his readers, visits from children and grandchildren, and, when the house gets a little too quiet, playing the drums.

John McNabb is a Welshman and an archaeologist, and a proud member of *The Sherlock Holmes Society of London*. He has published academic analysis of aspects of Conan Doyle's work, as well as its broader context. Mac also has a long-standing interest in Victorian and Edwardian scientific romances and the portrayal of human origins in early science fiction.

Paul Metcalfe has been a librarian for twenty-eight years, starting in public libraries, but is now the librarian at a technical college in rural Western Australia. He has been a lifelong Holmes fan since reading the original stories aged twelve, and now enjoys many of the later pastiches and Holmesian nonfiction as well. In 2005, he made the semifinals of the ABC television quiz show *The Einstein Factor* with the Sherlock Holmes stories by ACD as his special subject. He thinks Jeremy Brett is the television Holmes *nonpareil*, he collects old books and antiques, and is a strong advocate of the use of graphic novels to encourage reading. This is his first work of fiction.

Adrian Middleton is a Staffordshire-born independent publisher. The son of a real-world detective, he is a former civil servant and policy adviser who now writes and edits science fiction, fantasy, and a popular series of steampunked Sherlock Holmes stories.

Mark Mower is a long-standing member of the *Crime Writers' Association*, *The Sherlock Holmes Society of London*, and *The Solar Pons Society of London*. His pastiche collections include *Sherlock Holmes: The Baker Street Case-Files*, *Sherlock Holmes: The Baker Street Legacy*, *Sherlock Holmes: The Baker Street Epilogue*, and *Sherlock Holmes: The Baker Street Archive* (all with MX Publishing). His non-fiction works include the bestselling book *Zeppelin Over Suffolk: The Final Raid of the L48* (Pen & Sword Books). Alongside his writing, Mark maintains a sizeable collection of pastiches, and never tires of discovering new stories about Sherlock Holmes and Dr. Watson.

Will Murray is the author of some 75 novels, including some 20 posthumous Doc Savage collaborations with Lester Dent, and 40 books in the long-running Destroyer series. Other Murray novels star the Executioner, Tarzan of the Apes, The Spider, Pat Savage and the Mars Attacks characters. His book, *Nick Fury, Agent of S.H.I.E.L.D.: Empyre* (2000) foreshadowed the 9/11 terrorist attacks. Murray has penned nearly sixty Sherlock Holmes short stories. Murray's Holmes short stories have been collected as *The Wild Adventures of Sherlock Holmes*, Volumes 1 through 4. His novelette, "The Adventure of the Vengeful Viscount", in which Tarzan of the Apes, otherwise Lord Greystoke, hires Sherlock Holmes to solve a mystery, was approved by both the Estate of Sir Arthur Conan Doyle and Edgar Rice Burroughs, Inc. Murray is the author of the non-fiction book, *Master of Mystery: The Rise of The Shadow*, which is an exploration of the famous radio and magazine character, and a sequel, *Dark Avenger: The Strange Saga of The Shadow*. *The Wild Adventures of Cthulhu* Vols 1 & 2 collect Murray's Lovecraftian short stories. For Marvel Comics, Murray created the Unbeatable Squirrel Girl with legendary artist Steve Ditko. Website: *www.adventuresinbronze.com*

Orlando Pearson is an accountant. He commutes into London by day and communes with the spirits of Baker Street by night. He was born a short rather than a long shot away from 221b. He is the creator of the series, *The Redacted Sherlock Holmes*, which runs to eight collections of short works, two novels, and a book of plays. A new collection of short works is appearing later this year and a Mycroftian novel will come out in 2026. These accounts of real events were redacted one-hundred or so years ago at the time The Canon was being published. The liberality of modern times means we can now read of Holmes's exposure of the rigging of the home-insurance market, his identification of an alternative claimant for the British throne, and his investigation into someone even better known than himself who rose from the dead. Orlando's profile can be found at: *https://www.amazon.co.uk/Orlando-Pearson/e/B07DWP857S/ref=dp_byline_cont_book_1*

Tracy Revels *also has stories in Parts XLIX and L*

A professional author since 2007, **Josh Reynolds** has over thirty novels to his name, as well as numerous short stories, novellas, and audio scripts. Born and raised in South

Carolina, he now resides in Sheffield with his wife and daughter, as well as a highly excitable dog and something he hopes is a cat. A complete list of his work can be found at *https://joshuamreynolds.co.uk/*

Roger Riccard's family history has Scottish roots, which trace his lineage back to Highland Scotland. This ancestry encouraged his interest in the writings of Sir Arthur Conan Doyle. He has authored the novels, *Sherlock Holmes & The Case of the Poisoned Lilly*, and *Sherlock Holmes & The Case of the Twain Papers,* which was featured at the Museum of London Sherlock Holmes Exhibit in 2015. In addition, he has produced dozens of short stories, and has now joined the Sherlock Holmes 60+ Club, having exceeded Sir Arthur Conan Doyle's number of original Sherlock Holmes stories. All of his books have been published by Baker Street Studios and can be found at his website: *www.sherlockriccard.com* He credits his success to the encouragement of his wife/editor/inspiration and Sherlock Holmes fan, Rosilyn. She passed in 2021, and it is in her memory that he continues to contribute to the legacy of the *"man who never lived and will never die"*.

Dan Rowley *also has a story in Part LII*

Jane Rubino is the author of *A Jersey Shore* mystery series, featuring a Jane Austen-loving amateur sleuth and a Sherlock Holmes-quoting detective, *Knight Errant, Lady Vernon and Her Daughter*, (a novel-length adaptation of Jane Austen's novella *Lady Susan*, co-authored with her daughter Caitlen Rubino-Bradway, *What Would Austen Do?*, also co-authored with her daughter, a short story in the anthology *Jane Austen Made Me Do It, The Rucastles' Pawn, The Copper Beeches from Violet Turner's POV*, and, of course, there's the Sherlockian novel *Hidden Fires*. Jane lives on a barrier island at the New Jersey shore.

Andrew Salmon has won several awards for his Sherlock Holmes stories and has been nominated for the Ellis, Pulp Ark, Pulp Factory and New Pulp Awards. He lives and writes in Vancouver, BC. His novels include: *Fight Card Sherlock Holmes: Work Capitol, Blood to the Bone*, and *A Congression of Pallbearers* (collected in the *Fight Card Sherlock Holmes Omnibus*) *The Dark Land, The Light Of Men*, and *Ghost Squad: Rise of the Black Legion* (with Ron Fortier) and his first children's book, *Wandering Webber*. His work has also appeared in numerous anthologies covering multiple genres. His tales from the award winning *Sherlock Holmes Consulting Detective* series were collected in *Sherlock Holmes Investigates. Ace of Devils*, the second novel in the Eby Stokes series featuring the female pugilist turned Special Branch agent, is out now and he's working on the third book, as well as a myriad of other projects. To learn more about his work check out: *amazon.com/Andrew-Salmon/e/B002NS5KR0*

Brenda Seabrooke's stories have appeared in thirty-eight literary magazines, mystery anthologies, and magazines. Twenty books for young readers were published, and then two Sherlock's Dog books. She discovered that she liked writing about the world's greatest consulting detective and mysteries. Two collections of Sherlock Holmes stories were published by MX UK, and her stories have been included in "4 Best Mysteries of New England" (Level Best Books). She has received a grant from the NEA, a fellowship from Emerson College, and is an MWA runner-up. She has twice judged and once chaired Edgar mystery categories. Brenda is the former president of the Children's Book Guild of DC, a member of AG. *Viva* Holmes and Watson!

Peter Shumway is a retired computer professional residing in Pennsylvania with his wife, Patty. They have been married forty-one years and have two daughters and four grandchildren. In the early 1970's, Peter performed magic with Bill Baker's World of Magic, John Bundy's Magic Concert, and traded secrets with David Copperfield when they were teenagers. Peter read the original Sherlock Holmes stories while in college in 1979, and has enjoyed rereading them many times since. He published his pastiche *Sherlock Holmes and The Kiss of Death* in 2005 and *Gullible's Journey* in 2023. When he was offered the opportunity to write a short story for the MX Series, he picked up his pen yet again.

Shane Simmons is the author of the occult detective novels *necropolis* and *Epitaph*, and the crime collection *Raw and Other Stories.* An award-winning screenwriter and graphic novelist, his work has appeared in international film festivals, museums, and lectures about design and structure. He was born in Lachine, a suburb of Montreal best known for being massacred in 1689 and having a joke name. Visit Shane's homepage at *eyestrainproductions.com* for more information.

Award winning poet and author **Joseph W. Svec III** enjoys writing, poetry, and stories, and creating new adventures for Holmes and Watson that take them into the worlds of famous literary authors and scientists. His *Missing Authors* trilogy introduced Holmes to Lewis Carroll, Jules Verne, H.G. Wells, and Alfred Lord Tennyson, as well as many of their characters. His transitional story *Sherlock Holmes and the Mystery of the First Unicorn* involved several historical figures, besides a Unicorn or two. He has also written the rhymed and metered Sherlock Holmes Christmas adventure, *The Night Before Christmas in 221b*, sure to be a delight for Sherlock Holmes enthusiasts of all ages. 2024 saw the publication of *Sherlock Holmes for Letter or Verse*. Joseph won the Amador Arts Council 2021 Original Poetry Contest, with his Rhymed and metered story poem, "The Homecoming". Joseph has presented a literary paper on Sherlock Holmes/Alice in Wonderland crossover literature to the Lewis Carroll Society of North America, as well as given several presentations to the Amador County Holmes Hounds, Sherlockian Society. He is currently working on his first book in the Missing Scientist Trilogy, *Sherlock Holmes and the Adventure of the Demonstrative Dinosaur*, in which Sherlock meets Professor George Edward Challenger. Joseph has Masters Degrees in Systems Engineering and Human Organization Management, and has written numerous technical papers on Aerospace Testing. In addition to writing, Joseph enjoys creating miniature dioramas based on music, literature, and history from many different eras. His dioramas have been featured in magazine articles and many different blogs, including the North American Jules Verne society newsletter. He currently has fifty-seven dioramas set up in his display area, and has written a reference book on toy castles and knights from around the world. An avid tea enthusiast, his tea cabinet contains over five-hundred different varieties, and he delights in sharing afternoon tea with his childhood sweetheart and wonderful wife, who has inspired and coauthored several books with him.

Kevin Thornton has, by his own count - and remember he's a writer, not an arithmetician – been in seventeen of these volumes, including this one. That's not a bad record, neither near the top nor the bottom, metaphor for his life mayhap. A middling student of English in South Africa, he was taught by two Nobel Literature Laureates to little noticeable effect, and has since been a soldier in Africa, a military contractor in Afghanistan, a forklift driver in Ontario, a bartender everywhere, and a logistician in Northern Alberta, which is, naturally, why he now works as a Communications Consultant for an Indigenous Nation of Cree, Denesuline, and Metis people. It has evolved into a good life, improved immeasurably by a tolerant, beautiful, and loving wife, two sons who smarter than they let on, and a Belgian Malinois with all of the energy of that breed and none of the intelligence. He lives in Northern Alberta, not quite in the North Pole, Santa Claus neighbourhood, but near enough for it to be a local telephone call. He is content.

A Sherlock Holmes fan since reading *The Hound of the Baskervilles* at about age twelve, **Tom Turley** has been writing pastiches since 2006. Most have appeared in previous volumes of *The MX Book of New Sherlock Holmes Stories*. All except the latest three have been collected in two books available from MX Publishing and Amazon. *Sherlock Holmes and the Crowned Heads of Europe* (2021) is a collection of four historical novellas that involve Holmes and Watson in the events leading up to World War I. The four stories are also available individually on Audible. As its title indicates, *Watson's Wives and Other Tales of Sherlock Holmes* (2023) focuses primarily on the Doctor's marriages. It likewise will soon be available on Audible. Currently, Tom is at work on a Sherlockian novel. A retired historian and archivist, he resides with his wife Paula in Montgomery, Alabama.

DJ Tyrer *also has a story in Part XLIX*

Peter Coe Verbica lives in the redwoods of Northern California. He grew up on Rancho San Felipe, a cattle ranch, where he learned the value of a strong work ethic. He obtained a BA from Santa Clara University, a JD from Santa Clara University School of Law and an MS from the Massachusetts Institute of Technology. Readers can find ten of his short stories in *The MX Book of New Sherlock Holmes Stories* anthologies, edited by David Marcum. These include "The Disfigured Hand", "The Magic Bullet", "The Adventure of the Matched Set", "The Musician Who Spoke from the Grave", "The Dutch Imposters", "A Ghost in the Mirror", "The Deceased Priest", "The King of Spades", "The Hyde Park Blackmailer", and, most recently, "The Ambassador's Dilemma". An additional seven stories, including "The Lucky Strike", "The Mystery of the Five Keys", "The Man Who Didn't Smoke", "The Noble Heart", "The Curious Case of the Bald Prince", "The Lost Uncle", and "Death at Hampton Court" can be found in *The Missing Tales of Sherlock Holmes*. Mr. Verbica is the author of non-fiction articles as well, including "Rise of the Rothschilds: A Legacy of Lessons", featured in *Opportunity Now Silicon Valley*, "We are thinking about . . . Artificial intelligence and trading platforms" featured by Silicon Private Wealth, and "The Divine Leaven of Self-Sacrifice (written in honor of Lenah Sutcliff Higbee)" presented at the Mast Stepping Ceremony of *USS Lenah Sutcliff Higbee* (DDG-123). His free verse works, such as "Small Mound of Stones", "A Visit with Quentin", "Dreams of a Burning Man", "The Locusts", "Visitor 231", "A Thanksgiving Lesson", "Small Miracles", "Brazil", Gold", "Fear of Long Words", "Speak Easy", "Heaven", "The Home Which Dreams", and scores of other pieces appear in various anthologies and books across the globe. The author has also served as moderator and host of a popular speaker series, featuring the former CTO of the US Space Force; Deputy Director of the National Intelligence Agency on cybersecurity; the former US Ambassador to Ukraine on Eurasian security issues; the former US Ambassador to Thailand on US-China relations; a former USN Rear Admiral on the importance of civility in society; an expert on US tax law regarding proposed changes, and other speakers of merit, including the preeminent publisher of Sherlock Holmes-based fiction. Mr. Verbica currently serves as a Managing Director and Principal of Silicon Private Wealth, a Registered Investment Advisor where he helps "clients achieve their dreams through prudent and personalized investment planning." He won a top-two slot in the primary election for Board of Equalization in the State of California. He has served as President, Vice-President, and Chair for numerous

non-profit local and statewide non-profit and political organizations' boards. For more information, please visit:
www.peterverbica.com

I.A. Watson has written over fifty Sherlock Holmes stories, and is always surprised that there are still new things for The Great Detective to do, which is a real testament to the genius behind Doyle's most famous creations. His most recent Holmes activities though were in providing extensive notes for a talk about the character in a New York public library, which was quite a different creative challenge. In addition to the novel *Holmes and Houdini*, the anthology *The Incunabulum of Sherlock Holmes*, and the forthcoming *The Paralipomena of Sherlock Holmes*, I.A. Watson has provided entries to all twenty of the *Sherlock Holmes Consulting Detective* books, to about the same number of MX volumes, and another dozen or more in other eccentric places. In his spare time he produces other novels such as *The Death of Persephone*, *The Labours of Hercules*, *The Legend of Robin Hood*, *Women of Myth*, *The Transdimensional Transport Company*, and *Vinnie de Soth, Jobbing Occultist*. It is perhaps not traditional to use an "About the Author" paragraph to offer thanks, but I.A. Watson would like to dedicate this "About the Author" piece to Mr. David Marcum for his astonishing accomplishment with the MX Holmes series, and his tireless enthusiasm as one of the stoutest Holmesians. A full list of I.A. Watson's publications is available at:
http://www.chillwater.org.uk/writing/iawatsonhome.htm

Ashley Williford writes: "This is my first Sherlockian publication. I am a devoted Sherlockian and Ravenclaw and a member of my local Sherlockian scion society, *The Giant Rats of Sumatra* in Memphis, Tennessee. I have a hilarious three-year-old boy, Williford "Will" Roney, as well as two goldendoodles, Albus Percival Wulfric Brian Dumbledoodle (eight) and Merlin Aberforth Dumbledoodle (six). I am an Adult-Gerontological Acute Care Nurse Practitioner with a Doctorate in Nursing Practice, and I specialize in critical care. My favorite of my many hobbies include writing Sherlock adventures, hand embroidery, puzzles, games, reading, starting flowers from seeds only to abandon them after sprouting, and listening to absolutely everything Steven Fry narrates."

Marcia Wilson *also has stories in Parts XLIX and L*

DeForeest Wright III has a day job as a baker for Ralphs grocery stores. It helps support his love for books. A long-time lover of literature, especially of the Sherlock Holmes tales, he spends his time away from the oven hunched over novels, poetry, anthologies, or any tome on philosophy, mathematics, science, or martial arts he can find, sipping an espresso if one is to hand. He writes prose and poetry in his off hours and currently hosts "The Sunless Sea Open-Mic: Spoken Word and Poetry Show" at the Unurban Coffee House in Santa Monica. He was glad to team up writing with his father.

Sean Wright, BSI makes his home in Santa Clarita, a charming city at the entrance of the high desert in Southern California. For sixteen years, features and articles under his byline appeared in *The Tidings* – now *The Angelus News*, publications of the Roman Catholic Archdiocese of Los Angeles. Continuing his education in 2007, Mr. Wright graduated from Grand Canyon University, attaining a Bachelor of Arts degree in Christian Studies with a *summa cum laude*. He then attained a Master of Arts degree, also in Christian Studies. Once active in the entertainment industry, and in an abortive attempt to revive dramatic radio in 1976 with his beloved mentor, the late Daws Butler, directing, Mr. Wright co-produced and wrote the syndicated *New Radio Adventures of Sherlock Holmes*, starring the late Edward Mulhare as the Great Detective. Mr. Wright has written for several television quiz shows and remains proud of his work for *The Quiz Kid's Challenge* and the popular TV quiz show *Jeopardy!* for which the Academy of Television Arts and Sciences honored him in 1985 with an Emmy nomination in the field of writing. Honored with membership in The Baker Street Irregulars as "The Manor House Case" after founding The Non-Canonical Calabashes, the Sherlock Holmes Society of Los Angeles in 1970, Mr. Wright has written for *The Baker Street Journal* and *Mystery Magazine*. Since 1971, he has conducted lectures on Sherlock Holmes's influence on literature and cinema for libraries, colleges, and private organizations, including MENSA. Mr. Wright's whimsical *Sherlock Holmes Cookbook* (Drake), created with John Farrell, BSI, was published in 1976, and a mystery novel, *Enter the Lion: a Posthumous Memoir of Mycroft Holmes* (Hawthorne), "edited" with Michael Hodel, BSI, followed in 1979. As director general of The Plot Thickens Mystery Company, Mr. Wright originated hosting "mystery parties" in homes, restaurants, and offices, as well as producing and directing the very first "Mystery Train" tours on Amtrak, beginning in 1982.

471

The MX Book of New Sherlock Holmes Stories

Edited by David Marcum

(MX Publishing, 2015-2025)

"This is the finest volume of Sherlockian fiction I have ever read, and I have read, literally, thousands." – Philip K. Jones

"Beyond Impressive . . . This is a splendid venture for a great cause!"
– Roger Johnson, Editor, *The Sherlock Holmes Journal*,
The Sherlock Holmes Society of London

Part I: 1881-1889; Part II: 1890-1895; Part III: 1896-1929

Part IV: 2016 Annual

Part V: Christmas Adventures

Part VI: 2017 Annual

Eliminate the Impossible
Part VII: (1880-1891); Part VIII: (1892-1905)

2018 Annual
Part IX: (1879-1895); Part X: (1896-1916)

Some Untold Cases
Part XI: (1880-1891); Part XII: (1894-1902)

2019 Annual
Part XIII: (1881-1890); Part XIV: (1891-1897); Part XV: (1898-1917)

Whatever Remains . . . Must be the Truth
Part XVI: (1881-1890); Part XVII: (1891-1898); Part XVIII: (1898-1925)

2020 Annual
Part XIX: (1882-1890); Part XX: (1891-1897); Part XXI: (1898-1923)·

Some More Untold Cases
Part XXII: (1877-1887); Part XXIII: (1888-1894); Part XXIV: (1895-1903)

2021 Annual
Part XXV: (1881-1888); Part XXVI: (1889-1897); Part XXVII: (1898-1928)

More Christmas Adventures
Part XXVIII: (1869-1888); Part XXIX: (1889-1896); Part XXX: (1897-1928)

2022 Annual
Part XXXI: (1875-1887); Part XXXII: (1888-1895); Part XXXIII: (1896-1919)

"However Improbable . . . ."
Part XXXIV: (1878-1888); Part XXXV: (1889-1896); Part XXXVI: (1897-1919)

2023 Annual
Parts XXXVII (1875-1889), XXXVIII (1889-1896), and XXXIX (1897-1923)

Further Untold Cases
Part XL: (1879-1886), Part XLI: (1887-1892) and Part XLII: (1894-1922)

2024 Annual
Parts XLIII (1874-1888), XLIV (1889-1897), and XLV (1898-1917)

Occupants of the Canonical Realm
Parts XLVI (1861-1889), XLVII (1890-1898), and XLVIII (1899-1924)

The True Mr. Holmes: England's Greatest Hero
Parts XLIX and L (18XX-18XX) and (18XX-19XX)

The MX Book of New Sherlock Holmes Stories
Edited by David Marcum
(MX Publishing, 2015-2025)

Publishers Weekly says:

Part VI: *The traditional pastiche is alive and well . . . .*

Part VII: *Sherlockians eager for faithful-to-the-canon plots and characters will be delighted.*

Part VIII: *The imagination of the contributors in coming up with variations on the volume's theme is matched by their ingenious resolutions.*

Part IX: *The 18 stories . . . will satisfy fans of Conan Doyle's originals. Sherlockians will rejoice that more volumes are on the way.*

Part X: *. . . new Sherlock Holmes adventures of consistently high quality.*

Part XI: *. . . an essential volume for Sherlock Holmes fans.*

Part XII: *. . . continues to amaze with the number of high-quality pastiches.*

Part XIII: *. . . Amazingly, Marcum has found 22 superb pastiches . . . his is more catnip for fans of stories faithful to Conan Doyle's original*

Part XIV: *. . . this standout anthology of 21 short stories written in the spirit of Conan Doyle's originals.*

Part XV: *Stories pitting Sherlock Holmes against seemingly supernatural phenomena highlight Marcum's 15th anthology of superior short pastiches.*

Part XVI: *Marcum has once again done fans of Conan Doyle's originals a service.*

Part XVII: *This is yet another impressive array of new but traditional Holmes stories.*

Part XVIII: *Sherlockians will again be grateful to Marcum and MX for high-quality new Holmes tales.*

Part XIX: *Inventive plots and intriguing explorations of aspects of Dr. Watson's life and beliefs lift the 24 pastiches in Marcum's impressive 19th Sherlock Holmes anthology*

Part XX: *Marcum's reserve of high-quality new Holmes exploits seems endless.*

Part XXI: *This is another must-have for Sherlockians.*

Part XXII: *Marcum's superlative 22nd Sherlock Holmes pastiche anthology features 21 short stories that successfully emulate the spirit of Conan Doyle's originals while expanding on the canon's tantalizing references to mysteries Dr. Watson never got around to chronicling.*

Part XXIII: *Marcum's well of talented authors able to mimic the feel of The Canon seems bottomless.*

Part XXIV: *Marcum's expertise at selecting high-quality pastiches remains impressive.*

Part XXVIII: *All entries adhere to the spirit, language, and characterizations of Conan Doyle's originals, evincing the deep pool of talent Marcum has access to. Against the odds, this series remains strong, hundreds of stories in.*

Part XXXI: *. . . yet another stellar anthology of 21 short pastiches that effectively mimic the originals . . . Marcum's diligent searches for high-quality stories has again paid off for Sherlockians.*

Part XXXIV: *Mind-bending puzzles are the highlight of Marcum's fully satisfying 34th anthology, which again demonstrates that multiple authors are capable of giving Sherlock Holmes and Watson innovative mysteries to tackle while staying in character. Marcum's inventory of canonical pastiches shows no signs of being exhausted any time soon.*

475

An Investees' Anthology
Edited by David Marcum
(MX Publishing, 2022)

Selected Contributions to
The MX Book of New Sherlock Holmes Stories
by Members of
The Baker Street Irregulars

*All royalties from this collection are being donated
for the benefit of the preservation of Undershaw,
a school for special needs students located at
one of the former homes of Sir Arthur Conan Doyle*

Stories, Forewords, and Poems in this volume
have previously appeared in Parts I – XXXVI of
The MX Book of New Sherlock Holmes Stories

Featuring Contributions by:

Mark Alberstat, Marino C. Alvarez, Peter Calamai, Catherine Cooke, Carla Coupe, David Stuart Davies, John Farrell, Lyndsay Faye, Sonia Fetherston, Jayantika Ganguly, Jeffrey Hatcher, Roger Johnson, Leslie S. Klinger, Ann Margaret Lewis, Bonnie MacBird, Stephen Mason, Julie McKuras Nicholas Meyer, Jacquelynn Morris, Otto Penzler, Christopher Redmond, Tracy J. Revels, Steven Rothman, Nancy Holder, Mark Levy (and Arlene Mantin Levy), Nicholas Utechin, and Sean M. Wright (and DeForeest B. Wright, III)

MX Publishing

MX Publishing is the world's largest specialist Sherlock Holmes publisher, with over six-hundred titles and over two-hundred authors creating the latest in Sherlock Holmes fiction and non-fiction

The catalogue includes several award winning books, and over four-hundred-and-fifty have been converted into audio.

MX Publishing also has one of the largest communities of Holmes fans on Facebook, with regular contributions from dozens of authors.

www.mxpublishing.com

@mxpublishing on Facebook, Twitter, and Instagram

www.ingramcontent.com/pod-product-compliance
Lightning Source LLC
Chambersburg PA
CBHW032257020726
47495CB00001B/146